PENGUIN BOOKS

GREATEST LOVE SERIES BOOK 3

About The Author

Hannah is a twenty-something-year-old indie author from Canada. Obsessed with swoon-worthy romance, she decided to take a leap and try her hand at creating stories that will have you fanning your face and giggling in the most embarrassing way possible. Hopefully, that's exactly what her stories have done!

Hannah loves to hear from her readers, and can be reached on any of her social media accounts.

Instagram : Hannahcowanauthor
Twitter, Facebook : Hannahdcowan
Facebook Group : Hannah's Hotties
Website : www.hannahcowanauthor.com

HIS
Greatest
MUSE

GREATEST LOVE SERIES BOOK 3

HANNAH COWAN

PENGUIN BOOKS

PENGUIN BOOKS

UK | USA | Canada | Ireland | Australia
India | New Zealand | South Africa

Penguin Books is part of the Penguin Random House group of companies
whose addresses can be found at global.penguinrandomhouse.com

First published in the United States of America by Hannah Cowan 2023
First published in Great Britain by Penguin Books 2024
001

Cover designed by Booksandmoods @booksnmoods
Edited and proofread by @oneloveediting
Interior illustrations by Jordan Burns @joburns.reads
Printed and bound in Great Britain by Clays Ltd, Elcograf S.p.A.

The authorized representative in the EEA is Penguin Random House Ireland,
Morrison Chambers, 32 Nassau Street, Dublin D02 YH68

A CIP catalogue record for this book is available from the British Library

ISBN: 978–1–405–96626–9

www.greenpenguin.co.uk

Penguin Random House is committed to a
sustainable future for our business, our readers
and our planet. This book is made from Forest
Stewardship Council® certified paper.

Author's Note

Hi, everyone!

Before you dive into this story, I wanted to make sure that you know *His Greatest Muse* is the third instalment in a second-generation series. This means that there will be a *heavy* helping of characters involved in this story, both new and from the previous stories. A previous secondary character from my Amateurs In Love duet plays a big part in this story, and the impact of their actions will have more meaning if that duet is read prior to this story.

Keeping those things in mind, I have written this as a standalone to the best of my ability.

If I am a new author to you and you are interested in reading the books prior to this one, I have included a recommended reading list. If not, I have also added a family tree.

Disclaimer

Please note that this story is <u>very</u> different than what you are used to reading from me.

If you go into this with the expectations of Noah taking after his father or brother, you will be disappointed. He does not have a redemption arc in this book, nor does he seek one. His actions are at times harsh and unforgiving. He is a morally grey character in all its glory.

Please read the content warnings below before continuing.

Mention of recreational drug use, detailed physical violence (described on page), presence of a stalker, crude language, mention of blood and gore (described on page), parental abandonment (brief mention).

If you're comfortable moving forward, enjoy the ride ;)

Reading Order

Even though all of my books can be read on their own, they all exist in the same world—regardless of series—so for reader clarity, I have included a recommended reading order to give you the ultimate experience possible.

This is also a timeline-accurate list.

Lucky Hit (Oakley and Ava) Swift Hat-Trick trilogy #1

Between Periods (5 POV Novella) Swift Hat-Trick trilogy #1.5

Blissful Hook (Tyler and Gracie) Swift Hat-Trick trilogy #2

Craving the Player (Braden and Sierra) Amateurs in Love series #1

Taming the Player (Braden and Sierra) Amateurs in Love series #2

Vital Blindside (Adam and Scarlett) Swift Hat-Trick trilogy #3

Her Greatest Mistake (Maddox and Braxton) Greatest Love #1

Her Greatest Adventure (Adalyn and Cooper) Greatest Love #2

Family Trees

CHARACTER ORIGINS

SWIFT HAT-TRICK TRILOGY

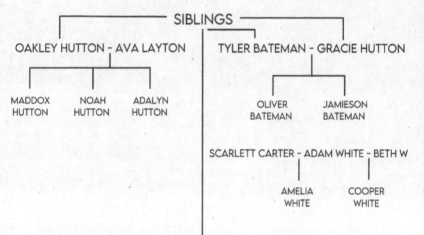

SIBLINGS

OAKLEY HUTTON - AVA LAYTON

TYLER BATEMAN - GRACIE HUTTON

MADDOX
HUTTON

NOAH
HUTTON

ADALYN
HUTTON

OLIVER
BATEMAN

JAMIESON
BATEMAN

SCARLETT CARTER - ADAM WHITE - BETH W

AMELIA
WHITE

COOPER
WHITE

AMATEURS IN LOVE SERIES

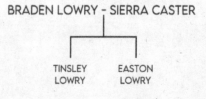

BRADEN LOWRY - SIERRA CASTER

TINSLEY
LOWRY

EASTON
LOWRY

Playlist

My Own Worst Enemy — Lit	2:49
Lifeline — Papa Roach	4:18
Iris — The Goo Goo Dolls	4:50
SLIDE — Chase Atlantic	3:56
HEARTBEAT — Isabel LaRosa	2:05
Loner — Maggie Lindemann	3:11
I'll Be — Edwin McCain	4:27
i'm yours — Isabel LaRosa	2:26
I Feel Like I'm Drowning — Two Feet	3:06
Fuck It — New Medicine	3:41
It's Been Awhile — Staind	4:25
Breaking the Habit — Linkin Park	3:17
High Enough — K.Flay	3:52
Beyond the Sun — Shinedown	4:14
Ride — The Vines	2:36
Deal with the Devil — Pop Evil	3:21
Bleeding Out — Imagine Dragons	3:41
All over You — The Spill Canvas	3:23
Drugs Or Me — Jimmy Eat World	6:26
Not Afraid — Eminem	4:08
Horns — Bryce Fox	3:38
So It Goes... — Taylor Swift	3:48
Cinnamon Girl — Lana Del Ray	5:01
Blood // Water — grandson	3:37
Addicted — Saving Abel	3:46
Fire Up the Night — New Medicine	2:58
Vicious — Bohnes	3:27
Fine Again — Seether	2:21

For Hayley, because without her I would have stopped after chapter 5.

And for every one of you who prefers red flags over green ones.

PROLOGUE

Noah

WHEN I WAS TEN, MY FATHER TOOK ME TO A THERAPIST.

He said it was because I was different. That I was just hard to understand. That he and my mother didn't know how to reach me.

I knew he was lying.

My parents took me to a therapist because they were scared of me. They feared me because they didn't understand me.

I've never been like my brother or sister. There's something wrong with me, deep, deep down in the shadowed crevice of my soul. Where there should have been light, there is darkness, a massive black pit of emptiness.

They didn't understand why I lacked the glimmer you should have found in the eyes of a musically gifted young boy with a bright future ahead of him, and they never believed me when I tried to explain.

They chalked it up to some illness that must have festered in my brain, but they were wrong.

I held no light because I had given it to her. The moment I laid eyes on my golden girl, I tore myself open and handed her piece after piece of me until there was nothing left but that eerie darkness that scared my family.

It is because of the girl with the glossy brown hair I imagine wrapping my fists in and the pale, unblemished skin I want to decorate in bruises the shapes of my lips and fingertips.

The owner of the charred, bloody organ that beats like a kick drum in my chest at the mere idea of her existence. Tinsley Lowry is my obsession. The reason I'm still here, living a life that gives me no joy, no satisfaction.

She is happiness personified. Everything fucking good on this earth.

She is mine.

And after all these years, it's time she knew what that means.

1

Tinsley

"Do you want a ride home, sweetheart?" Dad asks, a soft but firm hand splayed across my back as we linger outside.

The empty building that's going to be the third expansion of my dad's gym franchise stands before us on a plot of prime real estate in West Toronto. The space above the doors where the Knockout Training sign will go is an empty space of dark brick, and the windows on either side of the doors are still boarded up.

"Thanks, but no, thanks. My walk home is the only time I get a chance alone now that you have me slaving around this place."

"Slaving," he echoes, blowing a raspberry. "My apologies, princess."

"You could always let Hunter take over for you full-time already. At least it would be him busting my lady balls and not you."

"You know, there are thousands of boxers who would love to have your dear old dad as one of their trainers. I'm kind of a big deal around these parts."

"These parts? Have you started watching westerns again? I thought Mom hid all those from you after your last bender."

"She tried. But it seems you got more than just your fantastic sense of humour from your mother."

Our inability to keep a secret. We would make terrible politicians.

"Is that a compliment or an insult?" I ask.

"We'll have to leave that one up to interpretation," he teases, breaking away to lock the gym doors.

I stifle a laugh when the toe of his sneaker catches on a slight crack in the walkway—one that wasn't there this morning—and he stumbles, curse after curse slipping out. He shoots me an exasperated look over his shoulder before shoving a hand through his floppy silver hair and then flipping me the bird.

"It won't be so funny when it's you tripping next time."

"We both know I'm far too agile for that. You've lost your edge, Gramps."

After finally locking up the gym, he swivels around and walks back to me. "Smart-ass. Are you sure you don't want a ride home? I don't like you walking alone at night."

I look around at the dim, early evening streets. There are still crowds of people on the sidewalks and pooled together at the chirping crosswalks. The sun, while just barely, is still up.

"I wouldn't exactly call it nighttime."

His eyes tighten at the corners. "Tiny."

The nickname I've had for as long as I can remember doesn't make me laugh as much as it did when I was younger. Tiny is the last adjective that I would use to describe myself. I'm five ten, and while I might still look small in comparison to my six-three father, I'm far from it to other people.

"Dad."

He points to his head. "You're the reason for all of this silver, in case you didn't know."

"Me or Easton?" I know for a fact my younger brother is responsible for most of his greys.

He twists his mouth as if he's actually thinking about his answer before grunting, "You. Definitely you."

"I love you too, Dad," I sing.

Sighing, he pulls me in for a tight hug. "Be safe. And text me or your mom when you get home so we don't worry all night."

"Will do."

"Love you. See you tomorrow," he says, ruffling my hair and then stepping back, heading to his car. I wave as he gets inside and, after a moment of purposeful staring, as if to remind me to be safe again, drives away.

NH)

I HUM ALONG with the song playing in my earbuds as I jog up the darkened driveway with three heavy grocery bags in my hands. The sun set an hour ago, but the early June air is warm. In need of a good burst of fresh air after spending the day cooped up at my dad's boxing gym, I opted out of taking a separate trip to the store with my car and hit it on my walk home instead.

The front door of the house I share with my best friend, Noah, and his bass guitarist isn't locked—*surprise*—so I twist the knob with my elbow and walk right in.

"It smells like a frat house in here," I mutter, crinkling my nose.

The green-spotted bong on the coffee table is a centrepiece that I can't seem to get rid of for long, and the Ziploc baggy beside it is empty, only a thin coating of white left on the plastic. A pair of pink lace panties are hung on the doorknob to the right of the entrance. I speed walk past, deciding to keep my earbuds in so that I don't have to listen to whatever the hell is going on in there.

The kitchen isn't in much better shape, with a sink full of dirty dishes and an array of empty glass bottles scattered over the countertop. There's a pot on the stove that looks like it's full of Kraft Dinner, and I shudder at how old it must be.

I haven't been back here in three days. I've been staying with my parents while Noah's been gone doing a few radio shows this week to promote the upcoming tour. There was no way on earth I was going to be left alone to deal with Josh and his groupies while they partied. But after receiving not one or two, but *three* angry calls from our next-door neighbours this morning about the noise over the weekend, I thought I should come home and see what the hell Josh has been doing while I've been gone.

Clearly, not much different than what he does when I am here. He doesn't dare pull this shit when Noah's here, but when it's just me and him? It's a free-for-all.

I flip the lights and set the bags down on the counter before starting to unload the groceries into the fridge and bare cabinets, ignoring the mess as best I can.

Inviting Josh to live with us wasn't exactly my brightest idea, but when Noah's sudden rise to fame hit us all and his newly appointed manager found him a band, it sort of just happened. Josh was lonely after a tough breakup and was living out of a suitcase when Sparks found him. I felt bad for the guy, and we had a spare room. How was I supposed to know he would turn out to be not only a terrible bandmate but also the world's worst roommate?

Balling the empty grocery bags up, I shove them in the over-flowing trash can before emptying it and hauling it out the back door. The alley is just as dark as the front of the house, and I make a note to replace the burnt-out porch lights when that nagging discomfort of not knowing if someone might be watching you tingles the back of my mind.

I've just shoved the heavy black bag in the dumpster when the song in my ears transforms into a twinkling ringtone. I grin, letting the dumpster lid fall closed with a bang before digging into my pocket for my phone.

"Golden Girl," my best friend's gruff voice drawls.

"Hi, Mr. Dark and Twisty."

"You were supposed to FaceTime me ten minutes ago."

I head back inside, locking the back door as I grab a granola bar from the cabinet and go to my room. I'm relieved when I push open the door and see nothing out of place. Turns out Josh has a bit of decency left in him.

"Mm, that's right. I forgot about that agreement." I bite my lip to stifle my laugh.

"You forgot," he grunts. "Well, do it now."

I click my tongue. "You're bossy tonight. Everything okay?"

"I'm always bossy."

"Okay, okay. Calm down, I'll pull it up now." Flopping down on my bed, I adjust the pillows behind my back, pull the earbuds from my ears, and hold my phone out in front of me, flipping the call to video chat.

Noah answers instantly, and his face fills my screen. Well, actually, far more than just his face.

I clear my throat as his naked, tattooed chest comes proudly into view. He's sitting back on his bed, the wall behind him covered in torn-out pages of notebook paper with song lyrics filling them. His black hair falls to the middle of his thick neck and is messy like always. He has it pushed out of his face with a black-and-white bandana, and the black gem in his earlobe glimmers.

Deep brown eyes watch me intently, two thick brows creating deep slashes on his face. The lines of his jaw are harsh as he scowls, plump lips the prettiest shade of pink.

"Has anybody ever told you that you have pretty lips?" I ask, grinning.

"You're not distracting me with compliments you give me on a daily basis. Did you walk home alone again? Is that why you were late?"

I roll my eyes. "You're not in a very playful mood."

"Tinsley."

Amused at the way he growls my name, I keep pushing my luck. "Is now not as good as five minutes ago? I can always just hang up."

The camera moves closer to him as his eyes narrow. "Did you walk home alone again?"

"I'm fully capable of walking myself to and from places, thank you."

"I never said you weren't."

I squint at the wall behind him. "Did you cover your hotel room walls with notebook paper again?"

"The wallpaper was fucking hideous."

"Oh, you rebel, you." I waggle my brows. "You better clean up after yourself before Sparks reams your ass in the morning."

"We both know you're the only one who would dare try to *ream* my ass."

"And don't you forget it. But I hope you're not giving her a hard time. Poor girl has had to deal with you all on her own."

Noah's manager is a force to be reckoned with, but my best friend can be a scary guy. He's a shark, and despite how fierce she is, she's easy prey in his mind.

I'm still a bit unsure as to how she wound up with Noah Hutton, rock star and my Mr. Dark and Twisty, but one day, it was just us, and the next, a short, spikey-haired woman named Sparks was introducing herself as his manager. Due to the suddenness of Noah's music career, we all just kind of accepted her presence, knowing we didn't really have any other option at the ready.

She's still here a year later.

"If you're so worried about her, you should have come with us. I invited you."

I flip onto my side, scootching down the bed and holding my head up beneath my folded arm. Noah watches me intently as I get comfortable, his body perfectly still.

"If I wasn't training, I would have. You know how much I love watching you get sweaty onstage and sing until you lose your voice."

"I'm flying home tomorrow morning. Will you be home?"

"I'll be at the gym. Meet me there?"

"Yeah."

"Think you could bring me one of those smoothies I love?" I bat my eyelashes.

"What's in it for me?"

"My dazzling smile and a big hug?"

He tilts his head, eyes calculating. "Okay."

"Yes! You're the best." I yawn, scratching at the skin beneath the band of my sports bra. "As much as I missed your voice and handsome face, I need to change and go to bed. I'm exhausted."

He scowls, jaw tight. "Your dad is working you too hard."

"He's not. I'm training for my first real season in the pros. There's no level of training for something like this that doesn't feel like death. I'll take a break when I win my first professional title."

"And when you're on tour with me."

I blow out a long breath, far too tired to have this conversation again. "Are you asking me to come again or telling me?"

"Telling," he states, tone even, relaxed.

"Noah," I sigh. "I'm hanging up now."

"You can ignore this conversation as many times as you want to, but I'm not going on this fucking tour without you."

"And I'm not promising you anything right now. We don't even know the tour dates yet. Can we at least wait to discuss it until then?"

He tongues his cheek. "Fine."

"Don't make me hang up the phone in a bad mood."

"I bought you something today," he mutters, and I know this topic change is his way of apologizing. In over two decades of friendship, he hasn't changed.

"What is it?"

"You'll see tomorrow."

I snort a laugh. "How typical of you, you goddamn tease."

"You should be thanking me. Now you can go to sleep excited for tomorrow instead of pissed at me."

"This better be one hell of a gift."

"I know you well."

"That's the understatement of the century."

"Go to sleep, Tinsley. I'll see you tomorrow."

I blow a kiss at the camera, and we say good night. The moment his face disappears from my screen, a pit grows in my gut.

We used to go weeks, sometimes months, without seeing each other before he moved from his home in Vancouver to Toronto, but after having him here with me every day these past couple of years, it gets harder each time he leaves. I'm greedy, but when it comes to my best friend, I couldn't care less.

If he had any idea how much I hate turning down his offer to join him on tour, he would take it and run. So, for now, the only answer he'll get from me is a heavy maybe. That will have to do.

For both him and me.

2

Noah

SPARKS IS SPEAKING TO ME, HISSING SOMETHING ABOUT THE START date of the tour. I ignore her, picking at the bleeding skin beside my thumbnail instead. I've heard enough about this tour to last a lifetime.

Right now, my head is somewhere else. On someone else.

"For fuck's sake, just go in so I can go home. I've had enough of your psycho ass," Sparks snaps, waving a small hand in front of my face.

"Hands to yourself unless you want me to break your fingers," I threaten, still staring out the car window.

"Break my fingers and I'll break yours."

I turn my head and stare at her black-stained scowl. "Try it."

Curling my hand around the smoothie in the centre console, I open the door and then step outside. Sparks doesn't say anything before driving off.

There's a stupid fucking bell above the door of the gym, and it rattles when I step inside. I search through the mess of construction tape and power tools until I find her.

For the first time since I left a week ago, I feel my heart beat.

"Noah!" she shrieks from the makeshift boxing ring.

Her boxing gloves come flying off, hitting the floor. Wide,

silver eyes brighten, and a grin spreads her pink lips as she starts jogging toward me. Strides long and steady, she closes the distance quickly.

I don't let myself sway when she jumps into my arms. I've become too accustomed to her. To this move. Five times in the past two months, I've left her. Five times, she's come running to me the minute I've returned.

"Tinsley."

She buries her face in my neck. I cradle the back of her head and splay my hand over her back, the Styrofoam smoothie cup barely avoiding her skin.

"I missed you," she sighs.

"I'm here now. When are you done at this place?"

Stepping back, she adjusts the straps of her flimsy sports bra and sets her hands on her hips. My eyes strain with the effort it takes not to look her up and down.

"I have about another hour until lunch. Are you gonna stick around or go home and relax? I imagine you're tired."

"Is your father here?"

She snorts a laugh. "No. But you already knew that."

I hide my satisfaction well, having mastered that skill. Her father hates me. For whatever fucking reason. Probably because I'm the one person who could take her from him, and he knows it.

I've been trying it since we were teenagers. One of these days, I'll succeed.

"I'll stay."

She lights up, and I curl my fingers to keep from touching her smile. "Yay! Alright. Please try not to scare the construction workers off. They're on a roll today."

One glance at them shows that they're more interested in watching her nipples poke through her bra than working. A warning flashes in my eyes as I stare at them, and a beat later, they're back to work.

"Right. A roll," I grunt.

"Don't be an ass. I only have a few more minutes left before I can take a break. Wait for me?"

"Drink your smoothie first," I order when she takes a small sip and then tries to hand it back to me so she can get back on the mat. "All of it."

"Keep bossing me around and I'm going to dump it on your head instead."

I keep my mouth shut, and she wraps her lips around the straw, drinking the expensive-as-shit mango drink in large gulps. Satisfaction floods me.

After a handful of swallows, she shoves the cup against my chest with a sickly smile. "Happy, Dad?"

"Yes."

Her eye roll is all play, and *fuck* do I want to play with her. But that's not smart. Not acceptable.

I shove my hands into my pockets and rip the remaining skin off my thumb instead.

"I'm getting back to work. Thank you for the smoothie."

The familiar feeling of unhealthy desperation at the thought of her not being within touching distance shreds my insides as I ask, "Do you need a partner?"

NH)

"YOU'RE GOING easy on me. *Again*," Tinsley snaps, eyes brimming with frustration.

Her next punch hits my gut hard enough to seize my lungs. I grind my molars and shift my stance so she can't make contact with the same spot twice.

A growl slips from her lips when I don't hit back, choosing to wait for her next move instead. Her gloved hands thump against her hips as she seethes.

"I don't know why I bother sparring with you when you

refuse to hit me every single time! A punching bag would be a better partner than you."

I keep my expression blank. "By all means, go sulk."

Tinsley has been boxing since she was a preteen. I blame her father for that. But with years spent perfecting the ridiculously reckless sport, she's become the best of the best. To anyone besides myself, she has no tells. No way for anyone to guess what her next move might be.

I'm different.

I would go as far as to say I know her better than she knows herself. I've always been able to anticipate her next move.

The tightening of her pupils has me swooping to the right half a second before her arm shoots out. She spits air through her teeth when her glove slices through nothing but air.

"You're a dirty cheat, Noah Hutton."

I don't deny it. My eyes drift to the clock, knowing there's only a matter of time before her father wanders in. I want to be gone long before then. "If I hit you, can we leave?"

"Yes, fine. But I'm not going home until I've had a *proper* spar."

Nodding in an act of pained acceptance, I get into position with my arms in front of me. She grins, victory blazing in her gaze before morphing into something predatory.

"It will hurt," I say.

She rolls her eyes. "Only if you get past my defenses."

I never do. My next sequence of punches—the ones she taught me—are nothing in comparison to hers. She blocks them easily, as if batting away a fly. If I cared enough about this fucking sport, I would have been ashamed of myself.

Today, it doesn't take much to satisfy her in the ring. "Finally," she huffs.

Sweat clings to her everywhere. It's harder than it should be not to give myself what I want and gawk at her body. I shouldn't care about the consequences of dragging my eyes over her curves and finally satisfying the hunger that roars inside of me, and if it were anyone else, I wouldn't give a flying fuck. But Tinsley is not everyone else.

She's something entirely her own. An angel far too precious to be stared at by a demon in disguise. So, I yank my gloves off and walk away, glaring at the rubber floor.

"Do you know when the tour starts yet?" she calls behind me.

With slick fingers, I tug my shirt over my head and use it to wipe my face and neck. My scowl doesn't budge. "A little over three weeks."

A pause. "Oh. That's not long."

"You're coming with me."

"How can you possibly know that? I haven't gotten my schedule yet. Hunter only has a handful of fights set."

Right. Her new manager/trainer.

Frustration bubbles in my gut. This fucking argument again. "It will be fine."

My spine stiffens when I hear her walking toward me. She sighs, and a beat later, she touches my shoulder. I grind my jaw at the touch. It feels too good. Always does.

"I'll be with you whenever I can, okay? Plus, we don't want you to get too sick of me."

"If I was going to get sick of you, I would have already."

It's not as if I want to be this attached to her. I've never wanted that. Never asked for this dependency that I have for her. It just happened, as if the universe was punishing her for something she did in a past life by giving her to me. There's no other explanation.

She might be my salvation, but I'm her damnation.

I always will be.

"That's true, I guess," she murmurs, removing her hand from my back only to slip in front of me and grip my wrist when I start to tap the tops of my thighs. Her fingers can barely touch around the thickness of it, and a sick satisfaction tears through me.

I stare down at our hands, the heat from her touch seeping into my wrist bone. "I want you there. Don't make me go without you again." The words are gruff, my emotions far too exposed.

Tinsley blinks up at me, silver eyes shining with sympathy in a way I detest. "Let's just enjoy the next few weeks together, yeah?" she offers quickly, not missing my dwindling patience. "I've been missing seeing you play, and I assume you'll be playing around here while you're home, right?"

I nod. If I don't play, I'll be bored. And when I'm bored . . . I just don't fucking like it. Music empties my head. Quiets the world.

She smiles at me and drops my hand, taking a step back. "Perfect. I'm going to shower, and then we can go home? You brought my present, right?"

"Yeah. I'll meet you back here."

With a nod and a new pep in her step, she heads to the women's locker room, disappearing from my sight. I stand there for too long after, simply staring at the wall I know hides the showers as every instinct in me screams to follow her and make sure she's safe. It's possessive, ridiculous. *It's me.* I've never been able to shake the urge to protect her. Even when it comes to protecting her from myself.

It's why she didn't invite me to follow her to the shower. Why she never has and never will. The only danger to Tinsley is myself, yet I'll never be willing to eliminate the threat.

3

Tinsley

TO NO ONE'S SURPRISE, WE FIND JOSH PASSED OUT ON THE SOFA when we get home. The smell of sweat, booze, and something else that makes my stomach roll wafts off his clothes, filling the air. I crinkle my nose and leave Noah in the doorway, needing away from our roommate before I spew chunks.

I come to an abrupt halt when I hear a pained groan and then a thump. Spinning, I suck in a sharp breath as I take in the sight. Noah has yanked Josh off the couch, leaving him sprawled out on the floor, gasping in shock. With an eerie calmness, Noah crouches in front of him and cocks an eyebrow.

"Just leave him," I say on a tired exhale. The last thing I want after a day of training is to have to peel the two of them apart, even if Josh had it coming.

Plus, I want to put my new present away. The dainty golden chain sits heavily in the pocket of my shorts, and I'm itching to add it to the collection of jewelry Noah has gotten me over the years.

Noah lifts his eyes and looks at me, face blank. Then, he just shakes his head, glaring at Josh again.

"You smell like pussy and kush. I told you not to bring that shit here," he says, the words bitter and cold.

"I didn't bring it here. Do you see any pussy, asshole?" Josh smarts, one hand coming up to rub at his eyes. With a smirk, he adds, "And I don't mean Tinsley."

Noah's jaw pulses. His fingers curl where he has them holding his knees. "I would fucking hope you weren't referring to her as pussy."

I roll my eyes, huffing a breath. "Josh, can you just go shower, please. You really do stink. It's all over the living room."

He grunts and pushes to his feet, struggling far too much to gain balance. We really do need to get him out of our house and into one of his own. But would he even survive on his own at this rate? I'm sure having us here with him is the only thing keeping him from totally losing it.

"Thanks for the wake-up call, Mom and Dad," he mumbles. As he stalks off, he sways on his feet, knocking his shoulder into the wall before slipping into the bathroom.

"He needs to leave," Noah announces.

"I'll see if I can find someone who's looking for a roommate. It would be nice if you took him under your wing or something. Maybe he needs a friend."

"He's a mess. That's not my problem."

"Maybe not. But it would be the nice thing to do."

"I'm not nice," he states.

"No? You're nice to me."

He chuffs a dark laugh. "Am I?"

My brows pinch. "Yes. Do you no—"

A staccato rhythm of vibrations draws our attention to the coffee table, where he must have set his phone before tearing Josh off the couch. It bounces on the glass, and a lump grows in my throat when I see who's calling.

My eyes are drawn to Noah again, as if my body knows this will have upset him. The mix of anger and frustration in his expression as he glares daggers at the phone confirms that I was right.

"Are you going to answer that?" I ask softly.

"No."

"Do you want me to? Maybe it's important." His father doesn't usually call him unless it is, but I don't say that out loud.

He steels his expression, locking his emotions down again as he says, "Answer it or don't. But I'm not speaking to him." And then he's gone, storming out of view. I hear his bedroom door shut a few beats later, and then I'm rushing for the phone.

I manage to answer the call before it goes to voicemail. "Noah's phone."

"Oh! Hi, Tinsley," Ava, Noah's mother, replies, sounding disappointed.

I try to hide my surprise at hearing her voice and not Oakley's, clearing my throat before saying, "Hi, Ava. Noah's busy right now, but I can have him call you back. I just didn't want to miss a call that could be important."

"You don't have to lie to me, sweetheart. I knew calling from my husband's phone was a bad idea, but I left mine back at the hotel, and I was missing my boy. I'm sorry to bug you. I know you must be busy with all of your training."

Ava Hutton is one of the sweetest women I've ever known, and this is just one reason as to why I believe that. Despite how hard Noah fights to keep his distance from his father and, in turn, his family, Ava never stops trying to push through those barriers. Her son might not see her efforts, but I do, and I've been trying so damn hard to make him pay attention. I know how much it must hurt her not to have a close relationship with him.

"Hotel? What are you guys up to?" I ask, focusing on something other than why her son avoided her call.

"Oh, you know how Oakley is. He planned a surprise getaway for us. We arrived in Palm Springs yesterday."

My heart warms. "That's great. I'm sure you'll have a blast. Palm Springs is one of my favourite places. The beaches are to die for."

"That's exactly why we love it here. Maybe we'll buy a

vacation home someday. After we get our condo in Toronto, of course."

"You're buying a condo here?" I stammer, surprised. This is news to me. Does Noah know?

"We've been debating it. It's hard being so far away from Noah. It would make me so happy to get the chance to see him so often. To see the *both* of you."

My foot begins tapping on the floor as I start imagining how potentially bad their being here more often could be for Noah. But also, maybe . . . how good.

"You'll have to let us know when you start shopping around. I'd love to join you on the hunt. My mom too, I'm sure."

"That's an amazing idea! We can make a day of it," she gushes.

"Of course."

"Well, I guess I should go, then. Please let Noah know that I love him and want to talk to him soon. I miss him."

"He misses and loves you too, Ava."

My chest constricts when I hear her sniffle. "We'll talk soon, sweetheart."

We hang up, and I set the phone back down on the coffee table. Hopefully, I'll be able to convince her son to see her too. She deserves some time together. They both do.

NH)

"THIS IS ALL he has ready so far?" Noah barks, scowling at my laptop. The schedule my dad and Hunter sent me earlier is all but smirking back at him, goading a reaction out of him.

It's past midnight, but neither of us have ever been great sleepers. Late nights spent watching horror movies on our cheap, second-hand couch are sort of our thing.

"I'll be busier than last year. Don't worry," I tell him.

"That's not what I'm worried about."

"Then what is it?"

"I'll be on tour. *We* will be on tour. He should have all of your fights scheduled so we know what to prepare for."

The reminder isn't necessary. It's not like I could have forgotten.

Noah's sudden venture to fame has been a learning curve for all of us. I'm proud of him, *so proud*, but it's been hard. All of the time away, his busy schedule. It's a lot to get used to.

Noah didn't want this at first—I still don't know if he really does—but when a music producer as well-known and respected as Reggie Beckett offers you a shot, you don't turn him down. It was partially my influence, but mostly, this was all Adalyn's doing.

Noah's little sister is what she refers to as a social media influencer but what I call a goddamn badass. She's much more than a pretty face online. And she proved that more than ever when she used her contacts to get Reggie in touch with Noah, knowing just how deserving he was of having his musical talent shown to the world.

The rest is history.

I blow out a long breath. "Okay, that's true. But this is just how boxing is. It's why I haven't promised to go with you. The fights will be all over the place."

"Fuck's sake, just come. We can make it work. I'm tired of this argument."

I glare at him. "Stop making it into an argument, then. I'm not risking my career to follow you through yours. You're my best friend—why would you think that's the fair choice?"

He tangles his fingers in his hair and curls them, pulling on the strands. With his legs spread wide on the couch, eyes brimming with anger, and jaw clenched so damn tight, he screams danger. Hell, danger should be tattooed on his forehead. A warning sign to those who don't know him well. Luckily, I'm not one of those people.

Noah has never scared me.

I lean toward him and set my hand on his clenched thigh. The rips in his jeans have my fingers touching his bare skin as I toy with the loose denim strings. He stares straight ahead, completely silent, frozen solid.

"Being fair has never mattered to me," he says, each word more strained than the last.

"Well, it should now. Would you cancel the tour if I asked you to follow me around?"

"Yes."

I groan, tipping my head back and staring at the ceiling. "The difference is that I would never ask you to do that for me." When he goes to argue, I cut him off. "Look, it's only a few fights. There are what, twenty stops on the tour? I'll come to those. Every damn one."

"Twenty-one."

I exhale, exasperated. "Noah."

"Fine."

My brows meet my hairline as I stare at him, blinking slowly. "Fine?"

He shrugs, suddenly completely unbothered. It's unnerving how quickly his demeanour has changed.

"No more arguing about it?" I ask.

"It's done."

As he crosses his arms over his chest, I search his expression for any hint of what he's thinking, but it's no surprise when I find nothing. Not. A. Fucking. Thing.

"Perfect, then. So, we can finish our movie in peace."

He tips his chin in approval and focuses on the screen. And just like that, the conversation is over. Hopefully, for good.

4

Noah

THE BOARDROOM IS HOT. TOO FUCKING HOT.

Several pairs of eyes watch me. Curious, annoyed, worried. Scared. They still don't know what to make of me. I like it. Means they'll work harder to please me. With how much they make off my success, it's only fair.

Being in this room is tiresome. I don't know why I have to entertain these meetings when I have a manager. This should be her concern.

"There are twenty-one dates so far, including a couple of music festivals and opening acts, but once tickets are released in the next couple of days and we get a better idea of the demand in certain cities, we could always add additional ones. Is everyone in agreement?" the owner and CEO of Swift Edge Productions, Garrison Beckett, asks the room of stuffy execs.

They make sounds of agreement. But would they tell him the truth if they thought otherwise? Does a single one of these people have the nerve to disagree with their boss?

I stretch my legs out in front of me and watch the board at the front of the room change to show a list of dates and corresponding cities. With narrowing eyes, I search through them all, checking that Garrison didn't go back on his word.

Approval worms through me when I confirm that he didn't. Every fight Tinsley showed me on her schedule last week lines up with a show. I'll have Hunter match the rest of them.

Garrison adjusts the cuff of his black button-down and nods. "Great. A tour on the smaller side will be a good first step. Usually, we like to have this information released to the public at an earlier time, but circumstances wouldn't allow for that this time. We got lucky with the venues having such open availability." The last two statements are spoken directly to me, but I meet his hard stare with one of my own. I'm not sorry for demanding he bend to my will.

It was either work the dates for me or risk me not performing. We both know I'm not the one scared of losing this partnership.

"Has all of this information been sent to my inbox?" Sparks asks beside me.

Garrison looks to her, the annoyance he feels toward her way too obvious. He doesn't bother hiding it. His lack of respect for her annoys me.

It's because she's young and inexperienced in this industry. But so am I. What she lacks in experience, she makes up for in wit and nerve. The business suits and lined pockets don't intimidate her.

"Yes. It should be there already." He looks around the room again. "Any questions regarding these dates?"

I stifle a smirk when Sparks speaks up again. "Noah will have his own bus, correct?"

"We already discussed him sharing the bus with the band," Garrison replies stiffly.

"And you know he needs his own."

"Sharing would not work, Garrison," I add in support.

Annoyance flares in his odd-coloured eyes. Are they brown or green? They look like a shitty swamp.

"The tour isn't big enough in capacity to have two separate

buses for you and the band. That is something I will not budge on."

For now.

"Drop it, Sparks," I mutter under my breath when she goes to argue.

She looks at me, cocking a brow as if to ask if I'm sure. I nod.

"Right. We'll circle back," she tells Garrison.

He brushes her off and sets his hands on his hips. He's a tall, skinny guy bursting with arrogance. Maybe I should call him String Bean from now on. He'd hate that. It might take him down a few pegs.

"If nobody has any further questions, we can move on to—"

I zone out. The logistics of this tour don't matter to me. Getting paid for playing the music that I love isn't completely worth the screaming people and lack of personal space, but the look on Tinsley's face every time she watches me perform is. I do this for her, but she doesn't know that. I'm unsure what she thinks is the reason behind why I agreed to sign my life away to this company or why I continue to put myself in uncomfortable positions if not for her.

One day, she'll figure it out. She's too smart not to. The question is whether she will approve or not. Most likely not.

My mind slips to the bus issue. There's no way I'm allowing her to share a bus with the band. They're loud, pushy sex addicts. The alcohol and drugs they'll find on tour have no place in her living quarters. I'd kill the first one of them who stumbled onto the bus drunk or high. Does Garrison really want a death on his conscience?

"Noah."

I blink, my eyes so dry they're burning. Sparks is in front of me, thick folders in her hands. She rolls her eyes as I come back to the present.

"Meeting is done. Reggie is waiting for you at the studio," she says.

I stand, stretching out my back before glancing around the

room. It's emptied out. Garrison is lingering in the doorway, checking his watch impatiently.

"Let's go," I mutter.

Sparks shuffles ahead of me, leading the way. I grow a bit more respect for her when she glares at Garrison as we walk past him. He huffs a disbelieving laugh, shutting the door behind us.

When he clears his throat, Sparks and I stop, waiting for whatever he wants to say.

"We'll talk later, Noah. Everything needs to be finalized before you leave. I don't do disorganization. Especially not on tour."

The condescending tone of his voice grates on my nerves. "Fine," I force out through gritted teeth.

"Okay," he repeats. "Have a great rest of the day."

I don't reply before continuing down the hall. That's Sparks' job.

NH)

I NEVER WANTED A BAND. Obviously, I needed one, but that didn't change the fact that having a group of people I did not know, or *want* to know, be up in my business is annoying as fuck. Bringing more people into my life sounded like torture. A punishment. Over the past couple of months, it's proven to be just that.

It started with Josh and his incompetence and childish behaviour. He was hardly my bass guitarist for two weeks before I ordered Sparks to replace him. She said no, and I haven't been able to shake that annoying fucker since. He's living in my house, for fuck's sake.

Then there's Justice on drums and Dagger on electric guitar. They're easier to stand than Josh, but that's not saying much. Justice is always late for rehearsal because he's raising his daughter on his own, but he's quiet. Dagger has an ego big enough to carry him to the solo career he's been pining for. He won't admit it to us, but he wants what I have. Good luck to him.

The moment I enter the studio, I find Dagger already in the sound booth, tuning his guitar. The way he pets the thing feels intimate. I most likely look the same when I have my guitar in my hands.

My fingers curl in my pockets as I'm reminded of the lack of said guitar. I don't need it when we're recording, according to Reggie. *That's why we have the band,* he tells me every time I try to sneak it in. I don't see why I can't take Dagger's place. I'm a better player than him, anyway.

The grey-haired man hunched over the soundboard wearing a tiger-striped fedora is Reggie himself. He's never not been the first one to the studio on recording days.

"Why am I here, Reggie? Thought I was done with my part."

My presence doesn't surprise him. He glances at me over his shoulder and grins. "Can't I just wanna see you?"

"You enjoy my company that much?" I deadpan.

His laugh is rough. If I didn't know just how much the man laughed, I would have thought he never did. "It's hard to find someone as cheerful as you, son."

"I bet."

He laughs again and pushes out the chair beside him with his foot. "Take a seat."

"Tell me why I'm here first."

"Always so damn serious. I just want to play something for you."

"Fine." I sit in the chair, letting it hug my back. Crossing my ankles, I look at him expectantly.

He leans across the board and uses the intercom to tell Dagger to wait another minute before working his fingers across the buttons again with startling expertise. A heavy beat fills the room, followed by my voice.

I fall into the new song, memorizing it. Each note, beat, and breath. It swirls in my soul, leaving behind a fingerprint. Approval burns through me, lighting me up.

"It's good," I mutter, my fingers dancing on the arms of the chair in time with the beat. I imagine how it would feel to play this live, with my guitar in my hands, the strings plucking at my fingertips as the crowd roars. It's electric. The best feeling.

"Glad you think so. I want Garrison to add it to the set list."

I nod. "Good."

"Got a name yet?"

"No."

He pats my shoulder, and the song fades away. "You will. Let me know as soon as you do, and I'll send over the finished track."

"Yeah. Why is Dagger here?"

He's staring at us from behind the glass, his scowl deep, thick with jealousy. I smirk, tilting my head. His grip tightens on his guitar, fingertips white.

"There were a few beats I needed him to re-record." Reggie speaks into the speaker at Dagger. "Start right after the second verse, slower this time."

Dagger tips his chin in a barely there nod before relaxing, zoning into the music. His buzzed hair has started to grow out again, along with his beard. It's rough-looking, in an *I don't care way*. It's all an act, though. I'm sure of it.

"Did you see Josh this morning? He was supposed to be here two hours ago," Reggie says.

"No."

He was either gone or asleep when I left. His door was shut, and I wasn't going to knock to find out if he was home. He's not my responsibility.

"I worry about him."

"You worry about everyone. You should stop that," I mutter.

He looks at me, and the sympathy in his stare churns my stomach. I stiffen, taking a mental step back from him as the darkness inside of me tries to take hold.

"It's not a bad thing to worry about those in your life," he tells me softly. I hate that tone of voice.

There's no reason for anyone to feel sorry for me. To look at me with this disgusting sympathy. I chose to be this way. While most people seem to have convinced themselves there's something wrong with me, that isn't the entire story. I want to be like this. Want to not care about anyone. Why would I? I've already given Tinsley that power over me. My small reserve of care has been drained.

I've never hidden that from anyone. It's their fault if they're disappointed when they can't find anything left in me to take for themselves.

"Don't," I spit.

He blinks, feigning innocence. "Don't what?"

"Treat me like I'm broken. I get enough of that from my father."

"What do you mean?"

I immediately know I've made a misstep. That I've opened a door I should have kept locked.

With a twist of my body, I'm out of the chair and halfway to the door before he says, "You don't have to leave, Noah. I'm sorry, I was out of line."

"Get the song on the set list, Reggie," I order coolly, and then I'm out the door.

If I wanted to be counselled, I would have stayed with one of the five therapists my dad handed me to when I was a kid. All I want now is to see my golden girl. She's the only one who can calm the monster inside of me before he takes over.

5

Noah

BRADEN IS IN THE RING WITH TINSLEY WHEN I GET TO THE GYM. HE towers over her, pads on his waiting hands as he yells sequences of numbers in her direction. His daughter punches and swings her body every which way in time with his commands, eyes narrowed with concentration.

This is Tinsley in her purest form. Fierce, attention-grabbing, fearless. Each sharp breath pushed from her lips is perfectly timed, the rise and fall of her shoulders steady. She appears almost superhuman.

I cross my arms and watch them dance, my gaze never straying from Tinsley. Despite the gnawing feeling of jealousy in my gut at her training with someone who is not me, I don't step in. Don't make my presence known. Not when she's in her zone.

Despite his age, her father keeps up with her just fine. It's annoying as fuck because I would have loved to witness him get his ass beat by his daughter. I'm sure he's still praying for the day he gets to see her beat my ass too. The dislike between us is just too thick, too everlasting, to want much else.

I don't know when it began for him. The moment I was born or at the same time my father grew to hate me. There's no doubt that my dad played a part regardless. They've been friends for decades. I assume there aren't many more secrets between them than there are between my mom and Sierra, Tinsley's mother.

Not that any of that matters. The only approval I've ever wanted is Tinsley's.

"Good! Take a break and drink some water," Braden demands, patting Tinsley on the shoulder.

Tiny sets her hands on her hips and smiles, nodding once before he slips between the ropes and hops off the training platform. Her posture is slightly hunched as she catches her breath. My chest grows tight the moment she notices I'm here. Her silver eyes meet mine, coming to life as her smile grows into a bright grin.

"Hey!" she calls, waving me toward her. Unluckily for me, Braden follows her stare to find me waiting. He scowls, jaw tightening.

With my arms still folded across my chest, I stroll toward them, stopping when I can grip the ropes, leaning my weight on them. I look at Tinsley, aware that even without smiling at her, she can tell how relieved I am to see her.

"Hey."

"Noah," Braden grunts, hovering in the same spot as if he still doesn't trust me alone with his daughter. At least he has good common sense.

If it weren't for Tiny watching, I would have ignored him completely. But, not wanting to upset her, I glance at him and offer a weak "Braden."

"Phew, that's a lot of testosterone in the air. It reeks," Tinsley huffs.

Braden laughs under his breath. "Sorry, sweetheart. I'm going to make my rounds while you break." He glares at me with a silent warning.

"Sounds good, Dad."

I watch him finally walk away toward the pair of guys sparring on the training mats. Once he's out of earshot, I tighten my hold on the ropes and pull myself up and through them. It's alarming how beautiful Tinsley is from afar, but up close, she's devastatingly so. I clench my fingers before shoving them into the pockets of my jeans. Not the time to touch her. *Not my right.*

"What have you been up to this morning? Been busy?" she asks.

Instead of answering her right away, I search the platform for her water bottle and then silently pick it up. Her smile is soft when I hand it over.

"Thank you."

I make a rough noise in the back of my throat. "Had a meeting with the label today. The tour dates are set."

She sucks in a breath. "And?"

"You're coming with me." Simple as that.

"We just talked about this," she sighs, sounding exhausted. It hurts me to see her that way. I don't like it.

I take a stilted step toward her before stopping, rolling my jaw as I become frustrated with my lack of control. "I'm not demanding it of you again. I'm telling you that you can come. The dates work."

She gapes up at me. "This isn't some type of sick joke?"

"No."

A squeal, and then she's in my arms, wrapped around me like a koala. I hold her up with a tight grip on her thighs, savoring the feel of her flush against my front and her warm skin beneath my fingertips. Swallowing a groan, I watch her grin from ear to ear with such a pure happiness that I almost join her in the act.

She truly wanted to come with me. It wasn't obligation but a genuine necessity the way it is for me. How? I'll never be able to comprehend it.

"This doesn't look like much of a break," Braden barks. Tinsley stiffens in my arms as if suddenly remembering where we are before jumping down despite the way I tighten my grip. With a glare in his direction, I reluctantly let Tinsley step away from me.

She smiles innocently at her father. "Sorry."

"What has you so excited?" he asks.

I stand straighter. "She's coming on tour with me."

"How?"

"Our schedules are aligned. It's a damn miracle," Tiny sighs, grinning again.

Braden does the opposite. His frown is so deep it might become permanent. His displeasure is too satisfying.

"That's great, sweetheart." His petty attempt at sounding supportive isn't bought by anyone, especially his daughter.

She's far too sympathetic when it comes to those she cares about. It's her greatest weakness and one I've tried to wean her away from. I've been unsuccessful thus far.

As she moves toward Braden, I fight to keep my face blank. Watching her wrap her arms around him in a hug I know is warm and reassuring gnaws at me.

"Don't be sad. I'll make sure Easton is on his best behaviour for you and Mom," she says lightly.

He wraps her up in his arms and kisses the top of her head. Our eyes meet when he sets his chin on her crown and levels a glare in my direction. It becomes a competition to see who will look away first, neither of us wanting to lose. But once Tinsley starts to squirm out of his grip, his glare disappears, and we both look toward her instead.

"You could always come with us. I don't have all the details yet, but I'm sure we could make room for you on fight nights," she offers.

Unease ripples through me. *Not a fucking chance.*

Braden doesn't seem as displeased with the idea as I'd hoped. "We'll talk about it. Hunter and I have a meeting set for tomorrow, so I'm sure he'll fill me in."

The final words have a hint of bitterness to them that most likely has nothing to do with Hunter but with the news that, despite the odds, I've managed to make our schedules work.

Braden's lack of involvement wasn't personal on my part. It was calculated.

He would have tried to keep her from me.

"Alright," Tiny says. After a swift tug of her ponytail, she stretches her neck and starts to bounce in place. "Should we get back to work? You gonna join us, Noah?"

Yes. "No. I'm going home. Just wanted to tell you the news."

The corners of her mouth fall as she nods. "I'll see you at home, then?"

"Yeah."

I should go now, but my shoes are full of lead. It's the fucking string between us—that goddamn *tether*—that keeps me so attached to her. Some would call it love, but labelling it something so far beneath what it truly is is insulting. There's no term to describe what Tinsley is to me, and I've long accepted that.

A fist grips the organ behind my ribs so hard I swallow to hide a grimace. She's waiting, watching me like she wants to tell me to stay but knows better. Braden clears his throat, and that's all it takes. I spin on my heels, forcing myself not to look back as I leave.

NH)

Tinsley

NOAH STORMS out of the gym, and I know I've done a terrible job of hiding my disappointment when Dad gives me a sympathetic pat on the back. It's unfair to expect him to stay, but I won't pretend I don't want him to.

"Ready to go again?" he asks.

"Yep." I toss my water bottle on the mats and pull my gloves back on. He's glaring at the entrance of the gym when I look up again. "You have a terrible poker face, you know?"

He blinks innocently. "What?"

"He's my best friend."

"I'm aware of that, T."

"You need to be nicer to him. He gets enough hassle from Oakley. Don't add to that. Please."

Noah would pop a blood vessel if he knew I was pleading on his behalf to my dad, but when is enough *truly* enough? He moved here for me, away from all of his family and friends. My small family is all I have to offer him, and I don't want them to create a rift between us.

While I may not see Noah in the way I sometimes suspect he may see me, I wouldn't survive in any form of reality without him. It's always been this way between us. One breathing life into the other. It's unusual and hard to believe, but it's us.

The moment we met, it was like my soul recognized his. As if old friends were being reacquainted after decades apart. We're soulmates in its truest form, which is why I choose not to think too much about the looks Noah gives me when he thinks I'm not paying attention. He does a good job of keeping the feelings I suspect he has hidden from me, but I know him far too well.

It's not love. With Noah, I don't think it ever would be. He's not programmed that way. It's obsession and adoration. A need to protect me and a will to do anything to make that happen. It works with the way we are now. Best friends. But in a romantic sense? It would suffocate me. The part of my heart that pleads for a chance at a fairy-tale type of love would shatter. I've been battling the guilt that comes with thinking this way for a long time now, and it hasn't gotten any easier. I'm beginning to doubt if it ever will. For now, I'll just keep giving him what I can. It's been enough so far.

The shuffle of Dad's feet on the mats pulls me from my thoughts. I curl my fingers in my gloves and glance his way. He's frowning.

"Noah's relationship with Oakley is tough. I'm sorry I've added to that. I don't ever want to upset you."

I shrug. "It's not me you need to apologize to. Just stop with all the glaring and goading. If you keep pushing him, he will snap. I won't let you use that against him." *And if that were the case, it's Noah's side I'd be taking,* I want to add.

"Okay," he agrees with a sigh. "Alright."

Relief ripples through me. "Alright. Now, the quicker we get back to work, the sooner I get to go home. Hit me, Pops."

6

Tinsley

SITTING BESIDE ME ON THE COUCH, HUNTER PASSES ME HIS PHONE TO show me the final list of fight dates and correlating locations. The boxing match on the television provides comforting background noise as I stare at the screen in silence, my lips rolling. My nerves are making me uneasy.

It's my first season not in the amateur boxing league, and I have a lot to prove—to myself and everyone who's supported me since my earliest days. My father especially. I've worked incredibly hard for this opportunity, and getting to experience it alongside my best friend feels too good to be true. Like I should be preparing for the other shoe to drop. It's turned me into a nervous mess.

"Everything look good? I've left space for challenges and any fights required from the league, but for now, this is the final list," Hunter says, the rough tone of his voice a lot less terrifying than it was the first time I heard it.

Hunter Ramirez is one of the best. As a two-time heavyweight champion in the World Boxing Association, he knows the ins and outs of this sport. Retiring only two years ago, he decided to branch out into management, and with my father's contacts, we somehow wrangled him into working for me and the gym part-time. He may be more standoffish than some of the other managers we spoke to, but he gets the job done. I trust him to further my career, and that's a huge deal for me.

He leans over my shoulder and huffs, "Is your silence a good or bad thing?"

"Good. Very good."

A jerky nod. "Great." He takes the phone and shoves it between his thighs. "We'll start easy and work our way up. I don't want to push you too hard. Not when it comes to the other women in your weight class. Most of them have been doing this much longer than you have."

"You make me sound inexperienced. I lost two fights last year," I mutter stubbornly.

"Two fights in a much lower league."

"Fair enough."

"I don't say it as an insult, Tinsley. If I didn't think you were good, I wouldn't have agreed to represent you."

I smile softly, glancing at him. It's the first compliment he's given me, and by the harsh expression on his wide-set face, it feels completely out of place. The guy is intimidating as fuck, with his dark eyes and jaw that's in a constant state of tension, but maybe that's why I like him. His demeanour feels right at home with me and my family of misfits.

Noah doesn't hate him either, which is a total bonus.

"Thanks, Hunter," I say.

He bristles at the thanks before changing the subject. "I'll email you the list tonight."

"Great. You're a gem."

Appearing almost offended at the compliment, he awkwardly pats his thighs and hops off the couch. I stifle a laugh as he makes a beeline for the door.

"See you later! Don't forget about the meeting with my dad!" I shout when he opens the door and goes to leave.

A backward glance is all I get before he's gone. I blow out a breath and grab a water from the kitchen. The cool bottle feels soothing against my swollen, sore palms. Hours with my hands in wraps and gloves take their toll, but I wouldn't change the pain for anything.

The soft plucking of guitar strings slips beneath Noah's bedroom door, and my feet move on their own, taking me there. I nudge the door open and lean against the frame, attempting to keep my presence unknown for as long as possible.

Black hair falling over his face, he leans against his headboard, head dipped toward the black guitar in his hands. Longer fingers that I've seen bleed from the constant plucking of those strings move across the wooden neck in a caress so gentle it seems unnatural. He plays a tune I've never heard before, and my curiosity sparks. It's soft, sad, almost angry in the most beautiful way.

I lean my head against the doorframe and watch, happiness warming my blood. It's in these moments that I see a part of Noah he doesn't show the rest of the world. The gentle, calm part of him that lives in his music.

His lips part and move to form silent words as he keeps his eyes closed, lashes fluttering. It's selfish to want to hear the words he's mouthing, but I've always been selfish when it comes to both Noah and his music.

Suddenly, he lifts his eyelids and looks at me, the soft notes still filling the room. "You could have come in."

"I know," I whisper.

"Come here."

I push off the wall and sit on the edge of the bed. Long legs covered in dark denim drape down the mattress, resting behind me. I place my hands between his calves and lean back, turning to look at him more clearly. He stops tugging at the strings and arches a brow.

"Up here, Golden Girl," he demands.

My lips tug at the corners as I shake my head. Is it bad that it makes me happy knowing he wants me as close as possible?

"I'm good here. Your bed is too damn small for us both to fit that way."

"We have before."

"That was when you weren't so damn big." Back when he didn't have wide shoulders and thick, muscled arms.

"You should blame that on my trainer."

I snort a laugh. "Fine. As punishment, she'll stay seated where she is." His dark scowl makes me laugh harder. "If you keep scowling like that, your mouth will stay like that forever. Move over, rock star. I swear if you end up pushing me off the bed, you'll regret it."

He barely moves an inch, and I can't find it in myself to push him on it. With little trouble, I maneuver myself so I'm leaning back against his headboard, my legs crossed at the ankles, running alongside his.

"So, you gonna tell me what song you were playing?" I ask softly.

He tucks his chin to his chest and stares down at the guitar, beginning to play again, just a tease of the melody I heard. "Not yet."

"You've never kept a song from me before."

The corner of his mouth tries to lift, but he fights to keep a straight face. "That bothers you?"

"Of course it does," I admit, unafraid of him knowing how I feel.

"Be patient. I'll tell you about it soon."

"Soon," I scoff. "How soon?"

He clicks his tongue to the roof of his mouth. "That's right. You've never been a patient girl."

I'm surprised to find my cheeks flushing at the comment, from either embarrassment or how . . . *sexual* that comment sounded. *Get a grip.* I swallow, scolding myself for even letting myself go there. But it's impossible never to think that way when your best friend is Noah Hutton, so I cut myself some slack. I'm only human.

"I'm just going to keep bugging you about it until you give it up. We're not supposed to keep secrets from one another." I pout.

"It's not a secret if I'm planning to tell you later."

"Uh, yes it is. Who taught you how to keep secrets, because they did a terrible job."

His laugh is deep, dark. Angry. "I can tell you who never taught me a damn thing."

Oakley. I swallow again, this time finding my throat clenched tight. The mood shifts, taking a turn for the worse. "Have you called your mom back? She sounded like she really wanted to talk to you."

He stiffens, suddenly tense, full of so much resentment and hurt. I want nothing more than to be able to take some of his pain away. To fix what his family let break between them.

I exhale slowly while covering the fingers stroking the strings with my own, squeezing his hand. Leaning my cheek to his shoulder, I stare down at our hands, at how different they are. Noah's fingertips are tough, calloused and worn. The nails are bitten, the skin around them ripped and sore. My heart tugs at the pain he brings himself, the scars on the outside only a brief preview of what lies inside.

The scabs and bruises on my knuckles are the only scars I have. Both inside and out. It's unfair. I would have done anything to give Noah the life I had growing up, the unwavering understanding I received.

He shouldn't have struggled the way he did. His family isn't evil. They love him in their own way and have always wanted the best for him. I think, maybe, that's where they went wrong. They tried too hard to control him, to the point they pushed him away. Noah is a wild horse, and they tried to pen him up the way they had his siblings. But what worked for Maddox and Adalyn didn't work for him. He got spooked, and they lost him. Now . . . now he's too far gone, been alone in the wild for too long to ever come back to them.

Noah's voice cuts through the silence, the sound of it hoarse. "If I call, she'll ask to see me."

"Maybe not."

"You know better than to believe otherwise."

I sigh, rubbing my cheek on his bicep as I bring our hands to my chest, keeping them close. "She's your mother. And she loves you so much. Would seeing her be such a bad thing? If not before we leave, then once we're in Vancouver. Your show there is the night before my fight. There's no reason we couldn't stop in and say hello."

He links our fingers and grips them tight, as if finding strength in the embrace. His throat bobs before he mutters, "Fine. When we're in Vancouver. But I need you there with me."

"I said *we*, didn't I?" I tease, attempting to lighten the mood.

He nods and bangs the back of his head to the headboard, staring at the ceiling. His next words are strained, as if he isn't sure if he wants to actually speak them.

"I'll play you the song tonight if you give it a name."

Giddy excitement rushes through me. "Really?"

"It needs a name before I can release it. I have nothing. Been thinking about it for days."

He pulls his hand from mine and starts to play the song from the beginning, I stay tucked into his side and let the music flow through me. I shut my eyes and allow the notes to take me somewhere special, a place only he and I know.

We stay like this for hours, him finishing the song only to start it over and over again when I keep quiet, not ready for him to stop. By the time sleep comes for me, not only do I have a possible title for the song, but another piece of him has dug its way into my soul.

I dream of the soft, sad notes and the hint of his voice whispering words that I know I won't remember in the morning.

7

Tinsley

MY WORLD FEELS COMPLETELY AT PEACE AS I ACCEPT MY MOM'S HUG and breathe in her soft perfume. She sighs into my hair and rubs her hand up and down my back, her arms growing tighter around me with each passing second.

"Oh, I'm going to miss you so much," she breathes.

I give her a squeeze. "I'm going to miss you too. But I'm not leaving yet. Can we please save the tears for when I do?"

Reluctantly, she nods, dragging her hand up my back once more before pulling back, holding me in front of her by my arms. We're not big criers in my family, but when it comes to each other, we could fill buckets with our tears. I've already begun to prepare myself for our goodbye.

Mom's silver eyes, the same colour as mine, are glistening with unshed tears that twinkle in the foyer light. The sight is enough to make my nose burn and eyelids blink profusely.

"Knock it off," I chastise her, covering her hands and squeezing her fingers.

"Oh, boy. Look at what you've started, little fighter." Dad enters with a lingering kiss to Mom's cheek. He's still wearing his gym clothes, the Knockout Fitness logo a deep red on the corner of his T-shirt. He must have left work early to get home for dinner, which isn't an unusual thing for him. Not on family dinner nights.

"Hello, darling daughter. Long time no see," he teases before he's grinning at me and tugging me into a quick but comforting hug. "If the both of you start crying already, I'll be next, and I have a reputation to uphold, yeah?"

"That's right, how could I have been so selfish?" I ask.

"Self-awareness is the first step to recovery," he tosses back as we break apart and he steps behind Mom, wrapping his arms around her from behind.

Mom tilts her head back to greet him with a kiss, and he throws a hand in my face, blocking my view of them just before I hear an exaggerated smooching noise. I roll my eyes, shaking my head while glancing behind them at where my brother and Noah stand in the living room. My chest warms as I watch Easton take a quick peek up at Noah and say something to him that I wish I could hear. Noah has his arms folded across his chest, his posture stiff—uncomfortable—but not closed off. Not to Easton, at least.

I don't know why, but Noah has let Easton in, at least enough to allow them to be acquaintances, if not slight friends. It was only a few years ago, around the time my brother turned eighteen, that I started to notice the change between them. The sudden conversations they grew to have had me frozen in place the first time I stumbled upon one. There were no sarcastic, harsh words shared but ones of understanding.

Easton has always been more like Noah than me. He's shy and stone walled, the furthest thing from a people person. Their friendship makes sense, but knowing Noah the way I do . . . I just never saw it coming.

My feet move before I tell them to. The two men glance my way at the same time, their conversation coming to a halt. Easton doesn't look at me long before he's pulling his phone out and beginning to type, completely unimpressed with my interruption, but Noah, he doesn't look away. He holds my stare, even once we're an arm's length apart.

"What were you two talking about over here?" I ask, trying my best to sweeten Noah up with a smile.

His biceps flex as he shoves his hands into his pockets. "Can't say."

"What's for dinner?" Easton changes the subject, still not looking up from his phone. It's his number one trick for avoiding conversations with people. He's been doing it since he was old enough to have a phone.

"You've been home all day; you tell me."

"You're sassy today," he mutters.

"Sassy *and* hangry if Mom and Dad don't stop making out long enough to feed us."

That draws my brother's attention. He looks up at me, a slight grimace making his lips turn downward. "Try still living with them. They get worse as they get older."

"You could always move out," Dad throws over his shoulder. He's separated from Mom now, and I catch the embarrassed flush to her cheeks as she shakes her head at the two of them.

"Don't be pushing our son out of here too soon. I'm not ready for my nest to be birdless just yet," she scolds Dad.

"Why would he leave when he could have Mommy and Daddy still do his laundry and clean his bathroom?" I ask with a smirk. Sibling bickering has always been one of my favourite pastimes. Especially because it's far too easy to rile my brother.

Easton glares at me, finally putting that phone back into his pocket. "I do my own laundry, jackass."

"But Mom still cleans your bathroom? Does she fold your tighty-whities too? I hope you at least wash your own crusty socks."

Humour sparks in his stare, and I hear Noah scoff a rough laugh. "You're hilarious."

"Thank you, little bro."

"Can we not speak of your brother's socks, Tiny?" Mom pleads, nose wrinkled.

"He started it," I defend myself.

"I did not," he barks.

"Did so."

"Guys. You're both adults now, remember?" Mom groans, hands on her hips.

Dad chuckles, starting to usher all of us toward the dining room. "Let's eat, guys."

"Finally," I groan. Easton flicks the back of my ear and smirks, pushing my shoulder to step in front of me. I ignore him and, with a quick glance behind me, flash an encouraging smile at my best friend.

He's been here a million times, has come to a million family dinners, but still obviously feels uncomfortable around all of us. It's written in every tight muscle and harsh line on his face. I hate it. This should feel like a second home to him, my family his.

I linger behind the others and wrap my arm around his waist, leaning against him as we walk. "Are you going to tell me what you and my brother were talking about now?"

"He was asking about you. Wanted to make sure you would be taken care of while we're gone."

A smile grows on my face, despite my damn stubbornness at the belief I can take care of myself. "I don't need to be taken care of. You'll be busy, anyway. I'm not your responsibility."

It's the first time since learning of Noah's tour that I've allowed myself to speak my selfish vulnerabilities. I'm so used to getting his full attention for so long that I feel jealous of those he will begin to share his time with. Will he find someone he gets along with just as well as me? Will he become too busy to spend time with me?

I hate that I've thought this way, but at the same time, it feels impossible not to. For over two decades, it's only been us.

He frowns, looking down at me with a slight glare. "Not my responsibility," he echoes, the words deep and growly.

"You know what I meant, Noah."

"No, I don't."

"Don't make me embarrass myself further."

We've stopped walking now, stalled beneath the archway separating the living room from the rest of the house. The hum of voices coming from the dining room tells me everyone must be waiting for us, but it's just a passing thought.

Noah turns to me and wraps his fingers around my wrist. With a tug, he brings me crashing toward him. In an attempt to steady myself, my hands come up in front of me and push into his chest, probably harder than needed. He rocks back on his heels, not expecting me to lean into him, but keeps his grip on me tight as he steadies himself. It's not tight enough to hurt. More like a reminder that he's there, that he's holding me in place.

"What do you need from me?" he asks. The words are strained yet surprisingly soft.

"I don't know."

"Don't lie to me. Tell me and I'll do it."

I swallow, suddenly incredibly unsure about what I'm feeling. What *do* I need from him? A promise that he won't forget about me once he becomes a proper rock star? The idea of asking that of him seems pathetic.

Shuffling my feet, I meet his eyes, finding them dark and intense, the subtle rage that's brewing inside him clear. I drop my hands from his chest and exhale slowly, my wrist still locked in his grasp.

"Just promise me that nothing will change between us. That at the end of the tour, we'll still be best friends," I whisper, hating how exposed I feel.

A crease grows between Noah's brows as he furrows them, his pink lips curling into an even deeper frown. I flick my eyes back and forth between his, trying to decode the new emotion growing in them, but he blinks too soon, and it disappears, gone just as quick as it came.

His thumb presses to the underside of my wrist bone, keeping it over my pulse point, as if reassuring himself it's still thumping. "I will never let you go, Tinsley. *Never*."

His confident words settle something inside of me while also leaving a lingering feeling of something unnerving at the same time.

"Okay," I breathe.

He releases me then, slipping the fingers that were just wrapped around my wrist through his hair and leaving my skin cold. His black waves aren't held back by a bandana today, and I find myself liking the lack of one more and more each day. He has nice hair, smooth and shiny, and it feels cruel to hide it behind a bandana.

Lips smoothing into a line, he slides his hands into his pockets and asks, "Better?"

I attempt a smile. "Yeah. Thank you."

He looks unconvinced. "Are you lying again?"

"Tinsley! For someone who hangry, you're taking your damn time!" Easton shouts.

I huff a laugh and squeeze Noah's forearm. "Come on, before they come out here and drag us in."

I'm relieved when he doesn't fight me on it, despite not believing me. In all honesty, no words could make me feel better. I won't believe that we'll survive this next chapter of our lives until it's here. Actions have always meant more to me than words, and that's never been truer than right now.

But I can't help myself from going back to his previous words and wondering if they were a promise . . . or a threat.

8

Noah

AFTER DINNER, BARELY RESTRAINED ANGER MAKES PAIN BLOOM between my brows. Anger at myself and my failure to ensure Tinsley never had reason to doubt me. It's my job to keep her happy. As happy as I can. My chest aches, something rattling from within the deep pit of misery where my soul rests. It's painful, nauseating. My punishment.

Tingles break out on the back of my neck from where I know she watches me from behind the window with innocent, round eyes. I've been outside for a while, no longer able to sit at the table with her and her family while this eats at me. I'm alone with my self-hatred instead. A stupid move, considering my thumbs are nothing more than raw, bloody skin from how long I've been picking at them.

The burn doesn't register any longer. I'm too numb to anything besides this anger and frustration. It's been like this for as long as I can remember. The aftermath of disappointing Tinsley has always been so crippling I can hardly breathe. I brought it up to the first of my therapists, back when I was a child. He had stared at me with a curious glint in his eyes, like I was a puzzle he needed to solve. His two-hundred-dollar-an-hour advice was *"And why do you think you feel like that?"*

It was the last time I brought anything up significant to a shrink. The last time I bothered going to him at all.

Talking about my feelings has never solved anything. It's a waste of time. A way to alleviate the worries of those around you, not help yourself. I don't want help. Never have.

Commotion from inside draws my attention. Alarmed, I turn my body, peering through the back window at the family as they gather in the front room. Braden is speaking, though I can't hear the words nor who they're spoken to.

There's movement from the direction they're staring, and a thick wrist with a smartwatch appears, reaching out toward Braden. They shake hands, and Braden smiles at the unknown guest with a welcoming expression that has never been directed at me. It fills me with unease, not jealousy.

I'm at the back door in a blink, slipping back inside. Greeted with the lingering smell of baked ham, I tuck my hands into my pockets again, ensuring Tinsley won't see the mess they've become, and then head to the living room.

Blood rushes in my ears when I enter the room. An immediate blast of envy—of *rage*—threatens to strike me down. I straighten my back, cocking my head at the man with his hands on her. On *my* golden girl.

He's young. Our age, probably. With sandy-blond hair and blue eyes that are watching her too closely, his interest blatantly obvious as he touches her hand in greeting. Something lingers in my mind, telling me that I recognize him from somewhere. He isn't a stranger to me, or her, from the way he touches her.

With my insides twisted painfully tight, I close the distance between us, pressing close to her, *too* close, her shoulder brushing my chest. My nostrils flare as I breathe her in, a bite of pleasure mixing with that constant thrum of anger.

I carefully touch her back, my fingers spreading over the dip at the base of her spine, needing the contact more than my next fucking breath. She exhales then, leaning against my palm as if she approves of my actions while pulling her hand away from the intruder. I clench my teeth, fighting a shudder as her acceptance threatens to unravel me completely.

"Who are you?" I grit out.

It pisses me off that I don't know his name, just his face. If he's here, in this house, then it needs to be my priority to learn everything about him. A realization sparks when I tear my eyes from him and slowly look at Braden. Something dark and savage curls in my gut when I find him watching me curiously, calmly. It's then that I know for certain he called this intruder to his home. That this was a test. A pity attempt at seeing if I'll be able to keep myself under control, just days before I take his daughter away from him.

Well then. I trap a war cry in my chest, flashing him a savage grin. If he wants to play . . . we'll fucking play.

"You don't know Lucas? He's been working at the gym for a few weeks now," Braden says, slapping a hand on the dead man's back.

"I've told you to call me Luke. Only my grandma calls me Lucas." He corrects Braden with ease, as if he's done it before. Like they've spoken a million times.

Tinsley stiffens beneath my fingers, and my eyes narrow on her father. He must feel the venom in my stare because he doesn't look my way. The heat from Tiny's body seeps into mine, melting the ice in my chest as it builds. Over and over again. The cold is a comfort. The heat makes me wary.

"He's a martial arts instructor. Since we work on opposite sides of the gym, we've only spoken a handful of times," Tinsley clarifies. But for whose benefit? "What are you doing here, anyway?"

When I glance down to find her nose crinkled slightly— another one of her tells—I know she's glaring at Braden. When we were younger, she told me about the boys in school who used to tease her about that crinkle, making her attempt to hide it.

They stopped speaking to her when I flew over there that summer and began finding each one and hanging them from the flagpole in the schoolyard by their underwear.

"Don't sound so excited to see me, Tin," *Luke* teases, the sound of his voice utterly repulsive.

Suddenly, Easton barks out a laugh from where he sits on the couch. His dark eyes tighten in a scrutinizing stare. "Tin? Does she look like she's full of your grandmother's cookies, Lucas?"

Blondie pulls at the collar of his orange polo, his ears tipped with red. I make a mental note to buy Easton the gaming console he's been talking about once I'm done here.

"I'm just dropping a few things off for the boss here. I didn't mean to interrupt," he says, eyes fluttering around the room, never settling on one person.

"And have you?" I ask, my tone deceptively calm. The effort not to snarl the words at him takes far too much strength. I need to get Tinsley out and away from here before I rip his head from his body and let Braden win this little game.

"What?" It's the first time he's acknowledged me.

My fingers curl in the material of Tinsley's shirt as I work to keep my jaw from cracking from the pressure of my constant clenching. "Have you dropped off whatever it was you *needed* to bring *tonight*?"

"Uh, yeah. Braden was just introducing me to everyone—"

"Not everyone, it seems," I purr, my blood running hot. It feels like my insides are boiling.

"I think Noah and I should head home. You know how early I have to be up, Dad," Tinsley announces, cutting through the tension in the room. My temperature cools.

Braden frowns. "Already?"

"You'll have plenty of company to keep yourself busy for the rest of the night," she mutters pointedly. "We'll talk tomorrow. Mom, would you walk us out?"

I notice Sierra for the first time since I entered the room. She looks frustrated, eyeing her husband before looking to her angry daughter. "Of course."

Tinsley reaches behind her back and takes my hand in hers, startling me. I huff a curse, those delicate fingers clutching me tight as she pulls me behind her. My discomfort is still raging strong as we put our shoes on and let Sierra usher us through the front door.

Before the door can fall shut behind us, I look over my shoulder. Braden is scowling at me, a bundle of emotions burning in his eyes. I lick my lips and leave him with the image of my hand in his daughter's and the knowledge that he's upset both women in his life. The taste of victory dances on my tongue as I take the final step outside and let him disappear behind the door.

NH₃

"HE SAID he would leave you alone," Tinsley mutters, surprising me.

They're the first words she's spoken since we left her parents' house. That was over half an hour ago.

I drove us home in silence. If she wanted to speak, she could. My words wouldn't have done any good at that moment. I would only have hurt her.

"When?" I ask tightly.

"I don't want to hear a scolding once I tell you. I'm not in the mood."

I drop the car keys to the kitchen counter, watching as they fall. They make a loud clang, filling the house with noise. My fingers have begun to burn, the numbness wearing off now that we're home. I should wash them before Tinsley sees the damage.

My wounds would only intensify her anger. She's the calm one between the two of us, but when she blows, it drives me to insanity. Fuck, maybe I *should* show her.

Give me your wrath, Tinsley. Let it dance with mine.

The thought has my cock pulsing, growing rock-hard in my jeans, a rare occurrence in the presence of anyone else. It only wants one person. One golden girl. It's always been this way.

In the next breath, I'm watching her, searching for that familiar fire in her eyes. When I find it, my breathing grows ragged, a new ache in my bones.

"What?" she questions, hands on her hips. One eyebrow creeps up when I don't reply. "Fine. I asked my father to go easier on you, okay? I am sick and tired of the coldness between you two! We're leaving together in just a few days, and I shouldn't still be stuck in the middle of this pissing contest after twenty damn years! But apparently, my request fell on deaf, stubborn ears because what he pulled tonight? Oh, I want to hit him right in his stubborn face!"

The words sound harsh and angry but also tired. Her silver eyes are dull. Dim. Frustration builds at my want to spark them again.

"He doesn't trust me with you."

"He has no reason *not* to trust you with me."

Disbelief shifts something in my chest. Braden has every right not to trust me. I think deep down, she knows that, too, but doesn't want to admit it. I'm a wolf in sheep's clothing. A friend that craves her in a very unfriendly way. I want her in ways that would scare her father far worse than he already is. Yet, I haven't made my move. Something has been keeping me from taking what I want. What I fear I *need*.

But that shift inside of me, it begs me to do something—fucking anything—to silence her father once and for all. To be able to stake my claim and deny any of his further attempts to challenge me the way he did tonight.

"He won't be around in a few days. It will be just us," I rasp.

Anger begins to slowly leach from her face. "Just us and a million crew members, fans, your band members, and my team."

"It has always been just us," I push.

"For someone so grouchy, you do a good job of making me

un-grouchy," she huffs. Lashes fluttering, she meets my stare. My pulse quickens. "You're right. It's always been just us. I was silly to think that would change, even in the coming months."

She has no idea how true her statement is and what I'm prepared to do and give up in order to keep it that way.

9

Tinsley

"READY?"

I freeze in the hall, turning to Noah. The handle of my suitcase is slick with the sweat from my palm. I'm clutching onto the thing for dear life, as if it might somehow ground me. I'm confused by the clash of emotions in my chest as I shuffle my feet outside of my bedroom, frowning at my best friend.

I'm excited to leave Toronto, to start the next chapter of my life and take another step toward my dream. But even as I remind myself for the millionth time that I'll only be gone for a few weeks, a wave of homesickness swarms me. So much can happen in only a handful of weeks.

I don't know how both of my parents gave up their homes and families in Vancouver to move here all those years ago. And I certainly don't know how Noah did it. If I didn't have him or my parents close by, I don't think I could handle it. My world-class bravery only gets me so far, it seems.

"Tinsley." Noah says my name like a chastisement, and the rugged sound of his voice calms me like a homemade dose of Xanax. I grab onto the sound and use it to gather myself.

"Is it bad that I'm going to miss this place?" I ask him.

"Yes. It's a shithole."

"True. But it's also our home."

He contemplates that. "I guess."

"We'll have to hire someone to come check on it. I don't trust that Josh doesn't have house keys spread throughout the entire city for anyone to find. The last thing we need is the place burning down while we're gone."

"They can set fire to whatever they want, as long as it belongs to Josh," he grunts.

I suck the inside of my cheek. "Noah!"

He blinks at me, deadpan, those bulky arms folded across his chest. "You're telling me you weren't thinking it?"

"I would never think such a thing," I gasp.

His shoulder shrugs the slightest bit. "Me either."

I roll my eyes, moving toward him as the wheels of my suitcase roll across the bumpy laminate. While the banter may help distract me momentarily, we can't stand here forever. It's now or never. Time to put my big-girl panties on.

He watches me carefully, those dark eyes full of curiosity and intrigue. He won't voice the thoughts tossing and turning in his mind, no matter how much I wish he would. Even just once. I hold in my huff of frustration and step into him, leaning against his chest.

"I haven't been on a bus since I was in high school," I blurt out.

His chest lifts and falls with long, tight breaths. I realize it's because he's gone stiff, as if he's uncomfortable. Embarrassed, I go to pull back, thinking it could be because of me and my needy move toward him, when he suddenly reaches for me. A heavy arm anchors me to his body as he says, "Me either. I hate them."

"The close proximity, right?" Combined with the lack of personal space and tight confines with those he doesn't know well. My stomach tightens with concern. Will he be able to do it for the next three months? Will *I*?

"I told Garrison that I wanted us on our own bus. He's testing me. Making me sweat."

I swallow. "Is Sparks with us?"

His calloused fingertips slip past the hem of my shirt sleeve and press into my arm, a small slip of his self-control. The shiver I manage to fight off at the unexpected touch is a true testament of mine.

"Yes. She promised to keep everyone from overwhelming us, but it won't work. They don't respect her enough."

"That's nothing we can't fix. She's the big boss here. Maybe all she needs is a prime opportunity to show her power off to everyone. They'll see she has their careers by the balls before they even realize she's grabbed ahold of them. Maybe I could help with that."

He makes a deep, contemplative noise in his throat. His chest rumbles against my cheek, and I smile.

"By all means, have at it, Golden Girl."

The nickname has my smile growing into a grin. "You know what, Mr. Dark and Twisty? I think I just might."

A raspy, rare type of laugh escapes him then. It shakes the ground beneath my feet, the happiness it brings me taking me aback. It's beautiful, although rough and unused.

It's my favourite sound in the entire world.

NH)

THE TOUR BUS towers over us, blocking out the sun and painting the parking lot in shadows. A full-body shot of Noah onstage at one of his most recent shows in town has been plastered on the side of the bus, and I stifle a laugh, knowing he must be seething over it. The crowds of people rushing around us are nerve-racking, but I focus on not letting my discomfort show. It's not the time or place to have shaky knees.

Noah's near the end of the bus, talking to Garrison and Dad. The tension in his body tells me that the conversation isn't going well. I knew it wouldn't. Garrison won't give Noah what he wants, no matter how many times he asks, and I doubt my dad will fare much better.

It will be a new, interesting dynamic sharing living quarters with so many people that I don't know well, but if I can survive living with Josh, then this will be easy as pie. Plus, Noah would never let me stay anywhere I wasn't safe. That's something I'm certain of.

"Are you ready for this, sweetheart?" Mom asks softly, setting her hand on my shoulder.

I tear my eyes from Noah and focus on the familiar silver eyes in front of me. They're wet, glassy with tears like the last time we were together, and I frown, pulling her in for a tight hug. She smells like home, like comfort.

"Not really," I breathe into her shirt. "Maybe? I don't know."

She leans back enough to kiss the side of my head, then rubs up and down my arms. "You are. You're going to come home with a title belt and a million stories to share. Enjoy this, my girl. Don't fear it."

"You didn't give me your fearless gene, Mom. Apparently, you saved them for Easton."

She laughs, taking a step back to stare at me. There's so much confidence in her eyes, so much clarity, as if she knows my future and that everything will be okay.

"I'm far from fearless, Tinsley. I just don't let you see me when I'm feeling weak. Do you think that I wasn't scared to leave my life in Vancouver to follow my dreams? I was scared shitless, but I forced myself to do it anyway. Fear is inevitable; you just have to find the strength to tell it to kiss your ass and push past it. And you, my love, have that strength. I've seen it every single day of your life."

A mix of pride, doubt, and appreciation have tears filling my eyes. "Thanks, Mom." *I'll make you proud.*

She strokes a gentle hand over my hair. "Three months feels like a long time to be away from home, but we'll visit. You can't forget about your birthday and Christmas either. Time will fly by, you'll see."

I scoff a laugh, wiping my wet cheeks with the back of my hand. "I'm twenty-five. I shouldn't be so scared to leave home."

"I was the same age when I left, and I cried just as much."

"You had also just had your heart broken by Dad and were pregnant with me. It's not exactly the same," I tell her.

"Maybe not. But that doesn't change the fact I was terrified to leave home. Just remember that you always have a place to come back to after you've lived your dream. You have a family that adores you and that will be cheering for you each step of the way."

Warmth floods my senses, encouraging me to steel my spine, determined. "You're right. I'm going to make this season my bitch. Three months isn't forever."

Her eyes fill with approval and pride. "That's my girl."

"Thank you, Mom."

She waves me off, glancing to the sky for a brief moment, as if to collect herself. "We should wander over to your father and Noah. It's never good when they end up having to fight on the same side."

"Are they on the same side? I know Noah wants us to have our own bus, and I highly doubt Dad wants that. I'm surprised he isn't trying to push for a crowded bus."

We start walking in their direction, and Mom shakes her head, the corner of her mouth twitching with the tease of an evil smile. "Your father would rather you sleep in a cushioned box where he could stand guard and make sure nobody gets within a foot of you. But while that's not possible, I think we can all agree that he would rather you be with Noah than any of those band-mates of his. And in his defense, there's a man named Dagger! You have to understand his hesitation."

"Trust me, I get it. Dagger's name is the least scary thing about him, but he's here to work. I doubt he's planning on ways to terrorize us. I don't know how often I'll even be staying on the bus. Hunter mentioned wanting to book me a few hotels throughout the first couple of weeks to get me more comfortable with the whole travelling thing."

Mom reaches for my hand and squeezes. She uses her grip to bring me closer and then rests her head on my shoulder as we walk. With a sigh, she says, "Try not to stress about it. Everything will work out the way it's meant to."

"You sound like a fortune cookie."

"I am a sucker for some Chinese food," she teases.

"Sometimes I don't know who's worse with their unseriousness. You or Dad."

"Ow, that hurts."

She pinches my side, and I squeal, drawing Noah's attention as I slap her hand away. I roll my eyes at him when he cocks a brow, turning his back on my dad and Garrison, bringing the conversation to a dead stop. I glance at Dad and find him watching me and Mom, his expression softening. Garrison's scowl deepens before he stalks away, attention moving to the two buff men carrying parts of a dismantled drum around to the other side of the bus.

When Mom and I stop in front of Dad and Noah, Dad is quick to pull me under his arm for a hug. Over his shoulder, I see Noah continuing to watch us, his jaw growing tense. Guilt swells like a balloon in my chest. I offer him a small smile before giving my dad a final squeeze and breaking the embrace.

Noah's family isn't here to wish him off, which shouldn't make me as sad as it does. It's not like it makes sense for them to fly here to wish him luck just to fly back home after. The circumstances are different with him, and I try to remind myself of that, but it doesn't do much good. I feel like I'm waving my family in his face, and it makes me feel like the world's worst best friend.

I don't hesitate to move to his side, hoping my presence will help him feel not so alone. Easton said his goodbyes last night, and now that Mom has said hers, there's only Dad left. He'll be the one person I see most often, with his plans to meet me at my first fight and then every three after to train. Apparently, he doesn't trust anyone besides himself to keep me in peak shape. He will never admit that, though.

"I'm not going to get emotional because I'm going to see you in a week. But, just like I told Noah, I expect you to be in safe hands. I'm so proud of you, Tiny," Dad says, his voice soft and sure.

I flash a barely there smile. "Thank you. I couldn't have made it this far without you."

He shakes his head. "Yes, you could have."

Stubborn. "Either way, I appreciate everything you've done to help me."

"That's what family is for. You ready for this?"

My eyes find Noah's, and he nods, not a hint of doubt in his expression. His confidence in me—in *us*—makes me soar. Then, I look at Mom. She's watching me softly, and when she nods, I swallow a new lump in my throat.

"Yeah, Dad. I think we are."

10

Noah

My phone vibrates in my pocket as I follow Tinsley onto the tour bus. I grit my jaw and tense my fingers, ignoring it for the third time. It's my dad, and I have no desire to speak with him. To hear a weak good luck and congratulations that I doubt he would even mean.

"Oh, wow," Tinsley mutters, head swivelling to take in the interior of the bus.

Yeah. It's big. Big but *crowded*.

Three men and a sleeping child are sprawled on the couch and solo armchair, watching a loud movie on the TV hung on the wall. Bags and suitcases are piled in front of them, blocking the walkway to the kitchen and the rest of the bus. It smells like body spray and sweat. *Already*.

The lights are dim, some tinted red. There's a tablet on the kitchen counter, and it probably controls the lights. I don't reach for it. Red is fine for now.

Justice is the first to acknowledge us, daring to look away from the sleeping girl in his arms. His daughter. "Finally," he groans. "We were about to take bets on whether you'd wimp out or not."

"This is my tour. I would simply kick you off the bus, not quit."

"Nah, man. You need us here, whether you like it or not," he returns, grinning like always.

I cock my head, eyes tightening as I glare at him. "Need you? No."

His smirk pulls at the scar on his cheek. *How did someone who shits rainbows get such a nasty scar?* I don't care. "Hear that, boys? I think Noah's hinting that he *wants* us around."

"Fuck off." My glare intensifies.

"Do I get a hello? I *am* one of your new roommates, after all," Tinsley smarts, arms folded across her chest.

Her words instantly grab the attention of the other two guys. I swallow a growl when they boldly ogle her as if I'm not right here. Dagger's doing it on purpose, just to spite me. The way his eyes glitter with amusement has me clenching my jaw so hard my teeth have begun to ache.

"I'm sorry. You just make me so nervous that I forgot how to speak for a moment," he says, voice way too fucking smooth. He wouldn't be able to speak if I ripped his tongue out. The idea is appealing. "It's not often Noah brings such beautiful women around. He's been hiding the infamous Tinsley from Justice and me for months now."

Josh snorts a laugh, and I fling my glare at him, one eyebrow slipping up my forehead. He rolls his eyes.

"You know damn well that Tinsley is the only woman willing to be around Noah. And that's saying something because you won't be thinking of her as a woman once you spend enough time with her."

Tinsley gasps dramatically, seeming to ignore the dig. That's not the case for me. Desperate to keep myself under control, I give in to my instincts and settle a hand on the centre of her back, letting my palm fill with her body heat. *He just wants to get a rise out of you*, I remind myself.

Tinsley clucks her tongue and says, "Josh, honey, your

jealousy is showing. You know just as well as any of us that I'm the only woman he *wants* around him. Maybe one day, you'll have half the groupies Noah does. Don't lose faith just yet."

Justice and Dagger snicker at the insult while Josh glowers at her. I let my face split with a carnal smile as my cock throbs at her protectiveness. Fuck, this is why Tinsley's meant to be mine. She might look sweet, but there's a sliver of darkness trapped down inside of her that I would get on my knees and worship if she'd allow me to.

She turns slightly toward me, just enough that my hand slides to her waist before I pull it away. Lifting the arm that's holding her duffle bag, she says, "Now that we got that cleared up, I'm going to take my *womanly* stuff to my bunk instead of leaving it in a pile on the floor like a slob. Excuse us."

I follow her as she moves, not giving it a second thought. Justice and Dagger watch us as we walk, but when I glance over my shoulder, I find Josh staring at the TV again. He's the only one besides myself who knows Tinsley at all, and he's clearly unfazed by her presence. Even then, he barely knows anything.

"Which one is mine? I'm assuming you have your own bed back there," she says when we're alone in the hall, pointing lazily to the door at the back of the bus.

With bright curiosity, she quickly turns her attention to the rows of bunks on either side of us. She pulls each bunk curtain open, searching for one that's been left untouched. I almost laugh. *As if she would be sleeping out here with everyone else.* With Dagger, Justice and his daughter, Josh, Sparks, and Tinsley, each bunk would be full, leaving her with zero privacy.

I set my hand on the edge of the top bunk and lean into it at the same time she tries to pull its curtain back. The silky fabric slides between my fingers as I pinch it and pull, keeping her from seeing into the bunk. Grey eyes snap up to look at me, demanding answers.

"What are you doing? Let go so I can see if this is mine. It's the only empty one left."

I keep my grip on the curtain tight. "You're not sleeping in a bunk."

"What?"

"You're not sleeping in a bunk. You'll sleep in my room with me."

Her eyes go wide, lips parting slightly. She shakes her head and releases a disbelieving laugh. "No, I'm not."

"You are. I already told Garrison that you'll be sleeping away from everyone else."

"You did what?" Her tone is careful, deceptively so.

I sense her anger building and welcome it. Would she still get angry if she knew how hard it made me? "This doesn't sound like a thank you."

She laughs, but there's an edge to it. I'm tempted to see how sharp it can get. Would it cut me? Would it make me bleed?

"It's not a thank you! Did you actually decide where I was sleeping every night for the next three months without consulting me?" She pauses, leaving me time to reply, but I don't. My silence pisses her off further. "Of course you did! God, you can be impossible sometimes."

I curl my fingers in the curtain and dip my head toward her, lowering my tone. "I'm offering you privacy, Tinsley. I don't trust these people. Not around you."

She stares up at me, fire still burning in her eyes. Her top lip thins before rolling over her bottom one. I stay still, waiting for her next words like the desperate fuck I am.

"This was just about my privacy?"

"Yes," I lie.

As she leans toward me, her gaze tightens with scrutiny. "You're lying."

My pulse thumps in my throat, excitement sending a thrill through me. "Prove it." The words are throaty, desperate to even my ears.

A break in her expression. The corner of her mouth twitches. I stop breathing when she cautiously lifts a hand between us and presses the tip of her finger to the skin between my eyebrows. She gently drags it up and down, side to side. It's so warm my skin burns beneath it.

"You get a crease right here when you lie. It's easy to read you after this long," she murmurs before blinking and looking away, righting herself. *Remembering who I am.*

I nearly beg her to keep touching me when she drops her hand a second later. As she takes a stiff step back, I notice how close we'd gotten. I release the curtain and shove my hands in my pockets.

"If you're adamant enough about my right to privacy to go to your manager on my behalf, then okay, I'll stay in your room," she says, sounding composed once again.

I swallow a roar of victory. "Good."

"But," she starts, hands settling on her hips. Her chin tips up proudly. "I'm sleeping in there alone."

I go stiff. "No."

"Why not? I need my *privacy*, don't I?"

A dark sense of humour fills my mind. My little fucking cheat has me by the balls, and she knows it.

I barrel into her space, retracing her step back. The beast inside of me howls at our closeness and thrashes around in an attempt to get me to go further. To finally break these godforsaken chains I've wrapped around myself and yank her against me.

She sucks in a quick breath and drops her bag, surprised at my sudden closeness. Her head tilts back as she meets my eyes. I wonder what she sees in them. If she ever sees what truly lurks there, she'd run screaming.

I feel instant relief when instead of running, she smiles coyly and flutters her lashes, ignorant to the devastation that could have been. The rattling of chains in my mind begins to quiet as my beast calms at the sight of her smile.

"Fine. The room is yours."

She smirks knowingly. "Thanks."

I roll my eyes and grab her duffle bag from the floor. Side-stepping her, I lead us to the back room. The door is shut but not locked, and I shove it open easily.

"A bed fit for a rock star," she notes when we walk inside.

I nod. One king bed in a bus full of singles. There's more than enough room for the both of us in here, but I keep my thoughts to myself. She'll give in eventually, but for now, I'll sleep out there. With all of them. I swallow my disgust.

"There's a private bathroom in here. Use it. Don't use the main one," I demand. She turns her head, giving me a look that makes me add a tight *please* to my order.

"Got it. Will you be using this bathroom as well?"

"Am I allowed to?"

She laughs lightly. "Yes. Of course you are." Wandering over to the dresser, she starts to pull open the drawers. When she gets to the bottom one and finds my clothes, she looks over at me and asks, "This is all you brought? How very *un*-celebrity of you."

I lean a shoulder against the wall. "Keep teasing me, Tinsley, and I'll have you sleeping with Justice's drum set beneath the other bus."

"Ooh, how terrifying." She wiggles her fingers in front of her.

"How well will you fight with no sleep?"

She groans, turning back to my clothes. "What happened to quiet, sulking Noah Hutton? You're annoying me with all this banter right now."

My laugh is rough, but it has her flashing me a grin over her shoulder before she stands up and turns to me.

"I like hearing you laugh," she admits.

I immediately stop, then scold myself for stopping when it was making her happy. *Fuck.*

"Unpack your clothes. We should be leaving soon," I grit out, suddenly way too fucking tense.

Her expression forms one of understanding as I shut down. I'm already feeling claustrophobic knowing there's nowhere for me to run. Anxiety rises in my chest, and my heart patters quickly. Too quick.

I tear my eyes away and stare down at my hands, focusing on the ink that covers them. The designs swirl in my vision as I spin on my heels and stalk out of the room.

By the time I throw my body into the main bathroom, I've already repeated all of the reasons why I can't allow myself to be with Tinsley in my mind five times over, adding what just happened to the top of the list.

And only when I've splashed my face with cold water enough times to soak my shirt do I feel like I'll survive seeing her again.

11

Tinsley

THE FIRST FEW DAYS ON THE ROAD FLY BY. WE'RE ALMOST AT THE first tour stop, and I can feel the nerves rise around me with every kilometre we diminish between us and Edmonton, Alberta.

Noah spends his time preparing for his first show that's *not* in a dive bar or tiny theatre while his bandmates make one final push to perfect the way they perform his music. Everyone else . . . well, they try not to get in the way.

Life on a tour bus is the opposite of luxurious, but it's not terrible. Then again, it's probably easy for me to say that, considering I don't have to sleep in a bunk every night. With how sore I am by the end of every day, I don't know how I would have survived the next few weeks in such tight confinement. I'll never admit it to him, but Noah did me a huge favour by giving me a real bed.

Sweat drips from my nose and soaks the material of my sports bra as I punch the pads in Hunter's hands in a 1-6-3-2 sequence. My entire body aches from the hours spent in the gym today, but the pain fuels me, pushes me harder. *No pain, no gain*, Dad always says. It's the oldest saying in the book, but it hits the spot every time.

There's nothing easy about the level of physical activity I have to push myself to every day during training camp. It's gruelling and exhausting and not for everyone. The strain I'm putting on my body is undeniable. It's my reality, though, at least during these weeks leading up to my professional debut.

That isn't to say that I don't thrive off the sore muscles, frantic heart rate, and cramping fingers after a five-hour training session. I do. *I really do.*

Hunter is just as hard on me as my dad is, if not harder. In the past week, we've established a routine. I start my day with a run, either outside or on a treadmill, depending on where the bus stops come training time. Then, the real work begins at whichever gym Hunter's booked us time in that day. Hours of bag and pad work, conditioning and bodyweight training, and sparring with a man who doesn't hold back on me.

We take breaks every half hour, just long enough for me to gulp back water and shove my hands back into my gloves before he calls for me again. Warm-ups are long and tiresome. I think I have calluses on my palms from the handles of the jump rope he's so fond of. I've never done so many squats and pull-ups. Ice baths have become a new normal for me.

There are still two weeks to go before my first fight, and I've already begun to see the slight changes in my body from the days before we left and the past few on the road. A giddy excitement fills me at the thought of where I'll be after we've finished.

"Jab, cross, left uppercut, cross," Hunter calls, each command growing in strength.

My exhales tumble out of me, and my inhales are shaky and weak. A throb builds in my shoulders as my arms become heavier with each punch. I'm becoming sloppy, unfocused, as fatigue builds and builds. Hunter scowls at me when my uppercut barely makes an impact with his pad.

"We're done," he announces once I've hit the final cross.

I drop my arms instantly. They go down like lead balloons.

"Sorry," I rasp on a quick exhale. My lungs burn like a motherfucker, making it hard to suck in full breaths.

He slips off one pad and tucks it beneath his arm before patting me on the back. "You hit five hours. I pushed you hard today. Go home and eat something before you pass out."

"I don't want to eat another prepped meal in my life." The thought of microwaving another Tupperware meal makes my stomach roll. There's nothing like a bland chicken breast and broccoli mixture to make a girl want to never eat again.

Hunter makes a sound as close to a laugh as I think I've ever heard from him. "Get used to it. You can pig out once the season is done and your weight class doesn't matter anymore."

"I've been having dreams of a giant Big Mac chasing me down the street for two days now, begging me to eat it. Even my subconscious is struggling."

"You could always swap your chicken for salmon."

I crinkle my nose. "I hate fish."

"I know."

"Thanks for the amazing suggestion, then, Hunter buddy." With the little strength I have left, I tug off my gloves and toss them on the weight bench we used an hour ago. The relief is euphoric when I stretch out my fingers and begin to unravel my wraps.

"Anytime. Want me to fill the bath for you before I leave?"

I shiver, recalling the last ice bath I had. For a moment, I wondered if I was going to die in that tub, surrounded by pounds of melting ice in a sweaty, stinky locker room. It would have been a terrible way to go.

"Not today. I don't think I'd even be able to crawl in."

He nods. The keys to the gym jingle in the pocket of his shorts as he taps his foot. I narrow my eyes slightly on the jerky movement.

"Is there something else you want to say?" I ask.

Crossing his arms, he flashes me a small, tense smile of approval. "Good job today."

I can't help but preen under the compliment. Who wouldn't? Hunter is a legend, and he thinks I'm doing a good job?

"I think that's the nicest thing you've ever said to me."

His smile morphs into a scowl. I grin back at him, enjoying seeing him have a bit of fun. I've always been good at bringing people out of their shells. It's a talent of mine, I guess.

"Lock up after me again, and don't be late back to the bus," he grunts, and then he's retreating through the gym at a quick pace, as if he can't wait to be free of my presence.

"I was hardly late today! It's not my fault my Uber driver drove ten below the limit!" I call after him, but he's already gone, the door slamming shut behind him.

With a loud laugh, I shake my head and start to pick up the things I've littered all over the gym. Once my arms are full of ripe gear and towels, I head to the locker room. It's quiet in the empty gym, and to be honest, the quiet has always freaked me out a bit. Especially when I'm alone and in an unfamiliar place.

Hunter being Hunter knew the owner of this gym from his days in the ring and was able to get special privileges for us for the day. Everywhere we've stopped over the past three days, he's managed to find us somewhere to train from three till eight, but today has been the only time we've been alone and unbothered.

The lack of curious, gawking stares was a welcome change from the last gym we were at. You'd think after years of dealing with unwanted attention from men that it would be easy for me to ignore it, but that's not always the case.

I'm a woman training in a space dominated by men double my size. They don't know that I could knock them on their ass ten times easier and faster than someone of their own height and weight. Even had I not decided to make a career out of boxing, my dad still would have made sure I knew how to stand up for and protect myself.

I inhale and exhale a full breath, my heartbeat finally slowing. A glance out the front window tells me the sun has only just begun to set. It was hot this afternoon when I got here, and I'm already dreading walking back out into the heat.

Maybe an ice bath does sound appealing.

Shouldering open the locker room door, I quickly set my things down on a bench and grab everything I need to take a shower. Normally, I wouldn't bother showering at a gym, but it beats suffering with the water pressure—or lack thereof—on the bus.

The showers are small but clean, which is all I need to know. I turn the water on and strip out of my soiled clothes, tossing them in a pile in the corner before tossing my hair up and out of the way. The hot water pelts against my back the moment I step into the stall, and I moan, feeling my muscles relax.

I stay in the water for longer than necessary, my eyes shut and head tipped forward. Exhaustion hits me like a brick a beat later, and it takes everything in me to peel my eyes back open and start to lazily wash myself.

I've only started rinsing away my body wash when a bang ricochets through the gym, loud enough I can hear it over the rush of the shower. My blood runs cold as I jerkily reach behind me to turn off the water and grab my towel, wrapping it around my torso.

Hunter probably forgot something and just came back for it. It's the most comforting idea and the most realistic. I let the knowledge of that help calm me as I wait for another sound. A bang, or maybe even a familiar voice calling my name. When the seconds tick by with nothing but silence, I give my head a rough shake with the hope of flinging my worries away.

"Don't be that girl, T," I tell myself. Don't be the girl that runs toward the creepy noises like a complete idiot, like she doesn't have a care in the world for her own livelihood. "And *definitely* don't do it naked."

The door bangs a second time when I step out of the shower, the steam fogging the mirrors above the sinks. It's like someone cranked the temperature up around me. I'm suddenly too hot. Sweat begins to collect on my neck as fear attempts to sink its claws into me. But I refuse to let it win, even if I'm following in the footsteps of a horror movie heroine.

Drying off in a hurry, I throw a pair of sweatpants and a T-shirt on before gripping the door handle. My palm is sweaty as I squeeze the metal knob and turn it until it won't go any further.

I abandon my things in the room and pull the door open, peeking into the hallway. It doesn't look scary. There's more than enough light for me to see an abandoned pair of gym shorts on the floor and the small No Smoking sticker on the back door a few feet from the men's locker room.

The scolding I give myself for getting so nervous in the shower is one for the books. The gym is completely quiet, and I doubt more than a handful of people have a key to this place. Hunter wouldn't have left the door unlocked behind him.

I roll my neck and let my shoulders drop as I swipe the back of my hand over my forehead. I've almost started to smile despite myself when footsteps start to clunk toward me. I spin toward the sound, and my heart jumps to my throat. Movement from my peripheral has a scream building in my chest before flying loose as a bulky male figure comes into view.

It takes all of five seconds to recognize him and for my scream to die.

"You fucking fuckity fuck!" I shout, instantly dropping to a squat and covering my face with my hands. They're shaking, so I press my palms into my eyes to try and make them stop. It doesn't work.

I hear Noah rush toward me. He falls to his knees—so hard I hear them knock against the floor—and circles my wrists, pulling my hands from my face. There are spots in my eyes from pressing them so hard, but when they clear, I see the concern on his face. It flashes like a warning beacon. My heart tugs at his worry.

"What's wrong?" he asks, sounding like he's swallowed glass. Like he's on the brink of losing it.

I almost laugh at the ridiculousness of his question. There's nothing wrong. I'm just a scaredy-cat who's apparently scared of her own *best friend*. Ugh.

I try to compose myself. "I was in the shower and heard the door slam shut. I didn't know you were planning on coming here tonight, so I was hoping it was just Hunter forgetting something. I'm fine. Just a bit freaked out."

His eyes are cold and dark, brutally so. "He shouldn't have left you here alone. Something could have happened."

I shake my head and turn my hands so our fingers can interlink. Pulling them to my lap, I smile to try and reassure him that I'm okay. He's always been overprotective, and when he gets this look in his eyes, it's usually trickier than normal to calm him down.

"I'm good. You're here. Who's a better protector than you?" I tease. He doesn't reply, doesn't lose the tension straining his muscles. "The answer is nobody. Obviously."

"Anyone could have come in here. You were *showering*." He spits the word out.

"Nobody did but you. Wait, how did you get in here, by the way?"

He shrugs. "Got a key."

I should ask how he got one and who gave it to him, but I'm too exhausted to care. Instead, I lean forward and rest my forehead against his shoulder, breathing him in. He always smells like leather after he plays guitar, and tonight is no different. I don't think he's ever worn leather in his life. The smell comes from the guitar strap I got him for his fifteenth birthday.

Maybe I should get him a new one for his birthday this year, but something tells me he likes his current one more than enough.

"How do you feel about chicken and broccoli for dinner?" I

ask into his shirt a few moments later. It's a terrible attempt at changing the subject, but it's all I've got in me.

He flexes his fingers before tightening his grip. "I'd rather starve."

12

Noah

BREATHE IN. BREATHE OUT.

Pretend I'm alone. Focus on the beat. The kick drum pulsing through me. The low, throaty notes of the bass guitar. Feel the strings beneath my fingertips. Let the music carry me away.

I touch my chin to my chest and sway to the song. *My song.* When I squeeze my guitar pick between my fingertips, it digs into the skin, and I grab onto that pain. It settles enough of my distress that I can peel open my eyes and lift my head, finding Garrison watching from down in the pit. His scrutiny pushes me to wave back at Justice, giving him the go-ahead to lead into the song.

The drum line picks up, and the rest of the band follows his lead. It's loud. The mix of instruments behind me still makes me uncomfortable. We've played together before at small shows. Not a venue this size, though. The music echoes and plays back in my ear. I flinch but don't miss my cue.

The lyrics fly out on instinct, carried through the venue by the mic at my lips. I'm tense, and you can hear it in my voice. I tap my foot on the stage and somehow keep pace with the beat in my ear.

The disapproval on Garrison's face is obvious. I'm not

playing like I should. Even without him here, I would know that. I grip the neck of my guitar and press the body into mine before beginning to strum. The leather strap resting on my shoulder is heavy with the weight of the new guitar I got yesterday. It makes me feel unsteady.

With one last drumbeat, the song comes to an end. The silence that sits like stagnant water around me is uncomfortable. It seems my terrible performance was obvious to everyone.

"You hear that, Noah? That's the sound of a silent arena. If you keep playing like that, you better get used to that sound because nobody in their right mind will come to see you," Dagger growls, stalking toward me with his oversized, clunky boots dragging along the stage.

I hold still, keeping my expression blank as he closes in. The only sign of my rage is the snapping of a guitar string that I've tugged too hard.

"Dagger," Justice warns from behind me.

Dagger swivels his head toward him and snarls, "Fuck off, J. I'm not letting this asshole ruin our careers because he doesn't give a shit about his!"

"It's been one song. Chill out," Josh chimes in.

I flick my tongue to the inside of my cheek and watch the man in front of me. The vein thumping in his forehead exposes his inability to keep his anger in check. He's driven by emotion, by a burning, undeniable jealousy. I want to poke at that insecurity and watch him quiver. If only he knew in another world, I would have given him the keys to my castle and sat back as he destroyed himself trying to be worthy of it.

"You sound so confident that you have a career for me to ruin in the first place, Dagger," I say softly. When he whirls on me this time, his eyes are wild. "But you don't, and everyone knows it."

My lip curls as I lean into him and drop my tone so only he can hear me. "The next time you get in my face, I will make sure you can never play another song in your life." The obvious rise and fall of his throat has me pulling back an inch. "You're here to work *for* me, not *with* me. Now, get to it, doggie."

He reels back, jaw slacked before it tightens up. When he hesitates to step away, looking as if he has something to add, I flash the hint of a carnal smile and purr, "Woof woof."

Claps erupt from the pit, where Garrison stands waiting, watching. I fight an eye roll and turn to face him, brow raised expectantly.

His eyes trail over all of us as he says, "Congratulations. You've managed to create a spectacle of yourselves. Are you proud? Does it feel good? Because it shouldn't."

The soft clatter of Justice's drumsticks hitting the ground comes from behind me before Garrison continues his speech, pinning those dull eyes on the drummer.

"The first show is tonight, and not a single one of you is ready. I don't care how good you think you are because I promise you, you're not there yet. It's easy to replace a band. Remember that the next time you want to have a dick-measuring contest," he grinds out.

Easy to replace a band but not the guy who's paying your bills is what he doesn't say. He might have meant the warning for everyone, but I ignore it. If it were that easy for him to get rid of me, he would have done it months ago. We both know that.

"Am I understood?" he asks, voice so loud it echoes around the venue.

"Yes," Justice and Josh mutter while Dagger appears to be biting his tongue.

My lips twitch with amusement as he struggles to speak. Finally, he croaks a weak *yeah* in response.

Garrison shakes his head and calls out, "Start again. We're not moving down the track list until you nail this one."

And so, we begin again. And again. Until my fingers have gone raw and the lyrics burn like fire crawling up my throat. Only then do we move to track two.

NH)

"DRINK THIS," Tinsley orders, pushing a mug of tea into my hand later that night. I loop two fingers into the handle and accept it from her.

It smells like honey. "I hate honey." And tea.

"Don't care." She taps the bottom of the mug before starting to tip it toward me. "Bottoms up."

I narrow my eyes but let her control the movement of bringing it to my mouth. Taking a gulp of the hot liquid, I ignore my gag reflex as it travels down my throat.

She grins, satisfied for now. Stealing the mug back from me, she brings it with her as she sits beside me on the couch. I watch her get comfortable by tossing her legs over my lap and stretching out along the couch, head propped by the armrest. My hands are glued to the cushions on either side of me, no way to move them without touching her.

Before setting the mug on the ground, she gives it a cautious shake and says, "When you're ready for more, let me know."

I jerk my head in a nod. My fingers curl as she wiggles her legs in my lap, stretching and relaxing her calves over and over again. Her shorts are small, leaving her legs bare from the top of her thighs down to her ankle socks. I'm staring at them. At the smooth, creamy pale skin of her thighs. The muscles flex with each slight stretch of her calf, and before I can stop myself, I've rotated my right wrist and extended my index finger, brushing the back of her knee with the tip of it.

My chest thunders at the feel of her. I exhale out my nose, nostrils flaring as I keep my face blank.

"Are you sore?" I croak. My back stiffens at the lack of control in my voice. "From today. Training."

She cocks her head, smiling softly. "Are you worried about me?"

"Always."

My honesty earns me a glance at the slight pink tint that suddenly appears over the bridge of her nose.

"I worry about you too. Hence making you drink the tea that you hate."

"I was terrible today," I admit.

She knows all of my weaknesses. It's fitting since she's my biggest one. There's no reason to hide them from her.

Her expression twists with concern, and she reaches for me, snagging my hand from beneath her leg and setting it on her thigh instead. With a soft pressure, she holds my hand, watching me quietly, as if she's waiting for me to open up further.

For anyone else, I would tell them to mind their own fucking business, but for her . . .

"When I get onstage, my chest gets tight, and my head hurts. Music was for me. *Just* me. Now, it's for everyone else. It's not the same as before, and I can't get comfortable. Garrison was there today. *Watching.*"

For hours, he stood there watching, correcting us and demanding we do a better job. I've never played a show with a hoarse voice before. Tomorrow will be my first, but I don't tell her that. My little angel would destroy him on my behalf. She can't get involved with it.

"And he saw you weren't your best, which is why you sound like a frog when you speak. I'm sorry." She rolls her lips for a moment before her eyes flare wide, and she reaches an arm behind her, over the side of the couch. Her chest pushes toward the ceiling, and I bite back a groan at the flash of her nipples through her shirt.

When she pushes back up to face me, she's spinning a joint between her fingers. "I watched Josh stash a few beneath the couch the other day. Don't tell on me."

The way her mouth kicks up into a coy little grin makes my pants tighten, my cock stealing all the blood from the rest of my body. I meet her stare and slip my hand into my pocket to pull my lighter out. When I flick it back and a small flame begins to burn, I watch it reflect in her eyes.

"Outside. I don't want Justice's daughter around the smell," she says before hopping off the couch and heading for the door. I follow her, reaching up to adjust the tie of the bandana holding my hair back as we step outside.

The parking lot of the hotel we stopped at for the day is busy, but the bus is parked in a way that cuts us off from the cars. As we lean against the side of the bus, we face an empty field on the edge of town. Smoking weed is legal in Canada and allowed on a boxer's drug test, but I know Tinsley doesn't want a photo of her online with a joint in her mouth.

When she offers it to me, I take it, purposefully brushing our fingers as I pull back. Something curious fills her gaze before she blinks it away and smiles, nodding.

I put the joint between my lips and light it up. The first hit starts to ease the tension in my body, and the second has my head hitting the side of the bus. I watch Tinsley with a deeper intensity than I usually allow myself.

When she leans toward me, I hold the joint in front of her but don't bring it to her mouth.

"You sure?" I grunt.

She rolls her eyes. "Yes, Dad. I'm allowed to smoke pot every once in a while."

"It's not good for you."

"And it's good for you? We both need our lungs in prime condition, but I don't harp on you for smoking."

I scowl, jaw flexing. The smell of marijuana swirls in the air, so fucking potent. It would have stunk up the bus for days, and Justice would have been enraged that his daughter had to smell it.

It wouldn't have stopped me from getting high, but Tinsley would have felt guilty.

"You're more important than I am. Nobody would give a

fuck if I ruined my body with any number of drugs on the planet."

She slaps my arm and snags the joint from me. With an icy glare, she takes a puff and blows the smoke out in a perfect O.

"You're a jackass, Noah."

I wait for her to take a second inhale and then take the joint back. "I know." Another puff, and I take a step closer to her, my shoulder pressing against hers.

She sighs, turning into my body. Her arms come around my hips, hands locked and resting at the bottom of my back. I shudder, but she doesn't say anything.

To her, this is friendly. This is how best friends act.

To me, her touch threatens to undo every lock on the chains keeping me from devouring her.

"You know there *are* people who give a shit about you, even when you try like hell to push them all away. Your siblings, Reggie, your parents. *Me*."

I don't know what to say, so I keep quiet. My arms shake as I set them on her shoulders, pulling her against my chest, just . . . holding her. I take advantage of the moment and rest my chin on her head. *Just for a minute*, I warn myself.

The joint burns and burns, ashes falling to the ground behind her, and once it dies, I drop it to the pavement.

Minutes pass with her in my arms, but I don't let go.

13

Tinsley

WATCHING NOAH PERFORM IS UNLIKE ANYTHING I'VE EVER SEEN before. As he comes to the end of his final rehearsal before the show tonight, he's a sight to behold.

He doesn't need to dance all over the stage to command it. The sheer power in his voice and the confidence radiating from every line of his body as he plays his guitar is impossible not to recognize. Performing is what he was born to do. Even if he doesn't believe it.

After everything that Oakley has given Noah a hard time about, at least he was right about the music. It would have been a waste of Noah's talent not to pursue this opportunity.

I'm torn from my thoughts when someone settles beside me. They keep a safe amount of distance, and when I smell the familiar scent of pine, I smile, knowing who it is.

"He's magic," Reggie says, almost in awe. I wouldn't blame him if he was.

"He is. I haven't seen him perform in a few weeks, and watching him now makes me wish I had managed to find the time to when we were home."

I stomp down the brief swell of guilt that tries to sweep me under. We've both been swamped, and Noah would never fault me for putting my career at the top of my priority list. He'd most likely be pissed at me for thinking that way.

"He gets better every time I see him. I'm glad Garrison hasn't taken that passion from him."

I begin to laugh, but after only a second, it gets stuck in my throat. Noah's responsible for the ugly cough that follows as he moves his guitar to rest against his back and tugs the hem of his T-shirt up to wipe his forehead, exposing the hard, rippling slab of muscles beneath. My tongue sticks to the roof of my mouth as I gawk at him. Even from backstage, I can see the definition of the abs that were definitely not there the last time we trained together.

Reggie says something, but I can't distinguish exactly what over the sound of the thump in my ears. I'm suddenly hot, my tank top sticking to my neck, so tight it feels suffocating. Confusion muddles my thoughts. I should look away. It's not the first time I've seen Noah's bare chest—far from it—but for some ungodly reason, it's different this time. And I'm not talking about the new muscles. It's me. I feel different, and I can't pinpoint why or exactly how. Just that I am.

In all honesty, I'm probably just horny. It's been, well, *forever* since I've had sex. Long before Noah moved to Toronto, and that's a fact. The poor guy has just been subjected to my very inappropriate staring because he's hot and sweaty and muscly and I'm sex deprived.

This time, the guilt that comes is too much to ignore. It nips at me, making it easier to finally look away from him as my stomach turns over.

I partially blame the way he accidentally stroked behind my knee yesterday for this new train of thought. I'm far too sensitive there, and if I hadn't reached for a blunt to distract myself before he moved his finger a second time, I worry what I would have done in my horned-up state.

Ugh. *He can never learn about this.*

A large hand darts out in front of me, two fingers snapping

just inches from my nose. I blink rapidly and focus on Reggie. The damn guy is smirking at me, a knowing glint in his eyes that deepens the frustration in mine.

"Don't even say it. You saw nothing," I rush out, painting on my best intimidating scowl as I face him.

He barks a laugh and raises his hands in front of his chest, palms to me. "Saw what?"

"That's what I thought. Now, let's focus on Garrison for a moment."

"An expert subject change, Tinsley," he teases.

I ignore him and push forward. "You need to get Garrison to lay off a bit. He worked the guys so hard yesterday that Noah came back to the bus with a hoarse throat. He drank the tea I made him, Reggie. *With honey*! You know what that means."

Concern settles in the lines of his face. "I didn't know Garrison was with them last night. It figures, with it being their last night before the big show. I should have put it together when I heard Noah's voice tonight."

"If he keeps pushing them already, he won't have anyone in shape to actually do the tour. I know you two don't really talk, but it's worth a try. For Noah."

My best friend isn't much of a gossip, but when poked and prodded enough, he tends to appease my curiosity. The terrible father/son relationship between Reggie and Garrison is the only one I've ever heard of that could rival Oakley and Noah's. It quite possibly tops it.

If you weren't explicitly told that Garrison was Reggie's son, you would go your entire life without knowing. They both keep to themselves, not wanting anything to do with the other. It stems from decades of arguments and disapproving life decisions on both sides, but somehow, they're crazy enough to continue a business relationship. I guess it makes sense, considering the success the record label has had, but if I were in their shoes, I couldn't do it.

I've always had a terrible time pretending with people.

When I don't like someone, I don't bother hiding it. If you piss me off, I let you know. Life is too short to surround yourself with people you don't like or respect or just truly treat you like shit. Noah taught me that lesson back when we were just children.

"He won't listen to me," Reggie says, the words heavy with emotion.

"He kind of has to, doesn't he?" They're both owners of Swift Edge Records. Every action has to be approved by both halves of the company. And Reggie loves Noah. I trust that he doesn't want his son to ruin their chance at making him the next big thing in music.

If Garrison did, I can't see that going well for both the company and the relationship between him and his father.

"You're right. I'll speak with him. And once rehearsal finishes up, I'll talk to Noah."

"He won't tell you, but I think he'll appreciate that."

"Doesn't have to tell me. I read him well," Reggie says.

"A skill you've learned with your son?"

"You could say that. Believe it or not, but Noah's easier for me to read than Garrison."

"I don't envy you if that's the case."

He huffs out a breath. "Yeah, I wouldn't expect you would. Nobody should."

"I can always talk to him. Give him a bit of a shakedown, if you want," I offer with a wink and quick flex of my biceps.

His answering laugh is so pure it warms my chest. "Honey, we both know he wouldn't make it out of that talk alive."

"You're my favourite, Reg. Thank you for being so awesome. Noah is lucky to have you in his corner."

He sobers up and stares at me with soft, understanding eyes. It reminds me of the way my dad looks at me when I tell him something sugary sweet, usually when I want something from him. But with Reggie, the only thing I'll ever want from him is his continued support of my best friend.

"I think he's lucky to have us both, wouldn't you say?" he asks.

I grin and glance at the stage, finding Noah instantly. He's already watching me, and as I wiggle my fingers at him, he begins to head in our direction, rehearsal finished.

His hair hangs in his face, the bandana he had tied around his head earlier now tucked in the pocket of his jeans. A guitar pick twirls between his fingertips. The permanent scowl on his face makes him look like a broody teen, and I can't help but giggle at it. I want to press my thumbs to the corners of his mouth and tug it into a smile. His smile is one of my favourite things on this earth. I wish I saw it more.

"There's my money-maker!" Reggie calls.

Noah keeps a straight face, but he glances suspiciously between me and his producer as if trying to piece together what we were talking about.

"At least you recognize it," he mutters back.

"I may be old, but I'm not blind, son."

Everyone else would have missed the pain that ever so slightly cuts through Noah's blank stare at the term of endearment, but I don't. It screams at me. My heart gives a harsh tug in response. *I'm sorry.*

On instinct, I inch closer to him. His fingers are tense, curled into fists when I touch them. As I gently start to uncurl them, he releases a shuddered breath. They start to shake when I link them through mine, from pain or anger, I'm not sure.

Reggie doesn't pay much mind to Noah's lack of reply. He carries on as if he hadn't kept quiet.

"I know you must want to head back to the bus for a couple hours before the show, but I wanted to talk to you first. Well, apologize, really."

Tipping my head back, I stare up at Noah. "Should I go? I can find something to busy myself with until you're done."

He squeezes my hand, scowl deepening. "No."

"Okay." I squeeze it back.

"Garrison has been—" Reggie starts before Noah cuts him off.

"Stop. Don't apologize for him. I don't want it."

The anger in his words is powerful. It cuts through the air, chilling it.

Reggie flinches, looking stricken. "It's the right thing to do. It's not fair for him to punish you because . . ."

Because of me, he doesn't say. Garrison's jealousy of the relationship Noah has with Reggie is palpable. It's leading them all down a terrible road.

My chest begins to ache. I want to fix this. Fix all of it. Noah and Oakley, Noah and Garrison, Garrison and Reggie. Fuck. Everything has gone to shit the past few months. It's becoming too heavy of a load to carry around—for everyone.

Isn't there some sort of intervention for family drama? One of those would be very handy right about now.

Noah tongues his cheek. "I don't care about Garrison."

"But I do. I care for the both of you," Reggie pushes. I want to warn him to stop, but he continues before I get the chance. "I will be having a talk with him. We don't do harm to our artists. He knows better, regardless of who you are."

"Do not speak to him on my behalf. I am *not* your responsibility. You're not my father. *Stop* trying to take care of me," Noah growls before ripping his hand free and storming off.

I close my eyes when they start to water, listening to the receding sound of his footsteps. Inhaling a long, tired breath, I look at Reggie. He looks hurt, guilty. Torn.

"That didn't go how I wanted it to," he breathes out.

"Noah . . . he . . ." I groan, scratching the back of my head. "He'll come around. He doesn't know how to accept help from people."

Reggie's smile is weak. "I just want to care for him. He deserves to succeed. With or without Swift Edge."

I caress his arm, giving it a soft squeeze. "He knows that.

Trust me. Just give him some more time to accept that. You have to prove you're not going to disappear on him if he lets you in."

"I will. You can trust me on that."

With a growing appreciation for this man, I kiss his cheek and say, "I do. But if you'll excuse me, I'm going to go make sure he's okay. Just don't give up on him, okay?"

He nods, determination in his stare. "I won't."

14

Tinsley

TO NO ONE'S SURPRISE, NOAH DIDN'T WANT TO TALK. HE SHUT down, and I let him walk away to cool down on his own. That's just how he is. When he's pushed too far, he recoils like a wounded animal, and not even I can soothe him.

He always comes back, though. Whether that's an hour later or after days of regrouping, when I've missed him and worried too much to let him continue to wallow. Tonight, he forced himself out of his shell quickly. There was a show to play, after all.

Noah can't deny himself his music.

I'm not the only one thankful for that. The people who sold out his first show are too.

My skin is hot, burning to the touch as sweat clings to my neck and chest. I'm in the pit with Noah's sister, Adalyn, and her husband, Cooper, who have flown out to watch his first show. Together, we watch my best friend give the best show of his career thus far.

There's no way to compare tonight with any prior show. It's like he found some sort of power lever inside of himself and cranked it all the way up.

Noah's voice is raspy, dark, and soothing all at once. It's the most toe-curling, heartbeat-thrashing combination I've ever heard. There's something about it that defeats all of my worries and just makes me feel . . . *safe*. At home.

We're all beneath him where we stand, blanketed in darkness while the spotlights slip over his body. It makes him appear godlike. Almost as if we should be worshipping him. I suppose in some way, we are.

The heavy drumbeat kicks up, and for the first time tonight, Noah leaves his spot at the front of the stage and takes two slow steps closer to the edge. He seeks me out of the crowd, and our eyes connect. His pupils are blown, making him look downright feral. It rattles something inside of me, and I gulp, feeling my belly heat.

"That's my brother, bitches!" Adalyn screams, her mouth too close to my ear. I wince and whip my head in her direction.

"Ow!" I shout back.

She smiles sheepishly and mouths, "I'm sorry," before turning back to the stage and jumping in time with the music. Cooper tugs her against his chest after a few beats and buries his face in her hair, not giving a shit about the eyes of those around. When Addie leans her head back and nuzzles into his embrace, I look away, suddenly feeling like an intruder.

Addie has been one of my best friends since we were children, and I miss her deeply. Noah used to fight with her constantly, trying to get me to be just *his* best friend. He was not successful in that, and Addie has never let him forget that. Life was so different back then, without husbands and busy careers. Some days, I wish for nothing more than to spend a few more days as a kid.

I don't see enough of my surrogate family back in Vancouver. I'll make sure to spend the day with Addie tomorrow before she goes back home. The reminder that she isn't staying long has my chest constricting.

The increase of screams in front of me draws my attention back to the stage. My lungs squeeze so tight they begin to scream when I find Noah crouched down at the edge of the stage, the toes of his black boots hanging over it. He's staring at me, his shoulders tight, a heavy tension radiating off him as he sings the lyrics he wrote.

I suck a breath between my teeth and follow his dark eyes as they slip toward his sister and then come back to me. Unsure of what he's thinking, I just shake my head and smile. I drop my gaze to the microphone in his hands and find him gripping it so tight his knuckles are white.

The metal barricade keeping those of us in the pit from climbing the stage is cold beneath my fingers when I grab it and lean my body against the top, trying to get as close as I can to him. I know security will give me shit for this after the show, but right now, I couldn't care less.

Extending my arm, I hang it over the space between us and wiggle my fingers. Bodies push at my back and sides as the crowd clues in to what I'm doing. They all want the chance to touch him, and when he reaches his hand out toward me, the look of severed control in his expression nearly does me in. He doesn't want anyone else to touch him, but he's willing to risk it for me.

For the chance to touch *me*.

It's a big reach, but our fingers brush before curling and locking in place. An unease I didn't know I held settles at the touch, and I grin, tossing him a wink before pulling back and letting the crowd swallow me. He keeps his eyes on me as I move into the throng of people and try to catch my breath.

Only when I've successfully found Addie again does he slowly back away from the edge and move back to his abandoned mic stand. He slips the mic into its holder and picks his guitar up from where he set it two songs ago.

The leather strap settles against his shoulder, and a beat later, a familiar riff floods the venue. It's the one that leads into my favourite song: "Golden Girl."

NH)

Noah

I'M A LIVE WIRE.

Adrenaline has my cock harder than steel. The urge to fuck is a living, breathing thing inside of me. The crowd still rings in my ears, calling to me long after they've started to leave the venue.

We're in my dressing room. Justice is with his daughter on the couch. He's trying to play a cartoon on the television. Josh is asleep beside them.

Dagger looks how I feel. Like he's fighting not to erupt. Down on the floor, he's doing push-ups at a too-quick pace. The high makes him feel invincible. The sore muscles and fatigue will come tomorrow, and then he'll do it all over again.

I lean against the wall, my fingers tapping on my thighs. The hands on the clock hung on the wall move slowly. The meet-and-greet is soon. At any minute, they'll grab me.

Is that where Tinsley is? Waiting for me?

I still feel her fingers curled around mine. Still see the glow in her eyes as they held mine. She didn't back away from the wildness she saw in me onstage. It looked like she enjoyed it.

The idea of that drives me to insanity. My nails dig into my palms, and I keep pressing until one pops the skin. The pain eases some of my tension. It helps me focus.

Sparks whips open the dressing room door, finding me immediately. "Time to go."

"Keep it short. And no fucking touching," I warn. Meet-and-greets weren't part of the original deal. They're something I agreed to later.

"I've already warned them. Just trust me."

"Where's Tinsley?"

She sighs and ushers me into the hallway. It's empty but noisier than the dressing room. "Already there. She said she wasn't going to let you do the meet-and-greet alone."

I don't reply. My relief is too strong for me to form words.

"All you have to do is say hello and sign whatever they give you. Just no blank sheets of paper. It will only be ticket VIPs, and they've been briefed on the time they're allowed to take with you."

With a tug on my arm, Sparks stops us just before we reach the door to another room. My ears still ring from the show, and the noise inside is loud.

"If you need anyone to intervene, just signal one of us over. Are you ready?" she asks.

I would rather walk over a bed of nails. "Yeah."

"Great. Knock 'em dead, Rockstar."

Following her to the room, I wipe all expression off my face and look around. Security guards watch the line of people from the back and front, appearing alert enough. Sparks leads me to the front of the line beside a guard with his arms crossed and a concentrated stare scouring the room.

I keep searching for Tinsley, and once I find her, I take my first full breath since I was crouching onstage. She's standing behind me a few feet, too far away.

"Why is she back there?" I ask Sparks, accusation heavy in the question.

Sparks heaves a sigh and leans toward me to say, "Garrison wanted it that way. She can be here, but not too close."

I turn on her then, standing at my full height. Anger swells in my veins until they threaten to pop. "Do you work for me or Garrison?"

Anger fills her eyes, but she keeps a tight leash on it. "You."

"That's right. So, it should be me you take orders from, right?"

She huffs. "What if I told you that against my better judgment, when it comes to this, I agree with him? One photo of you and Tinsley together tonight, and it will be on the news by morning. You aren't capable of keeping your distance from her, and everyone knows it. Believe it or not, we're all trying to help you right now. You have a bigger following now than you did this time last year."

My laugh is shallow, humourless. "Keep her from me again and I will end you. Don't push me, Sparks."

With gritted teeth, she says, "Fine. It's your funeral."

"Wouldn't you rather it be mine than yours?" I flash my teeth and spin back to Tinsley.

She doesn't wait for me to ask before coming over. I barely restrain myself from grabbing her and holding her to me. *She doesn't want that, Noah.*

"You belong beside me," I growl at her.

She smiles softly. Her fingers flex at her side, but she relaxes them a beat later. "Don't be hard on Sparks. She just wants the best for you. Sometimes, you have to give people a chance to prove that to you."

"She should start with not listening to Garrison," I grumble.

"Stubborn," she chides with a look behind me. "The faster you go speak to all your fans, the faster we can leave."

"Fine."

The rush of adrenaline has slowed enough that my mind should be clearer, but my arousal has only grown with Tinsley's close proximity. I should have known better than to get close to her right now, but the thought of her staying away . . .

A few brief conversations and photos, and it's done. Then I can take Tinsley away from here. I'll settle then.

"He's ready to start, Sparks," Tinsley calls softly.

Sparks nods and tells security to start letting people come up. A black marker is handed to me, and I grip it tightly. Tinsley is close enough that I can smell her perfume. It makes my cock weep.

The first couple of people move toward me, and I grow stiff but fight the urge to run. It's two women. They're short and blonde. Nothing like Tiny. My lust begins to fade.

"Hi! Would you mind signing this for me?" one of them asks. There's a black T-shirt in her hands. The same picture of me that's on the tour bus has been printed on the material.

"What's your name?" I attempt to sound interested.

Her eyelashes flutter over and over again as her friend clutches a CD to her chest.

"Natalie," she squeaks.

With a tug, I take the shirt from her and sign it. Her eyes are wide when she takes it back and lets her friend hand me her CD. It's the first and only EP I've released with Reggie so far. After it sat in the top charts for two weeks, I got the call from Garrison about the tour.

The second girl is calmer as she waits for me to sign the CD. "Can you sign this to Sam? He's my boyfriend and really wanted to come tonight, but work, you know?"

I nod and sign it before handing it back.

"Can we get a picture?" T-shirt girl asks.

I swallow my refusal. Sparks would only tell them yes if I turned them away. "Yes."

It's awkward. They seem comfortable touching me. Like I'm a friend, not a stranger. I try not to be so tense, but as their arms move around my waist, I feel my stomach turn over.

Wrong. Very wrong.

The moment Sparks snaps the photo, I step back and away. Both women flash me a grin and then shuffle off together, words whispered between them. If they noticed my discomfort, they didn't care.

One after the other, the fans reach me. Some have merchandise they've purchased tonight for me to sign, while others brought things from home. Every single one has wanted a photo, but it's gone smoothly.

Until a woman wearing one of my concert shirts that's been

ripped down the front to expose her tits and a short leather skirt reaches me. I take a step back. She has gold stars on both her cheeks, and they become distorted when she grins.

"Do you have anything for me to sign?" I ask, noticing her empty hands.

Her grin turns to a smirk. The slit in her shirt grows larger when she grabs both sides of it and spreads her fists. One of her tits nearly pops out as she leans toward me and rasps, "Can you sign right here? Make it out to Golden Girl, please."

Before I have the chance to tell her to fuck off, footsteps clunk hard against the floor. When I look over and see Tinsley stalking toward us, her eyes glowing with outrage, it takes every ounce of my self-control not to howl in satisfaction.

That's it, baby. Come stake your claim.

15

Tinsley

It was going just fine. I was unaffected. Calm, cool, and collected. *Proud.* So. Fucking. Proud.

Then, it was as if a pair of knuckles had plowed right through my stomach and grabbed my insides in a powerful fist. It squeezed and squeezed until nausea rose, and a sudden, strange fury unlike any I've ever known stole my breath.

I felt myself unravelling with each forced hug and lingering smile I was forced to watch, one thread at a time. There was nothing left by the time the woman with the dangerous smirk sauntered toward Noah. I was a ticking time bomb, and the idea of detonating was almost thrilling.

But there was nothing thrilling about watching the woman push her chest in his face. I barely felt myself moving after I heard her ask for him to sign them with my name—*mine*! All I knew was that they were getting closer by the minute, and it wasn't them that were moving.

Noah's eyes bore into me, but I ignore him. Deep inside, I know this isn't his fault. My reactions and feelings are my own, even if I don't understand them. But right now, the voice in my head screaming at the sight of them is too loud to focus on the part that's trying to remain sane. I don't understand what's happening, and I don't have time to try to dissect it.

The woman baring her chest gawks at me, one of her dark brown eyebrows curling into her hairline as I close in. I can't get my legs to stop moving until I'm so close to her that the tips of our shoes touch. Noah is behind me, and I realize that I've stepped in front of him, acting like some weird, possessive bodyguard.

A hush falls over the room, but Sparks is talking, ordering people around. She's probably trying to clear the room before a scandal breaks.

Hot, laboured breaths scatter across the back of my head. Noah's moved closer to me, and something inside of me preens at that. It might as well be a spoken approval.

"You're sure pushy. The rest of us waited in line to meet Noah, so go back and wait your turn. Thanks," the woman snarks. Her smug smile might as well be a declaration of war.

I lean toward her and ask, "Why would I wait in line when I can have his attention whenever I want to?"

She jerks back and narrows her eyes. Finally, she pulls her shirt closed and covers her chest. "I didn't know he had a girlfriend."

"He doesn't. I'm his best friend," I clarify.

Am I reminding her . . . or myself? I scold myself. Her. Definitely her.

Noah makes a sound behind me, and I ignore him again.

The woman watches me curiously, searching for something. "So, what's the problem, then? I waited a long time for this, and I didn't bring anything else for him to sign. I already have an appointment set up tomorrow to get his signature tattooed."

"It's just not happening." I straighten my back, a petty part of me wanting to look at her beneath my nose.

She looks over my head at Noah, her lip jutting out. "Please?"

I wait for Noah to tell her to get lost. I'm expecting it, but as the silent seconds tick by, growing heavier, my stomach sinks. Embarrassment bites into me as I replay the last few minutes in my head. I've made a fool of myself in front of all these people for nothing. *Fuck my life.*

Confused with both my actions and Noah's, I sidestep the two of them and glance at Sparks. Sensing my stare, she looks away from the two security guards and shakes her head at me, obviously frustrated. I heave a breath and mutter a quick apology at the fan before taking another step away from them.

Noah grabs my wrist and tugs just enough to grab my attention. I don't want to look at him, but guilt forces me to lift my eyes. The woman who prides herself on being brave and strong crumbles. I expect him to be annoyed with me for cockblocking him, but it's concern intertwined with a flaming heat that I find in his waiting stare. It makes my knees wobble.

"Sign her chest and make her day, Noah. The bedroom is yours tonight if you want it. I'm sorry," I say, the words quiet enough only he can hear me.

And then, I pull my hand free and walk out of the room. The space between us helps me breathe again as I try to collect my thoughts.

I step into the hallway and lean against a wall. Bending at the waist, I grip my knees and exhale. My pulse is racing.

"Are you okay?"

I want to scream in frustration at the stranger's voice. *Leave me alone, please.*

"Fine. Just needed to be alone," I reply, squeezing my eyes shut.

"I'm sorry to bother you, then," the man says.

I don't reply, and footsteps sound as the person walks away. Being rude to someone, especially someone who's just trying to be nice, is not my thing. I'm not that type of person. But right now, I don't feel like myself at all. I feel like a stranger in my own body.

"Tinsley," Noah barks.

I haphazardly shove my hair out of my face and stand, staring at the wall across from me. "Can a person not get any goddamn alone time in this place?"

"Don't walk away from me."

"I'm not walking away."

I feel him getting closer. The power rippling off him is smothering. It wraps around me against my will, keeping me from running.

"You did. Back there," he growls.

"Would you have preferred an audience? Because I might like to look at boobs from time to time, but hers held no appeal to me."

Suddenly, his palm meets the wall beside my head as he moves into my space, crowding me. We're so close we could hold a piece of paper between us. Anger pulses off him, but I'm the furthest thing from afraid.

He releases a ragged breath and watches me, those dark eyes flaring. "Tell me something, Tinsley."

I swallow, and the arm beside my head flexes. It's thick, bulging with heavy ropes of muscle. Muscle I helped grow. The ghost of a touch moves up my side, over the swell of my hip and dip of my waist, tracing the length of my torso before his other hand presses to the wall. He boxes me in against the wall, a hungry satisfaction flickering across his face.

My hands form fists as I force myself to answer him. "Tell you what?"

"Did you want it to be you?" He tips his chin and moves a hand to my shirt, hooking the tip of his pointer finger beneath the collar. A surprising heat grows low in my belly. "Did you want me to write my name on *your* tits, Golden Girl?"

The crudeness of his question should be enough to have me shoving him back. If anyone else had asked me that, I would have done worse than a shove. But instead, I stand frozen, a throb building between my thighs.

What is wrong with me?

As if sensing my arousal, his face grows pained, but his eyes are hot, sinful.

"You feral little thing," he grinds out. "I wanted you to tear her apart. Waited for it. But you held back. Why?"

"I don't know."

"Liar."

"It doesn't matter." I try to sound firm, but the words are weak.

His jaw pulses before he says, "You are so far above her. She is nothing in comparison."

I want to shout my pleasure at his words, but instead, I shake my head. "Don't say that."

"It's the truth."

"It's mean."

He flashes his teeth and leans in, so close I feel his breath flutter over my nose. "You've always liked me a little mean." The flecks of gold in his irises are so pretty against the dark, angry shade of brown. I could drown in his stare and not even fight for air. "I like you a little mean too."

My breath hitches. Those eyes fall to my mouth, burning hotter and hotter.

His voice is nothing more than a groan. "No one compares. And I think I've had enough of waiting for you to realize that."

My heart jumps to my throat. "Did you do it? Did you sign for her?" I can't keep from asking.

"No. And there was no need to be jealous. I would never ruin your tits with a Sharpie, Tinsley. One day, I'll sign them with something much more potent."

And then as soon as he was here, he's gone. A rush of cold air hits my burning body, and I shiver at the sudden change. I'm forced to watch him walk away as I shake beneath the hurricane of emotions that threatens to strike me down at the knees.

What just happened? And why do I want it to happen again?

NH₃

THERE WASN'T much time for me to gather myself after my conversation with Noah. His sister found me in the hallway a handful of minutes later, and after dragging me into the family room she and her husband had been waiting in, I was forced to see him again.

Noah kept his emotions under wraps, like nothing had just happened. On one hand, I appreciated that. On the other, I wanted to scream at him to explain this all to me. I still do, an hour later.

"I can't even begin to describe how happy I am to be here and to see your pretty face again," Addie bursts.

She rests her head on my bicep and squeezes me, a happy sound escaping her. It's always been hard to be away from her, but at least back when we were teenagers, our families were constantly making plans with one another. We didn't go this long without being together. If my family wasn't out here, nothing would stop me from moving closer to her.

Leaning into her, I squeeze her back. "I missed you so much. You have to tell me about everything. I want all the details on what's been happening in your life these past couple months."

"Where do I start? Um . . ." She chews on her bottom lip and glances at Cooper.

I follow her stare and watch the smallest smirk tilt his mouth. Cooper is *not* a smirking type of guy. After knowing him my entire life, I know him pretty damn well. Although, he has surprised me more than a few times over the past few years.

Take accidentally marrying Adalyn, for instance.

"Tell me what happened!" I push.

Addie giggles. "Nothing yet! But we have decided on something pretty big."

"Stop teasing me, you witch. Tell me. I'm not above begging."

There's a rumbling sound from across the room. I risk a look to find Noah watching me beside Cooper. His arms are crossed, legs spread wide. It's a power stance, and I have to grit my teeth to keep from letting my eyes wander. The room feels too stuffy with him here. My fight-or-flight response is screaming at me to get the fuck away and find somewhere to gather myself.

I need time away from him, or I fear I won't be able to figure out what's going on. The thought of that terrifies me. Our friendship is too important to be unsure about anything.

I'm screwed. *Our friendship.* I think we just crossed a line that best friends aren't ever meant to cross. We have to forget about this and move on because he's too important to me to risk over whatever all of that was.

"Out with it, love. Don't make her crazy," Cooper tells his wife.

I throw my hand up and nod heavily at him. "Thank you!"

Addie flicks my arm. "Oh, relax. Or else I really won't tell you."

"Adalyn." Noah sighs her name.

She flings an eyebrow up her forehead and looks at him. "Oh, hello. Welcome to the conversation, brother."

"You should be nice to me tonight."

"Is that so? Are you going to be nice to me tonight?"

"Have I not been?"

Addie rolls her eyes at her brother, but I can see the amusement in them. She misses him deeply. "I suppose you have. I've yet to have to chastise you for anything. That must be some type of record."

"Tell us your secret, Adalyn," he mutters.

She doesn't need to be asked again.

"We're going to have a baby!" she squeals.

"We're going to start *trying* to have a baby," Cooper clarifies. The way he's looking at her has my eyes glistening. He's so in love with her, and I couldn't love them together more.

"Oh, my God! You're going to have the cutest babies." My

voice cracks, and then I'm crying. Such intense happiness fills me so full I could burst. "I love you two so much!"

Adalyn starts to cry beside me, and we hold on to each other, soaking our shirts with each other's tears.

"Happy tears?" I hear Cooper ask. The words are hushed, so I know they're for his wife.

"Yes," she croaks.

I jerk when a warm hand settles on my back. But after I get a whiff of leather, I relax back into the cautious touch. For right now, I don't try to dissect the events of earlier. I focus on my best friend and what the future holds for her.

Everything else can wait until later.

16

Noah

MY SISTER IS IN FOR IT, AND SHE KNOWS IT.

I freeze in my bedroom doorway not more than an hour later when I see my dad talking to Tinsley in the main part of the bus. As if he's welcome here. It's been months since I've seen him. I wish it was longer.

My hands are in fists. Each step toward him makes my chest throb. I used to be able to feel nothing unless Tinsley was near. My father took away that comfort. He makes me feel more than I want, and more often than not, none of it is good.

The band is nowhere to be seen. They probably ran when I was in the shower and my family showed up.

"Noah," Tinsley says when she notices me coming. She smiles apologetically, but she has nothing to be sorry for.

Adalyn pops out of nowhere and settles between Tinsley and Dad. She doesn't look sorry, but I know this was her idea. *Her fault.*

I stop moving when Mom appears behind my sister. Her eyes and cheeks are wet. She's crying like she always does when we see each other. I hide my discomfort behind a blank stare.

"Hi, Mom," I greet her.

"Oh, my sweet boy! I'm so sorry we missed your show, but

our plane was delayed and—" She stops sobbing long enough to rush to me and wrap her arms around my torso. I awkwardly hug her back. "Oh, it doesn't matter. I just needed to see you, whether we saw the show or not. We'll be at your next one, I promise. I wouldn't miss it for the world."

"You've seen me perform before." I try to placate her. Tears disturb me. Especially hers.

She shakes her head and presses her cheek to my chest. "Not like this, sweetheart. This is no comparison."

"Are you flying back to Vancouver tomorrow, then?" Tinsley asks.

"After lunch, yes." Dad's voice makes me stiffen. Mom notices, and a new patch of wetness grows on my shirt. I wish I didn't hurt her so often.

My show in Vancouver is three nights from now. It's the last Canadian stop before we start to wrap through America. We'll finish the tour on the East Coast of Canada, back in Toronto.

"You could have just waited to see me at the home show. You wasted money coming tonight," I mutter.

Mom lets go of me then, and I try not to show my relief. She frowns. "Seeing my son is never a waste of anything."

"Where are you staying tonight?" I ask.

"You don't need to worry about our accommodations, my love." Mom pats my arms and smiles softly. "Will you come to the house while you're in Vancouver? For lunch or supper? Whatever works best for you and Tinsley."

"I'll try. Tinsley is busy with training and—"

I feel my smug little boxer move to my side before cutting in. "We would love to, Ava."

I swallow a growl. "Lunch, then."

"Fantastic. I can't wait. I'll make all your favourites. Can I invite your brother and Braxton? Liam has gotten so big over the past few weeks, and I know he would love to see his Uncle Noah," Mom rushes out, sucking in a breath when she finishes.

"Maddox would show up whether you invited him or not," I grunt.

Mom laughs. "Is that a yes?"

"Fine."

"I'd like to show you something when you're home, Noah," Dad says.

I flinch. "We'll be on a time crunch. So, probably won't happen."

"Well, if you have the time, then."

"Maybe." Not.

My parents' house stopped being my home when he drew the line between us.

Dad's eyes take on an odd gleam as he stares at me. If I didn't know better, I would think they looked sad. I do know better, though.

He nods once. "Alright."

"You have to stop by my house, too, because I can't wait to show you the changes we've made to it. The landscapers we hired to build the pool in the backyard totally nailed my vision!" Adalyn exclaims.

She loves her house. It was Cooper's, but she moved in when they got married, and it fits her. I was dragged there once. It's very loud and pink. I didn't know they were putting in a pool.

"If we have time."

Her face falls slightly, but she hides her disappointment well. "Okay, big bro."

"Even if he doesn't, I will. I've been dying to see all of your renos," Tinsley tells her. She's being genuine. Her love for my sister is pure.

I've always been jealous of that love. Never hid it well.

Addie beams at her. "Sounds like a date."

"Where's Cooper?" I change the subject, noticing his absence.

"Let's just say that he may or may not be back at the hotel fast asleep. Your fans are intense—I think they overwhelmed him," my sister answers.

I blink. "Oh."

Garrison told us about the crowd already, right after the meet-and-greet. He will never admit that it turned out better than he thought, but I know the truth. He's relieved. I made him a fuck ton of money tonight.

Sparks didn't hide her pride. Despite the scene at the signing, she was happy for me tonight. She most likely is just happy not to have signed her life away to a failure.

Adalyn chokes on a laugh. "Yeah, oh. You're lucky the show was worth it. I don't think Cooper will want to come to the Vancouver show, though. PTSD, you know?"

"I'll have to stop by and check on him before we leave tomorrow," Mom says.

Adalyn waves her off. "I think between the both of us, we can handle a bit of exhaustion, Mom."

Mom looks at Dad. "Why did we end up with the most stubborn children?"

"Karma for our stubbornness, I suppose," he tells her.

She sighs. "Must be."

A knock on the bus door grabs our attention. When it swooshes open, Justice walks in with his daughter fast asleep in his arms.

"I'm sorry to interrupt, but I have to get her in bed," he apologizes quietly.

Mom's quick to move. She pushes through everyone to get to Justice and starts urging him through the bus.

"Come put her to sleep. Oh, she's adorable. How old?" she whispers.

We all step out of their way as they tear through the bus. The bunks are on either side of the hallway, and we watch in silence as she pulls back the curtain of Paisley's bunk and steps back to let Justice tuck her in.

"Your mom has a heart of gold," Tinsley murmurs, leaning into me. Smooth fingers curl around my forearm as she moves in closer and uses my bicep as a pillow. She doesn't pull away when the curious eyes of my family members fall on us.

I ignore them and glance down to find her eyes beginning to droop.

"You're tired."

She huffs a laugh. "Exhausted."

"Come to bed."

"Everyone is still here. It would be rude."

I love when she fights me, but right now, I want her to take care of herself. That means sleeping.

"Please." It's a rough attempt at a beg.

Her brows lift in surprise before she nods. "Okay."

When I look away from her, I notice everyone watching me. They always act surprised when I'm gentle with Tinsley, like they're waiting for me to grow too rough with her the way I am with others. It should sting, but their opinions don't mean anything when it comes to us. I've always believed that.

I would rather die than hurt her.

"We're going to bed," I announce.

Goodbyes come rushing at me. Mom hugs me again, and Adalyn sneaks one while I'm recovering. Dad doesn't try for one. We haven't hugged since I was a child.

Justice is in his bunk above Paisley's, leaving us alone. I don't know where Josh and Dagger are. As long as they're at the show in Vancouver, I don't care where they sleep tonight.

Once everyone is cleared out, it's quiet again. I don't feel as if I'm going to suffocate.

Tinsley releases a tired sound, and I quickly lead her to the back of the bus. She's worked herself hard, and it's late.

I push open the bedroom door and help her sit on the edge of the bed. Her mouth is tilted in a smile too soft for my darkness.

So much has happened today. Things I want to bring up but don't. Would she even talk about what happened earlier? Is she mad at me for it?

I should be mad at myself for losing control. Fuck, it was

worse than a loss of control. I pushed too hard. But I couldn't help myself. Watching her grow so jealous at the meet-and-greet made me feral. Every savage part of me came unleashed, and I wasn't strong enough to cage myself back up.

I press my back against the wall across from where she sits on the edge of the bed and suck in a sharp breath. Memories of earlier barge through my mind. My pulse kicks up, thumping so hard in my throat I wonder if she can see it.

She felt so good against me, soft and warm and *mine*. Fuck, my cock grows so hard it hurts, just like it did in that hallway. It would have been so easy to press between her legs and make her feel what she does to me. How badly she makes me ache.

She looked just as wild as I felt. I didn't misread that. I couldn't have. Something has begun to change in her. And I want to explore whatever it is. Learn what it will take to make it grow.

I told her I was done waiting.

I meant it.

It's finally time to take her for myself.

17

Tinsley

THE ROOM FEELS SO INCREDIBLY SMALL AS I STARE UP AT NOAH. HE leans back against the wall with a deceptive calmness. It's his eyes that give him away. The flaring of them as he watches me like a panther stalking its prey, muscles coiled and ready to pounce.

I know he has to be upset about his parents showing up tonight, but whatever has him so eerily still is overshadowing that pain and frustration. That in and of itself makes me nervous. A flapping sensation comes to life in my stomach.

I force my tongue to unstick to the roof of my mouth. "What are you thinking right now?"

"You don't want to know what I'm thinking."

"I do." Fisting the comforter on either side of my thighs, I nip at the inside of my cheek before adding, "We've never had problems talking to each other before."

He rolls his jaw. "You need to sleep."

My stomach fills with rocks. My worst fear is something coming between our friendship. I've been terrified of losing him my entire life, and this . . . this damn tension between us right now is fuelling that worry. If his inability to feel emotions the way I do wasn't enough to keep me from considering taking the terrifying leap into something more with him, what's happening to us right now—*already*—is.

One confusing encounter with him and things are changing. Becoming awkward and tense.

I drop my head back and stare at the ceiling as a ragged exhale escapes me. "You told me nothing would change between us on this tour. This is exactly what I didn't want to happen."

His scoff is mean. "This doesn't have anything to do with the tour."

"Doesn't it, though? This wouldn't have happened at home." I tip my head forward and tighten my gaze on him. He doesn't back down from my glare. If anything, it makes his intensify. "Don't break your promise."

He answers with two steps toward me. My lips part when he drops to his knees at the edge of the bed and places two shaky palms on my lower thighs. I freeze, my legs so tense they begin to burn.

The air fizzles as I focus on the heat of his hands. On the scent of leather and spice. On the growing throb between my legs.

He watches me with those dark eyes, suddenly so full of emotion I struggle to suck in my next breath. My blood feels electric, my skin buzzing. I tighten my grip on the comforter to keep from reaching for him.

When he speaks, I feel the words rip through my skin and bones before burrowing deep in my soul.

"You are the only one I will ever get on my knees for. That should tell you everything you need to know." Calloused fingers rub at the material of my jeans as if they're trying to burn a hole through them to touch my bare skin. "I've been patient. You've seen it. You know what I feel for you. What I think of you. I will not pretend you didn't light up for me earlier. You're mine, and you'll realize that soon."

My lungs scream at me to breathe, but I struggle to. It's already taking everything in me not to run and hide. Not out of fear of Noah but of the confidence in his words. He doesn't just think we'll be together; he seems sure of it. That's what scares me.

Have I really been that blind? Is there something I'm just not understanding? Am I that naïve to my feelings that I didn't see what he has been?

A knuckle traces the line of my jaw. It's just the ghost of a touch, but it helps me steady myself. I focus on Noah's eyes and watch the specks of gold dance in the brown. This is still my best friend. The one person I trust more than any other on this earth. I need to focus on that.

I want a fairy tale and a Taylor Swift song-worthy love. That's what I've always wanted. But if that's true . . . why am I beginning to feel such a pull toward the man who isn't meant to fit into either of those categories?

Have I just been reading the wrong stories and listening to the wrong music?

"I've scared you," he rasps.

I swallow to soothe my dry throat and shake my head. With a full breath, I uncurl my fingers from the blanket and shyly rest a hand atop the one he has on my thigh.

"I've always known that you cared for me that way. But I— I'm not—I just—you're my best friend, Noah. That means everything to me. You are so important to me," I push out. Frustration nips at me.

He doesn't look surprised by my words. "I won't push you. But I refuse to hide my feelings from you anymore. It's too hard."

Suddenly, a wave of sadness barrels into me. I tug my lip between my teeth and bite down to try and fight the burn in my eyes. My nostrils flare as I glance at the ceiling.

"Tinsley." It's nothing more than a rough sound.

"I'm sorry for hurting you," I whisper.

A deep, pained sound fills the room before he gently grabs my face between two rough hands and forces me to look at him. A lone tear slips out of the corner of my eye, and by the way Noah recoils, you'd think I had reached out and slapped him.

He's always been terrible with tears.

"Stop," he demands.

I choke on a watery laugh. "Most people are afraid of things like clowns or sharks. Not tears."

He scowls while taking his thumb to the inner corner of my eye to collect the tear. The lines between his brows become more prominent. "I'm afraid of nothing."

"Sure."

"You're afraid of ladybugs."

I scrunch my face, the sting in my eyes gone just as suddenly as it appeared. Just like he was hoping.

"They appear out of nowhere and infest your home. They're the worst type of pest."

"They're cute."

"You don't think anything is cute. Nice try."

"Liam is cute."

"Liam is a child. Of course you'd use him to back yourself."

"Cute is an insult unless you're speaking of children or animals," he smarts.

"Don't think that I don't know *you're* also afraid of onions. Keep bugging me about the ladybugs and I'll post a seriously ugly picture of an onion on your Instagram," I threaten.

"Do it and you'll pay."

I waggle my eyebrows and realize that he's still cupping my face. My grin slowly falls as we both realize how close we are. He swallows so loud it's audible.

It's so easy to forget about time and place with Noah. We just mesh. Falling into conversation with him is as natural as taking a breath.

"Do you want to lay in bed and talk about your guests?" The question falls out of my mouth before I can stop it.

When he tenses and I watch his expression close off, I know it was the right thing to ask. Yet, it also feels like the absolute worst thing.

His hands fall from my face, and he leans back on his heels before climbing to his feet. I scoot back on the bed until I'm resting against the headboard. There are a few beats of awkward silence before he nods and comes to the other side of the bed.

The bed isn't big enough for us to lie far apart. I can't tell if I'm truly upset about that when he sits beside me and our arms rest side by side between us. His pinky curls around mine on the mattress. It's a reassuring contact, the equivalent of a warm hug when it comes to Noah.

I let my leg press against his. "If you really don't want to talk about it, we don't have to. But it's not good for you to always hold your feelings inside."

"You should win a trophy for your ability to change a topic whenever you want to," he grumbles.

"There wasn't much more to say. For now, we leave it alone. You said you wouldn't push, right?"

He exhales heavily. With the hand he has free, he starts tapping at his thigh.

"You know why I don't want to see my dad. I want him to leave me alone. Why can't he do that?"

"Because you're family. Despite everything, your dad loves you, and you love him. It's just that neither of you know how to express that. And you're too afraid to. The past is dark for you two, but when is this fight too bloody to go on?"

His tapping picks up pace. "He loved me once, but not anymore. If he did, he wouldn't have said what he did that day."

I close my eyes, Noah's hurt becoming mine. There isn't much I wouldn't do to take all of these problems away. Every child should feel loved by their parents. It breaks my heart that Noah has gone for so long believing Oakley doesn't love him.

Growing up, I spent every summer break with the Huttons. They're my second family. I've watched Oakley raise his children, and there's no doubt in my mind that he loves each and every one of them. He and Noah were never close, but Oakley tried. Whether he knew what he was doing or had no clue, he didn't stop trying to understand Noah. Everyone saw that but the man beside me.

But everything changed that day. The explosion that happened between them destroyed not only their relationship with one another but several outside of it. So much damage has been done that if I ever succeeded in bringing back the father and son, things would never be the same as they were.

I believe with everything in me that Noah needs to make amends with Oakley in order to move on. There will always be a huge chunk of him lost and hurting until they figure their shit out.

"It makes me sad that you think that," I finally say.

"I have nothing else to think."

I uncurl our pinky fingers, choosing to hold his hand instead. It's so much bigger than mine, with tiny raised lines over the knuckles. It's almost offensive that he's hurt his hands so many times by throwing punches without gloves, considering my profession.

"When we go there for dinner, can you please just make sure you spend some time with your mom?" I ask.

His fingers stop tapping as he says, "She was sad tonight."

"She was also happy to see you. It's been months since you've seen your family."

"I miss her," he admits.

"You should tell her that. It would probably make her entire year."

A beat of silence, and then, "Can I hold you tonight?"

My chest warms. The question reminds me of when we were young and I would sleep over but had to stay in Adalyn's room. We always snuck out together and slept in Maddox and Braxton's tree house, ignoring his parents' rules. Despite being so young, he would ask me that question every time.

When I feel the smile on my mouth, I try to reach for some control, knowing we need to keep some boundaries right now.

"We shouldn't be sharing a bed."

"We've always shared a bed." He's stubborn.

"How about we stay here until we get too sleepy to stay awake?" I offer, meeting him halfway.

"Fine."

I should have known better because the moment the sneaky fucker tugs me close, I begin to grow far too comfortable to keep my eyes open.

Neither of us leaves the bed that night.

18

Noah

DAGGER IS ON MY LAST NERVE. HE'S TESTING MY PATIENCE. I WOULD have smashed my guitar over his head already, but that would be insulting to my guitar.

From the increased volume of his microphone, he must have coerced one of the sound techs to raise it before the rest of us arrived for rehearsal. I can't focus with him screaming behind me, his backup vocals louder than my main ones.

Josh has noticed the difference in our sound. He's been glancing at me every two minutes, expecting me to do something about it. I won't. Not yet. Let the arrogant fuck think he's got one over on me for now.

I sing the final lyrics in the last song on the set list and wait for Justice to bring it to an end before walking offstage. My throat is raw and dry. I swipe a bottle of water from the snack table and chug it back. Backstage is busy and loud, full of frazzled people rushing around in preparation for tonight. Someone replaces the water I took before disappearing again.

It's my home show tonight. Everyone expects me to be happy and excited to play here. I'm neither of those things. Vancouver is full of unrealistic expectations and cruel memories. Mistakes I've made over the years that nobody can seem to forget.

The media has been desperate for a story. Oakley Hutton's son and Maddox Hutton's brother, back in town. The one Hutton man with no connection to the NHL. Will he bring disaster with him again? Is there another Hutton scandal brewing in his cauldron?

Vancouver Warriors fans haven't forgiven me for what happened to my brother before I moved away. The misunderstanding that inevitably led to my brother leaving Vancouver to play for Ottawa.

All because of a fight between me, my brother, and a bouncer at a club I had played at that night. The club manager refused to pay me for the hours I put in entertaining his customers, so I took the money I was owed anyway. He sent someone out to make sure I couldn't leave with it.

My brother just so happened to be there at the wrong time. The bouncer shoved me against the hood of his truck, and Maddox wouldn't let me take the beating. He got involved, and once the media found out he was at the club, they swarmed us. With a bag of weed I stupidly made a show of having and the fistful of money I threw at the bouncer in an attempt to get him off my brother, it didn't take a lot of work for the media to turn it into a drug deal gone bad.

I haven't played a show in Vancouver since. If there wasn't a Knockout Training facility here, I would have convinced Garrison to skip the city altogether. But Tinsley deserves to train somewhere she's comfortable and be around people who care for her.

"It's a sold-out show tonight," Justice says, coming up behind me. "How you feeling about that?"

I toss my empty water bottle into the trash. "I should let Dagger take my place."

"Don't give him that satisfaction. How much do you think he paid someone to get his mic turned up?"

"More than he's getting paid to sing backup for me."

He laughs loudly and grabs a juice box from the table. I

notice the sloppy braids in his long hair when they flop into his face. "What are you going to do about him?"

I ignore the question, not wanting to talk about Dagger. "My sister used to braid my hair. She should teach Paisley."

"You did? I can't imagine you letting a little girl anywhere near your hair. But thanks, I think Paisley would like that. She doesn't get to spend a lot of time around women."

"What happened to her mom?" It's blunt and a bit rude, but there's no reason to beat around the bush. He can tell me to fuck off if he doesn't want to share.

He sips the juice from the small clear straw and moves closer to lean against the table beside me. This close, I notice that his grey shirt has a big, glittery pink stain on it. Garrison would rip into him if he saw it. Our boss is a clean freak.

A faraway look ghosts over the drummer's face. "Mel walked out on us a year ago."

I scowl. The taste of displeasure fills my mouth. My mother's biological parents walked out on her. There's no place on this earth for humans like that.

"Does she talk to Paisley?"

A bitter laugh. "No. And it's better that way. My daughter is worthy of more than a woman who could so easily leave her behind."

"You're right."

"I know this isn't the best environment for a little girl, but it's all I can offer her right now. I figure, at least we're together. You know?"

The pain in his voice is too much. I wince as I pat his shoulder weakly. He glances at me, brows knitted together, but doesn't press about the unexpected touch. I would have recoiled if he had.

"If there's . . . anything I can do to help, tell me." I force the uncomfortable words out.

"Thank you."

Retracting my hand, I tap at my thigh and blurt out, "You should have the bedroom. You and Paisley."

"What?"

I gulp, my neck suddenly hot. "On the bus. The bedroom. You should have it with her. Be together."

"Nah. That's your room. We couldn't take that from you."

"Take it. It will be ready for you tonight."

He opens his mouth, probably to argue more, but before he has the chance, I stalk away.

I'm still feeling uncomfortable and confused by the time I leave the venue and step into the Vancouver rain. Something is wrong with me, and I don't know what it is.

NH₎

THE DINNER TABLE is quiet as everyone toys with their food but doesn't eat. The scraping noise of metal on porcelain is grating. I want to get up and leave but force myself to stay seated.

We've been here for an hour, and Mom cried from the moment we arrived till the moment we sat down to eat. My teeth ache from how hard I've been clenching them in an effort to keep from speaking. I don't trust that when I do, I won't say something wrong.

"So, are you going to tell us how you've been, Noah?" Maddox asks.

Apparently, *he* wants me to say the wrong thing.

He's sitting across the table from me, his wife at his side and son on his lap. Liam is stabbing a piece of cheddar cheese with a tiny fork. When he continues to miss it, Maddox guides his hand to help him.

"I've been busy," I reply.

"I would hope that's the reason why I've barely heard from you in months."

Mom sighs from her spot at the end of the table. "You've been busy too, Maddox. We all have."

"Yet *I've* still made time to talk to my family," my brother says pointedly. He's staring at me, looking almost betrayed. That frustrates me.

"Have you? I don't remember seeing your name on my phone recently," I tell him.

"Would you have noticed if I had called? From what I hear, you haven't been answering anyone's calls besides Mom."

"Been gossiping with Dad, have you?" I make myself sound as unbothered as possible.

It was only a matter of time before I was accused of something tonight. I'm not surprised that this is what they chose to go with.

"That's beside the point," he utters.

The mountain of food that Mom set on my plate has grown cold. What little appetite I had before arriving has completely disappeared.

"Would you like me to apologize for not calling, Maddox?" I ask.

He scrapes a hand down his face. "Just forget it."

"I think we just wish you wanted to be more involved in the family," Dad says, finally acknowledging my presence tonight.

I drop my fork. It clatters on the rim of the plate. With a turn of my head, I find him staring at me, expression calm. I tongue my cheek to find my own sense of calm.

His brown hair and green eyes make him look so unlike me. We have so little in common, physically, emotionally, and personality-wise. I don't know how I'm his son.

"Involved in a family where half its members can't stand me. It's a wonder why I'm not nipping at your heels trying to be involved." The words are sharp enough to hide the hurt in them.

"Noah, you know that's not true," Mom croaks.

I push my plate away and feel Tinsley's eyes watching me. When her fingers brush my thigh, it's like the room falls to the back of my mind. I zero in on the touch and the way it steadies me.

She's the cure to my insanity. The flicker of light in the inescapable darkness. She's mine.

I reach for her hand and set it fully on my thigh. Then, I cover it with my palm and hold it there. She doesn't try to pull away.

"Can I talk to you in private?" Maddox asks a beat later. Green eyes hold my stare, almost pleadingly.

I want to say no, but a yes escapes me without warning. His expression relaxes a fraction before he hands Liam to Braxton and stands. It feels wrong to let go of Tinsley's hand.

As I follow him through our childhood home, I harden my shell, not wanting to let myself wander down memory lane. The past is the past. Those memories have no business in my present life. They'll only make my time here harder.

My brother doesn't seem to notice my efforts.

"They kept our heights ticked on the wall in the laundry room. Have you ever noticed that?" he asks.

Slowing his steps, he forces me to walk beside him.

"Is that supposed to mean something to me?"

He laughs, but it's a sad sound. "Apparently not."

"They're just marks on a wall."

"You're right."

I keep my walls up high. "If this is your attempt at bonding, I'm not interested. Childhood memories won't change how I feel."

He leads us toward the basement. The door is closed, but he pushes it open before flicking on the light. A set of stairs becomes visible. I haven't been down to the basement since before I moved out. My bedroom was down there. It's where I spent most of my time.

"Are you trying to get me to move back home? Because it's not going to happen."

He scoffs a laugh and starts to descend the staircase. "Yeah, right. I just want to show you something before you leave again."

. I follow him down the stairs but don't reply.

Everything is exactly how I remember. The gaming centre with the flat-screen and couch that covers the entire room from edge to edge. The bar with the neon green stools. The empty guitar stands.

My bedroom door is shut with the *keep out* sign still taped across the middle. My chest grows tight.

"Addie told me that Mom used to come down here all the time after you moved out. She did the same with my room after I moved out, but not to the same extent," Maddox says, suddenly beside me. "She would take naps on our beds."

"Mom has always been emotional with us."

"You're right. But she worries about you most."

I shove my hands in my pockets and mutter, "I never asked for that."

"You didn't have to. But you had to expect it would happen. They've always been different with you. It's not a bad thing, but you're different than Addie and me."

"Is there a point to this?"

His next exhale is longer than usual. "Yes. There is, smartass. Open the damn door."

When I do, the sight of my childhood bedroom makes my head swim. An explosion of emotions, both confusing and familiar, hits me when I take in the new posters and newspaper articles that clutter the black walls.

"When did Mom start doing this?" I step into the room, walking toward the wall that has my first printed poster hung on it. It's in a glass frame above my bed.

"Mom didn't do this."

The second frame has a photo of me playing in the backyard for Adalyn's sixteenth birthday. I force my eyes off it and turn to Maddox, suddenly too fucking curious.

"Was this you, then?"

He shakes his head, mouth pulling into a sad smile. "It was Dad."

"Don't," I warn, the word coming out venomous.

"It's true."

My tongue is heavy in my mouth. I don't reply.

"You might think he doesn't love you, Noah, but he does. You two hurt each other, and neither of you knows how to make it right. Maybe you don't even want to. But eventually, this has to come to a head. And when it does, please don't run. If anything, please just fix this for the rest of us," he pleads.

I struggle to do more than nod. He knocks his knuckles on the wall and nods back.

"Right, well, come up when you're ready. Just take a look around and try to start believing that you aren't as unloved as you believe you are. I, for one, love the shit out of you, little bro."

The blow from those words makes me rock back on my heels. I swallow past the dryness in my throat and open my mouth. Nothing comes out. Maddox doesn't seem offended by my silence, but even if he was, I don't think he would have said anything.

He walks out a beat later, and I reach up to grab the back of my head, feeling too many emotions. I don't know how to sort through them.

I stand there and suffocate instead.

19

Tinsley

I BOUNCE MY LEG UNDER THE TABLE AND TRY TO JOIN IN THE TENSE conversation Braxton is having with Oakley and Ava. Liam is blabbing a string of words that don't really sound like words, and I want to grin at him but can't bring myself to. I'm far too anxious to relax in that way.

"You should have been the one to take Noah downstairs, Oakley," Ava reprimands her husband. The sight of her tired, red eyes makes my heart ache.

"He didn't want anything to do with the idea of going anywhere with me when I mentioned it the other day. Maddox needs the time with him just as much as I do," he replies. Is he trying to convince himself of that as much as he is the rest of us?

"That's not true," I butt in. Three sets of eyes are flung in my direction. I grow taller in my chair and hold Oakley's gaze. "He may need Maddox, but he needs you more. I know you're not naïve enough to believe Noah will ever come back to you on his own. If you don't take that first step, soon there won't be anything left of your relationship to come back to."

He flinches at my words before scrubbing a hand down his face. When it falls to his lap, his mouth is downturned in a heavy frown.

"It's not that easy," he says.

Fire ignites in my gut. "You're right. And it shouldn't be easy. This is your son we're talking about. He's worth the effort, don't you think?"

"She's right. I miss our son, Oakley. I miss him so much," Ava whispers.

Pain slashes across Oakley's face as he looks at his wife. Remorse is heavy in his stare. Some wicked part of me likes seeing it. Maybe now, he'll actually fix this.

I've never known Oakley Hutton to be a chicken shit. He's lived a successful career as a professional athlete, and I know that takes more than just skill. It takes endless courage. Yet when it comes to his son, something keeps holding him back.

Not for the first time, I wonder if something more happened between the father and son than I'm aware of.

The sound of footsteps draws our attention. Maddox comes into view. Alone.

"Everything okay?" I ask. Why isn't Noah with him?

Maddox lifts a shoulder. It's a tired movement. A defeated one. My anxiety skyrockets.

I jump to my feet and start toward where Maddox came from. "I'm going to find him."

Nobody tells me not to. They know better than to waste their time. Mumbles sound behind me as I walk quickly, but I tune them out. Like always, when it comes to Noah, nobody else matters. It's always been us. Best friends from birth until the end of time.

Reaching the bottom of the basement stairs, I take a long look around the room. Memories, *so many of them*, rush at me from every direction. Movie nights, girl talks with Adalyn and Ava. Long hours spent helping Noah write songs and perfect chords that fit those songs we created like a glove.

I sigh and head toward the open door of Noah's room, expecting to find him there. I don't doubt the door is usually kept shut.

When I find him standing in the centre of the room, his fingers tangled tightly in the hair at the back of his skull, I close the distance between us. The black walls around us are so different than they used to be. Once decorated with ripped notebook paper and shelves of Noah's favourite records, they're now covered in . . . well, Noah.

Unable to help myself, I pause at his back and slowly, carefully, slide my arms along his sides, holding him in a hug that I hope he finds some comfort in. His sudden inhale as I clasp my hands at his front, resting them against his abdomen, is the only reaction I get.

I press my cheek to the space between his shoulder blades and close my eyes, inhaling his scent. "I saw Maddox come up alone."

"Does it bother you that I'm not like my brother?" he asks, surprising me.

I hide my confusion. "Not at all. Why would you ask me that?" No response. "I've never wanted you to be anyone but yourself. Is this because of your dad?"

"Does it matter?" His voice is so cold, detached.

"Of course it does. Your feelings *matter*, Noah."

"To you," he rasps. "They matter to you."

My chest tightens, his words wrapping a fist around my heart and squeezing. How can he sound so surprised by that? Fuck, that makes me sad.

"They always have."

He leans back into my touch, a deep sound rumbling in his chest, the vibrations warming my hands. My fingers tighten around themselves as I keep myself from stroking his abdomen through his T-shirt. The moment is all wrong, but fuck, I want to do it. Clearly, it wouldn't be the first time I've ever touched his chest, but if I gave in to my curiosity right now, feeling the way I am, it would be *so* very different.

Little by little, he's giving some slack to the tight rope wrapped around his restraint. The knowledge of that shouldn't affect me nearly as much as it does. I can't take advantage of that.

Suddenly, I remember his promise from the other night.

You're mine, and you'll realize that soon. Like every time I've repeated those words in my mind, I feel myself grow antsy with the urge to find out just *exactly* what being his would be like.

But I don't allow myself to think about that too much. Not when I know he's so clearly struggling. This much hurt inside of one person is bound to destroy them. It's too heavy to carry alone. Hell, it's too heavy for even two people, but I'd endure the weight of it for him.

"I gave the bedroom on the bus to Justice and his daughter."

My eyes grow wide. "You what?"

"Shouldn't have done it without asking you. You can be pissed at me."

I roll my forehead to his back and release a breathy laugh as I squeeze him tighter. "You want me to be pissed that under all of this thick, spiky exterior of yours, you're really just a big-ass teddy bear?"

His reply is deep and growly and makes me giggle. "That's insulting."

"If you say so," I sing.

When he spins around and encloses me in his arms, I howl a laugh despite my surprise. If I didn't know better, I would think the jutting of his bottom lip is almost a pout.

He narrows his eyes on me and holds my hips beneath his big hands. The touch makes me feel small in comparison to him, which is not something I'm used to. His thumbs and forefingers slip above the waistband of my jeans and disappear beneath the hem of my shirt. My laugh trickles off as my pulse thrums in my ears. Little tingles erupt from beneath his fingertips, making my skin beneath them buzz.

"I'm not a teddy bear," he grunts.

I glance down to where he holds me, at the gentleness of his touch. Lifting a brow, I ask, "No? 'Cause you seem pretty soft to me right now."

Eyes flaring, he digs his fingertips deeper into the swell of my hips before he yanks me toward him. I suck in a breath when he shifts his groin and presses against me, right into the ridges of my abdomen.

"There's nothing soft about me, Tinsley."

My tongue is in my throat. I've swallowed it. The rigid length of him juts into me, so long and thick I wonder how I've never noticed it before. My pulse has fallen between my legs, thumping so heavily I wonder if he can sense it.

The corner of his lips tugs into a dirty smirk as he leans down and purrs, "Cat got your tongue, Golden Girl?"

"I swallowed it, actually," I squeak, suddenly so damn flushed.

A rough, deep laugh traces my temple before he brushes it with his lips. With a subtle push of his hips, he grinds himself against me. His eyelids fall shut over those dark eyes, and his touch turns bruising, hard enough that I'll feel him there long after he pulls away. Yet, I don't tell him to stop. I don't want him to.

What's wrong with me?

"You drive me fucking crazy," he grinds out, as if he's angry with me. "Tell me to stop."

I shake my head. "I can't."

And then we're moving. Air bursts from my lungs when my back hits the wall, the following thump sounding so loud in the silent room. His jaw pulses as he stares down at me, the iron-tight grip he has kept on his control finally bursting to pieces on the floor. I notice the palm cupping my skull and the fingers tangled in my hair when he grips it and drops his forehead to rest against mine.

He cushioned my head from hitting the wall.

I gulp for air, trying to fill my burning lungs. The air smells like him, leather and spice and an all-consuming dominance. My head empties of everything but Noah. With each breath I fight for, he fills me, until all I know and feel is him. His anger, lust, and obsession.

One breathing life into the other.

That's how it's always been.

I drop my head back against the wall and bite down on my lip to stifle a whimper when he buries his face in my neck and groans. It's a wild, angry sound, and it has me rubbing my thighs together, the ache between them growing to be too fucking much.

"I'd devour you. Take and take until you had nothing left for me. I'm not right for you."

I can barely pull a sentence together. "You don't scare me."

As if to try and prove a point, he smacks the wall beside my head so hard I'm positive they heard it upstairs. I don't so much as flinch. A thick sense of approval has fire blazing in his eyes. The flames grow brighter with each second we watch each other, my newfound confidence driving me to reach for him. With one sure movement, I push the bandana out of his hair and thread my fingers in the thick strands. I've played with his hair before, but it's never felt like this. Like with each tug of it between my fingers, I'm in some fucked-up way embracing my power over him. Like I could shove him to his knees and use it to pull him between my legs.

It's wrong.

It's also *right*. So fucking right.

My grip grows tighter, to the point I know it must hurt. His responding grunt sends me for a spiral as he shoves his erection against my stomach again. I give his hair a brutal tug, and he throbs against my belly.

"I should terrify you," he breathes, lips parted over my pulse point.

My head is swimming. All common sense has drowned in the darkened cave of my mind. There's nothing here but this insatiable want and need boiling my blood. It's dangerous. Reckless. Stupid. I don't care.

"I know," I whisper.

"So run. Before I don't let you," he warns with a sharp nip at my throat. The burn that follows only stokes the flames between us.

"I'd just let you catch me."

A flash of disbelief flickers across his face before it's gone, replaced with something dark and dangerous. His stare drops to my mouth, his tongue darting out to wet his.

That's it, Noah. *Let me play with the monster inside of you.* Just for a minute.

And just when I think he might do just that, a hesitant knock on the door has the beast slipping back into the shadows. The heat cools in his stare, a mask falling back in place.

It's a shock to my system. All at once, I feel reality set in, the consequences of what could have just happened between us making my head spin. A cruel cold sweeps over me when Noah backs away and glances at the door. I want to demand he come back, and that terrifies me. With a shaky hand, I attempt to smooth the knotted hair at the back of my head.

"Did you need something?" Noah asks, sounding purely curious.

The lack of aggression in his tone has me following his stare. I go red from top to bottom. I've never been one to get shy easily, but there has to be nothing more embarrassing than getting caught pressed up against a wall by the mother of the man doing said pressing. Especially in his childhood bedroom.

Noah's mother is pink-cheeked as she stares at the ceiling, seemingly not sure where to look. Her hands are clasped at her front, thumbs tapping.

"It had been a while since you left, so I just wanted to check on you and make sure everything was okay. It's the mama bear in me. Can't ever turn it off, you know? Even after having three children, I just can't seem to let things be," she rambles nervously, still staring at the ceiling.

I hit my head against the wall and wince at both the pain and the mortifying situation.

Noah scowls at me but speaks to his mom. "Is there something on the ceiling?"

She whips her head in his direction and laughs softly. "Well, aren't you full of questions today." Taking a quick glance at the frames on the walls, she frowns ever so slightly. "Come finish eating, my love. Your food is cold, but I can microwave it. I also stocked up on your favourite snacks this morning."

Ava has always been the type of parent who has so much love to give that I don't know how she manages to contain it all. She reminds me of my mother in that way.

I fight off a frown as a wave of homesickness rolls over me. Only a few more days and my parents will be at my first fight. I like Hunter, but it'll be nice to have my dad there to train with me beforehand to help ease my nerves. Same with Mom.

"I'm not that hungry," Noah tells Ava.

She scoffs, waving him off. "You aren't leaving this house without food in your stomach. Now, come on. I don't have much time left with you."

Noah hesitates, his expression far too blank, so I move first. When I shoot him a begging glance as I walk past, he reluctantly trails behind me. The smile on Ava's face when we join her is bright enough to light an eternal void.

If every member of his family were as loud with their love as Ava is, I think most of their problems would disappear.

20

Noah

Tinsley is in my arms the moment I step offstage. Her laugh is airy and clean. It blankets my heightened emotions and dampens the thrill of adrenaline pumping through me.

Home. Is that what she is to me?

"You were amazing! You all were," she says.

I tuck my face into her neck and huff, "Don't compliment them."

She smells so good. Like fruit and something deeper, sexier. Having her this close only reminds me of what occurred earlier in my childhood bedroom. Of how close I was to rutting her against a fucking wall like a beast at the sight of her attraction. She wanted me then, not quite to the extent I want her, but it was something. Haven't been able to forget it since. Probably never will.

She wiggles in my grip, and I reluctantly let her go. When she slides down the front of my body and feels my hard cock, I almost smirk at the squeaky noise she makes.

"Are you ready for your first official after-party?" she asks, appearing slightly flushed.

Before I can tell her how I would rather walk into traffic,

Sparks comes up behind me, knocking her shoulder against me. "He can't wait. Isn't that right, Noah?"

"I have never been so excited for anything," I deadpan.

Tinsley grins knowingly. "How long do we have to stay?"

"Long enough for everyone to know you were there." With a pointed look at me, she adds, "That means no hiding. Take a few pictures and smile at least once, for me."

"Anything else?" I ask.

She rolls her eyes. "Be careful on your way out. I have a security team ready to leave with you and a car waiting, but the media has migrated to the back door. They've drawn a crowd too. This could wind up being a PR nightmare, and unless you want Garrison to become even more of an overbearing nuisance for the duration of this tour, I need you to be smart and ignore them."

"How long will it take for them to clear out?" Tinsley asks, almost hesitantly, as if she's dreading the answer. We both are.

Sparks grimaces. "Longer than I would like."

"Great." All of the work we've put into avoiding the media was fucking pointless. They're sharks with the scent of fresh blood, and Sparks has tossed me overboard with a bloody nose. "We're leaving now, then."

Tinsley glances at me, chewing anxiously on the inside of her cheek. "Are you sure? We can wait. Isn't it better to be fashionably late to a party? Especially your own?"

"You might take them by surprise if you leave right now. They'll be expecting you to try and wait them out a bit," Sparks says, agreeing with me for once in her life. She turns to wave at the three guys waiting off to the side of the backstage area. The biggest of the three tips his chin at her and then says something to the other two before they all head our way.

With a brief introduction and lesson on following rules, the glorified mall cops lead us away from Sparks and toward the side door we used earlier. Shouts from outside assault the door, the volume of them surprising.

The big mall cop with the wannabe punk-rock hair faces us, his back to the door. Expression stoic, he barks orders at the other two guys whose names I don't care to remember and then turns to me.

"Stay between the three of us out there. It's not just reporters out there; there are fans too. Head down, mouth shut. Clear?"

I swallow my agitation at his tone. "Do your job and we'll be fine."

"What he means is that yes, we're clear," Tinsley cuts in, running a hand up my back. A warning? If it is, I want to ignore it just to see what she'll do to me.

Mr. Wannabe straightens his shoulders and nods. It's the last look at him we get before he pulls open the door and leads us outside.

I nearly trip. The press is everywhere. Screams, questions, and flashes come from every direction. I think fast, tucking Tinsley beneath my arm and plastering her to my body as we push through the crowd. My heart beats heavily in my chest. Too many people. Too fucking close.

There's been no time to come back to earth after the show. I'm still high on adrenaline, still slipping back inside my body. How did all these people get back here?

We're sucked into the crowd with only one bodyguard in front of us. I don't know where the other two are. It's too loud to try and listen for them.

Someone shoves me from behind, and I tighten my grip on Tinsley as we stagger forward. With a whip of my head, I have a man with a camera pinned beneath my stare, my lip curling with silent warning. I want to hurt him for threatening Tinsley's safety. Make him drop to his knees on the filthy pavement and apologize.

"Don't. Keep moving!" she shouts at me. I dismiss the man and focus on her, nodding.

But the rage doesn't go anywhere. It grows with each touch and picture taken against our permission as we push through.

My chest constricts, refusing air into my lungs. Anxiety scratches at me the longer it takes to get free.

"Noah, are you a naturally angry person?"

"Please take a photo with me!"

"Are you on drugs again?"

"Where is your father tonight?"

A muffled cry coming from my arms turns my blood to ice. I look down at Tinsley and find a foreign hand too close to her. Find three light pink lines running down her forearm, red pooling from within them.

My mind goes quiet. Still.

And then, it's too loud. Everything in me screams that something isn't right. I don't realize I have the man's shirt in my hands until I've pulled him so close I can smell the liquor on his breath. There's interest in the eyes that stick to Tinsley despite my closeness to him. I shake him violently, even as arms begin to tug me back. A savage snarl escapes me when he continues to ignore me, watching what's mine.

I can hear the voices of people I know screaming at me to let him go. They tug at me harder, their efforts beginning to pay off. I'm jerked to the side, and I bring him with me. Every feature of the man before me has been memorized, locked away for safekeeping. The dirty grey hair and odd-coloured eyes. Too bright. Too blue. He's slim and tall. Old enough to be my parents' age.

When I feel someone yank on my arm hard enough to elicit a hiss of pain from me, the man finally looks me in the eye. I recognize the way they glimmer, brimming with the two most dangerous feelings one can feel.

Obsession.

Lethal rage.

I welcome the darkness that fills me then. Let him witness it and the promise we make him. Only then does he begin to understand how very wrong he was to approach her.

"Noah! Please, we're almost there!"

I feel a gentle sweep of fingers across my jaw, and then the arms clawing at me drop. The weight of hundreds of wandering eyes is heavy as I stand there, the man still in my grasp. It's the bossy guard who grabs him from me. With a disapproving glare in my direction, he shoves the guy back into the crowd and starts cutting through bodies for us.

I don't give a fuck about his disapproval. He can think what he wants, but nobody touches Tinsley. Only someone with a death wish would hurt her. There's a smear of blood on her arm from where she must have tried to quickly wipe it away. I can't focus on anything but the sight of it. Her cry of pain echoes in my mind.

"Now, Noah. Let's go!" she yells, trying again to get me to move. Slowly, I raise my gaze from the scratches up to her face. An encouraging smile tugs at the corners of her eyes. "Almost there."

I reach for her again, angry with myself for letting her go in the first place, and then let her lead me by the hand the rest of the way. It's easier to get through now. Several people have backed away. I don't look to see if they've grown afraid of me. They should be.

One of the bodyguards opens the back door of the black SUV, and I usher Tinsley in first, then crawl in after her. Once the door is slammed shut behind me, I twist my body and reach across her lap to grab her arm.

The driver doesn't say a word before pulling the SUV away from the venue. Tinsley watches me examine her. It's so silent my breaths are like claps in the night.

"I'm okay," she murmurs.

I grunt in response. Cupping her elbow, I brush the tip of my finger along the edge of the first scratch, careful not to touch the broken skin. It's not deep, but it's not nothing either. She acts tough, but she's fragile. Easy to break. The dried streak of blood on her arm is an example of that.

"They're just scratches. I've bled from much worse. Have you forgotten that I get hit and punched for a living?" Her voice is light and teasing. The gentleness doesn't help. Each word is a blow. They make me more eager to lock her away somewhere safe, where nothing and nobody can touch her.

Ripping my stare from her, I look over the seat at the GPS on the dash and bark at the driver, "Take us to the hotel. We're not going to the fucking party."

Tinsley huffs. "Yes, we are. Don't take us to the hotel."

The driver uses the rear-view mirror to glance between us. He makes no move to change the address on the dash.

I smack the centre console. "Hotel. Now."

"You're being ridiculous. And *rude*. Take us to the party." Tinsley's glaring at me now, fire turning the silver in her eyes a molten grey.

I set one hand on her headrest and the other on the door beside her as I move into her space, hiding her from the driver's sight, giving him my back. She isn't fazed by me, doesn't back down. When she straightens and closes the distance between our faces until I can almost taste her lips, I suck a breath through my teeth and curl my fingers into the leather seat.

My cock turns to stone, so fucking wet with precum my underwear sticks to me. Arousal heats my blood to the point of boiling. One tip of my chin and I'd finally know what she tastes like. Know what sounds she'd make as I tucked her lip between my teeth and bit down hard. A punishment for driving me to such insanity and desperation.

"We are going to the party. Do you understand me, Noah Hutton?" she growls.

I'd take any order from her right now. Do her bidding as if it were my own.

I spit a jagged curse when she sets a firm hand on my upper thigh and *squeezes*. My vision blurs. *Too high.* The warmth of her palm seeps into the tip of my cock, the squeezing pressure she's using bringing pure ecstasy. Pleasure spikes through my groin as my hearing blows and my muscles turn to cement.

My jaw throbs from how hard I'm clenching it, fighting to stay silent when I want to scream for her. I throb beneath her hand over and over again as I spill into my underwear.

She doesn't pull away. *No.* My filthy fucking girl tenses her fingers, even as my cum fills the material beneath them. The widening of her pupil-blown eyes tells me she knows exactly what just happened. What her touch—even accidental—was able to bring out of me.

My hearing slowly returns. Each second that passes is another with her hand on my cock. I don't move. Don't want to scare her away. I'm unashamed of what happened. But even I can tell how fragile this moment is. She doesn't look afraid of what happened, though.

Her lips are parted, so ruby red and glossy, begging to be sucked and bit and *filled*. Fuck, I ache to fill that pretty mouth.

I'm a freak. There's always been something wrong with me, and she knows that. She's long accepted it, even when everyone else warned her it wasn't a good idea. So, when I remove my hand from the headrest and shove it past my waistband, I don't hesitate to coat my thumb in my cum. Watching my golden girl, I pull my hand back out and lift it to her mouth. I offer her my thumb, the tip shiny and slick in front of her lips.

A shiver thunders through her as she stares at my thumb, and that's it. My control snaps like a taut cord.

I push my thumb past her parted lips to the second knuckle and then push down on her tongue. "Suck."

Determination flares in her stare before she presses down harder on my cock and does exactly what she's told. A loose groan slips free at the feel of her warm, wet mouth. *Fuck.* I want this mouth on me. I want to shove it so far down her throat I can feel the shape of it when I choke her until she's light-headed. I want to shoot my cum down her throat, filling her belly.

"Taste what you do to me, Tinsley," I rasp, head dizzy.

Her tongue swirls over the tip of it, grabbing every last drop. I roughly press my nose to hers, rubbing them together. When her blunt teeth nip at my thumb, I let loose a gravelled laugh and slowly pull it out.

The driver clears his throat. "At the risk of being yelled at again, I should be taking you to the party still, right?"

Tinsley

I STILL TASTE HIM MINUTES LATER WHEN WE PULL UP IN FRONT OF the club. Taste him, feel him, crave him. *Want him.* The thrill inside of me is one I've only felt after a winning match. Noah elicited that response from me. No, he *commanded* it, coaxed it out of me with dirty eyes and an arrogance that shot directly between my legs. I can't remember ever being so turned on.

I've never been outgoing with my desires. Maybe that stems from my overall lack of love life or just simple insecurity. Not many boys flocked to me much growing up. Not only was I looked at as one of the guys because I was more concerned with training than flirting, but on the rare chance a boy showed me any serious interest, Noah was there to scare him off the moment he stepped foot in Toronto to visit.

Somehow, I'd managed to lose my virginity to a guy in twelfth grade a few weeks before graduation. I knew it was my last chance before Noah returned for the summer, and I refused to go my entire life a virgin. In the end, a very disappointing and painful five minutes was all it turned out to be. But even if I had wanted more with the guy after school ended, my shadow returned that summer.

A hulking, grouchy man shadow who that very summer

punched a guy in the face when he asked me for my number. Honestly, I didn't mind the overprotectiveness much. Noah was always everything to me, and I knew I was everything to him. We had each other, and that was more than enough. But I can't pretend that the smallest part of me doesn't feel as if maybe I've missed out on a lot of experiences that I should have had as a teen but never bothered trying. Like staying out past curfew to kiss boys or experimenting with my sexuality.

Isn't that what you're supposed to do in your twenties? Make a million mistakes and get your heart broken? I'm not unhappy in the slightest with how I've lived my life up to this point, but I am curious. And that's all on me. I had ten months of the year to put myself out there and try new things, but I spent them at home on the phone with my best friend every night instead, waiting for when we would be together again.

It was weird to those who didn't know us and even to some who did. My other half lived across the country. I should have gone out and lived my life to the fullest without him, but something inside of me always rebelled at that idea. If I couldn't do something with Noah, then I wouldn't do it. Simple as that. And I knew he was the same.

Never did I imagine we would be here, doing the things we've done over the past couple of weeks. It's all wrong. Best friends don't have heated moments in their childhood bedrooms or make each other come in their pants in the back of rental cars. My face heats at the reminder of what followed that shocking event.

For something so wrong, I can't help but realize how right it feels. Like peeling off a blindfold that you never realized you were wearing. I want to be scared at what's happening between us, but I don't think I've ever felt safer. That's the terrifying part. It sounds naïve. My father would be the first to tell me that. Strangers would question if I should be put in an asylum.

But Noah wants me, and there's no doubt in my mind that if I gave in to him, he would never let me go. I'd be the most treasured person on this earth, set on a throne made from his blood, sweat, and tears. Our friendship has always been destined for forever; *nothing* could change that. Yet, I know there's something holding me back. The tiniest thorn in my side reminding me not to take the leap.

Would I be happy? Could he truly give me the kind of love I need? Not just obsession and protection and desire but genuine love. I don't know if I could sacrifice that for him. Not yet. I'm not ready to say whether or not it would be worth the risk.

"Tinsley."

"Huh?" I ask, snapping my head to the side to look at Noah. He's frowning. "Sorry, I was just thinking."

"About what?"

Shuttered camera flashes bounce off the SUV's tinted windows. I wince, nearly reaching for the fresh scratches on my arms. They don't sting anymore, but I don't want another set to match.

"They won't touch you." It's an angry promise.

He's too far away from me, sitting properly in the opposite seat. I want to yank him back, want to feel his muscles grow stiff beneath my fingers again. I slowly release a breath and grapple for some sense of calm.

"We should go, then."

He rolls his jaw. His eyes are watching me, brimming with a deceptive gentleness. "Guess so."

Neither of us moves. It's hot in here despite the air conditioning blowing against my sweat-slicked skin. My clothes feel too tight and heavy. I shut my eyes and clench and unclench my fingers. When I open them again, Noah is still watching me, but he's closer, leaning across the middle seat between us as if he couldn't stand the distance any more than I could. He's still too far away but close enough I feel like I can breathe again.

Dark eyes trace the lines of my face before he strokes his knuckles along my jaw. "Don't stray too far in there. I'd hate to have to tear the place apart to find you."

I lean into the touch and grin. "Don't act as if you wouldn't like chasing me."

"I've been chasing you for two decades. Never been able to catch you, though. The idea does appeal to me."

The underlying dare in his words makes my stomach tumble in the best way. "Game on, then, Mr. Dark and Twisty."

"I hope you know what you're doing," he warns, the start of a smirk growing on his face.

I wink and, with a quick thank you to the driver, hop out of the car. The air feels like it's gotten muggier since we left the venue, and I groan as it sticks to my skin. I doubt the club is any cooler. At this rate, I'm positive I'm going to just combust into a ball of flame the moment we step inside.

The sound of Noah's door shutting has me rushing to meet him. He's readjusting the red-and-black bandana in his hair when I bump him with my shoulder and nervously watch the crowds of people hanging around the entrance as they turn to stare at us.

Being watched by this many people will always be uncomfortable for me, even if I'm not completely new to the experience. Even as an amateur boxer, I've dealt with people watching me. And Noah has always been a musician, regardless if he was playing in dive bars or arenas. It's learning how to handle crowds to this extent that's going to be a challenge for the both of us.

"Come on, superstar. The sooner we get inside, the sooner we can leave," I encourage.

He nods and closes off his expression. "An hour."

"An hour," I agree.

And then we head inside.

TURNS out an hour can feel a lot longer than you think when you're not having fun.

I've never been one for sulking, but for the past forty minutes, that's become my newest personality trait. By the time we stepped inside the club and were ushered toward the VIP section, swarms of people were already trying to grab Noah's attention. Screams and chants are still ringing in my ears as I watch another woman wave a poster from her spot on the lower dance floor.

Noah, I want The Devil Inside Of ME!

He's too busy leaning over the red VIP rope signing CDs to notice. I'm grateful for that. The wording of the sign is fitting, considering *The Devil Inside* is the title of his album and tour, but the hidden meaning behind it makes me want to puke almost as much as it makes me want to maul him in front of everyone in this damn club. I'm acting ridiculously possessive, but I'm beyond caring. I've never been able to understand how Braxton can be okay with the things said to Maddox both online and in person. I'm already beginning to lose my mind, and Noah isn't even mine to be possessive over.

"I've never seen you glare at someone like this before. It's kind of scary," Sparks shouts from beside me.

"I haven't been glaring."

She makes a sound of disbelief. "Yes, you have. You've been sending a death glare to that poor woman for the past five minutes. I'm surprised she hasn't noticed yet."

"Can you blame me? Look at the sign. How did that even get in here?" I place my hands on my hips. "It's offensive."

"It's not illegal to bring a small sign into a club, Tinsley. Would you like me to go down and snatch it up?"

"Yes, actually," I deadpan, meeting her stare. "That would be great."

"It's hard to believe there was a time when I worried about you with how much time you spent with Noah. Turns out you're just as savage as he is."

Would it be wrong to feel pride at that? Probably. "That's the nicest thing you've ever said to me."

"I've been a real bitch to you, then."

"Add a boss to the bitch, and you're on the money."

Her eyes twinkle, warming her usually cool features. It's nice to see her not so guarded for a change. I can't help but want to get to know her a bit more, considering she isn't going anywhere.

"Thank you for getting him here tonight. I know he didn't want anything to do with this," she says, attention drifting to Noah.

I'd have to be blind not to see the tension in his body as he watches the line of people continue to grow, regardless of how many of them get their items signed and move on. He refused to host a meet-and-greet, so I know how much this has to be stressing him out. There wasn't supposed to be a signing of any sort tonight, but when Sparks arrived after us with new orders from Garrison, there wasn't much we could do to stop this from happening.

"When can I get him out of here?" I ask.

She glances at the smartwatch on her wrist. "I can get the driver back here in a few minutes."

Some of my worry eases. "Thank you. I'll go tell them to close the line."

"And have Noah come at me for letting you out of the VIP section? No. I'll get the line closed, and once he's finished, you can steal him away. I'll give the driver your number so he can call you when he arrives."

"Thanks," I say on an exhale.

She shrugs me off. "Just doing my job. I'll see you both tomorrow." I don't get a chance to reply before she's heading toward the red rope and slipping out of the secluded section.

Noah must notice his manager begin to move through the line because he whips around to look at me, lifting a questioning brow. I toss him a wink and close the distance between us. He's started to sign over the sadistic Devil portrait on his album cover when I reach him.

The red marker in his hand drifts across the CD and leaves behind a messy scribble before he hands it back to the man waiting. When I notice the marker shaking in his grip, I set my hand on his back and hope the subtle touch is enough to help soothe him somehow.

Leaning up on my toes, I move my mouth to his ear. "Sparks is closing the line. Then we can leave, okay?"

"Can you stay with me?"

Something wraps around my heart and tugs. "Always."

The next person in line steps up and excitedly shoves a poster toward him, not even bothering with a hi. I wince and watch Noah sign it before giving it back. There are only a handful of people left, and one by one, they come and go until the line is gone.

I don't waste a second before grasping Noah's hand in mine and tugging him toward an area quiet enough we can speak without shouting. The smoke machine from beneath the DJ's booth pushes tendrils of smoke around our feet. I'm too busy watching it wrap around Noah's black boots to prepare myself for his next move.

I belt out a surprised squeal when he twists in front of me and lifts me into his arms before stalking straight through the club, past the woman with the stupid sign. With wide eyes, I quickly latch onto him and try not to let my face flame too much under the shocked and curious stares of everyone around us. I want to believe he would have done this even if what happened earlier was a figment of my imagination, but that would only make me both blind *and* delusional.

In Noah's world, this is as big of a declaration as any number of sweet words he could have said to me.

"You're making a scene," I tell him, my face buried in his throat. The scent of leather still lingers, bringing with it a sense of familiarity in such an uncomfortable place.

He adjusts his grip on my thighs, the tips of his fingers brushing the swell of my ass. "Let them see. I'm beyond caring."

I'm glad nobody can see my face because there's no way to stop my grin. It's like a switch was flipped inside of him these last couple of weeks, his promise to me holding true. Everything I thought I knew about how I felt for him is changing, beginning to grow into something unknown. I want to poke and prod at it until I can figure out why it's only just now appearing after years of nothing.

Is it me? Are they even new feelings, or have they always been there, lying dormant beneath my fear and worries? So many questions with so few answers.

The cool feel of the door against my warm back has me shivering as Noah walks us outside. The sudden stillness of the empty street is staggering compared to the bustle inside the club.

"Sparks said she would call the driver and have him meet us," I tell him, the words still spoken into his throat. Despite the fact we're alone outside, I can't get myself to move away.

"Fuck the driver. I want to take you somewhere."

My reply comes instantly.

"Let's go."

22

Tinsley

"ALRIGHT, YOU CAN LET ME DOWN NOW, YOU GOOF," I TELL HIM once it feels like we've been walking for hours.

It's silent in this part of town, with no nosey reporters or fans lurking about. We spent long nights in this neighbourhood when we were teenagers. It was a place we could just *be*, without the opinions and voices of those always around us. It's different now, though. Changed.

The vacant lots we used to lie on and watch the sky have long since begun to fill with new, lavish houses, and a middle school with a fancy logo and walls of glass has been built where an old, abandoned pawn shop used to sit. When we passed a big stone sign with the words Beachwood Hills engraved in its centre on our way in, I felt a piece of my soul die.

In the time we've been gone, our safe space has been overrun by outsiders. I'm not sure how I should feel about that.

Noah doesn't fight me as I squirm in his arms and drop to my feet. "It hasn't felt like it's been that long since we've been here," I say softly, the silence threatening to swallow my words up.

"A year," he replies. Before Adalyn hooked him up with Reggie and his life changed.

The old sidewalks that used to be a tripping hazard have been replaced, not a single chip or divot in sight. A line of countless street lights hangs over the road, making it feel bright and safe. I wouldn't doubt every one of these houses has a state-of-the-line security system watching us walk down the street right now.

It feels like my parents' neighbourhood in Toronto. The safety should be a good thing, but half of the fun of hanging out in this neighbourhood was the thrill of never knowing what was lurking in the shadows. It's stupid, but when your best friend is Noah Hutton, you learn not to be afraid of anything.

Anyway, the worst we ever saw in this neighbourhood back then was a few harmless homeless people or a family of raccoons. If my father had ever learned that we were spending our nights together out here, he would have never let me come back.

"Do you miss it?" I ask, walking alongside Noah.

"I don't miss this place. I miss being here with you."

"Me too. Is that why you wanted to take me here? To reminisce?"

He makes a noise in his throat. "This isn't where I was taking you. We're not there yet."

I furrow my brow, glancing around. The layout of the neighbourhood is too different now for me to recognize how far we've wandered.

"If you forgot our place, I'm going to leave you here alone and go back to the hotel," he grumbles.

And then I'm grinning at him, my stomach tumbling. "It's still here? I just assumed they tore it down when they started rebuilding the neighbourhood."

He grunts. "Over my dead body."

My pace quickens. His dark laugh twirls in the night air as I move ahead of him, watching him over my shoulder. I probably look ridiculous. I'm far too old to be skipping along the road searching for a place I thought would have been long gone by now, but I couldn't care less. I hope the people who live here watch their driveway camera footage tomorrow and laugh.

"Don't tell me you threatened them to make them leave it alone."

"I didn't threaten them."

"So, they just left it alone all on their own? In the midst of completely redoing the neighbourhood?"

"Guess so."

I spin to face him fully, walking backward. "You're lying to me, Noah Hutton."

He shrugs one shoulder with a coy nonchalance. I blow out a frustrated breath and stop on the street so suddenly he nearly collides with me. My hands shoot out in front of me and meet the thick wall of his chest in an attempt to keep us from hurting ourselves. Amusement dances in his eyes as he stares down at me, revealing the playfulness inside of him that's been trapped down and hidden for so damn long.

"Prove it, Tinsley Lowry," he dares, the words sounding dirty and rough. A shiver travels down my spine. Is that how he would be in bed? Filthy? Not afraid to make me scream?

I force a shaky laugh into the night. "My full name is such a mouthful. Please never use it again."

The arching of his brow is enough to tell me that he isn't oblivious to my subject change. Thankfully, he doesn't push it. He takes a step back and nods to the alley on our left, tucked between the last house on this street and a corner store. The street lights don't reach past the first few feet of the gravelled alleyway, making it nearly pitch-black. I retreat to his side and straighten my back, putting on a brave face.

"Scared?" he asks.

I scoff. "As if. It's just been a while since we've been there. I don't know what kind of beasts you've stored in the shadows since we've been gone."

"None that would harm you, Golden Girl." He presses a

hand to the centre of my back, fingers softly tracing my spine as he adds, "They'd bow to you, just like I would."

I lean into his touch. It's impossible not to. It strokes something inside of me, something carnal. Savage.

"It's not hard to believe you're a songwriter," I breathe, watching the shadows in the alley, waiting for something to crawl out of them.

"No?"

I shake my head, a blasting sensation of need growing hot in my gut. His fingers strum a rhythm on my spine, a silent song filling the air.

"You say things that only a writer could. Such simple words but ones that carry heavy meaning. It's just . . . natural for you. It's how your brain works."

"My brain is a mess."

"A mess of beautiful words."

He grips my waist and settles at my back, thighs cupping my ass. Knuckles stroke down my spine, the silent strum disappearing. His touch is controlled, the burn of it seeping so deep within me I feel him light my soul on fire, the flames roaring out of control. I want more. And more and more. All of it. No fear, no worry. *No interruptions.*

Show me the beast.

Let me see if I can handle it.

"Tinsley." My name is a warning and a promise.

I step back into him, eliminating any space between us. The whimper that escapes when I feel him hard against me sounds unrecognizable, as if it came from someone else.

"Noah." His name is a declaration and a plea.

Teeth nip at the tip of my ear hard enough to sting. I'm entirely unprepared for the order he utters next but shockingly into the idea.

"Run. If I catch you, you're mine."

NH,

Noah

SHE'S STILL, frozen as my order registers.

Then she's breaking out of my hold and running into the alley. The darkness sucks her in, welcoming her in its grasp. Her sneakers dig into the rocks as she moves through the alley, the sound of her footsteps growing quieter and quieter the further I let her get from me.

I know this area well. We both do, but she's forgotten some of the layout in our time away. She'll find the house, though. It's a permanent fixture in her life, regardless of how they changed the neighbourhood.

When I don't hear her anymore, I start for the alley. The light from the street fades as I step onto the gravel, my boots crunching the rocks and dirt. My heart thumps hard and heavy in my chest, adrenaline beginning to fill my blood at the prospect of catching her. I know where I'll find her. It's not truly a chase, but it doesn't seem to matter. The only thing that does is what I'll do when she's in my arms again.

No more waiting for her to see what was right in front of her. No more searching for the right time or place. She's realizing it now. *That she's mine.*

My eyes adjust to the dark quickly as I move through the shadows, staring straight ahead, where I know she'll have gone. The curve in the alley that leads to the house is brighter than the rest of it, but not by much. I get a glimpse of the spray paint on the trash bin behind the renovated corner store. They couldn't be bothered to replace it, even with Tinsley's terrible drawing of a raccoon-shaped animal with fangs and a half-missing skull covering the front side.

I freeze when I hear the faint sound of footsteps nearby, too slowly paced and sloppy to be Tinsley's. It's too dark for me to see anyone, even as I look around, the sting of protectiveness nipping at my gut. If there's anyone else here, they don't belong near her.

The footsteps disappear as quickly as they came. Silence fills the alley again. I don't wait for them to come back. The house is close, and I push through the rest of the way until I reach the end of the alley. Gravel changes to grass and weeds before becoming concrete.

It's exactly as I remembered, falling apart and untouched. The abandoned house we found a decade ago is an eyesore, fucking hideous in this upgraded neighbourhood. The Sold sign is still on the lawn, a continuous reminder to the developers that attempted to tear it down that they lost.

The front steps are broken, the wood rotted and snapped. The porch isn't much better. I did replace the windows when I bought the house, not wanting animals to get in. Did she notice them when she ran inside? The lock on the door is the same, and the key is still beneath the broken flowerpot on the porch.

I've been paying the electricity bill since I purchased the house last year. She wouldn't have thought to turn the lights on. There was never power when we used to sneak in, just dirt and peace. It was a foreclosure property, and when it went to auction, I beat the developers to it. I bought it for too much, but they weren't touching it. Any price would have sufficed to keep it for Tinsley. I never told her I bought it. It never seemed important.

Carefully, I walk up the porch steps and open the door, breathing in the familiar smell of dust and wood. The floorboards creak beneath my boots as I walk inside, moving around the old furniture on instinct.

"Tinsley," I call, excitement blooming in my stomach.

The kitchen is at the back of the house, closed off with walls and archways, while the living room is open to the hallway. When I look inside, all I see is furniture covered with dirty white sheets. A creak from across the house has me pushing through the hall, tearing into the guest bedroom. The door was left open, and as I step inside, I know instantly someone else is with me.

She comes flying at me, her body colliding with mine and sending us both into the wall. My back slams against it, and my lungs scream with the impact. Brown hair whips around her head as she holds me against the wall with an arm beneath my chin and her legs stomped between mine. Her silver eyes fucking glow in the dark, making her look more and more like a goddamn angel here to send me down to Hell.

I want to touch her, I ache for it, but when she grins proudly and purposefully rubs her body on mine, I curl my fingers into my palms and squeeze instead. I'll let her be in control this time. Let her revel in her win. Because this may be the only time I allow her this opportunity.

She leans in so close I can taste the vodka from the only drink she had earlier on her breath. I tense my jaw and glare at her lips, at the mouth I want to feast on and mark as mine.

"So, what do I get for catching you?" she asks lowly, teasingly.

"What is it you want?"

Take anything. *Everything*.

Those silver eyes flare, a million emotions flashing through them before one sparks brighter than the rest, lingering on me. A rough growl rips through me when I recognize that emotion and let it register to her.

The moment it does, I finally get what I've been waiting my entire life for.

She leans in as I grip her face in my hands and take her mouth in a brutal, hard, soul-shaking kiss. A kiss that changes everything.

23

Tinsley

NOAH KISSES ME LIKE A MAN WHO'S DREAMED OF IT HIS ENTIRE life. Like he fears he might die without tasting me, and I respond just as eagerly. Rough lips, the angry bite of teeth on sensitive skin. It's a rush, the kind I imagine you would get when throwing yourself off a cliff and diving headfirst into icy waters. The burn and then the chill. The pain and then the bliss.

Even as he buries his hands in my hair and yanks savagely at the roots, the pain heightens the pleasure building inside of me, turning me inside out. I want more of it, am desperate enough that I would beg for it if we could tear ourselves away from one another long enough.

I reach for his body and drag him closer until he's pressed flat against me, chest to chest. His hips pin me to the wall as he presses between my legs, the thick length of his cock already hard and digging into my belly. My ears go fuzzy as I drag his swollen bottom lip between my teeth and bite down, eliciting a groan of pain from him. I feel that groan like a zap to my clit, and there's no stopping my responding whimper.

He hisses between his teeth and tears his lips from mine, only to place them over my throat before sucking and nipping at my neck until I'm positive I'll be covered in marks later tonight, if I'm not already.

"The sounds you make," he grinds out. "Want to bottle them up."

I exhale a shaky breath, baring my neck further, giving him complete access to whatever he wants. It's second nature, a decision I make without having to put much thought toward it. Maybe I'll regret the marks tomorrow, or maybe I won't. Right now, I never want him to stop.

He warned me that he would take and take until I had nothing left, but in this moment, I'm prepared to give him everything he desires. It feels too right, like this is what we're meant to be doing and we've both finally accepted that. *I've* finally accepted it, as crazy as that may be.

The house is dark and silent, making our sloppy kisses and panted breaths echo through the rooms. I feel like I've spent hours in front of a furnace, warming myself to the bone. But in reality, I feel this way simply because of Noah. His touch and kiss and words. The feel of him all over me, exploring and learning.

Why haven't we been doing this for years already? The thought is fleeting, but I catch it before it disappears. It spears right through my chest.

"More," I whisper, my brain scattered.

Long, skilled fingers drift up my stomach with a gentle touch, *too* gentle. I arch my back, attempting to force them to press harder into my skin. It's not gentle that I want. Not from Noah.

Never from Noah.

"More what?" He asks it in a way that makes me think of how a predator toys with its prey. Like it's fun for him to see me helpless and at his will.

A ragged moan is pulled from me when he pinches my nipple through my shirt and gives it a rough tug, dark eyes boring into me, watching my reaction. If he could hear the thoughts in my mind, he wouldn't be cautious of hurting me. He'd know how badly I want him to push me out of my comfort zone, to help me feel something that I've gone my whole life without knowing if I like it or not. We've already gone this far, crossed so many lines.

"Don't be gentle with me. Show me what you like. I feel like I'm going to explode." It comes out in a whoosh. I wait for the embarrassment to come. It doesn't.

"Don't ask for things you don't know if you truly want."

Another twist of my nipple, and I'm parting my lips in a silent cry, the area between my legs hot and slick. I shake my head and try to keep my eyes from rolling back, focusing them on him.

"I'm sure. I'm so fucking sure, Noah. I shouldn't be, but I am. Give me something. I know it's there; I've seen glimpses of it."

The air around us is tight, *alive*. His throat works with a swallow as he drops his stare to my chest, at the way it's moving with a scary quickness. I want to rip my shirt off and coax the darkness out of him, beg it to come play with me. I've never feared that side of Noah. Not once. Doesn't he know that by now?

Deciding that I won't allow him to put this boundary between us, I move my hand between our bodies and cup the bulge in his jeans, the same one I'd felt twitching for me earlier. The reminder makes me throb, my underwear ruined beyond repair.

I tighten my hold on his cock and watch the shift in him. The final wall between us crumbles, leaving him exposed completely. Excitement sings in my blood, the anticipation of what's next providing a high too strong to be experienced by any drug known to man.

"There you are," I breathe, my eyes darting between his. They're pupil blown, the dark brown flooded with a harsh black. He pushes his hips in answer, pressing himself into my palm. "It's about time."

The air in my lungs is forced out when his hand snaps up to grip my face, smooshing my cheeks in a tight hold. They tingle from the pinch and the force of them pressing against my teeth. Quick, harsh breaths hit my face when he leans in and bites my mouth, both of my lips throbbing from the pain as I stand there, allowing him to get this final test out of his system.

When I refuse to so much as flinch at the pain, he releases my lips and whispers, "Tell me how badly you want me to touch you."

He's still gripping my cheeks, keeping my swollen lips too close together for me to speak properly. Is this another test? Another way for him to ensure that I want him the way I say I do? When I search for that uncertainty in his expression, I find it hidden behind a familiar bravado.

That look is the reason I attempt to speak through my pursed lips, knowing how utterly embarrassing I must sound. "Let me show you."

He throbs in my hand, and I almost come right there. The tightness of my jeans has become uncomfortable. I want him to pull them down to my knees and take away this ache. By the hunger flaring in his stare as he watches me and feels the desperation in the way I cling to him, he has to be thinking the same thing.

Finally, he releases my face. As blood rushes to my cheeks, the feeling of his fingertips lingers. I nearly preen at the heady sense of approval that coats his features.

One thick black brow curls as he says, "Show me, then."

I furiously tug at the button on my jeans and jam down the zipper before shoving my hand past the band of my underwear. The tip of my finger slips over the hot, smooth skin of my pussy, finding it just as wet as I expected. Without breaking eye contact, I dip it lower and tease my opening before making a slow, long circle around my clit. I swallow back the pleasure that sparks from the soft touch, and Noah's lip curls with distaste before he's wrapping his fingers around my wrist and yanking my hand from my pants.

"I told you to show me, not get yourself off," he chastises.

My eyelids droop as I watch him lift my middle and pointer fingers to his mouth and, with a deep, rough groan, push them between his lips. He sucks on them for one, two, three seconds, taking his time as his tongue strokes each finger. Fuck, if this is any hint at what he might do between my legs . . . I'm going to pass out.

"Noah, plea—" The words die on my tongue when a thunderous knocking noise sounds on the front door.

A bone-chilling rage slips over Noah. A possessive hand curls around my waist as he frees my fingers and presses them to my belly. With a blank expression, he buttons up my jeans. I wait for him to speak, to tell me that it was just the wind, but there's not much more than a light breeze outside, and we both know it.

"What was that?" I whisper.

"Don't know. I'll be right back."

A surprising rush of genuine fear ripples up my spine, cold and harsh. I curl my fingers in his T-shirt, tugging when he goes to leave. "Alone?"

He covers my hand with his and uncurls my fingers one by one. "Yes."

"I'm the fighter. Let me come so you don't get your ass beat."

He scoffs loudly, not giving a shit about the potential creeper hanging around outside hearing him. "Not a fucking chance. You're insulting my trainer if you don't think I can protect myself."

"I'm your trainer."

"I know," he deadpans.

Sighing, I pat his chest and say, "Fine. I'll be listening for any sign of distress."

I expect him to leave right away, but he lingers, rolling his jaw. Prepared to ask if he's okay, I part my lips only to have him kiss me, sending my concern evaporating into thin air. My eyes flutter shut as I melt into him, moving my lips over his in a rhythm that comes as naturally as breathing. He pulls away too soon and, with a brief glance, leaves me in the bedroom alone. Arousal is still hot in my blood, but it's beginning to cool, allowing me a moment to get a hold of myself.

I listen to his boots clunk on the floorboards before the door creaks, letting me know he's opened it. I'm not sure why I'm so nervous all of a sudden, considering that I just ran through a dark alleyway and into an old, abandoned house by myself, but maybe this is different. I knew Noah wouldn't have sent me into danger when he told me to run from him.

The door slams shut a beat later, and I grow stiff against the wall, straining my ears to pick up on any sign of him before those heavy boots begin to move across the floor again. I deflate like a balloon, my limbs loose again when I see him enter the room.

There's something different about him as he comes into view this time, and it's not just the bulging vein in his forehead or the promise of murder in his eyes. It's the crumpled stack of papers in one of his fisted hands and the recognizable red drawing on the front of the CD in the other.

I'd have to be blind to not recognize that drawing. It's mine. I drew it for Noah seven years ago in this very house.

24

Noah

SOMEONE WAS IN THIS HOUSE BEFORE US.

The stack of notepaper and the old CD that were left on the porch could have only come from one place—the upstairs bedroom. The last time I saw them, they were beneath the window Tinsley and I sat beside nearly every night she was in town. Song lyrics I can recite from memory are scrawled over both sides of the papers in my right hand, and the old CD with the rough sketch of the same album art that I demanded be on my most recent one is in my left.

Seven years is a long time. But not long enough to make me forget when Tinsley brought a blank CD to this house, sat beside me on the hard floor, and told me that I was going to be someone someday. That I was going to sell enough records to tour the world. Then, she drew a pathetic excuse of a Devil on the white slip in the front of the CD and titled it *The Devil Inside*.

She didn't know at the time that I was going to take both the name and drawing and make something real out of them. For her.

Nobody knew about the songs, the album, or the house. We made sure of that. Whoever wandered in here earlier and took our things to toy with us was either stupid or brave. Neither will fare well for them if I ever find out who it was. There was no sign of them outside, so they dumped the shit and ran. At least they had the smarts not to linger, their sick joke completed.

Tinsley looks uncomfortable, freaked out. Seeing her like that makes me want to punch something. Preferably the person who made her feel this way.

My want for her is still raging. The sudden surge of protectiveness I felt at the knock on the door has toned it down, but only slightly. Wanting her is a constant ache that I've learned to accept as normal.

"Where did those come from?" she asks, wide eyes darting back and forth between my hands.

"Outside."

"Outside," she echoes softly. "Outside where?"

"On the porch."

"What the fuck?"

"It's probably a prank."

She looks up at me, mouth gaping and eyes blazing. "A prank? That's not a prank, Noah. Those are our things!"

"I know."

"You *know*? Well, by all means, continue to look like you couldn't care less while I freak out about what kind of weirdo searched through this house and stole our stuff only to what? Gift it back?" She throws a hand in the air and begins to pace the floor, each step making the wood creak. Jerkily, she twists her body to face me, looking fear-stricken for a brief moment. "What if they're still here?"

"They're not," I tell her. Truthfully, I don't know if they are. Most likely not if they were just able to be outside.

"You don't know that."

"Would you like me to check?"

She thinks about it, chewing on that still-fat bottom lip. I want to be the one chewing on that plump skin, making it throb the longer and harder I dig my teeth into it. Her reactions from earlier tell me that maybe she'd like that too.

"No. I don't want my potentially last memory of this house to be of a creep hiding in the bathroom. I want it to be of you. Of us just being here together," Tinsley admits. It sounds almost shy, so unlike her. "We can figure all of this out later."

She doesn't know this won't be the last time we're here together. It might be a shit hole, but it's mine now. Hers, if she'll take it.

With a slight cock of my head, I narrow my eyes on her, desperate to figure out what thoughts she's keeping from me. The darkness betrays me, casting too many shadows over her that hide the little things I want to know. Like is her face warm and pink? Is her chest still moving too quickly?

The rapid fluttering of her eyelashes as she stares back at me, one palm flat against her belly, has me wondering if I already know the answer to both of those questions.

Would she look away if I told her that I could still taste her cunt on my tongue? Or would that force her closer to me, desperate to offer me another taste?

"Tell me what you're thinking about." It's a harsh demand. I'm unable to give anything warmer. What's left of my control is pitiful.

"You're going to pretend you don't already know?"

I chuckle roughly, the beginning of a smirk tugging at my lips. "Have you ever wondered what it would feel like to wear a pair of tight jeans with a flaming red, sore ass?"

A trembled exhale. "Are you threatening to spank me, Noah?"

"It's not a threat."

I'd have to be blind to miss the hint of excitement that caresses the soft lines of her face. She wets her lips and starts to retreat further into the room, keeping her eyes fixed on mine.

"A promise, then?" Her voice is so soft.

My palm tingles. "Yeah, Golden Girl. A promise."

The window behind her has a view of the fenced-in back-yard. It's barren, grass overgrown, boring. But the clouds part in the sky behind it, revealing bright stars that begin to flood the room with light, illuminating her figure.

She's an angel; even the stars believe it to be true.

It's too bad the Devil is about to paint her red.

"Where are you going?" I ask, eying her movements. She's almost at the wall with nowhere else to run.

"Nowhere."

"No? You're not scared?"

"Of you?" she breathes.

I begin to move toward her, my steps slow, taunting. "Of what I want to do to you."

She watches as I let the objects in my hands fall to the ground beside my feet. I have no use for them with Tinsley in front of me.

"And what is it that you want to do to me?"

"Everything."

Three steps and I'm in front of her. She exhales, hands moving to press flat against the wall on either side of her. I follow the length of her body with my eyes, a needy noise building in my chest when they snag on her tits. Two thick, hard nipples are locked away behind too many layers, rising and falling with the rapid beat of her heart. I want them in my mouth, draped over my chest, pointed at the ceiling. *Fuck.*

A squeal flies from her lips when I grab her hip and spin her toward the wall. With long brown hair flying over her shoulder, she glances back at me, so beautifully shocked as her hands find purchase against the wall in front of her. I grind myself against her ass, fingers digging so deep into the curve of her waist that I hope I see bruises tomorrow.

I don't stifle my warning growl when she pushes her ass against my cock, drifting it side to side, almost like she's begging me to punish her. With a steady hand, I reach around her front and pop the button of her jeans before shoving them past her knees. A thin strap of black lace is tucked between her ass cheeks, leaving the round, muscled flesh bare for me. The band around her hips is thin, too easy to rip apart. I hook my finger beneath it and tug before letting it snap back. She hisses at the sting, making my cock throb, the tip wet.

"Gonna tear these off of you." I drag the words up my throat.

She wiggles her hips in response. I fill my palm with one of her ass cheeks, kneading it for a few beats before curling my fingers and biting into the skin with my nails. There are so many things I want to do to her. But it's too hard to tease her. I'm too fucking desperate. The teasing will have to wait.

I grip the string beneath the band of her thong and follow the length of it with my fingers, pulling it free as I move down her ass. When I reach the bottom curve, I press my knuckle to the thicker material cupping her pussy and curse at how wet it is. I dig my knuckle in and move it left to right, forcing her panties to sink into the sensitive flesh.

"I only hear empty threats," she grinds out.

I watch her closely as the string of her thong is yanked viciously into my fist. The lace panties cut through her wet flesh as I pull, digging in painfully as the string finally tears in my grip. We both watch it fall to the floor.

"Oh. Never mind," she whispers, her expression both excited and nervous. "Well? What's next?"

I don't respond. Can't. I'm transfixed by the sight of her cunt. Puffy and pink. So fucking wet. Savage hunger saws through me as I grab at her waist and try to calm myself. It's helpless. I'm too weak, my control now belonging to the beast she's so desperate to know.

"No." I choke on it, forcing it out. "Say it and I'll stop."

Her laugh is bright, disbelieving. "Not going to happen."

I drop my forehead to her shoulder and beg, "Tinsley." My fingers have drifted across her stomach, already dipping over her pelvis.

When I force myself to stop with my fingers ghosting the strip of hair above her pussy, she nods rapidly. "Fine. Yes. Okay."

The words have barely registered before I'm touching her. I glide a finger through her lips and dip it inside her entrance. She's so fucking wet that it slides deep with no resistance. No fight.

"*Fuck*," I spit, pulling my finger out before shoving it back in. She cries out, but not in pain. "Knew you'd be wet for me. Didn't think you'd be gushing, though."

"Your mistake." A gasp tumbles from her lips when I bring my other hand down hard on her ass. The clap screams through the house. "Oh, shit," she moans, head falling forward, hitting the wall.

I add a second finger inside of her, the fit nice and snug. She's perfect, just for me. *Only* for me. That I'm fucking sure of. I won't let it be any other way. Not anymore.

I've never shied away from my possessiveness. I embraced it a long ago. If that meant scaring off anyone who looked at her with even the slightest touch of interest around me, that's what I did. She's not a virgin. I know she's only been with one guy. I sent him running with his tail between his legs when she told me about him.

"You're mine, Tinsley. Need you to hear you say it." When her reply isn't instant, I swat at her ass again and watch as it bounces back, warming beneath my palm. "Now. Or I'll fucking leave you here with an empty, greedy cunt."

Her glare is vicious. I snarl back and spank her again, this time twisting the two fingers inside of her at the same time. She cries out, slapping the wall as she pushes back into my grip.

"You dirty fucking girl," I grunt. She tightens around my fingers, trying to keep them inside when I go to pull them out. "Say you're mine and I'll let you come. I'll make you drench my hand and drip drown your thighs."

Her pussy quivers around my fingers, hips pushing her back into me over and over again, the movements growing quicker as she tries to get herself off with my fingers. It's one of the most beautiful things I've ever seen. But I can't have her doing my work for me. She doesn't deserve to come that way.

I abandon her ass for her pussy, shoving my other hand between her legs in search of her clit. With a sweep of my thumb across the swollen bud, she's jerking in my arms, muscles shaking.

"Two words, Tinsley."

She sucks in a breath, eyes bloodshot as they openly devour me. I can see how close she is. It's written all over her face. I narrow my gaze, curling my fingers and flicking them deep, coaxing that building release out of her. She's become a whimpering mess, pleasure building so hard and fast that she's unable to give me the words I'm demanding from her. It pisses me off, but not enough to make me stop.

I'll give her this. It's my fault for driving her this far. Should have waited, slowed down. Taken my time.

She reaches behind her and slaps at me before grabbing my arm and yanking. "Please." It's a muffled, desperate noise. "I'm yours!"

I never stood a chance.

With a harsh exhale, I roll my thumb over her clit again and then give it a light, testing pinch. She nods her head frantically, lips parting on a silent cry, so I do it again, harder this time. Silver eyes flash a warning, and then she's gasping.

"I'm coming," she cries, voice shaking.

I decide then that I want to hear those two words every day. Want to witness this experience over and over again. Want to be the one that makes it happen. It's everything I thought it would be. More than.

When her knees begin to shake, I pull my fingers out and slide one arm around her middle to steady her. Her chest shakes with a soft laugh, and I stiffen, confused.

"Relax. I'm just . . . surprised and unexpectantly exhausted, I guess," she murmurs, head tipping back to rest against my chest.

A flurry of uncertainty hits me. I need to provide aftercare . . .

right? That's what she needs. In a rush, I wipe my hand off on my jeans and then maneuver her in my arms so I can pull her pants up her legs. I don't feel bad as her sore ass rubs against the roughness of her jeans. She deserved every one of those spanks, and she knows it.

I've always tried to be gentle with Tinsley. But I'm not a calming person. If that's what she needs from me right now, I will fail. Will she regret this because of that?

"If I can hear you thinking, then so can the creep upstairs," she says, teasing me.

"If he can hear me thinking, then he just heard you scream for me too," I reply.

Her eyebrows waggle as she does up her pants and then reaches for my hand, intertwining our fingers. I stare at them, my chest tight.

"At least he'll always have one hell of a show to remember me by."

"He doesn't need to remember you," I grumble.

Her smile makes her look happy. Pride swells in my chest. I did that. Right?

"Come on, Mr. Protective. I'm starving. It's too late to be thinking about what all of this means right now."

I know it's not the time to fight her on that. With a silent nod, I let her lead me through the house. She only stops once on the way out—to pick up the papers and that goddamn CD.

 25

Tinsley

I'VE BEEN BOXING SINCE I WAS A PRETEEN. I WATCHED MY DAD FIGHT every Friday night for most of my life and had practically lived at our first family gym in the heart of Toronto growing up. There was never any doubt from myself or anybody else that I would follow in his footsteps when I got old enough.

It wasn't always what my mother wanted me to do when I grew up, but there was no denying my passion or talent when it came down to it. She gave me her support like she always had, even if every time I stepped into the ring, she would worry herself half to death about what might happen to me.

My dad never chose to go pro. He told me he didn't want to be away from our family travelling for fights and that the pressure would have taken the fun out of it. I've always believed that that was the reason. I would have hated it if he was gone all the time. While I'll never tell him that I'm grateful he didn't take that step in his career, I am. We wouldn't have been as close as we are if he wasn't around as much as he was. I know damn well that I wouldn't be as skilled without his training.

The jump rope in my hands whips through the air as I bounce in place, staring forward at my name on the poster taped to the locker room door. My heart beats quickly but steadily as I focus on my breathing, keeping it as even as possible. It's not the first time I've seen the fight poster, but seeing it here, in this locker room, just minutes before I face my first opponent as a professional boxer? It feels like the first time.

"How long have you been jumping?"

I grin at the sound of Dad's voice and let the rope slap my heels as it comes to a stop. He's leaning one shoulder against the wall, looking just as burly as usual, if not the teeniest bit harsher. But once I start in his direction, he's flashing me that loose smile and holding his arms open.

His hug fills me with a comfort that I've missed so damn much on this tour. I squeeze him harder than usual before stepping back and pointing excitedly at the fight poster.

"Did you see the poster yet?"

"I did. I had Hunter send us one after the first print. Your mom already has it hung in a frame in the living room."

My chest warms at the mention of her. "She's here, right? And Easton? What about Grandpa?"

"Your mom and brother are already in their seats. But Gramps couldn't make it, kiddo. His hands are getting worse."

"First, I'm not a kid. Second, how is he doing? I should have visited him before I left."

My grandfather was such a big part of my childhood. Not only is he a total badass ex-boxer like Dad, but he always let me do everything my parents didn't. A couple of years ago, his finger joints started to swell and hurt so bad he stopped being able to use them to do much of anything. It turns out that the warning they give boxers about the potential of arthritis rings very true. My grandfather's worsening case of osteoarthritis rings like a warning bell in my mind. It's not enough to make me give this up, though. That either makes me stupid, reckless, or both.

"I think he's more pissed off that he can't be here for you than much else. Don't beat yourself up about it. He's just proud you're here doing what you love," he reassures me.

I nod, putting on a brave face. This isn't the time for sadness. I have to focus.

"Be honest with me," I mutter, shaking my hands out nervously at my sides. "Are there a lot of people out there?"

He sets his hands on his hips and dips his chin. "A shit ton."

"Great," I breathe, dropping my head back to stare at the ceiling. "God, I don't want to get my ass beat on live television."

Dad belts out a laugh. "My daughter has never gotten her ass beat. She's not going to start tonight."

"Have you watched Jules fight? She KO'd her last two opponents!" I exclaim, staring at him in disbelief.

With a shake of his head, he holds me by my shoulders and meets my stare. His features are relaxed, not a single worry there for me to see. Why doesn't that make me feel any better?

"Her last two opponents were strong but slow. You've always been quick on your feet like me. Invite her to dance, and watch how long it takes for her to tire herself out. It's the oldest trick in the book, but it never fails. You are going to win, my littlest fighter. Don't doubt yourself." His voice is so confident, so sure. I force myself to believe his words.

"Tire her out, then aim to kill. Got it."

"That's the spirit," he teases. Smoothing his hands over my biceps in a soothing motion, he smiles softly. "I'm proud of you."

I tuck those words into my chest for safekeeping. "Thanks, Dad."

"Now that we've taken care of that," he starts while taking a seat on the long wooden bench splitting the room in two. "Noah's been taking care of you, right?"

My face flames at the innocent question. If he knew just how good Noah's been taking care of me, he'd haul me out of here and forbid me to see him ever again.

The past week has been . . . odd. So different from how things used to be. Ever since that night in the old house, Noah hasn't left me alone for longer than absolutely necessary. I like it. I love being around him and experiencing a new side of our relationship. It's just that now we've crossed over from being just best friends to best friends that kiss—*a lot*—and I don't know what that really means for us. There's still so much we have to talk about and things that we have yet to decide, but I've been avoiding all of it.

It's easier when we can just be Noah and Tinsley, no questions or expectations. Once we start to dig into all the little details, things could get messy. There are questions that I just don't have the answers to yet. He's been frustrated with me for being so weird and cagey, but for right now, I just need to focus on this fight. Maybe once it's over, I'll be ready to talk about what happens next. I don't think he'll give me much more time to hide, anyway.

"Yes. But you already knew that," I finally say, hoping my father can't read into the blush on my cheeks.

His eyes have tightened at the corners as he reads me. I hold my breath. "How has it been so far? I can't imagine you've enjoyed sharing a bus with a bunch of messy guys."

"You say that as if I'm any neater than they are. I've only had to pick up a couple pairs of dirty socks off the floor so far. The bus isn't so much messy as it is cluttered."

He frowns. "Hunter said he would get you put up in a hotel whenever you wanted. You don't have to stay in a cluttered bus, Tiny."

I release a long exhale, letting my shoulders sag with the movement. "What I'm trying to say is that it isn't so bad. I don't want a hotel room. As crowded as it may be, I'm actually having fun."

It's the truth. Even Dagger has relaxed a bit. Well, that or he's just begun to ignore we all exist instead of berating us for being in his space. Either way, it's been nice. I've gotten to know Justice and his daughter a little bit more too. We've made plans to braid Noah's hair together the next time Addie can make it to a show and join us. I'll have to break that news to Noah closer to that day. Possibly a few minutes prior so he doesn't have a chance to say no.

Finally, Dad nods in reluctant agreement. "I believe you. That's great, kiddo. We've been worrying about you, that's all."

"You don't need to. I'm doing fine. Great, even."

"Alright, alright. I'll try to relax."

I take a seat beside him and lean against his shoulder. "Can I ask you something?"

"Always."

Staring down at the silver shorts draped over my thighs, I shove aside my nerves and ask what's been on my mind since Vancouver.

"Did you know that Oakley has been keeping articles about Noah in his old room? I always thought he was disapproving of the choices Noah made with his career, but it seemed like the opposite."

He's silent for a beat. "I didn't know about that. But I'm not surprised. Oakley is proud of Noah and what he's accomplished, despite what the both of you think. He wants the best for his son just like any dad does."

"Then he has a terrible way of showing it. Even you should be able to admit that. If he tried even a little bit harder—"

Dad twists to face me and takes my hand. "Sweetheart, it is not your responsibility to mend Oakley and Noah's relationship."

"No? Then whose is it? Because me and Ava seem to be the only ones upset enough by it to want to try. It just makes me so *mad*. Things were never perfect between them, but they used to be better!" I shout, pulling my hand away and resting it on my lap. Dad's frown deepens.

I know Oakley unknowingly made Noah feel less than his siblings because he just didn't know how to treat him. Noah made it hard. He loved to fight with his dad, to test how far he could push him. His siblings were so different than him, and Oakley truly never stood a chance. There were no right or wrong sides when it came to the two of them. But I put most of the blame on Oakley because at the end of the day, he's his father. I'll always believe he should have tried harder when things fell apart. He should have made sure Noah knew that no matter what, he was loved and a valued member of their family the way Ava did.

Yet, out of everything I know, I'm missing a vital piece of the puzzle. The details of what happened that final day, the one that broke the last fragile piece of their relationship that had kept them together through all of the bad.

Noah refuses to tell me, and I'd never ask Oakley. But I know that my dad knows. I'd bet my uncle Ty does too. Maybe I'll have to ask him. He's never been able to tell me no. I think that's because he's secretly always wanted a daughter but got stuck with two sons instead.

"Tinsley, I'm sorry, but you need to let this one sort itself out. This is a Hutton family problem. It's not our mess to get in the middle of."

I laugh humourlessly. "That's a cop-out."

Dad sets his chin on my head and wraps an arm around my shoulders, forcing me close. His following sigh speaks volumes. "It is. But it's all I can give you."

"No, it's all you *want* to give me. There's a difference."

"Would you want me to tell your secrets to Noah if you kept them from him on purpose?"

I roll my eyes. "That's a redundant question. I've never kept secrets from him."

"You're definitely your mother's daughter," he relents with a kiss to my head. "That attitude couldn't have come from me."

I scoff a laugh and shove his shoulder before slipping out from beneath his arm. Standing from the bench, I run a hand over my head and tug at the band in my hair, tightening it. "*Right.* Never from you."

"Maybe you got it from your uncle. That guy has more attitude than anyone I've ever met."

"How does it feel?" I deadpan, holding in a laugh at his confused expression.

"How does what feel?"

"Living in la-la land. At this point, it must be the greatest place to ever exist because you seem content to live there forever."

His laugh threatens to shake the locker room walls. It makes me laugh along with him, my stomach locking from the strength of it. The part of me that had been in desperate need of some time with my family finally feels a bit more at peace.

"Maybe you're more my daughter after all," he states a couple of moments later, once we've both sobered up.

"Insult or compliment?" I throw back, letting the past few minutes go. Again, this isn't the time to get upset.

Dad doesn't have a chance to answer before there are two hard knocks on the door. Excitement swells in my belly as I rush to let Noah in. I wasn't positive that he would be able to finish rehearsal in time to catch the beginning of my fight, but I should have known better.

I'm smiling before I even get the door open. "You're here."

"I am," he mutters.

With a powerful push of his arm, he swings the door shut behind him and stalks toward me. Like two magnets, we're drawn to each other, our bodies moving on their own. His hands cup my face, and then he pulls me in, kissing me hard and desperate, like we hadn't only seen each other this morning.

"Noah," I gasp between kisses. "My dad."

He growls against my mouth, nipping at my lip as if to punish me for trying to speak.

I tug at his shirt and yank myself back, scolding the devilish part of me that demands I shut up and kiss him again. "We're not alone," I whisper.

He narrows his eyes on me, annoyed. Reluctantly, he pulls himself back just enough to glance over my shoulder. Without turning to follow his line of vision, I know he's staring at my dad.

Finally, he speaks, his voice rough and sore-sounding. "I don't care if he's here. I've been without you all day."

A simple statement that makes me feel a very *unsimple* way. My hand shoots out on its own, curling around his ink-covered forearm, the grip possessive.

"I missed you too," I murmur. Our eyes catch and hold as the words settle. The way he's looking at me lights a fire in my gut, burning deep.

He traces my mouth with his thumb. "Are you nervous?"

"No."

He almost smiles. "Good girl."

"You should get ready to go, Tiny," Dad says, cutting through the tension that's built around Noah and me with swift efficiency.

The angry huff that escapes Noah is sexy as hell. If Dad weren't here, I'd ask him to do it again. I've never found that noise attractive before.

"He's right. It's almost time." I speak low for only Noah to hear. "I'll see you when I win?"

He nods once and then takes my mouth again, gentler this time. It's a good-luck kiss. I melt into it, using it to motivate me.

"Yes. I'll be here," he mutters against my lips.

It's all I need to hear. I'm ready to kick this woman's ass. And once I'm done, I'll figure out how to explain what's happening with Noah to my father before he starts a second fight.

I just have to hope he waits that long.

26

Noah

Braden wants to kill me. The curl of my smile tells him that I find the idea interesting, if not pitiful.

Sierra opted to take the seat beside me in the crowd, putting distance between her husband and me. It was a smart move. We're front row beside the fighting ring, surrounded by loud, obnoxious people discussing their bets for tonight. Tinsley's name is sung throughout the arena, a guaranteed win in the minds of the majority. She wouldn't believe me if I told her that.

I've been to more of her fights than I have shitty dive bars. This environment has yet to feel at all enticing. Watching Tinsley fight is painful for me. She rarely loses, but that doesn't mean she doesn't bleed. Bleed and cry and hurt.

"I'm glad you got the time off to come tonight. I know it means a lot to Tiny," Sierra says, offering me a familiar soft smile. It's her daughter's smile.

"I wouldn't miss it." *Obviously.*

"I know, but still. It says a lot about you."

Braden scoffs beside her. His wife swats at his thigh as I bite my tongue to keep from telling him to fuck off.

"You've always been good to her." Leaning toward me, she

adds in a lowered voice, "Even if my stubborn husband can't see that."

This entire conversation is weird and uncomfortable. Braden must have been blabbing to her about what he saw in the locker room. Tinsley's mom has never given me this much of her attention before, and she sure as fuck hasn't told me that I'm good for her daughter either.

I don't know how to respond. Discomfort makes my skin itch below the surface. When the fuck is this fight supposed to start?

Easton adjusts himself on my other side and mutters, "Stop terrifying him, Mom."

"I'm not scaring him! Am I scaring you, Noah?"

My muscles are stiff as I grunt, "No."

She's not scaring me. Just poking at my inability to be around people I'm not comfortable with. They're not strangers, but they're not *not* strangers either.

"See?" She pokes her tongue out at her son. It almost makes me laugh.

Sometimes I forget how similar she and Tinsley are. Maybe I just try to ignore it. If I started to pay attention to those types of things, I risk growing close to others. The idea is not appealing to me.

Thankfully, I'm not forced to continue to speak to anyone. The lights cut in the arena before flashing rapidly as a deep, throaty bass guitar is pushed through the speaker system. I swallow the lump in my throat as the familiarity of the song hits me.

It's my song.

The main track of the album.

Smoke shoots from the stage into the air. It fills the arena, sticking to my legs and crawling up my chest. The light show continues as the music grows louder. It's dramatic, but I don't look away. Don't risk the chance of missing her run out. She's dreaded the show that comes before the fight, so it won't be long now. In Tinsley fashion, she's probably backstage, begging the crew to hurry this the fuck up.

"Jesus Christ," Easton shouts, hands gripping his knees. He seems just as uncomfortable as I do.

My discomfort only grows worse when my voice carries through the crowd, Dagger's guitar lifting it in a way critics declared was *beautifully haunting* just days after the album was released. I watch the end of the platform for Tinsley, mentally flicking through the ways I'm going to make her pay for surprising me with the decision to use my song as her entrance track. I fucking love that she used it. But I hate surprises. She knew that. Maybe that's why she did it. To test how far she could push me before I'll punish her again.

I'll add this to the growing list of things she's done to deserve it, right beneath avoiding talking about what happened a week ago.

A man with a microphone appears in the ring amidst the lights and smoke. The music continues to play in the background, but the sound of the man's voice stifles it. It's a bunch of boring welcome bullshit. I only tune in when he introduces her.

Tinsley "Fast Track" Lowry. One hundred and sixty-five pounds. Five foot ten.

Fast both on her feet and in the league, jumping past competitors who should have been her superiors had they held half the talent she does.

Hunter helped with the name. He insisted she have one when she fought against the idea, declaring it too "showboaty." This entire league is.

I swallow my tongue when the grey lights spin and focus on the tunnel full of shadows. She's there, bouncing on her toes. A silver robe that looks as if the edges were dipped in black paint drapes her frame. It shines, glossy beneath the lights as she moves, a matching set of gloves on her hands. She hits them together over and over again.

Her hair is hidden beneath the hood of her robe. The hood

casts shadows over her face, but still, I find the determination in her stare. It's enough to have my hands clenched, desire thickening my blood. So few things scare her. It's incredible.

"That's my girl!" Braden shouts, standing from his seat.

He's wrong. She's *my* girl.

She comes jogging down the platform now, with Hunter and her medic close behind. When she parts the red ropes and slips inside the ring, her narrowed stare drifts through the crowd, searching. I push to my feet and wait for our eyes to meet. When they do, the arena grows muffled, the screams and music disappearing. My hands are still in fists, and when she looks at them, she smirks.

I lift a brow and cock my head. She makes a show of looking at the ceiling, where the music is coming from, and then pursing her lips and kissing the air. My responding glower is a preview of what's to come as soon as she's out of that ring.

Her head falls back with a laugh I wish I could hear. Then, she's focused again. We all become invisible to her. The only thing she sees is the ring and a win with her name on it.

NH)

IT TAKES five rounds for Jules Collins to begin to lose steam. She has a dangerous punch, muscle mass making up for the height she lacks. It's an advantage she has over Tinsley.

Tinsley's bleeding from her forehead, a small gash having opened up after taking a hard hit at the beginning of the round. Her medic is poised and waiting outside of the ring, a small red bag in her hand. Two minutes feels like an eternity when I have to watch her fight injured.

Blood drips from the gash, but she stays focused, not letting it distract her even as it affects her vision. Her teeth are gnashed painfully hard around her mouthguard. Each move she takes is calculated, her hits skilled beyond belief. I swap my attention between her and the ref as the round ticks down.

Finally, the round finishes, and she collapses on a stool in the corner of the ring. Hunter and the medic slide between the ropes and rush to her. I can hear her telling the medic to leave the gash, swearing the next round will be the last one. Hunter scolds her and nods at the medic. The next minute moves in fast-forward. I've cut my palms with my nails by the time they finish putting pressure on her gash and swab it with what I know has to be epinephrine to stop the bleeding. Tinsley will need the cut closed after the fight, which she'll hate.

My golden girl didn't so much as flinch when there was a hand pressed to her cut skin. I'm in awe of her. She was born for this. Boxing to her is what music is to me. I want to be by her side while she wins fight after fight. I *will* be.

When the next round is about to start, Hunter smacks her on the arms before leaving the ring with the medic. Tinsley stands and twists in my direction. Her eyes are tired beneath all of that drive to win. I push myself to smile at her. It's the least I can offer her right now. Her shoulders lift and fall with the weight of her exhale, but she smiles back despite her exhaustion.

My anxiety returns when the ref calls both Tinsley and Jules to the middle of the ring and makes them knock gloves. Another bell rings, and they circle each other again. This time, Tinsley is on the offensive. The strategy she made before coming out tonight is working.

Each punch is solid and quick, not leaving enough time between them for her opponent to both protect herself and return the effort. Tinsley is relentless, fucking ruthless. My heart thunders in my chest as I watch her send Jules rocking backward with an uppercut to the jaw. Arousal floods me, turning my cock rock solid when she repeats the move twice more and finishes the fight.

Her mouthguard goes flying across the ring as she takes two steps back and drops her arms, not bothering to watch Jules drop cold. She's already waiting when the ref blows his whistle and grabs her by the arm, lifting it into the air. Hunter dives into the ring and screams his congratulations, but she's ignoring him, looking at me.

I keep my face blank, not trusting how I'll appear to others around us if I let my true feelings show right now. The darkness inside of me cries out in outrage at the distance between us. It wants to be alone with her, somewhere nobody will hear or find us. I'm tempted to give it what it wants. Far too fucking tempted.

"Knew she'd do it!" Sierra exclaims, clapping above her head. "Seven rounds and a KO!"

"She's got my uppercut, that's for sure," Braden boasts.

Sierra holds his hand, bringing it to her chest. "But thankfully not your giant head."

Tinsley's parents are as blatantly in love as my parents are. I don't know how to be like them. But I think that's what Tinsley wants from me. She just has to realize that what I have to give her is better. Stronger. Not such a fleeting thing. Anyone can fall out of love. Nobody and nothing can alter the way I feel about her.

"When will she be ready to leave?" I bluntly interrupt their pointless bantering. There are more important things to do.

Easton laughs under his breath and looks expectantly at his parents, his phone clutched in his hand. He's become addicted to it recently. Whenever I see him, he's staring at it.

Braden's the one that answers me. "Half an hour, maybe. She'll be interviewed first."

"Where?" I ask.

His eyes narrow on me. "Behind the ring. Maybe outside the locker room. Wherever they want."

"Who's doing the interview?"

"What's with the third degree?"

I ignore his attitude and turn to Sierra, knowing that Tinsley would want me to at least say goodbye to her. "Nice to see you." The words are weak and stiff.

She pretends not to notice. "It was nice to see you too. Will you please tell Tiny that we'll catch her before you guys leave?"

"Okay."

"Bye, Noah," Easton says, not looking up from his phone.

I turn and leave them. Searching through the crowd, I spot my way out and take off. The next fight is going to start soon, and I want to be with Tinsley before that happens. My show tonight is set to start in two hours, and we have to be gone long before that. I don't want to get stuck here in the middle of the next match.

Sparks was worried someone would recognize me here, and I didn't care at the time, too obsessed with getting here as soon as possible. Now, I worry that would only derail my plans even further. I don't look like the other people here. Maybe I should have tried to blend in. Worn a shirt that covers the tattoos on my throat, at least.

If I believed in any higher power, I would thank them when I make it through the arena unnoticed and, with a flash of the pass around my neck, slip past the guards at the locker room entrance. It's louder back here than before the fight. The press is swarming, and in the centre of their madness, I find her.

It doesn't matter how many of them I have to shove my way past or how every random touch from a stranger makes me choke back bile because once I reach her side, I feel complete again. Like I'm exactly where I'm supposed to be.

27

Tinsley

My toes slap the floor as I stand in place and bounce my leg, high on adrenaline and the win of my first fight. I'm antsy, my blood singing. The thumping in my chest is scary fast, but I can't help but grin despite it. *I fucking won.*

I'm floating too high to care when a recorder is roughly jabbed in my face and a man with a lanyard that tells me his name is Brad from *Sports Weekly* demands, "Tinsley, tell me how it feels to win your first professional match."

My smile doesn't budge, even when another handful of men and women dressed far too fancy to be fans come bustling into the locker room. Security follows behind them, expressions tight and focused as they ready themselves for anything. Even when I was a bit unsure about giving interviews after the fight, I gave the approval to Hunter. It's now or never. Dip my toe in slowly now or wind up drowning later on.

I focus on the man in front of me. "It feels like an out-of-body experience. I'm incredibly proud of myself and my team for what happened out there."

A woman budges past the man and smiles at me. Her recorder is moved toward me with much more grace than his was.

"I'm Tilly from Upper Cuts. How is your face feeling? Do you have anything to say to Jules?"

I suck back a laugh. "My face is fine. She was lucky with that one. And no. I said everything I wanted to in the ring."

"How has it been working with Hunter Ramirez? Were you aware of the success of his career when you hired him?" another man asks, shouting from the swarm of reporters, not bothering to introduce himself.

"Hunter has been incredibly amazing to have as both a trainer and manager. His experience just adds to his ability to help me grow," I answer. Speaking of this trainer of mine, where is he? He was supposed to be here already. Eyes drifting to the door, I squint past the bodies and watch the door open.

Noah steps inside and searches the room, body tense, discomfort flaring in his gaze. I fight back the urge to run to him and take some of the discomfort away. He's never liked crowds, never been able to relax around strangers. I've always been the one to help with that. To guide him through these situations. He'd never ask me to do that for me, but he's never had to.

Finally, our eyes catch across the room. He pauses for a brief second before picking up his pace. The reporters turn to gape at him as he cuts through toward me. We've never hidden our friendship from the media, but it's not often they get an opportunity like this where they can have access to the both of us together in a media-friendly environment. Luckily for us, these reporters work for sports centres, not online gossip sites or music pages. That should help minimize the damage tonight.

If Noah's realized what's going to happen now, he doesn't let on. Instead, he comes to my side like that's the only place he wants to be and presses a subtle yet possessive hand on my lower back, toying with the band of my shorts. I lock my muscles to keep from shivering.

Having him here with me right now means more than I imagined it would. He has another sold-out show to play tonight and should be at rehearsal right now, but instead of risking the chance of missing my fight, he moved up his rehearsal to earlier today. It ruined everyone's schedules, but there was no changing his mind. For the millionth time in my life, I'm left wondering how I got lucky enough to have this man in my life.

"Hi," I say softly, quiet enough I hope the recorders in front of us won't be able to hear. The media's attention is so focused on the two of us that if a bomb went off outside, I doubt they would be able to tell.

He curls his fingers in my shorts, subtly tugging me closer until our hips meet, and then mutters, "Hey."

A collective sense of interest and desperation for a good story travels through the faces around the room. One by one, they begin to realize what a rare chance they've just been gifted. Lingering adrenaline still thrashes through me, but that doesn't stop my nerves from beginning to swell.

The pretty reporter in front of me blinks her wide, blue eyes and pulls herself together before everyone else. Her grip grows the slightest bit shaky on her recorder as she swerves off her predetermined course.

"Noah Hutton, did you watch the fight tonight?" she asks.

I bite my tongue to avoid giggling at the question. Noah hesitates with an answer, and I know that if I looked at him right now, I would find him biting his own tongue to avoid telling her something sarcastic.

"Yes," he replies instead.

The reporter grins. "Did you come for Tinsley?"

Those fingers gripping my shorts tighten, tugging them until the front part of the band digs into my belly. "Yes."

"Are you going to make it to your concert tonight? You wouldn't let yourself miss it, right?" This from another man, one who hasn't spoken yet.

Noah finds him in an instant, his dark eyes pinning him in place. "We'll make it."

We. Not I.

"How are you liking Seattle? It's got to remind you of home," the same man pushes.

Noah grows even stiffer. "You're here to talk to Tinsley. Not me. Do that, yeah?"

I hear what he doesn't say. *Mind your fucking business.*

"Actually, I think that's enough for tonight." It's Hunter's voice.

I didn't see him before, but as he moves to stand on my other side, the reporters take a respectful step back, appearing to not want to crowd him. Annoyance sparks in my chest at that. Why does Hunter deserve the space, but I don't?

"Thanks for coming to talk to Tinsley, but we're done now. You can talk to her when she wins her next fight," he tells them, appearing so damn confident in front of everyone. One day, I'll be the same. But until then, I'm grateful to have him to keep them away when it becomes too much.

A few of them grumble their frustration, but they slowly begin to exit the room, the security guards hot on their tails. Despite the lack of gossip they got tonight, there's a story waiting to be written from what they *did* get from us. It won't be the first time I've been in the tabloids with Noah, but in the past, it's always been him in the spotlight. This time, I will be.

"You should have waited for me before starting, Tinsley," Hunter scolds, facing me with his arms crossed.

I lift a brow and replicate his stance. "Maybe you should have told me that, then. Or at least been here before they started letting themselves into the locker room. Don't make me unhappy with you when I was just feeling grateful."

He backs off a little. "Point made."

"Great, because I'm too exhausted to argue with anyone tonight. All I want is to take a shower and get out of here."

His eyes drift to the cut on my forehead. It throbs, the pain starting to cut through the numbness brought on by the rush of adrenaline. "You need to get that closed up as soon as you're done here. No arguments."

"Stitches?" I ask.

"No. Just a butterfly should work. She got you good, but not that good."

"So, just patch me up here, then. Don't make me go to a clinic tonight."

Noah finally releases my shorts. His palm cups my side instead, a strong, heavy arm pressed against my back. I sigh softly and lean against him, burying my cheek in his shoulder.

"Don't forget about the celebratory party tonight in *your* honour. You can't show up with a half-cleaned cut because you didn't want to go to the clinic," Hunter says.

"Hunter," I groan, unashamed to be acting stubborn. He's not the one who just fought. "Please don't push this. I'll get it closed, but I'm not going to a clinic. I'm already going to this party even though I don't want to, so please don't push on this."

He huffs a reply. "Fine. I'm not up to a fight tonight either. Just go get cleaned up, and I'll have Marie come in and get you fixed up when you're finished. Don't miss this party, Tinsley. I'm serious."

"I won't. Fighter's honour." I press my hand to my chest. "Thank you!"

He flashes a quick look at the towering man beside me. Noah nods at him, and I roll my eyes at whatever they just silently agreed on. God, I'm surrounded by overprotective men. It's a blessing and a curse.

"You two are ridiculous. How about you go have silent man talk outside and leave me to get cleaned up." I clap and wave my hands at them when they continue to stand there. "Now."

Noah tightens his gaze and stays right where he is while Hunter lets out a rough laugh and, with a single wave of his hand, leaves the room.

Once it's just me and Noah, the room grows hot, like Hunter cranked the thermostat before disappearing.

I set my hands on my hips and meet his stare. "Well? I need to shower."

"Then shower." His voice is so chilled that it threatens to drop the temperature in the room back down.

He watches like a silent predator as I move for my gym bag. "Did you want me to shower with you in here?" I ask, doing my best to avoid looking at him.

"You can't hide from us forever, Golden Girl. One taste isn't enough for me," he says slowly, each word spoken in a way that feels like a stroke of his tongue between my legs. Hot, desperate, dirty.

"I'm not hiding." *I definitely am.*

He laughs darkly. "You are. I've let you."

Glancing at him over my shoulder, I ask, "What are you wanting to talk about, then? Does Mr. Dark and Twisty want to talk about his feelings?"

I'm pushing him. Why can't I stop doing that? Am I really such a glutton for punishment? Shit, I am.

I'm a punishment whore.

"Feelings," he echoes, spitting the word as if it's revolting. "I don't want to talk about feelings. I want to stop pretending that you aren't hiding from me. I want you to accept what's happening with us."

"I have. In case you forgot what happened an hour ago, you kissed me in front of my father, and I didn't slap you. He's not going to just forget about that."

"It was time he knew that I'm not going anywhere. He's been pushing me too far."

"He's known that for two decades, Noah."

"Then he doesn't care. I'm done with him throwing men at you and hoping they fucking stick. You're not available for other men. Just. *Me,*" he growls.

Ignoring the heat that's begun to build between my legs at his possessive words, I turn my back to him and grab my gym bag. My pulse kicks up as I drop it on the bench between us, fingering the zipper. It's already half-open, my clothes hanging out through the opening. My brows knit together. I swear I zipped it when I changed before the fight.

"Have you been back here at all?" I ask Noah as I begin to unzip the bag the rest of the way. I've never been much for folding clothes when I pack, but I've never been this messy before. It looks like I balled everything up and shoved it inside in a hurry. *Which I didn't do.*

"Don't change the subject."

"I'm serious, Noah." The words are shaky.

"I wasn't back here before the fight."

"Were my parents?"

"I don't know." That ice in his voice has gotten more prominent. Scary, even. I hear his boots hit the floor as he moves toward me.

With the bag fully open, I start to pull out each piece of clothing and lay them one by one on the bench. Shirt, shorts, socks, bra. My blood chills when my fingers meet the bottom of the bag, nothing left inside besides a small cosmetic bag full of my shower things.

"Do you know how easy it would be for someone to get inside this room during a fight?" I ask, my head beginning to throb.

Noah wraps a hand around my bicep and gently turns me to face him. His jaw is tight, teeth grinding. I chew on the inside of my cheek as nausea swirls in my stomach.

"Why are you asking me these questions?"

I look down at my bag and then back up at him. I'm embarrassed to say what I'm thinking. Maybe I just forgot what I brought with me today. Maybe I'm just on edge from the fight.

"Tinsley. Tell me."

It comes out in a rush. "Some stuff is missing from my bag. Two things. Two personal things. I don't know if someone took them or if I just never even brought them in the first place. Fuck, I don't know."

I release a shaky exhale when he cups my cheek and forces me to meet his stare head-on. There's so much rage in his eyes, but I know that despite our previous conversation, it's not aimed at me. Still, as it burns into my chest, I welcome it. There has to be something wrong with me because recently, I've begun to enjoy when he gets like this—all protective and dangerous—not just accept it like I used to. Now, it makes my heart race and my toes curl in the dirtiest way. It's probably not normal to find the idea of watching someone rip apart anyone who has ever done you wrong appealing. Yet, I can't deny the effect Noah has on me in seemingly every possible way.

It's obvious to me now that I would let him do anything, even destroying someone in my honour. Maybe I would even encourage him or join in, depending on the circumstances. God, that's fucked up.

"What's missing?" He's not going to let it go.

Swallowing, I clench the side of the bag in my hand. "My hairbrush."

A tick of his jaw as his fingers press into my jaw. "And?"

"My underwear."

28

Noah

I'M ROUGHER THAN I SHOULD BE AS I GRAB THE BAG FROM HER AND shove my hand inside. I need to see for myself that she didn't just miss something. A simmering blast of rage makes my fingers tremble when they brush the bottom of the empty bag, finding what she did. *Nothing.*

"I always bring extra underwear with me. I didn't forget them," she mutters lowly, as if trying to convince herself.

I already believe her. Did the minute she grew quiet. It wasn't that she didn't want to finish our conversation but that she could no longer focus on it. She was too afraid.

Without replying, I tear out of the room. The pathetic excuses for security guards standing outside the door gape at me as I whirl on them. Their eyes go wide as I shove one of them against the wall and hold him there with an arm to his throat, pressing and pressing until finally, fear fills his expression. He's bigger than me, yet as I snarl in his face, he flinches like I'm double his size. Like I terrify him. I should.

"Who did you let into this room?"

The other guy slips behind me but makes no move to pull me off this one. I feel feral, and I most likely look the same.

The throat beneath my arm tries to bulge with a swallow, so I press harder, making it impossible. "Nobody," he gasps.

I dig my heel into his toes and lean my body weight into it. His face twists in pain. "Try again."

"We were here all day. Nobody got in besides Hunter and the fighter," the guy at my back says in a pathetic attempt to save his partner a set of broken toes and a shattered larynx.

My top lip curls as I spit, "*The fighter* has a name. I suggest you use it."

"Noah." Tinsley's voice is an electric shot to my chest. "If they didn't see anybody go in, then they didn't see anybody go in. The media is still lingering. Don't give them a story."

"Fuck the media," I mutter.

The guard in front of me is red in the face, his breathing growing frantic. I twist my face in disgust. This is the kind of security that was entrusted to protect her? I find the idea repulsing.

Warmth envelops my elbow as she cups it and tries to steer me away from the guard. I tear my eyes away from him and focus on her. She's a flash of light that cuts through the red mist in my vision. I let it move through the rage, breaking it up until it floats away like fog.

Her lips part with a smile, and a small flicker of pride pushes through the underlying anxiety in her silver eyes. "Let's go. There's nothing else to be done here."

I slowly release the pressure on the guard's throat and grunt, "We can watch the security feeds."

She nods. "I'll have Hunter grab them."

"Fine. Get your bag so we can leave."

Her brows slip up her forehead. Despite the tense situation, she's still strong-willed. "I think you're missing something in that statement."

I roll my eyes but correct myself. "*Please*, grab your bag."

While the guard gasps for breath, I watch her smirk with

approval before slipping into the locker room. Once she's gone, I drag my scrutinizing glare between the two men.

"Tinsley Lowry just saved you both a lot of pain. If you forget her name again, I don't care where you are, that pain will find you," I threaten, my tone deceptively soft.

Before either one can mutter something that I don't give enough of a shit to listen to, I'm following my girl like a dog on a short leash. Tail wagging and all.

NH)

TINSLEY DISAPPEARS into the bathroom when we step onto the bus. She was silent most of the way back, only speaking to tell me that she didn't want to think or talk about what happened tonight. The quiet has never pissed me off more than it did then.

I need to fix whatever is happening to her. There are too many questions with no answers. Each one angers me more. If taking Tinsley's things has become someone's idea of fun, they're going to regret it. Are all of the things happening recently connected? The visitor at the house in Vancouver, and now her missing panties? I'm unsure. I hate being unsure. Especially when it comes to her.

If these events are connected, that creates a bigger problem. First Vancouver, now Seattle. They're not isolated events. They're moving with us from city to city. Hunter is meant to collect the security tapes in the morning. Answers will come then.

I tug the bandana out of my hair and rake my hands through it. It's overgrown. Too long and annoying now that it curls at the top of my shoulders. Leaning over my knees, I drop my head and shake it, sending my hair flying. It feels good to ease some of the tension in my neck.

I fall back against the couch cushions and exhale, staring at the ceiling. It's almost showtime. My phone vibrates for the hundredth time on the counter. Sparks looking for me, no doubt.

She can wait. Tinsley deserves some patience, and she's going to get it from me. Rock stars are supposed to be late for their shows. Maybe I'll fit in more now.

"I'm almost done!" Tinsley shouts from the bathroom.

I want to go to her. Fuck, I yearn to be in the same room, watching her get ready. But she's been violated today. I won't add to that by crowding her the way I know I will. Watching her the way I do, like she's my salvation. Like I might go up in flames if I don't get my hands on her soon.

She didn't ask me to join her either. If she wanted me to, she would have asked.

The reminder has something close to discomfort trying to worm its way into my chest before I push it away.

"How much longer do I have?" she asks.

"However long you need."

She groans loudly. "Noah."

"To make it there when Spark would prefer, we have to leave in ten minutes."

"Shit!" A clatter in the sink. "Give me two."

My control is slipping as time moves at a snail's pace. Our unfinished conversation from earlier left me unsatisfied. I'm nowhere closer to having her accept what's happening with us than I was before. I need her to fully understand what I want from her and what I want to *give* to her. Kissing and touching aren't enough. It's nowhere close.

I need everything. Mind, body, soul. I want to make good on my promise and devour her. Ruin her for anyone but me. From the moment we met, she was meant to be mine. Completely. Now that she's realized "just friends" was never supposed to suffice for either of us, I don't want to wait any longer.

"What do you think?"

I jerk my head in the direction of her voice and go wooden. Standing in between the kitchen and lounge room, she smiles at me almost timidly and pinches the bunched material at her waist. My cock grows painfully hard as I take her in. I smooth my hands down my thighs and grip my knees.

"Come here," I rasp, nostrils flaring.

She curves a brow but doesn't argue. Doesn't tell me to say *please*. I would have given the word to her a million times if it hurried her pace. With slow, teasing steps, she starts toward me. Her crimson silk dress caresses her hips as she moves, the bunched material at her waist making the swell of her curves more prominent. One shoulder is bared, a metallic gold strap on the other. Long, lean legs exposed to the middle of her upper thigh. Her eyelids are brushed with black, and her lips are the same shade as her dress. A butterfly bandage pinches her cut skin together on her forehead.

Fuck. Me. She looks like a She-Devil. My perfect match.

The moment she gets close enough, I dart my arms out and grip her ass, squeezing it hard as I pull her onto my lap. She gasps, grabbing onto my shoulders to steady herself before she crashes into my chest.

Her knees dig into the couch on either side of me, keeping her hovered above my thighs, her pussy just inches from pressing against the bulge in my jeans. There's too much fucking space between us. With my hands full of her round, firm ass, I pull her forward, closer.

"Drop, Tinsley," I growl, letting my head fall to the couch back so I can stare up at her as her face hovers above mine.

She wets her lips and then sucks the bottom one into her mouth. I slide one palm along the curve of her ass before slipping it beneath the silk and cupping the smooth, bare skin I find.

"I didn't want panty lines," she murmurs when I find the lack of so much as a thong.

Lust makes my blood sing. A pulse beats in my ears, as loud as a kick drum. My thoughts drift to a place of filth and desire. Nothing exists besides her.

Without another thought, I push the dress up over her ass

and settle it on the curve of her hips. Her eyes don't drift from mine the entire time. They're wild, my favourite shade of molten silver.

"You were going to my show with a bare pussy?"

The corner of her mouth twitches. I abandon her ass and roughly cup her face before digging my thumb into that smart mouth and pushing her lips apart.

"Don't forget the party afterward," she purrs, taking my thumb between her teeth and biting down until it begins to throb.

One look between her thighs and I'm spitting a curse between us. They're wet, her pussy gleaming with how needy she is. Forcing my eyes away, I find her staring down at my lap, where my cock is trying to tear through my jeans to get to her.

I shift my hips and revel in the way her eyes eat up the movement. "You look desperate for it, Tinsley. Is that why you decided to flaunt my pussy for anyone to see?"

"Last I checked, you're the only one looking at *my* pussy."

I flash a carnal grin and surprise her by reaching a hand between her legs and cupping the slick, hot flesh there. She shudders in my grasp, nails pricking my shoulders as she tightens her grip on them. My palm grows wet as she gushes for me. There's no hiding her response to my touch.

Squeezing the back of her neck with my other hand, I bring her face close and press my lips to the shell of her ear. "You can deny it if you want, but your cunt knows who it belongs to."

A low, desperate noise falls from her lips, and then she's finally dropping into my lap. I puff out a shaky breath and yank my hand from between her legs, needing to feel her heat against my cock, even over my jeans.

"Shit," she breathes, lurching her hips forward.

A sudden surge of pleasure makes me bite down on my tongue so hard I taste metal. I'd blow in my pants again if it meant having Tinsley grind on me, but I can't let her continue. She's been pushing me all fucking day, just begging for me to punish her. Avoiding conversations, surprising me with her entrance song to get a rise out of me, and now not covering her pussy beneath that short dress? She doesn't get to come, even if it pains me to starve us both of that experience.

Setting my hands on her hips, I still her when she tries to rock forward again. "No."

"No?" she asks, anger flaring to life in her eyes. "No what?"

"You're not getting off. Don't deserve to."

A bitter, livid laugh. "Fuck you."

"Not yet. But you're going to do something else for me."

Bewilderment dances across her face. "You're high if you think I'm going to do anything for you now."

I tug at the gold strap on her shoulder, letting it fall to her arm. Her tits aren't big, but they're perfect, and when I pull the top of her dress down, exposing them, I fucking groan at the sight of them. Cupping one with my palm, I dip my head and bring it to my mouth. I suck her nipple deep, grazing it with my teeth, teasing her with a bit of pain. She cries in response, pushing her chest into my face as her fingers thread through my hair, tugging harder with each nip of my teeth.

"Noah," she whimpers. Taking advantage of only having one hand on her waist keeping her place, she lurches forward, chasing a release I refuse to give her.

With a pop of my lips, I release her nipple and swat at her ass. She squeals, jerking in my hold. My heart jumps when a dark look swirls in her gaze, a look I recognize from the mirror.

"Get on your knees," I demand. My voice sounds like I've swallowed glass and can't stop bleeding.

"How about *you* get on *your* knees, you teasing jackass."

I chuckle so roughly her skin lifts with goosebumps. "Get. On. Your. Knees. Before I shove you down and make you choke on my cock."

Softly, she runs her fingers through my hair. I don't buy it. The blunt feel of her nails dragging down my scalp is a warning hidden within the façade of a soothing touch.

"We both know you were going to make me choke regardless," she says wickedly. "Maybe I want you to."

I watch her slink down my body, each inhale I pull into my lungs burning like hellfire. A clunk on the floor sounds, and I know she's fallen to her knees. Thin, delicate fingers that lead to knuckles I've seen deliver jaw-shattering blows trail up my thighs. A sick thrill races through me at the thought of those same fingers clenched around my cock.

"Take it out, Tinsley. Stop playing games."

"I will when you stop calling me by my name." The words are venomous.

I drag my hand over her head and cup the back of it. My hold is steady, firm. A warning that I can have her mouth full whenever I want to. Whether she takes me out of my jeans or continues to test my patience.

"What would you prefer I call you, then?"

An expression I haven't seen before darts across her face. Something wanton, *filthy*. "I don't know."

Oh, I want to explore that look. Want to watch it expand until it fucking explodes. I don't wait for her to undo my jeans. I can't. Her breaths quicken as I pop the button and shove them down my thighs.

She parts her lips and stares at the outline of my cock in my briefs. They're wet with precum, and I know she sees that. Enjoys it, even. It's for her. All of it. Everything.

Her fingers wander higher up my thighs, past my jeans and to my inner thighs. I grow tense and stare at her with an intense, heavy sense of desperation. "Tell me what you want me to call you."

"Anything," she whispers on an exhale.

The first brush of her finger along my shaft has me spitting a garbled "mine" through gritted teeth. She moans an illegible reply and, in one rough motion, has my underwear at my thighs and my rigid length hitting my stomach.

"Holy fuck." She sucks air through her teeth, eyes darting all over my lap. "When did you get those?"

"Long time ago."

The pelvic piercing is nothing more than a small metal ball at my groin. It gives me no pleasure, but she'll enjoy it. The two holes in my tip are for the Prince Albert I took out yesterday. She'll like that one, too, when I decide it's time to put it back in. I didn't want it to scare her. Knew it could complicate things like this when she realized she didn't know how to work around it. Nothing was getting between her and me once we got through the fucking tension that's been hanging over us for days. I wasn't risking the piercing.

"I've never . . ." Her thumb draws a line over the hole on the underside of my tip.

I swallow, but my throat is too dry. I choke on air instead. *Enough.* With the hand holding the back of her head, I guide her forward. Hot breath fans my shaft before she finally wraps her hand around me in a cautious grip. I jerk into her fist, unable to control myself. It's too much. Too much pleasure I already feel like coming.

If that's the case, I'm coming in her mouth. Down her fucking throat. I can cover her skin in my cum another time, once I've felt how her lips feel around me.

"In your mouth," I hiss softly, guiding her closer. "You can explore later. I'm too fucking close."

Her lips hover over the head, tongue flicking out to lick at the single bead of precum pooling there. "Better my mouth than your pants," she teases, and that's my last goddamn straw.

Her gag fills the room when I thrust past her lips. Fingers grasping for anything to hold on to, she holds my knee and uses it to push herself up, gaining more leverage. She jerks my cock in time with her mouth. It's hot and warm and wet as it works me, just like I know her pussy will be. It's a taste of what's to come. Soon.

"That's it," I grit out, tugging on her hair.

A swirl of her tongue beneath the head and I'm curling my toes into my socks. She traces every ridge with that dirty tongue, as if attempting to learn every inch of it. I want to tell her not to rush. That she'll have plenty of time to memorize my cock. But I can't speak. Too tongue-tied.

Her eyes are running when she finally looks up at me. The black beneath them has smeared down her cheeks. She looks beautiful like this. Depraved. Hungry. *Feral*.

"An angel," I groan. "You're a filthy fucking angel."

She whimpers in approval around my shaft, sending shock waves down my spine. Pleasure builds and builds, making stars blast behind my eyelids. Pushing forward on her knees, she pulls me deeper in her mouth, gagging when it goes too far. She can't take more than the first few inches, but she'll learn how to take it all. I'll teach her everything she'll ever need to know. We can teach each other.

When she pushes past her gag reflex and swallows me as far as she can, the rush of pleasure shoots me off.

I fill her mouth with spurt after spurt of cum, keeping her face buried in my groin when she tries to pull back on instinct. When some of it escapes her lips, dripping down her chin, I swipe it up with my thumb and push it inside along my cock, filling her too full. The twisted part of me wants to howl with satisfaction when I've stretched her mouth too much and more cum spills out. It wants to punish her for that, too, even if it was my fault.

"Drink it all," I coo, slowly relaxing my grip on her head.

A flutter of her lashes, and then she's making a show of pulling off my dick, sticking her tongue out and moving it side to side. "Gone."

"Not completely."

Gently, I swipe away the mess of cum on her chin and hold my hand between us to show her. Her cheeks deepen in colour as she stares at my wet fingers.

"Come up here, baby," I tell her as I pull my pants up.

Surprise warms her gaze. It takes me a moment to realize what sparked that look. When I do, I don't have the urge to take it back. It's odd. Very unlike me.

She's quick to move back onto my lap. A soft exhale falls between us when she settles there, her hands finding purchase on my chest, thumbs dragging over my T-shirt. Her tits are still bared, dress still resting up on her hips. She looks undone. Freshly fucked, but without the fucking.

"We're going to be late for the show." Her voice is soft, tired.

"Fashionably late."

She huffs a laugh. "Right."

A beastly urge blasts through me when I go to wipe my hand on my jeans. With her legs spread over my thighs, I give in to that urge and bring my hand to her centre and drag my cum-slicked fingers through her lips. I swirl the tip of my finger over her clit, and she collapses against me, whimpering into my throat.

"If you're going to walk around bare, you can at least wear my cum on this pretty pussy. Can't have you forgetting who it belongs to, can I?" I rasp.

"Noah," she begs, trying to rub against my hand, seeking more.

I pull my hand away. It physically pains me to leave her unsatisfied. "No. Next time you want to be a brat, you'll remember this." Teeth pull at my throat, biting hard. I laugh loudly, smoothing a palm over her head. "You've always had fangs, Tinsley. I'm not afraid of them."

Fixing the top of her dress, I tuck her chest behind a wall of silk and slide the strap back up her shoulder. I want to stay here with her forever. Want to pull her inside my body and keep her there. She cradles herself against me, her arousal forgotten, and I'm reminded of why I decided to keep her all this time.

Tinsley was custom-made for me.

 **29**

Tinsley

I'VE MADE A GRAVE ERROR.

Teasing Noah seemed like a cheeky idea, an easy way to rile him up. But I'm paying for that now. Have been for the past three hours. I grit my teeth and try to clear my mind of how badly I want to get back at him for this.

It doesn't help that while still being way too damn turned on, I'm being forced to watch him perform again, hours after his concert has ended. As if that isn't making me drip down my thighs every five fucking seconds. I'm sure the people around me think there's something wrong with me from how often I'm rubbing my thighs together in hopes of easing the ache between them.

Nope. Just horny beyond goddamn belief.

I'm angry at how hot he is. At how easy it has become for him to hold my attention and have me panting after him like a dog in heat. It makes me even angrier that I can't pinpoint what it is about him that makes me this way because *everything* seems to.

I was never into long hair, dark eyes, and tattoos. I never thought I wanted to fall for a tortured soul. Happy eyes and a charming smile are what I always gravitated toward. Oh, how naïve I was to believe that that was really what I yearned for. I had myself convinced I wanted that because there was only ever one man who didn't fit into that mould. The one I knew I shouldn't let myself have. If I could go back in time, I would smack myself silly. *So much wasted time.*

Sweet words and pretty smiles don't make someone a good person. Their actions do. The things they're willing to do and risk to ensure you're happy. Noah might not be everyone's idea of a good person, but to me, he's never been anything less than the best, even if his actions aren't typical. Nobody is perfect, and Noah just happens to be less so. Perfect is overrated, anyway.

My mouth tips up in a sly smile when I zone back into the party. Without my knowledge, Hunter managed to convince Noah to play a couple of songs at my victory party. While my stomach was swooping at that news, Noah was flashing me filthy looks on his way to the stage. He thought he'd gotten another one over on me, but he was dead wrong. This is a victory party in my favour, is it not?

I sink into the crowd muddled along the small stage and sway to the skin-chilling rasp of his voice. It makes my toes curl and my breath quicken. I've listened to that voice change over the years and been there when it developed the sound it has now. It's beautiful but brutal. A voice that you hear in your mind late at night when it finds you in the silence.

He grips the mic stand and, with an unwavering stare, pins me to the place I stand. The words he's singing are tortured, but they make me warm, as if he's singing about love instead of heartbreak. I steady my breathing and find that smirk from earlier, flashing it at him. He might have the power to keep me too enthralled to walk away, but I have power of my own.

The dance floor is full, bodies closely huddled together. It's easy to fall in sync with the dancing around me. I've never been a great dancer, but I know how to move my body in a way that grabs attention. And as I swirl my hips and dig my fingers in the damp hair at the base of my skull, Noah tracks my movements, his eyes flaring dangerously hot. I bite my tongue and lift my eyebrows coyly.

His hold tightens on the mic stand, the stomp of his foot on the stage growing more forceful. I watch the darkness swirling in his eyes expand as his stare darts behind me. An expression so brutal it threatens nothing less than absolute destruction twists his face mere seconds before two hot hands cup my hips from behind. The next lyrics Noah sings are snarled into the microphone. A series of excited screams come from the people around us as they assume that's the way he's supposed to sing the words. I know better.

Excitement makes me shiver. I don't shove the hands off me, but I don't move into the body behind me either. I want to see how this plays out. He can consider it payback for teasing me by forcing me to watch him sing onstage *twice* in one night.

It takes everything in me not to recoil at the feel of hot breath on my ear. The person behind me smells like cherries and tequila. Two of my least favourite scents. I can't blame them for continuing to dance behind me, considering I haven't stepped away, but that doesn't make the feel of a random person's dick rubbing against my ass any less gross.

The song is coming to an end. As familiar lyrics drift over throaty guitar notes, I know I'm about to be eaten by the big bad wolf sooner rather than later. Unknotting my fingers from my hair, I drift them down my front, between my breasts and over my belly button. I purposely dodge the hands on my hips, and Noah doesn't miss that. It doesn't calm him down, though. With a hiss of the final lyric, he's abandoning the mic stand and hopping off the stage a song early. The crowd parts for him while I swallow and jut my chin, waiting.

Taking the baring of my neck as an ill-timed invitation, the guy behind me moves in. By the time I peel myself away, it's too late. I prepare to have to yank Noah off the guy, but he completely ignores him, as if he was never there in the first place. Instead, he moves right for me. My stomach drops at the expression that twists his face into something that has the people around us taking a step back. I knew it was coming, begged it to, but now . . . maybe that wasn't such a good idea.

I'm in trouble now.

"Noah—" I start.

"Come," he snips. He wraps his fingers around my wrist, but they're so gentle that it feels wrong with how angry he is.

Curious eyes follow us as we rush through the rental space that was transformed for this party. I don't know what this place is usually used for, but it works pretty great for a party space. Hunter did a good job. It's a shame I'm not going to be here much longer to enjoy it. At least I've already done my rounds.

"Where are we going?" I ask when we turn down a darkened, empty hallway. The bright, neon lights from the other room snap at our heels. They flash across Noah's back, painting him in red and blue and green.

Loud music muffles the sound of my heels clacking on the floor as I struggle to keep up with his fast pace. I don't dare ask him to slow down.

My lungs empty with a sudden exhale when he suddenly whirls around and starts toward me, boxing me in against the wall. Top lip curled, he forces our foreheads together and covers my hip with his hand, replacing the memory of that man's hand with one that features only him.

"Do you have any fucking clue what you do to me? How easy it is for you to drive me to insanity?" he hisses, roughly bumping the bridge of my nose with the tip of his.

In one needy action, I have my fingers jammed through the belt loops in his jeans, using the leverage to yank him close. He breathes a throaty laugh, digging those long fingers into my curves.

"Do you not think it's the same for me?" I ask. My tongue feels loose, like I've downed an entire bottle of vodka when I haven't had a drop of alcohol in weeks. "Watching you up there drives *me* to insanity. Everyone looks at you like you're a god.

But they're all wrong. There's nothing holy about you, is there?"

His nostrils flare. "No. There isn't."

I flex my fingers and push them beneath his shirt. As I guide them across hot, hard, tattooed skin, I watch him react to my touch. Each breath he takes sounds pained, stressed. Like he's holding back again, refusing to give us both what we crave. I want to get my hands on him properly and explore without a single boundary between him.

"I want you to rip the halo off my head, Noah. There are very few things I've done in life that I've loved as much as being on my knees for you," I murmur, lips brushing his jaw.

A savage noise escapes him then, cutting through the thumping music as if it was never there at all. The hallway isn't private by any means, but Noah doesn't care. When he falls to his knees and frantically pushes my dress up over my hips, I don't care either. If anything, the idea of someone catching us drives me to dig my hands in his hair and roughly pull his face between my legs.

Yes, yes, yes. *Finally*.

"Fuck," I curse at the first curious stroke of his tongue through my slit. My back curls, and my head slams against the wall as I throw it backward and moan.

He presses a hand to my belly while diving the other between my legs. Parting me open for him, he stares at me as if looking for any sign of discomfort before thrusting his tongue inside of me and applying a soft, teasing pressure to my clit with his thumb. I carve my nails into his scalp hard enough I want to feel the ridges left behind when we're done. He growls against my pussy and trails his hand from my belly to my thigh, moving it to his shoulder and giving him more room.

Starving. That's what he is. He eats my pussy like it's the only thing he's ever wanted to taste. After being teased all fucking night, this is exactly what I needed.

The first breach of his finger inside of me has me crying out, the achy feeling of emptiness finally easing slightly. I'm so wet it's easy for him to add a second finger, seeming to sense that one wasn't enough before I can voice that to him.

"So good," I breathe, grinding into his face.

He leans back just enough our eyes clash and hold. I part my lip to beg him to come back, but then he's keeping his eyes on mine and pursing his lips before spitting between my legs. All thought disappears from my mind like smoke in the wind. It's filthy. Something I never would have imagined I'd like. But I feel my knees shake in response, the heel beneath my unsupported leg teetering. He shifts so he's fully supporting the leg thrown over his shoulder, steadying me so I don't collapse.

"For years, I've wondered how dirty you might be, Tinsley. What fantasies you might have," he grits out, his fingers gaining speed as they thrust inside of me. The hall echoes with the sound of how turned on I am for him.

"Don't call me Tinsley," I hiss.

Not right now. It doesn't sound right. Not earlier, and not now.

He blows on my swollen, throbbing clit. "Then tell me what you want me to call you."

I know he knows. He has to by now, but he won't say it on his own. It's not anything to be ashamed of. I know that. But it's something I've only fantasized about.

"Don't make me leave you like this again, Tinsley. You're close, aren't you?" He curls his fingers and makes contact with my G-spot for the first time. I try to clamp my legs together at the swell of pleasure, but he denies me that, turning his face to bite at the inside of my thigh. "Tell me and I'll let you suffocate me in this greedy cunt."

The heat of his mouth hovering over my clit has me blurting out, "Please! I'll fucking beg you."

A low, dark laugh. "Sluts do love to beg, don't they?"

My eyes roll back in my head. He sucks my clit into his

mouth and slips a third finger inside. I go off like a firework. Sparks flicker behind my eyelids as my lungs scream for air.

"Oh my *fuck*," I gasp, pulling his hair so hard it has to hurt him.

When I manage to suck in a single breath, it's thick with Noah's scent. It rips through me, adding to the insanity that's shredding me apart right now. Wave after wave of spine-numbing pleasure continues to move through me long after the initial blast, and when I manage to peel my eye open, I realize that's because he hasn't retreated.

Eyes full of an unspoken challenge, he pulls his fingers from my pussy and replaces them with his mouth. Lick after lick, he continues to feast on me until I'm a whimpering, crying mess, half out of my body.

"Please," I beg, my voice sounding like it belongs to someone else. "I can't. Too much."

"You can," he growls.

"I can't!" Tears blur my vision. I've never orgasmed back to back before. But I can almost taste the release as it drifts in front of me. But I can't reach it. Can't get there.

Noah pulls his mouth from my entrance and slams three fingers back in its place. I jolt, my back sliding up the wall.

"You're going to be my good slut and soak my face again. I'm not going to stop until you do," he demands.

Magic.

It has to be some type of sick magic.

My second orgasm crashes into me more suddenly than the first. It's stronger, harder. Nearly painful as it goes on for so long my thighs have begun to cramp by the time it finally begins to trickle off.

I'm boneless. My hearing is blown, fizzling in my ears. Everything happened so fast, and now I'm falling back to earth without a parachute.

After lowering my leg from his shoulder, Noah swipes at his mouth with the back of his hand and moves up my body. He holds me against him with big hands as he fixes my dress and blows a long breath into my hair.

"Are you going to behave now, Golden Girl?" he asks, the hint of a tease in his tone.

I can't help the laugh that escapes me. Even if I could, I wouldn't. I want him to hear it. "For tonight."

His chest rumbles with a throaty sigh. "You're everything I knew you would be."

My heart skips and swells in my chest. I bury my face in his throat and slide my arms around his middle. It's a full bear hug, one I hope expresses the words I can't yet say. The ones I don't know how to articulate.

"So are you," I breathe.

 30

Tinsley

PAISLEY ROCKS ON MY LAP TO THE BEAT OF HER DAD'S DRUMS IN THE studio. It's been a long day for such a little girl, but she's a trooper when it comes to life on the road. I swear she doesn't have an impatient bone in her body. If I'd been this chill as a kid, my dad probably wouldn't have put me into martial arts as a way to drain my energy.

Her bright blonde hair is in two uneven pigtails today, and they flop back and forth as she bops her head excitedly. Justice glances over at us from his place behind his drum set and gives his daughter an adorably wholesome grin. His love for her is so bright and refreshing. So warm.

Technically, Paisley and I aren't supposed to be in the recording booth with the boys, but Noah took one look at my pout and fluttering lashes this morning and told the studio manager to kick rocks. Reggie being here has helped too. He'd never turn me away.

Paisley relaxes against my chest when Reggie tells the band to go back and redo the last chorus. They nod in response.

"Thanks, guys. We're almost done today," Reggie says into the mic. His sympathetic smile is a comfort, even through the glass separating us. That man is a miracle worker.

My eyes find Noah for the millionth time today. He's already watching me, a softness gleaming in his eyes that I've grown attached to over the past week and a half. Ever since my victory party.

I don't know what it was about that night, but he's been different since. More at peace, if that's even possible for him. Somehow, we've grown even closer than we used to be. Like by removing the remaining boundaries between us, we've fallen completely in sync. It's been good. Really, *really* good. Labels have never been my thing, and I know they aren't Noah's, but he's mine in every way that matters. I no longer fear that. It was stupid to in the first place.

I've been avoiding the conversation with my father about what happened in the locker room, though. Not because I'm ashamed of anything but because I know what he's going to say, and I don't want to hear it. There isn't a single thing he could say that would make me change my mind. I might not have a damn clue what being in a relationship with Noah is going to bring, but as long as we keep going in the direction we are right now, I'm buckled up and ready for the ride.

I wiggle my fingers at Noah and grin. He doesn't smile back, but the small tip of his chin has the same effect.

"He has a crush on you," Paisley whispers, her amusement thick in the words.

I cock my head at her and tap her knee. "You think so?"

"I know so. My daddy said that my friend Brody had a crush on me because he was *always* staring at me. He told me that I had to tell him to eat dirt and leave me alone, but I don't think you should do that to Noah if you have a crush on him back."

I lean forward and softly ask, "Do you want to hear a secret?" She nods frantically. "I totally do have a crush on Noah."

Her gasp is adorable. "Are you . . . boyfriend and girlfriend? Like in the kissing movies?"

"Just like in the movies." The kind featuring a tortured bad boy instead of a Prince Charming.

She releases a dreamy sigh and nuzzles her cheek into my shoulder. The move reminds me of when Adalyn would cuddle me when we were little. I always wanted a little sister, but instead, I got a brother who would have rather carved his eyes out with a rusty spoon than come to his big sister for a cuddle when he was sad. I love him anyway, even if he makes it hard sometimes.

"That's a wrap for today, guys. Good job," Reggie says.

Dagger's the first one out of the booth. He hauls ass, disappearing as Paisley hops off my lap and starts for her dad. Justice crouches and lets her wrap her arms around his neck. Josh gives me a nod and Noah a risky slap on the back before following Dagger.

I meet Noah by the exit and step into his body on instinct, letting him tug me close. Tipping my head back to meet his waiting eyes, I say, "You sounded good today. The next album has to be almost done by now, right?"

"Two songs left," Justice answers for him. He follows us out of the booth with Paisley on his back. "I don't know what you're doing to him, T, but please don't stop. He's never been more focused than over these past couple weeks."

I pat Noah's stomach and laugh. "I'll try my best to keep him inspired."

"That's all I can ask," Justice says.

"Let's not act like Noah's the only one here who's been succeeding. Tinsley here hasn't lost a single fight so far," Reggie speaks up from his place at the soundboard.

We've all missed him these last couple of weeks. It's nice to have him around while they nail down the rest of this album. He's the band's father figure, and sometimes I think that despite their ages, the guys need one of those around here from time to time. Especially Dagger. He's an impossible person to try to get to know. His stubbornness might rival Noah's.

"Don't flatter me, Reggie," I tease.

"It's not flattery, sweetheart. I haven't missed a single fight on the television. We even got the proper channel and every-thing." He puffs his chest at that last part. I nearly swoon.

"Don't tell me that you've been forcing your sweet wife to watch my fights!" I scold half-heartedly.

"She likes them, I swear. You should have seen her last night when that Becks girl nearly knocked your tooth out." He blows out a harsh breath. "I thought she was going to throw the remote at the television."

Noah's abs tense beneath my fingers at the reminder. It was a tough fight. Probably the hardest I've had thus far, but it made the win that much sweeter. I felt invincible. Hell, I still did when I walked into the gym this morning. Hunter had me regretting that arrogance after a few deadlifts.

I flash my teeth quickly to show they're all still there and then say, "We're all good. A little bit of a scare always makes for good television."

"Why can I never watch Tiny on TV?" Paisley asks her dad, tone biting.

"You're too young, bug," he answers.

She huffs. "That's not fair."

"You get to see her in person when not many other people do. Isn't that even better than on the TV?" Justice asks.

She contemplates that for a long moment, a dainty finger tapping her chin. "I guess."

"That's my smart girl."

"How about we have that hair-braiding date soon? Maybe this weekend when Noah's sister comes to visit us?" I offer, hoping to steer her away from the current topic.

When her eyes light up, I know I've succeeded.

"Yes, please!"

I glance up at Noah, and my stomach swoops when he kisses the side of my head. It's the closest thing to approval I'll get, and it's even better than words. I'm such a sucker for him that it's almost embarrassing.

"Well, now that that's settled, what do you say we go back to the bus and make some lunch?" Justice asks his daughter. She's quick to approve of the idea, and then he turns to us. "You guys coming?"

"Please. I'm starving," I groan. Noah nods in agreement.

Reggie claps his hands a single time, drawing our attention. "You guys get out of here, then. I'll see you tomorrow."

"Do you want to come?" Noah's deep voice cuts through the room, surprising Reggie enough that his eyes flare wide.

My heart throbs. It takes everything in me not to kiss the fuck out of my guy and tell him that I'm proud of him for taking such a giant step. A couple of months ago, he never would have offered to spend time outside of the studio with Reggie.

"Are you sure?" Reggie asks. He runs a hand over his silver hair. Noah's reply is a stiff nod. "I'd like that, then."

"I hope you're into cold cuts, beer, and frozen yogurt, Reg, 'cause that's about all we got unless Tiny shares her premade meals. Wouldn't recommend those, though," Justice says as he starts leading us out of the studio.

"I'll live."

Noah and I leave Reggie to lock up the studio but slow our pace behind Justice. I grab Noah's hand and thread our fingers. He drifts a thumb across my knuckles, back and forth, back and forth.

"Paisley says you have a crush on me," I tell him once we step outside.

"She's seven."

"But is she wrong?"

"Yes."

I scoff in disbelief. "Right."

"I've never had a crush on you. That term is worthless in comparison to what I feel."

My chest tightens, a sudden warmth growing beneath my skin. "Do you have a term of your own that's more fitting, then?"

I'm fishing. I can't help it. When you grow up hearing your

parents say I love you to each other multiple times a day . . . to think of a life without those words is a bit harder to comprehend. I'm realizing that it's not the words that are important and more the actions that say what you don't hear, but it's going to take some time to not yearn for them still, even if we're not at that stage yet. I'm too unsure of the depth of my own feelings to be considering these things, but I can't seem to help it.

"Not yet."

That's better than a no.

Reggie's footsteps follow behind us down the sidewalk to where the bus sits at the end of the road. It's hotter than Satan's ass crack in Vegas today, and it takes less than a minute for my neck to grow damp and my hair to frizz. We've been in several beautiful places so far on this tour, but Vegas is not on my favourites list. Not only is it disgustingly hot, but it's also far too busy for those of us who love a boring, quiet night from time to time. I think Noah has pulled out handfuls of his hair already, and we've only been here for two days.

"Garrison never told me why you insisted on staying in the bus instead of a hotel while you were here. I can't imagine it's been very luxurious. A hotel would have been a nice break for a couple of days," Reggie mutters, coming up on Noah's side. "I would have made sure you got a room at the Bellagio or something."

"Wasn't necessary," Noah grunts.

Reggie looks across at me as if I'll tell him something different. I shrug. "The bus has been just fine."

And crowded. And loud.

The truth is that Noah would have agreed to a hotel room had Garrison not attempted to shove it down his throat the way he did, all high and mighty about the fact his name would get us the best place in town. He should have known better. So, while the tour crew and Josh and Dagger were put up in hotel rooms for the two nights we're here, we've been staying in the bus with Justice and Paisley. It has been nice to have a quieter bus, but it doesn't compare to a five-star hotel with a king-sized bed and a shower with amazing water pressure.

Maybe I'd be thinking differently if I didn't have to sleep in a bunk below Noah every night instead of *beside* him. God, I would do questionable things if it meant we could spend the night in the same bed. We've been like horny teenagers this past week, but there's only so many times a girl can get eaten out in a dark hallway or empty dressing room before she wants something more.

"Well, next time, you should consider the hotel. You deserve the luxury for a couple of nights," Reggie says.

"We will," I reply before Noah can tell him to leave it alone. He squeezes my hand softly in punishment, and I swallow my laugh.

The bus comes into view then, and my steps falter when I see Justice turning him and Paisley away from the door, his head frantically swivelling as if in search of something. *Us*, I realize when he looks in our direction and starts jogging across the parking lot.

"What's up with him?" I ask, but nobody answers me.

My stomach drops to the pavement when he stops directly in front of Reggie and croaks, "Take Paisley back inside. I don't want her around for a little while."

"What's going on?" Reggie asks, automatically alert at those words.

With a wince, Justice awkwardly glances between me and Noah. His face is red, and considering his endurance with playing the drums for hours on end, I don't think it's from the short run across the parking lot.

"Fucking hell. Just go to the bus," he tells us.

"That's a toonie in the swear jar, Dad," Paisley chastises.

Reggie takes a step toward them and settles a hand on Justice's shoulder. "Tell me what's going on."

Justice shakes his hand off. "You don't—just please take Paisley inside. I don't think they will want you to see this."

"Who?" Noah asks slowly.

A pause. "You and T."

That's all Noah needs to hear before he's moving. I offer Reggie an apologetic glance before following after him. Justice hands Paisley over to Reggie, and then I hear his footsteps behind me.

"Noah! Slow down," I shout. He ignores me.

The next few seconds happen in slow motion. I watch Noah tear a piece of paper off the bus door and pick something blue up from the stairs before kicking the side of the bus and turning his back to us.

"Noah!"

He jerks at the sound of my voice. I close the remaining distance between us and press into his space. He pulls away from me when I try to grab his arms and make him look at me. Fear pangs in my chest.

"No." His voice is hoarse.

I furrow my brows and slide my hands down to his wrists, squeezing hard and bringing them between us.

"Tinsley. No," he spits, trying to yank his arms back again. I tighten my hold and drop my eyes. When I see what's in his hands, I wish I hadn't looked.

"What the fuck?" I whisper.

31

Noah

I'VE ALWAYS HAD VIOLENT TENDENCIES. I STRUGGLED TO KEEP THEM under control, to not let them control my life. Didn't want to scare anyone the way I did my dad the first and only time I fed into them, when I was fourteen and beat the trunk of a tree until I shattered my hand after getting suspended for shoving one of Adalyn's bullies into a bathroom stall and flushing her hair in the toilet.

He was mad at me. Preaching about the proper way to behave when you're upset. Calm and smart. It didn't make sense to me. We were raised to protect our family always, regardless of consequences. I was doing that. Adalyn was brave, but it was going to take more than a snippy retort and an upturned nose for those girls to leave her alone. They were jealous of her. Of our family. I took care of it.

It was the threat to keep me home over the summer with a babysitter when we were supposed to go to Toronto that sent me over the edge. He knew it would. I lashed out. After a trip to the emergency room, I spent the entirety of my suspension in a stuffy office with a therapist who cared far too much about me.

I've never feared the consequences of protecting the few

people that matter to me. I'm hard-wired that way. The one thing right about me.

But when it comes to Tinsley, that protectiveness is far beyond normal. It's a living, breathing thing inside of me. A swell of black in my chest that spreads like poison, curdling my blood. If my father could feel what I feel right now, clutching silk in my fist and staring at the fear in Tinsley's eyes, he'd run.

Bile crawls up my throat as I watch her grow repulsed at the items I'm holding. I want to burn the world for putting that look on her face. And I will. After I get her inside of the bus and out of the eye of anyone who might see us here.

"Inside." The word is a slap in the silence. Misunderstanding who I'm speaking to, Tinsley nods absently and goes to set her foot on the first step. I circle her wrist, halting her movements. "Not you. Justice. We need to make sure it's safe."

She grabs the handle and pulls. It doesn't budge. "It's locked."

"Here." Justice is already handing her his key. We all have them. Has anyone lost theirs? Left it for someone to take?

It's not worth risking. I push past both of them and, after shoving the panties into my pocket, take the key from her and open the door. My boots clunk on the floor as I tear through the hallway and search every bunk, the bedroom, and bathrooms. I don't know what I was expecting to find, but there's nothing. No one.

When I return to the front of the bus, Tinsley's sitting on the couch, her legs tucked to her chest, toes hanging over the edge. A cloak of discomfort hangs off her shoulders. She's been violated more than once these past few weeks. The sting of bile returns, this time harder to swallow down.

Justice is standing across from her, by the television. I should feel bad that he saw all of this before I did, but I can't find it in me to care. I'd rather him than Tinsley.

"What's on the paper?" Tinsley croaks, eyes on my left hand.

Rage thunders in my chest as I uncurl my fingers and extend

the photo toward her. My jaw pulses with the ache of clenching it so tight.

Her fingers shake when she takes it from me. The terror in her eyes gives way to revulsion the longer she stares at it. An expression as sharp as the tip of a blade twists her features before she drops the picture to the couch, darting her stare to my bulging pant pocket.

"Give me my panties, Noah," she orders.

"No."

The photo is enough. I don't want her seeing what happened to her underwear. My palm stings, fingers burning from the reminder. *Dirty.* My skin is dirty.

Her lip curls, teeth flashing. "Yes. Let me see them. I need to."

"No," I snarl, meeting her seething tone with one just as dark and terrifying.

Slapping a hand out, she reaches for the abandoned photo and shoves it into the space between us. I refuse to look at it. Don't need to. It's engrained in my mind.

Us in the hallway at her victory party. Her head thrown pack in pleasure, mine between her legs. An X slashed over my body with angry words beneath it written in red.

Stop. Letting. Him. Touch. You.

I knew something was off. Felt it in my bones. Knew someone had gone into her dressing room that day. Saw it with my own eyes when we watched the security footage later. A tall male body, black clothes, hood up to hide his face, leaving us fucking nothing to go off. I should have been more careful. She's mine to protect. My responsibility.

My fault. My fault. My fault.

"Now," she hisses.

"Maybe it's better if we just get rid of them," Justice offers weakly.

She acts as if he doesn't exist. I do the same, too focused on Tinsley. Narrowing my eyes on her, I flare my nostrils with my next exhale. She won't let it go. Stubborn. So *fucking* stubborn.

The silk burns my skin when I pull them out of my pocket and dangle them between us. The new stain on the crotch turns my stomach. Her eyes fill with venom. She swipes a hand out, but I yank mine back.

"You're not touching them."

"Fuck you I'm not. They're mine."

"Not anymore. I'm burning them."

"No, you're not. We're keeping them and using them as evidence."

I slide a brow toward my hairline. "Are you planning on telling the police about this now?"

She refused involving anyone after the locker room incident. Garrison approved of her silence. I did not. I have money to keep mouths shut for a little while, but she insisted on keeping it to ourselves. To see if that was the end of it. It wasn't. I fear it was only the beginning.

We can use the DNA if I haven't tainted it with my own when I grabbed them from the step. It was a sloppy decision to leave his cum inside of her panties and hand them over. Did he think we wouldn't use it? Or did he want us to? It's no longer a sick joke. It's crossed that line. The photo of us is further proof of that. He's following us. I suspected that but was never positive until now.

A stalker.

Someone watching and wanting what's mine, growing angrier and more possessive with each day that passes.

Tinsley pales at my words. "We'd have to tell the police if we wanted a DNA test."

"Can someone please fill me in here? Who put your things outside the bus, Tinsley? What's going on?" Justice asks, arms crossed.

"I don't know. Someone took my underwear from the locker room when I fought my first fight, and I hadn't thought about it much since then. I thought it was just a creepy fan," she rambles.

I stare down at the silk draped over my finger for a second

more before dropping them onto a dish towel that was left on the kitchen counter. With my palm open, I fight the urge to burn my tainted skin.

Lifting my stare, I focus on Tinsley. When she feels me watching her, she meets my eyes with dull ones before I speak.

"It's been more than that. In Vancouver, I thought I sensed someone in the alley by the old house. Then, the shit on the porch. The fight. The photo. It's not a coincidence. Someone is stalking you."

She rubs at her face and whispers, "How would they have known about the house, Noah?"

"I don't know." They shouldn't have. Nobody does but us. It doesn't make sense. Isn't right.

"You have to go to the police." Justice keeps adding his fucking opinion as if it matters. I have to rein in my frustration with that. He's trying to help. But it isn't his place.

"How long would it stay a secret from the public if we did that? I don't want this coming out and affecting your career or this tour," Tinsley says. Her voice drops. "My career."

"I don't know. Maybe a couple of weeks." I won't lie to her.

She huffs, determination masking her lingering worry. "It's not worth it, then. Not yet. All I have is a pair of underwear and a scratched-up photo. That doesn't prove anything."

"That's not a good idea," Justice says.

This time, I spin on him, spitting, "Enough."

Tinsley pushes to her feet and threads her hands through her hair. She tips her head back and exhales a heavy breath. "This is my decision. I refuse to live my life in fear. Bringing the police into this right now won't help. It will only air out our secrets. This isn't anything I want the public to know yet, and that's my right."

I nod. "Okay."

"Okay? That's it? You nearly smashed Dagger's guitar over his head when he stared at Tiny for too long, and that was harmless. You're really just going to let her walk around with a sicko watching her and do nothing?" Justice exclaims, disbelief blazing in his eyes.

The scowl that tugs at my mouth is dark, unforgiving. I flex my fingers to try and soothe the urge to drive my knuckles into his face. "You think that I'm going to do nothing?"

I crowd his space, a sick sense of pleasure washing over me when he opens his mouth and then snaps it shut.

"I will end anyone who comes close to her. If she doesn't want the police involved, then I will be the one protecting her. Don't question me again. I'll break your spine instead of using words to explain myself."

With a flex of his jaw, he nods once and steps back.

"I appreciate you caring, Justice. But this isn't even up to Noah. I'll be smart, but I don't want cops around until I have something good enough to give them. If it goes that far," Tinsley tells him.

I want to touch her. Comfort her. Want to go to her and feel her skin. But my hands are tainted by the man who wants to take her from me. I move to the sink and turn the tap as hot as it will go. The hand soap is slimy on my palms, but it's not enough. Even as I shove my hands beneath the steaming water and start to scrub, they're still dirty. They begin to throb and burn the longer I keep them in the water. The pain moves through my system and runs gentle fingers through my mind, settling me little by little. Cleaning me.

A curse from behind me, and then I'm jerked from the sink. Another gentle touch but on my skin instead. I close my eyes and inhale Tinsley's smell as she holds my hands.

"They're clean," she murmurs. "You don't need to melt your skin off."

I shudder at her touch and drift closer. "Are you sure you don't want to run the DNA?"

"It's not worth the risk right now."

"I'll keep you safe, Golden Girl," I rasp, opening my eyes. We're so close I feel her breath on my lips, her taste teasing my senses. I'm too weak to refuse my desires when they involve her any longer. It's been weeks since I've had that ability.

I dip my chin and take her mouth in a kiss that seals my promise. She releases a soft noise and steps into my body, crunching our hands between us. Her tongue glides along my bottom lip, and I pull it between my teeth, biting softly.

With a breathy laugh, she pulls her tongue back between her lips and presses her face into my throat, nuzzling in. I lift a throbbing hand and cradle her head. Then, I begin to plan how to keep her safe at all times. No matter the cost.

32

Tinsley

My dad swings his left arm too far out, and I duck out of the way with a grating laugh. He's been off his game all day. Sparring with him has always been a healthy challenge for me, but right now, I might as well be using a punching bag.

"I know you're old now, but I didn't think you'd grow so weak already," I say, tucking my shoulders in and landing a hard, solid sequence of punches to his abdomen.

He rolls his jaw and resets his stance. "I'm not on my game. Being ignored for weeks by my only daughter will do that to a guy."

"I wasn't ignoring you." And it was only two weeks.

Gold gloves flash in front of me as he throws a jab. I catch it seconds before he's pushing a cross with his other arm. I block the move and huff a breath at his increase in speed. His right hook is strong, and I rock back when I successfully block that too. It's been a long few hours, and it's starting to wear on me.

"You were," he grunts.

My arms go up in front of my face as we reset. "I was postponing a conversation I didn't want to have."

"What is that conversation, exactly?"

I grit my teeth and throw a jab-cross instead of replying. He blocks and returns the sequence. "Noah and me. You don't like it."

"Are you finally admitting that you're together?"

I tilt my head and stare at him with an *are you serious* expression. "Are you finally admitting that you would have a problem with it if I said yes?"

He takes a step back and smacks his hips with his gloved hands. *Guess we're done sparring.* "You're old enough to make your own decisions, Tinsley. You've never needed my approval for anything before."

"Just because I never needed it didn't mean I've never wanted to hear it. I'd have thought you'd be at least a little relieved to know that I'm dating someone whose priority is my well-being."

I almost crinkle my nose at the term. Dating seems so insulting.

"You are dating, then?" he asks, expression tight.

"You could call it that."

Shooting a rough breath between his lips, he begins to pull his gloves off, letting them hit the mat one after the other. The silver in his hair, mixed with his surly scowl, makes him look far older than he is. If he had any brown hair left on his head, it would have turned grey from this conversation alone.

"He looks at you like you're his lifeline. Like he can't breathe without you," he mutters a beat later. I gnaw on the inside of my cheek, swatting away the flutters that grow in my stomach at his observations. "A relationship like that can consume you, my littlest fighter. It can make you lose yourself. That's what I've always been afraid could happen. You are too special of a person to conform to someone else's idea of who you should be."

I frown. The large space of the gym suddenly feels too small. It's always confused my dad how close Noah and I are. *Inseparable.* I've heard that term my whole life.

He doesn't understand our bond. And in his defense, most of the time, I don't even understand it. It goes *beyond* understanding.

It just is. And this feeling of rightness is not going to go away. If after two and a half decades it's still here, it's obvious that it's a forever type thing. I've just finally accepted that and let myself have what I think I've always wanted. Whether my dad tries to make sense of that or chooses to disapprove is up to him.

"Have I changed, Dad? Or am I still the same little girl I was when we would make fresh lemonade for Mom's office every Saturday morning? I'm still me." I slip my gloves off and set them on the mats beside his. Gold and silver. The perfect pair. Dad watches me with silent concern but appears to be content enough with listening to me speak. "Noah has always been here. He's always been my other half, and I've continued to stay true to who I am, no matter that fact. I don't know how to explain our relationship to you without sounding like a naïve little girl."

He shakes his head. "You've never been naïve. Try and explain it to me. Please."

Rocks fill my throat despite how many times I try to swallow. Fuck it. *Here goes nothing.*

"We're connected. Somehow. Where he goes, I go. I'm my best self when I'm with him, and I help bring out things inside of him that nobody would ever be able to witness without me. I feel like I'm breathing polluted air when he's too far away. The only time I can take a full, clean breath is when he comes back to me. I don't remember a time in my life where it wasn't like that. I don't think there ever was. And I know how that must sound to you, but I can't change the way I feel, even if Noah isn't the type of person you imagined me with."

My words smack into a wall of silence. It doesn't feel uncomfortable, though. Just . . . heavy. Dad's still staring at me, but the concern in his expression has shifted. No longer curious, he appears almost shocked, as if he didn't expect me to unload on him the way I did. Despite our close relationship, we've never spoken about boys or relationships before. He's always been too protective for me to even contemplate bringing up a crush to him. This all has to come as a surprise. At least it's out there now.

Maybe he can try and understand how I feel instead of putting his preconceived notions of Noah first.

"You okay?" I ask after a few more beats of silence.

He blinks a couple of times before glancing around at the gym. He's fidgeting. My dad isn't usually a fidgeter. I'd say this isn't the time or place to tell him about my stalker. The last thing we need today is for him to go into cardiac arrest.

"Dad?"

His head snaps back at my voice this time. A soft, apologetic smile pulls at his mouth. "I'm sorry, Tiny. I'm just a bit out of my comfort zone here. I've never heard you speak about anyone like that before. It's me that's been naïve, I think. I should have seen this coming years ago."

"You would have if you hadn't let everything that happened with him and Oakley cloud your judgment."

He tries to hide the guilt that flashes in his eyes, but I find it in an instant. "I think it was a lot of things. Oakley and my love and worry for you are just the main reasons behind my lack of understanding. I'm your dad. I'm always going to want to protect you from the things that could hurt you."

"Noah isn't going to hurt me. The way you and everyone else tend to treat him does."

"I'm sorry, sweetheart."

I close the distance between us and give him a hug. He wraps me up in his arms and presses a kiss to the top of my head. I'm surprised at how receptive he was to what I had to say. It's progress. A bit of weight off my shoulders.

The rest of it will remain there until we figure out who's been taking my things and watching us. Watching *me*. A sense of wrongness floods my senses at the reminder of what's been going on these past few weeks. It's only been three days since we found my underwear and that scratched-up photo outside the bus, but they've been three incredibly tense days. We're constantly waiting for something else to happen, and I don't want to live my life looking over my shoulder all the time. I wake up on edge, and it only gets worse as the day goes on. We haven't told anyone else about what happened, and I want to keep it that way for as long as possible.

"Thank you, but I think Noah's the one who deserves the apology. He's never going to be perfect, but he makes me really, really happy. He's my unconventional kind of perfect," I say.

Dad tightens his arms around my back, squeezing me softly. "I'll apologize the next time I see him."

I roll my lips to hide a smile as I back out of his arms and scratch the back of my neck. "About that—"

"Tinsley?" Noah shouts. He's perfectly on time, as if I accidentally summoned him here.

Dad stiffens, eyebrows fastening together. "Coincidence?"

"We have plans after training," I answer innocently.

"Right."

Noah stalks into view, and I feel all of the tension leave my body. I grin and wave, not paying much mind to the irritated expression on his face when he glances at my dad. My excitement to see him makes everything else hard to care about. Maybe he's rubbing off on me after all.

God, that sounds dirty. In a good way.

"Hey." I bounce my leg to keep from running to him.

He looks back at me, and his features settle. "Finished already?"

"We got a bit distracted. Four hours will have to cut it today. Right, Dad?"

I widen my eyes at him and jerk my chin, silently telling him to get on with it. I'm grateful when he turns to Noah and attempts to make himself look less intimidating. Noah just stands in place, one brow twitching as they stare at each other.

"I'm sorry for the way I've treated you recently. If you make my daughter happy, then that will have to be good enough for me."

My eyes pinball between the two men as a sticky silence drapes over us. I exhale a massive sigh of relief when Noah dips his chin and, despite the tension radiating from the hard lines of his body, attempts a grimace-like smile.

"Thanks."

"You're welcome," Dad replies quickly. He wants out of here, and I have to stifle a giggle at his discomfort. It's not often I get to see him this way.

"Thank you for taking over for Hunter today, Dad. I'll see you later?" I ask.

We got to Salt Lake City, Utah, this morning, and we're staying for two nights while the band finishes recording the album. Swift Edge Records has studios all over America, serving as a constant reminder that Noah wasn't signed to some mediocre label but one of the best. I'm grateful for the two-day stay as that means my dad gets to hang out with us longer. Garrison put him up in the same hotel that I convinced Noah to stay in tonight. *With me.*

My neck grows hot as I let my gaze wander over my rock star. He looks incredibly sexy in those tight black jeans that I know are cupping his ass just right. The grey acid-washed tee hung over his shoulders hides the thick ridges of abdominal muscle that I haven't had a chance to get properly acquainted with these past couple of weeks. He's all about touching me when we're alone, but when I try to take my time with him, he always has other plans. I want to change that as soon as possible. Tonight, hopefully.

His hair is overgrown even for him, and I know the length has been bothering him. I'll give it a trim once Paisley gets a chance to braid it in all of its current glory. Fit with red lips, dark under eyes, and dangerous brown eyes, he's all mine.

He doesn't play until tomorrow, and I have big, big plans for him tonight. Starting with a trip to a small tattoo parlour that Sparks told me about this morning.

Dad shakes me out of my head when he gives me a goodbye hug. "Yeah, I'll see you later. Stay safe tonight."

I reluctantly tear my eyes from Noah and return Dad's hug.

As soon as he pulls away, Noah's moving in, clearly just as impatient as I am. His hand settles between my shoulder blades before drifting down, fingers caressing my spine.

My shiver is involuntary. "Love you!" I squeak at Dad when he starts to leave us.

"I love you, Tiny," he calls over his shoulder, and then he's gone.

I hardly have a chance to take a breath before Noah's spinning me around and kissing me until the only thing left in my mind is him.

It's peaceful. Like coming home.

33

Noah

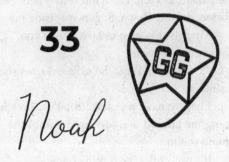

"God, do you have any non-tattooed skin?" Tinsley grumbles, pawing at my body.

It was when she shoved my shirt up my chest and couldn't find enough bare skin to ink anything more than a single letter that she started to become growly. Her scowl deepened after she spun me around and repeated her check on my back. It was the same result. Not including my face, there's only one part of me that I've kept void of ink, and I'm disappointed in her for not remembering. She's seen the small section of blank skin more than once. Touched and sucked it.

The tattoo shop she brought me to is a dive. It's dark and smells like mould. If it were a male artist, I would have taken her and left already. If she wanted a tattoo this badly, she could have come with me any of the times I got mine. Her sudden change of mind is surprising. I've done several of my own tattoos. I could have done hers. In private. At home.

"Fine. We're tattooing your face, then," she huffs. Even after she's backed away a step, her perfume lingers, making my cock stiffen. It's always fucking hard now. I don't remember the last time it was fully soft.

"Okay," I agree.

She blinks repeatedly. "Actually?"

"Why does that surprise you?"

"Because it's a face tattoo."

"I've done tons of face tattoos," the lone artist in the shop puts in. She's tall and edgy with a buzzed head that's been dyed pink. The two holes in her earlobes are interesting. I wonder if they hurt or whether she didn't feel them stretching like that.

The black leather table she's begun to set supplies onto is one of the only two in the shop. The shop I go to back home is similar in size but better. If this artist ruins Tinsley's skin, this place won't last much longer.

"Just don't give me a prison tattoo," I deadpan.

Tinsley rolls her eyes and smirks. "I don't know, I think you're rugged enough to pull it off. And Garrison would most definitely have a stroke."

"Tempting."

She taps a blunt nail to the skin above the arch of her brow. "I'm thinking right here."

"I'll get one there if you do."

"Really?" Excitement turns her cheeks pink.

"Yes."

"Do you know what you want to get?"

Your name. "A star."

"There meaning behind that?" the artist asks.

Wheels spin on the floor when she sits on a stool and swivels herself over to a small table. She picks up a tablet and starts sketching something.

Tinsley stares up at me with a look I don't deserve. It's too soft, too warm. How can she look at me like that? As if she doesn't see the shadows that fill my soul. Like they don't scare her when they do everyone else.

She's too good for me. But I'm bad enough to take her anyway.

"It's something from our childhood," she answers the artist on my behalf.

A star was the only image I could draw in reference to Golden Girl. It's stuck since. Stars are drawn into my skin all over my body. Some are hidden, some aren't.

"Sick. And what am I doing for you?"

"I want two. One on each temple. Devil horns on one side and a halo on the other."

My chest fills with a disbelieving laugh. I lick my bottom lip and drop to my ass on an empty stool. When I pat my thighs, she comes to me without hesitation, perching on my right thigh. I grip her hips and move her to my lap, threading my arms around her stomach.

I slide the hair away from her neck and press my mouth to her pulse. A breath gets caught in her throat. "Is the halo for me?"

"It wouldn't be very fitting," she breathes.

I hum against her skin. My thumbs fan out on her belly, rubbing back and forth. She fidgets on my lap, pushing back against my dick. I cover a groan with a dark laugh and grip her knees, snapping her legs together.

"You should get a pointed tail instead of Devil horns."

She turns her head, bringing my lips to the underside of her jaw before I pull back. "Why a pointed tail?"

"Because you're a fucking succubus."

Her laugh makes my toes curl into my boots. "I'll stick with the horns. I don't think my parents would appreciate the explanation for the tail."

"They won't appreciate you tattooing your face at all."

"You're not wrong."

"If you guys want to come have a look at these images, I can start printing off the stencils," the artist says.

Tapping Tinsley's knees, I urge her from my lap and swat at her ass the moment it appears in front of me. I stifle a groan at the way it shakes in her too-tight jeans. What panties is she wearing beneath them? *Fuck.*

"You okay?" she asks over her shoulder when she catches me

staring, her voice dripping with fake innocence. The curl of her smile tells me she knows why I'm sitting so stiff on this fucking stool.

"Let's leave," I mutter.

She winks and grabs my hands, yanking me up. "Nope. It's time to pop my tattoo cherry, baby."

This time, I don't hide my groan.

NH

TINSLEY UNDERESTIMATED HOW MUCH a face tattoo would hurt. I went first and wasn't good enough at explaining the feeling of the needle in my flesh to properly prepare her. I've gotten so many tattoos that I've become numb to the pain of them. But even as the artist begins to ink the final curve of her second tattoo, it becomes obvious Tinsley is not any more used to the bite of the gun as she was when we began.

With gritted teeth and wet eyes, she keeps her attention on me and not the gun buzzing in her face. I stroke the inside of her knee like I have been for the past half an hour. Goosebumps dance over her throat, drawing my attention to the small mark beneath her jaw. *My* mark, uncovered for everyone to see.

It matches the hidden ones on her hips and thighs left from the hard, desperate press of my fingers. I can't seem to help leaving them. And she likes seeing them. Tells me it often. They're a reminder of the way we play in the dark. Desperate. Without boundaries.

If it weren't for our constant pathetic lack of privacy on the tour bus, my mark would be inside of her too. I want her in every way, fucking crave it. I'm going out of my mind without it. But I'm used to holding back with her. Waiting to get her alone long enough to give light to our twisted desires will be worth it. I plan on being excruciatingly thorough when the time comes.

It's not plausible to risk being caught simply because it's tiring to wait.

The chime above the shop's entrance alerts us to someone walking inside. Tara—the artist who finally told me her name before sticking a needle in my face—turns off the tattoo gun and swivels to look past my body at the door. I follow her stare, my muscles tightening.

"We're not open for walk-ins right now," she tells the man that lingers in the entryway.

He's tall, with a long, thick beard that probably smells like shit, considering his dirty clothes and oily, greying brown hair. The black hoodie hugging his torso in an uncomfortable way is so stained that it looks acid-washed, and his jeans are torn at the knees, but not in the way mine are. His hands are in the front pocket of his sweatshirt, and something dark flares inside of me, urging me closer to Tinsley.

Tara eyes the stranger with a mix of curiosity and annoyance. "If you want to get a tattoo, you should call the shop first. We book up really fast."

Unless your name is Tinsley Lowry. Then, you can get a spot whenever you please.

"Oh, I'm sorry," the man mutters. His voice turns my blood to ice.

My golden girl must sense the change in my demeanour because she curls her fingers over the ones I've been using to stroke her knee and squeezes. I want to look at her and reassure her but can't tear my gaze from the man. There's something familiar about him. Something that unsettles me. That feeling only expands, growing teeth when his odd-coloured blue eyes dart to Tinsley and remain there for longer than necessary. The familiarity of that stare has a snarl slipping from my lips.

It's the guy that scratched her outside of the club in Vancouver. The one whose eyes gave him away that night as they bored into *my* Tinsley. The reminder of him sends me spiralling.

I can't ignore the nagging bite in my chest that tells me he's not meant to be here. That he's a threat to her. With everything going on with this sick fucking stalker, I can't risk him getting anywhere close to her. Fire grows in my gut as I work to paint a clear picture in my mind.

I'm off my stool and halfway across the shop before I realize I've moved. It's more than aching to seek retribution for the marks he left on Tinsley that has me accepting the siren call of my shadows. It's everything coming together in a messy, desperate conclusion. He shouldn't be here. Utah is a far trip from Vancouver. Was he in Vegas, too? Seattle?

What he lacks in smarts, he makes up in speed. He's out the door before I reach him. Tinsley calls my name and tells me to wait, but I'm already following him outside. It's dark out, but the sun hasn't fully dipped yet. I pause outside the shop and look left, then right, unsure which way he went. It's the angry curses shouted by a woman on my right that have me pushing in that direction.

My boots are heavy, too heavy to give me the speed I need to catch him. Curling my fingers into my palms, I push myself harder. I run through the gap of people on the walkway and find a woman adjusting herself a few feet away, as if she were just bumped into by my dead man. I rush past her and grit my jaw, catching a black hood a few feet ahead. They're moving too quickly to be on a casual walk, so I follow them. I'm unfamiliar with this city. I don't have a single fucking idea where I'm going. None of it matters.

I follow the hooded man until he runs across the street and slips into a crowd of people exiting the subway. I slow my steps and shove a hand through my hair. There are too many people to find him in the mass of bodies.

The prickle on my skin from someone watching me turns my frustration into blistering rage. He's close, and I can't fucking see him. I need to know if he's the one behind all of this. Need to fix it if he is. Keep her safe. The world spins beneath me. Warmth fills my palms. I'm bleeding. Cut myself with my own nails. The pain doesn't soothe me.

"Noah! Jesus Christ, Noah!"

I snap my head in the direction of her voice. She can't be here. Not when I can't see him. Hands brush my back, and I spin, lip curled back in warning. I find her. My eyes fall shut, the fire in my lungs extinguishing. *Breathe.*

"You can't just take off like that, you dick bag!" she scolds, clutching desperately at my body. I focus on her touch. "Who was that guy? Do you know him?"

I shake my head. Words won't form on my tongue.

"You left your phone in the shop. I thought you might have gotten lost and then trampled by fans or something."

I don't speak. Instead, I tug her into my arms and hold her too tight. She doesn't understand what's going on, but I can't tell her. Not yet.

We've never had secrets, but today, I keep one that could destroy everything.

34

Tinsley

NOAH LINGERS NEAR THE HOTEL ROOM DOOR, FIDDLING WITH ALL the locks as I wander inside. He's keyed up, so much anger brimming beneath his skin. The inside of my cheek is raw from gnawing on it the entire Uber ride home. This isn't how I planned tonight to go, but I refuse to let this ruin my plans.

I ghost my fingers over the ink on my face and wonder how different my past twenty-five years would have been if I had the same nerve I do now. I got two tattoos today. On. My. Face! They're small and delicate, but they're still tattoos. *I'm a certified badass now.* And despite what happened afterward, I will acknowledge that fact.

My dad is going to lose his shit when he sees my face tomorrow. It's probably fucked up for me to be excited to witness that impending meltdown, but as a near perfectly behaved child growing up, it's been a long time coming.

I roll my lips and trace the room with tired eyes. I've never stayed somewhere so fancy. When Garrison told us this morning that Reggie insisted we be put up in a hotel this time, I half expected the jackass to find the worst room possible out of spite. This is definitely not the worst. The bed is massive and thick with a heavy comforter. There's a fully stocked bar and a bathroom fit with a soaker tub and a glass shower that could probably fit an entire football team. It's a taste of what the future holds for the both of us if we manage to survive everything that's happening right now.

"Are you going to be dark and twisty all night?" I ask, moving to the tall windows. The curtains are open, welcoming the moonlight into the room. Neither one of us bothers to turn the light on.

I don't hear him closing in on me, yet the feel of his hands cupping my shoulders doesn't shock me. With a soft exhale, I lean back into his touch.

"I thought you liked me dark and twisty."

"Mm, I do. Just maybe not right this second."

He presses against my back, hands drifting down the length of my arms. I swallow the swell of emotion that builds in my throat at the gentleness of his touch. It's ridiculous to get emotional over a brush of fingers over my arms, but this is Noah. We haven't said in words what tonight is going to bring, but we both know. This soft side of him won't last, and while I want nothing more than to coax that beast out from inside of him, I love these moments. They're rare, and that's what makes them so special to me. It's why I've begun to fall in love with him despite everything I thought I wanted from a relationship. These little moments are worth more than three words. They're better.

"Are you going to tell me why you really ran after that guy today?" I whisper.

"No." He drags his knuckles back up my arms, raising goosebumps along the way. "Not tonight."

I hear what he chooses not to say. *Not until I have to.*

"Do I need to be worrying?"

The pressure of his touch grows for the briefest second before evening out. "No."

I don't have to look at him to know it's a lie.

"Okay," I breathe. The backs of my eyes sting before I grab

hold of myself and blink it away. I had a feeling deep in my gut that he ran after that man for a reason. A reason that I wished I was wrong about but now know that I was right.

There's a face to my stalker now. A confirmation that he's still following us. Following me. He's not going to let it go. Noah probably only angered him more by chasing him through the street. It's going to get worse, and there's nothing I can do to stop it.

Still, I won't let him take tonight from me. Everything is changing around us, but Noah and me . . . that's permanent. Forever. Tonight is ours.

Noah chokes on a groan when I push my hips back against his groin, making contact with the length of him, already hard for me. The hands on my arms still before I grab them and drag them over my front. His fingers spread around my breasts, cupping them with a firm grip. My nipples are tight, scraping the material of my shirt. I want the boundary to disappear. Want him to pull and pinch and bite them until my legs turn to jelly.

"If there was any chance you could escape me, Tinsley, it will cease to exist the moment I feel you gripping my cock."

The warning falls on deaf ears. I'm already too sure of this decision to be swayed.

"It's brave of you to assume it wouldn't be the other way around. That I'd ever let *you* escape *me* after this," I murmur.

Abandoning my left breast, he threads his fingers in the hair at the base of my head and tugs at the roots, exposing my throat. He drops his face to my neck and breathes deeply before parting his lips on my hot skin. He tastes me and groans, digging his dick into my back.

My eyes shut as I drop my head against his chest and reach behind me to grip his thighs, desperate to touch him. When he sucks at my throat, the hand on my breast drifts. Suddenly, my nipple is pinched between two of his fingers, forcing me to cry out. I jerk against him and arch my back at the spark of pleasure between my legs. It's only a tease of what I know I'm in for tonight, and I'm desperate for more.

Sensing that growing need inside of me, he twists my nipple and orders, "Take your clothes off, Tinsley."

I don't have to be told twice. Forcing myself out of his grasp, I take a step forward and face him. He looks pissed off. But I know he's not. He's holding himself back, not wanting to devour me before we get started. Seeing him like this does something to me that nothing else has ever been able to come close to. It makes me feel sexy and powerful and in control despite the promise of danger that lurks in his eyes.

He'd crawl to me like a dog if I told him to. The image of that makes my stomach swoosh.

"All of them?" I ask coyly, fingering the hem of my shirt.

His eyes darken. "All of them."

I tug my shirt over my head first, then work on my jeans. When I'm left in my bra and panties, I slowly reach behind my back and slip my fingers beneath the band, watching him. His nostrils flare as he stares at the red lace bra hiding my chest, poison filling those dark brown eyes.

"Finish," he snips.

I wet my dry lips and unclasp the bra. It falls from my chest to the floor, and he clenches his fists as his eyes fix to my nipples. His uneven breaths fill the room, giving me the confidence to keep going.

Dropping my hands to my hips, I push the red thong down my legs and step my feet out of them before crouching to pick them up. They dangle from my pointer finger, the soiled patch in the middle of them facing him. Mischief has the corner of my lips tugging up as I throw them to him.

He swipes a hand through the air and catches them. My heartbeat stutters when he clenches the lace between his fingers and brings the wet material to his nose. The following moan that drifts through the room has more of an effect on me than him tugging on my nipples did. And when he lowers his hand

and shoves the thong into the pocket of his jeans, I nearly collapse.

He smirks, as if reading my mind. "Get on the bed."

I'm crawling onto the bed in an instant. The thick mattress sinks beneath my knees as I move toward the headboard. I can feel the heat of his stare between my legs as I crawl, and it only makes me hotter, so goddamn wet I'm sure I'm dripping.

"On your back. Legs spread."

"What if I don't want to get on my back?" The snarky words slip free before I can swallow them.

I should have expected him to spank my ass, but the strength of the hit sends me rocking forward on my hands. The burn is a ghostly caress on my clit. I'm throbbing, so turned on it should be illegal considering he's barely touched me.

"What was that?" he grits out.

I glance over my shoulder and lock my eyes on his towering figure at the edge of the bed. He's shirtless, having discarded the damn T-shirt while I was too busy mouthing off. Black ink covers every available inch of thick muscle. It's an intimidating sight to most people, but not to me. How can it be when amongst the harsh words and dark drawings, there are stars of all shapes and sizes woven in? The shooting star nestled between his pecs is the one I focus on. I've seen it a million times, but it means more in this moment than it ever has.

I was such a fool.

"Get on your back before I put you there myself," he commands.

It's such an appealing suggestion that I wiggle my ass and wait for him to follow through. The second smack makes me gasp, the burn intense. I don't have a chance to find another breath before he's tugging me by my ankles and spinning me onto my back. My chest shakes with the impact of the movement, and I grin, enjoying this far too much.

His eyes are two balls of flame as he watches me spread my legs and rest my palm on my pelvis, an inch from my pussy. The confidence I get from his approving stare has me bending my knees and pulling my legs up, exposing myself further.

"Now what?" I coo, tapping the mattress.

"Play with my pussy while I take my fucking jeans off."

I throb at the gruff sound of his order. I'm too turned on to care that he referred to it as his. He can have it. Fuck, I want him to have it.

I dip my hand between my legs and find the slick lips of my pussy swollen with need. I'm moaning before I even touch my clit. The noise I make when I do find that spot is almost inhuman. Something beyond pleasure ricochets through me when I swirl one gentle circle around it.

I don't realize I've closed my eyes until I hear his voice.

"How does it feel?"

My vision is blurry when I peel my eyes open and stare at him. He's naked, all pale, inked skin. I gush arousal when I find his cock jutting between his legs, long, hard, and so fucking thick. I've never seen one so big. And I've definitely never had one that big inside of me before.

"Not as good as when you touch me," I whimper through my dry mouth.

"I know. Keep going. Fuck your fingers."

The air grows thick and heavy, pressing against my skin. I don't bother fighting any longer. The tip of my finger sinks into my entrance, providing little relief to the ache inside of me. I need more, even after adding a second finger. My hips lift off the bed with each stroke along my inner walls, and frustration makes my eyes burn as the feeling of emptiness only grows worse.

"Noah," I whine.

He answers me by wrapping a tattooed fist around his cock and squeezing before giving it one long stroke. He's still keeping his piercing from me. I glare at his hand, a wave of possessiveness growing in my chest. I angrily pull my hand from between my legs and push onto my elbows.

"Absolutely not," I hiss. He blinks to try and hide his surprise, but I see it. I'm unfairly angry at him for touching himself instead of letting me touch him. "That's mine."

His hand freezes. A strained breath is blown from his mouth. *He likes my claim.*

I rush toward him. Leaning over the edge of the bed, I grip him by the back of his neck and bring him down on the mattress. He catches himself above me and locks our eyes. I can see his every emotion like this. He's letting me, I realize a beat later. It goes against every protective ward he's scarred into his soul to give me this power over him, but he's doing it anyway.

I yank his mouth to mine and sink into the ecstasy his kiss sparks. Warmth flows through my veins, mixing with the arousal already there. If I didn't believe in any greater power in the universe, this right here would change my mind. Because there's no other plausible explanation for the bond we share. The way we form two halves of the same soul. One half dark, one half light.

I sink my nails into his lower back and curl my legs around his waist. I'm done waiting. Done messing around and teasing. There's time for that later. Right now, I think I could die without feeling him inside of me.

"Now, Noah. Please. I don't want to wait anymore. Please don't make me wait," I rasp into his mouth. He swallows the words, his fingertips leaving invisible marks on my cheeks and jaw and neck as he touches me.

I shift my hips and feel the first touch of his cock against my entrance. The tip is already wet as it slides over my clit. I bite down hard on his lower lip and don't release it until he opens his eyes again.

"Please," I whisper again.

His throat moves with a swallow, and then I feel a hand move between our bodies. I shudder in relief at the first pass of his fingers over my entrance. He dips two fingers inside and holds them there as he watches me.

"I'm not a virgin," he mutters.

I swallow, confused. "That doesn't matter to me."

His fingers move inside of me, slowly working in and out. "I tried to fuck someone else years ago. Just wanted to see if I could. If it would work."

My chest grows tight at the thought of him with someone else. In a woman's bed that isn't mine. Her hands all over him, touching the tattoos he got for *me*. I clench my jaw at the jealousy that tries to poison my mind.

"I've never gotten hard for anyone but you. Not one fucking time. I let that woman try, but even closing my eyes and thinking of you could only get me hard enough for her to work half of me inside. I'm not programmed to be with anyone but you. I've never tried again."

My thoughts fade like fog in the wind. "What?"

He pulls his fingers from me, and I suck in a sharp breath when I feel him notch his cock at my entrance instead. Hovering there, he drops his forehead to mine and says, "I apologize for not waiting. Should have known it had to be you. It's always been you."

I cry his name when he thrusts forward and, in one powerful thrust, buries the entire length of him inside of me. It's a rough contradiction to his sweet words. It's Noah.

"Holy shit," I moan, tightening my thighs around his waist as he holds still for a brief second. When he starts to move, shifting his hips back, I choke on a cry. "So big. I don't know if I can—"

He nips at my jaw and growls, "You'll take it. It's yours, isn't it?" I nod rapidly. Satisfaction turns his expression wicked as he shoves his cock all the way back inside. "That's right. So fucking take it."

The stretch is intense but not painful. I'm so goddamn full that I don't know how to breathe. I don't care about the missing piercing. It would have been too much tonight. Each slide of him inside of me adds a spark to the building flame in my belly.

"That's it. My good little slut. So perfect," he groans, softly cupping my cheek.

I preen beneath the praise. It adds a new intensity to his thrusts. Makes each one feel harder, stronger. My pulse is erratic and loud in my ears. He might claim not to be a virgin, but he is. That night with someone else didn't count. Tonight does. And I want to make this as good as I can with my own limited experience.

Using surprise as my advantage, I roll him to his back and swallow the sound of disapproval that tries to crawl up my throat when I lose the feeling of him inside of me. A few minutes and I'm already addicted to his dick.

Yeah, that sounds about right.

"I wish I could give it to you," I whisper as I take the smooth, wet length of him in my hand and hover above his hips. Dragging the tip along my pussy, I tease him the way he teased me.

His jaw pulses as he asks through clenched teeth, "Give me what?"

"My virginity."

Darkness flares in his eyes before he's thrusting up and impaling me on his cock. I collapse on top of him, my breasts smooshed to his chest, unable to hold myself up on weak arms. His hand wrapping around my throat makes my eyes bulge, exhilaration electrifying my blood. He uses his hold on my throat to lift my head so our eyes meet. I manage to force myself up with a hand to his chest before I run out of oxygen.

"Your virginity might not be mine, but this pussy knows who it belongs to. You won't bleed for me, but I'm the one who gets to stretch you out and break you in."

It's the perfect answer. Those words bury themselves in my chest and give me the strength to lean back and take control the way I wanted to when I put him beneath me. I drag my hips forward to apply pressure to my clit but feel something cold and hard beneath it instead of warm skin. A curse escapes me when I glance between us and focus on the piercing at the base of his shaft. The metal ball rolls beneath my clit, bringing with it an unsuspecting rush of pleasure that turns me boneless.

A dark chuckle caresses my skin before he's taking advantage of my weak muscles and wrapping an arm around my waist, bucking up into me. I let him, accepting that he's going to win this battle. He has too many advantages.

"Got that for you," he breathes.

I throw my head back and grind again. "It's so good."

The promise of a climax rears its head as I fall into the rhythm of his thrusts and the grind of my hips. Working perfectly in time with one another, it doesn't take long for him to stiffen beneath me and start helping me rock over his pelvis.

"I need you to come, Golden Girl. Can't get there until I feel you gripping me nice and tight," he grunts, squeezing my ass so hard his nails prick into my flesh.

"Almost there."

We're both sticky with sweat, but as I flatten my palm to his chest and finally feel his abs flex in time with his thrusts, I couldn't give a shit. I swirl my hips in a circle, and light flashes behind my eyes when his dick rubs my G-spot. He picks up on my reaction to that feeling and moves his hips in a way that allows him to keep hitting that spot. My muscles turn to lead as I stiffen and finally welcome the blast of pleasure that turns me to liquid.

It's hard and fast, so powerful I don't think I breathe until it starts to ebb. I've never come like that before, but I already want to again, even as I collapse to his chest and begin to lose all the energy I had left.

Noah slaps my ass harder than he's ever done before and groans his release against my cheek. Warmth fills me as he comes, and I grin despite myself, knowing that this is the first time he's ever done this with someone.

"Fuck," he curses, going lax beneath me.

I kiss his neck and jaw and chin before reaching his lips. Our tongues meet for a moment as I sigh into his mouth and reluctantly pull back.

When he starts to soften inside of me, I lift myself off him and flop to my back. My cheeks go red when he moves down the bed and stares between my legs. I want to squeeze them shut out of embarrassment, considering I don't know what I must look like down there after being shoved full of monster dick, but he doesn't look grossed out. He actually looks . . . turned on by it. It's not until I start to feel something wet seeping from my entrance that I realize he's watching his cum leak out of me.

I jerk at his touch when he drags a finger through my pussy before slowly pushing it inside. I'm too sensitive to get much enjoyment from it, but seeing the awe in his expression is more than enough to keep me from telling him that. Right now, this isn't about physical enjoyment. It's all mental.

"You're mine, Tinsley." It's a reminder for the both of us.

I smile at that and nod, a lazy contentment filling me. My heartbeat begins to slow to a healthy speed as I watch him step off the bed and head into the bathroom. The tap runs for a beat before he's back, moving between my legs with a wet cloth.

"I can do this," I offer.

He shakes his head and swipes the cloth through my swollen skin, cleaning the mess he made. The pressure is a little too much with how sensitive I am, but I don't tell him that. He's so concentrated on doing this for me that I don't want to spoil the moment.

As soon as he's finished and disposed of the cloth, I curl onto my side under the comforter and wait for him to join me. He looks out of his comfort zone, but after sliding on his boxers, he climbs in beside me. The small star above his brow snags my attention even in the dark of the room.

"Are you sore?" he asks, snaking an arm around my waist.

My eyelids flutter with exhaustion as I hum. "A little. I will be tomorrow."

We've never slept like this beside each other before. Not

intentionally, anyway. Tonight is full of firsts for us. I never want to forget anything about it. Want to remember it for the rest of my life.

"Sleep," he says, bossy even after sex.

I laugh softly and scoot closer to him until my head is tucked beneath his chin and my leg can curl around his hip. Exhaling, I press my lips to his chest and mouth three words before closing my eyes and letting sleep take me.

35

Noah

I LOVE YOU.

That's what she mouthed against my chest. I didn't mistake it for something else. It's not possible.

I love you.

Three words I thought worthless have been running through my head on repeat for three days. Words that have never meant anything to me. Still don't. Or maybe they do. No, they don't.

I glare at the wood floor of the tour bus and remind myself that they don't count for anything. They form nothing more than a weak statement. But Tinsley said those words. There's nothing weak about her.

Disgruntled, I lock those thoughts away again, knowing they'll escape from their cage whenever the fuck they wish to. Small fingers tug roughly at my scalp, the sound of ripping hair making my scowl deepen. The floor is hard under my ass. I've been forced to sit on it for an hour now while Paisley attempts to braid my hair. It's not going well. I'll be fucking bald before she gets the hang of it.

"I can hear you growling over the movie," Tinsley teases. She's beside Paisley on the couch at my back, her leg kept in a tight hold beneath my armpit. I'd prefer her in my lap, but the kid's presence had her turning the offer down.

My sister is on the floor beside me. She arrived this morning. Hasn't left my side since. It's weird. She keeps batting her eyes at me like she's had something stuck inside of them all day. It's answers she wants. About me and Tinsley. But I won't give them to her. She can ask my golden girl for the details.

"My hair is being ripped out. It fucking hurts," I grunt.

"That's a toonie in the swear jar," Paisley sings.

I blink twice. "I'm not putting money in a fucking swear jar." She's been up my ass about it for weeks. A toonie here and a goddamn loonie there.

"That's two toonies now, right, Dad?"

Justice has the nerve to reach over his daughter and pat me on the head like I'm a goddamn house pet. I almost bite my tongue off to keep from snapping back. "I think we should charge some sass tax on top of that, don't you think?"

Tinsley laughs, and I pinch her ankle in punishment. It just makes her laugh harder. Adalyn lifts herself onto her knees and leans over my head. When her fingers move alongside Paisley's, the grip on my hair loosens.

"He has been extra sassy today, hasn't he?" Addie asks. "I think we can loosen the grip on his hair a bit, though. Maybe that will help."

"He's been *so* sassy tonight!" Paisley shrieks. Her hold on my hair only relaxes for a milli-fucking-second before she's tugging again.

I part my lips to tell her it hurts when Tinsley leans forward and brushes her lips against my cheek. The pain in my scalp disappears. Her closeness fills my senses. "You're doing well with her. Despite the swearing, of course. I'll make this worth your while once you're finished. Only one more braid to go."

I tighten my grip on her leg, my next exhale shuttered. My cock stiffens at the promise before I'm jerked by the roots of my hair closer to Paisley. I suck back my displeasure. Whatever

Tinsley has planned will be worth this pain. If it isn't, she'll be the one to answer to that with my handprint on her ass.

I've never let anyone besides my mom, sister, and Tinsley touch my hair. It's always been long, and Adalyn didn't grow up with many girls her age besides Tinsley. I was always her hairstyle test subject, even when I complained about it and told her to fuck off. She was never this rough, though. Justice hasn't taught his daughter how to be gentle yet, apparently.

If it weren't for Tinsley flashing her smile at me when she asked me to do this tonight, I wouldn't have considered it.

"Easy, girl," Adalyn tells Paisley, carefully working her fingers beneath the little girl's and beginning to lead her through the braid again. "Pulling hard might make the braids sit closer to the scalp, but they're more painful. We have to find a comfortable middle ground so that we can't even feel that we have our hair in braids when we finish."

"He keeps moving when I try and tuck the end piece, and then I lose it," Paisley huffs. "I have to pull it hard."

I blow air through my nose. "I keep moving because you're ripping my hair out."

"That's more money in the sass jar," Justice says.

This night isn't real. "There's a fucking sass jar now?"

"Another toonie!" Tinsley adds.

"How about I just grab your wallet and empty it into the jar? I think I see it on the counter there." Justice stands and knocks his knee into my shoulder as he walks past. He swipes my wallet from the counter and opens it up before riffling through the pockets. "Do you really carry this much cash with you?"

"Not all of us are poor," I throw back.

He rolls his eyes and pulls out three one-hundred bills. Spreading them in his fingers, he starts to fan himself with them.

"This should be enough to cover tonight, don't you think?"

"Clean him out. Maybe that'll teach him to mind his manners," Adalyn says. Justice makes no move to take more.

I continue to stare deadpan at him. "You might as well take it all. There's still another side of my head to braid."

The thousand dollars in my wallet is nothing compared to what's sitting in my account right now. It's his if he wants it. Money has never mattered to me.

He tightens his gaze, attempting to read me. I don't give him anything *to* read. Finally, he looks away and sets my wallet back without opening it again. The colourful bills in his hand get shoved inside a clear jar before he comes back to the couch.

"You're too nice. I would have taken it all. How did you end up playing drums for my brother again?" Addie asks him.

He settles on the couch before answering, "Luck. I was playing at the same dive bar Noah was set to sing at, and Sparks found me practicing in a back room. She was either incredibly desperate or had impeccable taste."

"Desperate," I grumble. A flick on the side of my head has me attempting to look back, only to have my hair yanked again. *Fuck.*

"Sparks has always had good taste, believe it or not. Before Reggie showed interest in Noah, she was still hanging around his surly ass, trying to convince him to try for a chance in the industry. If Tinsley weren't in the picture, I think Sparks may be the second most believing person in him," Addie replies. "Obviously, I'm in a league of my own. I always knew my brother was going to succeed."

A knot builds in my throat. The money, the fame—it's all because of my sister. Because of her annoying inability to let things be as they are. She's a meddler, and she meddled hard when it came to my career.

"I like Sparks," Paisley notes, telling us her opinion again. She's a talker like her father. *Lucky me.*

I zone into the feel of her fingers on my head to see how much longer I have to sit on this goddamn floor for. Seems like she's on the other braid now, about halfway down. Adalyn isn't helping her anymore. And I don't think I've lost any more hair.

Circling a hand around Tinsley's ankle, I stroke the exposed skin between her sock and leggings. Not for the first time since I was forced to the ground, I let my mind wander to the last time we were in this position. Me on the floor before her, my head between her legs. The desire to kick everyone out of this bus and take her on the couch makes me ache. I swallow a groan and press my other hand against my thigh.

It's a punishment from God himself not being able to spend every day and night alone in bed with her. We've fucked like crazed animals the past few days. In the gyms, after fights, and before shows. Our bunk reeks like sex and the scent of her perfume.

"I'm done!" Paisley shouts. The hands disappear from my hair.

"It looks great, LeeLee," Adalyn praises.

I wince at the nickname.

"Thank you for teaching me." Pride is thick in Paisley's voice.

A hand runs a gentle route over my head before Tinsley says, "I don't think Noah's hair has ever looked better."

"You should grow it out forever. Like Rapunzel," Paisley says.

I reluctantly release Tinsley's ankle and stand, my ass aching. "No."

Paisley follows me, narrowing her eyes. "Is there something wrong with Rapunzel?"

"What?"

"You don't want to have hair like her. Why?"

Is she serious? Standing behind the girl, Tinsley sucks her lips in to keep from laughing. This child is fucking weird. Maybe I shouldn't have given her my bedroom after all.

"I don't like her hair," I answer her stiffly.

She gasps. "You should have to put a million dollars in the swear jar."

"What did I tell you about forcing people to like everything you do, Paisley?" Justice asks, the words shuddered with the weight of a hidden laugh.

I glare at him. He's enjoying this. They all are.

"When I was a little girl, Noah cut all the hair off of my Barbie dolls. He just doesn't like blondes, sweetheart. It has nothing to do with Rapunzel. She's my favourite too," Adalyn steps in.

"You're making me sound like a serial killer," I snap, exasperated. "I cut all their hair off because you told Tinsley I had an STD when I was twelve."

Tinsley claps her hands. "Oh, right! I remember that."

"I did not! I was an angel child." Adalyn swirls a finger over her head.

"What's an STD?" Paisley asks.

Nobody answers. Justice groans and sets a hand on her head before starting to push her away from us, toward the hallway. Looking at us over his shoulder, he flips us his middle finger and tells his daughter, "It's a grown-up word. Now it's time for bed."

"Then why does Noah get to use it?" she retorts, and the girls burst into fits of laughter, calling goodbye to their new favourite fucking person.

I feel the corner of my mouth twitch before I force it to stop. That kid is too much. Her personality is too big for this bus. Justice shouldn't have to raise her here.

"I'm going to bed." I give Tinsley a pointed look. She arches her brow in response, speaking to Adalyn about something I don't care about.

She better be in bed with me by the time I've gotten comfortable in that godforsaken bunk. It's just tall enough for me to be able to hover above her and wide enough she can fit beside me. If it were any smaller, I would have burned the bus to the ground and demanded another with more room.

"Goodnight, Noah," Addie calls as I stalk down the hallway.

"Have a good sleep on the couch," I reply, tone snipped.

I shove open the bathroom door and step inside. My expression sours further at the state of my hair. It's split down the middle into two crooked braids. I look ridiculous.

The dark circles beneath my eyes don't help my appearance. I've always had them, but they're worse somehow. It's the late nights and early mornings. The stress and lack of answers in the recent days.

I run the tap and lean toward the sink. Cupping the cold water in my palms, I splash it on my face and close my eyes. My mind is so loud today. It goes beyond the braiding lessons. Far beyond.

I want to know more about the man watching Tinsley. It's been three days of nothing. Of silence and waiting. But I know he's out there. Maybe he's following the bus right now as we pin down the interstate. I clench the sink and stare at myself in the mirror. Discoloured blue eyes flash back at me instead of familiar brown ones. The same ones I see in my nightmares, bright with the promise to take her from me. I'm on edge, looking for a fight with anyone over anything.

My pulse thunders in my throat. I'm unravelling further with each day we wait for him to appear. What will he do next? How far is he willing to go?

My head whips to the side when the door slowly opens. With her messy brown hair slipping out of a loose hair tie, Tinsley looks at me, a knowing expression slipping over her face as she takes me in. Guilt tears through me for putting that sad gleam in her eyes.

"What can I do to help you right now?" she asks once she's slipped inside and shut the door.

I put my back to the sink and wait for her to come to me. When she steps into my body and wraps me in her arms, I finally take a deep breath. The noise in my head begins to quiet, finding a temporary peace in her closeness.

"You're doing it."

"You're worrying yourself to death, Noah. We can't live like this."

"There are too many unanswered questions."

She sighs into my chest and nuzzles her cheek between my pecs. I pull her as close as I can, wishing I could just shove her inside of my body. She'd be safe there. Well protected. It's not just her heart she's walking around with. It's mine too. If something happened to her—*fuck*. It's not possible. Never going to happen. I'd give my life for hers. Any day, any time. She'll be okay. Has to be. I'll make sure of it.

"Baby," she murmurs. Soft hands cup my face. Warm silver eyes find mine, hooking their talons deep so I can't look away. I wouldn't bother trying. "I'm okay."

I feel weak. Pathetic. Emotions I've never had a problem hiding are storming through me, impossible to get a grasp on. I'm drowning in my own thoughts. My fear.

My touch is desperate as I grab her hips and then her waist and shoulders. Her pulse flutters beneath my fingers when I brush them over her throat and jaw. She stands still, letting me touch her, her stare never wavering. I blow out heavy breaths, some of them shaky, others hollow.

"For now," I croak.

"For always," she corrects me.

I stay silent when she drops her hands to button of my jeans and undoes them before shoving them to my knees. After doing the same to my briefs, she moves to her pants and does the same. Cautiously, she takes one of my hands from her neck and brings it between her legs. Smooth and warm. Perfect. Mine.

Mine.

"Feel me, Noah. Take me because I'm yours," she whispers. "I'm not going anywhere. No matter what."

My chest is tight, each breath I draw in feeling like fire in my lungs. But I fight through it, spreading her pussy and circling her entrance, finding her already growing wet. My cock responds, already hard from her promise earlier but throbbing at the idea of being inside of her. I grit my jaw and fill her with two fingers, wedging them in through the tight positioning.

"You are mine. Your eyes, your smile. This cunt. Everything. Is. *Mine*." My voice is so rough it sounds pained. Maybe I am in pain. A pain I don't understand.

"Yours," she coos.

Gripping my cock in a tight fist, she glides her thumb over my slick tip and closes her eyes. I nearly shoot off when she begins to stroke me, each flick of her wrist slow and controlled.

"Need inside you," I grit out.

We didn't use a condom when we had sex the first time, and we never will. The morning after, she told me she was taking birth control. I was glad I didn't have to convince her to let me fuck her without anything between us.

She nods and releases me before spinning to face the mirror and spreading her legs. Hands finding the sink, she watches me in the mirror and licks a line over her bottom lip. One glide of my cock head through her slit, and I'm burying myself deep. My exhale shoots through my nose as I breathe through the pleasure.

Made just for me, her pussy moulds around my cock, dripping juice down to my balls. I press my chest to her back and find her eyes in the mirror. She's stunning, eyes glowing bright enough to light the caverns of my black soul. Pink blooms across her cheeks, and she moans low in her throat when I pull out to the tip and slam back in.

I cover her mouth with my palm and lick up the side of her throat. "Shhh. Unless you want everyone to hear us." Those innocent eyes flash, forcing a chuckle up my throat. "You like that idea."

"I want everyone to know what you do to me."

A carnal satisfaction threatens to have me rip the door open and give her what she wants. If we were anywhere else, with anyone else around, I would. If I knew she would approve of it right now. But it's the lust talking. She wouldn't be okay with it here.

"Soon, I'll take you somewhere the world can hear you scream for me," I promise. *Where he can hear you scream.*

Our angle at the sink allows me to tug her hips back and thrust harder, going deeper than I have before. So deep she has to tear her teeth into her lip to keep from screaming at the new sensation. I bury my face in her hair and tense my jaw so hard it could splinter as I continue to fuck her, already on the edge.

"Noah—" she whimpers on a raged inhale. "Close."

I know. Her pussy quivers around my shaft, tightening up like she's trying to keep me buried deep. My balls pinch, drawing tight when she breaks.

She's an angel when she comes. A goddess.

I've never seen something as beautiful as her expression when she reaches nirvana. I could come from the bliss in her eyes alone. The freedom in her parted lips and the disbelief in the fall of her head when it grows too heavy to hold up. I want to give her this every day. Want to be the one to help her feel this way over and over again. I *will* be that one.

I paint her inner walls with rope after rope of cum a beat later, thrusting hard and fast, filling the bathroom with the sound of slapping flesh. It's loud, but what little care I had about everyone else doesn't exist right now. She holds me deep as I finish, and when I sweep her hair from her neck to kiss the sweat-slicked skin, she shivers.

Blinking, I meet her eyes in the mirror. She's smiling softly, sleepily. "There he is."

"I didn't go anywhere."

"Not physically. But your eyes were haunted. They have been all day. I just never had the chance to get you alone."

"I'm sorry."

She shakes her head, and I pull out, careful not to be too rough. I've learned several things about sex since our first night together. She's sensitive after we're finished, and I have to be gentle, careful. It's a big change from how we are when I'm fucking her. It can be hard then, but it has to be soft after. I have to take care of her and make her feel comfortable and safe. It makes me feel important to tend to her like that. To know nobody else has before.

I reach for the roll of toilet paper and rip off a bunch before reaching between her legs and carefully dabbing at the cum that trickles from her swollen skin. Her stare prickles the side of my face, but I focus on cleaning her. When I'm done, I toss the toilet paper and help tug her pants up her legs. The elastic band snaps on her hips, and she giggles.

"Thank you."

I fix my pants and then kiss her, slipping my tongue inside her mouth when she parts her lips in surprise. Should have kissed her before. Fucking love kissing her. Could do it until I die.

"Kiss me in bed, Mr. Dark and Twisty," she mumbles against my lips. "Our bed."

In a flash, I reach down and hook her legs around my hips before carrying her out of the bathroom and doing just that.

Love.

I've never understood it. Thought the term worthless. I still do, but maybe . . . maybe it means more than I thought it could.

36

Tinsley

I swipe the drying blood from my nose and sniff despite the pain that follows. My winning streak came to an end tonight. It was bound to happen, but fuck me, it stings. The chip in my confidence is nothing in comparison to the ringing in my ears and throb behind my eyes, but it still sucks.

It wasn't a close fight. I got my ass handed to me, and Hunter made sure I knew every single one of my missteps the moment we got to the locker room. His failure speech wasn't needed. I already knew where I went wrong out there.

My attention wasn't on the fight long before I stepped into the ring. It was fixated on the text message I received the moment I got to the gym this morning. For the first time since I started boxing, I took one look at my screen and lost my perfect balance, falling face first on the tile floor. My knees still ache from taking the brunt of the impact, and the bruises that began to discolour my skin soon after are only a reminder of him.

The message was sent from an unknown number but held a very friendly tone. Like in my stalker's mind, we've been friends for years. My throat clogs as I stare at the metal tub filled to the rim with ice. It was Hunter's parting gift.

> Unknown: I'm so proud of you, Tiny. I'll be watching tonight.

Anger rolls through me as the message flashes in my mind. I blocked the number instantly, but I'd been able to try and push the thoughts of him behind everything else these past few weeks, and I was successful for the most part. But I'm unable to do that now. I've been in a constant state of distress since I received his text—despite the fact I immediately blocked the number after—and it cost me my win. And my pride. The aches and pains in my body are an added punishment. From the way I was pummelled during the last round, it's a miracle I could even get up on my own afterward.

The cut in my bottom lip stings as I lick the dryness away. "Fuck," I hiss.

It's easier to strip out of my shorts than it is my tank top. I pull the hem to just below the band of my sports bra before stopping, the pain in my abdomen too much to lift my arms any higher. I twisted my shoulder, but it wasn't dislocated when Hunter looked me over. Sure feels like it, though.

"Tinsley." Noah's gruff voice comes from behind me. I chew on the inside of my cheek and don't turn around. The door clicks, and then he's walking toward me. "You should have waited for me to help with this."

"I didn't think I would need help."

"You fell on your shoulder. It took all your weight."

"Thank you for the reminder," I snap. My stomach pinches as regret follows the rudely spoken words. "Sorry."

"Don't apologize to me."

His fingers touch my lower back, their warmth bleeding into my sore muscles. He exhales, long and hard, and takes my shirt from me, slowly lifting it over my torso. It's too early for there to be bruises, but they'll be there soon. I'm going to be one giant bruise by the time I wake tomorrow.

Once my shirt reaches my neck, he helps work it over my

head and drops it to the floor. Palms cup the tops of my shoulders, holding me in place as he drops his mouth to the underside of my jaw. He kisses me as if he worries I might shatter beneath his lips. I let the gentleness of his care fill my belly with flapping wings.

"Can you help me into the bath? I don't trust myself not to wind up on the floor again."

I notice my misstep as soon as I sense the shift in his posture. Growing stiffer, he turns me by his grip on my shoulders and stares down at me with flashing brown eyes. I inwardly wince.

"What do you mean, *again*?"

"I fell earlier." *When I got the creepy text from my stalker that I haven't exactly told you about yet.* "It's not a big deal."

He drops his hands to his sides and furiously looks me up and down, inspecting me for injuries that I didn't sustain during the fight. The dim lighting in the locker room helps to hide my bruised knees.

"You don't fall."

I roll my lips and limp to the tub. With my hands gripping the edge, I lift my left leg and shove it into the water, knowing it'll only be worse if I move slowly. An angry huff hits my back before Noah's helping me put the other leg inside. After stabilizing myself with a hold on both sides of the tub, I submerge the rest of my body beneath the water.

Breathe in. Breathe out. Don't hold your breath.

The shock of the cold gets easier with time, but it never fully goes away. Not in my experience. You just learn how to handle it. The first thirty seconds are torture. The next thirty are easier. After that, my muscles start to relax.

"Move forward," Noah orders once I've mastered my breathing.

My lips pop open in shock. I look over and find him standing beside the tub in just his briefs. He's so handsome. "You're coming in?"

"Yes. Move forward."

The water sloshes as I scoot forward and tug my knees to my chest. It splashes over the edges of the tub when he climbs in behind me and hugs my back to his front, his legs settling along the outside of mine. A low grunt is his only verbal response to the shock of cold.

I got him in an ice bath once before, after hours' worth of begging, but it took him less time to hop back out than it did for him to get in in the first place. He's never crawled into one with me since. Until now.

"Cold?" I tease.

He drapes his arms over my shoulders and cups my breasts, no doubt feeling how hard my nipples are. "Not as cold as you, apparently."

"You're telling me your dick hasn't shrivelled up and tried to crawl into your ass looking for warmth yet?" I snort.

One arrogant press of his groin to my back proves how wrong I am. His dick is definitely very much there and apparently not affected by the cold as much as it is the feel of my tits in his hands.

"Would you look at that," I mumble.

He removes his hands and clasps them together before hanging them between my boobs. "Stop trying to distract me and tell me why you fell earlier."

"If I tell you, then you have to promise that you won't lose your mind and will remember to breathe."

I didn't want to do this tonight. My level of exhaustion is one reason why, but more than that, if I tell Noah about the message, it'll become that much more real. It won't be a secret anymore. Things will only get worse. Of course, I'm not so naïve that I thought I could hide it forever. Just maybe until tomorrow.

His biceps bulge and strain against my neck. "That's not reassuring."

"Promise me."

"Fuck, fine. Just tell me."

I swallow my fear and lean completely against his torso, my

hands gripping his knees. "I got a text earlier. An unknown number. I assume that it was—"

"Him."

Fuck. A single word has never been so sharp. So deadly. I turn my cheek and kiss his pec, feeling the rapid rise and fall of it. "He called me Tiny. That nickname—it's wrong for him to use. He shouldn't even know it."

"I'm going to kill him."

It's the most honest thing I've ever heard someone say. That in itself terrifies me. Not because I worry for my stalker but because I'm worried for Noah. I know without a doubt that if it ever came to it . . . fuck it all to hell, he'd do it. He'd ruin his life to protect me and not feel an ounce of regret.

I can't let it get that far. "We have to tell someone else about this. Maybe ask for their help. If he can find my phone number, then I don't know if this is something the police can ignore. With everything else that's happened, maybe we'll be able to build a strong enough case to force them to help us."

"What did the message say?"

"That he was proud of me. And that he'd be watching the fight."

A ragged exhale, and then he buries his face in my hair, inhaling deeply. "Cops won't do shit unless he proves that he's a physical threat to you. I won't let it get that fucking far."

I nod weakly. Having trust in his ability to protect me can only get me so far. We don't know what this man is capable of or what he's willing to risk in order to get whatever it is he wants with me. I won't be able to live with the guilt of anything happening to Noah because of that. I want him safe. Far, far away from this mess.

"Okay, then maybe Reggie can help. Sparks and Hunter should know, too."

"Hunter will tell your father."

"Maybe that's not the worst thing." I fight off a grimace.

Noah's legs press into mine, forcing them shut. He wraps

himself around me, forming a shied that vibrates with fury and lethal promises.

"I won't let Braden take you from me. I might already be a terrible person, but I'm prepared to cross every existing moral line in my attempts to keep you close. It won't matter to me if he's your father."

It's wrong to be turned on by the intensity of his claim over me, but when I begin to throb between my legs, I realize maybe I've always been a little wrong. A little perverse. There's a reason the universe chose me for him, right? If I bring light to the dark corners of his soul, maybe it's the opposite for him. Maybe he basks some of my light in shadows. We have to find our balance somehow.

"I'm not a child. He doesn't control me. I make my own decisions."

His thumbs tap an anxious rhythm on the tops of his hands. "What will your decision be?"

I nuzzle into the feel of his skin, so warm despite the frozen water. We've soaked for long enough. My toes are numb, and my teeth have begun to chatter. Yet, I can't bring myself to step out just yet.

"You. Always you. But I'm also not going to let something happen to you. If it gets to that point—"

Water splashes violently onto the floor as Noah spins me between his legs and tugs my knees to bring me as close as possible to his body in this new position. My toes curl at his sides to avoid touching the cool steel at his back. Sitting like this feels much more intimate, with his cock nudging my centre and eyes so focused on me. I rest my palms on his shoulders and take in his expression. Layer upon layer of raw emotion fills his gaze. It's hard to witness how heavily all of this is affecting him. How desperate he is to make it all go away.

He grabs my chin and strokes one finger along the curve of my bottom lip. "You will not make decisions on my behalf. Promise me."

I frown, trying to shake my head despite his grip on my face. "I can't."

"You will not put yourself in danger for me. You will not push me away. I won't let you. Promise me, Tinsley," he demands.

No.

He doesn't notice when I let my right hand drop beneath the water. And when I cross my fingers beneath the ice and lie to him, he doesn't notice that either.

"I promise."

37

Noah

TINSLEY DOESN'T LIKE TO ADMIT IT, BUT SHE LOVES HER BIRTHDAY. She likes to be spoiled and sung to in front of burning candles. For the past twenty-five years, she's never wavered from that.

She's also never gotten better with telling us what she wants for her birthday. It's a constant guessing game every August 14. I always succeed, but the others aren't as lucky. The days before her birthday are the busiest for me. My phone vibrates more on those days than during the rest of the year. Everyone wants to spoil my woman. That's the only reason why I don't ignore them all.

> Braxton: On a scale of 1 to 10, how many pairs of workout leggings does Tinsley own?

> Easton: Got her those shoes you sent me.
> Thanks.

> Little Sister: Just wanted to let you know I don't need your help like everyone else. Tell those assholes to get lost xoxo

> Mom: Just landed at the airport! Can't wait to hug my favourite two people <3

Mom: I got the goods, BTW. Thank you for helping me with this <3<3

Braxton: *Sigh* why do you have to be famous and busy now? I got her a gift card. Excited to see you guys!

I reply to my mom and lock my phone screen. The tattoo gun digs into my groin, and the man holding it mutters a weak apology while continuing the design. With my pants shoved down my hips, hugging the shaft of my cock and exposing my pelvis to the guy, I'm fucking uncomfortable. But not as uncomfortable as when the owner of this tattoo shop tried to convince me to let her ink me instead of the guy.

I wasn't letting a woman that wasn't Tinsley get anywhere close to my dick. Especially not with a needle. If she found out, she'd take me back here and use that needle on the woman. It would be sexy as fuck to watch, but only until she turned that needle on me.

"This is my first pelvis tattoo," the guy informs me.

No fucking shit. If I had any less of a pain tolerance, I would have dislocated his jaw by now.

"Okay."

"Who's Golden Girl?"

"Mine."

"Your what?"

"Mine. That's it."

He pulls the gun from my skin and looks at me with an expression between confusion and discomfort. "Territorial. I get it. She must be a dime, then."

"A dime that's worth more than any sum of money you'll accumulate in your entire life."

He frowns and returns to the shooting star on the left side of my piercing. The opposite side has already been inked with a matching star and Golden Girl woven through its star dust.

We're nearly finished. They won't be healed by her birthday tomorrow, but she'll enjoy the sight of them regardless.

It takes another twenty minutes for him to finish the last star. I take the wrap from him and apply it myself before yanking up my pants. It costs far too much considering the mediocre skill of the artist, but it was a last-minute booking close to home, so I toss more cash than needed on the front desk and leave.

Being back in Toronto, I'd have thought I'd get an in with my usual artist, but apparently, not even a celebrity status gets you in with Rocky when he's fully booked.

My pocket starts to vibrate as I walk home. Tinsley is there with Sparks and Josh. Everyone else has gone back to wherever they came from while the tour breaks for a couple of weeks. We've been on the road for six weeks. The break was needed.

Being home is weird. Our house is the same as we left it. That's not a good or bad thing. It's never been somewhere I wanted to stay forever. Tinsley doesn't like it. We don't need the cheap rent anymore. Finding somewhere else should have been a priority long before we left for tour. It will be my priority while we're back. She deserves somewhere better while I start organizing work on the house in Vancouver.

I look at the name on my phone and answer the call. "I'm on my way home."

"Hello to you too, my amazing but grumpy man," Tinsley sings in my ear.

Walking across the street, I avoid the crater in the road and silently slip between two buildings. The backways through Toronto are easier for me to navigate. Less traffic, less noise. I could have driven home, but being cooped up in a bus for almost two months had me itching to walk. Fresh air, the freedom to go where I please. I missed it.

"You sound like you want something, birthday girl," I tell her.

"Me? Never. And it's not my birthday yet."

My lips twitch. "Out with it."

"It was actually Sparks' idea."

"Is that supposed to help your case?"

"Whatever. Can you grab some ice cream on your way back? The stuff from the corner store with the gre—"

"I know which. I'll grab it."

She sighs softly. "Thank you. How far away are you? I miss you."

I swivel my head in search of a street sign and find one a few feet to my left. "About ten minutes."

"Okay. Be safe."

With a reluctant goodbye, I end the call and put my phone away. I should have been selfish and brought her with me tonight. It's not like she didn't spend enough time with Sparks and Josh on tour.

If she were here with me, I wouldn't have been thinking about seeing my dad and Braden together tomorrow. In Braden's house. Dealing with them one-on-one is bad enough, but together? The tightness in my chest is only going to grow. This already constant thrum of discomfort is bound to become unbearable.

This is for her. Every year, I've done this. Put up with their disapproval. She'll be happy with them around. That's what's important.

Focus on what comes after an uncomfortable situation. Is it relief? Pride in yourself that you were able to push through the discomfort without running?

The voice of my fourth therapist drifts through my head as I turn down the sidewalk toward the corner store beside the entrance of our neighbourhood. The first three shrinks were worthless. But the fourth . . . he at least attempted to figure me out. He failed but came closer than any of them did both before and after.

For some reason, I clung to that one piece of advice he gave me. It was the most useful information I received in my adolescence. I've repeated it in my mind more times than I can count over the past decade. If I were a better person, I would find that shrink and thank him for trying that day. But I don't even remember his name. I don't care to learn it either.

The familiar white sign is bright over the dark street. From the first night we moved into the dump that is our house, we've spent too much fucking money at this place. The common corner store price markups plague this place like it does every other. It's the same overpriced, stale food that you'd find at every other shitty place like this, but it's ours. Tinsley will probably drag me here even after we move. She's sentimental that way.

The door jingles when I walk inside. The aisles are set up the same way they were before we left, and I head for the back of the store. Two freezers hold the ice cream and frozen dinners. I find the carton of ice cream with the green lid and bite back a smirk.

Mint chocolate chip is her favourite. I hate the taste of it.

Black licorice is my favourite. She hates the taste of it.

I grab a carton of both and head back. The kid working the till is staring down at his phone, looking half-asleep, but when he senses me, he shakes himself awake.

Eyes bulging, he loses his grip on his phone, and it falls to the counter with a clatter. I lift one brow and stare at him as I set the ice cream down.

"You—you're Noah Hutton. Oh, my God. You're Noah Hutton. I love your music, dude. Like seriously, so much. Holy shit," he rambles, his fingers flying out of sight as things begin to rattle to the side of the till. When he shoves a pen and blank piece of receipt paper toward me with shaky hands a beat later, he adds, "Can you sign this for me? Please. My friends aren't going to believe this."

I keep my expression steady as I take the pen and paper from him. "Name?"

He blanches. "Shit. Right. My name's Sheldon."

"Okay." I sign the paper and set the pen on top of it before sliding it across the counter.

Snatching it up, he clutches the paper to his chest. "Thank

you. I know you must get this a lot, but you're so talented, dude. I'm a huge fan. I tried to get tickets to your next show here, but it sold out too fast. Are you adding another Toronto date?"

My skin prickles with discomfort. It's not the kid's fault. This is all me. I'm not built for these situations. Never know what to say. Compliments should make me feel good. But from strangers, they make me itch, desperate to abandon the conversation.

"Thank you," I croak. My neck grows hot. "Just one show currently. I can bring up adding a second to my manager."

His face lights up. "Yes!"

I swipe a hand across my neck, finding it wet with sweat. "Can I pay for this now?"

"Oh! Yes, of course. I'm so sorry. It's not every day you get to meet one of your favourite artists, you know?"

I don't know. "It's okay."

He eyes the two tubs of ice cream. "Which one is for you?"

"Are you planning on telling the world my favourite flavour of ice cream?"

His laugh reminds me of my brother's. "No. I just assume one is yours and one is for Tinsley, right?"

My hackles rise before I force them back down. She's all over my social media. And Adalyn's. This is common knowledge. Not dangerous.

"I just really like ice cream," I grunt, not willing to risk letting him know anything about Tinsley.

He lets it go and changes the subject as he scans the ice cream. I shove a twenty-dollar bill in his hand, refusing change, and watch him put the cartons in a plastic bag. It's obvious that he wants to talk more, but I've let this go on long enough. I'm rattled and anxious. My head is on a swivel as I rush outside and push toward the house.

The street is so silent it feels wrong. I don't know if that's in my head. My heart is pumping too quickly. I'm too out of it. Helplessly on edge. I need to be beside her. I've been gone too long, and the beast in my chest is unhappy with the distance between us.

My feet drag on the sidewalk, but there's another sound nearby. More footsteps. Faster. Clunkier. *Frantic.*

I turn too late.

Blue eyes flash in front of me before I'm gasping, pain blasting through my jaw. He swings again, this time forcing us into a hidden alleyway. I stumble and dodge his punch, rage straining beneath my skin. The man keeps his hood up, shielding his face in the shadows. I grit my teeth and harness the pain that follows to drive my arm out with more force. My fist sinks into his abdomen, making him bend in half, gasping for breath.

"You're a dead man," I growl, reaching for his hunched figure.

He shoots forward then, sending the hood flying back, exposing his face as we collide. I didn't need to see his face to know who it was. The eyes gave him away. I'll never forget that shade of blue. Not even in death. His and mine.

I hit the ground first. My lungs pinch, leaving me gasping for breath at the hard impact. He takes advantage of that, diving on top of me. His knuckles meet my face, and my head whips to the side. I focus on the flash of his scarred, uneven knuckles before the hit. On the hiss of pain that escaped him directly after.

Warm metal fills my mouth, leaking from my lips and dripping down my chin. The inside of my cheek burns, but the pain doesn't register. I reach for him, my nails ripping through the skin of his neck as I push. He drops his hands to my throat and attempts to wrap them around it. I grip his wrists and squeeze, snapping my torso off the ground before he can grab hold of my throat.

The man tumbles beneath me. I spit the blood filling my mouth into his face and bare my teeth as my fists fly. One, twice, three times, my knuckles hit his jaw. I spit again, blood and spit coating his cheeks.

"Tell me your name!" I roar, squeezing his throat with one hand while the other grips his swollen jaw.

He shifts beneath me. I realize in an instant that I haven't pinned him properly. His hands move between us, searching and searching. The soft sound of a switchblade flinging open into the calm breeze is all the warning I get before I'm falling to the ground. Gravel crunches in my ear. Fire flares in my side. Flames upon flames spread through my torso. My lips part in shock, the starless sky glaring down at me.

Footsteps, heavy breaths. Blood rains down on my face. "I'll tell Tiny happy birthday from you."

More footsteps. Receding. Another set, fainter. Maybe it's all in my head.

My fingers shake as they move to my right side. Warm and sticky. Wet. Blood seeps from the wound, steadily coating my hand. Too much blood, I realize when my vision swims. Adrenaline has my ears thumping with my pulse. Heat makes way for cold. A cold so similar to ice baths.

Tinsley.

I reach for my pocket and bend forward, groaning in pain as the flow of blood on my fingers increases with the movement. My grip is weak on my phone, but I pull it out and manage to type my password. When I find the right contact and hear the dial tone, I let it fall to the ground beside me. For the first time, I'm thankful for the sneaky location tracking app he got Tinsley to install on my phone before we left for the tour.

My voice is a garbled mess when I try to speak. Braden's voice is the last thing I hear before the lights go out.

"Noah?"

38

Tinsley

"You could go outside and smoke like a civilized person, Joshua," Sparks grumbles from the couch. She waves a hand through the fresh cloud of smoke floating toward her and coughs.

He rolls his eyes and rolls the joint between his fingers. "Using my full name, really?"

"You've been smoking outside for the past six weeks. I thought we had you house-trained by now. Silly me."

"Yeah, silly you."

I watch the two of them silently from my oversized, black, fuzzy chair in the corner of the room. It was an early gift from Sparks, and I haven't gotten out of it since the moment I found it in the living room this morning. My heart hurts a little at the thought of it stinking like Josh's weed, but I'm sure I could always steam clean the smell out.

Checking the time on my phone for the thousandth time, I tap my kneecap in a nervous pattern. Noah said he would be home in fifteen minutes. That was almost an hour ago. Both of my calls since have gone unanswered. The gnawing in my gut feels a lot like a warning that something isn't right.

"Have either of you heard from Noah?" I blurt out.

Sparks waves more smoke out of her face and looks at me. "No. Why?"

"He's late."

"Don't be a clinger, Tinsley," Josh mutters.

I narrow my eyes on him. "Don't be a douche, stoner."

"Don't be jealous because Noah wouldn't text you even if you were the last person alive," Sparks snaps at him.

He takes a lazy drag of the joint and shrugs, blowing it out slowly. "I wouldn't text him then either."

Sparks makes a face. "As if."

I check my phone again, seeing only two minutes have passed. My gaze flicks to the front door. "I think I should go look for him."

"Do you want me to come? If he got himself in trouble, he'll need me, anyway," Sparks offers.

Josh scoffs into his blunt. "You guys are ridiculous."

"And you're stoned and very fucking annoying right now. How about you go to your room and stay there?" I snap.

His eyes widen. "Hiss, kitty."

"And you wonder why Noah tried to get me to fire you two days into knowing your sorry ass. Smoke yourself silly on this break, Joshua, because you won't be touching drugs at all once we get back on tour," Sparks promises. Offering me a supportive smile, she jerks her head toward the door. "Shall we?"

I nod, a sense of appreciation for her forming in my chest. "Thank you."

"'Course. You've called him, I'm guessing?"

"Twice. No answer both times."

She twists her mouth and claps her hands on her thighs before pushing off the couch. "Let's go, then."

I heave a sigh and uncross my legs to stand when my phone starts to ring. My heart jumps to my throat, relief a living entity inside of me when I see Noah's name on the screen.

When I answer the call, my words come out in a rush. "Noah, you had me worried sick!"

There's a long pause. "Sweetheart."

"What happened?" I whisper. My dad has Noah's phone. He's calling me from it. "Why do you sound like that?"

"Are you alone?"

Something cracks in my chest. "No."

"Can you give the phone to whoever is with you? Just for a minute." He's pleading with me. Begging. The tremor in his words is all wrong.

The crack spreads.

"Tell me. I know something happened. I felt it. Just tell me."

A hand touches my shoulder. Rubs it slowly. I tighten my outer shell as my insides chew themselves up. The house is suddenly suffocating. The smell of marijuana makes my stomach roll.

"You need to get to the hospital. Don't you dare think about driving yourself. Ask whoever you're with to bring you."

I bite down on my tongue to trap a sob. Pressing a hand to my stomach, I squeeze my eyes shut and nod. *Noah*. Oh, God. *Noah*. My throat tightens, squeezing and squeezing. I can't speak. Pain deep in my chest rocks me back on my heels.

"Dad—" The word claws its way up my throat.

He curses softly. "I know, baby girl. I'm here. We can stay on the phone for as long as you want."

"How bad? What happened?" How bad is he? He has to be okay. I would know if he . . . if he wasn't okay. I'd. *Know*.

"He was attacked, and he's being taken into surgery soon. You need to be here by the time they're finished and he wakes up."

That trapped sob escapes. The hand on my shoulder moves to take the phone from me, and I let it. Without the weight of it against my cheek, I move frantically around the house, shoving everything off the kitchen counters and tearing through bags on the table in search of my car keys.

This was my stalker.

He hurt Noah bad enough he needs surgery.

I'll kill him for this.

My unshed tears dry, the sobs in my chest drifting to nothingness. A cold feeling of unrelenting vengeance fills their place.

I find my car keys in the junk drawer and grip them so hard they prick my palm. Sparks is standing by the door, hand on the handle, when I head in her direction. Josh hasn't moved from his spot on the couch, but the blunt is gone.

Sparks extends her arm and offers me my phone. The screen is open, still on the call. One look at the contact name and I'm swallowing the emotion in my throat and storming outside, not stopping until I reach the car parked along the curb out front.

Sparks' footsteps sound on the sidewalk, but I force them from my mind. Moving onto the street, I throw my hands into the air, spinning and spinning as I look around the neighbourhood. He's watching. He has to be.

My shout pierces the night.

"I'm right here, you sick fuck! You should have had the nerve to come get me instead of touching him. Now, I'm going to tear you apart! That's a promise."

NH)

THE MOMENT I see my parents in the waiting room, I'm sprinting. That bravery I had out on the street is gone. Like throwing a towel over a stove fire, the flames of revenge are snuffed out, leaving me hollow. Nothing but that crippling pain drifts in my chest.

My cheeks are wet, my knees weak. Dad reaches for me first, tucking me into his body and holding me tight. I let the sobs shred my throat then.

The events of the past few weeks shake through me. The fear, worry, disgust. The questions still unanswered. And now Noah. My everything, here in this fucking hospital because of me. It's too much. I feel like there's a bag over my head, and it's getting pulled tighter and tighter. I'm tired of trying to yank it off. So tired.

Dad's hands run over my head, smoothing my hair. I feel Mom at my back, rubbing circles along my spine. Their comfort should help. But it doesn't.

"Shh. I've got you."

I soak Dad's shirt, hiding my face from the people around us. It's all wrong. Everything is wrong. I love my dad, but the arms I want around me are somewhere else in this hospital, in a room surrounded by doctors. He's not here.

Because of me.

A hot flash of guilt tears another fit of sobs from me. "I—I made him g-go. It wasn't s-s-safe, but I asked him to stop."

"Honey, this isn't your fault," Mom murmurs.

I shake my head furiously, crushing my nose to Dad's chest. "I want to know what happened."

"Can we sit and talk?" Dad asks softly.

"Okay."

The bright white lights above us burn my sore eyes. Sheepishly, I glance around the waiting room. It's quiet, still. Empty besides a few people spread through the bulk of plastic chairs. They don't look at me. Don't judge me. They're all struggling with whatever it is that brought them here.

"This way." Dad keeps me close as he leads us toward an empty row of seats. Mom grabs my hand.

I collapse onto the hard plastic chair, and they flank me, one on each side. Dad's arm goes around the back of my chair while Mom pulls our hands to her lap. My leg shakes, the only visible sign of my anxiety.

"Where are Oakley and Ava? Do they know he's here?" I hiccup.

"They'll be here any minute. I called them after I called you," Dad says.

They're here for my birthday, not to witness their son in the hospital. "You called them?"

"Noah was stabbed in an alley, Tinsley. He called me, and I got there as soon as I could." He pauses, swallowing thickly. "I found him and called an ambulance. He wasn't awake when I got there, but he woke when they started applying pressure to his wound. I called you first because he told me to. As soon as we got in the ambulance, I called Oakley and then your mom."

My vision blurs. I stiffen every muscle in my body to try and fight the agony in my soul. "How bad is it?"

"The knife missed anything vital, but it tore through a lot of muscle when it was pulled out. They're trying to fix as much damage as they can. But he should be okay."

"They told you that he'd be okay?"

"They said that he got lucky. The bleeding is under control, and the damage is minimal considering what could have happened."

A small flicker of relief settles inside me at his words. It's not enough, though. Not by a long shot. It's time to come clean about everything and ask for help. We should have done it weeks ago. Keeping it to ourselves almost cost me the other half of my soul.

"I need to tell you something, Dad," I mutter. He shifts his body and stares down at me, his brown eyes more haunted than I've ever seen them. "And you're not going to like it. But I need you to listen to me."

"I don't like anything about this situation already, sweetheart."

Mom strokes her thumb over my hand. "What he means is that we're listening."

So, I tell them everything. From my missing underwear and the things left on the porch in Vancouver to the threatening picture and text messages. I tell them about every time I felt watched or saw that man appear in the same place we were. And about every secret and conclusion we've made on our own.

And then I do it again when Noah's parents arrive. As Ava buries her face in my shoulder and cries. First in fear and then relief, and then fear again. I watch Oakley storm out of the hospital and then come back an hour later with his hand wrapped in gauze and a broken expression on his face. I sit in silence and listen to my dad tell the police to give everyone some room when they stop by asking questions nobody is prepared to answer yet.

When Maddox and Adalyn arrive, I watch them get lied to. I watch as our parents decide they don't need to know the details of why Noah is here. And like a coward, I let them.

Because I don't want them involved. I don't want the police involved either.

What I want is a plan for how to find this man. And then I want to do to him what he did to Noah.

I meant every word I shouted in that street. I'll make him regret coming near either of us.

39

Tinsley

IT TOOK TWENTY-SIX BIRTHDAYS FOR ME TO WANT TO SKIP ONE. To simply pretend it wasn't happening. I wish I could jump ahead a couple of weeks to a time when Noah isn't asleep in a hospital bed, his hand too cold in mine. Where he isn't covered in bruises and cut skin and hooked up to machines pumping fluids and pain medication into his veins.

Midnight came and went before he got out of surgery. He was brought to a recovery room for a while before they finally moved him into a room reserved for people with money and a need for privacy. We had some semblance of peace for a while before the press was tipped off to Noah's whereabouts. They don't know what happened, just that he's here, and I can only hope it stays that way.

It's just past two, and he hasn't woken up yet. The nurses say it could be a little while and that I should go home and get some rest while we wait, or at least get something to eat. I can't stomach food right now, and the thought of leaving him and not being here the moment he opens his eyes is not a possibility for me.

I'll sit in this chair at his bedside for days if I have to. But I am not leaving him.

Glancing down at his hand, I find the knuckles swollen and bruising. I trace the ridges of each one with the ghost of a touch and worry my lip. He got a few good hits in if the state of his hand is anything to go off.

I scoot my chair closer to the bed until I can lift his hand to my lips and lean my elbows on the mattress. The white sheet is tucked beneath his armpits, covering his torso. His hair is hanging in his face. He'd hate that. I'll cut it for him as soon as he can sit up. I should have done it days ago.

The nurses have cleaned his face and torso, but the scrapes on his cheeks and neck create a vivid enough story of what happened in that alley. I don't need to see the rocks they dug from his skin or the dirt they washed away to know he spent those minutes of pain on the ground.

That's how my dad found him. On the ground. Bleeding. Unconscious. Alone.

I'm angry that he didn't call me but relieved he didn't at the same time. My father was the best person he could have asked for help, even with their differences. I wouldn't have been able to think past the sight of him hurt. My dad did.

"I'm sorry," I whisper, kissing his fingers one by one. "If I hadn't been so selfish, you wouldn't have gotten hurt."

I don't hear the door open and another person join me until Oakley says, "That's not true."

I'm too exhausted to show any physical signs of surprise. The skipping of my heart rate is more than enough. I didn't notice how shaky I was until I start to lower Noah's hand to the mattress, refusing to release it.

I gave Ava and Oakley time with him alone before coming in. But as selfish as it is, I won't give them any more. He's my person, and I will be by his side the way I know he would be by mine.

"I don't need pity. There's no way you and Ava don't blame me for this," I tell him, my words weak.

"We don't blame you for anything. None of this was your

fault. You didn't force anyone to hurt Noah, and you didn't hurt him yourself."

I tear my eyes from Noah and look at his father. He looks like shit. A sick part of me revels in that. There's a chance he could have lost his son last night. Is he thinking about that?

"He was targeted because of his relationship with me."

"Maybe. But that still isn't your fault."

I heave a sigh. "Why are you even here, Oakley? I know it isn't to try and absolve my guilt."

"My son was stabbed. I wouldn't be anywhere but here."

His eyes fill with pain. Pain and regret and guilt. So much guilt it's hard to stare at him without feeling the weight of it. He's struggling, and now isn't the time to ream into him for what's happening with him and Noah.

"That's good."

"You don't believe me," he notes. There's a resigned accusation in his tone but no aggression.

"Do you blame me?"

"No." With a couple of unsteady steps, he stands beside me, peering down at Noah. His throat bobs. "I failed him. He deserved a better father. One who tried to understand him the way I never did. That's something I will carry with me for the rest of my life."

I lift Noah's hand to my lips again and blow on his cold fingers in hopes of warming them. My words caress his skin. "I won't say he made it easy on you. But why did it have to be easy? You should have loved him regardless. That's what family does. We love each other for the good and the bad. The hard and the easy."

"Is that what you think? That I don't love him?"

"I don't know what I think. All I have is what I know, and I don't know that you've ever shown your love for him in the ways he needed to see it. At least not for a long time now."

He flinches, and I feel the weight of it. "Is that how he feels too?"

I trace my eyes over Noah's face. The swell of his swollen top lip and bruised under eyes turn the tide inside of me, making it harder to breathe. So much pain lives inside of him, and now he looks every part as broken on the outside. My next exhale is shuddered.

"You have to fix it. Fix *everything*. I don't want to see him like this anymore. He will never tell you that he craves your love and attention, but he does. There's a break inside of him that you caused. I don't care what you have to do to heal it, but if you don't . . ." I pause, considering if I'm really about to threaten a man whom I've always seen as family. The longer I stare at Noah, the clearer my answer becomes. "You won't see him again once we leave this place. I'll make sure of it."

Keeping my attention fixed on Noah's peaceful expression, I don't see Oakley move until he's directly in my line of sight. He's on the other side of the bed, bending over the rail and sweeping his fingers through the hair hanging in Noah's face. After pushing it out of his eyes, Oakley pulls out a familiar black bandana from the pocket of his hoodie and uses it to hold his son's hair back. His movements are steady and knowing, as if he's done this so often it's muscle memory. The sight of that specific bandana makes my head swim. I haven't seen it since Noah left home. He used to wear it every day, but he thought he'd lost it.

"He loves that bandana," I croak.

A sad smile pulls at his mouth. "I know."

"You've had it this whole time."

"I have."

"He'll be happy to have it back."

He nods and runs his palm over Noah's head a final time before stepping back. "Will you let us know when he wakes up? I took Ava and Adalyn back to the hotel so they could shower and try to sleep, but I'll need to get them the minute he's awake."

"Yeah. Of course. You're staying here, then?"

He runs his palms down his thighs. "I am."

There's a minute of awkward silence before he speaks again. "I do love him. More than I could ever explain to either of you. Things have just gotten so bad, and . . . I never closed the gap between us. I let him slip further and further away from me because I didn't know how to fix what we broke. But I'll try."

They're the words of a broken man. One staring down a dark, unfamiliar road with no idea how to get back home. I want to help guide him, but I just don't know the way either. He has to meet me halfway. Then I'll help.

"That's a good start."

He stares at me, and I meet his eyes with a bravery I dredge up amongst the hurt and worry swirling in my stomach. After a few seconds, he dips his chin and breaks contact. I watch him round the bed and pause at the foot of it.

"I'm glad he has you, Tinsley."

"I'm glad I have him too."

He smiles at that before slipping back out of the room, closing the door behind him.

I close my eyes and drop my head to Noah's forearm, whispering, "Please wake up before I have to have another awkward conversation like that with your dad, you douchebag."

NH)

MY NECK ACHES when I wake. A tight pinch screams in my shoulder.

I blink the sleep from my eyes and find the room dark, the lights having been turned off. As I shift, I feel a blanket fall down my arm. Head foggy with sleep and confusion, I almost miss the stretch of Noah's fingers beneath my palm.

I ignore the pain in my body and whip my head up to find him awake. His eyes sear into mine, even in the dark, and a shudder racks through me as my chest grows tight with emotion.

"Come here," he croaks, the words rough and scratchy.

My lips part, but no words follow.

He watches me with an intensity that makes my heart lurch. "Come. Here."

Finally, I shake my surprise and leap into action. The pitcher of water on the small rolling table is full and waiting. I push out of my chair and rush toward it, quickly pouring some into a plastic cup and dropping a straw into it. When I hold it out to him, he opens his mouth and lets me guide the straw inside.

"You're awake," I whisper in disbelief.

The intensity of his stare doesn't waver as he gulps down the water. Even in this fucked-up situation we're in right now, my stomach flaps and sings beneath of weight of his attention.

"When did you wake up?"

He finishes drinking, and I set the cup back on the tray. "I'll tell you when you get in this bed with me."

Pulling back, I drop my gaze to his shirtless torso and the white bandage wrapping around his side. It's the first time I've seen what's been hiding beneath the blanket they tucked him in when they finished surgery. The faint dark marks ruining the perfect white have me in a state of panic. It's blood.

"Did they just change these?" My fingers graze the tape along the edges of the covering. He grabs my hand, holding it tight. My eyes flick up to his.

"Get in bed with me, Golden Girl."

Hearing the nickname fall from his lips is too much. I almost break, ready to give in to his every want and desire. Instead, I force myself to say, "The bed is small. I don't want you in any more pain than you already are."

"Not having you beside me is painful."

"Do you want me to call your parents? Or the nurse?"

"No," he grits out before softening his tone. "Not yet."

"Fine. But you have to move over. Slowly. Don't pop a stitch or—"

"Stop worrying."

Yeah fucking right. I nod meekly as he shifts, the crease in his forehead the only sign that he's in pain. It takes me a couple of minutes to climb on the bed, but once I'm curled up beside him, the heaviness in my gut starts to ebb.

We're positioned awkwardly on the small bed. One of my arms is beneath me while the other lies along my side because I don't want to risk touching his wound. He's on his back with his bicep beneath my neck and his hand curled over my shoulder. I can't imagine it's comfortable for him, but he doesn't say anything. Neither do I.

He turns his head and nuzzles his face into my hair. "Happy birthday, baby."

Tears burn my eyes. I blink them away. "Thank you."

"Don't cry. I fucking hate when you cry."

I tuck my face into his shoulder and laugh. "How do you know I was going to cry?"

"Is that a joke?" he grunts.

"I'm all out of sorts right now. Be gentle with me."

He kisses my head. "I'm not gentle with anyone."

"You are with me."

A deep rumbling noise comes from deep in his chest. "You're mine. It's not the same."

"You had me terrified, Noah," I say on an exhale.

"I know."

"It was him, right?"

The bicep beneath my neck grows hard, and I snap my attention to his bandage. No new red spots.

"Yes."

I fill with dread. Noah lifts the arm resting at his side and brings it across his body before grabbing my hand and linking our fingers. He rests them on his sternum, over his heart. I choke back a sob at the familiarity of the touch.

"How bad does it hurt?" I ask.

"It doesn't."

The IVs in the hand wrapped around mine are making sure of that. I don't remember half the names of the medications that are pumping into him right now.

"Are you tired?"

"Are you?"

"That doesn't matter."

He squeezes my hand. "Sleep with me."

"I'm sorry," I blurt out. "For asking you to go get that ice cream. I'd rather have gone myself. I'd rather it be me in this bed instead of you."

"If you were in this bed right now, I would be in prison. This is the way it was supposed to be," he growls.

I ignore that. "He hurt you because of me. I will never forgive myself for that."

Cold fingers prod at my jaw, forcing me to look at him. Brown eyes clash with my silver ones. "There's nothing to forgive. I would die for you. That's never going to change."

"Stop." Fear wraps its thin fingers around my throat and tightens and tightens— "Nobody is dying."

"He will." It's a dark promise.

"Are you trying to make me an accomplice to murder right now?"

"Never. Now, sleep, birthday girl. We're done talking about this. When you wake up, you can have the gifts I got you."

"I don't want a birthday this year," I tell him.

He adjusts his arm and eliminates the gap between our bodies. I carefully rest my cheek on his bare pec, and his heart-beat thumps a steady beat in my ear, reassuring me that he's okay. His fingertips draw lazy patterns on my back. Exhaustion barrels into me.

"Too bad."

I kiss his chest, letting my eyes close. "You hate birthdays."

"I love yours."

My lips spread in a small, lazy smile. That sounded a lot like an I love you.

40

SEVEN YEARS AGO

MADDOX SITS ACROSS FROM ME IN THE KITCHEN, WEARING A *Vancouver Warriors hoodie and matching track pants. He finished hockey practice an hour ago and stopped by in an attempt to get me to make him one of my refuelling smoothies. I caved the moment he asked and went right to work pulling the old container of protein powder out of the basement pantry.*

"This is really good. Thanks, Dad."

The slurping noise that fills the kitchen as he drinks the last of the smoothie is enough to let me know I haven't lost my smoothie-making skills since retiring from the league. That seems like a lifetime ago.

"I'll give you the recipe so you can make it yourself, unless there's another reason you came here today. Like, maybe missing your old man," I tease.

He smacks his lips in a way he knows I can't stand the sound of and hops off the kitchen stool to load his cup into the dishwasher. He's twenty-four now and playing in the NHL, so it's nice to know he hasn't lost his manners.

"I do miss you, Dad. I miss everyone."

"How do you like the new place?"

His eyes light up. *"It's really nice. Quiet and has a killer view."*

He bought a new construction penthouse, so I think really nice is an understatement. It's gorgeous and far bigger than his last place.

"That's great, Dox. I remember the first place your mother and me got after we moved in together. It was nowhere as nice as yours."

He snorts a laugh and then sobers up, rubbing his lips together. *"I wanted to invite Noah out soon. Think he'll come?"*

"I do." Hopefully.

"Is he home right now?"

I lean forward and brace my elbows on the edge of the kitchen island, staring at my eldest son. While my relationship with Noah has always been on the rockier side, it's gotten worse as the years have gone on. The boys' relationship has unfortunately turned down the same road. They're such vastly different people that it's hard for them to relate to one another, and neither of them seems willing to find a way to work that out. Hopefully things will change sooner rather than later. Before the rift between them has grown too far to jump across.

"He wasn't home when I got back from the gym a half hour ago."

He nods and closes the dishwasher before sitting back on his stool. *"Did he tell you that he turned away that internship interview with the record company I got him in touch with?"*

I blow out a breath, shaking my head. *"No. He didn't."*

"What is it going to take for him to put himself out there? He's fucking amazingly talented, Dad. It feels wrong for him to continue to turn down these opportunities."

"He's only seventeen. More will come along for him."

At least, I hope so. I don't want to see him push and push until there's nothing left. We all have to remind ourselves that he has his entire life ahead of him. There's no reason for him to rush into anything yet, even if it kills us to see him make certain choices.

"Yeah, more that he'll continue to turn away."

"You and your brother are different, Maddox. You can try to deny it, but you like the spotlight that comes with doing what you love—

hockey. Noah doesn't like the spotlight that would come from a career in music. He's turning down those opportunities for a reason."

"He's not just turning them down. He's wasting them."

I scratch at my jaw, tugging on my beard. "Noah has always been like that." He fears what he doesn't know. Putting himself out there means he'd feel insecure.

"So you agree that it's a waste of talent."

I pause. It's not that easy of an explanation, but . . . "Yes."

"God, I want to shake some sense into him. He could have the beginnings of a music career already if he just fucking tried. Anyone else would have taken advantage of the chances he's gotten."

The front door slams shut, interrupting us. Heavy footsteps thump through the house, toward the basement. Maddox shoves a hand through his hair and stares at me, his expression tight.

"Guess he's home now."

NH)

ROCK MUSIC BLARES beneath the floorboards in the kitchen later that night. Even through my thick socks, I can feel the vibrations of it crawl from my toes to my fingertips. Noah invited people to the house tonight, but by the number of voices at war with the music, it sounds as though he invited every single student from his high school instead of the small number he had initially told his mother at dinner.

The clock on the microwave reads just over 1:00 a.m. An hour past his curfew. I take a long sip from the glass of orange juice in my hand and contemplate whether or not I'm going to be the bad guy that storms downstairs and tells a bunch of teenagers to get out of my house. Noah would hate me for embarrassing him like that, and we're already on the rocks too much lately. A throb grows between my eyes at the reminder of our fighting.

Every day, there's something we're at each other's throats about. His grades and my nosiness. His staying out all the time and my lack of patience. We never meet eye to eye on anything, and I've begun to realize we may never again. That doesn't stop me from wanting to try, though. Even if I get bitten each time I attempt to dig into his life and emotions.

"What are you doing down here?" Ava asks, sliding her arms around me from behind. She kisses my spine and runs her hands up and down my chest.

I cover her hands and follow her movements. "Contemplating party crashing."

"Come watch a movie with me instead. Let them be."

I set my glass down on the counter. "It's late, Ava. And it sounds more like a rager than a friendly get-together."

She laughs against my back. "I'd rather them be here than out somewhere else. They're safe here. We know where Noah is."

"We gave the same rules to Maddox and Adalyn. 12:00 a.m. curfew. No exceptions. They never broke that rule, so why should we let Noah?"

I'm struggling to understand how to parent Noah. I want to be fair and understanding, but it goes against my instincts to only allow certain things for one kid and not for the others. Maddox and Adalyn have always been understanding when it came to their brother, but how many times can they watch him get away with things that they would have been punished for before they get fed up?

I won't let rifts grow between our children. I'd rather have Noah punish me than have his siblings grow annoyed with him over our decisions.

"Noah is at home, my love. He's listening to music with his friends, not out at a seedy bar partying with strangers and doing LSD," Ava murmurs.

"LSD is oddly specific."

"Mm, well, since you're already thinking worst-case scenario, I figured I'd add my piece."

"You think we should let it go on? For how much longer?"

"Adalyn is asleep upstairs, and Maddox hasn't lived at home for years. The basement door is locked from up here, so everyone can only come and go from the outside entrance. Noah has a key to get upstairs and promised there wouldn't be any alcohol around. Let him have some fun. If it will make you feel better, we can go check things out."

I nod firmly, liking that idea a whole lot. "Please."

"Come on, then, overprotective Papa Bear."

She steps back from me, and I spin to face her, taking in the coy smile that parts her lips. Her hair is wet from a shower, leaving damp spots on the shoulders of my T-shirt she has on. The sight of her bare legs beneath a pair of loose-fitting shorts has me contemplating telling her I'll go to the basement by myself, but it's a safer choice to have her come with me. Just in case.

"You're beautiful," I tell her.

Even after two decades together, my words paint her cheeks pink. "You're not bad yourself. Even if you are a suck up."

I grin and bend down to steal a quick kiss before tucking her beneath my arm and leading us to the basement door. She twists the lock and peels open the door, letting the music blast past us into the hallway.

"Okay, maybe it's a little loud," she notes.

I don't tell her I told you so. With her close behind me, I lead us down the stairs and into an absolute disaster zone. The music was a warning sign I shouldn't have ignored. My jaw falls open, then shuts tight enough my teeth ache as I dart my eyes around the space.

My grip on Ava tightens as I pull her closer and sift through the strangers in our house in search of Noah.

This isn't a party. It's a giant fuck you for something I must have done wrong. No alcohol, he promised. Bull. Shit.

Ava tears herself out of my grip and shoves her way through the teenagers, not a care in the world that she's smaller than most of them and could easily get hurt. I follow her, realizing a breath later that she's already found our son.

He's sitting in the corner of the game room with a pair of earbuds in his ears and his eyes closed. It's as if the party means nothing to him. As if it's not happening around him. In our house.

"Noah James Hutton!" Ava shouts. Nobody blinks an eye, most

likely not even catching her voice over the overpowering rock song playing.

I turn and find the large speaker on the counter beside the bar. It's almost hidden behind empty beer bottles and chip bags, but I manage to catch it. Five steps is all it takes to reach it and abruptly cut the music.

Silence falls before a mix of confused and angry voices take over. I cross my arms and bark a loud "Party's over. Get out before I call your parents!"

My eyes are laser focused on my son. On the lazy flutter of his lashes as he opens his eyes and takes in the rush of people moving toward the door that leads to the backyard. He must sense that someone's watching him, because suddenly, he's meeting my stare with one full of fury.

Ava storms toward him and slaps her hands on her hips, saying something to him that I can't hear. He has the decency to level off his fury in front of his mother.

It takes several minutes for everyone to leave, but once they do, the tension in the large space is almost suffocating. I attempt to calm my frustration and disappointment before joining my wife and son. It's not easy, but I manage it.

We've trusted Noah to have friends over at the house before. For most of his life, we've encouraged him to do it. I grew up in a very easygoing, trusting household, and I took that, and we raised our children the same way. But this is the first time any one of them has betrayed that trust. I would be an idiot to believe that came out of nowhere.

"Was this your concept of having a couple of music friends over?" Ava asks him, slicing through the silence. "I don't think I've ever seen you hang out with any of those people!"

"Sorry," he drawls.

"You're sorry? Something could have happened to you! This is our home, Noah, not a shack in the woods! Why would you— Oh, my God! Are you high?" she shrieks, dropping to her knees in front of him and grabbing his face in her small hand. Turning his head side to side, she sucks in a sharp breath. "Pot? Or something worse?"

He tears away from her grip and snaps, "Why do you care what I do with my life?"

Ava flinches, surprised at the tone. "What is that supposed to mean?"

"Stop pretending to care!" Pushing his body up the wall behind him, he comes to a stand and slips around Ava, leaving a wide berth between them. "Just leave me alone."

I'm moving before he can get to the safety of his bedroom. Lifting my hand, I press the tips of my fingers to his chest, stopping him from going any further. I notice what Ava must have now that he's closer. The red in his eyes that goes far beyond the excuse of exhaustion.

"Where did you get it? You're seventeen." I struggle to keep my voice level.

His lip curls as he takes a step back. I let my hand fall. "It's none of your business."

"I beg to differ. As long as you live here, your business is mine. That includes how you got your hands on marijuana."

"Let me waste my life away, Dad. Nobody said you had to give a shit about me. I'm sorry I'm not more like Maddox."

"Don't make this about your brother," Ava scolds.

He turns to her. "He has enough to say about the way I want to live my life that he might as well be in this conversation." He flings his eyes to me next. "Why don't you call him? Speed dial number one, right?"

"What happened with you and Maddox?" Ava asks, slowly moving closer to us.

"I'm guessing you heard us talking earlier," I say.

Noah's laugh is cold. My stomach sinks at the hurt that drifts through the cruel noise. "When you said I was a waste of talent? Yeah, I did."

Ava looks at me from behind Noah, alarmed. I shake my head, trying to settle her. He heard a portion of that conversation and took it the wrong way. The party makes sense now. It was his way of trying to hide his hurt.

"You misunderstood what we were talking about. Nobody thinks you're a waste of talent," I clarify.

His expression closes off fully. "Explain what you meant, then."

"We want you to do more with yourself. You're turning opportuni-ties down that others would love. By continuing to put yourself in situations like these ones, you're wasting the talent that lives inside of you."

"There's that word again," he spits.

Ava tries to diffuse the situation and sets her hand on Noah's shoulder. He shrugs it off and steps even further from us.

"You're not wasting anything, honey. That's a bad way to put it," she murmurs.

"Stop, Mom. Just stop. I don't need this. I don't need any of you."

"Noah," she whispers, pain twisting her features.

"I can't live like this anymore!" he shouts. Like a terrified animal, he lifts his hands up and takes quick steps back. "The pressure to live up to Maddox. The disappointment in Dad's eyes every time I make a decision that he doesn't approve of. I'm never going to be the son you wanted."

I swallow, fighting the urge to go to him and wrap him in a hug. "You're high. Let's talk about this in the morning."

"I'm high because it's the only way to stop thinking about what a fucking failure I am. I invited those people over to piss you off because I wanted to watch you suffer the way I am. I'm getting out of this fucking house as soon as I can. Away from you. I can't stand being around you."

The hate in his tone strikes me at the knees. Ava's mouth is open, but no words come out. I cough, trying to dislodge the rock stuck in my tightening throat.

"Noah—" I begin.

"Don't bother. I've already started looking for places in town."

When he stalks past me, I reach for his arm, but he slaps it away. I've never seen so much anger and hatred in his eyes before. Such betrayal. I stare where he used to stand and blink slowly, disbelieving, as his bedroom door slams shut. A piece of me chips away, leaving behind an ache that I don't know how to soothe.

This burst wasn't just from today. It's been building for years. From things I didn't even know I was doing. Ava brushes her hands down my shoulders, and I let her try to bring me comfort, even though we both know I don't deserve it.

41

Noah

PRESENT

WHEN I WAKE NEXT, IT'S MY DAD SITTING AT MY BEDSIDE. EYES groggy, I blink to bring him into focus. Regardless of my lack of empathy for him, I can admit that he looks like shit. Must feel like it too. He's alone in the room with me, hunched in a plastic chair beside my bed. Fingers clenched in the blankets beside my leg, it's as if he wanted to touch me but decided against it.

"You're awake," he blurts out when he notices that I'm awake. I stare back at him, and he laughs humourlessly. "I know I'm not who you wanted to see."

"You're right." My voice is scratchy, still fucked from how long I was asleep.

"She's been guarding your door for the last few hours, if that helps. Nobody has been able to convince her to go home."

If I was a better man, I would have had my dad tell her to go home. But I'm no good man. I want her here with me, even if she's dead on her feet.

"We don't do small talk. What are you doing here?"

Dad sucks in a breath, disappointed but attempting to hide it. "You could have died. I wanted to see you. Talk to you."

"It took me getting stabbed for you to want to speak with me?"

"I've never not wanted to speak with you, Noah."

I swallow a laugh. "You've gotten funnier over the past few years."

Pain washes over his features. "I don't know how to do this with you."

"Do what? Speak?"

"Apologize. Try to have a conversation that isn't filled with resentment. I've done so many things wrong when it comes to you. So many things that I wish I could go back and change."

I clench my jaw, pissed off when my chest pangs in response to his words. "You *can't* go back."

"I know. But I can apologize for everything and try to move forward with you instead of against you. It was never my intention to allow things to become so broken between us. You're my son, Noah. I love you. I've loved you since the moment your mother told me she was pregnant."

Love. There's that word again. It's still too hard for me to process that term and the supposed meaning behind it. When Tinsley said it, I couldn't help but believe it. If there is such a thing as a single term to combine a cacophony of different feelings, the term would suffice instead of describing each one. She's worthy of my understanding toward it. My father, however, is not.

"I don't believe in love."

He blinks, taken aback. "Why?"

"That doesn't matter."

"Yes, it does." He's stubborn like Maddox.

I adjust my position on the bed and sit straighter against the mattress at my back, wincing at the tugging sensation in my side. The extra pillow someone shoved behind my back while I was sleeping has slid halfway out of its spot, but when I go to rip it all the way out, Dad's already moving. He urges me forward just enough to put it back in place and starts fidgeting with the blankets at my waist.

"That girl out there loves you. Are you saying you don't think that's true?" he asks, not letting the subject die like I wish he would.

"What we feel for each other goes far beyond the basic term. But yes, she uses it. I know the depths of her feelings, so I accept the word. But you? I don't know your definition of the word, nor have I seen that definition in your actions," I tell him bluntly.

Green eyes tightening quizzically, he takes me in. It's a long moment before he speaks again. "That's fair. I have done a piss-poor job of showing you my love. I'm so, so sorry for that."

"Apologies mean nothing to me."

Again, he looks pained. It's a relieving sight. He's finally getting it—that I'm a worse version of that teenager he let push him away seven years ago. I've spent so many years resenting this man. Hating him for giving up so easily. Words are such pretty, fleeting things. Actions make an impact.

He tucks the blanket beneath my stiff thighs and sits back in his chair. His eyes drift over my side, still bare with only a bandage covering my wound, and he winces. I tap my fingers against the bed rail and wet my dry lips.

"Let me prove it to you, then. I know it took me too long to do this. It shouldn't have taken you getting hurt for me to reach this point. But don't for one second think that I haven't missed you or hurt over the distance I let grow between us, because I have. The day you moved to Toronto, I cried for the first time in over a decade. I've been a terrible father to you, but I want to try and fix that. It's going to take a long time to repair what I broke, but I'm not afraid of that. I can't lose you again. Won't."

My stomach turns over. There's an unfamiliar sheen to his eyes that makes my skin prickle with discomfort. They're tears, and ones not from my golden girl. I've never seen my father cry. I thought him incapable of it until now. His words are the prettiest I've ever heard, but I don't allow myself to believe in them.

There was a part of me that shifted into the wrong place when he allowed the final rope to snap on the bridge keeping us together, and it would be too painful to allow it to shift again.

It's always easier to cast aside the promises of someone you don't trust. Not so easy when it's your father. Feels wrong to disregard them.

"Did Mom put you up to this?" I rasp.

His brows furrow as his head moves side to side. "She wants us to be a family again, yes, but that didn't have anything to do with me speaking to you today. I want to be a family too. I want my son back. I've never been more terrified in my life as I was when Braden called to tell us you were hurt and in the hospital."

Something painfully cold wraps around my rib cage. Doubt? Pain? "Mom had an emergency C-section with Adalyn. Maddox almost lost his career."

"Those things did happen. But neither were as scary as thinking we could lose you."

Two soft knocks on the door make the cold feeling inside of me dissipate, replaced with an overwhelming warmth. I divert my stare from my father and place it on the door as it opens, revealing my woman. Even with exhaustion heavy in her expression and the lines of her body, she's stunning. We lock eyes, and everything is right again.

She smiles sheepishly at me. "I'm going to get some lunch from the cafeteria. Do you want anything? Jell-O? Pudding?"

There are already two Jell-Os on the table beside my bed. She's been up for a while, it seems. I decide not to complain about her leaving my arms while I was asleep, considering that apparently, having her take care of me makes me almost as hard as taking care of her does.

"Jell-O is fine," I tell her.

She beams at me, pleased with the approval. "Be right back." Then, with a quick glance between my father and me, she lifts a brow at me.

I fight the urge to order her to come back to bed with me and dip my chin to tell her it's fine instead. She lingers in the doorway for a brief moment before slipping out, leaving the door cracked open. The sound of footsteps receding down the hall lets me know she's not eavesdropping.

Dad is watching me when I look at him again. There's a soft expression on his face that looks a lot like awe. It's not the first time he or anyone else in my family has looked at me like that. Always when I'm with Tinsley.

"How long has she thought you like Jell-O?" he asks.

"Since we were children."

When she was seven and I was six, to be exact. The first time she told me that raspberry Jell-O was her favourite snack, and I lied and told her it was mine too, just so we would have something in common. I've been eating it with her ever since, even though the gelatine sits terribly in my stomach.

"I remember the first Christmas your grandmother made Jell-O salad for dessert and didn't tell you what it was made out of before you ate a massive spoonful. You spent the night in the bathroom throwing up."

"It's not the first time that shit has made me throw up."

"Yet you still eat it."

"For Tinsley."

He smiles almost sadly and leans his elbows on the edge of the mattress. "That's love, Noah. It makes us do the stupidest things. Like eating something we know will make us sick just so we can see them happy. I'm sorry I never taught you about something as important as what it means to love someone."

I push away the tingle of emotion his statement attempts to fill me with before it has the fucking chance. I'll accept his apology today and let him prove himself. But that's all I'm willing to do. There will be no forgiveness yet. No father-and-son moments. With no expectations, you beat disappointment at its own game. And I hate to lose.

Instead of thinking about it any further, I change the subject to something safer and comfortable, despite still being in relation to Tinsley. Everything is about her, just the way I like it.

"If you want to start making things up to me, I need you to do something right now."

He's quick to agree. "Anything."

"Plan a birthday party for Tinsley. As good of one as we can have in this fucking place."

His expression shifts to something that looks too similar to pride. I choose to ignore it. "Consider it done."

NH)

KEEPING TINSLEY out of my room was the hardest part of the day. Her parents had to drag her out of the hospital with the promise of a hot shower. She turned them down at first, but when Braden told her she stunk and she looked at me for confirmation, my nod—albeit a lying nod—was the deciding factor. Her supposed smell wouldn't have bothered me even if it was real. I just needed her to leave so my room could be transformed for her.

My father worked overtime to do as I asked. There's a two-tier silver-and-black cake on the table beside the stack of Jell-O and birthday presents. Bundles of balloons float along the ceiling above a Happy Birthday banner he's currently hanging.

My room is big, on a floor guarded night and day. A request I learned came from Dad the moment he arrived at the hospital. Mom said it came from a place of worry, but it could have been for privacy. The lack of trust I have in him is alarming. Maybe even a bit unfair.

Tinsley's been gone for a while now. I'm growing more agitated as the minutes go by without her here. *This will make her happy*, I remind myself. I refuse to allow her to miss a single birthday, especially on my behalf. It's not the same as celebrating on the exact day, but that won't matter to her.

"They should be up here any minute," Dad says. With a

finishing strip of tape on the edge of the birthday banner, he steps down from the chair he was using as a step stool and pats his hands on his thighs.

I nod. "Thanks."

"Anytime."

As he starts busying himself with cleaning up the garbage from the decorations, I look for the bag Adalyn and Mom brought for me. The nurses changed my bandage this morning and confirmed to my nerve-racked mother that I'm healing well. I want to put a shirt on so I don't look like a fucking slob for Tinsley.

"Can you get me a shirt?" I ask.

He nods quickly. The black duffle bag beside the window is so full of shit the zipper is hard to undo as he crouches in front of it. "Is this one okay?" A plain black T-shirt dangles between his fingertips.

"Yeah."

Bundling it in a fist, he struggles to zip the bag up before walking toward the bed. I watch as the want to help me get dressed drifts across his mind, but he lets the thought slip away, handing me the shirt instead. His eyes grow haunted as he retreats.

"Thanks," I mutter.

"You're welcome. Is there anything else you need before everyone else gets here? Anything I should add?"

"It's fine as it is. She's going to like it."

His mouth lifts at the corner as he looks around the room. "Yeah, she will."

Taking advantage of the distraction, I tug the shirt over my head and work to get my arms through the holes. My left arm goes in easily, but a searing pain makes my vision go black when I try to push my right one above my head.

"Fuck," I grunt.

Footsteps slap the floor while my vision slowly starts to come back. Fingers prod at my side, checking the bandage for blood, most likely, while I swallow a snarl. Seemingly satisfied with the bandage, Dad releases a heavy breath and pulls at the shirt, bending my arm in a way that doesn't pull on my stitches as he slides it through the hole.

He rubs a hand up and down my back once my shirt is all the way on. My muscles lock up at the unfamiliar yet terrifyingly comforting touch. I grit my teeth to avoid jerking away. He's already felt my stiffening, though. His hand drops instantly.

"I'll go check where they are," he says softly.

"Okay."

"Thank you, Noah. For . . . letting me do this."

"It's for Tinsley." But it ridiculously means something to me.

He smiles knowingly. "She'll love it."

I don't know what to say back, so I keep quiet. Thankfully, it isn't long before my hospital room starts to fill. Mom, Adalyn, and Maddox show up first. Maddox eyes me and Dad oddly, as if looking for some sort of sign as to how things are going. He won't get anything from me. I do wonder if he'll try to get me alone and speak with me sometime before he goes home. Our relationship is far better than the one I have with Dad, but that doesn't mean much.

Everyone paws over me, concerned with my injury and my feelings and if I need anything. It's too much. I feel suffocated. Each moment that passes with me watching the door like an abandoned dog, I grow more and more desperate for her. By the time that door finally opens for the final time and she steps inside, I'm starved for her. Goddamn ravished.

I grip the blankets on either side of me in tight fists when she glances around the room and then at me, eyes wide and so fucking bright. Amazement twists her features into something magical. The look in her eyes is a hot poker of arousal in my gut. I'm suddenly grateful for the blanket over my lower half that Dad refused to let me take off.

She's quickly abandoning everyone else in the room and rushing toward me. The moment she's close enough, her hands are on my face, drawing me in. Our lips meet in a blast of longing and pure, unfiltered want for one another. It's a terrifying explosion that doesn't just linger on my mouth but wraps itself around my chest and squeezes and squeezes until I'm sure it'll ruin me. I want it to. Would beg to be ruined by the taste and feel of her.

Time, place, company. Nothing matters but her. I've always put Tinsley at the forefront of my mind. It was immediate, on instinct. But she's finally doing the same. I'm to her what she is to me. It's fucking electrifying.

I push my fingers through her hair and breathe her in in large, greedy inhales. A flurry of satisfied noises works up my throat before I trap them down. The opinion of those around us don't matter to me, but they do to her. I don't particularly think she'd enjoy her family hearing how desperately I want their daughter right now.

If I could tear my eyes away from her, I'm positive I'd find Braden trying to slit my throat with his eyes for so much as kissing her in front of him.

Our audience disappears from my mind the moment her eyes open and she strokes her thumb below the bruise surrounding my eyes.

"Thank you," she whispers.

I reply by kissing her again.

42

Tinsley

MY ATTENTION KEEPS DRIFTING FROM THE PILE OF GIFTS AT THE FOOT of the bed to Noah, the rock star who's refusing to let me leave the warmth of his body. There's a tiara on my head with the title Birthday Girl written in hot pink, glittery letters across it. I haven't stopped grinning since I walked into Noah's room over an hour ago. It feels wrong to be happy despite the brutal reality nipping at our heels, but I can't help it.

This party is everything to me.

For tonight, our lives are normal. Well, almost normal. The machines that continue to pump medication into Noah's veins are almost as hard to ignore as the cuts and bruises marking his pale skin.

The rhythmic tapping of his fingertips on my bicep tries to pull me back into the conversation taking place around me. I focus on something else, though. Noah's tapping a beat to one of his songs, the one still without a title. He's been singing it every night on tour, but it remains incomplete until I decide on a name.

"What did you get Tiny, Noah?" Addie asks, her blue eyes bright and bushy-tailed like always. She winks at me, and I return it, grateful for the reminder. I've been forced to open his last, and I know that was on purpose.

He knows he got me the best one and wanted to make sure everyone else knew it.

The biggest gift of them all is wrapped neatly in silver paper with a black bow on top. My eyes immediately find Oakley sitting across the room, sandwiched between Ava and my dad. The small chairs they got brought into the room look ridiculous beneath the massive frames of him and Dad, but they take what has to be serious discomfort like champs.

Oakley smiles knowingly at me, and I laugh beneath my breath. Noah's terrible with wrapping gifts. It's usually easy to recognize which are his, even in a giant bundle of presents, so I know that it was his father who wrapped this one.

"Open it," Noah tells me.

"You don't have to tell me twice."

Mom giggles. "There's my girl."

She and Dad got me a custom hoodie with Fast Track written across the chest and a list of all my fight wins so far on the back. I had to suck back tears at the thought that went into that gift. I've always loved special gifts like that the most. The ones that take thought and care. That's what makes this one so special to me. It's a reminder that regardless of the shit going on right now, I've been kicking serious ass as a professional boxer. I refuse to let anything take that from me.

Adalyn is the one who shoots out of her seat and brings me the silver present. I take it with an excited grin and set it in my lap. Tugging the bow first, I watch it come apart and then brush it away. I slip a finger beneath the corner of the wrapping paper and pop it up before tearing it away.

The box beneath the paper is a simple black one with a matching top. Noah's stare digs into the side of my face, watching my reaction instead of the busy movements of my fingers. The rumble of satisfaction that grows in his chest when I pull the lid off and gasp at what's inside makes goosebumps spring to life on every inch of my skin.

"You needed ones to match your robe," he murmurs, lips brushing my jaw.

I hesitate to touch them. The silver boxing gloves are too perfect, too beautiful, to risk smudging with fingerprints. My fingers hover above them before carefully tracing the ink-splotch designs that have been splattered over the silver. They're a perfect match for my shorts and robe. A completed set.

"Show us!" Mom claps.

"They're yours. Touch them all you want," Noah rasps, the words just for me.

So, I do. My fingertips glide along the curve of one before I lift it up and stare at it with blurred vision. Blinking back tears, I make out the words Fast Track inscribed along the wrists. My heart skips too many beats as I quickly grab the second glove and look at the exact same place.

Golden Girl.

"Noah," I croak.

"Those are gorgeous, Tiny," Ava says.

I tuck both gloves to my chest and shift my body so I'm facing Noah. He's already watching me, and when our eyes connect, I make out every emotion running through his mind. I'm feeling the exact same ones.

"I'm sorry there was no party yesterday," he mutters.

I frown. "This is perfect. It's everything I wanted."

He searches my eyes for any hint of a lie, but there is none. "Okay."

"I feel like we all just lost the best-present-giver title again this year," Adalyn notes.

I exhale a laugh and find her in the room. She's pouting, but there's nothing unhappy about her right now. My best friend is the sweetest, most supportive person I know. Even now, when our lives are so drastically different and we're thousands of kilometres away from one another every day, I know that I can count on her always. I've always known how lucky that makes me, to have not only one best friend who would do anything for me but two. Having her here today is everything I didn't know I needed.

"We always lose that title," Maddox corrects her.

His sister blows a raspberry. "Good point."

Maddox is the only one not sitting. Instead, he's standing to the side, leaning against the wall. His leg hasn't stopped bouncing since the moment I entered the room, if not long before that. Maddox isn't a fidgeter. He's the cool, calm, and collected sibling. The one with confidence and pride to spare. That's most likely why I flagged his odd movements. Well, that and the fact he hasn't stopped staring at Noah's side for longer than a second.

If I didn't know better, I would have taken his anxiousness as him missing his family back home. But I've been around him long enough to know that's not it. While he might miss his family in bundles, this goes beyond that. It's what happened to Noah that has him out of sorts. Noah and the torn pieces of their relationship that neither of them has bothered to repair yet.

"It's a loss we take in stride," Mom says.

My brother snorts. "Speak for yourself."

"You're turning green, Easton," Noah replies coolly.

I roll my lips to hide my smile when Easton flips Noah the bird. "I'd rather be green than get stabbed. How'd you do that, anyway? Did my sister piss off one too many Noah Hutton fangirls, so they came at you with knives?"

The room goes cold with silence as our families gape at his gall. He's never feared digging into Noah, and it goes both ways between them.

Anticipation fills my belly at Noah's delayed response, and one look at him confirms that he's understood my brother's attempt at comedy and isn't about to bury him beneath insults like everyone else assumes he might. He's too calm, with his mouth tugged ever so slightly in a coy smirk.

I set my new gloves gently back inside the gift box and place it on the end of the bed before snuggling back into Noah's side.

Everyone watches me curiously, and a sweep of my stare across the room reveals that out of every person here, Oakley's the one that isn't tense at all. He's calm as he watches me and his son on the tiny hospital bed, completely disregarding the tension coming from those around us.

It's a small win, but one I tuck close to my chest.

"Ah, so that's what happened. You sent the women your sister shooed away from me on a kill mission to take me out of the picture. Once they cut me up into ribbons, you'd be their second option. It was a valiant effort, Easton," Noah says.

Dad clears his throat in an attempt to hide his laugh. Easton's eyes flare with something hot and daring before Mom's voice snuffs out the flames with her words.

"If we ever left you two boys alone, you'd burn someone's house down."

"Just the house? I'm thinking the entire neighbourhood," Oakley adds.

I turn my face into Noah's side and smile. The black shirt he's put on smells like him and helps hide the scent of hospital that continues to linger in the room. It's been a long day, and I feel the weight of exhaustion creeping in.

"Do you want cake now?" he asks me, ignoring the conversation that continues to move around us.

I smooth a *totally* innocent hand down his thigh and flare my fingers to cup his knee. "Would it be rude of me to say that I don't?" He stops breathing, his muscles locking up. "Maybe we could have it later? Just you and me?"

"Just you and me," he echoes, the words strained.

I hum. "I want to thank you for all of this. But I think it would be better if I did that without everyone watching."

"Tell them to go."

"Yeah?"

"Yes. Before I do it."

That would be a terrible idea. Everyone would leave here scarred for life.

I wait for the current conversation to trickle off before saying, "I really appreciate all of this, but Noah's exhausted. I don't want to push him too much so soon."

A rare laugh escapes him at the excuse I come up with. It makes my stomach flutter uncontrollably.

With a shared understanding filling the room, everyone begins rushing around to say goodbye and happy birthday. It takes a long few minutes before the majority of everyone has cleared out with promises to come back tomorrow and lingering hugs. Noah's parents are last to leave after Ava kisses Noah's cheeks and orders him to text her before he goes to sleep. Oakley didn't try to hug Noah, but he didn't need to. The emotion in his expression was more than enough to portray that he wanted to but wouldn't push.

Later, I'll ask Noah about what happened with his father while I was gone, but the minute the door closes, leaving us alone for the first time in hours, that conversation is the last thing on my mind.

With two dark brown eyes hooked on me, I move down the bed and straddle his thighs one leg at a time. They're rock solid beneath my body, so strained and tight. I find his gaze and hold it, letting the desire he's feeling pool low in my belly, mixing with mine.

"You didn't have to do all of this for me," I whisper.

Setting my hands on his shoulders, I lean forward, touching our foreheads together. He butts his nose against mine and nips at my mouth. The sting warms my blood, making it sing.

"Wanted to. You deserve this."

"How are you feeling? Are you in any pain?"

Hands falling to my waist, he drags me up his lap. "No."

"None at all?"

His cock is hard between us, and with a cautious rock of my hips, I drag my centre along the length of it. The breath that tears from his lips is far from pained. The pleasured sound of it has me soaking my panties, so completely gone for this man.

"You know where I ache, Tinsley. I haven't felt my side all day."

I shudder, grinding over him a second time. The pressure on my clit makes my head spin. He puffs an exhale across my mouth.

"We shouldn't risk you tearing your stitches."

"Fuck my stitches. They can replace them," he grunts.

"Noah." My laugh is quiet, breathy. "I can help ease your ache without busting your stitches."

His eyes flare, darkening to a brown bordering on black. "Go on, then."

With his approval hanging in the air, I push myself down his legs until I'm straddling his shins. Holding his heated stare, I pull the blanket from his waist before doing the same to both his sweatpants and underwear. The view of his cock leaves me breathless, as if I'm seeing it for the first time all over again. In a way, I am.

The two designs that now mark the skin of his groin have my heart stalling, my lungs two chunks of ice. The last section of un-inked skin is now etched with my name in a branding of sheer possession.

"Happy birthday," he coos.

My eyes flick up. "When did you do this?"

"Do you like them?" He ignores my question.

"Yes." I touch my pointer finger to the edge of the shooting star on the right. It's still ringed with red and a bit swollen, so he had to have gotten it really recently. "Are you sure you won't regret them?"

"Don't ask stupid questions," he growls.

I touch the left tattoo, this time running my finger over the top of it. "You still haven't put your piercing back in."

"I was a bit busy."

The bluntness of his statement makes me snort a very unattractive laugh. "Fair enough."

"You're stalling."

"You're impatient."

"I have you bent over my lap with my cock in your face."

I smirk, drifting my touch toward said appendage. It shouldn't be possible, but he's grown even harder since I tugged his pants down. My tongue darts out as if it has a mind of its own and swipes at the pearl of liquid on the tip. His taste fills my mouth at the same time I'm wrapping a fist around the shaft and squeezing on the first upstroke. He's hot and smooth in my hand, and my body reacts to the feel of him, a sharp throb growing between my legs.

"I fucking missed you," he grunts, his cock jerking in my fist.

I look up at him through my lashes as I lick him again, sweeping my tongue along the underside of the head and then over the slit. His fingers dig through my hair and over my scalp before gripping the strands and pulling, encouraging me to take him into my mouth.

Considering what he did for me today, I don't make him beg. I shift forward and slowly work him between my lips. His shuddered curse when I get halfway down the shaft encourages me to open my throat and attempt to take him all the way. I end up gagging when the tip hits the back of my throat—still unable to accomplish my goal—and he throbs in response.

"That's it, baby. Choke on your cock," he orders through clenched teeth.

I release a needy moan around his shaft and pull back, hollowing my cheeks and sucking hard on the tip before diving back down. Over and over, I work him into my mouth, jerking what I can't reach with my hand. His breathing grows frantic, the grip on my hair so tight it burns and makes my eyes water, but I don't stop. His response to me only makes me go faster and suck harder. My tongue explores the ridges and bulging veins along the length of him, memorizing the spots that have him thrusting his hips to meet my every downward glide.

His cock muffles another of my moans, and then he's trying to take control with a hard thrust that pushes him deeper than

I've been able to take him before. Spit runs down my chin as I gag and dig my fingers into his slicked shaft.

"Going to paint your throat with my cum, Golden Girl. Want your belly full of it."

I rub my thighs together and abandon my grip on his length to cup his balls. One soft roll of them in my palm and he's forcing my face into his groan and coming down my throat in harsh, throbbing pulses. It goes on for several seconds, until I've swallowed so much of it so quickly that I can't keep up. Some leaks from the corner of my lips, but he's catching it with his thumb before it can drip down my chin.

"Unbelievable," he says on an exhale. "You're unbelievable."

I pull back when he begins to soften and take a gulp of air before he's pressing his thumb into my mouth, on my tongue.

"Swallow all of it, Tinsley," he commands.

With a roll of my eyes, I make a show of sucking on his finger and then sticking my tongue out for him to see. "Happy?"

"Very."

"Good. Now, let me check your side. You weren't exactly keeping still." I shoot him a glare and then switch my attention to the bandage covering what I know is a deep, jagged wound. When I see it hasn't turned red, I relax. "I should have the nurses come in and check you over."

"Absolutely fucking not. They can stay away from us until the morning. Longer, if possible."

"I hope you haven't been rude to them today. They're keeping you in one piece for me."

The thought of him getting an infection or winding up back in surgery makes me break out in a cold sweat. It's not something I can consider right now. I'm barely holding myself together as it is.

"They're overbearing."

With quick movements, I have his pants back up and the blanket around his waist. "Well, I'm grateful for them. They gave us time alone just now, didn't they?"

"It's not enough."

"I know."

His eyes tighten at the corners with defiance. The hint of arousal skips through them, and I can't help but wish for more too. The ache between my legs is insistent and beyond annoying, but I refuse to put his body under any more stress. I already risked enough just now. Plus, seeing him experience that blast of pleasure is more than enough for me.

"It won't be long until the police force their way back into the picture," I add in an attempt to change the subject to one that can dull my blinding lust for him.

His features darken at the mention of them. "I don't have anything to say to them. I've contacted a PI. That's all there is right now."

"Are you sure that's how you want to handle this? Do you trust this PI? Who is it? When did you get in contact with them?"

His throat bobs with a hard swallow as he shakes his head. "We're not talking about this tonight. Not on your birthday."

"It's hardly still my birthday."

Lifting his arm expectantly, he scowls at me. "We'll figure it out tomorrow."

I don't move toward him yet, and he doesn't drop his arm. "Promise me? Because we can't keep putting it off."

"I promise," he grumbles.

Satisfied enough with that, I settle beneath his arm and smile when he begins tapping that same beat against my skin again.

43

Braden

I FLAG THE MAN THAT GLIDES PAST ME INTO NOAH'S ROOM AND SIT straighter in my chair. With his head held high and hands in his pockets, he appears at ease, but I've spent enough of my life reading opponents in the ring to know better. I've never seen him before. He's a stranger to me, and that's a good enough reason to follow him. My daughter is in that room, and with the threat of a stalker hanging over her, I won't risk anything happening under my watch.

Stretching the sore muscles in my neck from sitting here for two straight days, I follow the man into the room, trying to muffle my steps as much as I can. When I reach the doorway, the sight of him standing at the edge of Noah's bed, staring at the couple splayed across it, makes me clear my throat, announcing my presence.

"Who are you?" I bark.

Three sets of eyes glance my way. Tiny worries her lip while Noah stares blankly. The stranger examines me, curiosity curving a thick brow. His hair is long and flops in his face. It would make him appear young if his bright blue eyes didn't hold such heaviness. He can't be much older than either of the kids in here.

"You must be the father," he greets me with a smooth nonchalance.

I cross my arms. "And you must be lost."

"I think I'm in the right place."

"Name. Now."

He turns his head to look at Noah with an exasperated expression. "Tell your father-in-law to relax. I'm not the enemy."

The term makes me stiffen. I'm not fucking ready for that yet. Not by a long shot. Tinsley is never getting married.

"I'll relax when you tell me your name. You're not a cop, so what are you?"

He curls his lip at the mention of the police, and another red flag waves in my mind. I don't like this at all. My every instinct screams for me to take Tiny and run, but she doesn't seem scared. A bit nervous but not fearful.

"It's Alec. That will have to suffice for now."

I chuckle, but it's hollow. "I don't think so."

"Dad, just listen to what he has to say," Tinsley pleads.

I meet her stare, finding her own anxiousness too obvious to ignore, and nod reluctantly. "Fine."

Alec pulls his hands from his pockets, a cell phone in the left one. "I've been talking to Noah here since shortly after he woke up, but I figured I'd come introduce myself formally once I had some concrete proof for you all."

Noah doesn't deny it. "Alec is who I thought was a PI for hire. Turns out he makes a better liar than a detective. Fortunately for us, he didn't lie to me about who Tinsley's stalker is."

I freeze, gawking at the newcomer. Did Tinsley know Noah was looking for a PI? That he supposedly hired one? From the subtle awkwardness radiating from her, I'm inclined to say no.

"How do you know who it is?" I ask.

"Let's just say that he pissed off the wrong group of people. We've been looking for him for a while now but lost his trail a few weeks ago when he dipped into America. He popped back up on our radar when he arrived back in Toronto," Alec explains, flexing his tattooed fingers as our eyes meet. "It would appear that you have a history with him as well, Braden."

My blood runs cold with dread. Tinsley sucks in a breath, but I can't bring myself to look at her right now. This stranger knows my name, but that's not what's most concerning.

It's that I could have somehow been the one that put her in this danger.

"Tell me what you know," I demand, taking a step toward him.

His eyes latch onto the movement, and his fingers twitch, as if wanting to reach for something. "I have the footage from the store Noah stopped at before he was attacked. It doesn't show the stabbing, but it catches enough leading up to it to confirm the man's identity."

"Show it to us," Noah hisses, the words cruel, unforgiving.

For the first time in my life, I find myself grateful for his anger. It means he'll keep my daughter safe. Deep down, I've always known that, but I refused to acknowledge it. If I did, I wouldn't have been able to hate him and pretend that he wasn't in love with Tinsley.

Alec is quick to unlock his phone and open it to a dark video. He offers the slim device to Noah, and I move to stand beside my daughter. I'm completely unprepared for what I fear I'll see on the screen. A thousand prayers to the man upstairs wouldn't be enough to settle my nerves. Each second that passes with us watching the black screen feels like an eternity. My palms are slick as I wipe them on my thighs and set an arm on the back of the bed, behind Tinsley's head.

Noah's grip on the phone makes his fingertips turn white before he's pressing Play. The screen brightens slightly, just enough to make out the dimly lit street outside the corner store at the entrance of their neighbourhood. For several moments, nothing happens. Not so much as a bird flies in front of the camera. But in a blink, that changes. I recognize Noah as he steps into the store and disappears.

"Forward the video ten minutes," Alec instructs.

Noah does, and the same empty street fills the screen until he stops, playing the video at normal speed. We watch the screen as he steps out of the store with a plastic bag in his hand, and then Tinsley adjusts herself on the bed. She presses her mouth to Noah's arm and whispers something I don't make out. It's most likely an apology. One she's been repeating since I called and told her something had happened to her best friend.

Nausea swirls in my stomach at the reminder of the state I found Noah in, but I force myself to focus on the screen again. I'll see it all again in my nightmares tonight.

In the video, Noah walks down the street and out of the frame of the video. It's not two minutes later that another figure appears, following him at a slow pace. My lungs tighten, the air inside of them getting choked off.

The stranger turns to check behind him, and the world stills as the camera catches a grainy view of his face. I yank my arm from behind Tinsley and stumble back a step.

"Dad?" she asks, alarmed at my jerky movements. "Do you know who that is?"

Alec makes his presence known again with a rough laugh. "You're white as a sheet, Braden. Have you seen a ghost?"

I try to speak, but no words come out. Alec doesn't wait for me to collect myself before he's speaking again, disgust ringing in my ears.

"His name is Cole Travis, Tinsley. And I think he's infatuated with you because you remind him of your mother."

NH)

TWENTY-SIX YEARS AGO

"You're right about Cole. He isn't worth it. I'm sorry that I let him get to me like that. Usually, it's easier to ignore his shit," Sierra tells me.

"You say that like dealing with his shit is a common thing."

She lifts a shoulder, avoiding my scrutinizing stare. "He just likes to push his boundaries. It's an ego thing."

My shoulders pull tight, scowl deepening. "It's not a damn ego thing, Sierra. What kind of boundaries does he push? Has he touched you?"

The unmistakable flame of anger flickers across her face before she can hide it.

"Tell me what he did. Now." I seethe.

Sierra's fingers tap her hip. There's worry in her eyes. "Can you promise me that if I tell you, you won't hunt him down and stomp him into the ground?"

"No."

"Then I won't tell you."

I laugh once. The sound is anything but humorous. "Simple as that, huh?"

She nods. "You're not getting involved."

"I'm already involved. You're my girlfriend. We're going to have a baby together, dammit!"

I want to pull my fucking hair out right now. Not smashing Cole's face into a brick wall at this very moment almost feels like a punishment of some sort. And the longer Sierra keeps me shut out, the more this feeling of rage heightens, and the harder it becomes to ignore.

I've always been an act first, think second kind of guy. I'm a fighter; I like to feel the surge of adrenaline in my veins before throwing a punch and the burn in my knuckles that follows.

Sitting back and letting things play out on their own is not something that I ever planned on doing. Especially not when it comes to Sierra and that butt plug of a boss of hers. He's crossed the line one too many times.

When Cole is introduced to how I deal with boys who fuck with my girl, he won't have anybody to save his sorry ass. It'll be just me and him.

"Yes, we are going to have a baby together. But that doesn't mean that I need you to fight all my battles for me. I've got it handled," Sierra says, exasperated.

My stare hardens to stone. "Handled it how? By sitting back like a good little worker bee and letting him continue to make you fucking uncomfortable?"

"Don't talk down to me because I won't let you act like a caveman out to save my honour."

I run a rough hand through my wet hair, tugging on it and expelling a harsh breath. "I'm not trying to talk down to you. I just don't want you to keep quiet about this. If he didn't touch you, then tell me right now, and I'll drop it. But if he did, he needs to be dealt with. He can't continue to put his filthy hands on you. He won't stop unless I make him." My voice softens. "Guys like him, baby, they don't just have a change of heart and leave you alone. He won't stop until he gets what he wants, and that's not okay."

Something I said seems to resonate somewhere in that pretty head of hers because some of the stiffness in her shoulders melts away, and her eyes finally clash with mine.

Her inhale is shaky. "Before you got here, there were a couple of times where he touched me. Just lingering brushes on my arms and sides when we would pass each other in the halls or get pushed together in a crowded meeting."

"Fuck. And? There's more. I can hear it in your voice."

"There was only one time . . . that he tried for more." She has to pause to clear her throat, blinking a few times. "I was looking for extra sugar packets in the breakroom for my coffee. They're in the bottom cupboard, so I was bent over or squatting, I don't remember. But I felt hands on my ass, squeezing it roughly. I shot up instantly and just froze. My thoughts were scattered all over the place. It took me a few seconds to turn around and see that it was Cole. He had the biggest fucking grin on his face, like he had just won a gold medal for touching me like that. Some intern walked in before Cole had a chance to say anything or touch me again."

A ball gets lodged in my throat before sliding free and tumbling

*through my insides like I'm a living pinball machine before it lands
with a splat at the bottom of my stomach.*

"I'm going to break each one of his fingers," I promise.

NH)

COLE'S CHAIR *scrapes across the floor when he stands abruptly. His jaw
is clenched so tight I'm surprised he hasn't broken any teeth. Who
knows, maybe he's leaving that honour for me.*

*"Can I talk to you outside, Sierra? This can't wait for Monday
morning."*

*My arm slips around her waist as she stiffens. "We really need to
go. Maybe you can email it to me."*

*That's apparently the wrong thing to say because Cole's eyes flash
with something violent, making me push Sierra behind me. My brows
climb my forehead, this fucker's entire existence a complete thorn in my
side.*

*"Oh, like you emailed me about being pregnant with this incompe-
tent, wannabe fighter's baby instead of telling me face to face? Why
would you get yourself into this mess, Sierra? He's nowhere near good
enough for you."*

*His words settle in my stomach like shards of glass. He's so angry,
so bitter, that I can almost smell his hatred in the air. Flat palms glide
over my back, drawing my attention long enough for me to notice the
several sets of eyes watching us with such curiosity it makes my skin
crawl.*

*"You know what, big guy? I think taking this outside would be a
great idea," I growl, gesturing toward the exit.*

*I grab Sierra's chin between my fingers and lift, making our gazes
lock before I'm capturing her mouth in a claiming, demanding kiss. A
shiver moves through her when she kisses me back just as hard. With a
nip to her lips, I pull back and glide my thumb along the top of her
cheekbone.*

"Don't have too much fun without me," she says before slipping away.

With Sierra gone, I turn my attention back to Cole. Hatred swirls in my blood, making it bubble in my veins. "Either you can walk yourself out of the building, or I can drag you out in front of all of these people. Pick."

He stares back at me with a grin that has my stomach swirling.

"You're quite demanding, Braden. Sierra didn't strike me as the type to enjoy being bossed around, but maybe that's what I was missing. Perhaps I was too nice."

"Don't talk about her. This is the only warning you're going to get."

NH)

COLE'S HANDS find his hips, his fingers curling. He shakes his head furiously. "You're not going to touch me, Braden."

"I'm not?"

"Not unless you want me to press charges, you're not."

I can't help it. A booming laugh scrapes up my throat, and my head falls back.

"Do you know what a hypocrite is, Mr. Big Shot?" I ask with a wicked grin. Cole blinks at me, unimpressed with my question. "See, if you were to press charges against me for whatever it is I'm going to do to you, then it would be completely plausible to expect Sierra to press charges against you for sexual harassment, don't you think?"

He takes a brave step forward, fists shaking at his side. There's no hiding the outrage burning in his eyes. I've just struck a chord deep inside of him, one that he didn't want me knowing he had.

"I didn't sexually harass her!" he roars, taking another step closer.

"You touched her without permission, you fucking scumbag! She's never given you any reason to think you could lay a single finger on her. But you did it anyway. You took what you wanted because that's what you thought you deserved, right?"

I don't give him time to answer.

"Well, now I'm going to break every single bone in your hand so that you won't forget what happens when you touch somebody like that without their permission. The next time you think of doing this again, you'll feel the pain of your bones snapping and hear the tremble in your cries like it's happening all over again. Because it will happen again. Mark my words, Cole Travis. Touch somebody else the way you did Sierra and I'll come back here and fucking end you."

I stalk toward him, watching with the same unwavering smile as he fumbles back a step, and another, and another until he collides with a brick wall.

"You gave her a promotion, so she owed it to you, right?" My voice is shaking, but I'm not sure if it's from the outrage burning inside of me or the pain I feel thinking about him touching Sierra.

"She didn't tell you no. So in your fucked-up mind, that meant yes, right?"

Against my better judgment, my arm shoots out in front of me, and my knuckles collide with the bricks beside his head. He gasps, eyes bulging while I suck a pained breath through my teeth.

Fuck. I can't wiggle my fingers.

I'm towering over Cole as I tightly grip his right wrist with my non-aching hand and lift it beside his face, pinning it against the scuffed brick. The maneuver is a bit uncomfortable and leaves my entire side open and vulnerable if he decides to fight back, but I'm not about to try and test the extent of my hand injury. I definitely broke something.

"You're not really going to do this," Cole stammers, struggling a bit against the wall. I tighten my grip on his wrist until I know that he'll have bruises the shape of my fingertips in the morning.

NH₎

I slip the cold brass over the knuckles on my left hand. It's not the first time that I've felt this type of heaviness on my hand, but it's never been on my nondominant hand.

My fingers tingle like they know what's about to happen and can't hold back their excitement. I roll my shoulders back and close my left hand into a perfect fist.

"I warned you what would happen if you so much as talked to Sierra again, but I never would have given you the chance to walk away so easily if I had known what happened while I was gone. Now you'll pay for what you did to her."

Cole's scream vibrates through the night when the brass knuckles make contact with the back of his hand, crunching the bones, leaving his hand utterly useless.

"Get the fuck out of Toronto, Cole. I never want to see you again."

44

Noah

PRESENT

Cole Travis.

I burn the name into my memory and let the beast inside of me howl impatiently as he waits to feast on him. A cold, lethal rage rattles my chest, growing stronger with each piece of information I learn about Tinsley's stalker.

Alec is nothing more than a stranger to me. A man pretending to be what I sought in order to get information. Yet, he's provided vital information that I've been waiting on for weeks. Given an answer to my most important question. I don't care much for his life's story, nor for the events that led him to us. Eliminating Cole is more important, and Alec will help me accomplish that, even if I have to risk working with someone I don't trust. Someone who appears to be too similar to me. A predator trapped beneath his own skin. I'm not unnerved easily, but there's something about him that has me on guard constantly.

I tugged Tinsley between my legs a few minutes ago. With her back to my chest and my legs bracketing hers, I feel in control. She's protected fully in my arms. Safe.

There's no doubt in my mind that Cole needs to face greater retribution for what he's done than spending a few years in a prison cell. I want to destroy him. Make him cry out my name as I tear him limb from limb. Murder has never intrigued me. I'm not a psychopath. But just because it's never intrigued me doesn't mean that I'm against it. I've never feared the consequences of taking someone's life. Truthfully, I blame that on my lack of a conscience for most actions.

When it comes to those who have managed to breach the walls of my stone heart, I would commit any act to keep them safe. Murder included. A threat against Tinsley is a threat against me. And I won't hesitate to eliminate it if given the chance.

"How do you know about Cole's supposed relationship with Braden?" I ask Alec.

Tinsley's father now sits on a chair at the end of the bed, most likely because he's too weak in the knees to stand. He spaced out for several moments after Alec revealed Cole's name to us all, and I was waiting for him to collapse once he came to. His guilt-stricken expression is pitiful and worrisome but not revealing of whatever inner monologue is rolling through his mind.

I don't care for this look of his. It won't fill in the several blanks that still remain.

Alec crosses his ankles and leans back in his chair. Eyes bright in colour yet so incredibly dull and lifeless watch me. "It isn't a supposed relationship. I'm sure you'd love to explain, Braden."

"What does this have to do with Mom?" Tinsley asks weakly. There's a weight to the words that I wish I could pick up and carry for her.

Braden inhales slowly and begins to explain their past with Cole. Each bit of information he shares fuels my beast's demand for violence and revenge. Everything leading up to now begins to fit into place with minimal effort once he admits to his actions in that alleyway before Tinsley was even born. The blanks begin to fill with answers I wasn't expecting.

I'll gather the rest of the information from the man himself. When he's the one bleeding out in front of me, unable to fight back.

"So, he didn't leave Toronto," Tinsley mutters.

I unfold her hands from her lap and move them to my knees, needing her to touch me as much as I ache to touch her.

"No. I don't think he did. I'm unsure what he did leading up to these last few months, considering I'm not fucking old enough to have witnessed what happened between him and your father, but it wasn't hard to dig into his history," Alex says before focusing on Braden. "Did you know he went to the police that night and attempted to have you arrested?"

Braden grits his teeth and gives a single shake of his head. "No."

"Well, lucky for us, he did. The record of his statement was easy enough to find, while buried under two decades' worth of tossed reports."

"If he reported Dad, why wasn't he ever arrested? Or at least questioned by the police?" Tinsley asks.

Alec's smirk is so similar to mine it's disconcerting. "Most likely because of the nice big bruise he left on the cheek of a night shift nurse in the emergency room not even an hour after leaving the station. Her following statement was a thick red X over his. He received a slap on the wrist for the marked-up face he gifted her and then went on his way."

I tighten my hold on Tinsley, completely wrapping myself around her frame. "What did he do to make you dig into his past this deeply? Forget to walk your dog?"

"He stole and ruined something of ours. Something worth a lot more money than his pathetic life. And we intend to cash in. Consider it a win-win. You help me find him, and I'll let you have a few minutes alone with him before I finish with him."

I dig my teeth into my tongue and let warm blood fill my mouth. He's not Alec's to finish off. He's mine.

Braden bends in his chair, resting his elbows on his knees. "Who is this 'we'?"

"Again, it's none of your concern," Alec deadpans.

I swallow the pool of blood in my mouth and then clear my throat. "That's not going to work. Give us the information we want, or this conversation ends here. You can fuck off and try to find him on your own. Haven't done a great job of that so far, have you?"

"You're feisty, Scowls," he muses, a predatory smile spreading his lips. "You won't get anything out of me. But you're more than welcome to try. It would be a waste of our time, however."

A waste of time, but entertaining, nonetheless.

"How do you plan for us to help you find him? He seems to be the one finding us," Tinsley says, trying to help guide the conversation. My sweet girl, always working to protect us all.

Dipping my head, I press my mouth to the warm skin behind her ear and inhale. She relaxes into my embrace, her head lolling to the side, exposing more of her throat. I nip at the shell of her ear before forcing my attention back to Alec.

The look he's giving my golden girl has a vicious snarl escaping me. "Fuck. No."

He feigns ignorance. "What?"

"You're not using her to get to him. Over my dead body," I spit.

Braden jumps out of his seat, the lines of his body brutally hard. "You want to use my daughter as bait? That's why you're here, isn't it?" Alec blinks slowly, calmly. Braden bares his teeth. "Get out. We'll be fine without you."

Tinsley shifts in my arms, pulling away slightly. It's too fucking far. I curl my fingers into my palms to keep from yanking her right back.

"What do you need me to do?" she asks on an exhale.

No. My hand uncurls, reaching out, the tips of my fingers

turning her face toward me. I feel the violence swimming in my eyes, but she bats it away as if it doesn't mean anything to her.

"You are not getting involved in this," I snap.

Her stare tightens, lips flattening. "I'm *already* involved. This is my decision. Not yours."

"You're wrong. I'll do everything I can to keep you away from this."

She leans in, close enough our noses touch, and growls, "Try it."

"Tinsley, you know better than this," Braden cuts in.

Her gaze lingers on mine for a few more seconds before she turns harshly in my arms, facing her father with a spine of steel. "I've never let others make my decisions for me, and I'm not starting now. I don't need either of you to give me permission to do this. I'm going to do it anyway, and you're either going to accept that or continue to be stubborn assholes about it. Either way, you're *not* telling me what to do."

Is it wrong that my cock is hard right now? Fucking hell, I've always liked her fire. But this isn't a simple fire. This is an inferno raging inside of her with nowhere to go but out, aimed at me and her father and anyone daring to tell her no. I welcome the burn with open arms, knowing she'll be the one healing me afterward.

It goes against everything inside of me to let her do this. To sit back and watch as she willingly puts herself into danger. But it's either give her what she wants or lock her up so she has no choice but to let the idea go. I would never cage her, so that leaves me with no choice but to agree. To risk her well-being with the hope of putting an end to this sick fuck's attempts at taking what's mine.

I'm naturally a selfish prick, and I can't pretend letting her have her way doesn't benefit me, even slightly. If only the risk wasn't so steep.

I look past her at Alec. "Tell me what you want her to do."

NH)

THE POLICE LINGER in the hallway an hour later.

Alec is gone, having disappeared after laying out his picture-perfect plan for us. It's well thought out for him but leaves too much room for error in regard to Tinsley. If everything goes the way he wants it to, she will be in danger for minutes before we intervene and get her out of harm's way. My head throbs, a million negative outcomes tearing at my mind.

My father stands alone at the edge of my bed, worry creasing his forehead as he waits for me to speak. He wants answers. Ones I won't give him. He refuses to let me speak with the police on my own, and that complicates things. Forces me to involve him even slightly.

Where Braden has a more curved moral code, my father's is pin straight. He's clean where Braden's dirty and I'm filthy. I can't involve him in what we have planned. Not even Braden has been pulled as deeply into the plan as I have. Despite everything that's happened between us, I won't risk either my father's honour or Tinsley's over this. Mine would never forgive himself, nor me, for what I want to do. What I've already promised my beast we'll do.

Tinsley doesn't know that I don't plan on letting her stick around after she's played her part. She wouldn't have agreed if she did. At the end, it will be me, Alec, and Cole.

"I need you to let me talk to them. Don't say anything. Just go along with it," I tell him.

He grips the end of the bed. "I don't understand."

"How badly do you want me to forgive you?"

"Noah . . ." He trails off, worry beginning to strain his features. "What are you doing?"

"I'm going to tell them that I don't know anything about why I was attacked. And then when they leave, you're going to tell

Mom and everyone else that I did the opposite. That the police
are handling everything."

"You want me to lie to them? To your mom?" he croaks.

"Yes. I do."

I watch him think it over, struggling to agree blindly to my
wants. He's too honourable. It's a trait he gave to my brother but
not to me.

"I don't suppose you'll tell me why you're doing this?"

"No."

"I can't lose you, Noah. We couldn't survive losing you." So
much sincerity rings in his words that it floods the room.

I double blink, surprised by the way his words flop heavily in
my chest. "I'll be fine."

"You always are."

"I want to trust you," I admit, my throat tight. "If you do this,
I will try to."

Miraculously, that seems to be enough for him. A dip of his
chin, and then I'm telling him to open the door for the cops, a
dozen lies poised on the tip of my tongue.

45

Tinsley

"WE REALLY NEED TO FIND A DIFFERENT PLACE TO LIVE," I GRUMBLE, stepping through the doorway behind Noah.

It's his first time home since the accident three days ago. We're both on edge but excited to be out of the hospital. Stinking like disinfectant, I take in the lack of wandering eyes around us and relax the slightest bit. Josh and Sparks have been here the entire time we've been gone, and I'm grateful they were willing to do that for us. For me, especially.

If the house was full, Cole wouldn't have come inside. He wouldn't be waiting to ambush us the moment we opened the door. God, the thought of him here makes me feel ill. Thinking of him *at all* sparks that response.

With my emotions overloaded, I shut the door behind us and lock it, double-checking it's actually locked before moving back to Noah's side. He's still weak and sore but, with permission from the doctor on shift this morning, has been healing well enough to go home. I've been like a fly in his ear since, unable to leave him be for all of five minutes.

"We will," he replies.

Josh is passed out on his bed in nothing but a pair of boxers with his bedroom door wide open, and Sparks is out of sight.

The living room is clean, and when we step into the kitchen, I notice it's free of Josh's usual mess as well.

"I was half expecting to find this place a disaster," I say.

Noah watches silently as I pull open the fridge and find it full. I don't think it's ever been this stocked. Fruit, vegetables, milk, and juice. It's obvious our parents have been here multiple times since we've been gone.

"My mother was here," Noah notes.

"Both of our mothers were. Don't tell me you're surprised by that."

"I'm not."

I laugh when I spot my leftover birthday cake on the top rack, wrapped in cling wrap with a candle resting on top. "Fancy a piece of cake for lunch?"

"Only if I get to eat it off your naked body," he mutters, the words so damn blunt.

"Liar. You don't like cake."

"You're right. I don't want any of that fucking cake. I want you."

Heat crawls up my neck as I close the fridge and turn to face him. The desire in his eyes is almost enough to distract me from the fact that he's still injured. It would be reckless to have sex so soon. So selfish . . .

"It's not safe."

"I don't want safe."

"Noah." My voice is soft.

"Baby," he rasps.

One foot after the other, he prowls toward me. My back meets the cool door of the fridge, and then he's boxing me in, forearms kissing my cheeks. The hint of his usual scent lingers beneath the smell of hospital, and I breathe it in greedily, desperate for more. It settles something inside of me that's been restless for days.

"You shouldn't call me that," I whisper. "It makes it hard to think."

"I don't need you to think right now."

The whites of his eyes are so small compared to his pupils as they feast on me, a million tiny fangs nipping at my skin. I exhale and arch my back, bringing our chests together. The light brush of my nipples against his hard body threatens to sweep my legs out from under me.

This man undoes me with a simple glance. And when he watches me like this . . . it takes all my strength not to let myself get washed out by the waves of his unyielding tide.

"Baby," he repeats against my mouth.

Warmth pools in my gut, slowly slipping lower and lower . . . "Josh is too close. I don't know where Sparks is."

"The prospect of an audience has never stopped us before."

He smooths a possessive hand down my side, cupping my curves. The heat from his palm seeps into my bones when he grips my waist and yanks me against him. I reach for his lower back and dig my fingers into the thick muscle before sliding them down, over the ridge of his ass. Giving it a squeeze, I catch the quick flash of a smirk on his lips before my leggings and panties are tugged down to my knees.

"Noah!" I whisper-hiss, my eyes flaring wide.

He ignores me, hitching one of my legs around his waist and grinding against my wet, bare centre. "Not waiting any longer to be inside of you again. I'm fucking you right here."

I moan my approval the second he's dropping his pants and dragging one thick finger through my pussy. I'm already wet, which isn't in the least bit surprising. Noah could spare me a second's glance, and I'd be soaking my panties for him.

The first breach of his finger inside of me has me stifling a whimper by digging my teeth into my bottom lip. He flashes me a dark grin before adding a second finger and pressing his palm against my clit, moving it side to side. Shocks of pleasure twist up my spine, flooding my senses.

"You don't have to hide your sounds from me. Let them

know we're home," he coos, pressing hungry kisses to my cheeks and jaw.

I shake my head. "No." Yet the idea makes me throb around his fingers, gripping him tight.

He captures my mouth, kissing me with a desperation that you would expect after going months without the taste of the one you love. I focus on the movement of his lips on mine, returning the ferocity.

The first stroke of his tongue along mine is met with a glide of his cock through my slit. My eyes snap open as I bring one hand to his neck and twirl my fingers in the hair there while gipping his ass with the other, encouraging him to move.

He notches himself at my entrance and opens his eyes to watch me as he thrusts inside. A growl gets stuck in his throat when he buries himself fully. My lips part in a silent cry, the feel of him inside me shooting me into oblivion. So full of him, physically and mentally. He's everywhere. In everything.

It's him, it's him. *It's him.*

I choke on the words that try to claw their way up my throat when he starts to move, starting soft and growing more powerful. My stare drops to his side and the bandage that's hidden beneath his shirt. I want to tell him to stop, to let me help so he doesn't strain himself, but the moment he's covering my throat with his hand, that worry is overrun with a hot flash of pleasure.

The thought of him disregarding his own safety in exchange for the bliss we bring each other in these moments turns me to goo. It's fucked up. *Sick.* But I'm dripping down his cock anyway, release building so quickly inside of me that I worry I'll wind up passing out from it before he joins me. Each thrust fills the kitchen with the sound of my arousal, and I no longer care if anyone hears. Let them.

Suddenly, my throat is constricted, his hand tightening its grip. The anger that swells in his eyes should scare me, but it does the opposite. I soften my expression and don't fight against the tears that build in my eyes from the lack of oxygen in my lungs. It happens so quickly, and I let it. Let him use me to feel the emotions he's been denying himself since he was attacked. Maybe longer than that.

I'm a willing servant to his needs. Trust is the footing of every relationship, and I have never trusted anyone the way I do Noah.

"Want to lock you up somewhere and keep you safe," he spits.

Unable to speak, I simply cup his face and hold his stare, letting him take and take from me. Harsh slaps fill the room with each snap of his hips. My vision shudders, and then he's releasing me, letting me gulp breath after breath as a sharp pressure grows against my clit.

"Let me keep you safe from this," he begs.

"I can't."

He grits his teeth and twists my clit, eliciting a cry from me that's impossible to muffle. I barrel into an orgasm with no chance of stopping it. It sweeps me under, and I sink beneath the weight of it, drowning in ecstasy. When his thrusts turn savage before beginning to slow, I feel his warmth fill me and grow weak against him.

"Please, Tinsley." They're deep, exhausted words.

Tears burn my eyes. This time, a lack of oxygen isn't the reason behind them. I want to tell him that I'll do what he wants me to. But I won't lie to him again. I will never forgive myself for what happened to him, but I can try and make up for it. That starts with our plan and my part in it.

I pull his face closer, until we're breathing each other's air, and then whisper, "I love you."

Pain fills his eyes and travels across his face. I feel that same pain travel between us and crawl inside my chest, making a home for itself there.

He stills, still buried deep and throbbing, and sucks in a deep inhale.

"I am *never* letting you go. I will follow you into the afterlife if that's what it takes, but you're never spending a day in this world or any other without me. We're bound together. I know you know that. We're forever. *Inseparable*." His fingers climb up my neck and trace the lines and curves of my face. As if he doesn't already have them memorized. "Remember these words when you're risking everything."

NH)

FRESHLY SHOWERED and in clean clothes, I park my ass at the top of the bed and watch Noah tie a pair of sweatpants around his waist. Of course, they're grey, as if I needed to get horny while I'm sore between my legs. Each shift of my body has me aching, the feel of him still lingering. It's incredibly sexy, albeit a bit annoying.

"You chose those pants on purpose," I accuse.

He arches a brow at me before stalking toward the black guitar beside the bed. Excitement swells in my belly as I watch him pick it up and move to the bed.

"Just grabbed the first pair of pants I found."

I roll my eyes. "Liar."

"Do you want me to play for you or not?"

"Oh, I do. Very, very much. Give me the private Noah Hutton experience."

"Only for you," he replies while getting comfortable beside me.

Bending his right leg, he rests the body of the guitar against his stomach and grips the neck. It's a second nature position for him, and I don't dare speak as he begins to tune the strings and quickly dives into a melody that I recognize on the first note.

I rest my chin on his shoulder and watch the graceful movements of his fingers across the strings. The familiar rasp of his voice fills the room, bringing a much-needed sense of temporary peace to our lives.

"Golden Girl" flows seamlessly into another song, the one without a title. Two words appear in my mind, but I'm not sure enough about them to voice them out loud as a potential title. Instead, I focus on the lyrics and notes and the story they tell.

I don't need to give it a title to know it's about me—*us*. Our story and forever love.

When the time comes, it won't be just Noah's declaration from earlier that I'll remember. It'll be these lyrics and the piece of his soul that he put inside of them.

46

Tinsley

MY MOM SETS A BOWL OF RED JELL-O AND WHIPPED CREAM ON THE table in front of me. I stare at it and shake my head, grinning as she pulls out the chair beside me and sits.

"I'm not a little girl anymore, you know," I tease, poking the centre of whipped cream with a spoon.

"You'll always be my little girl." She rests her elbow on the table and drops her chin to her palm. When I make no move to eat the Jell-O right away, she sighs. "Just let me baby you for a bit right now. Eat it."

I dig the spoon into the jiggly red mass and slice through a section before bringing it to my mouth. Once I've swallowed it, I poke my tongue out at her.

"Happy?"

Her grin is blinding. "Yes."

"How did you have time to make this, anyway? I only told you I was coming a few minutes ago." As I was driving home from a workout at the gym with Noah tailing me in his car.

His worry has grown to a near-suffocating level, and it led me home in need of a breather. I love that he's so protective of me, but I won't allow myself to continue to feel helpless because of some freak. I knew Noah wouldn't follow me inside my parents' house if he didn't absolutely need to, so here I am.

After learning about Cole and his past with my parents, I've been wanting to see Mom. To talk to her about this. But she can't be involved, and that puts a massive boulder in my path. I'm trying to work around it right now, but I don't know how. How am I supposed to pretend a man who once terrorized her hasn't now moved on to do the same to me? At a far larger scale.

"It's the premade stuff," she admits, waving away her pinkening cheeks.

I smile softly before eating another spoonful. "Thank you. It still beats the Jell-O they had at the hospital."

"How is Noah doing?"

"For only being back home for one day, I'd say he's doing really well. Hasn't popped his stitches yet, so that's a small win."

She laughs while tucking her hair behind her ears. It's the same brown colour as mine but much thicker. We've always looked similar. Silvery-grey eyes, brown hair, the same swoop of our noses and dip in our chins. She used to call me her mini-me, and I loved the nickname because it meant she liked our similarities as much as I did. I'm sure she only stopped calling me that because I grew into my own person. Sometimes, I miss it.

My mother is a woman I've looked up to my entire life. She's strong, fearless, outgoing. A successful businesswoman, kick-ass mother, loving wife. She wears so many hats that I used to wonder how her neck didn't hurt from the weight of all of them.

I never knew much about her struggles in life before I was born. Easton and I were both told about the broken relationship between her and our grandparents when we were young, but that was it. I guess it makes sense for her not to tell us about a creep from her past who everyone thought had been dealt with. It may be unfair, but I can't help but wish that she had.

"I thought your father was going to collapse when Noah called him," she says.

"Collapse from fear or happiness?"

She frowns. "That's not funny."

"I'm not trying to be funny. You know how Dad feels about him."

"He loves Noah. He's as close to family as anyone can be outside of blood. That cold front your father places in front of himself when Noah's around is simply because he's protective of you. He worries you'll get your heart broken because of how deeply you love that boy. For decades, it's been that way. Your father doesn't understand when to let go when it comes to you."

How long has she known that I love him? Before I did?

"Dad doesn't need to let go. He just needs to drop that *cold front*, as you call it. It comes off as mean, and it hurts my feelings when I see the way it affects Noah, even if you all can't notice that it does the way I can," I argue, stabbing my spoon into the Jell-O. It bounces in the bowl, and I exhale a heavy breath.

She rubs my back in small, soft circles. "I know, my love. You're right. And there's still time for that. It will all work itself out."

"Do you really believe that, or are you just trying to make me feel better?"

Her laugh sounds like home. "I truly believe that, Tinsley."

"Then I'll try to believe it too."

"How are *you* doing?"

"I'm okay," I lie.

She sees right through me. "Tinsley."

"How should I be doing? I haven't stopped feeling guilty for five minutes about what happened to Noah. We all know he was only attacked because of me. What if he had—" I cut myself off, unable to say it as I stare at the table.

Mom leans forward and touches my chin, urging me to look at her when I refuse. When I do, I wish I hadn't. I don't want anyone's sympathy. I want revenge. Blood spilt. I've never felt such anger. It threatens to choke me.

"You'll forgive yourself. I'm not going to tell you that you shouldn't feel guilty because that won't help you. It's not that easy. Feel that guilt until it dies out inside of you. But don't let it burn you alive."

"I won't," I promise, unable to give anything more than that.

There's a moment of silence before she asks, "Have you heard anything from the police yet?"

I fight off a nervous swallow. "It's only been two days."

"I know. I'm just hopeful, that's all. You know how I get. I worry about you."

"I'm sure we'll hear something from them within a couple of days." The lie sounds guilty even to my own ears. I pray she can't hear it too.

It won't be the police taking care of Cole; it will be us. Me, Noah, and Alec—a new, surprising ally. Dad has a small part to play, but it's enough that I feel disgustingly guilty for him having to lie to Mom. It feels like a criminal offense to lie to her about this. Especially knowing her history with my stalker. *It's better this way*, I remind myself. If she doesn't know what's truly happening, we can protect her from the pain of it.

"I hope so. It's so unfair for this to be happening to you. Look at you—you're my beautiful, happy, successful daughter who's out in the world living her dream. I want this person to pay for threatening to take that away from you," she declares.

I let her anger find mine as it grows stronger, potent in the air.

"Me too, Mom."

We'll make him pay for what he did to her, to Noah, and to me. He'll pay for his actions over and over again until he can't anymore. Until we've broken him so deeply it will be impossible for him to put himself back together again.

LETTING a man like Alec into our home feels an awful lot like welcoming a wolf into a fox's den. If the fox's den already had its own wolfish bodyguard on retainer.

The new relationship between Noah and Alec is dangerous yet fragile at the same time. Like glass before it shatters into shards sharp enough to flay skin. I find myself holding my breath when they're in the same room, anticipating the first blow.

It's been two days since Alec waltzed in with his plans for how to handle Cole. Two days of waiting to enact such plans. Of staring at the blocked number on my phone that I won't ever forget belongs to Cole, trying to get myself to just unblock it and get a move on. I don't want to need someone involved with this outside of Noah, but Alec wants the same thing we do, and he has the means to get us there. Even if I don't trust a damn thing about him outside of that.

"You're a boxer, right?" Alec asks me, his voice smooth as warm butter.

"Yes."

With a slow drag of his eyes, he looks at Noah sitting beside me on the couch. "And you're in a boy band?"

"Do you intend to play twenty questions with us all night, or are you finally ready to get this fucking done with?" Noah asks between clenched teeth.

Alec clicks his tongue to the roof of his mouth. "Didn't your daddy ever teach you about patience?"

"He was too busy teaching me not to talk to strangers. Imagine if I had used those lessons the day you barged into my hospital room. You'd still be looking for Cole behind dumpsters and crack houses," Noah remarks.

Alec smirks, but it's deceptive. The kind of smirk I've seen a million times on Noah's face in the company of someone he can't stand. "I love when you get feisty. It turns me on."

"Okay, that's enough," I interrupt. If we don't do this soon, I worry I'll lose my confidence and chicken out. I'll never admit that to anyone, though. "Can I text him now?"

The arm Noah has wrapped tightly around my upper back flexes. Alec drapes his large body over my new fuzzy black armchair and nods.

"Have at it."

Suddenly, the weight of what we're about to do crashes into me. My fingers begin to shake as I swipe open my phone and find the blocked number already loaded and ready.

Long, tattooed fingers wrap around my wrist, steadying me. I swing my gaze from Noah's hand over mine to the man himself. Dark eyes are already waiting. I fall into the depths of them, my breaths shallow.

"Do you want me to do it?" he asks, and I know he doesn't just mean the texting. He means all of it. Every part I'm set to play tonight.

"No."

His brows slide down toward his eyes. "You're shaking."

"I'm terrified," I admit, quiet enough I know Alec won't be able to hear.

The fingers around my wrist flex, Noah's control growing thin. "So don't do this. Let me take care of it. Take care of you."

"You always take care of me."

"I was born to do that."

I shake my head, my stare intense. "You were born for so much more than that, Noah."

"You're wrong, Golden Girl."

Stubbornness may be a Hutton trait, but it's also a Lowry one.

"I'm going to do this with you. You're not the only one of us who was born to take care of the other."

He closes his eyes and leans in, touching my brow with his. "Do you believe in soulmates, baby?"

I brush my mouth across his. "From the moment I first saw you."

He tugs the phone from my hand, and I let him. Dropping my eyes between us, I watch as he unblocks Cole's number and opens a text conversation. My chest grows tight when he offers it back to me, nodding slightly.

"Ruin him, Tinsley."

I type the message and send it before I have the chance to change my mind.

> Me: It's time to officially meet. Or are you too scared to step out of the shadows?

47

Noah

EVEN WITH MY EYES OPEN, I SEE HIS SHADOWED FACE IN THE DARK pits of my subconscious. The sick twist of his lips before he spit blood into my face. I feel the hot brand of the knife in my side and the brutal twist of the blade when he yanked it free. Each memory is another reason to end his pathetic life. He sealed his fate the moment he began to watch her. When he grew to want her.

I will get answers from him tonight to every single one of my questions. He'll tell me even when he's choking on his own blood. I won't have it any other way.

Tinsley's phone is in my palm, her brief conversation with Cole illuminating the dark cab of the car. The headlights and radio are off. Only the air conditioning blows, but it does little to cool me. Sweat drips down my spine and between my brows. I'm vibrating, anticipation so thick in my blood it could clot my veins.

> Unknown: Tell me when and where. I'll be there.

> Unknown: I want to see just you. Leave him behind.

Tinsley: Okay.

Then she sent him a location and ended the conversation despite his following messages. The ones I deleted just as quickly as they came in.

The building in front of us is still under construction, but the sign on the front was hung recently. Knockout Fitness. One of the newer Lowry boxing gym expansions.

"The alarms are off. Tinsley has the keys. Try not to burn it to the ground," Braden warns from the back seat.

He's leaning forward between the two front seats, one hand on each headrest. I can almost smell the fear wafting off him. It's not a misplaced emotion. He has reason to be scared tonight.

"Thank you, Dad." Tinsley turns to face him. She squeezes his hand and kisses his cheek. "Go home and be with Mom."

I watch him from the rear-view mirror. The heaviness in his eyes is unusual for him. It tugs at his mouth and makes him appear older. He's not used to having information withheld from him, and his daughter and I are keeping too many secrets. It's blind faith and a shared want for revenge that had him agreeing to let us use his gym. If everything goes to plan, we won't be here for long. No blood will be spilt on his floors. But it's a safe space for Tinsley. Somewhere she can feel in control meeting her stalker for the first time.

He must have some idea of what we're going to do tonight, but he hasn't shared those ideas. I wouldn't confirm them if he had. We're going to do what the police wouldn't dare do to Cole unless they were paid to do so. The money that would take isn't worth losing the opportunity to be the one to punish him. Prison isn't enough. It never will be.

"I love you, sweetheart. Call me when you're finished here. Or before. If you need anything, I'll be by my phone."

"I will. I love you too."

Heaving a sigh, he nods once and then smooths a firm hand down her hair before pushing open the back door. He lingers with one foot outside. Our eyes catch in the mirror. "Take care of her, Noah. I'm trusting you with her tonight. Don't make me regret it."

"I'll always take care of her," I reply.

His throat bobs. "And keep yourself safe. My heart can't take finding you like that again."

Silence. My brows furrow, confusion slashing through me. Is he concerned for me? It sounds wrong.

"We'll take care of each other, Dad," Tinsley says, covering for me.

He holds my stare for a beat longer before accepting her answer and stepping into the night. The back door shuts softly. I watch him walk to his car parked behind mine, not looking away until he gets in and starts the engine. A minute later, he pulls up beside us, casting one last look at his daughter before driving away.

"I hate lying to everyone," Tinsley whispers.

I set her phone in the centre console and pull mine free from my pocket. The first message on the screen is from my dad, the second from Mom.

Dad: Can I see you tomorrow? Maybe we can go for lunch, just the two of us. Be careful tonight, please. I love you.

Mom: Your dad insisted on staying in Toronto for a couple of extra nights! What is that about? Call me in the morning, my love. xoxo

I don't like the small swirl of emotion in my stomach as I read their messages. It feels uncomfortable. I've always found it hard to be guilty about anything. It's one of my many flaws. Got me in trouble my entire life. But this new emotion has to be guilt. It's biting, unrelenting. Similar to the feeling of regret I get when I upset Tinsley.

Soft fingertips stroke the skin around my elbow. "You should reply to them."

"Should I feel guilty lying to my parents?" I ask.

"Do you?"

"I feel weird," I admit.

She moves her touch down my arm to my hand and then holds it. When she pulls our joined hands to her lap, I shift closer to the console. I don't need light to find her beautiful face in the dark. She's the only thing I can see.

"Well, I know that I feel guilty. I have rocks in my belly just thinking about having to lie to them. They grow heavier and heavier when I actually do, though. Tonight is no different. It feels wrong, but at the same time, it's the right thing to do. It wouldn't surprise me if you're feeling the same way. Especially because you and your dad have just started connecting again. You aren't lying to him, really, but you're keeping him in the dark. We both are," she explains without judgment.

I roll her words over in my mind. Her explanation is a good one. It makes that biting sensation in my stomach dull slightly.

"It's almost time," I note, not wanting to talk about myself any longer.

Tinsley accepts my change of subject. "It is."

"Are you ready?"

"No."

I'm not ready to let her go either. I glare at the building across the street, wishing it would go up in flames despite Braden's warning. She needs to be inside before Cole shows up. It will give her the upper hand.

Alec is here too. I can't see him, but I can sense he's close by. It's a warning in my head. The one I get whenever he's around.

Two apex predators have never been able to coexist in the same herd. We're on borrowed time. I want him gone and out of our lives by the end of the night.

"I'll be outside. You won't be alone with him for long. Once he lowers his guard, we'll be there," I promise her while picking back up her phone and calling my number. I answer, connecting the call that will allow me to hear everything said between the two of them inside.

She takes it from me and shimmies it into the pocket of her jeans. "I can protect myself. I'll be good until you come in."

"That's my golden girl. He's worthless compared to you."

She nods, but it's stiff. I give our hands a tug, and her body follows, resting over the console. Cupping her jaw, I pull her face close until our noses bump. She smells like the shot of whiskey she took before we left home mixed with her perfume. I take a lungful of the scent and let loose a quiet moan before kissing her.

My cock strains behind the wall of my jeans at the hard kiss. I'm fucked up enough to want to take her before she goes inside. To have her meet Cole with *my* cum leaking from her swollen, used pussy. Would he be able to smell me on her? See her puffy lips and know it was me who just fed on them?

Our kisses grow desperate, a feral tinge to them that only we can ever understand. We're about to do this together. Side by side, we'll eliminate the current threat to her.

She's just as excited to make Cole beg for mercy as I am. To see the life bleed from his eyes as he cries for a miracle that only we can grant him.

My twin flame.

The other half of my soul. My perfect match. I should have known this side of her was there, buried deep down, crying out for me to uncover it. I'm ashamed it took me so long to feed life into it again.

"You're mine, Tinsley," I groan into her mouth. "Never his."

"Yours," she sighs, swiping her tongue along the seam of my lips.

My beast roars in outrage when I pull my mouth from hers. Its control has been shredded to ribbons over the past few days. The power that comes from his outrage burns at the edges of my very core. I promise him that I'll satiate his need for his queen when we're finished tonight. He's about to meet the monster that hides inside of her, and it might be too much for me to handle without losing my mind.

"Go before I keep you in this car. I'll be listening." The words claw at my throat so deep I should taste blood.

A new confidence flares in her eyes. My cock throbs in answer to it.

"I'll see you soon," she answers.

Without lingering any longer, she undoes her seat belt and climbs out of my car. I can't look away from her. The confident sway of her hips as she crosses the street and prowls toward the front door of Knockout Fitness is intoxicating. That's my fucking girl, afraid of nothing.

Only after she's used her father's key to get inside do I drop my gaze to the phone in my lap. Her previous words flow through my head, urging me to open the conversation with my dad.

Me: *Lunch is fine.*

I send the message and type one out to Alec.

Me: *She's inside. Don't mess this up like all of the other times you've gotten this close to him.*

Alec: *Don't worry, Scowls. There won't be a next time after tonight.*

I drop my phone and reach behind my head to tighten the tie of my bandana while I stare at the front of the gym. The countdown has begun, Tinsley's call silent. It's up to her now.

NH)

Tinsley

THE HEAVY DOORS of Knockout slam shut behind me when I step inside. It's so silent in the empty building that my footsteps echo, each one as loud as a thunderclap in the night. I try to ignore that thought and focus on getting a light turned on. The moment I reach the switch and fill the front room with light, it doesn't seem quite as scary.

I wander around the gym for the first time in weeks. It's so different from when I was here last. Construction has finished, and all that seems left to do are the floors and the finishing touches. It feels wrong to bring Cole here. To taint the new space with poison. But it was the first place that came to mind. It's somewhere I know. A place I feel powerful.

I'm a boxer. I grew up in the original Knockout Fitness. This may only be a replica of that place, but the strength I grew to harness in that place still ripples through me here. Cole won't have the upper hand. I will.

As the minutes tick by, I wait for him. Some of my confidence ebbs away in exchange for paranoia the longer I stand in the centre of the gym. I feel exposed, each exhale sounding more and more hollow. I'm about to take my phone out to ask Noah if he's noticed anyone outside when the door rattles.

My blood runs cold. Sweat collects at the base of my spine.

I thought I was ready for this, but when the first foreign footstep clunks on the cement floor behind me, I freeze. Fear shackles me. My breathing shallows, a relentless tightness sawing at my chest.

Squeezing my eyes shut, I curl my fingers into my palms and steel my spine. I dive for the images in my memory of Noah in that hospital bed and the gut-wrenching worry I felt when I got the call he had been hurt. The stolen panties, the photo of me and Noah with that harsh red X across it. I remember it all.

Physically, I'm on my own right now. But Noah's listening from my pocket, ready to come running in at the first tell of something going wrong.

Letting that calm me even the slightest bit, I force myself to turn and face Cole when the door slams shut. I've seen him before. More than once. I heard his voice backstage at Noah's show when he was asked to sign that woman's chest and saw him at the tattoo shop and on that pixelated security footage. But this time is different than all the others.

Suddenly, fear is the last emotion rolling inside of me. A

vicious anger swells, filling me from the bottom up. Even as it threatens to choke me, I embrace it.

Bile burns my stomach when he smiles at me beneath the shadow of his hood. It takes every ounce of my willpower not to send him soaring back through the door, a dent the size and shape of my fist in his face.

Instead, I paint on a timid smile and swipe my palms on my thighs, embracing the part I have to play.

"Hi."

48

Tinsley

COLE TAKES A STAGGERED STEP FORWARD, AS IF HE CAN'T HELP BUT get closer. My skin crawls as my feet grow heavier, anchoring me in place. The haunting shade of blue in his eyes remains as unsettling now as it was the first time I saw him. He watches me with a heady sense of recognition and familiarity.

"Hello, Tiny," he says. Disgust coils in my gut as I recognize the thick sense of desire in his voice.

I push that feeling deep down and lock it away. A mask slips over my face, transforming me into someone entirely new. A persona I can't wait to set fire to once this is over.

"I was nervous you changed your mind and didn't want to meet." My bottom lip slips into a pout.

"No! No, no. I just wanted to make sure it was safe. For you," he rushes out.

"That was really sweet of you. Thank you for doing that for me . . ." I trail off, raising my fingertips to my lips. "I still don't know your name."

He grins, and years ago, it might have been a handsome smile. But now, it's nothing more than a glimpse of crooked, yellowing teeth hidden behind thick facial hair.

"Cole. My name is Cole. And it's my job to protect you. Always."

"It's nice to officially meet you, Cole. It's been a long time coming, hasn't it?"

He rocks forward on the balls of his feet as he nods. "You look beautiful. I love that colour on you."

"This?" I pinch the blue blouse between my fingertips and flutter my lashes. It's a silky material, the colour as similar as possible to the panties he stole from me. "I knew you'd like it."

He takes my words as an invitation to boldly check me out, his wide eyes roaming up and down my body. I hide my discomfort behind a sultry smile.

"I do. You've always looked best in blue."

I take a risk and ask, "When was the first time you saw me in it?"

"You have questions," he sighs.

"Can you blame me for that? You've hidden from me, and I'm curious as to why."

He shakes his head, edging closer. When he stills, we're less than three feet apart. I catch a whiff of him, and it takes every ounce of my self-control not to gag. Up close, he's even scarier than I anticipated. The heat radiating off him intensifies my discomfort, given my already alarming body temperature.

A dark voice murmurs in my mind, pleading with me to take advantage of the proximity and wrap my fingers around his throat. If this were a normal situation, I would have been terrified of myself for thinking this way. But this isn't normal, and I'm not fully myself. Instead, I tell that voice to be patient.

"I couldn't risk your parents seeing me. They would have kept us apart. And that friend of yours, he was always there when your family wasn't, guarding you like a dog. A *mutt*," he spits. As I keep my mouth shut, his expression lightens again. A switch flips in his mind. "But I was always there. I've been here, watching and waiting for you your entire life. You've grown into such a magnificent woman, Tinsley. So beautiful."

He extends a long, bony finger toward my ear, tracing its curve. My mask remains firmly in place. His words have done far more than disgust me. They've confirmed that he never left Toronto. He's been waiting for decades.

"Why would my parents have kept us apart? I'm sure they would have seen how perfect we are for each other," I argue.

"Your father would never approve of me."

"Why not? Because of our age difference?" I feign ignorance.

His frown is so deep that I half expect the lines of it to start to bleed. "I was reckless when I was your age. I knew your parents then. Thought your mother was meant for me. Your father wouldn't allow that and attacked me for pursuing her. I lost everything because of it, but still, I couldn't let her go, even then. She was pregnant with you. Once they brought you home, I knew I had to stick around. Watch over you. It was just this feeling in my gut. You believe me, right?" He thumps his fist into his chest.

"Of course I do."

"Good. Good. I regret waiting so long. If I had introduced myself sooner, you wouldn't have left with Noah. Wouldn't have let him *touch* you." His words grow in volume, each one filling with more and more venom. "I could tell you didn't want him that way. He's forced you to be with him and to fear me! You can admit that to me, Tiny. I'll always believe you. It's why I tried to get rid of him! Nobody else believed you when you told them that!"

Pain surges through my chest. I see the man who dug that knife into the man that I love. Who tried to snuff the light out of his eyes and take him from me. Nobody is allowed to take Noah from me. *Nobody.*

"You're right. He did. I'm so grateful for you." I taste the bile in my throat. Each word burns. Lie after lie after lie. "He was standing in the way of us."

His head nods frantically in agreement, a manic, proud smile stretching across his face. The space that separates us vanishes when he pulls me against him, taking my shiver of repulsion for one of desire. He groans in my ear, drawing in a deep breath of my scent.

"Even the smell of your cunt can't come close to the way you smell right now. I can't get enough."

The mask I wear threatens to shatter under the weight of my fury. I close my eyes, allowing him to believe he has power over me. His cold fingers trace my waist and move downward, his heated breath assaulting my face.

Tension coils within me when he presses his crotch to my middle and his hard dick grinds into me, but I steady myself. He doesn't truly have any power over me. I'm stronger than him, smarter too. I'm in this position because I'm allowing it. Every single one of his rough touches is happening in an attempt to give him a false sense of safety. To avoid even the slightest possibility that he could escape us and continue to terrorize everyone that steps foot in his path.

Had he not evaded Alec for so long, I wouldn't have been so concerned with him slipping past us. But his unpredictability makes him dangerous.

I swallow and set my hands on his hips. He digs his groin into me harder and exhales a pleasured noise when he notices my touch, but I shove that into a locked box in my mind, never to be revisited again. Dragging my fingers over the front of his dirty jeans in search of a weapon before doing the same to his back side, I stumble over the hard object in his back left pocket. A knife like the one that hurt Noah, I assume.

Something white-hot tears through my chest and paints my vision red. *Pain*. It's a pain so deep and powerful the world around me blurs into a distant, hazy backdrop. I have no choice but to surrender to it as I gasp for a relief that seems agonizingly out of reach.

Feeling the ridges of the same object responsible for Noah's injury is enough to have me tearing the invisible mask from my face. Cole's oblivious to my search while grinding into me, desire blocking his senses. I'm grateful for that.

In one quick movement, I pull the switchblade from his pocket and flick it open, taking in the mix of shock and betrayal that morphs his features when I press the tip to his side and push it in just enough to pierce the skin.

"Fuck!" he howls. His first instinct is to push away from me, and I let him, watching as he stumbles backward half a step, his jaw gaping as adrenaline tells him he's okay, but the cold burn surrounding the blade does the opposite.

The weak punch to my jaw comes faster than I anticipated as I push the blade deeper into his side and thrust my hand upward, tearing through his muscle the way he did Noah's. Warm, sticky blood flows over my fingers. I pull the knife out of his side and push my body back, managing to dodge his next hit.

"Why would you do that?" he cries, diverting his attention to where he's bleeding and pressing his palm against the wet material of his shirt.

"Why?" I choke out, my voice dripping with venom. My grip on the knife handle is weak, his blood making it slippery. "You are a delusional, crazy bastard! There is something so, so wrong with you. I'd never want anything to do with you, you psychopath. I want you dead for what you did to Noah. That wound is only a small taste of what we're going to do to you tonight."

For the first time in my entire life, I think I feel true, undiluted fear when his hurt morphs into something dark. I stagger back and find myself enveloped in an overwhelming sense of dread. He seems to forget about the pain he's in and instead focuses on the pain he wishes to bring me for this display of rejection.

On reflex, I duck to the right when his fingers flex and he shoots a hand in my direction. My jaw still throbs from his hit earlier, even if it was a weak one. The wound in his left side is dripping blood onto the cement, but it's not enough for me. I want it gushing, draining his veins.

"You have to make everything so hard, Tinsley," he chastises me, following each step back I take with one forward.

"I didn't do anything. You did. You did all of this. I know what you did to my mom. Know that my dad beat your ass in an alleyway because of it. You were supposed to leave, but instead, you fixated on me. A child!"

Disgust fills his eyes, turning them a wicked blue. "I didn't want you as a child. That came after, once I saw the woman you became with age. Your mother was nothing more than a mule carrying you for me. I see that now. We're meant to be together. Why can't *you* see that?"

The door is still shut behind him. Noah's absence is a distraction. He should be here by now, seeking retribution for the damage this man has caused the both of us.

I hold the knife in front of my chest, somewhere Cole can't help but notice it. "No. We're not. You're nothing more than a low-life creep who gets off on watching from the shadows, but today, that ends."

"It doesn't end when you say it does, Tinsley. That's not your decision to make," he growls.

My laugh is bitter. "I'm not alone in wanting you gone, Cole."

"What are you talking about?"

"You shouldn't have touched Noah. Not only did you do a terrible job of keeping him from me, but you drew the attention of someone who's been looking for you for a long while now." I pin him beneath a brave glare and watch as he digs into my words, digesting them. "You think you know me, but you don't. Not even in the slightest. If you did, you'd know that I'd do anything for Noah and that he'd do anything for me. You can't keep us apart, even in death. But now . . . you're going to pay for the damage you've caused."

Cole curls his lip and darts his hand out in front of him in an attempt to grab my face. His nails sink into my chin before I dart out of the way. He's too slow, his adrenaline beginning to lull. With a wince, he blinks hard and sways on his feet.

"You're meant for me!" he bellows, his voice wavering as it echoes through the gym. So absorbed in his emotions, he fails to notice the door flinging open, and two tall figures stalk inside. My stomach soars at the sight of Noah. "I *will* have you. Everything I've done has to be worth it!"

Noah's voice is low and chilling. "The only thing you'll have when I'm finished with you is my name on your bloody lips, Cole." He approaches us, each step deliberate and commanding.

The moment he sees the growing pool of blood on the concrete beside Cole, his eyes lock onto me, flickering with approval. I want to run to him, want to bury my face in his chest and let him take me far from here, but we're not finished yet.

When Cole lunges at Noah, I act before thinking. Any semblance of control I've clung to evaporates at the thought of him hurting Noah again. I refuse to witness him in pain again at the hands of Cole. We collide, and Cole's voice rings out, a mix of surprise and agony, before we crash to the ground, him pinned beneath me.

Finally, I allow the dark voice in my mind to control me. I wrap my fingers around Cole's throat, lifting his head only to slam it back down. I dig my nails into his skin and grin when he grips my wrist and slaps at my face, fighting me for breath.

Fear dilates his eyes. The sight is enthralling. I lean down, hovering my face above his and whisper, "Don't. Ever. Touch. Him. Again."

49

Noah

IN JUST FIVE WORDS, I'M RENDERED POWERLESS. NOTHING BUT A meat suit for my beast as he pushes toward my consciousness and attempts to take control.

Tinsley is a dark angel. Her beauty might be one of the greatest wonders of this pathetic world, but it pales in comparison to how magnificent her soul is. Something no one dead or alive would ever be worthy of worshipping. It's bright yet dark. Soft yet hard. The perfect push and pull between good and evil. Right and wrong.

Yet, despite all of that, she's mine.

I get to worship her every moment of every day. She protects *me*. Loves *me*. Would risk everything for *me*. In the exact same ways that I would for her.

I've never been prouder of her than in this moment, watching as she chokes the life out of the man who terrorized her and attempted to force us apart. She's vicious, fucking lethal in the way she grins while squeezing his throat, turning his face blue from the lack of oxygen. I should tell her to stop, but my lips are sealed shut. It feels like a waste to stop her now. I'm enjoying the view far too much. *So proud of her.*

"Enough. Let him go," Alec commands, towering above Cole's head, staring down at him with cold eyes.

Tinsley digs her fingers deeper into Cole, and he chokes a plea through dry lips. "No."

"Get her off of him before I remove her myself." The words are spoken to me. A hard demand that has me coiling inward.

I take a protective step toward Tinsley, casting a shadow over her. "Touch her and it'll be my nails in *your* throat. I don't play with my food the way Tinsley does."

"Get her off. Now. Or was it always your intention to christen this building with a murder? I'm sure her father would give you his blessing, then."

The reminder of not only her family but also where we are has her snapping out of her blood lust. Fingers flying from where their nails left deep, blooming red crescents in Cole's throat, Tinsley shoots off his body. She crashes into my chest, shaking from head to toe, but not from fear. Something entirely different.

Instinctively, I wrap her in my arms, but instead of hiding her face in my chest, she twists in my grip and faces the scene, wanting to be a part of this. I want to force her to face me so I can look her over. The call was so muffled it was hard to make out specifics of anything more than words before we rushed inside. If this piece of shit hurt her . . .

But with adrenaline running rampant in her system, she's nearly rabid, desperate to watch what comes next, so I let it go. For now.

She doesn't even flinch when Alec hauls Cole up onto his feet, gripping his hair to make their faces level. The way she shudders in my grasp makes me believe she likes to see him suffer, bleeding onto the floor. *Fuck.*

"We've been looking for you for far too long, Cole. It's grown tiresome," Alec says.

At the sight of the inked designs on Alec's forearms, all traces of colour seep from Cole's face. A foul scent fills the air. My gaze shifts downward to find a damp patch expanding on his pants, trailing along his inner thighs. Alec notices, too, and crinkles his nose. "We've barely begun, and you're already pissing all over yourself. At least try to make this interesting for us all."

"I—I know wh—who you a—are," Cole stutters.

His knees are visibly shaking. He's so weak Alec must be keeping him upright by his hair. It's a wonder he hasn't ripped it from the roots yet.

Alec's smile is cheek splitting. "Good. I've always hated introductions."

"Stop playing with him. I'm tired of waiting," I grunt, twisting my fingers in Tinsley's hair, urging her head back so I can bury my nose in her hair. My cock is throbbing against her back, and fuck me, she pushes back into it, accepting every twisted part of me.

"Let's go, then," Alec whispers in Cole's ear before spinning them both and shoving Cole in front of him. The moment he releases his hair, the scum is crashing to the floor, his knees hitting the cement so hard they crack.

He cries out, and Alec laughs, the dark pitch of it swirling around us like smoke. Tinsley jolts in my arms, and when I glance down at her, she's fixated on Cole's hands, splayed on the concrete, supporting his weight.

It's not the hands she's focused on but the mangled mess of knuckles on his right hand. He's using what strength is left in his arms to hold himself up off the ground. His elbows are locked, and his head hangs between his shoulders.

My golden girl slips from my grasp, moving to stand beside Alec. I grind my molars, keeping my mouth shut.

Alec sends her a long, smirking glance, giving her space as she steps up in front of Cole. Her silver eyes narrow on his pathetic stance. The power swelling in her expression is a sight to behold.

"My father is responsible for the state of that hand, right?" she asks, though we all know the answer.

Cole doesn't speak. The anguish stretching his features answers for him. He feels betrayed by her. Delusional doesn't begin to describe what is wrong with him. *Sick* is closer. *Perverted* is even better.

"My mom deserved better than what you put her through."

I inch closer, wanting to be at her side when she loses control once again. Fucking *needing* to.

"I won't make the same mistake my father did by letting you go and giving you a chance to change the way you live your life." The emotion in her voice is quickly overrun by pure, spitting rage as she looks down on him. "There is no changing you. You are a pathetic, broken excuse of a man who never deserved to live a day on this earth."

A stifled cry spreads his lips before a sickening crunch sings through the air. One by one, Tinsley crushes his fingers beneath her shoes, snapping bone and cartilage. I'm moving quickly when I hear the first of his vocal cries. I tear a thick strip from his shirt and shove it into his mouth, muffling any noise that could potentially have us filling a jail cell alongside him.

"You could have done that once we were no longer in a place so public," Alec half-assedly chastises her.

She ignores him, hovering her foot over Cole's wrist bone, about to press down when I grip her arm, tugging her back.

"Not here," I murmur.

Flashing me her pupil-blown gaze, she jerks her head in a nod and sets her foot back on the cement. Without sparing another look at us, she starts for the back door and snaps, "I'll be in the car."

We don't hesitate to collect Cole's broken body and follow after her. My headlights flash in the alleyway behind the gym, where I hid it before coming inside, and I catch a glimpse of Tinsley sliding into the passenger seat. Alec releases a muted chuckle, doing something that elicits a pained whimper from Cole.

"Seems you picked the wrong girl, buddy. She'd do well in

Crimson Bay," he tells him. As he maneuvers around me, dragging Cole with him, he adds, "So would you, Scowls."

"Crimson Bay sounds like a fucking make-believe city," I mutter.

He shoves Cole the rest of the distance to the car, and we watch as he topples over the trunk, his forehead slamming into the paint. "Been saying that for years."

"Are you finally going to tell me what Cole stole from you?" I ask.

With the hand not holding Cole to the car, Alec tugs a handful of zip ties from his back pocket and shoves them at my chest. "Help me restrain him. We don't need you somehow escaping again, do we?" He thrusts his palm into the back of Cole's head, propelling his forehead toward the trunk again.

I take a black zip tie and hand back the rest. "You didn't answer my question."

I've never zip-tied anyone before, but it's simple enough. Cole's broken fingers are a horror to look at, and I enjoy that too much. He howls into the fabric between his lips when I use them to pull his hands together, tightly binding them without cutting into his wrists.

Alec steps back and hauls Cole off the trunk before I pop it open. The car dips as we force Cole inside, sealing him in.

"Contraband. Worth a fortune," Alec finally divulges. "He didn't know he stole from us at the time, but it doesn't matter. We aren't the forgiving type,' Alec finally says. Feeding me what he thinks will be enough information to placate me. He couldn't be more wrong.

"Who is 'we'?"

He dismisses my question with a shake of his head, his tattooed hand gliding over my car as he heads to the back door. It's an expensive car, but he appears unimpressed by it. More questions plague my mind.

"Get in the car, Noah. It's time for you to finish this and take your woman home."

I exhale a long, tight breath and let it go. He opens the door and slides inside, but before he can close the door, I catch Tinsley's waiting stare from the passenger seat. The determination in her eyes is enough to have me slamming Alec's door shut and joining them inside, ready to end this.

NH)

TINSLEY IS the first one out of the car when we pull up outside of a fucking decrepit-looking barn nearly an hour later. I fly out after her, rushing around the hood of the car and reaching her side before she has a chance to take off into the barn on her own.

"Be careful here, Tinsley. I don't even know where we are." The absence of road signs beyond the city limits has left me on edge, a deep-seated distrust churning in my chest.

I take her hands in mine, feeling the obvious shake in them. Bringing them toward me, I rub them over my sternum and trap her stare.

She breathes out softly. "Did you hear everything earlier?"

A possessive, furious roar builds in my chest at the reminder of his sick words and declarations. "Yes."

Dropping my gaze to her rolling lips, I freeze. The shutting of the trunk is muted behind the racing thump in my ears. Our first moment face to face since I let her walk inside the gym alone, and I'm noticing she isn't how I left her. The two deep, bloody gauges on the tip of her chin running along the underside and over her neck make my stomach roll.

Nail marks. From him. On her skin.

Alarm transforms her expression before she's attempting to pull her hands free and step back. To hide those scratches from me.

"I took care of it, Noah," she says.

My brain goes silent, only two words ringing out. One demand.

End him.

Tinsley's voice fills the night behind me, but I've given up control. For the first time in my life, I hand the reins to my darkness and step back, giving it space to wreak havoc.

To do what needs to be done. For her.

Always for her.

 **50**

Tinsley

I FORGOT ABOUT THE SCRATCHES.

I didn't notice if and when they bled. With everything else going on, they seemed insignificant. My first mistake was overlooking them. My second was attempting to hide them from Noah once he locked onto them. All I did was confirm that something was indeed wrong and that he wasn't imagining it.

I never wanted to get in the way of his revenge, but the glaze that slipped over his eyes just now tells me that he's fallen down a hole that he's spent a lifetime avoiding. All because of me.

I've had my fun with Cole. I felt that intoxicating surge of power when I crushed his fingers beneath my foot and filled his eyes with pleas that he wasn't able to speak aloud. My fingers are stained with his blood from when I dipped the blade of his knife into his side, tearing through skin and muscle. It's crusted beneath my nails, splattered over my clothes.

Noah deserves that same feeling of power and retribution for the wrongs committed against him. But not like this, when he's half-crazed and acting out of a need to defend me.

In the blink of an eye, he has Cole out of Alec's arms, dragging him across the gravel surrounding the barn. The field is empty, and we're alone. So, when Cole starts to splutter apologies that we'll never accept, Noah allows it. He doesn't put back in the gag that must have been removed when Alec pulled him out of the trunk.

"You're not a killer," Cole gasps, his probably shattered knees scraping against the stones, leaving a trail of blood behind them.

The bleeding from his side has slowed. It no longer soaks his shirt. Someone must have covered it, and that someone wasn't Noah or me.

"You don't know me," Noah snarls, his gaze unwavering.

"I've watched you for just as long as I've watched Tinsley!"

His stupid, stupid statement has me and Alec both picking up our pace behind them. Noah finds the barn door slightly ajar and shoulders it open wider to drag Cole inside.

When they disappear into the shadows, a knot of anxiety forms in my throat. Alec curses beneath his breath and hurries past me. The gleam of the gun handle he has tucked in the waistband of his jeans causes me to stumble into his back. He whips his head to glare at me before taking in my expression.

Whatever he finds in it has him muttering, "It's not for you. Relax."

I struggle to find words as fear begins to grip me. For both Noah and me and the mess we've caught ourselves in.

But then Cole screams. I'm forced to set aside my thoughts and worries and follow Alec inside without collecting all the answers I want, focused on finding Noah.

The darkness is heavy inside the barn. It floods every corner, keeping all but the centre hidden from view. Moonlight shines through the small cracks between the wooden planks in the ceiling, illuminating a single metal chair that Cole occupies.

His hands are behind his back, but his legs are free. Once I get close enough to get a good look at his knees, it becomes clear that he couldn't use his legs to run even if he tried. They're ripped open, full of gravel and fragments of bone.

"You've seen these before," Noah purrs.

I hear my heartbeat in my ears as I stare at him. Alec slows and blows out a loud, exaggerated breath.

"You brought toys, Scowls," he praises.

Noah ignores him. The moonlight gleams off his knuckles. Off the brass that now wraps around them. I quickly close the distance between us and fold my fingers over the brass knuckles, drawing a hiss from his throat when our skin touches. His muscles are bunched, preparing to strike. I won't tell him to back off, but this plan has never been more important than him.

"I'm right here, Noah. And I'm not afraid of you," I whisper. His expression shudders. "Take your power back."

He searches my eyes for something, seeming to find it a beat later. My confidence in him? My love? Regardless of what it is, it seems to solidify something inside of him.

"I love you," I murmur.

His brown eyes flare, ablaze with unwavering devotion to me. When he speaks, his words steal my every thought.

"I love you, Golden Girl."

Frozen with disbelief, I go limp as he lifts our hands to his mouth. He presses a ragged, rough kiss to my fingers before dropping them. With a lingering look at the marks on my chin, he curls his lip and turns to Cole.

Subconsciously, I give him space, drifting back into the shadows. I'm not scared of him or what he's about to do. He's still inside of himself somewhere. I accept that he needs this moment. For him, for me, for my parents, and what could have been our future if we hadn't succeeded tonight.

I'm ready to watch his darkness chew Cole up with venomous fangs and spit him out on the ground. Then, when it's done, I'll beg it to play with me. To coax mine from the shadows and have him repeat those three words to me over and over again until I no longer fear they were just a figment of my imagination.

The air chills when Cole sobs for mercy. He broke so easily that it feels unjust. Less satisfying. His wide-eyed gaze locks onto Noah's dark, menacing stare, searching for a sliver of mercy that doesn't exist. Seemingly accepting what's coming, Cole closes his eyes and drops his chin to his chest.

He still screams when Noah drives the brass knuckles into his jaw, one swing after the other. His head snaps side to side with the blows. Every punch is a testament to Noah's anger and pain. The fear that he was shackled with the past few weeks. Looking over his shoulder, second-guessing everyone everywhere.

The crunch of bone turns my stomach, and I look away when Cole's nose contorts, no longer resembling a nose at all. Alec steps beside me as blood sprays across the dirt, shimmering in the moonlight. Cole's cries become softer with each strike of Noah's fist until they're broken whispers.

"You asked for this, Cole. Every time you thought about her. Every time you stepped outside in search of her. When you hurt her. This is what was coming for you the entire time. Me and you. An inescapable end," Noah snarls. His arm falls to his side. Blood drips from the knuckles, soaking into the dirt. The brass hits the ground a beat later.

Cole's left eye is swollen shut, the corner of it bleeding. When I lower my gaze, I sway at the gruesome state of his face. His lips are split, broken, and when he tries to speak, his words are garbled.

Noah's chuckle is dark, ruthless. Despite the scene around us, my belly swoops at the sound of it. God, my head is fucked up.

"I should kill you."

"Should but won't," Alec interrupts. He begins to clap, turning this into a bigger spectacle than it already is. "Are you satisfied? Because I'm not. Not even close."

Noah looks at him over his shoulder, the storm breaking in his eyes. "Do you plan to kill him?"

"It's time for you to go."

I tense. Noah senses my discomfort and flicks his stare to me but speaks to Alec. "You're dismissing us?"

"It's been a pleasure, but we don't particularly like witnesses."

"We?" I echo.

"Don't look so offended, sweetheart," Alec says with a quirk of his lips. His gaze remains icy. "Our time together has been a highlight in my life, but you had to know you weren't going to be here much longer than this. We both held up our ends of the deal. You brought him to me, and I helped you get your revenge."

Noah's face is drawn taut, like a rubber band stretched to its limits. A dangerous edge hovers around him. "Just make sure he never gets near us again."

Alec lifts his pinky, extending it toward us. "Want me to pinky promise?"

"We don't exist to you once we leave here," Noah warns. He comes to my side and hovers there, guarding me. I step into him, resting my hand on his chest. "And you don't exist to us."

"You say the prettiest things, Noah. But you wouldn't be allowed to walk out of here right now if I didn't plan on forgetting about your existence in the next ten seconds. So, please." He waves toward the barn door and stares down at Cole. "I *would* like to play with him a little before he passes out from blood loss. So . . ."

I shake my head, my emotions so jumbled from today that I almost laugh from the nonchalance with which Alec regards this entire situation. It's as if this is normal for him, and that makes him that much more dangerous.

"Thank you," I tell him.

His grin winks at me. "Try not to attract any more fucking creeps, Tinsley."

Noah moves then, shielding Alec from my eyes with his large body. I take a steadying breath and roll my forehead between his pecs before stepping back. Our eyes meet the moment I look up, and for the first time in weeks, the world feels steady beneath my feet again.

"Come," he mutters softly.

His hand falls to my lower back as we walk through the barn, not sparing another glance at Cole's broken body or the man who I feel in bones will be his Grim Reaper.

The faint rumble of an approaching car makes our steps falter. As I peek out of the barn, the glow of headlights illuminates a sleek, black car coming to a stop on the opposite side of the gravelled road.

The driver's door opens slowly, and a man steps out, dressed in black, his movements methodical, calculated. His sharp, cold eyes scan the barn, missing nothing. They're the kind of eyes that consume everything in their path, never satisfied. A shiver trails down my spine when he stares at me. There's an unsettling confidence in his stride as he closes the distance between us with a sense of purpose and something heavier. Darker.

A new danger is coming for Cole, and I intend to be gone long before he falls victim to it.

Noah takes my hand, squeezing it tightly. We should be running, but our strides keep a solid, calm pace as we exit the barn. The man pauses when we pass one another. One look at the thick scar marking his cheek, and I'm meeting his stare, shockingly unafraid of him as he disappears into the barn. After what I've done tonight, maybe he should be afraid of me.

I wait for that thought to terrify me. To feel wrong, like I've made a mistake tonight and crushed my past self beneath the same shoes that did Cole's fingers. But those feelings never come. Only relief and a dark, brutal intensity thrumming inside of me that begs I take Noah behind the barn and drop to my knees for him.

I feel more like myself right now than I ever have, and I want Noah. Right here and now, the both of us now free from Cole's lingering threat. No more fear. No more looking over our shoulders.

Just us.

He rounds the hood of his car and opens the door for me. My

stomach flutters at Noah's gesture, confirming that I'm not in my right mind. I shouldn't be calm enough to swoon over a sweet gesture. Seeing the blood on Noah's hands—the same blood that stains my skin—shouldn't make my nipples pebble, brushing my bra with my every staggered inhale.

I slide inside the car and wait for him to get in beside me, my lungs tight and thighs rubbing together. The ache between them is intense, scarily so. With each inhale, the air in the car starts to thin, intensifying the burn in my belly.

By the time he's sitting in the seat beside me, I'm gasping for breath, my neck arched and head tipped back against the head-rest. I've never felt this way before. Driven by a lust so intense I feel like I could black out at any given second. I'm trapped inside my clothes.

"*Tinsley*," he mutters, his voice deep and husky.

My fingers have begun to shake again as I fumble with the button of my jeans, frantically trying to get it undone. I'm so wet my panties are soiled, maybe my jeans too.

When Noah's hand covers mine, stopping my movements, I whimper in refusal and attempt to pull it free. "I can't wait."

Just the feel of his skin is enough to have me shuddering, waves of pleasure crashing into me.

"Your hands are covered in his blood."

My eyes burn with tears of frustration. "Clean them!"

"Shhh, baby. Just wait." He thumbs the tears from my cheeks before turning the engine over and pulling away from the barn.

Rejection races through me despite the fact I know I'm being unreasonable. We can't stay here. It's not safe. But I want him. Right now. All over me. In any way he wants.

"How do you not feel the way I do? Like I can't breathe without my pussy aching," I gasp.

The gravel road makes the car vibrate, and my fingernails dig into the centre console as it only intensifies my gut-wrenching arousal.

The confines of the car shrink as we speed away, the urgency inside of me mixing with the raw, magnetic pull between us. Noah's grip on the steering wheel is firm, and there's a wildness to his eyes that lights me on fire.

"I've wanted to fuck you since I watched you stealing the life from Cole in your father's gym. I'm lethal with want for you, Tinsley. My control is hanging on by a thread, but I won't risk your safety."

"We don't need our hands to fuck, Noah."

Without warning, Noah swerves the car onto the side of the road, the headlights briefly illuminating the surrounding trees before he cuts the engine, plunging us into darkness. The silence that envelops us is almost surreal. The only sounds are the faint chirping of crickets outside and our ragged breathing filling the car.

I turn to face him, unclipping my seat belt. His expression twists, and my heart jumps in answer.

"Get out."

51

Noah

My golden girl all but dives out of the car.

I twitch with the need to chase her. To pin her down and fuck her until we're both sated. It might take hours, days even, but I won't stop until our beasts are at peace once again, no longer tearing us apart inside with their poison-tipped claws.

Peeling my door open, I slowly step into the night. Tinsley's breathing heavily in the dark, not bothering to pretend she isn't suffering from an adrenaline-induced lust fit. I snap my head in the direction of her ragged exhales and curl my fingers over the top of the door when I spot her.

"I can't wait any longer," she moans.

Her body is laid out on the hood of my car like a five-course meal reserved solely for me. She's watching each step I take toward her, head tilted to the side, her cheek flat against the car. Hard nipples stab through her shirt, pointed at the star-flecked sky. Her thighs are parted and dangling over the hood, beckoning me between them.

Accepting her invitation, I move between her legs, watching her tremble. My hands start at her knees, gliding up over the tight denim moulded to her legs. "You were made for me."

"We were made for each other," she corrects me.

"Did I scare you?"

She shakes her head and wraps her legs around my waist, forcing me further between them. My hands jerk to her hips, pinning them down.

"Never. Did I scare you?"

I lean over her, letting my lips touch the sliver of exposed, creamy skin just above her jeans where her shirt has ridden up. She quakes beneath my touch, gasping her pleasure.

"You could never scare me," I promise, trailing the words up her stomach. She's so warm, her sweet scent strong as it fills my lungs. Goosebumps brush my lips.

She preens beneath my praise. I push her shirt over her chest and cup her tits in my palms. Her bra is red lace, the colour so similar to the blood beneath my nails, and I dig my teeth into the right side, tugging at her nipple. She grasps at my hair, yanking hard, the way she knows I like it. The pain shoots to my hard cock, making it seep in my boxers.

"Yes," she breathes, hips jerking against my chest.

"Tell me how you're feeling," I demand.

Nuzzling my face between her tits, I nip at the soft, warm skin and then suck, overrun with the urge to mark her.

"Powerful." She twirls a finger over the stud in my ear before returning to my hair. "Invincible." I drag my mouth to her other nipple and suck it between my lips over the lace. She moans, holding me in place by my hair. "Aching for you."

"Aching where?"

"My pussy, Noah. I ache so deep."

A noise of satisfaction builds in my chest. Keeping my face in her chest, I reach between our bodies and pop the button of her jeans. With a harsh tug, I have her bottom half bare beneath me, her jeans stuck at her ankles.

One after the other, I slip her shoes off and drop them to the ground. Her jeans come next.

Her cunt is swollen and wet, glistening in the moonlight.

Puffing out a low, needy noise, she pulls her knees to her chest and shifts on her elbows to watch for my reaction.

"Is that all for me?" I groan, licking at my dry lips.

"Is what all for you?"

A rough laugh escapes me at her attempt at toying with me. "You don't want to play with me right now."

"Don't I?" She drops her knees to the hood, her feet touching, spreading herself open for me. I stop breathing. "I've waited long enough to play with your shadows, Noah. Don't you want to play with mine?"

My mind explodes in flashes of white before I'm on my knees before her, rubbing them in the dirt. My fingers dip into the flesh of her thighs as I yank her to the edge of the hood and seal my mouth over her. I spread her with my tongue and slide it into her opening, wanting to drown in her arousal. She cries into the night, clamping her knees to my ears. I grip her ass cheeks, spreading and kneading them as I feast on her.

"How far are you willing to go to appease my darkness, Tinsley?" I whisper the dare into her inner thigh, following it with a sharp bite of her sensitive skin. She flinches but gushes at the pain. I drag my tongue up her slit, cleaning it up.

"Noah, please." She begs so beautifully that I almost let it go.

"Not good enough."

Flicking my eyes up, I catch her wild, savage gaze and hold it as I wrap my lips around her clit and suck. She's dripping down my chin, and I groan in appreciation. I want to shove my fingers deep and stretch her out, but I refuse to. Not until we're home and clean.

"How. Far. Tinsley?" I repeat myself. But she can't answer me. She's too far beneath the waves of pleasure to attempt it.

Her arms fly out across the hood, her back arching, offering her tits to the stars. A dark possession wraps around my chest with long, black tentacles at the thought of even the stars getting the opportunity to worship her the way only I can.

I punish her with a bite to her sensitive, throbbing clit. Her answering whimper is stifled, and I don't fucking like that. She needs to scream for me. My beast demands it.

"Come for me, my desperate little slut. Come for me and nobody else. *Me*," I spit out. "That's the only way you'll get my cock."

"Noah!" she gasps, the word pulled from deep in her chest.

My knees shake in the dirt when she opens her mouth and lets her pleasure fill the night. In awe, I watch as her chest heaves with each scream, her skin dewy and flushed. Knees press hard against my ears, nearly choking off her sounds, but I rip them away and hold them to the hood.

My grin is wicked against her pussy as it quivers against my lips with the aftershock of her climax. I keep fluttering my tongue over her clit, ignoring the way she hisses at the overstimulation.

"I'll stop when you answer my question," I grunt.

Her eyes narrow, pupils as small as pinheads. "I'll answer your question when you fuck me."

"That's not how this is going to work."

She grabs a chunk of my hair and yanks in punishment. "Noah."

"Baby," I purr before suctioning my lips around her clit and sucking hard again. She wiggles her hips in an attempt to get out from under my body.

Her heels dig painfully into my shoulders in a frantic attempt to get me to retreat. I snarl, shaking my head.

"Fuck me already," she orders through a clenched jaw.

"No."

I'm content with my head between her legs, feasting on her pussy. Could spend the rest of my life right here, tasting her morning and night.

She tries to push her body up the hood of the car. With a smirk, I take her hips in my hand and flip her to her belly before she gets too far. Gasping, she reaches above her head and stretches her fingers over the paint. They screech along the hood as I tug her over the edge, her bare ass perched over it. I swallow my approval and slap both hands down, capturing the muscled flesh in my palms, spreading the cheeks apart before spitting onto her exposed hole.

She whips her head around, looking at me over her shoulder with a flustered expression. "You're not fucking my ass."

"Not here. Not tonight. But I will eventually."

I'll be the one to take that virginity. Over and over again. With my fingers, my tongue, and then my cock, when she's ready.

I almost miss her subtle nod. The approval fills me with a wicked sense of pride. "Are you ready for my cock, Golden Girl? I can't stretch you first. I'll tear you up."

Lust glazes her eyes. She pushes her ass back, and I tighten my grip on it. "I want that. Want you."

My head falls back at her words. "Say it again."

"I want you, Noah." She reaches one hand behind her, and I grasp onto it. "I want all of you. Even the parts you try to hide. Give them to me."

With my free hand, I push my jeans and boxers to my knees and shift my hips to line us up, my cock drifting across her puffy, slippery lips. When the wet tip nudges at her entrance, she freezes, feeling my piercing.

"When did you put it back in?" Her voice nearly vibrates with excitement.

I stroke a hand along her spine, fingers splaying out. "This morning."

"Jesus," she breathes out, squeezing my fingers. "It's cold."

"It might hurt because you're not prepped. I've never—" I choke when she ignores my warning and presses against my cock, her tight cunt sucking the head inside. "*Fuuuck,*" I groan.

"So big. Oh my God—"

I push forward, slowly burying inch after inch of me inside of her. She's so fucking wet that I slide inside with little resistance, despite how tight she is. My chest is constricted, claws scratching just below the surface. Want to fuck her hard, but I'm holding back. I won't hurt her.

When I'm buried as deep as possible, she rolls her hips and whimpers when my piercing brushes the most sensitive part of her. I note the reaction when I retreat and then shove back in, angling myself so the metal hits that spot again.

She gushes over my shaft and slicks my balls. I strengthen my thrusts, and her following scream tightens every inch of my body. She's writhing on the hood of the car, each thrust jerking her forward.

"Let go. Fuck me like you mean it." It's a hoarse demand. It undoes me. I give in, too weak to fight against my urges any longer.

The moment I grab a fistful of her hair and yank her head back, she's moaning even louder, the sound so perfect I throb inside of her. My groin slaps her ass, and the sound of each hit carries over the dark, empty road like a rumble of thunder.

I tighten my grip on her hair and pull her body all the way back until my chest hits her back. The new position makes her take me impossibly deeper, my piercing dragging across her walls. She mewls desperate sounds and cups her tits, rolling her filthy fingers over her nipples.

"You stabbed a man tonight. Did you do that for me?" I grind the words into her ear.

A strong shiver rushes through her before she begins to nod, the movement seeming to go on forever. "Yes."

I bring my free hand to her front and cup her throat. Her pulse is rapid beneath my palm. "You looked so beautiful with your fingers around his throat. Did you feel beautiful, Tinsley?"

"Only when you looked at me," she coos.

The rumble of her words seeps into my skin, and I pick up the pace of my thrusts, making the car rock from the intensity of them. Tinsley's pussy clamps down on me, squeezing me so tight I begin to see stars behind my eyes.

"Tell me you're close," I beg, a knot of pleasure spreading in my groin.

"So close, Noah. I just—I want—" She breaks off, her nails clawing at my bare thigh when I thrust in and roll my hips before pulling out. "Tell me you love me again."

The new term settles inside of me, growing warm behind my rib cage. I furrow my brows and ignore the feeling.

Tinsley is not just a part of my life; she *is* my life. Bound by something beyond comprehension, we are forever. I live for her, and I would die for her.

By her understanding of the term, yes, I do love her. I will never believe that love is a word worthy of what I feel for her, but if she needs to hear it expressed in a singular form, I will give her that. I'll tell her every moment of every day if it makes her happy. I swore a long time ago that I would do everything in my power to keep her, and I plan on doing that.

She's mine. In the past, present, and future. And that will never change. I'll make sure of it.

Tilting her head to the side, I bring my mouth to her ear and whisper, "I love you, Golden Girl."

Her climax barrels into her at full speed.

"I'm coming! Fuck, I'm coming!" she screams, shoving her head back against my shoulder. Her body begins to shake, growing weak under the strength of her release.

"I love you," I repeat, pleased with the way the words bring her such intense pleasure. They're new, alien, but as they echo in the night, they feel right. The realization settles me, confirming I made the right choice by speaking them out loud.

As Tinsley comes undone in my arms, I chase after my own climax. With a few final, powerful thrusts, I lose myself inside her, thick ropes of cum spilling deep, marking her as mine in the most primal way.

She collapses onto the hood, the car groaning beneath her weight, and I follow, covering her trembling body with my own.

Our breaths are ragged. My heart thunders against her back. We both stay silent. Until she stiffens beneath me.

I was dreading this moment. For the reality of what we've done to settle on her shoulders. Her conscience. I don't have anything to make peace with. I don't *need* peace when it comes to Cole. Does she?

"We really did all of that, right? I didn't imagine it?" Her voice is raw, thick with too many emotions.

"We did."

She turns her head to look up at me, her eyes glistening with unshed tears. My hackles rise. Discomfort turns my stomach.

"You're crying." I try to stumble backward, away from her, but she reaches for me, settling a hand on my chest.

"I'm not upset with you, Noah. I'm emotional because I just can't believe it's over. He's really gone."

Relaxing slightly, I wrap an arm around her waist, tugging her into my body. I can feel the faint tremors running through her.

"Yeah, baby. He's gone."

Never to be seen again.

52

Tinsley

Noah holds the front door open for me but doesn't let me slip by without swiftly swatting my ass. Grinning, I look up at him. He's the picture of nonchalance, but the subtle twinkle in his eyes tells me that he's more than aware of his actions.

"Watch it, Mr. Dark and Twisty," I warn with a brush of my fingers along his chest.

The corner of his mouth twitches, and then I push into the house, feeling the weight of his eyes on my back. My spirits soar when I take in the bunches of people around me and voices filling the Hutton house to the brink. I take in a deep breath and exhale slowly, embracing the madness.

"If it isn't Tinsley 'Fast Track' Lowry! Back at last!" my cousin Jamieson hollers. He's my dad's half-brother, Tyler's, youngest son, which is an incredible mouthful, but the truth nonetheless.

He's the joker of the family, the opposite of his grumpy older brother, Oliver, and uncle Ty too. More like his mom, Aunt Gracie, he makes it a habit to pick up the slack from the other two guys with his sunshine personality.

"It's just Tinsley to you, Jamie," I reply.

He smiles, his eyes drifting behind me. "You even brought a celebrity with you. Is it someone's birthday?"

Now at my side, Noah palms my back. He dips his chin in a stunted greeting. "Jamieson."

"Noah." Jamie scowls playfully.

"You're going to get punched," Uncle Ty tells his son, speaking up from his spot beside him on the couch. His wife is perched on the armrest, somehow refusing to show any signs of aging with her smooth skin, silky blonde hair, and youthful smile.

Oliver is there as well, but he's glaring at something on his phone. The white Vancouver Fire Department logo on his T-shirt stands out on the navy fabric, drawing my eyes instantly.

I tilt my head. "What's your problem, OlliePop?"

"If you were a single mom with no support, can you tell me why you wouldn't want to accept help from someone who has offered *multiple* times? Are all women so damn stubborn?" he grunts.

Noah's fingers dip beneath the waistband of my shorts, tugging at it. "She'll never be a single mother. What the fuck kind of question is that?"

I bite my tongue to keep from laughing. Even two weeks after the night in the barn, he hasn't become any less protective. It's really no surprise, considering he's always been protective, but witnessing it right now, in his parents' living room, aimed at family, is enough to have my shoulders shaking with the force of my stifled laughs.

Oliver simply rolls his eyes, shrugging it off. "I'm not talking about Tinsley, you brute."

"Are we not going to talk about how Noah clearly made his move on her, though?" Jamie questions.

Oliver blinks, focusing on the possessive hand now cupping my waist. "Am I supposed to be shocked or something?"

"You're so boring," his brother mutters.

"And the two of you together are headache inducing," Tyler sighs. Offering me a tight, apologetic expression, he adds, "Good for you two. You look good together. But you always have."

"He's right. I love the two of you together so much," Aunt Gracie agrees.

"I should have taken Maddox up on that bet when we were teens," Jamie says.

Adalyn comes bouncing into the living room, a flurry of pastel purple hair and a peachy smile. Her husband is hot on her heels, eyes on her and only her.

"You should have because you lost four hundred bucks," she says.

The rest of the family follows behind her, and Noah grows tense beside me at the onslaught of people. It's the first time he's seen everyone for months now, but even though his injury has healed well, I know it's making him even more tense. He doesn't want sympathy from anyone. I don't think he'll find it here. They know him well enough not to put him in an even more uncomfortable position in this environment.

I've always known that the Hutton family had money, considering Oakley's career in the NHL, but the size of their home has always seemed . . . too much to me. However, now that all of us kids have grown up and started families of our own, their house truly is the perfect size. Anything smaller and we wouldn't fit as comfortably.

The first of the Hutton third generation comes barrelling between Adalyn's legs, his tiny legs carrying him into the living room. Liam grins brightly when everyone's attention falls on him. A yearning grows in my chest when he takes one look at Noah and squeals, changing direction.

"Nah! Nah!"

Noah removes his hand from my waist and drops to a crouch as Liam reaches him, his arms outstretched. The grumpiest, stone-walled man I've ever known envelopes his nephew into his arms and holds him close. The toddler tries to get his arms around Noah's shoulders but hardly reaches the tips of them. I swallow a ball of emotion in my throat and look away from them, my eyes snagging on Maddox.

With his hands in his pockets, his shoulder pressed to the wall, he meets my stare, a sheen over his eyes. A feeling of acceptance travels between us. I'll forgive him for hurting Noah on one condition: he never does it again. Not to this extent.

Seeing Noah in the hospital changed a lot of things for a lot of people. I don't believe that it should have taken something like that to shake some sense into them, but I'm just relieved something did. That's the only thing that matters.

Over the past two weeks, Oakley and Noah have made leaps and strides in their relationship. Things are still stinted, but every day, the two of them grow closer. Healing one another. The future is bright for them, and I feel blessed that I get to have a front-row seat to their growth.

Braxton sidles up to her husband and, like every single person in the house, watches the scene unfold with soft features. It doesn't last long, not with Liam being a toddler and, in turn, having the temperament of one, but I'll never forget it.

Ava is rushing toward the two of us when Noah stands, and Liam runs off. She pulls us both into a hug, her arms hardly long enough to wrap around one person, let alone two. "How was your flight?"

"Short. No turbulence either," I answer. My parents aren't here, but I know they wish they could have been. Dad's set to open the gym in two days, though, and I am so proud of him for that.

When we break apart, Noah's placing his hand back on my waist and holding me close to him, as if just by being here, I'm bringing him the comfort he needs to get through today. I love being that person for him.

"It feels like forever since we've had everyone here at once. My heart is so full today," she admits.

Looking around, I note the missing faces. "Where are Adam, Scarlett, and Amelia?" My brows furrow when I don't see Oakley either.

Cooper's family is usually always here first because his

father is Ava's best friend, and those two can't go long without being at each other's sides. It's always been adorable. Oakley's absence is odd but not worrying.

"They're on the way. There was a problem at WIT," she answers.

White Ice Training, Adam's hockey training facility.

"Dad was there too?" Noah asks, attempting to play off his curiosity.

Ava notices what I do and glances at me knowingly before focusing on her son. "He wouldn't miss seeing you, honey. He'll be here any minute."

He nods. I lean over to brush a kiss to his cheek and whisper, "You should talk to Maddox."

His hold on me tightens. Sparks erupt beneath his fingertips, a reminder that my love grows for him every single day.

"Don't let them eat you alive," he replies, voice quiet, the words just for me.

I speak in the same tone. "I'm proud of you for being here."

His stare grows warm, turning my insides to goo. When he looks at me like this, I don't need words. They're worthless in comparison.

After a few beats, I force myself to look away and flush when I catch the way Ava's watching us. Like she couldn't possibly be happier. Finally at peace.

"I'm going to talk to Maddox," Noah tells her.

"I think that's a great idea, sweetheart."

With a lingering look, Noah moves from my side, invoking a dull ache behind my rib cage that always swells when we're apart. I ignore it because as much as even a breath of distance between us hurts my soul, I know this might be one of the most important conversations of his life.

He's mine for the rest of time. I can spare a few minutes.

NH)

Noah

I STOP in front of Maddox, and he nods instantly, already knowing what I want. Braxton smiles at me and rubs my brother's arm before he kisses her quickly and turns to lead us out of the living room.

We move through the kitchen and toward the back patio. It's hot outside, but even with the air conditioning, so is the house. There are too many people. Even when I was a kid, I didn't like the big dinners my parents hosted. It was too much for me. I couldn't take it. At twenty-five, I still can't handle it.

Maddox opens the patio door and steps outside. Our house backs onto a few acres of land, making it private. The back deck was redone when we were kids and started getting slivers all the time. Some of the stain has faded since then, making it look worn.

We're both tense when we sit on the top step. I pick at the skin beside my thumbnail and stare at the long grass curling around the bottom step, touching the toes of my socks.

"How are you feeling?" he asks.

"I hate that question."

"I know. But I want to know the answer, anyway."

"I'm fine. I don't feel it anymore."

He leans forward with his elbows on his knees and nods. "Good. You haven't been pushing too hard now that you're back on tour?"

"Tinsley won't let me play guitar yet," I grumble.

His laugh hits me in the gut. It's so carefree. I used to be jealous of his ability to be so relaxed. I'm not anymore. Tinsley likes me the way I am. That's good enough for me.

"Sounds about right. She loves the fuck out of you, brother."

"I know."

"Do you love her too?"

I roll my jaw. "What is with this family's obsession with that term?"

"I think most people enjoy talking about love. It's not just us," he defends.

"I don't want to explain myself to you, Maddox. I already did to Dad."

"Fair enough. You care about her, though. You always have. If you didn't, there's no way you'd have gotten that fucking face tattoo in her honour. Good God, you're fearless. Both of you are."

I ignore the dig at my tattoo. "I more than care about her. The way I feel about her goes beyond your comprehension level."

He snorts. "Ouch. I forgot how ruthless you can be when it comes to Tiny."

"You always liked to bother me about that."

"I'm your big brother. Did you expect anything else?"

"I expected nothing from you. Maybe that was the problem." When he remains silent, I wince, recognizing my error. "Sorry."

He turns his head and stares at me, his green eyes sad. "Don't apologize. I was a shit brother to you."

"You and Dad are similar in most ways."

"We are. I always thought you were jealous of that, so I was a douchebag to you more often than not. In a perfect world, I would have gotten over myself and attempted to get to know you better instead. But this isn't a perfect world, and I didn't do that. I let you drift away while criticizing your life choices instead. It was wrong of me. And I'm sorry."

His confession settles on my chest like a foot, pressing down until it hurts. A good or a bad hurt, I don't know. It makes my head swim.

Sensing my reaction, he goes on. "You don't have to forgive me today, or ever, really. But I know you and Dad have been talking, and I'm jealous of him. You're my brother, and I don't know much about you other than what I've known since we were kids. I want to be a part of your life—I always have—and . . . I almost lost that chance forever. You were bound to do amazing things with your life, and you're doing them. I'm proud of you, little brother. So fucking proud. You can think about this for as long as you want, and I'll be here. I'm not going anywhere ever again."

Maddox waits patiently for my response, his eyes never leaving mine. I swallow hard, searching for the right words.

"I want to move on. With both you and Dad."

His face breaks out into a relieved smile, and for the first time in years, I like the sight of it. "I've missed you."

I don't reply, but I don't need to. He doesn't seem to mind. We sit in silence, the weight of years of resentment slowly lifting from our shoulders. I've been carrying this burden for so long it feels odd to have it begin to ebb, little by little.

Maddox breaks the silence with a chuckle. "I always used to tease you about Tinsley, but we've all seen how much she means to you, especially over the past few weeks."

I nod, my gaze drifting to the house. "She's everything. I won't waste any more time with her."

Maddox claps a hand on my back, his smile growing wider. "That's the spirit. Embrace what makes you happy, and don't let anything or anyone stand in your way. I didn't start to understand the meaning of that until I lost Braxton."

"Now she's stuck with you."

He laughs. "Yeah, that she is."

As the sun sets in front of us, an odd sense of . . . peace washes over me. The tension that had fucked with my relationship with Maddox is finally dissipating. The sun feels warmer on my skin.

The sliding of the patio door is the only warning that someone else has joined us. We look back and find Dad. I'm surprised when I don't go rigid with discomfort when he sits beside me and clasps his hands between his legs, keeping quiet, just being here. With me and Maddox. The silence is enough. More than. I don't need him to add anything.

"We're proud of you, Noah," Maddox says a few minutes later, his voice filled with genuine admiration. "You've always known who you were, even when nobody else accepted you for it. You deserve to be happy with your girl."

"Thank you," I mutter.

He shoves my shoulder with his. It sends me careening into Dad, knocking his as well. "You're welcome."

And with those final words, I rise from the step, needing to be back at Tinsley's side.

Where I belong.

EPILOGUE

Noah

THE CROWD ROARS, CHANTING MY NAME. THE MUSIC SWELLS BEHIND me. My earpiece dangles from my left ear from when I tore it out after the first song. I don't want tonight to be muted. I want to be present for the last show of the tour. The last show for months to come.

I don't like being sentimental. It's not an emotion that comes easily to me, but I will miss performing. The rush and thrill of having thousands of eyes on me, watching, listening to my music. Worshiping.

Justice carries the beat with a passion that doesn't go unnoticed in the crowd. He's always the best musician of the three, but tonight, he's beyond the best. He's magic.

Dagger tries to outshine Justice, but even with his skill, it's not possible. Josh plays like he always does. Like this is any ordinary job. Like he can't wait to finish and go home. If I cared enough to get to know either of them on a personal level, I would ask why he doesn't care about the opportunity that Sparks handed to him. But I don't, so I won't.

I find Tinsley in the crowd. She's been flush to the pit barricade all night, alternating between reaching for me and flashing her homemade sign above her head. I smiled when I saw it the first time. Couldn't help myself.

Noah Hutton Is My Boyfriend.

I've fought the urge to demand she be brought to the stage all night. She wouldn't want that, though. She wanted to get the complete fan experience tonight, and apparently, she could only have that by getting crushed and pushed around by a hot, sweaty crowd.

She grins at me, and just like my first show in Edmonton, I crouch at the end of the stage and take her hand in mine. Her palm is slick with sweat. So is mine. I want to tug on her hand and force her up over the barricades but reluctantly let her go when the song trails off. Having her eyes on me while I perform is enough. Knowing she's here and happy settles me.

The Toronto crowd is the loudest we've had on this tour. And they don't hide their approval of Tinsley. The security guard I've placed beside her is on high alert when my fans try to paw at her, shouting things I can't hear but don't need to. Her blush is enough to tell me it isn't anything upsetting.

I move back to my mic stand and slip the mic into place before tugging my guitar from across my back and leading the next song. The lights dim to a deep red that fans out over the stage. Justice thumps the bass drum as I play the first set of notes, and Dagger follows. Josh waits for his entrance, weaving his stare through the crowd.

I find Reggie lingering backstage, smiling at me. He's been sticking close to us the last few weeks of the tour, and I haven't hated it. His company is enjoyable. I like him, and he seems to like me enough to stick around. Garrison hasn't been around as often, but when he is, I pretend he isn't. That seems to work for the both of us. I plan on continuing to enjoy Reggie's company, and I think he'll do the same. When he tips his chin at me, his eyes soft, I know I was ridiculous to doubt him.

My voice carries through the venue when I lean into the mic and say, "It took months for Tinsley to give this song a name, but she finally did. This is 'Sinister Attraction.' Our song."

Eyes locking in the crowd, I sing every word to her. As if we're alone, just her and me. Even at a sold-out show, she's the only one I see. The only one I play for.

The one my heart beats for.

NH)

Tinsley

MY ABDOMEN SCREAMS when my opponent's glove makes contact. I hiss out a breath and reposition my body to prepare for her next attack. Sweat drips from my forehead and down my nose. My back is drenched. But that's all background noise.

I zone into Skylar's sharp, calculated movements, tracking them. I've made it to my first career title fight. I'm skilled, talented. She won't beat me. I'll win this thing, and then I'll come back next year and defend my win every single day if I have to. It's mine. Nothing will take it away from me. Not even a woman who's pushed me to the sixth round with showing no signs of tiring.

My speed isn't helping me tonight. She's just as fast. When I win, it will be because of my skill and drive. My inability to give up.

My hands fly in her direction, making contact with her rib cage and the left side of her jaw. She shakes both hits off and returns them. I dodge her gloves and bounce in place. The timer ticks down, and I advance on her despite the force of the hits that fly. My chin, stomach, jaw. She's relentless, eyes blazing with a drive to win.

I don't look for my family in the crowd. Don't search for Noah to see if he's watching and if he's proud of me. I already know the answers to those questions. *No distractions*, I promised myself before stepping into the ring tonight. It's just me and Skylar and a certified Tinsley Lowry title win.

She snarls in my face, and I fight the urge to grin. Alarm shifts across her face when her back makes contact with the ropes. I've cornered her, and she has nowhere to go unless she can take me down.

My jaw aches, and my chest burns from her hits, but I take that pain and use it to strengthen my punches. She defends my first few hits, but I've learned everything there is to know about her fight style since we stepped into the ring. After six rounds, I find a crack in her stance and attack.

My body screams in outrage when I take two quick steps back and allow her to hit me. It's a risky move, but it's one I've watched my dad do several times in his career. Let them believe you've run out of steam. Instill a false sense of control and then snatch it back.

The hits don't register over the adrenaline rush inside of me. She's tapped into her last pocket of energy and is giving me her all. I'm only partially tuned into the crowd, but I wouldn't be able to miss my mother's shouts even if someone filled my ears with glue.

"Tinsley! Fight back!"

I don't look at her. She didn't pay as much attention to Dad in the ring as I did. He's my teacher. I know every single one of his moves. He taught them to me.

A dark smile curls my lips when Skylar gives me my opening. One staggered exhale signals her first lowered guard. I slip beneath it and power forward. One after the other, I bring my gloves to her face. Blood squirts across my throat, her nose crunching. She shakes her head, trying to clear the fog slipping across her mind, but I'm there before she can succeed.

Just like I managed to do in my first fight, I deliver one final uppercut, and it's lights out for her. She drops to the mats, and then it's over.

The crowd screams, and I let the ref grab my arm, thrusting it into the air as I drop my head and catch my breath. When I lift it again, a pair of dark brown eyes are waiting. White noise fills my ears as we stare at each other, an invisible string tethering us together. It tugs at my chest, and I wave, wanting him up here when my team slips through the ropes and rushes toward me.

I'm halfway out of my mind when Noah follows my family into the ring. He takes me in his arms, and I let myself go limp in his hold, knowing he won't drop me. *He's always got me.*

Tears run down my face, and my chest shakes with the force of my sobs, but I just let myself feel. Feel the pride and happiness and just how lucky I am to be where I am right now, surrounded by so much love and support and a victory that I've always dreamed of claiming.

This is my life now. And I've never been more grateful to be alive.

NH)

HOURS LATER, the early October sun sets behind the fence of my parents' backyard. Yellow leaves cover the ground, and the wind nips at my bare arms, but I can't bring myself to go inside and change yet. I'm content with soaking in this peaceful moment. It's such a contrast to the fight earlier.

My brother sits on the chair opposite me on the back porch, his nose buried in his phone. Dad is adding a log to the flames in the stone fire pit, and Noah disappeared inside a minute ago, leaving his spot on the couch to grow cold in his absence. I watch Mom settle at Dad's side and set a hand on his back as he keeps the fire going. They share a long, soft look, and I smile, my chest warming.

"If you don't get that phone out of your face, Easton, I'm going to toss it in the fire," Dad threatens a moment later.

"I'm twenty years old," Easton replies, the words blunt.

Dad doesn't so much as blink at his attitude. He's always had the patience of a saint with my brother. According to Grandpa, that's probably because Dad was a shithead when he was a teenager.

"And I'm about to toss your twenty-year-old ass into the leaf pile if you don't listen to me."

Easton slowly puts the phone away and slides a look toward Dad. It's clear he's unimpressed with the demand, but at least he can read the room well enough to know that now isn't the time to start an argument.

"Thank you!" Dad calls.

My brother has always been hard walled, but he's grown more so as he's aged. I can't help but wonder why.

I stand from my spot and perch on the arm of his chair. He blinks up at me and attempts to smile. It's a valiant effort, and I don't hesitate to wrap my arms around his shoulders and give him a half hug. He's still beneath my arms, but with a vast level of experience with men who aren't very open with their emotions, I don't let the fact he doesn't hug me back deter me.

"I love you, little bro. You know that, right?"

He awkwardly pats my arm. "Love you too."

"Does that mean that you gonna tell me who you're always texting?"

"No."

"Worth a shot." Pulling back, I ruffle his hair and move back to the wicker couch.

"Where'd your shadow go?"

"I'm not sure, actually."

"Maybe Dad finally scared him off."

I snort a laugh. "As if."

We both look behind me when the patio door slides open and

Noah steps outside, a heavy plaid blanket in his hands. He meets my stare, his eyes heating.

When he reaches the couch, he drapes the blanket over my shoulders before taking the seat beside me again. He sets his hand over my thigh and squeezes.

"Better?" he asks.

I nod, leaning my cheek on his shoulder. "Much. Thank you."

"Did you bring me one, Noah?" Dad asks, abandoning the fire.

He pulls a patio chair from the opposite side of the deck and settles on Noah's right side. Mom takes the seat beside Easton and tucks the bottom half of her face beneath the top of her sweatshirt. I know her well enough to know she's hiding a smile.

Noah draws patterns on my thigh, appearing relaxed. He's still quiet around my family, but ever since my dad helped us with the Cole situation, he's begun to find a sense of ease with them. It's been the same with his family. I've always been proud of Noah, but somehow, I've managed to be even more so as of late.

"No. Easton would love to get you one, though," Noah replies smoothly.

Easton scowls. "Why did we let you in the house again? I thought we had a no-rodents rule."

"That's a good one. Did you see it on the back of a cereal box?"

I turn my head and press my lips to Noah's arm. A wave of happiness drifts through me, settling in my chest. There are very few things in life that matter as much as family, and having everyone I love together like this . . . it makes me feel whole.

Noah kisses the top of my head, and I grin, our future so bright it's blinding.

EXTENDED EPILOGUE

Noah

FOUR MONTHS LATER

The blindfold around Tinsley's eyes keeps the familiar street hidden. She loves surprises. This will be the biggest one I've ever kept from her.

It's been a long time coming. A lot of money and communication that made me want to rip my hair out in chunks. I thought it would never end. But, finally, it's ready for her.

"I think I know where we are," she squeaks from the passenger seat.

"No, you don't."

"I do."

"How?"

"I just feel it in my bones."

"No, you're trying to trick me into telling you."

"Never. That's not me."

Right.

We pass the neighbourhood sign, and I breathe through the anxiety that threatens to shackle me. It's so vibrant here. A place full of life and noise. You start a family in a place like this. Raise your kids. It wasn't like that in the past, but this isn't the past. It's the now.

"Do you want kids?" I blurt out. Scowling at myself for changing the conversation so drastically, I tug at the tie of my bandana.

I've wondered about her opinion on children for a while. I'd give her anything she wanted. But I think I'd be a shit father. She hasn't mentioned children for years. Not since we were kids ourselves. I know she wants to focus on her career. I'll support that decision. Her opinion might change in the future, though. I need to be prepared if it does.

"Are you taking me somewhere we'll end up with a kid when we leave?" she asks.

I blow out a breath. "No. Just curious."

Risking a glance at her, I watch her roll her lips, eyelashes moving behind the blindfold.

"Maybe. I haven't given it much thought. I'm not ready for them yet, that's for sure," she confesses.

"But when you are?"

"Do you want children, Noah?"

I tap the steering wheel. "I'm asking about you."

"And it isn't just my choice. Unless you're planning on leaving me, that is." Her voice has grown threatening, and I almost laugh at her anger.

There's my little Devil.

"Never," I promise.

"Then I want to know what you want as well."

I turn the car down the road on the left, the one that will lead us to our destination. Can I imagine our kids running down these streets in the summer?

What if we have the same relationship I had with my dad growing up?

"I want you to be happy. If that means babies, then we'll have as many babies as you want. If that means no babies, then I'll give you whatever else you want. Seeing you happy makes me happy. That's what I know for certain."

Her eyes are covered, but I know she's facing me without having to look. "I love you, Noah. Of course I would like to have a family with you. But I'm not focused on children. I want us both to experience our lives together before I even contemplate them. You're twenty-five, and I'm twenty-six. We're still young. And I would never make you do anything you weren't comfortable with just because you think it would make me happy. We're a team. You and me. Right?"

I swallow dryly. "Right."

"I want you to be open with me. Especially about something as important as children. Tell me what you're thinking."

Our house comes into view, the street in front of it packed with vehicles. My—*our*—family is here, waiting for us.

"Our kids would hate me."

She doesn't miss a beat. "They would love you just like I do."

"What if I don't love them properly?"

Releasing the gas, I press the brake, pulling in behind my father's truck. When we've stopped moving, I hold the steering wheel with both hands and stare out her window at the house.

It's been redone, renovated from the outside in. I kept the same structural outline, but most of the frame had to be redone. It was falling apart. Now it's sturdy. Safe.

It was renovated with her likes and dislikes in mind. I kept the same porch design and room layout. Memories are written on the walls of our bedroom upstairs. They fill this house. Now, she can make it a home.

"Can I please take this blindfold off? This isn't a conversation I want to be having when I can't even look at you," she pleads.

I reach across the console and pull the tie free, letting the blindfold fall to her lap. The moment she sees the house, she's tipping her head back and laughing angrily. My stomach turns at her reaction, unsure how to take it.

"You impossible man," she murmurs. When our eyes meet, hers are glassy, the corners wet. I catch the first tear that falls with my thumb and then do the same to the next. "It's our house."

"It is."

"When did you do this? How?"

I run my thumb over the dip in her upper lip. "I bought the house when the others in the neighbourhood started to sell to developers. It's ours. It was never meant to be turned into something cookie-cutter. After our last night here, I started with the renovations. I know you want to stay in Toronto, but we can have this house when we come to Vancouver. No more hotels or staying with anyone. Just us."

"Just us," she echoes. "In *our* house. A house I expected to be gone by now. One full of memories of us."

I watch her, not speaking. Disbelief travels across her features, and then she's shaking her head.

"And you think you couldn't love our children? You may love differently than others, but you love even stronger. Fiercer. I would be the luckiest woman in the world to have you be the father of my children someday." She points to the house but doesn't look away from me. I feel the affection in her eyes all the way to my toes. "I will never stop being grateful for you, Noah. You're my other half. Our future is endless. Regardless of whether we have children or not."

I don't have the words to reply. My lips find hers instead. I kiss her hard, trying to portray my emotions in the easiest way for me. Physically.

She smiles against my mouth, understanding me. Knew she would.

"Don't think I haven't noticed your dad's truck in front of us," she whispers. When I open my eyes, she's already looking at me. "You're not about to propose, are you?"

I keep my expression flat. "Maybe. Maybe not."

I'm not, but marrying her has never scared me. It's always only been a matter of time.

"Yeah, right."

"You've never cared about marriage," I say.

"It's a waste of money and time," we recall in unison. She's been telling me this for years.

Dropping her voice an octave, she says, "But I wouldn't exactly be opposed to being your wife, Noah Hutton. If you want that too, that is."

Then—without letting me reply—she's opening the car door and stepping into the bitter February air, leaving me to watch her ass sway in a pair of tight jeans as she walks away.

Thinking of Tinsley taking my last name has always made my dick hard. But now . . . now it becomes a necessity. Number one on my to-do list.

NH

My dad pats my back when he joins me in the kitchen. With a long neck in his hand and his baseball cap on, he looks younger than usual. Like the man in the old photos of him and Mom.

He leans against the counter and stares at the women in the living room as they reset a board game on the floor. I do the same, but I'm only watching one woman. Mine. She's been talking to my mom and sister all night, giggling that fucking giggle, driving me out of my mind. I want to tell everyone to leave and carry her to our bedroom. We can paint the walls with her cries.

Dad seems to sense I'm struggling and tries to distract me. "This is a beautiful house, Noah. You've done a great job."

It's dark and warm. Bright during the day but dim at night. Pieces of her and pieces of me while capturing her taste above everything else.

"She likes it."

"She loves it," he corrects me.

"Toronto is home for us. But this is a good place to stay when we visit."

"Is that something you want to try to do more?"

He's digging, and I can understand why. A recently added portion of my previous tour starts next month, and Tinsley's first fight follows my first show. We'll be gone often. Our new place in Toronto is nice because we don't have a roommate. But we come to Vancouver often. It's like when we were kids. For a long time, I never came home. Never wanted to visit anyone besides Mom. Things are different now.

I want to come home more. This house will help with that.

"Yes. Tinsley wants that too."

"Have you given any more thought to performing at WIT's fair this summer?"

Cooper's father asked me to last week. His arena always puts on a fair in the summer, but he's never wanted me to perform before. I told him I'd think about it.

"My music isn't for kids," I mutter.

He chuckles. "Fair enough. Just think about it and let him know. We'd love to have you do it anyway. Skip the curse words, and they'd be none the wiser."

The calm in his voice—the lack of expectation or judgment regardless of my decision—has me agreeing before I can stop myself. His responding grin hits me hard. I leave him in the kitchen directly after, my skin itching.

Tinsley finds me in the spare bedroom a minute later. She wraps her arms around me from behind. Her touch soothes my restlessness.

"Was that a good or bad conversation with your dad?"

I cover her hands with mine as they splay over my pecs. "Good. It overwhelmed me."

"It's okay to get overwhelmed. The two of you are still getting to know each other again. I'd say that's normal. Can I help?"

I lift our hands from my chest, hovering them over my lips.

Taking in the view of our backyard, I remember the last time we were here. The way the moonlight illuminated her figure as we stood in front of this window. How easily it was for her to tame the monster inside of me that fought for control.

Our story isn't a fairy tale, but it's ours. I'm not a Prince Charming, and she's not a damsel in distress. We're above that. A king and queen of our own making.

"You've already helped me, Golden Girl. I love you."

She presses her cheek to my back and whispers, "And I love you, Mr. Dark and Twisty."

THE END

THE END

The Devil Inside
Track List

♡ ⏮ ▶ ⏭ ⊕

Golden Girl	3:14
Fading Embers	4:18
Chains Of Insanity	4:50
Ressurection Road	3:56
Fury Unleashed	2:05
Whispers In The Dark	3:43
Eternal Desires	4:27
Fractured Bonds	2:26
Outsider	4:03
Sinister Attraction	3:41

Coming Soon

Did Alec and Mr. Dark and Mysterious peak your interest? Book a ticket to Crimson Bay in 2024 for the release of my first dark romance novel.

Until then, Reggie will be back in my upcoming stand-alone novel releasing in February. It's time to stumble into Cherry Peak, the hometown of the infamous country star Brody Steele...

Thank you for reading *His Greatest Muse!* If you enjoyed it, please leave a review on Amazon and Goodreads.

This second-generation series is far from over!

His Greatest Mistake – Maddox and Braxton

Her Greatest Adventure – Adalyn and Cooper

His Greatest Muse – Noah and Tinsley

Book 4 – Oliver Bateman and ? (TBA)

Book 5 – Jamieson Bateman and ? (TBA)

To be kept up to date on all my releases, check out my website! www.hannahcowanauthor.com

If you have not read all of the original love stories in this world, now is the time to do so!

Lucky Hit — Oakley and Ava

Between Periods (Novella and BH prequel)

Blissful Hook — Tyler and Gracie

Craving The Player — Braden and Sierra #1

Taming The Player — Braden and Sierra #2

Overtime – Matt and Morgan

Vital Blindside — Adam and Scarlett

Acknowledgements

There will never be a couple that touches me as deeply as Noah and Tinsley have. This one was a labour of love and tears and stress and even more tears during the hardest moments. I doubted my ability to give Noah and Tiny a story that I was proud of, and that I knew you would love. Somehow, I think I've accomplished that seemingly impossible task.

Hayley, my best friend, my Australian sister. I couldn't have done this without you. You put up with so much from me during this writing process. The days spent talking me off the ledge and inflating my head to near explosion with compliments when I desperately needed them, are the reason for this THE END. This book is for you. The whole fucking thing. I love you x infinity.

To Phoebe, Katie, Becci, Rose, Sierra, Nicole, Jordan, and Nikki, my incredible alpha readers but also my beautiful friends, thank you. I will never be able to give you the appreciation you deserve, but I'll try every damn time.

Publishing a book takes a village, and I am so incredibly grateful for every member of mine. Sandra, Booksandmoods, Taylor, Mitch, Shannon, all of YOU. Thank you.

Xoxo Hannah

He just wanted a decent book to read ...

Not too much to ask, is it? It was in 1935 when Allen Lane, Managing Director of Bodley Head Publishers, stood on a platform at Exeter railway station looking for something good to read on his journey back to London. His choice was limited to popular magazines and poor-quality paperbacks – the same choice faced every day by the vast majority of readers, few of whom could afford hardbacks. Lane's disappointment and subsequent anger at the range of books generally available led him to found a company – and change the world.

'We believed in the existence in this country of a vast reading public for intelligent books at a low price, and staked everything on it'
Sir Allen Lane, 1902–1970, founder of Penguin Books

The quality paperback had arrived – and not just in bookshops. Lane was adamant that his Penguins should appear in chain stores and tobacconists, and should cost no more than a packet of cigarettes.

Reading habits (and cigarette prices) have changed since 1935, but Penguin still believes in publishing the best books for everybody to enjoy. We still believe that good design costs no more than bad design, and we still believe that quality books published passionately and responsibly make the world a better place.

So wherever you see the little bird – whether it's on a piece of prize-winning literary fiction or a celebrity autobiography, political tour de force or historical masterpiece, a serial-killer thriller, reference book, world classic or a piece of pure escapism – you can bet that it represents the very best that the genre has to offer.

Whatever you like to read – trust Penguin.

NATIONS DIVIDED

JACK EMERY 3

STEVE P. VINCENT

First published by Momentum in 2015

This edition published in 2017 by Steve P. Vincent

The moral right of the author has been asserted.

A CIP record for this book is available at the National Library of
Australia

Nations Divided

Cover design by XOU Creative

Edited by Kylie Mason

Proofread by Thomasin Litchfield

 Created with Vellum

For those fighting for peace with words,
rather than guns

PROLOGUE

Rashid Sirhan opened his eyes at the sound of her voice, blinking quickly as he tried to adjust to the harsh overhead lighting. "Sorry, just napping."

The nurse smiled kindly, the usual twinkle in her eyes. "I've got your pills, Mr. Sirhan. I'm glad you finally got some sleep."

The young nurse filled his palm with a rainbow assortment of drugs, like his father used to with candy when he was a child. He shook his head at the thought, stuffed the pills into his mouth and washed them down with some water. The pills certainly didn't taste like his childhood, but instead felt like one more insult heaped upon many others as he'd grown old.

"All done?" Her voice had an edge of menace. She'd probably had problems with other patients today.

"Mission accomplished." Rashid opened his mouth to show her, then closed it. "I'll look forward to my lollipop."

She ignored the jibe and he closed his eyes again. As he relaxed and tried to ease back into sleep, Rashid heard the nurse push the drug cart to the next bed. Before he had the chance to drift off, he was gripped by a coughing fit, a dry and raspy reminder that he was down to one lung. The cancer that had plagued his body also destroyed his rest.

Just as his coughing subsided, Rashid heard a loud chattering sound from a few rooms away. The sound was unmistakable, akin to a half-dozen small firecrackers exploding in quick succession. Even before the squeals and shouts had started, he'd figured out what was happening: a standard-issue Israeli assault rifle was firing on full automatic. The IDF was here.

Rashid kicked off the covers and rolled out of bed, bracing as he landed hard on the ground. He'd be damned if he'd make himself an easy target or let the shrapnel from a frag grenade catch him in bed. Coughing again, he ducked low and listened. The gunfire relented for a moment, ripped off again, then stopped once more. The pattern – shoot and pause – hinted at one gunman.

Glancing around for a weapon, any kind, he ignored the noise and chaos around him as others fled the gunfire. He settled on a metal kidney dish and struggled to his feet, knowing this would be his last stand. Refusing to die on his knees, Rashid stood tall as the sound of the gunfire moved closer.

The door to the ward swung open. Rashid squeezed the kidney dish tighter as a male patient and a nurse ran through the door and towards him. The woman fell as gunfire found her, leaving a spray of blood in her wake. A second later, the man dropped as well.

The gunman walked through the door, dressed from head to toe in the uniform of the Israeli army and the triple chevron that revealed him to be a samal – a sergeant. Rashid stood as proud as he could, unwilling to let the Israeli see him take a backward step.

While Rashid had launched rockets into Israel before,

likely killing civilians, he figured you had to be a special kind of killer to shoot up a hospital. Or the closest thing Gaza had to a hospital, anyway. He wasn't sure how many had died, but as he lifted the kidney dish Rashid felt anger course through him.

The Israeli sergeant's features betrayed no emotion as he brought the assault rifle up. Rashid swallowed hard and threw the kidney dish at the Israeli. The projectile hit the other man on the chest and then clattered to the tiles, the lamest possible resistance. Rashid didn't care. He hadn't run away.

It wasn't much fun living with cancer anyway.

ACT I

1

As dignitaries descend on New York City for the signing of the historic peace agreement between Israel and Palestine, many remain skeptical that a deal will be finalized. Though both camps say that all issues are close to being fully resolved and that the massacre at Gaza's Al Amal Hospital has brought the parties closer to a deal, the world has seen too many false starts on this issue to be certain of an agreement. Until pen touches paper, the stakes will remain high and nobody has more to gain, or lose, from the agreement than President Bill McGhinnist, who has worked tirelessly to resolve this issue before the end of his first term.

New York Standard

Jack Emery's eyes darted back and forth across the page, consuming the news for the day. He licked his finger and turned a page with one hand while he fumbled for his coffee with the other. The shock from the story on page five caused him to knock over his coffee cup, drowning the *Post*'s scoop about a Supreme Court justice being photographed at a titty bar.

"Damn it." Jack reached for a napkin and mopped at the spill, trying his best to save the rest of the newspaper.

"Nice work." Celeste Adams' voice was heavy with sleep. "Good thing you never listen to me about the advantages of reading the news on your iPad."

Jack looked up. Despite the mess, he couldn't resist a smile as she leaned against the doorframe, wearing panties and a tank top. "Hey."

"Hey." She pushed herself off, walked toward him and reached for his plate. "Why'd you let me sleep so late?"

He swatted at her hand and his smile turned into a frown when she stole the remains of his bagel, biting into the last morsel. A smear of cream cheese remained on her lip. He stood, took her hands in his and kissed her deeply, using his tongue to lick at the cheese. She laughed and pulled away. They looked at each other for a second and then shared another kiss.

"Too cute to wake." Jack gave her hands a squeeze, pulled away and made a show of eyeing her up and down.

She gave him a gentle slap on the rear, then rounded the table and took a seat. "Any of the papers survive your drenching?"

He considered the mess. "Not sure. They all look a bit moist."

"Gross. That word should only be used to describe cake."

Jack laughed as she grabbed the *New York Standard* and started to flick through it with the practiced eye of someone who'd edited the paper the previous afternoon. She never knew how to disconnect from her work, though it wasn't like he could talk. He left her with the paper, walked to the kitchen and put a bagel into the toaster for her.

He thought about the strange situation that existed between them. Though Jack felt their relationship was equal to the one he'd had with his ex-wife – loving and supportive and exciting – sometimes it felt neither of them ever switched off from work enough to enjoy it. Celeste was living in a townhouse in New York and working as managing editor at the *Standard*, while he was living in Washington and working for President Bill McGhinnist. It had been that way for three years. He traveled to New York every second weekend, where they spent their time together feigning normalcy until he caught a late flight out of JFK on Sunday night. It was hard, but worth it.

The bagel popped. He gave it a liberal spread of cream cheese then picked up the plate and walked back into the dining room, stealing a glance over her shoulder at the story she was reading as he placed the plate down. It was yet another story about Israel and Palestine. The papers had been full of them for weeks.

"It'll work." Jack placed a hand on her shoulder.

"I'm not sure." She grabbed his hand and held it to her body as she finished reading the story. Then she reached for the bagel, took a bite and started to talk with her mouth full. "There have been so many letdowns it's hard to get too excited. Bringing them all into town was a ballsy move."

He nodded and sat beside her. They'd discussed the Israeli–Palestinian peace agreement deep into the night. Both of them were hopeful – but neither convinced – that the two sides would agree on the final few sticking points and get it done. Things had moved a long way since the massacre at the hospital in Gaza a few months prior, but the deal was a complicated one to negotiate.

"It'd be huge for McGhinnist. It's been a slog these past few years. He needs a big win leading up to the election."

"Plenty of presidents have tried, and failed, to crack the Israel–Palestine nut in their time, Jack." Celeste squeezed his hand gently. "If he's relying on this to get him over the line then it might be best to start preparing for life after the White House."

"He'll win." Jack's tone made it clear he didn't want to discuss the possibility of Bill McGhinnist losing the presidency.

"Just don't get too invested, okay?"

Jack nodded. It wasn't the first time she'd told him to be careful since he'd taken the job as special advisor to the President. While McGhinnist had no shortage of big ideas and a decent record of steering them through Congress, his popularity had taken a hit in recent months. Given America was still healing from the near takeover of the country by the Foundation for a New America and the full takeover by FEMA, Jack couldn't blame the public for some political fatigue. Yet he still felt the situation was unfair. McGhinnist had halted the blanket monitoring of US citizens and limited other impositions in place since 9/11, but those successes were yesterday's news – McGhinnist needed a new win.

The peace would be that.

Jack had spent nearly a year working with McGhinnist and US negotiator Karl Long to help shepherd the peace agreement between Israel and Palestine through complex negotiations and, at times, fraught decisions. Over countless meetings and phone calls, the sides had worked out problems large and small until, finally, they'd reached agreement on all issues but one: Israeli settlements on land claimed by Palestine. Despite this, McGhinnist had made the gutsy decision to schedule a date for the signing, hoping it would help to force a resolution on the last issue. McGhinnist had even authorized Long to throw out a few carrots if it meant getting a deal.

He'd be lying if he pretended not to care about the politics of it, given part of his job was to leverage wins like this into political gain for the President. But Jack's primary responsibility, and the sole reason he'd agreed to work for McGhinnist in the first place, was achieving good policy outcomes. The peace agreement was one of those. Any political benefits were a bonus.

"McGhinnist needs this to show he can build something positive. He needs to prove he can do more than just remove the excesses of others. This feels different. It feels good. He's going to get it done."

"Well, I hope you're right. He's proven before that he can take on big policy issues and win." Celeste pushed her plate aside. "Do you have much work to do today?"

"Not particularly. The President flies in later tonight, but he's straight into meetings with Karl." Jack thought hard to make sure he hadn't forgotten any appointments. "All clear."

"Glad to hear it. I get the feeling this might be the last break you get for a while, so I want you to make the most of it." She stood. "Now, are you coming or not?"

Jack's eyes widened as she walked slowly out of the kitchen. With each step, she exaggerated the movement of her hips slightly. She raised her tank top over her head and tossed it on the floor, then paused and dropped her panties. As he watched her walk to the bedroom, Jack grabbed the last bite of the bagel left on her plate, stood and followed her.

It was good to be home.

∾

SAMIH KHALADI WAITED at the crossing as dozens of cars blitzed through the intersection. He loved New York City, though not for the reasons most people did. It wasn't about the skyscrapers, the bustle or the attractions. What moved him was that so many people – all kinds of people – could live so closely together in relative harmony and safety. It was chaotic, but it worked.

The lights changed and he crossed the street with his

pair of security guards in tow, doing his best to stay a step or two ahead. If he had the choice, he'd go without the security entirely, but President McGhinnist had insisted the negotiators be escorted at all times when they were outside. Given Samih was representing Palestine in the peace negotiations, he had little choice.

He slowed as he caught sight of a Starbucks, then smiled and turned to his security. "I'm just going to get a—"

"Mr. Khaladi?" One of the guards interrupted, as the other looked at his watch. "We need to return to the UN building, sir. The lunch hour ends soon."

Samih sighed. He hated being on a schedule. It wasn't the guard's fault, but it was annoying. "Okay, but first let me grab a coffee."

"There's coffee back at the meeting, sir." The guard was insistent. "I really must insist that we turn back."

Samih felt his face flush. "The entire world will wait for me today if they have to. I'm one of the people trying to end the most intractable political conflict on the planet. I want a coffee, from here, so please wait outside for me while I go inside to get one."

Samih exhaled loudly and the door to the Starbucks felt his displeasure, as he pushed it open with some force. His security didn't seem happy and Samih didn't like throwing his weight around, but he wanted a few more minutes before returning to the pressure cooker. He waited in line for just a moment and then he reached the front.

"How're you today, sir?" An attendant struggled to feign interest. "What can I get for you?"

Samih swallowed his irritation and did his best to smile. "I would like a coffee please."

The man stared at him blankly. "Which kind, sir? You're supposed to know your order by the time you reach the front."

Samih's eyes narrowed as he considered the menu. "An Americano. A large one."

Samih paid and moved to the end of the counter, struggling not to laugh at the inanity of the exchange. After being involved in negotiations over land borders, migration of peoples and security issues – all incredibly high stakes – he'd had to be stepped through ordering a coffee by a college kid. Thinking about it cheered him up.

As he closed his wallet, he glanced at the photo he kept inside and felt a pang of regret. All he wanted for his people was peace, for them to be able to enjoy fast food, entertainment, shopping malls and sporting games without the threat of extremist violence or Israeli gunships. He wanted a nation for them. All that remained was closing the deal and hoping it was accepted. Only a few short years ago, Samih would have been at the front of the line of Palestinians decrying this agreement. Worse, he'd have advocated and committed violence to stop it from being signed. He'd been caught in a cycle of hate that served nobody and only left people dead. It was why he kept the photo of his brother close.

After his brother had been killed by an Israeli airstrike in retaliation for an attack Samih had ordered, Samih had faced a choice. In his anger, he'd considered further attacks, but he'd mourned and seen another way. Forming a breakaway group of Hamas, he'd banded with the Palestinian Liberation Organization to take the battle to the unreformed extremists. The conflict had been bloody – moderates and hardliners engaged in open warfare on the streets, with Israeli gunships occasionally adding their own fire and noise to the mess. The moderates had won, at huge cost. Samih had been offered leadership of the new, unified Palestinian authority but had declined in order to focus on helping to secure a lasting peace.

"Sir?" A Starbucks staff member touched Samih on the arm. "Sir? Your coffee is ready."

Samih shook his head. He was always prone to deep reflection on the past, but it seemed to be happening more often lately. He took the coffee. "Thank you."

He walked outside and didn't wait for his security to fall into line. The walk back to the UN building was uneventful. As he walked, he thought about the draft agreement. Though it didn't give his people everything they wanted, or deserved, it was the best deal that could be achieved. A good deal, peace and a state were better than waiting forever for the perfect deal.

The agreement had to succeed.

Back inside the building, Samih juggled his coffee as he returned to his seat with the other delegates. Everyone had the same goal: resolving the last issue. Samih represented the Palestinians and Ben Ebron represented the Israelis, as they'd done for years, aided in the negotiations by the US Special Envoy for Israeli–Palestinian Relations, Karl Long.

The last person to enter the room was in some ways the most important – Liliana Garza, Secretary-General of the United Nations. She'd obliged US President Bill McGhinnist's demands for the signing ceremony to be scheduled and for the talks to be finalized. Samih watched Garza as she walked to the head of the table.

"Gentlemen, I trust you enjoyed lunch?" She held her arms wide, a typically welcoming gesture from her during the tough negotiations. "If we're to sign an agreement tomorrow, we have this session to resolve the final issue. We left off at—"

"Compensation for displaced Israeli settlers." Ebron cut the pleasantries short, his voice sharp. "Israel is committed to finding a way through this issue and finalizing the agreement, but it mustn't be at the expense of our own people. There needs to be a strong package that I can take to my government."

Samih's lips pressed together but he kept quiet. Though he found it hard to comprehend that the final sticking point after three years of negotiations could be payments to Israelis who'd annexed the lands of his people, he knew that without compensation there would be no peace. He'd learned the hard way that one wrong word could destroy much painstaking work.

Garza took the interruption in her stride. "I've had my staff working the phones during the lunch hour. United Nations member states have agreed to contribute forty percent of the compensation amount. The rest of the world has done its part, now it's the turn of the others in this room."

Samih was surprised by the news, but smiled sadly. "This is an area where the Palestinian people can make little contribution. We are not a rich people."

Ebron flared. "Unacceptable. The Palestinians must contribute—"

Samih held up his hand. "However, upon achieving statehood, Palestine will set aside one percent of government revenue until one-tenth of the total is paid."

Ebron's mouth fell open slightly, before he seemed to catch himself and right his composure. "That's a welcome gesture, Mr. Khaladi, and one I didn't expect."

Samih smiled. He'd planned on just that and the effect had been powerful. For the diminutive state of Palestine to make a financial contribution to resettling Israelis was a game changer. Samih had long argued the presence of the settlers was illegal and that no compensation should be paid, but in the interests of peace a concession had to be made. He hoped it would be enough.

Long tapped his signet ring on the table. It had stopped bothering Samih, because it appeared be a habit. "The

President has authorized me to increase the contribution of the United States to twenty-five percent, but that's as high as we're going to go."

"A very generous offer." Samih nodded.

"Twenty-five percent remains." Ebron sighed as he looked at each of them, as if the pressure of expectation was too much.

"Mr. Ebron?" Garza's voice was gentle. "Do you need a recess to consult with your government and consider Israel's position?"

"No, that won't be necessary." Ebron sighed. "It burns me to my core that Israel must contribute financially to the displacement of its own citizens, but the pressure of tomorrow's deadline and the aftermath of the Al Amal massacre leave me little choice. I agree."

"Wonderful." Garza beamed. "Any costs borne out of this agreement will be more than paid for by the peace and prosperity that also flows from it."

"It's agreed then?" Long's eyes widened as they flicked between Samih and Ebron. "We have something to sign?"

"The agreement is suitable for Israel, if a little expensive." Ebron placed his palms flat on the table. "I hope this can be the end of it."

Now Samih felt the weight of expectation. He looked down at his notes, trying to think of any negatives for his people that he might have missed. He'd already gained the agreement of his leadership on the draft text, with the exception of the issues worked out during this final day. There was nothing in the last few resolutions that would prevent the deal being closed. It was good enough.

"Well?" Long's voice had an edge.

Samih looked up. He rested his elbows on the table with a smile. "My friends, this is an important day. We've achieved peace."

The ever-serious Ebron leaned back and spun around

on his chair, while Long slapped the table and sported a wide grin. Samih closed his eyes and allowed himself a moment of reflection. This occasion had been so long in coming, he never thought he'd see it. Thousands dead, generations ruined, years wasted. He hoped his people would welcome the peace on offer.

"Excuse me, Mr. Khaladi?"

Samih opened his eyes. Ebron was standing in front of him. "Yes?"

"I'd like to shake your hand."

Samih stood, feeling all the weight of his sixty years, then shook the proffered hand. "This is a momentous day, my friend."

"It is." Ebron nodded and pulled his hand away, clearly not used to being so personable.

"We will sign the agreement tomorrow." Garza joined them, the relief in her voice clear. "Twenty-eight days after that, there will be peace."

"ZED ESHKOL IS professor of history at Yeshiva University, a position he's held for nearly forty years. He lectures in Jewish history and his specialty is the politics surrounding the creation of Israel following the Second World War. He's considered one of the world's leading thinkers on the causes and consequences of conflict between Israel and its neighbors, including the Palestinian people."

When the crowd started its applause, Zed planted his cane on the ground, pushed on it heavily and climbed to his feet. Letting the cane support him, he shuffled slowly to the stage. At the bottom of the stairs he paused, making a mental note to talk to the staffer who'd selected the venue. Zed wasn't as spry as he used to be.

"Thank you, Ariel." Zed spoke softly, short of breath,

once he'd reached the top of the stairs. He patted the man on the shoulder.

Ariel beamed. "No problem, professor. Good luck with your lecture."

As Zed moved to the lectern, he reflected that, while Ariel had promise, he needed to be molded. He adjusted the microphone, handed his cane to another staffer and gripped the sides of the lectern as if his life depended on it. After checking his notes were in place, he looked up to the packed theatre. That audiences still came to see him speak was a thrill to him.

"Thank you all for coming. My thanks also to Ariel, who's organized a great program for us." Zed smiled. "I do wish I wasn't here tonight, though, or that we at least had a better reason to come together, but here we are. I'll speak for just a few moments, then we'll enjoy supper and reconvene for questions and discussion."

Zed looked down at his notes and used the pause to catch his breath before speaking again. "Quite simply, my friends, the peace agreement that will be signed tomorrow is a betrayal of Israel and the Jewish people, who gained their freedom and a state of their own after one of the darkest episodes in human history."

Zed looked up at the crowd. He usually didn't like mentioning the Holocaust, but there was no way to avoid it this evening. "I'll not speak of the Holocaust again, though many of you know that I survived it, but please be clear that the situation facing us tomorrow is the most desperate since that terrible chapter in our history.

"Israel has existed and grown despite being under the dark cloud of conflict. Every citizen has military training, its armed forces are potent, Mossad is rightly feared and a nuclear stockpile is the ultimate deterrent. Indeed, Israel has defended itself against aggression many times, often in desperate circumstances. It has never been belligerent, but always vigilant."

Zed paused and looked around the theatre. For a hastily convened event, the turnout was excellent. It gave him hope that, while the vast majority of the world and the American public wanted a deal between Israel and Palestine, there was still a cohort of the faithful. Over nine decades, he'd learned that where there was a glimmer of hope, there was the possibility of deliverance.

He continued. "Through it all, Israel has showed remarkable restraint in dealing with this aggression. Sometimes against better judgment, it has tolerated and negotiated when others would have struck, resorting to retaliation only when it's absolutely necessary. Israel invested in the Iron Dome, to stop rocket attacks, rather than spending more on jets and rockets to flatten the attackers."

Zed started to cough. Turning away from the lectern, he raised one hand to cover his mouth, but made sure to keep the other in place. He felt as if knives were stabbing him in the chest as his body clenched with each cough, though he did his best to calm himself and bring it under control. A few members of the crowd shouted out for someone to help him.

Someone gripped his arm and he heard Ariel's voice. "Professor, are you okay? I'll ask for an early recess."

"No!" Zed coughed again and then looked up to Ariel, his voice sharp. "Just give me a moment."

"Okay, professor. Take your time, at least."

Zed kept his back to the audience as he brought the coughing under control. Finally, the worst of it subsided and he returned to the lectern. "My apologies for the interruption, ladies and gentlemen. I frequently find that my body is my toughest critic these days."

The crowd offered sympathetic smiles and laughs. He

continued. "Israel's restraint hasn't been enough. For decades the world has judged and threatened Israel, twisting the arm of its leaders to show ever more restraint, make deals and repudiate its right to exist, peacefully, within its own borders.

"Yet while Israel has attempted to co-exist with its neighbors and the Palestinians in the hope of peace, it's never enough. Israel's enemies aim for total annihilation while the world expects capitulation to the demands of cutthroats and criminals.

"Thankfully, strong Israeli leaders long resisted those demands. But now, weak leaders are happily slitting their own throats. A massacre perpetrated by a madman, sad though it was, has pressured Israel's leaders into signing an agreement that is evil. It will split an Israeli state that should always be strong."

Zed paused. He'd thought long and hard about the next part of his speech. "The United Nations and the USA are revisionists who helped to grant Israel its freedom only to convince the country's leaders, now, to abandon much of that freedom – to act, to defend itself, to exist within its own borders.

"This agreement mustn't be signed. It represents the eradication of an Israeli state at the height of its power, the betrayal of our people and a disgrace before God. Every free-thinking Jew the world over needs to stand against this travesty, or history will judge this generation as the one that killed the dream of Israel!"

Zed felt an enormous wave of pleasure and relief wash over him as applause roared. He smiled slightly and gripped the lectern until the noise receded, then waved a hand lazily in the air and signaled for a staffer to bring his cane. It would take him an eternity to get down the stairs again.

By the time he'd managed the journey and taken a seat,

most of the rest of the crowd was busy getting supper in the foyer. Zed wasn't interested in making small talk. Instead, he wanted time to himself before the questions started and other eminent speakers joined him on stage. But he never got the chance.

A man approached and leaned down to speak to Zed. "Professor Eshkol? I'm David Kahlon. May I have a moment?"

Zed smiled softly, unable to help himself but careful to hide it. Men like these were as regular as clockwork. "Of course."

Kahlon nodded and sat. "Professor, I wanted to pay my respects on behalf of the Jewish Home. Many of my colleagues share your views."

Zed laughed. He'd closely followed the statements of Jewish Home – one of Israel's major conservative political parties – about the peace agreement. "It's a shame the government does not. I think it's important that those with a public voice continue to advocate sanity."

"Couldn't agree more, professor. I've been asked to sound you out, again, for your interest in becoming a citizen of Israel and running to join the Knesset."

Zed shook his head softly. This felt like the thousandth time he'd been asked to join the Israeli parliament. But he was old, tired and comfortable. He'd had his chance at the spotlight after surviving the Holocaust and helping to establish Israel, but had chosen instead to make his contribution in academia.

"Professor?" Kahlon pressed.

"Your request just takes me back some years." Zed smiled. "I think you know my answer. I'm an old man."

"But—"

Zed held up his hand. "No. Please respect my decision. I'll continue doing all I can to speak against this peace process, and to support the right conservatives with my voice during Israeli elections, but that's the sum of my contribution. I'm not a man for the limelight, Mr. Kahlon. Now, please excuse me."

There was a tinge of regret in Kahlon's smile, but they shook hands and he left. Zed forgot about him quickly. He had a lecture to finish.

2

On the day the peace agreement between Israel and Palestine is to be signed, sources from inside the White House have revealed that the United States is considering an unprecedented level of military support to Israel over the next month. The same source stated that the President is nervous about the agreement holding over the twenty-eight–day countdown period. Following the leak, several key Republicans have spoken in favor of the deployment, though others joined with Democrats to condemn yet another US military adventure in the Middle East. Despite the mixed views, it appears that the McGhinnist administration will let nothing stand between the division of Israel and Palestine into two states.

New York Standard

J ack stared at the croissant, tempted to devour it against all protocol and his better judgment. He'd been sitting in the New York Grand Hyatt dining room with a half-dozen others for nearly an hour, waiting for the President and his guests to finish their private meeting and arrive for breakfast. Polite group conversation had devolved into a series of rolling battles, with existing acquaintances talking quietly among themselves while they waited. Jack was struggling not to contemplate his empty stomach and the pastry that promised so much.

The President had ordered the entire hotel booked for VIP attendees at the peace conference. McGhinnist was also staying at the hotel, leaving no doubt as to how seriously he was taking the event. The Secret Service and NYPD had locked down the building, with only official vehicles and a select number of credentialed visitors allowed inside the cordon. The security was extreme, but then so to was the event. Jack knew that one bomb or crazed gunman would be all it took to end this thing.

"Reckon we'll hit an hour?" Jack turned to the President's National Security Advisor, James Tipping, doing his best to get his mind off food.

Tipping turned to Jack and smiled, as if his mind was returning from considering some deep question. "I'm going to eat the table soon."

Jack laughed. Though they'd been friends since Jack had joined McGhinnist's administration, Tipping was a man of few words – a very private guy. Tipping lived in Georgetown and McGhinnist had brought him over from the Bureau upon becoming president. Jack respected Tipping's intellect deeply and the other man was good for a drink. He couldn't say the same about all of his colleagues.

"How's Celeste?"

"Busy. This agreement is as much work for her as it is for us." Jack let out a long sigh. "It'll be good to see it done, though Celeste might sell less papers."

"Should have stayed in that game." Tipping frowned. "I'm not really sure why you left journalism to join our merry band. What exactly is your role, Jack?"

Jack had heard it all before and knew where this was heading. Tipping had a sharp sense of humor. "Special Advisor to the President."

Tipping snorted. "I advise on national security. Others advise on economics, foreign relations – all sorts of things. What do you do, Jack?"

Jack kept his voice flat. "I advise."

Tipping guffawed and Jack shared the laugh, knowing there was some truth to the other man's jokes. As McGhinnist's fixer and sounding board, Jack's role description was fairly vague and he was constantly stepping on toes. It meant a few people were just waiting for him to slip up, even some of those inside the White House.

Jack was about to speak again when the woman sitting one along from Tipping, Republican senator Diane Yates, craned her head toward them.

"Excuse me."

Jack sighed but did his best to smile. He wasn't in the mood for the senator or her opinions, but such was the price of a compliant Senate. "Yes, senator?"

Yates glanced at Tipping and then locked eyes on Jack, her features cold and sharp. "I couldn't help but overhear your conversation. I understand your role in the administration, Jack, unlike some of your colleagues, but I can't fathom how you can think the path the President is taking with Israel is wise."

Yates had been dead against the peace from the start, demanding America walk away from any solution that displaced Israelis. Given her status as Senate Majority Leader, she had to be listened to, humored and invited to the important dinners. She hadn't gotten her way, but she'd gone down swinging. Luckily, Jack knew which buttons to push.

"State Department and DOD analysis shows that if we

can secure the peace, then we'll be able to reduce our military and diplomatic footprint in the region by forty percent." Jack looked to Tipping, who nodded. "Given the President's commitment to tackling the deficit, I think you'll agree that's a handy saving."

Yates shook her head. "Well, that's true, but—"

"Not to mention the way we've been able to use this deal to get Iran on side." Tipping completed the one-two alley-oop. "We've got Tehran eating out of our hand right now, which is something the Democrats never managed. They let Iran acquire nukes, which we've managed to keep them from using."

Yates harrumphed and turned away. With a shake of his head, Jack smirked slightly at Tipping, thankful for the save. Yates could go on for hours if she built up enough steam, but having the National Security Advisor shoot down her protests had prevented that.

The door to the dining room opened and Jack stood with the other guests as McGhinnist walked in, joined by Ben Ebron, the Israeli negotiator, Samih Khaladi, the Palestinian negotiator and Karl Long, the US Special Envoy for Israeli–Palestinian Relations. They appeared in good spirits after McGhinnist had insisted on a morning meeting with the negotiators, prior to the signing.

"Sorry everyone, we were held up." McGhinnist's voice boomed in the enormous dining room. "Sit, please."

Despite McGhinnist's words, protocol dictated that every guest stand until the President was seated. Once he was, everyone sat and polite conversation resumed. Jack scanned the new arrivals for any hint of stress or gripe, but Ebron, Khaladi and Long seemed fine. Jack had been concerned when McGhinnist had told him about the unscheduled meeting, but it appeared to have gone well.

McGhinnist cleared his throat softly. "Before we eat, I wanted to express my sincere pleasure at having our guests here, along with some of my colleagues. Everyone here has had a part to play in negotiating peace, though we have not yet achieved it.

"In private, we've discussed the pressure on everyone to walk away from this deal. Israel faces political backlash and Palestine still has militants in its midst who may try to derail the peace. But we must remain strong as allies and as friends, because we've come too far to fail."

Jack's eyes narrowed. Even though there'd been a huge breakthrough in the negotiations and the deal was ready to be signed, McGhinnist was still urging vigilance and caution. After the signing, there was to be a twenty-eight-day countdown to peace, after which the state of Palestine would exist. Jack knew the President was nervous, but he wasn't sure where the speech was heading.

McGhinnist stared straight down the table. "After discussion, and after all parties reiterated their unbridled commitment to this agreement, I've signed off on the US force deployments that had previously been discussed. These measures will bolster the chances of the agreement surviving the next month."

Jack thought he could feel the steam from Senator Yates's ears as he caught Tipping's eye. The National Security Advisor nodded slightly, indicating that he'd tried to talk the President out of the deployment, but that McGhinnist had won out. They both turned back to the President, eager to hear the details of what was going to happen in the coming weeks.

"Significant naval assets will be deployed into the Mediterranean to warn off Israel's neighbors from trying to thwart the process. As well, American theater missile defense assets will be deployed inside Israel, to prevent any rockets launched by rogue Palestinians from landing and derailing this agreement.

"In return for these measures, I've gained agreement

from Israel that it will hold an entirely defensive military posture, while Palestine will redouble its efforts to keep militants in check. All sides must work at this, because one incident could destroy all of our efforts."

McGhinnist sat back and there were nods all around the table. As the food was served, Jack couldn't help but think it was going to be a good day.

JACK CLAPPED HALF-HEARTEDLY with the rest of the dignitaries as Samih Khaladi finished his remarks and stepped back from the lectern. The Palestinian chief negotiator had given a stupid speech about how, while buying a coffee, he'd reflected on the simple pleasure that statehood conferred on citizens. Jack had tuned out, bored and focused on his own problems, but clapped when required.

He let out a long, slow breath, realizing that he needed to cool down. As soon as he'd finished at the breakfast he'd logged on to the *Standard* online, only to find that Celeste had written a story confirming the US deployments to Israel, even before McGhinnist had announced it at the breakfast. Someone from inside the White House had leaked the President's decision.

Not that a leak within the White House was necessarily a problem. There were plenty every day, most of them intentional, but this one wasn't and the downstream reporting had painted the deployments as a sign that the President had doubts about the durability of the agreement. The peace process didn't need any more kindling on a bonfire that was piled high, waiting to be sparked.

It had made him furious at Celeste. But instead of recognizing the danger, he'd called her, ranted, and lost his cool about the leaks and her decision to publish confirmation of the deployments. Her voice had been cold when she'd told him, in no uncertain terms, to mind his own job while she minded hers. He'd hung up in a huff and not really cooled down since.

As Jack sighed again, the Israeli negotiator, Ben Ebron, stepped forward. He placed his notes on the lectern and adjusted the microphone.

"I'll be brief, because everything I wish to say is contained within the pages on that table over there. Israel wants peace and we want Palestine as a neighbor."

Jack was glad that Ebron left it at that. The more that was said and the longer it took, the more chance there was that a loose thread would be pulled and the whole thing would unravel. Jack wanted the agreement signed and for the next month to pass in boring normalcy. This issue had taken up way too much of the administration's attention. It was time for the payoff.

He watched as Ebron and Khaladi walked to the signing table. As they sat and posed for photographs, Jack spotted Celeste across the room. She was standing with some of her staff, eyes glued to the signing and unaware that he was watching her. He knew she'd only done her job, but he was still furious at her for printing the leak. He knew he shouldn't, but he stalked over to her anyway.

"Got a minute?"

She turned, a look of surprise on her face, then frowned. "Can it wait?"

"Not really." Jack gestured with his head away from the group.

She nodded and followed him to the back of the room, clearly annoyed, but that was nothing compared to his pent-up anger. Jack glanced up at the stage, where Khaladi and Ebron were preparing to sign. Once they were on their own, Jack turned around and faced Celeste, who had her arms crossed over her chest and a look of irritation on her face. This was going to be a street fight.

"What's the problem? You just embarrassed me." Her voice was a low hiss. "It's hard enough having my boyfriend on staff at the White House, now this?"

Jack kept his voice low even as his temper flared. "You don't think you're making *my* job harder? You're printing leaks from inside the White House! Half of the administration now thinks I'm whispering sweet somethings into your ear for a blowjob, Celeste!"

Her eyes narrowed and Jack felt the temperature between them drop to below freezing. "You're embarrassing yourself. I'm walking away now."

Jack wanted to keep talking, but he let her go. He stalked his way back to the front of the room, where Ebron was signing the document. He couldn't take his mind off Celeste. Though he'd known that confronting her would achieve nothing, it was too late for second thoughts. He'd be able to patch it up, but it might take some time.

As Samih Khaladi lifted his pen and put it to paper, he looked up to the crowd with a wide smile. Despite his anger, Jack smiled as Khaladi turned to Ebron and shook the Israeli's hand, even as camera flashes bathed the men in light. At their insistence, McGhinnist joined the pair, forming a formidable triad of influence. It was hard not to appreciate history in the making.

Once the flashes started to die down, the President moved to the lectern. Jack was surprised – McGhinnist wasn't scheduled to speak and, though McGhinnist sometimes liked to freelance, Jack would prefer he didn't do it during one of the most sensitive political events in the history of the planet. He looked around and caught James Tipping's eye. The other man shrugged.

"I don't want to take the limelight, because this day very much belongs to Israel and, in twenty-eight days, the state of Palestine. But I do want to congratulate my friends Ben and Samih for achieving what many people considered impossible." McGhinnist beamed and held his arms out wide. "You're all witnesses to—"

"*Gun! Gun!*"

Jack's mind raced and his eyes swept the room, as Secret Service agents continued to shout over the top of the President's speech. A moment later a gunshot boomed from somewhere near the stage, well in front of Jack. Though Jack couldn't see the gunman, he could see McGhinnist wince and grip his arm as a second shot sounded.

Chaos erupted as several agents jumped on the President and brought him to the ground, heralded by the shots of Secret Service agents and the shouts of others in the room. Jack inched forward as those near the front turned and surged away from the stage. Fighting the crowd, Jack joined Secret Service agents and NYPD officers in pushing toward the President, needing to know if he was alive.

By now the gunfire had ceased, but the scene was still manic. When he reached the stage, the President and the negotiators were nowhere to be seen, having been evacuated, but several Secret Service agents remained, weapons drawn. Jack glanced at the front of the stage, where a man was lying dead, blood starting to pool around his corpse.

Jack made his way to the table, where the signed peace agreement was still in its leather folder. A small speck of McGhinnist's blood flecked the edge of the paper, which was otherwise untouched – the scratchy signature of Ben Ebron intact next to the elegant curves of Samih Khaladi. With a smile of relief, Jack closed the cover, lifted the folder and moved to the edge of the stage.

"You shouldn't be here, sir." One of the agents peeled off

and grabbed Jack by the arm. "Come with me, I'll help you keep that thing safe."

Jack nodded and let himself be dragged forward. It was hard to believe that only moments before the room had been filled with celebration and goodwill. Now it was abandoned, except for men with guns and the detritus of those who'd fled: paper, water bottles and other trash. He shivered involuntarily. He needed to find Celeste.

The Secret Service agent led him outside, where NYPD officers were gathering everyone into a guarded area. He knew without asking that all would remain here until there was certainty that the threat had been contained. The thought of being inside a ring of serious-looking people with guns was fine with Jack at the moment.

Jack caught sight of Celeste. He thanked the agent and moved closer, hugging her tightly as she collapsed into his embrace. "You okay?"

"I thought we were done with getting blown up and shot at." She nestled into his chest. "At least this time the guys with guns are on our side."

Jack laughed, despite the seriousness of the situation. He broke the embrace and turned to the agent. "Any word from the President?"

The agent nodded. "He took one in the hand. They're evacuating him to New York Presbyterian to get it dealt with. We're lucky the guy was a terrible shot."

"He'll be okay." Jack smiled and clutched the folder, which had the peace agreement inside.

It was going to be a long twenty-eight days.

ARON BRAFF SHIELDED himself against the wind and rain as it whipped at his face. Taking the final few steps toward the cellar, he grunted as he pulled open the heavy door. The wind conspired against his effort, howling in apparent protest as he stepped into the cellar and eased the door closed, bracing to stop the wind from slamming it shut.

The stairs were in near darkness. Though his eyes adjusted as he descended, he'd been here so many times that he could do it blindfolded. When he reached the bottom of the small staircase, it opened into an expansive room lit by dozens of candles of all shapes and sizes and dominated by a hardwood table, at which the others were already seated.

"Please excuse my tardiness." Aron strode forward and took his place at the head of the table. "It's this cursed weather."

"It doesn't matter." Miri Shaked smiled warmly, her features as bright as the candles. "We have twenty-eight days, what difference will twenty minutes make?"

"Well put." Aron stared at his hands for a few moments. He never thought he'd have to convene the meeting. He looked up again. "So, it's done."

The others offered a mix of reactions. A few were stone-faced, resolute and ready. Others seemed angry. A few were upset. After so much effort to safeguard Israel by thousands of individuals over decades, its final guardians were now needed: a mix of loyalists who'd each given much during their official service to Israel and would give more still in the next month.

This was the inner circle. Though Aron didn't know everything, he knew that there were other cells just like this one all around the world. Some were lackeys, ready to do the grunt work of their mission, while others were very senior – experts and influencers in different fields, with different expertise and one unifying goal.

"I don't need to tell any of you how serious this situation is. It threatens the death of Israel as we know it." Aron looked at each of them in turn, trying to spot any weak links in the chain. He doubted there were, but he had to be sure. "You all know what we're about to commence. If you have issue, you may leave."

"We're here for the same reason you are, Aron." David Lubelsky's voice had an edge and his shaved head seemed to glow in the candlelight.

Aron swallowed hard. These individuals had been selected, prepared and now activated in the same way he had and it was unfair of him to question their resolve. He'd take exception at his own being challenged, so it was no surprise that Lubelsky had taken issue with his words.

"Of course. Forgive me. I'm still astounded that it's come to this." Aron ran a hand through his hair. "I thought someone would walk away from the table."

"We all did, as has happened a million times before." Shaked shrugged. "But it's done. The agreement is signed and we have our orders."

Aron nodded and glanced at each of them. The scene was eerie and potentially overly dramatic – a candlelit basement in the middle of the countryside. But theirs was a high-stakes game against adversaries capable of finding small needles in large haystacks. Preventing that required the utmost care, considerable expertise and techniques long thought outdated.

"You're right." Aron held out his hands to encompass the group. "We must invoke the Samson Option."

Shaked nodded. "Yes."

"Regretfully." Lubelsky closed his eyes.

The discussion moved down the table and each of them had a say, but it was a formality. They knew what needed doing. The Samson Option had never been intended for use, designed instead to threaten potential enemies and show them that no matter how hard you hit Israel, no matter how beaten she was, she'd always win.

The doctrine was simple – any threat to the territorial

integrity of Israel sufficient enough to compromise its existence must be met with indiscriminate nuclear fire. The Jewish people understood their past and the Samson Option was insurance against the future. If the Jewish state ever faced extinction, it had the power to destroy the world.

Aron and his colleagues considered the peace agreement such doom, and they would make sure to take the world down with them before Israel went meekly into history. That Israeli politicians had been conspiring in the death of their own state complicated matters, but it didn't matter and their doctrine was clear: massive destruction targeted at any threat to Israel. Even Israelis.

"Very well." Aron placed his elbow on the table and rested his head in his hands. "We should get started."

"I'll get the equipment." Shaked stood and moved toward a locked metal crate at the side of the room, which she busied herself with opening.

As he waited, Aron sat in silence with his eyes downcast. Though he knew what had to be done and that he had the most important role to play, he felt the enormity of the weight on his shoulders. In a short while they'd become the most wanted people on Earth. He knew that the treacherous government in Jerusalem would hunt them. As would others.

"It's ready." Shaked flicked a few switches. "It's not the most high-tech setup, but it will do the job."

"And it won't be able to be identified? We can't be traced here or tracked once we distribute this?" Aron needed to be sure.

"No."

"Okay." Aron nodded. He picked up a balaclava from the table and slid it over his head. "Everyone ready?"

The others donned their own masks and then stood. They crowded around his chair, facing the camera. When the group was loosely assembled, Shaked made sure everyone was in shot before pressing a few buttons and moving quickly to join the group. As she moved past him, Aron felt a pat on the shoulder. He interpreted it both as a message of good luck and to get on with it.

He looked straight down the camera and spoke clearly. "I'm a former Mossad agent. The others around me served Israel or the Jewish people in one form or another. We speak as one to a nation of many and a world of more, who don't realize the gross mistake that's about to be committed."

Aron paused and swallowed hard, making sure he kept his voice even and his pace slow. "We are the final bastion against any who'd destroy the Jewish state. Long a home, a refuge, to its people, that state is soon to be carved up by smiling traitors and enemies who conspire to destroy that home.

"My colleagues and I will ensure the survival of Israel, or the destruction of its enemies: the Palestinians who want to steal Israel's land and prosperity; the Knesset and the administration of Prime Minister Schiller who are in a hurry to abandon their people; and other states who are ready to pick the bones."

Aron leaned forward. "To the Israeli Government, we demand that you abandon this false peace, which spits on the sacrifice that generations of Jewish people have made to form and protect Israel. If the government won't act, it's up to Israelis to make them listen. Take to the streets and show your displeasure.

"To the Palestinian people, skulk from your holes and shout to the world to abandon this peace. Though we have problems with Israel, our anger is also directed at you. If it goes ahead, you will all feel the sweet taste of peace turn to ashes in your mouth.

"Finally, to the United States Government. You're as much to blame as anyone for this. You've used your influence to push Israel in one direction, now you must use that same influence to push it right back in the other. In gambling terms, you're committed. You're all in."

Aron looked left and right at his colleagues, watching them nod, before he continued. "Our demand is simple: that the deal be abandoned and that the status quo be maintained. If this occurs, we won't be heard from again. If it doesn't, the consequences will be devastating.

"Jerusalem. Mecca. New York City. Each location will be attacked with nuclear weapons should our demand not be met. There will be no negotiation or communication. Trying to find us would waste resources and time better spent unwinding the agreement. We're invisible. Until the countdown strikes zero."

Aron went silent and stared at the camera. As Shaked walked over and stopped the recording, Aron took several deep breaths. It wasn't every day you started the countdown clock on a nuclear attack. Several of the others patted him on the back or offered words of encouragement, but he barely heard them. He was lost in his own head for several moments.

Finally, he stood, walked over to Shaked and tapped her on the shoulder. She nearly jumped at the interruption and then turned and smiled.

"Okay?"

"Perfect." She beamed. "I'll cut it right away and get it ready to go. We can then release it to the world. An hour of work, at most."

"Wonderful." Aron smiled and spoke loudly to the whole group. "We carry the fate of our homeland in our hands, though what we're doing won't be easy."

Aron just hoped it would be enough.

3

Just one day after the signing of the peace agreement between Israel and Palestine and the process appears to be in tatters. United States President McGhinnist was wounded in an attempt on his life at the signing ceremony, for which no group has yet claimed responsibility. In addition, last night, a group of extremist Zionists threatened to use nuclear devices to destroy Jerusalem, Mecca and New York City if the agreement is enacted. These events have sapped much enthusiasm for the peace process, sparking protests across America and the Middle East. Despite these pressures, the signatories have so far remained resolute in their support for the agreement.

New York Standard

Jack had felt uncomfortable about his place at National Security Council meetings for the past three years. Though it was part of the job, his status on the council was murky. He was an advisor – not a formal member – who attended at the behest of the President. While some of the permanent members had welcomed him, others barely tolerated his presence.

Given McGhinnist was absent following the shooting, Jack felt even more out of place. He cleared his throat. "How seriously do we have to take the threat?"

Frank Howard, Director of National Intelligence, glanced at Jack with barely restrained contempt and then addressed the whole group. "Seriously enough, given the stakes. While we have no intelligence on this group, if they do have access to Israeli nukes the shit could fly. We need to find out if they do."

James Tipping gave Jack a small nod of support and then turned to Howard. "We don't know *anything* about these guys?"

"Nope. They're new on the radar. Monitoring Jewish extremists hasn't been a priority in recent years." Howard's eyes narrowed and he glared at Jack. "Though I should note that if we hadn't done such a thorough job of dismantling our intelligence eyes and ears in the past little while, we might know more."

Jack couldn't resist. "If those eyes and ears hadn't been monitoring American citizens en masse, we may have avoided that outcome."

Howard hissed. "Why exactly are you here, Ja—"

"That's enough!" Bill McGhinnist's voice boomed.

Jack's eyes shot to the door. As everyone stood, the President approached the table with the help of an aide, anger radiating off him. That he was here at all was incredible, given he'd been shot less than a day earlier. It showed the severity of the Zionist threat and how important McGhinnist considered the peace agreement.

Howard started to stammer something. "Mr. President, I—"

"Jack is here because I want him to be. I may be wounded, but I'm still the President. Now, can we focus?"

Jack smiled as McGhinnist sat. In the aftermath of the United Nations attack, he'd been evacuated to the New

York Grand Hyatt with other members of the administration and the negotiators. He'd flown back to Washington overnight and an NSC meeting had been called for the morning. McGhinnist's presence was a surprise, though apart from a heavily dressed hand he appeared fine.

"So what do we know?" McGhinnist looked down the table, his tone making it clear he wanted to focus on business, not squabbles between his staff. "James?"

Tipping nodded. "After the attack on you at the signing ceremony, there was no increase in global flagged chatter. However, near midnight eastern time, every major news channel in the world received a video file containing a threat from a group of self-styled Zionist extremists."

"I saw that." McGhinnist sighed. "So let me see if I've caught up: The peace agreement is bad because it takes away Israeli territory, is the death of Israel itself and an attack on Israeli Jews? If the agreement stands, they'll hit Jerusalem, Mecca and New York with nukes. If we abandon the deal, all is well. How'd I do?"

Tipping smiled. "Perfect, sir."

"Okay, let's park that for a minute. Anyone claiming responsibility for the attack on me?" McGhinnist shifted in his seat and winced in pain.

Tipping shrugged. "We can't be sure the Zionists are behind your shooting, but it would be a pretty big coincidence if the events aren't connected."

"So one assault – on me – and one threat. They're wanting us to look at what they did and listen to what more they can do."

Jack leaned forward. "They've certainly made a statement."

"Where to from here?" McGhinnist eyed each member of the council.

"It's questionable whether this group has the clout they

claim to, Mr. President." Howard spoke carefully. "We need to substantiate the threat."

Jan Wilson – the White House Chief of Staff – scoffed. "We've got twenty-seven days. We don't have time to substantiate it, we just need to stop it."

Howard started to protest, but Tipping chimed in, "Jan is right. We need to assume they have access to the weapons. The most likely source is Israel."

Jack winced at the thought of Israeli nukes blowing up Mecca. Whatever damage the nukes caused would pale in comparison to the shitstorm that was unleashed on whatever remained of Israel. It mightn't be a world war, but it'd make anything recent look like a fireworks display. It was moments like this he felt the weight of his job. He couldn't imagine how McGhinnist felt.

"Right, that's a fair assumption. So our first job is making sure all nuclear weapons – particularly those in Israel – are doubly secured." McGhinnist looked to the secretary of defense, who nodded and then pressed a button on the phone in front of him to put it on speaker. "Get me the Israeli PM."

It took a few moments for the council secretary to speak over the phone. "Mr. President, I'm told that the PM is in bed. His assistant asked us to make a time."

McGhinnist sighed. "I need to speak with him now, Madeleine."

There was another pause before she spoke again. "Connecting, sir."

"This is Mikael Schiller speaking." His voice sounded heavy with sleep, surprising given the events of the past few days.

McGhinnist smiled "Mr. Prime Minister, you're on the line with the members of my National Security Council. Thanks for taking our call."

"It's fine, Mr. President." The voice on the other

sounded a bit reserved. A bit cautious. "How are you feeling?"

"My hand hurts like a bitch, but I'm on my feet and it could have been worse, thanks for asking."

The warmth in McGhinnist's voice when he was talking to others always surprised Jack. Though he was a former FBI Director and had a reputation as a bit of a hard ass, in conversation with others he had a wonderful rapport. Jack didn't doubt that McGhinnist's temperament had contributed to the negotiation of the agreement that now threatened to unravel.

Schiller coughed lightly. "What can I do for you?"

McGhinnist seemed to steel himself. "Mr. Prime Minister, we're enormously concerned about the Zionist threat."

"As are we. But rest assured that Israel remains committed to the agreement at the same time as we attempt to eradicate this cancer."

"We may not need to go on the offensive, Mr. Prime Minister, if we can ensure they never get their hands on nuclear weapons."

There was a pause. "Can you explain what you mean?"

"My National Security Council is convinced that the Zionists' likely source of weapons is from Israeli stockpiles. If we can safeguard those until the countdown expires, then the threat will be mostly dealt with. Unless, of course, they already have the weapons or an alternative supply."

Schiller spoke carefully. "We've no evidence of such. In fact, we have very little intelligence on this group, though we're working to get it."

"Same story over here." McGhinnist sighed. "It appears the best form of offense may be a good defense."

"Israel's stockpiles are safe. We've done a full audit." Schiller was speaking slowly, carefully, as if he had something to hide or was feeling his way through the conversation. "We've doubled security at all installations and are conducting enhanced background checks on anyone with access to the weapons."

Jack still found it incredible that Israel had revealed its nuclear stockpiles as part of the peace process. Israel had been pressured on the issue throughout the negotiations and, while Schiller hadn't taken a backward step in maintaining his country's right to the weapons, he'd made public more information about Israel's capability than any leader in its history. It had been a sign of goodwill.

"Hold for a second please, Mr. Prime Minister?" McGhinnist muted the call as he scratched his forehead. "I'm not convinced he's telling us the truth. Even if he is, it's not quite enough to reassure me that the nukes are wrapped up tightly. But what can we do?"

There was silence around the table, no one keen to offer a solution to a very high-stakes problem. Short of spying on the Israeli Prime Minister, there was no way to be certain that his country's nuclear stockpiles were safe. But taking Schiller's assurances at face value was a gamble and Manhattan was a large pile of chips to lose if they got it wrong.

Howard leaned forward. "There's not much we can do, sir. If we were getting questions about our weapons, we'd politely tell the questioner to fuck off."

As he looked at the pursed lips around the table and the silence rang like a bell, Jack was astounded at the lack of imagination. "Why can't we offer US troops? We're already deploying some to puff our chests and make sure both sides play nice. Just extend the protection to the nuclear stockpiles."

McGhinnist smiled and pressed mute on the phone again. "Mr. Prime Minister? Thanks for your patience. I've got an offer for you. I think you'll find it's one you shouldn't refuse."

ZED MOVED his pawn slowly and deliberately, glancing up at his opponent. "Your move, Ariel."

Ariel looked down at the board with a smile on his face. "Lame move, professor. You're usually better competition than this."

Zed closed his eyes. He was unbelievably tired from the excitement of the past week or two. The peace agreement between Israel and Palestine had been signed, despite his best efforts and the shooting of the President of the United States. Now the world was on a countdown to peace between the two peoples. The two nations. He'd invited Ariel to play chess to get his mind off it.

He really was a good student. He'd taken his censure after the lecture Zed had given with a smile and no ill feeling. This was the part that Zed enjoyed, the reason he didn't retire: he couldn't give up the chance to shape bright and inquisitive young minds. It was the source of his joy and the secret to his professional success.

"Professor?" Ariel spoke softly and placed a hand on Zed's knee.

Zed opened his eyes. "Sorry, I'm very tired. Can you repeat your move?"

Ariel smiled and pointed at the board. "Of course – rook takes pawn."

Zed nodded and gave a thin-lipped smile, though in truth he was a bit disappointed. Ariel had been lured into the exact move that Zed had hoped he'd make, putting one of his most important pieces in danger to take out a marginal one. He'd taught the young man for two years now and he had great potential, but he was still prone to making simple, hotheaded mistakes during chess games.

"You still have some to learn, Ariel. Each piece plays a part, from the king to the lowly pawn." Zed waved a hand across the board. "Each soldier wants to make his mark, without necessarily seeing the whole situation. The general, on the other hand, must weigh risk and reward of all moves. Without emotion."

Ariel started to speak. "I—"

Zed held up a hand as he looked up from the game. "Wait a moment."

His assistant had peered into the office. "Professor Eshkol?"

"Yes?"

"You've got a call on the private line. Should I ask them to call back?"

"No, that's alright." He looked back at the board, moved his rook and smiled at Ariel. "Knight takes queen, checkmate."

"Nice one, professor." Ariel shook his head. "Do you want me to leave so you can take your phone call?"

"I trust you, Ariel. Reset the board. This shouldn't take long."

Ariel smiled and started to replace the pieces as Zed stood. He walked to his desk, picked up the phone and pressed the button for the private line. He knew who'd be calling. It was odd to have Ariel in the room while he took the call, and he'd have to be careful about what he said, but it was important to show the young man that he was trusted.

"Professor?" His contact's voice was garbled by the electronics that made him anonymous to everyone but Zed – a necessary precaution. "Is it safe to speak?"

"Safe enough, my friend." Zed collapsed into his office chair with a long sigh. "What can I do for you?"

"A quick update, that's all. The United States is going to use the forces they're deploying inside Israel as extra security for nuclear sites. The original plan was for a very public show of force, but now they'll actually be defending critical sites – including the nukes."

As his contact detailed where and what forces would be deployed, Zed felt cold anger lump in the pit of his stomach. He'd known about the deployment, but assumed it would be bluster. This was another symbol of the loss of Israeli sovereignty. It was one more insult heaped upon a people being asked to suffer so much already.

"That is most disappointing." Zed waited until the other man had finished speaking. "Thank you for letting me know."

"No problem, professor." He thought he could hear a hint of warmth through the electronic mess of a voice. "I'll speak to you soon."

Zed hung up the phone without further word. There was no need for any pleasantries. He leaned back in the chair slightly and closed his eyes again. The US deployment was the final exclamation mark on the shout of outrage being perpetuated on Israeli Jews. He'd thought of the Zionist threats and he wondered how the deployment would impact their plan.

He opened his eyes again and reached for the phone, casting a glance at Ariel as he spoke. "Get me Celeste Adams at the *New York Standard*."

After a moment, a warm-sounding British woman spoke. "This is Celeste Adams."

"This is Professor Zed Eshkol, professor of history at Yeshiva University." Zed paused briefly. "I was hoping to share some information. Anonymously."

"Go ahead, professor. Anything you tell me will be in confidence, though whether we print it or not depends on the evidence."

Zed smiled. He knew as much. Following the attacks on democracy and the media in America in recent years, many of the country's leading news outlets had developed a fresh zeal for factual reporting and strict verification. He supposed they were tired of being used as mouthpieces for powerful individuals and corporations. Most of them, anyway.

"Professor?" Adams prompted.

"Excuse me." Zed chuckled. "The US military is deploying inside Israel to protect against rocket launches and discourage any incursions."

"I know all of this, professor. I—"

"Do you know they're also deploying to defend Israeli nuclear sites, following the Zionist threat?"

She inhaled sharply. "Do you have the details of units, locations or timelines that I could print?"

"I do, but it's best you get them from the horse's mouth. You'll receive a call from your usual source inside the administration at the turn of the hour."

"Okay, professor." There was a pause. "Say, I've got a gap in my opinion page for tomorrow. How'd you like to fill it to go alongside the exclusive?"

Zed thought for a second. Though he wanted to stay at arm's length from the story, if he took up the offer he wouldn't have to discuss the deployments specifically. He could reiterate again that the peace process is an unfair imposition on Israel. He'd promised the conservatives who'd approached him at the lecture nothing less.

"Okay, Ms. Adams. I respect the influence and the veracity of your newspaper. I'll write you a piece in the next few hours. My assistant will email it through."

"Wonderful, professor. Look forward to reading it. Goodbye."

Zed returned the phone to its cradle and scribbled a few notes on his notepad. When he was finished, he raised his voice.

"Louise?"

"Yes, professor?" His assistant stuck her head inside the office. "Something I can help with?"

"Take this note." He tore it from the pad. "I need it typed up quickly and ready when I leave this afternoon."

She looked down at the paper. "Uh, professor? I can't read it. It's just a combination of letters and numbers."

"Don't concern yourself with that." He smiled. The message was code, using a cypher that had been unbreakable for thirty years.

As she shrugged and walked off, he struggled to his feet. With a deep breath, he moved slowly back to the chess board, thinking about the piece he had to write. It needed to be sympathetic to the Zionist cause. He'd reiterate – again – that the sensible course of action would be abandonment of the agreement and maintenance of the status quo. Nothing else would maintain the integrity of Israel.

But first, he had another game to win.

JACK REACHED UP, stuck a finger into his necktie and gave it a tug. He let out a long sigh as he pulled the restrictive silk away from his neck and then undid the top button of his shirt. Taking off his tie was one of his favorite moments of the day, but when you worked at the White House you had to play by the rules, and the rules said suit and tie. He was just glad that, in Bill McGhinnist, he'd found a boss who felt largely the same way.

Jack raised an eyebrow at the President, who was in the process of removing his own tie and had his feet up on the Resolute desk. "Beer?"

"Love one."

Jack nodded and walked out of the Oval Office. He made it as far as the desk of the President's senior secretary, who kept a bar fridge stocked for exactly these moments. He opened the fridge, perused the bottles and selected some Hawthorn Brewing Company Amber Ale he'd ordered from Australia. He cracked them open, returned to the office and placed one in front of McGhinnist.

"Thanks, Jack." McGhinnist raised the bottle in salute. "Here's to twenty-seven more days before this thing is clear of our desks."

"Cheers." Jack smiled and then took a long pull of the beer.

McGhinnist sipped his own beer, then put it down. "This one is pretty good."

"There's some advantages of having a slightly troubled drinker on staff."

McGhinnist laughed and then, somehow, it turned into a sigh. "You know, every night when we do this, I remember what it's like to be a normal guy."

"You're not a normal guy, Mr. President."

"Thanks for ruining it." McGhinnist smiled. "If you keep calling me that in private, I'll need to put an end to these sessions."

Jack chuckled. "What else would I do with my evenings in Washington? I don't like many of the other people here."

They shared a laugh and settled into a comfortable silence. Their evening beer had become an important way for them to blow off steam after what were always manic days. Jack felt his role often led to disagreements with the President or other senior members of the administration, so he was sure these sessions were a message from McGhinnist.

"I don't think I could get rid of you if I tried." McGhinnist took another sip of beer, then gestured toward his injured hand. "Besides, I need someone to open the beers for me while this thing is broken. And to tell me to put American troops in the middle of all this."

Jack laughed. McGhinnist had taken a huge risk in using US troops to defend Israeli nuclear sites. If there were casualties, or if the Zionists squirrelled the nukes out from under US guns, then the pressure on the President would be immense. If one of those bombs actually went off, the shit would really fly, but it still seemed like the best way to safeguard the nukes.

Jack was about to speak again when there was a slight knock on the open door. Both of them looked up at once to see the President's press secretary, Janice Gilbride, standing by the door with a frown on her face and a piece of paper in her hand. Jack wasn't sure how long she'd been listening to their friendly banter. Not that it mattered. His closeness to the President was no secret.

Besides, it looked like she had bigger things on her mind. She coughed lightly. "Mr. President, do you have a few minutes?"

McGhinnist smiled and waved her in. "Of course, take a seat and Jack will get you a beer. He was just going to get more."

Jack laughed. "I was?"

"Sure." McGhinnist shrugged.

"I'll pass on the beer, thanks." Gilbride pursed her lips. "I've got some bad news, Mr. President. You're not going to like it either, Jack."

Jack looked to McGhinnist in time to see his eyes narrow and then looked back at Gilbride. "What's the problem?"

She clasped her hands together in front of her. "The *New York Standard* has an exclusive on the deployment of US forces to guard Israeli nuclear sites."

Jack's hand loosened on his beer and he cursed as it fell onto the carpet. He leaned down to pick up the bottle to prevent further spillage, not concerned about the liquid. He was too outraged at Gilbride's revelation, so convinced that she must be wrong, that he found himself speechless for a moment. She'd clearly guessed correctly that this would be a big deal.

"This is above my pay grade, guys." Gilbride smiled in sympathy. "But I sort of need to know if it's true."

"It is. We've got a leaky faucet in here." McGhinnist's voice had an edge. "The deployments weren't secret, but using the troops to defend nuke sites is."

"Right." Gilbride nodded.

McGhinnist sighed. "Your girlfriend likes ruining my day, Jack. We need to do something about that."

Jack faked a laugh. "Any suggestions?"

"Take her to a secluded getaway and ravish her for the next twenty-seven days? Ask her nicely? The hell if I care."

"I think the threat of extremists with nuclear weapons outranks a leak to the *Standard*." Jack bit his tongue and held back the rest of what he wanted to say.

"True, but I don't like having my every move to resolve the former chewed up and spat out by the latter. These leaks are restricting my ability to act, Jack."

"There's more." Gilbride took a seat on the sofa. "A senior Yeshiva University history professor has written an opinion piece slamming the deployment. He's a leading voice within the Jewish lobby, so you can expect some more heat from that front, if there wasn't enough already."

"I'm not worried about that so much. I'm worried that anything I say or decide is being leaked."

Jack saw a hint of vulnerability in McGhinnist, as if the weight of the office was pressing down on his shoulders. "Any idea who is doing it?"

"None." McGhinnist shrugged. "If I knew, it'd be taken care of already."

"Anyway, I'll leave you guys to chew over this one, didn't mean to interrupt." Gilbride handed McGhinnist the printout and stood. "Goodnight."

"Oh, sit down, Janice." McGhinnist nearly spat, then his face softened. He started to read the article, then screwed it into a ball and threw it onto the carpet.

"We'll need to respond in the morning." Jack leaned forward and rested his elbows on his knees. "But it shouldn't matter. The defense of the Israeli nukes is the key and the boots will be on the ground by tomorrow. The leak and the criticism is a minor annoyance that's worth wearing if we can safeguard those."

"I'm not convinced." McGhinnist stared at him. "We need to respond strongly to defend our actions."

"Okay—"

"In fact, Janice? I want to go to New York in a few days to defend the decisions we've taken. I want to shove my point down this guy's throat in person."

"I don't think that's a—"

"Don't want to hear it, Jack." McGhinnist shook his head. "Make it happen, Janice."

Gilbride winced at the damage control that would be required. "Of course, Mr. President. I'll make the arrangements. Do you want the press corps there?"

"Every last one of them." McGhinnist sighed and jerked a thumb at Jack. "Including his girlfriend."

Jack nodded, taking the hint. Even though he'd had some tough moments with McGhinnist, it had never felt this personal. Celeste was just doing her job and he was just doing his, but it was making things tough. Someone in the White House was leaking against the peace agreement and those leaks were flowing straight to her. He hoped New York would put the issue to bed.

He doubted it.

4

The first United States troops have started to arrive in Israel, as large protests sweep across the Middle East and America. The troops have been stationed at a dozen locations across Israel, including several nuclear sites, in a very public display of force. Any benefit or stability the US hoped to gain from the deployments looks to have been quashed, with an estimated 100,000 Israelis taking to the streets in protest against the peace agreement and the US deployment. Meanwhile, US President Bill McGhinnist will speak this morning at Yeshiva University in New York about the peace agreement, the deployment, the protests and the damaging White House leaks.

New York Standard

J ack winced as he sipped the terrible campus coffee, which was too hot and had all the flavor of bubble wrap. As he peered out from the side of the stage, he figured that the Yeshiva University student theater was nearly at capacity. Scanning the crowd, he spotted Professor Zed Eshkol in the front row making small talk with colleagues.

"Desiccated old fossil, isn't he?" Gilbride spoke softly. "Hard to believe he can cause such a stir. He's become a lightning rod for the crazies."

Jack gave a short laugh. "Hopefully the boss can get a knockout, or at least go the distance out there. Is he ready?"

"Yep." She smiled.

McGhinnist strode past them to the lectern flanked by American, Israeli and Palestinian flags, a clear sign that Yeshiva University didn't necessarily agree with the views of its controversial professor. Fat lot of good such gestures made, though, when Eshkol was given a platform to spout his rhetoric. It was a mistake for the President to be here, but McGhinnist had insisted.

Jack looked at Gilbride. "Fingers crossed, Janice."

"And toes."

Jack nodded and turned to McGhinnist. The President had started his speech, acknowledged the VIPs and made some opening remarks. He was standing, tall and proud, like he owned the room. His arm, still in a sling, did nothing to detract from the sense of gravitas that his booming voice created. Jack could hear the anger at the leaks and Eshkol's opinion piece in McGhinnist's voice.

"Let me be clear." McGhinnist's voice thundered. "The United States unequivocally supports the peace agreement. America has a proud history of resisting extremist ideology and I reject the threats and demands of the Zionists outright. We won't waver in our support for this cause."

Jack nodded at the high notes in the speech. He hoped McGhinnist could leave the stage with the matter settled, the peace agreement stable and any support – tacit or otherwise – for the Zionist cause destroyed. The President would give a powerful performance, like always, but Jack wondered if this issue could be put to bed so easily. Nobody could blame McGhinnist for trying.

"America's interest in this agreement is solely to help secure a lasting peace and a sustainable arrangement between Israelis and Palestinians, which respects the former's right to exist but also recognizes the legitimate claim on statehood by the latter.

"The deployment of US forces was to encourage stability over the next month. But following the Zionist threat, it has become all the more vital. Those troops are now an essential protection against extremists getting their hands on nuclear weapons. Our troops will be the first line of protection against an atrocity.

"I should add, also, that these deployments have the full support of the Israeli and Palestinian leaders. To prove our intent, I've authorized for the media to be given access to all US assets in the region during the countdown to this agreement. The US has nothing to hide."

Jack grimaced. He wasn't sure that giving the international press access to the troops would calm things down, but it might help show the crazies that the deployment wasn't a covert invasion of Israel and the Middle East. Such a step wouldn't be necessary if Celeste hadn't printed the leak, but Jack couldn't blame her. That he'd have done the same thing didn't make it easier to swallow.

As McGhinnist concluded the speech, Jack sighed with relief. The President had nailed it. He watched as Gilbride went on stage and called for questions from the assembled media and students. A wave of nostalgia hit him as he reflected on the number of times he'd been on the other side of the equation – the journalist asking the hard question.

A young man took the microphone for the first question. "Mr. President, I'm a student here. I appreciate you talking straight. I'm in favor of the agreement, but not at the cost of Jerusalem and New York City. Why aren't you taking the nuclear threat more seriously?"

McGhinnist started to answer, amidst a few boos directed at the questioner. "Thanks for your question and let me be clear: while we're guarding Israel's stockpiles we'll also be actively looking for these terrorists. If we find them, we will deal with them."

Jack nodded and listened to the next question, something about Israel being robbed of its nukes as well as its land. He sighed and tuned out. His years in the White House and in the press had given him an eye for a story, and there was nothing here. McGhinnist and Gilbride could handle this. His time was better spent assessing the mood in the crowd.

He moved to the back of the theatre and took a seat. The questions continued to roll, but he was only half listening. He was more interested in the fear and distrust that charged the room like a superconductor. This wasn't a friendly crowd and it had been a mistake to come here. As the President finished up and Jack prepared to stand and leave, someone sat beside him.

"Hi."

He turned to face her, a thin smile on his lips. "Hi, Elena."

"Spotted you skulking about." She reached over and grabbed his arm, her voice barely a whisper as she gave it a squeeze. "It's good to see you, Jack."

He felt a range of emotions battle it out in his head. Though she'd acted under threat of harm to her fiancé, now husband, it had taken Jack a long time to forgive Elena Winston for her betrayal. Under duress, she'd given up information about Jack's resistance to Richard Hall. FEMA had used Elena's disclosure to crush the resistance, leaving many of its members dead or in prison. At the last, though, she'd been a vital ally in revealing Hall's atrocities. She'd walked a long road since, a hard journey Jack understood well. Deep down, despite the hurt he still harbored, he was glad she was well and working.

"You too." He gently pulled away from her grasp. "What did you think of the speech?"

She shrugged. "I thought the speech was fine. But I don't think it will change any minds in this room."

"I can't disagree with you." Jack sighed, running a hand through his hair. "Where are you working these days?"

"With Celeste at the *Standard*." Elena's eyes narrowed. "I'm surprised she hasn't mentioned it."

He grimaced. "She might have. It's been a busy few months."

She gave him a quizzical look. "Ah, trouble in paradise?"

Jack just stared at her for a moment, then shifted his gaze to the stage. A pair of staff members from Yeshiva were wrapping up, but he paid them no attention. Elena had put him in a dark mood, despite the success of the President's speech and through no fault of her own. He'd never felt worse about the current job he had, his relationship with Celeste or the prospects of either surviving.

For the first time, he felt as if the countdown that the signed peace agreement had heralded wasn't just toward peace and potential nuclear devastation. It felt like a doomsday clock for Jack as well.

ZED WATCHED as the university staff left the stage, ending the formal part of the event. McGhinnist's speech had been fine – as usual – but that was hardly surprising given he was a moderate and well-spoken. A competent administrator, he'd also proven to be a likeable man who could show policy vision and form coalitions for change. He was what America had needed as a balm to its traumas.

No, the only thing that made the President dislikable to Zed was his fascination with Israel and Palestine. Zed had thought a few times that, in another life, the two of them might have been friends and McGhinnist could have been a political ally, but it wasn't to be. They had competing visions for Israeli–Palestinian relations, an issue Zed could not compromise on.

Zed kept his face passive, but inside he was smiling at the thought of the intellectual differences. It had led their paths to cross in a way that Zed couldn't abide, which made the President a foe. McGhinnist had come to the wolf's den dressed as a rabbit, trying to convince the wolves that it was a good idea for them to cut off their own tails and stop eating meat.

It hadn't worked. Trying to persuade a room full of Jews that Israel should cede territory to people who'd tried to blow them up for decades was fruitless. Though some present might sympathize with the Palestinians, Zed felt confident that the vast majority in the theatre would fall on the side of common sense – maintaining the status quo.

Zed leaned on his cane heavily and groaned with determination as he struggled to his feet. As he moved toward the President, Zed could see McGhinnist speaking to senior university officials. The sycophants – many of whom shared Zed's views in private – were too busy sucking up to the President to prosecute the agenda that everyone at Yeshiva and all Jews should share.

Zed was just glad he was old enough to ignore all that rubbish. His roots went so deep at Yeshiva that even the strongest storm would leave him standing. He joined the group and coughed loudly. The dean of the history faculty turned in alarm and then made space for Zed, doing his best to suppress a frown at being interrupted.

"Thank you, Dean Benski." Zed smiled as he joined the group. "I must have missed the note that we'd be meeting with the President after his speech."

The dean took the interruption in his stride. "President McGhinnist, this is Professor Zed Eshkol. He's one of our stars."

McGhinnist smiled broadly, his famous white veneers shining bright. "Pleased to meet you, professor. Glad you were here to listen."

Zed nodded. "Mr. President, I'd like to thank you for coming here to defend your position on the peace agreement and your troop deployment."

McGhinnist held the smile, but any warmth disappeared from his eyes. "*Our* deployment, Professor Eshkol. America's."

"Of course, forgive me." Zed nodded and waved a hand. "That's what I meant. Though many of us don't agree with it."

"Or the agreement that will finally bring peace between Israelis and the Palestinians, apparently."

Either McGhinnist had deliberately invited him to dissent, or the President didn't possess half the intellect that Zed had previously credited him with. Zed smiled. "The so-called 'peace' will be a tragedy, Mr. President, which will do more to harm the Jewish people than any foe has managed since the creation of Israel."

"Is land really that important to your people, Professor Eshkol?" McGhinnist raised an eyebrow. "So important that you'd risk peace and accept more rockets raining down on Israel, more suicide bombings and more deaths of women and children? Both sides have some to lose but more to gain."

Zed felt anger rise inside him. "You don't know how hard 'my people' fought to gain a homeland, Mr. President, or how much they suffered. You could rain a thousand rockets a day on Israel and it wouldn't compare. I don't agree with the extremist threats, but I do support their goal."

Dean Benski coughed lightly. "Even though some might disagree with the agreement, Mr. President, it was wonderful to have you here today."

Zed shook his head as the dean and the university president cut into the conversation, obviously trying to suspend any further bristling. It took all his self-control not to laugh in their faces. They were bureaucrats, concerned about public image and politics, but not the guillotine hanging over the heads of their people. They weren't even worthy of contempt.

He took a step back and left the university officials to their campaign. There was nothing else to be gained by pressing further. He was about to turn away and shuffle back to his office when he saw someone else approaching from the corner of his eye. It was almost enough to make Zed smile, given how much he knew of the other man's exploits.

"Mr. Emery." Zed took a pained step toward the younger man. "It's a pleasure to meet you."

Zed had done his research. In many ways, Jack Emery was the lynchpin of President McGhinnist's administration. It was clear that he was handed the hard nuts to crack, and so far every job Emery had been entrusted with seemed to have been sorted to the satisfaction of the President. Usually Zed wouldn't care, but Emery's attention was on the peace process and he could be a problem.

Emery's eyes narrowed slightly and flicked between Zed and the President, who remained in conversation with university officials. "Professor."

Zed held out his hand. "Please, it would be a pleasure to shake the hand of the man who's saved this country from itself several times."

Emery looked down at his hand, clearly suspicious, but eventually shook it. "I wouldn't go that far, professor. I just played my part."

"You're modest. You've played an enormous role in protecting America, which isn't even your home country."

Emery smiled. "So you say, professor. You'll have to excuse me, I've got some work to do. It was so nice to meet you."

Zed held his gaze. "It was nice to meet you, Jack. Please also thank your girlfriend for allowing me the opportunity to write about the peace process."

Emery's eyes went from cold to flaming hot in the space of a second. It seemed like he might say something emotional and let his anger out, but after another moment Emery nodded and walked toward the President. Zed smiled. He knew he was being petty, but he had enjoyed the indulgence. Living was no good if you couldn't have fun once in a while.

JACK HELD the precariously balanced trio of drinks as Celeste and Elena each took a cocktail, then he sat and raised his beer bottle. "Cheers."

They clinked and he took a pull of the beer. It had been a long day in New York, spent riding shotgun to McGhinnist at Yeshiva and other engagements, so he'd decided to have a night off with Celeste. He hadn't expected that she'd invite Elena as well, since he was due to fly back to Washington in the morning. He didn't mind, but it showed that Celeste was irritated at him.

"Good job today, Jack." Elena took a sip of her martini. "The President handled himself well. I think it'll calm things a little."

Jack nodded. "The diehards will still think we're

invading Israel and selling it to the Palestinians, but I think we might sway some of the moderates."

Jack hoped so, anyway, if only to shove it down the good professor's throat. He still felt a little bitter about his run-in with Eshkol, whose views had gained quite a bit of attention and caused the President all sorts of trouble. Amid the nuclear threat and the stress of the countdown, Eshkol's agitation and the leaks were a thorn that stuck in Jack's craw.

Worse was Celeste's decision to print both. He turned to her. She had her drink to her mouth and her eyes on him. When he smiled she turned away, so he rolled his eyes, took another swig of beer and sat back in his chair. He wondered why she'd agreed to go out if she was still mad, but clearly Elena had been invited to mitigate that.

Elena seemed to be doing her best to carry the conversation. "How seriously should we take the nuclear threat? Do we need to head for the hills?"

"Hills? Near Manhattan? Fat chance." Jack gave a laugh. "We're concerned, but there's no proof the Zionists have a nuke. We're working to find out, though."

The conversation continued in pained fashion. They discussed the day at Yeshiva, plans for the weekend, the weather – everything except the elephant in the room. Jack didn't want to bring it up and was trying hard to swallow his anger, but he was finding it difficult. He loved her and understood being a reporter, but he'd never had the two cross with his business in such a way.

A cell phone started to buzz and Jack's eyes darted to the table. Both of the women looked as well, clearly hungry for some way to extricate themselves from the conversation. Celeste won the lottery and picked up her phone. She looked at the caller ID, smiled and stood to answer it. Jack tried to hear some of what she was saying, but she'd stepped too far away and the music in the bar was too loud.

Elena laughed. "Your ears burning or something?"

His eyes shot away from Celeste to Elena. "Sorry?"

"You're acting as if you can glean who she's talking to by intensity of stare."

Jack groaned. "Sorry."

"Now you're repeating yourself." Another laugh. "It's not me you need to apologize to. You're both being idiots, but someone needs to break the impasse."

Jack nodded and looked away. She was right, but his anger at the leaks and Celeste's decision to publish them were clouding his judgment. It took some effort to remind himself, just like he used to with Erin, that work was a means to an end. As obsessed and caught up as he got with his jobs, it was only worth doing if there was someone to share it with. He looked at Celeste, who was walking back.

"Sorry." Celeste placed her phone on the table as she sat. She turned to Elena. "Francine has a great story in her hands."

"Awesome."

"Something good?" Jack offered.

Celeste turned to him with narrowed eyes, clearly trying to figure him out. "Yeah. Might be on the front page."

Jack tried to resist, and nearly succeeded. "Need a quote from the White House?"

Her eyes narrowed further and she gave a barely perceptible shake of her head. "You're unbelievable."

"Sorry, I shouldn't have said that." He held out both hands with palms facing outward.

"Hey, Jack? Fuck you." She bathed him in the remains of her cocktail, balled her fists and stormed off.

Jack took the cocktail napkin that Elena was holding out for him. "Sorry about that."

"There you are with that word again." Elena laughed and patted him on the back. "Nice work, charmer."

As he wiped his face, he surveyed the damage. His

white shirt was splashed with color and his face felt hot. "That was dumb."

"Yep."

Jack sighed again as he reached for his beer, took another swig and then started to peel the label off. The crack had been stupid and he'd be paying for the comment for days, but sometimes he couldn't help himself. He laughed quietly to himself and shook his head. The relationship he had with Celeste was far more caustic than the one he'd had with Erin before she died.

"What's so funny?" Elena took a sip of her wine.

"Just thinking about my wife." Jack looked at her. "It's been five years now."

"You've found someone else now, Jack. A keeper at that." She smiled.

"Yeah."

"You just need to recognize when you're on dangerous footing."

"That's what everyone tells me." He laughed. "It's funny, I'm dealing with terrorist threats by day and relationship ones by night."

"Which one is the more dangerous, Jack?" She had a look of concern. "Just how at risk are you guys?"

"I don't know." Jack shrugged. "You want another drink?"

"Sounds good. On one condition."

Jack raised an eyebrow. "What's that?"

"I help you find a clean shirt at Macy's once we're finished."

5

Several days after the announcement of US troop deployments to Israel and as the last boots arrive on the ground, the world's media is being given an unprecedented look inside Israel's nuclear facilities. The Israeli Government has stated repeatedly that it has nothing to hide and that US troops are a welcome addition to their own security. All sides remain united in support for the agreement and it's hard to criticize the media access being granted to Israeli bases, US fleet assets and to the leadership of the US, Israel and Palestine. The sum result is a clear attempt to safeguard Israel's nuclear weapons, prevent any rogue elements from causing mischief and ensure the success of the peace agreement.

New York Standard

Samih smiled at the United States Army Ranger in charge and pointed at a security point that had been erected outside the base. "Is all of this necessary?"

The ranger – a captain – smiled. "Probably not, sir. But

our orders were to beef up the defences. We've done that. We could hold up an army."

The Israeli prime minister, Mikael Schiller, wore a grim expression in spite of the captain's easygoing nature. "It won't be an army, captain. Any attacks will come from extremist elements within the Israeli Government, army or security services who've aligned themselves with the Zionists. That's why you're here."

The captain nodded. "If they attempt to touch those weapons, my men and I will take care of it."

"A worthy objective, captain." Samih stopped and took in the enormity of the facility. "My people thank you for your service in helping to secure this peace."

The captain grinned. "All in a day's work, sir."

Samih smiled at the ranger's bravado, though he did not doubt that the US forces had the muscle to back up their words. The tour had just begun, yet standing inside the nuclear facility already felt extremely awkward. Until recently, Israel had denied it had nuclear weapons or that this facility existed, but the exposure of the nuclear assets had been one step on the long path to peace.

Now, Samih was walking a path through well-manicured lawns on a base containing weapons of disastrous potential. He'd nearly refused the invitation, content to let Israel deal with its extremist threat with the support of America, but after some reflection he'd decided it was important to show Palestinian support. His own people had been plagued by such elements, after all.

There was another reason for him to be here. The US deployment was a big deal – 5000 troops – and its purpose could easily be misconstrued. The only way to avoid that was to show support for the deployment and maintain consistency in referring to it as temporary. Once the countdown expired, the troops would depart, leaving Israel and Palestine to determine their own fate as neighbors.

"Thank you for your time, captain. We'll continue on alone." Schiller nodded at the young captain. "I hope you enjoy your time here."

"You've got a beautiful country, Mr. Prime Minister." The captain smiled. "We'll help make sure it will still be here in a month."

Samih winced as he resumed his walk with Schiller. Once they were out of earshot, he spoke. "Will all of these men be enough?"

He sensed Schiller assessing him, but Samih kept his eyes forward.

"The Americans? They've certainly given us a lot of support."

Samih nodded. He'd thought the scale of US deployment complete overkill, but overwhelming force was clearly McGhinnist's intent. In addition to the special forces troops, significant air and naval assets had been deployed to Israel. As well, the famed Iron Dome missile defense shield had been bolstered by US anti-missile interceptors. The President clearly wanted to leave no doubt that America took the protection of the nuclear weapons and the agreement seriously.

He hoped the show of force would also stifle any ambition – by Israelis, Palestinians or any of their neighbors – to cause trouble. Truth be told, Samih had been more worried about a few stray rockets fired by his own people derailing the peace than a fanciful threat to steal nuclear weapons, but it was nice to have the security blanket. With luck, the countdown to enactment of the agreement would be peaceful and the two-state solution would finally be realized.

"I hope we can both spend the next twenty-two days fretting about potential threats, rather than dealing with real ones, Mr. Prime Minister." Samih ceased his walk and turned to Schiller. "The Zionists are as much a threat as the last rogue members of Hamas, but we must resist both."

"A hard task." Schiller rubbed his head. "Though your extremists are in hiding, at least you know who you're dealing with: their names, their doctrine, their capability. The collective knowledge about the Zionists appears to be zero, and I can't be entirely sure they lack the capability to carry out their threats."

"I understand." Samih placed a hand on the other man's shoulder. "If you need any support that is within Palestine's meager resources, we will help."

Schiller smiled and spoke after a long pause. "Interesting concept, isn't it? Helping each other? After how much treasure has been expended blowing each other up, I really do wonder whether Israelis will still fear Palestinian rockets and whether Palestinians will still fear helicopter gunships when all of this settles."

"I hope that we can focus on the more mundane – education, healthcare, housing, economic development." Samih smiled. "Reconciliation."

"What do you mean?"

Samih sighed. "The righting of decades of wrongdoing by both sides. I hope we might finally resolve that."

"A worthy sentiment, Mr. Khaladi." Schiller's smile froze in place. "Both sides have made sacrifices for this peace. I hope it's all worth it."

Samih nodded as they resumed the walk. He cast a glance at a second US security post, and decided to leave the point at that. Though he'd negotiated the deal with Ben Ebron, Mikael Schiller was another beast entirely. Samih had his doubts about the Prime Minister and thought he might try to walk away from the peace at the first opportunity, so it was vital to keep reinforcing its importance.

He'd held his own people in check, despite some of

them still wanting to lob rockets at Israel. It had taken bullying, bribery and cutthroat politics to convince most of them. For the rest, he'd simply reverted to threats. But it had worked. He doubted that any Palestinians would go against a unified leadership, risking Palestinian statehood and making themselves a pariah.

No, he was more concerned about the Zionist threats. Despite his doubts about their ability to follow through, he had to admit that it felt good to see the nukes secured by the United States. Though many of his people called him a fool for trusting America, nobody could deny the role President McGhinnist and his administration had played in negotiating the peace.

For the first time in a large number of years, Samih felt he could relax.

JACK SMILED at the chirping of the birds and the gentle touch of the breeze blowing through an open window. It was a rare luxury for him to wake up with nature, rather than the ringing of a phone or the morning news bulletin that was his alarm, and it felt nice. Rarer still was Celeste nestled against his chest, still asleep as he dozed. He'd never known her to sleep so soundly.

He'd forgotten about the simple pleasures of home. Yeppoon was a postage stamp–sized town in the middle of Queensland, Australia, but it was warm for most of the year and you could sleep with the bedroom window open. He couldn't think of a better place to get away from the pressure cooker of Washington and the bustle of New York City.

The holiday was aimed at patching up their issues. The incident at the bar had been the catalyst. He'd returned home to Celeste crying and with her knees hugged to her chest. She'd thrown a tissue box at him and unloaded on him about the impossible situation he'd placed her in. At the end of it, she'd given him an ultimatum: they had to resolve their problems or they were through.

They'd quickly plotted a trip away. Celeste had taken leave, while Jack had approached McGhinnist, hoping for something similar. He'd been surprised when the President had agreed, saying he'd caught wind of their fight and that he could afford to go without Jack for a while. The hard work on the privacy legislation and the peace agreement had been done.

Jack was uncomfortable about being away, but with broad support for the looming peace, US forces in Israel and no sign that the Zionists had any weapons, he'd swallowed his doubts. At home, in Australia, he hoped they might be able to iron out some of the creases that had appeared in their relationship. It was going well so far.

He hugged Celeste tight as she started to wriggle in his arms. "Not a bad way to wake up, is it?"

"Hey. Not bad at all." Celeste pulled away, opened her eyes and smiled at him. Her eyes were bright and her face seemed clear of stress. "It's nice to be back."

"Under better circumstances this time." He laughed. Years ago, while battling the Foundation for a New America, Jack had sent Celeste to Yeppoon to protect her. His parents had taken her in for several weeks while he'd fought Michelle Dominique. They'd never really spoken about her experiences in Australia.

"Yeah, with you, for starters. And without a psycho chasing me across the globe." She smiled. "This doesn't mean I forgive you, I hope you realize?"

"No?" Jack propped himself up onto one elbow. "I thought business-class airfares and some time away would be just the ticket."

She laughed. "I'm not that cheap."

Jack smiled. He sat up, pulled back the covers and shuffled to the end of the bed, then took Celeste's left foot in his hands and started to rub. "Now?"

"That's a start." She closed her eyes and moaned softly with pleasure as he kneaded. "It was nice of you to bring me here, Jack. Thanks."

He grunted and kept rubbing her feet. Coming home hadn't been his first plan, but she'd told him it was the best. The visit had surprised his parents. Though he called them once every few weeks, they'd long ago stopped asking when he'd visit. His father hadn't even mentioned how long it had been when he'd picked them up from the airport.

They'd drawn the line at staying with his parents, so he'd shelled out for the most expensive rental apartment in Yeppoon, inches from the water. They'd shared a few meals with his parents but spent more time together at the beach or shacked up in their apartment. The TV had stayed off and they'd focused on little but each other. It had been great. He'd felt the tension melt away.

"What do you want to do today? I've pretty much shown you all the sights, unless you want more beach time."

"Well, I—"

He looked over at the nightstand as his phone blared, interrupting her. It was a text message, not a call, and there were only two people whose messages would override the do-not-disturb setting – the President and the woman naked in bed with him. He kept his eyes on the phone for a split second too long, feeling Celeste tense and the mood in the room chill.

"Jack?" There was a hint of warning in her voice.

Though they were working at their relationship, they were still relatively vital players in two important endeavors. They'd agreed to avoid all but the most important calls from work, given they couldn't completely inoculate themselves from some of the necessary ones.

While McGhinnist could still get hold of Jack and Celeste's staff could get her, the phones had been mostly silent. Until now.

"One second." He stood, walked over to his phone and checked the message. "Looks like US forces are now in place at all sites."

"Great." Her voice was flat. "You've had your fun, now come back to bed. You've still got to do the right foot."

"I can give all my attention to you now I know all the nukes are safe." He let out a long sigh as he stared at the phone, relief flooding through him.

"You're surprised?"

He turned to her, a playful smile on his face. "Look, you may have heard it from your man on the inside already, but some of us have to hear it officially."

She rolled her eyes and threw a pillow at him. He dodged it and returned to the bed, this time at the top end. They nestled close to each other, all thoughts of the day cast aside. She let out a long, slow breath. It was a clear sign that she'd dropped her annoyance at him answering the phone. He smiled and squeezed her tighter.

He woke up a while later. As his eyes flickered open, he realized that they'd fallen asleep and started to snooze again. He shifted slightly in place and coughed. She moved at the same time, turned onto her side and let out a short, sharp laugh when she felt him pressing into her. Before Jack could respond, her hands were roaming and forcing him onto his back.

He locked his hands behind his head. "This is nice. I think we're safe."

~

ARON BRAFF PULLED his trench coat closed at the front, did up the buttons and raised the collar. Satisfied, he buried his hands deep into his pockets, the heat from his breath leaving a trail in the crisp evening air. The cold had been bearable earlier in the evening, but as the hour grew later, the iciness in the air had increased. He could handle the cold, but this was something else.

He'd never been to Russia before and would be in no hurry to return. It was cold and drab. Everywhere. And the only thing worse than the surroundings was the people, who were as dark as their country. He'd known some Russian Jews in his time, fellow citizens of Israel, and he now understood a great deal about their makeup. No, Russia's only redeeming feature was the quality of the shopping.

He ran his gaze along the windows and rooftops on both sides of the narrow alley. The squat, Soviet-era apartment buildings that surrounded him rose to four or five stories, but he could see no sign of anyone watching him. Russians had learned centuries ago not to come to the window when there was a strange sound or muted conversation outside their homes late at night.

Satisfied, Aron looked down at his watch with a sigh. They should have been here by now. The delay was unacceptable, but he was a captive buyer. Quite simply, there was nowhere else on earth he could purchase the three nuclear weapons he needed. Whether he liked it or not, he was beholden to his supplier's timetable and their tardiness.

Luckily, he didn't have to wait long. He heard the low rumble of a powerful engine long before he had to raise his hand to shield his eyes from the headlights. He kept his hand in place as he heard doors open and then slam shut, unable to see because of the headlights shining in his eyes. The ice underfoot crunched with approaching footsteps and the van headlights finally switched off.

Aron lowered his hand. Without the headlights the

alley was lit in dim streetlight, but it was enough to see the men in front of him. "Mr. Kotvas?"

"Yes." The older man standing behind three larger, younger Russians spoke with a rough voice. "Please be quiet for a moment."

Aron nodded, held his arms wide and waited as one of the Russians stepped forward to frisk him. As he did, the other two kept their weapons raised, but it was no sweat. He wasn't carrying a weapon and he'd been told about the procedure. Apart from them being a few minutes late, the meeting was going to plan. When the Russian finished he barked something in his native tongue.

"Okay. Now we do business." Kotvas nodded. "Are you sure you can afford the price, Mr. Braff? Things will be not fun for you if you're wasting my time."

"Three devices for eight million dollars." Aron waved a hand toward the four metal briefcases stacked at his feet. "Four million paid, the balance at my feet."

"Good." Kotvas's voice was as coarse as gravel in a cement mixer. "I don't appreciate time wasters."

Aron was tempted to point out that his own time had been wasted by their lateness to the meeting, but refrained. They were armed and there was no point complicating a straightforward meeting. Moving slowly, he kept his eyes on the Russians and they kept their weapons trained on him. He lifted the first briefcase and handed it to Kotvas. The Russian supported the case while Aron unlocked it.

"One million dollars?" Kotvas glanced inside the case when Aron opened it.

Aron nodded. "Count it if you like."

"Not necessary. We're all professionals. This way."

Aron nodded and followed Kotvas to the rear of the van. Two of the goons followed, while the other stayed with the cases. One of Kotvas's men opened the van, then Aron peered inside and smiled. Though they were old, each RA-

115 device was the size of a backpack and very powerful. Each could level about twenty city blocks in Manhattan, cause chaos in Jerusalem or flatten Mecca.

"Fully functioning." Kotvas's voice was now cheerful. "As promised."

"Excellent." Aron smiled. "I think our business is concluded."

They walked back to the front of the van. Aron cast a glance at his cases, which were exactly where he'd left them. Kotvas's men were professional, if nothing else. He held out his hand to Kotvas, prepared to conclude their business, but had to wait as the other man stared down at Aron's hand. Kotvas was clearly unable to mask his slight distaste, but he eventually shook.

"Suicidal Jews." Kotvas laughed as he took his hand back. "I'd have thought your people would have had their fill of violence."

Aron stared at Kotvas but said nothing. Eventually the other man shrugged and waved lazily to his men. Aron turned his head and saw they were scooping up the briefcases and carrying them out of the alley. The cash had bought him the van as well as the nuclear weapons inside, a bargain really. He took a step toward the van, ready to hit the road and get out of Russia.

"Not so fast, Mr. Braff."

Aron turned. Kotvas had a pistol trained on him, as did another of his men. The other two Russians and the briefcases were gone.

"You don't want to do this."

"We're taking your money, Mr. Braff, and the weapons." Kotvas laughed. "There's no way I'm placing these weapons in your hands. Crazy fucking Jews."

"We had a deal." Aron took a step toward the two armed Russians. "Please don't waste my time. You were already late to our meeting."

"Not another step." Kotvas shouted. "Come quietly, we'll take you out of the city and you'll get a quick ending. Nice and clean."

Aron took another step. "No, I—"

"Resist, Mr. Braff, and we'll make it hurt." Kotvas fired a shot at Aron's feet. "Choose."

Aron sighed. He'd come here to conduct a business transaction – clean and hassle free. He'd paid the deposit, arrived with the balance and had intended to drive away with the product. In return, Kotvas had been late and now he was trying to double cross Aron. It was a gross breach of faith. Rage burned in the pit of his stomach.

Aron kept his eyes on Kotvas as he whistled loudly. Less than a second later the alleyway exploded with noise. Aron ducked low then surged forward as a series of loud booms sounded from overheard, followed by several smaller pops as the Russians returned fire. The younger of the armed Russians dropped and Aron grunted as he took a hit to the chest. He kept moving, despite the pain.

He heard several additional booms. The two Russians carrying the cases would be down now, victims of the rifles that his colleagues were well versed in using. Only Aron and Kotvas were left. The old Russian snarled as he squeezed the trigger and Aron felt another round hit him. He gasped for air but took the last step toward the Russian.

Aron brought his fist down on Kotvas's arm. The gun fell to the ground with barely a whisper, a contrast to the scream from the Russian's mouth when Aron's knee connected with testicles. The Russian bent over slightly and Aron brought his elbow up to slam into Kotvas's face. Kotvas's eyes went glassy and Aron used his momentum to push the Russian onto his back and leap onto him.

As he straddled his prey, Aron pinned Kotvas's arms with his knees and gripped his throat. Though the Russian was old, he made every effort to dislodge Aron. Every ounce of Aron's strength went into squeezing the throat, even as Kotvas bucked and tried to free himself. Aron cast a glance around, making sure the gun was safely out of reach. Only then did he look at Kotvas's face.

The Russian's eyes were bulging as Aron drove his thumbs harder into the man's esophagus. Aron saw the pain and the fury and the surprise at the fact his plan had gone south. Kotvas started to go purple as he thrashed, but he was too old and Aron was too experienced. Aron's fury manifested in a cold, steely focus to bring death to this man.

When it came, Aron climbed off Kotvas, wincing at the smell of the man's evacuated bowels. He could already see his colleagues gathering up the bodies of the Russians, kicking fresh snow over the blood and cleaning up the scene. The police had been well paid to stay away, Aron was sure, but never would the Russians have expected this. It would make an interesting tale in the newspaper.

Aron let out a long sigh as his colleagues completed their work. As they did, he slowly undid the buttons on his trenchcoat, pulled it open and inspected the damage. The two rounds he'd taken had impacted the vest but not penetrated, though he felt like a horse had kicked him. He wondered if he'd cracked a rib or two.

He waved at one of his colleagues. "Ready to go?"

The other man nodded. "Cargo secure."

Aron walked over to the van. His colleagues had retrieved the cash and the nukes. As he climbed inside and the ignition fired, Aron cast a quick glance back at the alleyway. He closed his eyes and felt around his ribs as the vehicle started to move. It hadn't exactly gone to plan, but it was good enough. He'd done his job and the fate of his people was still in his hands.

6

The New York Standard Online *is attempting to confirm claims on social media that Zionist extremists are in possession of three nuclear weapons. The tweets, which claim to be from representatives of the group, contain pictures of what appear to be small 'backpack nukes' alongside a Russian newspaper that confirms the date. Comment is being sought from the White House, the Pentagon and the State Department, as well as from Russian, Israeli and Palestinian officials. To date no comment has been forthcoming.*

New York Standard

J ack forked a heap of bacon, ran it through the drizzle of egg yolk and delivered it to his mouth. If there was one thing he missed from his childhood, it was his mother's breakfasts. They even made the company tolerable. He put down his knife and fork as he chewed, slipped a hand under the table and squeezed Celeste's leg. She patted his hand and they smiled at each other.

"You should eat better, Jack." His mother's voice broke

their moment. "You're both leaving it late to have children, so nutrition is very important."

Jack squeezed Celeste's leg again, in apology, and then shot his mother a look. "I told you, there's no certainty we're going to have kids. That's not our lives."

His mother bristled at what he'd said. She pursed her lips, clearly wanting to say something, but kept quiet. He'd heard it all before, about working too hard and living too little, but this wasn't the time. He and Celeste were having one last meal with them before heading down to Sydney for a couple of days. Celeste wanted to see the bridge.

They ate in silence before Celeste's cell phone rang. Jack glanced at her as she looked at the caller ID and then up at him. She gestured with her head toward the living room and he nodded. It was important, whoever it was. Or maybe she'd asked a friend to call her to bail her out of breakfast with his parents. Either way, he wasn't going to try to stop her.

"I'll just be a minute. Sorry. It's work." Celeste smiled at his parents and stood as she answered.

He locked eyes on his mother, daring her to speak even as Celeste's voice grew faint as she vanished into the other room. "What?"

"She's a nice girl." Joan smiled. "We liked her when she visited a few years ago, and we like her now."

"Yeah, I—"

His mother held up a hand. "But we're not sure you understand the importance of family, Jack. You missed the boat with Erin. Don't do it again."

He sighed and looked to his father for support, but received nothing. His mother was like a broken record. Whatever your achievements, if you failed to spit out kids then watch out. He shrugged. "If it happens, it happens. We've discussed our options but we're not on a timetable. It has to be right."

"You are on a timetable, Jack." Joan's eyes narrowed. "I know you lost Erin and that that was hard, but you're both in your mid-thirties."

"Look—" He never got the chance to finish. His own phone started to ring. It was the President. Jack pointed at it. "Sorry."

He ignored the look on his parents' faces and moved into one of the bedrooms. As he walked, a series of beeps played in his ear. It took about ten seconds for the phone to do its thing and the beeps were followed by a long bleeping tone. He'd been told upon commencing his job with McGhinnist to always wait for that sound, because it meant the call he was on was encrypted.

"Hi Jack." McGhinnist's voice was tense and he sounded tired. "Hope it's not a bad time?"

"Your timing is perfect." Jack sat heavily on the bed and cast a glance around, habitually checking to make sure he was alone. "What's up?"

"I've got bad news." McGhinnist's voice cracked a little with stress. "We have confirmation that the Zionists have three small nuclear devices."

Jack's eyes widened. Coming directly from the President, it was as good as fact. "Are we sure?"

"The CIA got word thirty minutes ago." McGhinnist snorted. "Not that it matters, but the Kremlin reached out and told our people."

"They did?" Jack was surprised. America hadn't exactly been on great terms with Russia for a long while.

"Yeah. President Ivanov called me a half-hour ago. He wanted to make it clear that the Russian state had nothing to do with the exchange." McGhinnist paused. "The Zionists made the deal with some Russian mafia guys, the deal went bad and they escaped. The Russians are trying to find the bombs."

"Makes sense. Ivanov doesn't want us thinking it's him

and raising hell." Jack changed tack. "How big are we talking?"

"Big enough to take a chunk out of Manhattan, I'm told." McGhinnist paused. "This thing just got a whole lot harder."

"Ivanov will find the nukes before they leave Russia." Jack wasn't confident, despite his words. "Or we will."

"Neither Russia nor the NSC are hopeful of that outcome, Jack. The Zionist posts about the bombs on social media were an estimated ten hours after the exchange. They could be anywhere. I'm surprised your girlfriend hasn't got the scoop already. Whoever is leaking to her must be slipping."

Jack ignored the jibe and stood. "Need me back stateside? Though I think I know the answer."

"Yep, it's going to be all hands on deck." McGhinnist gave a small laugh. "Hell of a way to ruin a vacation, huh?"

"I'll be back as soon as I can."

Jack hung up the phone, stood and walked back to the dining room. Celeste was just returning with her phone in hand. Her face was ghost white. "You too?"

Her eyes were glassy. "Yeah, I have to get back."

"What do you know?"

"Enough." She shrugged. "We're running the confirmation."

Jack frowned. The leaker, again. McGhinnist hadn't been far off. How the fuck could her source find out and called her minutes before the President had let him know? Whoever was leaking was close to the action. He nearly said something, but took a few deep breaths and let his anger subside. Now wasn't the time. They had a long flight back together.

"It was nice to see both of you again." Celeste addressed his parents. "I hope next time we can stay longer."

"Us too, dear." Jack's father ran a hand through his hair

and patted his wife on the arm. "Safe travels."

Jack nodded as his parents stood, their breakfast not yet finished. He hugged his mother tightly for several seconds. Once they were finished he held out a hand and his father shook it with a nod and a smile. The farewells complete, Jack stood back as Celeste and his parents hugged and then they all walked out to Jack's hire car.

"Jack, mate." His father spoke softly. "I know you don't like it here, but we still care about you, your mum and I."

"I—"

"Just listen. You can come back as often as you like or not at all, but I want you to look after her. She's stuck by you."

"I know, Dad."

"Okay." His father nodded. He'd said his piece.

Jack and Celeste climbed into their car. They'd return to their apartment, quickly collect their things and then drive to the airport. With luck, they could book some flights for later in the day. It was a long way back to the east coast of the United States, and the jetlag would be a killer, but at least they'd get to fly at the front of the plane.

Celeste gripped his leg. "Jack, I'm publishing the story. I don't want to hear anything about it. I have to do my job. That's it."

"I know." Jack smiled. "I wasn't going to say a word."

He didn't say that he was done arguing. While he mightn't yet be ready to propose to her, like his parents so clearly wanted, he valued his relationship too much to keep beating his head against a wall. Instead, he was going to put all of his energy into catching the leaker. He glanced over at Celeste. She was clearly unconvinced, staring at him with narrowed eyes, but she nodded. That was it.

"Shame I won't get to see Sydney Harbour." She sighed. "Seems a waste to come all this way and miss it for a second time."

Jack looked over at her once more and flashed a sly smile. "Third time's a charm?"

ZED POUNDED the lectern with his fist. "It's impossible to reconcile the utterly meek surrender we're currently seeing with the history of the Jewish people!"

He coughed violently, took a step back and reached for a glass of water. Silently cursing himself, he took a sip, realizing that he'd pushed it again. He was giving one of his most well-known lectures and, as always, it made him emotional. For a middle-aged man that was fine, but he was old man with mobility issues and a bad heart and needed to take it easy. Or so his doctor said.

"So, the last thing to note is that—"

"Excuse me, professor?" Ariel spoke softly behind him.

Zed frowned and turned. There was nothing he hated more than being interrupted mid-lecture. It deflated the entire exercise. Though Ariel was one of his students, Zed glared at him. Even if Zed resumed speaking within a moment, the students wouldn't remember the finely crafted narrative, laden with evidence and capped off with a compelling ending. They'd remember the interruption.

"What is it, Ariel? This had better be important."

"I think you'll want to see this, professor." Ariel approached the lectern and held an iPad in front of Zed.

He took the device. He hated them, these tombstones to the decline of the daily newspaper. The news used to have impact – gravitas – as the sole point of truth for the intelligent man for hours worth of current events. Now, more information was being created every few hours than in the entire history of humankind. It made comprehensive understanding and reflection impossible.

Zed read the screen and his eyes widened. His anger

melted away and he felt silly for being angry at all. It was a great day and Ariel had done precisely the right thing. He looked up at his younger student and gave him a broad smile and a pat on the back. Ariel frowned, clearly confused, but nodded and walked away from the lectern even as Zed's mind started to spin. He turned back to the class.

"I'm sorry." Zed wasn't really looking at them, his mind racing. "An urgent matter has come up. You're dismissed. We'll pick up tomorrow."

There were murmurs from the students, but Zed's mind had already moved on. Though he was in his twilight years, he was still an institution at Yeshiva. A few complaints would wash away like grease from Teflon. He had bigger things to worry about, if what Ariel had shown him was true. But given the *Standard* was reporting it, Zed believed it was.

He grabbed his cane and waved at Ariel to collect the rest of his things. He moved as quickly as he could back to his office, thinking the whole time about what he'd read. The Zionists having nuclear weapons was a game changer. Even if they were only small devices, it was still enough potential devastation to put the Samson Option into play.

Zed reached his office, closed the door and slumped in his office chair, exhausted. After a few long breaths to steady himself and ward off any coughing, he reached over for the only photo that sat on his desk. Thousands of people had asked him about it over the years, who the men in the photo were and when it was taken, but he'd never divulged the secret to anyone. Not even his wife.

He was the architect of the Samson Option, the last defense of Israel. Its purpose was complete destruction of any attacker, even if Israel itself had to be flattened to achieve it. Only through foes having complete certainty that Israel was committed to this policy could it work. In recent decades, weak leaders had prevaricated and opened the hen house just a crack. Zed had seen the potential for the wolf to peer inside nearly half a century ago. He'd convinced others – fellow Samson architects and other influential Israelis and Jews. They'd made a pact to do whatever was necessary to invoke the Samson Option if and when it was needed, whether or not it was government policy.

Though Zed was the last of those in the photo left alive, each of the original members had recruited others. Nobody knew everybody, or even many, which was the whole point. One of the men Zed had taught, and then recruited, was Aron Braff. He'd gone on to have a career with Mossad before joining the private sector, but they'd never lost contact. It warmed his heart that Aron had succeeded and that at least some people were prepared to fight for Israel and against the stupidity of the agreement. He'd been hoping that Braff would succeed, but it had been a long shot. Zed didn't want Braff to have to use the nuclear weapons, but it was important that the world knew the stakes.

He checked his watch. The timing was not quite perfect, but it was close enough. Braff had left it late, but he could be forgiven for some tardiness, given his success. Zed reached over and thumbed his way through his Rolodex. When he found the right number, he picked up his phone, dialed and waited. It rang for a long time until eventually it was answered by a groggy female voice.

"Hello?"

"This is Zed Eshkol calling Captain Cohen."

There was a pause and a sigh. "Professor, Joseph is sleeping. It's early."

Zed smiled. "Oh, of course, of course. Please excuse my waking you."

Another sigh. "It's okay. Looking after yourself?"

"Of course, my dear. Now I won't keep you any longer. Pass on my best."

"Goodnight, professor."

Zed hung up the phone. He'd introduced Joseph Cohen and his wife when they'd both studied at Yeshiva. Another of his recruits, Cohen had gone on to have a great career in the military. Zed regretted he was unable to speak to the man, but the message would do. Sometimes playing the doddering old fool got the message across fine.

He was counting on it.

~

Captain Joseph Cohen clasped his hands behind his back as he stared at his professional future – HMS *Vigilant*. He was a disciplined man, but considering the rarity of the circumstances, he allowed himself a moment of pride and a wide smile. It wasn't every day you prepared to set sail in a Vanguard-class nuclear submarine under your command.

"It's all yours, Joseph." Admiral Graham Sinclair gave Joseph's shoulder a friendly squeeze. "I told you it would be."

Joseph's first assignment in the Royal Navy had been aboard an attack submarine commanded by Sinclair. Though they'd served apart at times, Sinclair had risen through the ranks and Joseph had followed, serving diligently wherever he was posted. It was patronage, but Joseph wouldn't have it any other way. He'd based his entire career plan on it.

He turned and saluted the admiral. "Thank you, sir, for your kind words and for the trust placed in me. I won't let you down."

"I know you won't, Joseph." The admiral returned the salute briefly before lowering his hand. "We're in tough times, but you'll do just fine."

Joseph nodded and Sinclair gave one more smile, then turned on his heels. Nothing else needed to be said. He had no doubt that Sinclair had played a large part in him gaining this posting, which also reflected well on the admiral. It was how the game worked. He'd waited many years for a command, working his way up and serving for nearly a decade as an executive officer aboard HMS *Vanguard* until, finally, he'd been sent the papers. Now he had his own command.

He turned back to the submarine, *his* submarine, and let out a long breath. He'd spent some time with the crew working up the boat and readying it for sea, but this was his first time stepping aboard as an operational commander. He started to walk up the gangplank. Once aboard he made his way to the bridge, where the crew all stood at sharp attention. He returned their salutes, glad that the boat was formally his.

"Welcome, captain." His executive officer, Tim Jennings, smiled broadly. "The ship is ready to sail."

Joseph matched the smile and nodded, before starting to work on getting his boat out to sea. The process was automatic and he didn't have to think about it. It was his first time as captain, but his thousandth as a submariner. As they ran through the procedure, he couldn't help but beam with pride. He was joining an exclusive club – the four men in charge of Britain's nuclear deterrent.

The *Vigilant* would relieve another submarine and Joseph would sail his boat to the middle of the Atlantic. There, he'd remain under the waves, waiting for the order to launch and end the world. It was the notification that no submariner aboard a boomer ever hoped to receive, though they'd trained all their professional lives for the moment.

Joseph wasn't quite so bleak about it. Such doomsday weaponry was useful, if only to remind everyone that certain actions were above the laws of man and necessitated a god-like retaliation. He'd insisted on a religious man as his executive officer. It was vital that he could trust his second-in-command to follow the orders of men and the will of God. Even if it was a different brand of God.

He turned to Jennings. "Ready?"

"Ship uncoupled and crew at stations, captain."

"Away with it then."

Jennings nodded, barked orders at several of the crew and then turned back to Joseph and spoke with a low voice: "No escape now, sir."

Joseph gave a small, throaty laugh. "Hell of a time to be sailing on my first command, given this stuff in the Middle East. But I'm glad you're beside me, Tim."

They shared a look and a nod, then turned as one to watch the crew going about their work. The submarine was sailing slowly, above water, out to the ocean. Only there would it dive below the surface and assume its deadly station, as Royal Navy submarines had done since accepting the role of nuclear deterrence from Bomber Command in 1969.

"I need to go to my quarters for a moment." Joseph spoke softly to Jennings then raised his voice to address the whole bridge crew. "XO has the deck."

"XO has the deck."

When Joseph reached the door of his quarters, he entered his passcode. The door unlocked with a click and he pushed it open. The captain's quarters were hardly luxurious, but there was a decent bed, a small dining table, some storage space and even his own bathroom facilities. It would take a while to get used to all the extra space, no matter how modest.

For now he ignored it all, except for the safe on the wall, used to house his orders and any personal valuables. He quickly opened it, took some papers out of his pocket, placed them in the safe and then locked it. As he did, he thought about another safe, which was in the operations room and housed the main nuclear launch codes.

Inside *that* safe was *another* safe, dedicated to one thing: holding the Dead Man Letter. Joseph had never read the letter. Nobody had. The British Prime Minister wrote one to each ballistic missile submarine captain. In the event that the PM and her designated second were killed, and certain other conditions fulfilled, the letter contained orders from beyond the grave to retaliate, submit to an allied navy for orders, or to use his own discretion in responding to an attack.

Joseph couldn't open the safe containing the Dead Man Letter without Jennings' assistance. Chances were he'd never have to, either. The safe remained locked until it was needed. If a new PM was elected, or a new captain appointed, the letter was destroyed and the process started again. Over and over until, one day, one captain in one submarine would be forced to tear it open and ponder the end of the world.

He sighed deeply and closed his eyes. Though he was excited by his first Royal Navy submarine command, going out of contact with the world also daunted him. Though he'd be undersea with 134 other sailors as company, it felt like he was alone. It felt different. While he'd lived in the UK and served in its navy for decades, he had other loyalties. As a Briton, he was excited. As a Jew, he was scared.

He just had to trust others above the ocean to do what was necessary to safeguard Israel and the world from the countdown to madness. If that occurred, nobody would be any the wiser to his dual loyalty. If it didn't, the consequences would be dire.

ACT II

7

Twelve days into the countdown to peace between Israel and Palestine and, so far, the agreement is holding. The United States is doing all it can to keep the situation calm, but with agitation from all sides increasing and Zionist extremists in possession of nuclear weapons, the chances of holding the fragile peace together for two more weeks appear slim. So far the United States has resisted calls for the deployment of more troops to Israel, stating that those protecting nuclear assets and providing missile defense are sufficient.

New York Standard

Jack reached into his wallet and handed seventy bucks to the driver. "Thanks buddy, keep the change."

When he opened the door and walked around to the trunk, he saw that Celeste already had it open and was grabbing her bag. Jack caught her eye and smiled as he hefted his own case. She smiled back as she extended the handle on her case and took his hand. He wheeled his case alongside her as they crossed the street.

"I'm glad we both got some sleep on the plane." Jack sighed. "Going back to work after that sort of flight is tough."

"Yeah. And you've still got to get to Washington in the morning. I've just got to get downtown."

They'd flown out of Brisbane, Australia, and spent just over a day in transit, lasting the whole flight without any tension. He was about to speak but the words caught in his throat when he felt Celeste tense. Looking at her then following her eyes, he pulled up short as the door to her townhouse opened and a man in a black suit and sunglasses walked out.

Jack didn't sense danger, but he'd worked around Federal agents enough to know their swagger. "I'll see what this is about."

She clearly wasn't impressed, but she nodded as she let go of his hand. "I'll look after our cases."

He took the steps two at a time and stood in front of the suited man. "I'm Jack Emery. What's this?"

"I know who you are, sir." The agent made no move to get out of the way. "This is a joint Secret Service and FBI investigation. You'll need to wait outside."

Jack took a deep breath. He had to keep his cool. "What's the investigation looking at?"

"Classified."

Jack should have seen that coming. "Who ordered it?"

"Classified, sir."

"Then I'm going to need to see your warrant, Agent …"

"McClellan, sir." The agent dug into his pocket, flashed his FBI badge and handed Jack the warrant. "We good here?"

It had to be about the leak. Warrant in hand, Jack took a step back and pulled out his cell phone. "Excuse me, Agent McClellan, I need to call the President."

McClellan's expression didn't change. "Do what you need to do, sir. We're nearly done in here."

Jack took a step back and dialed. The phone was answered in seconds by the President's secretary. "Clara, it's Jack, I need to speak with him."

"One moment, Mr. Emery. I'll see if he's available." Her voice was pure sugar, as always.

Jack tapped his foot impatiently while the hold music played in his ear. As he waited, Jack tried to peer past Agent McClellan, who was blocking the door. He also looked down at Celeste, still waiting with their bags at the bottom of the stairs. A look of grave concern clouded her features. He flashed her a smile as the call finally connected.

"Jack? What is it? I'm in with Senate leadership in five minutes." McGhinnist sounded as tired as when Jack had last spoken to him. And irritated.

"My house is being searched by the FBI and Secret Service."

"I know. Everyone is getting the same treatment, Jack."

"But—"

"No." McGhinnist interrupted. "Everyone is getting the same treatment. I want to find out who it is and crush them. I don't think it's you, for what it's worth."

"Fine." Jack sighed. "But can you at least tell them to let me inside? Celeste is worried they're searching her stuff too."

"They know all about the First Amendment." McGhinnist paused. "Put one of the agents on."

"The President wants to talk to you."

Jack handed the phone to McClellan and after a moment the agent glowered and moved aside. Jack stepped into chaos. All the drawers in the hallway hutch had been rifled through and there were papers scattered up and down the hall. He froze in place, even as he felt Celeste's arm slip around his waist. He squeezed her hand and then turned to her. Her face was a mix of anger and shock.

He walked into the master bedroom, where several men in suits were rifling through their things. They paid him no heed until he spoke. "Having fun guys?"

"We're nearly finished, sir. This is the last room." One of the agents paused and looked up at Jack with a smile. "We'll be out of your hair in a minute."

Jack nodded and stood with his arms crossed, until one of the agents opened Celeste's underwear draw. He took a step forward. "Hey, come on, I—"

"*Do not move.*"

Jack turned. The agent who'd smiled at him a second ago now had a pistol trained on him. "What the—"

"Sir, you need to take a step back. You can stay inside the room, if you like, but you're not to impede our search in any way."

Jack nodded and raised his hands as he took a step back, his heart beating fast. The agents searched through Celeste's smalls with no further protest, but when she entered the room, Celeste looked at the agent and then at Jack with pure venom. She kept her mouth shut, despite the outrage that he was sure she felt. This was the second time she'd had her home raided by the police.

Finally, as suddenly as a sharp gust of wind, the agents nodded to each other and headed for the front door, taking with them a small box filled with some of the contents of the house. Worse, the agents had Celeste's laptop. She started to protest but they simply kept on walking. A black SUV pulled up in front of the house, they climbed in and the vehicle drove off.

Jack and Celeste were left hugging each other in the detritus of their home.

"I'm not super happy with your boss right now." She

had her fists balled by her side. "They took my computer. They might get the identity of my source."

"They might." He took a step toward her, wrapped her in a hug and they squeezed each other tightly.

She shook her head. "If they do, my person inside the White House will be exposed."

Jack couldn't resist. He smirked. "Your *other* man inside the White House will expose himself any time for you, my love."

She punched him softly on the arm, a smile breaking out across her face. "I'm being serious. They'll be locked up."

"Yep."

"What can I do?" She pulled away. "You're probably excited that you're about to catch them, but I need to help protect my source."

"Nothing, except reporting this search on your front page tomorrow. That's the best you can do." Jack paused. "I've got to get back to Washington."

SAMIH DOUBLED over and winced at the pain. It felt like every muscle along his spine was being pulled, making him crooked, even though he knew he'd been standing up straight. With hands on his knees, he took a few deep breaths. If there was one thing worse than getting old, it was getting old with back pain. He cursed himself for forgetting to take his medication this morning.

"Are you okay?" Ben Ebron leaned in and placed a hand on Samih's back. "Do we need to return to the hotel?"

Samih turned to the Israeli negotiator and smiled, even as a few of their security detail shot them a look. "No, I'm fine."

"Okay." Ben smiled. "Shall we continue?"

"Of course." Samih stood taller and sucked in a sharp breath.

"You're a soldier, my friend."

Samih laughed. "Those days are long over. For good reasons – the peace we've signed won't allow it and my body isn't up to it."

He'd spent years shooting at Ben and his countrymen, thinking that was the only way to fight, to rebel, to achieve. Only later in life had he come to see the incredible power of politics. Now he knew that sustainable change came from iterative improvement, not revolution. From compromise, not demands. It had been a hard pill to swallow.

As fears of the nuclear threat had grown, so too had agitation in the streets. It had started with protests and escalated into near rioting in some places. Samih and Ben Ebron had been discussing the growing tension privately for the past few days. Though politicians could call for calm, both negotiators felt they had a special responsibility to inform the public about the peace.

Samih didn't blame the protestors. They were scared. They were worried about nuclear fire being unleashed by Zionist extremists. Identical protests were taking place in Mecca and New York City. Here, in Jerusalem, there was an extra level of fear even assuming the Zionists could be stopped. The protestors were confused about what the future would hold next to a newly constituted Palestine.

As the men walked, their security detail ringed them at a respectful distance and local police kept the protestors behind the barriers that divided the street. It was a microcosm of Israel and Palestine. One side calm, safe and orderly and the other chaotic, suppressed and crowded. The one other constant, along with the security, was the camera flashes of the assembled media.

Samih took a few steps closer to the protestors behind

the barrier. They cried out and shouted at him, but he stood calmly as several tossed empty bottles at him. When one man took it further still, Samih calmly wiped the spittle from his face. He knew that – because of his role in the negotiations – everyone was watching him, looking for proof that Palestinians couldn't be trusted.

He saw a couple, young and beautiful, with a little girl eating an ice-cream on her father's shoulders. The venom they shouted at Samih and the signs they waved with fury ruined their picture-perfect image. Samih decided at that moment that, more important than the peace agreement and statehood, he had to convince that one family that he and his people wanted peace.

"Careful, my friend." Ben Ebron walked beside him and put a hand on Samih's arm. "You should stay back a little bit. It's not safe."

"It's okay." Samih shook his head. He walked up to the family, ignoring the violence that threatened to explode. He looked at the mother. "Hello."

She started to wave her placard even more furiously in his face. "Go back to your home and don't steal ours! Don't steal from my child! You've no right!"

Samih smiled as her sadly. "I don't want to steal from your child, just achieve peace and a future for the children of Palestine."

Samih took a half-step back when the father thrust forward. The crowd gave a roar and the fence started to buckle. Samih glanced up at the girl on her father's shoulders. She was no longer sucking on her ice-cream, and she looked terrified. Samih reached out to her protectively, but the father slapped Samih's hand away. The police and security detail were shouting.

"Samih, come on, they're surging!" Ben's shout could barely be heard over the noise of the crowd. "Let security do their job!"

Samih kept his eyes locked on the family, even as the fence buckled. He wouldn't be intimidated. He balled his fists and closed his eyes, ready to be attacked by the crowd. If his best wishes and peace wasn't enough for them, there was nothing else he could offer. He counted one second, then two, and was surprised when instead of a punch or a kick, he felt a hand clasp his.

He opened his eyes, looked to his right and smiled when he saw Ben Ebron standing beside him. The two men clasped hands and raised them over their heads. Some of the protestors stopped, but others pushed forward harder. When they were less than three feet away, Samih winced. The first of the security detail had thrown themselves into the fray, and local police were close as well.

The crowd came to within a foot of Samih and Ben before they started to turn, less keen on charging trained police and armed security guards than a pair of old men. Samih found the family in the crowd, his eyes locking onto them as they tried to remain calm in the push. Samih let go of Ben's hand when he saw the child drop her ice-cream cone and then reach out for it. When she fell he moved.

He was among the crowd in a second. The police saw him and did their best to stop him, but he paid them no heed as he made a beeline for the child. He felt one blow on his back, winced, but kept moving. Finally, he reached the girl. Her mother was screaming hysterically a few yards away, unable to reach her daughter. The girl's father was nowhere to be seen, swept up in the crowd.

Samih stood over the girl as the police and his security detail kept the other protestors away. The child looked up at Samih with wide, moist eyes, which nearly broke his heart. Camera flashes from the gathered media sparkled like stars. Samih leaned down to the girl's level. As the noise and the fury swirled around them, he had eyes for nobody but her.

Though tears streaked down her cheeks, she seemed only dazed by the fall from her father's shoulders, though she did have some grazes and cuts. He helped her to sit up. She searched around frantically and finally saw the object of her obsession: her ruined ice-cream cone, spilled on the ground and trodden on by dozens of feet.

"Here you go." He dug into the pocket of his pants and pulled out his tin of breath mints. He popped the lid and held them out for the girl.

Her eyes widened as she looked down at his hand, then up at Samih and back down at his mints. Quick as a viper, she snatched the tin from his hand. She removed one of the mints from the container and held it out to him. As the cameras continued to flash, Samih reached out and took hold of her hand. He closed it around the tin, making it clear it was hers.

She beamed. "Thank you."

"You're welcome, little one."

JACK TOSSED his White House staff ID onto McGhinnist's desk. "Well, my security pass still works. I assume I'm not the leaker?"

"Don't be dramatic." McGhinnist stood with a sigh, picked up the pass and shoved it into Jack's chest. Hard. "Everyone was checked."

Jack pocketed the pass and did his best to swallow his anger. He couldn't blame McGhinnist for ordering extra checks and trying to pry loose the leaker, who'd grown from a minor political annoyance into a major national security threat. Nevertheless, Jack's understanding didn't extend as far as tolerating secret searches of his home.

He'd flown from New York to Washington at noon. Though he'd intended to resign, the time in transit had cooled his head a little and now he was satisfied that he'd made his point to McGhinnist. The suggestion that he might be the leak made him laugh, but it also infuriated him after how much he – an Australian citizen – had done for this country.

"You done?" McGhinnist raised an eyebrow.

"Sure." Jack paused, but was unable to resist. "So, did my girlfriend's underwear drawer hold any secrets?"

McGhinnist smirked. "I hear she has some fantastic lingerie."

Jack rolled his eyes. "Did we at least find something for all that effort?"

McGhinnist shrugged. "They're still sifting through what was seized, but there's no smoking gun. I want to strangle whoever it is."

Jack nodded. McGhinnist was clearly as furious as he was with the leaker, but while Jack was angry because it had impacted his personal life, McGhinnist must be pissed because of the effect on every decision he was making. It was hard enough being president without the additional guarantee that everything you did would be on the front page.

Jack followed McGhinnist to the Situation Room, where the members of the NSC were already gathered. They stood as the President entered the room. McGhinnist moved to the head of the table while Jack took his place among the rank and file. He knew that McGhinnist had given the council twenty-four hours to come up with options to deal with the Zionists. Their time was up.

"What're our options?" McGhinnist remained standing and leaned on his fists, impatience clear on his face.

"Mr. President, unfortunately the Zionists escaped Russia. We don't know where they went and we don't know who they are." James Tipping paused. "We *do* know that they have three devices and their timetable and list of targets has been made fairly clear. We need to work back from there."

"We may not find them at all." McGhinnist sighed and sat. "Two weeks isn't much time to find a few tiny needles in a huge haystack."

Tipping nodded. "We've tasked all assets globally to finding them: satellites, humint, sigint. Anything not already engaged in a critical task will be devoted to finding them. But I'd say the chances of success are low. We should begin to consider other options."

"We could up our DEFCON level." Admiral Bryson Tannenbaum – Chairman of the Joint Chiefs – chimed in. "It'd increase our readiness to respond to any attack by the Zionists, but it'd also panic the public."

McGhinnist shook his head. "Maybe, but I don't want to go to a war footing just yet. We have time to power up our shields later. For now, our activity needs to be measured and aimed at finding them."

"Or we could just suspend the peace process?" Jack shrugged. "The stakes are high, but we can wait until the Zionists have been dealt with and then restart the clock, with the agreement of the Israelis and Palestinians."

McGhinnist stared down the table and straight at Jack. "The agreement is enacted in eighteen days. That gives us two weeks to find the nukes, deal with the agitation and prepare for the worst if an attack does happen."

Jack couldn't begrudge the President his refusal to delay. The negotiations had taken years, on top of the decades of groundwork. Achieving peace would be the crowning foreign policy achievement of the McGhinnist administration and a great step forward for the Middle East. Apparently nothing, not even the threat of nuclear devastation, would derail the President from this track.

Jack tuned out as the discussion of various options continued. This wasn't where he made his money.

McGhinnist had military and intelligence experts to chew over those issues with him, as well as a fair mind for that stuff himself. No, Jack helped the President in other ways – outside the strict lines of responsibility inside the administration. He did what others couldn't.

"Excuse me, Mr. President." Jack stood suddenly, thoughts rushing through his head.

"Okay, Jack." McGhinnist nodded. He was used to Jack's occasionally weird hunches and gave him the space to follow them. Sometimes they panned out.

Jack left the meeting room. In the time it took to return to his office – a hundred yards from the Oval Office – he pored over the plan in his head. He thought about what he knew: the leaker was smart, they'd remained hidden despite efforts to discover their identity and they'd made no mistakes. He was convinced that law enforcement would never figure out who it was. Not in time.

But he might. If there was one thing the leaker had shown, it was speed. Whenever the administration made a decision it was communicated to Celeste and the *Standard* in no time. He smiled. It was perfect. He only wished he'd thought of it sooner. He booted his computer and started working on a briefing note for McGhinnist and the rest of the administration.

McGhinnist stuck his head into Jack's office just as he finished keying in the final point, hours later. "What got into you back there?"

Jack looked up from his computer, dazed. He took a sip of water and leaned back in his chair with a smile. "I think I've figured out how to catch the leaker."

"Is that so?" McGhinnist stepped inside and closed the door. "That would be great, because I didn't get much to help fix our other problem."

Jack nodded and hit print on the briefing. Once it spat out of the printer, he handed it to McGhinnist. As the

President read the document, Jack paced the room and explained his plan in detail. McGhinnist was used to reading and listening at the same time, but he looked up when Jack reached the juicy bit. He glanced at the ceiling and then let out a long smile.

"You like it?" Jack sat on the edge of his desk. "It may not work, but I think it's got a pretty damn good chance."

"I like it." McGhinnist handed the paper back to Jack. "Send it to Clara and she'll distribute it to the council."

"It's a risk, sir. The media will be in a lather if this leaks." Jack took the paper and moved back around to the other side of the desk.

McGhinnist shrugged. "If a nuke goes off in Times Square, we're done for anyway. We need to focus on solving problems, not PR. Do it."

8

The President's National Security Council received a briefing yesterday on the threat posed by nuclear-armed Zionists, a copy of which has been obtained by the Standard. *Inside the briefing was a range of options to be considered by the council to deal with the threat. These options included: delaying the implementation of the peace agreement, attempting to negotiate with the Zionists, or conducting pre-emptive strikes on the Zionists if their physical location or that of their nuclear weapons can be determined. The White House declined to comment on the leak or on the contents of the briefing.*

New York Standard

J ack smiled as the sun started to rise, a cup of coffee in one hand and the newspaper in the other. He lifted the cup to his mouth as he scanned the front page of the *New York Standard*. He'd read it upon waking and it was a bombshell. He didn't need to read it again, but wanted to double check before he took action that was irreversible.

As he read, he took a few more sips of coffee. Once he was done, Jack let out a long sigh. It was true. It was time. After he'd laid some bait, the rat had chomped down on the cheese for a second or two before the trap had decapitated him. He'd had a feeling that his plan would work, but he'd been shocked by the outcome. It just proved that nothing was for sure in this business.

He sighed and turned back to the barista manning the coffee cart. "Thanks, Ramez. I'll see you tomorrow."

Jack tossed the paper into the trash, gulped down the rest of the coffee and trashed the cup too. He waved to Ramez, turned and crossed the street to his car. As he climbed inside and drove the short distance to the White House, he dialed a number on his cell phone and put it to speaker. The phone rang for a short while, then a man with a deep voice answered.

"This is Mike Seccombe."

"Mike? It's Jack Emery."

"Hi, Jack." Seccombe sounded surprised. It wasn't often that Jack reached out to the head of the Secret Service. "What's up? You okay?"

"I'm fine." Jack paused as he tooted the horn at a car. "Listen, Mike, I need you to have a word to the President and then detain James Tipping until I get in."

Seccombe laughed. "Sure, Jack, no problem. I'll just slap some cuffs on the National Security Advisor because of some prank."

Jack sharpened his voice. "It's no joke, Mike. He's the leak. We need to do this quietly before he figures out we're onto him. If I'm wrong, it's on my head."

"Damn right." Seccombe paused for a long few moments, then Jack could hear him exhale loudly. "Okay, Jack. I'll talk to the President."

The line went dead and Jack let out a long sigh. When he'd drafted the briefings the previous afternoon and had them distributed to all the members of the NSC, he'd inserted a small difference in each brief, stamped them Top Secret and waited. He'd known the *Standard* would pick up on the story, and the identifying detail would reveal the leaker.

He hadn't expected this morning's article to point at Tipping, but Jack had triple-checked the leak had the same detail as the briefing handed to the National Security Advisor – his friend. There was no doubt. As he pulled into the White House entrance, waved his pass and waited as his car was checked for explosives, his thoughts shifted from the betrayal to containing any further damage.

Jack pulled into the staff carpark, climbed out of the car and walked briskly toward his office. Seccombe and the Secret Service should have Tipping in custody by now, so Jack was keen to brief McGhinnist before their detainee kicked up a stink. The President wouldn't like it, but when Jack showed him the evidence, it would be undeniable.

He made it fifty feet inside the building when he turned a corner to see Seccombe and two agents. He pulled up short. "What?"

"He's gone, Jack." Seccombe's face was flushed red. He'd obviously lost it at his men, who stood around looking sheepish.

"Fuck!" Jack kicked at a potted plant, which toppled over. "When was he last seen?"

"Talking to Admiral Tannenbaum over breakfast." Seccombe shrugged. "Not sure what spooked him, but he's fled."

Jack knew. Tipping and Tannenbaum would have discussed the newspaper story. Tannenbaum would have revealed, confused, that his briefing lacked some of the detail of what was reported and Jack's game would have been revealed. Tipping was smart and would have realized then that he'd been played. Jack wouldn't be surprised if the other man was long gone by now.

Jack clenched his fists and his gaze fell upon Seccombe. "I need you to find him, Mike."

"We'll do our best. I'll be in touch." Seccombe nodded and then stalked off with his men in tow.

Jack let out a long sigh as he considered the art on the wall. He reflected that the beauty of this place sometimes outshone the dark shadows within its walls. The hard decisions, conflicting agendas and, occasionally, the acts of outright bastardry that were committed in the name of power. Tipping had committed several such acts. Jack needed to find him.

He went to the Oval Office and pushed the door open. Jack was one of the few with a standing invite to interrupt the President for matters of great importance. This was one of those. McGhinnist looked up from his desk, surprised at the interruption, and raised an eyebrow when he saw the look on Jack's face. He waved Jack toward a chair as he pressed a button on his telephone.

"Clara, we'll need something stiff to drink in here, please." McGhinnist cut the intercom. "What's wrong, Jack?"

"It's Tipping." Jack sat heavily on one of the sofas and then pounded a cushion with his fist.

"Mike said you'd found out it was him." McGhinnist sat opposite him and frowned, processing what Jack had said. "So your plan worked?"

"Yep." Jack shook his head. "He leaked it, Celeste published it and I asked Mike to detain him. But the fox has already fled the henhouse. He's gone."

"How?"

Jack was about to say more but they were interrupted by the President's assistant, opening the door with a tray of glasses and a bottle of Lagavulin – a favorite of

McGhinnist's. She didn't pour, but simply left the tray on the coffee table in front of them and left. Jack poured drinks for both of them and then handed McGhinnist a glass.

"I don't know how he got away, but it looks like he's up to his neck in it." Jack took a sip and savored the sharpness. "He might even be with the Zionists."

"It's possible." McGhinnist shrugged. "If nothing else, I'd say it's damn likely that he's worth having a chat to about some missing nukes."

Jack felt hot anger rising inside of him. An hour ago, he'd felt betrayed by Tipping. To discover that his friend was behind the leaks, the trouble in his relationship and maybe had something to do with nuclear-armed Zionists was nearly too much. But the fact that he'd escaped made it even worse. Jack couldn't sit around. He needed to act.

"What's on your mind, Jack?" McGhinnist stared at him as he took a sip of his own drink. "Spill it."

"I want to go after him, sir."

"You're kidding." McGhinnist put down his drink and shook his head.

He certainly wasn't. He felt personally betrayed by Tipping's actions and wanted nothing more than to find the man and confront him. Though there might be some danger, Jack doubted it. Tipping was flushed out and on the run, without resources or support. Jack had been in more dangerous situations over the past few years and come out unscathed. Besides, he was good at chasing down clues.

"I'm dead serious."

McGhinnist rubbed his chin. "Okay. But there's conditions."

"Name it."

McGhinnist opened his eyes. "You don't move anywhere until we have a solid understanding of where he is or where he's going to be."

"Fine." Jack shrugged. "Easy."

"And the whole reason I'm sending you is because it will be quiet. While you're looking, keep out of trouble. I'll have some covert teams doing the same, but I want to keep this as low-key as I can. The last thing I need is more headaches to deal with, like you getting arrested or something."

"Done, I—"

"There's one more condition." McGhinnist's face was as hard as granite. "And you're not going to like it."

Aron paused and glanced around for what felt like the hundredth time since he'd landed in Saudi Arabia. It was all for naught – there was nobody looking at him and he'd checked that he didn't have a tail – but he was feeling unusually conspicuous. He wasn't a nervous person, but he felt out of place this close to the most holy Islamic location on the planet, with a nuke strapped to his back.

Though he'd made it out of Russia with the rest of his team easily enough, this time he had no support and had to be very careful. Posing as a tourist was the easiest way to get around, aided by fake travel documents and a cheap camera to hang around his neck. The tourist angle also helped to explain the giant backpack he was carrying around.

He hefted the sixty-pound backpack with a grunt. His body was still in great shape, despite the fact he'd left Mossad several years ago, but the weight of the bag was testing his frame as much as the paranoia was taxing his mind. He felt as if a giant neon arrow was pointing at him, telling others that he didn't belong here. He just had to hope that his training and his body held up.

The sooner he reached his destination, the less likely it

was that he'd be captured. But it was still important to fit in. He lowered the hood of his sweater, lifted the camera from around his neck and took a few shots. If he was stopped at the airport, it would be useful to have some photos to show a nosy officer. He was a diligent tourist, after all.

He reviewed the photos, smiled and pulled the hood back over his head, then walked the short distance to the home of his contact. It was a rendered concrete building of four stories and zero elevators and, of course, his contact lived on the top floor. He sighed, walked through the entrance and started to climb the stairs.

By the time he reached the top, sweat was starting to bead on his brow and the straps from the backpack were cutting into his shoulders. He removed the hood, wiped his forehead and knocked on the door. He heard movement from inside the house, heavy boots walking on a wooden floor. He kept still, his hands in clear sight as one lock after another clicked and the door opened slowly.

"Who are you?" The barrel of a shotgun appeared through the crack of the door. "What do you want?"

Aron had expected such treatment. He was an outsider. "A friend sent me to deliver a package. It's quite urgent."

The shotgun stayed pointed at him for a split second longer than he felt comfortable with and Aron was just starting to wonder if he'd been betrayed when the weapon dropped and the door opened fully. A man pulled Aron inside, slammed the door shut behind them and bolted the five locks. Only when he was finished did he place the shotgun down.

Aron eased the backpack to the ground and then walked over to the man with his hand outstretched. "It's wonderful to meet you."

The other man grunted. He shook Aron's hand, but didn't appear thrilled to be doing so. "You're late."

Aron checked his watch. It was true, though barely. "Not a hanging offense, I hope."

The other man glared. "When you're floating on a tiny yacht in a giant storm, precision is everything."

Aron nodded. Given he had been told the other man was completely trustworthy, he could excuse some odd behavior if assured of results. Not that it was Aron's place to consider such guarantees. He played a small part in an enormous game of strategy, and this man played an even smaller part. They were moved around the board by a master.

He remembered his time at Yeshiva University, where Professor Zed Eshkol first captured his attention. Over several years, Aron had come to agree with the professor's views and with his sincerity of belief in Israel. Finally, the professor had taken Aron under his wing, confided in him about the special work of the Zionists and granted Aron his place in it all. He trusted Eshkol's leadership.

He just hoped the professor had chosen his men wisely, because this man from Mecca was one of three being entrusted with the future of Israel.

"Here it is."

The other man moved toward the bag and peered inside. "Armed?"

Aron smiled back. "Of course. It's set to go off one minute after the expiry of the peace agreement countdown. If the parties decide to step back from the agreement, then we disarm them. The bombs have been modified to allow remote disarming by satellite. There's nothing you have to do except keep it safe."

Secretly, Aron hoped the bomb would never go off, because it would mean that some wonderful historical treasures were saved, millions of lives were spared and sanity had prevailed. All it would take was for several powerful men to determine that the status quo was acceptable. If Israel was saved, then Aron was happy and so were the Zionists. The bombs would stay silent.

The decision to detonate the bombs wasn't Aron's, nor were the conditions placed on their use, but he fully supported the man tasked with such impossible decisions. He was done here. There was plenty to do without worrying about parts in the plan that weren't his responsibility. In his mind, he'd already moved on to the next target.

"Very well." The other man seemed satisfied. He closed the backpack and hefted it over to the corner of the room, out of the way.

They shook hands again. If the clock expired, then this apartment would join the priceless historical assets and hundreds of thousands of people vaporized to pay the price for the folly of Israeli and Palestinian leadership. If the agreement was abandoned, like Aron expected, then his man would bury the weapon in the desert.

He pulled the hood back over his head.

ZED LOCKED his hands together and laid them at the top edge of his desk. With a shout, he dragged them along the entire surface, reveling in every piece of stationery or other office paraphernalia that hit the floor. Some items smashed, while others just formed part of the messy chaos that achieved nothing but helped to soothe his rage.

Once he reached the end of the desk, he collapsed into his chair, exhausted. Lungs burning, he closed his eyes, trying to bring his anger, his breathing and his blood pressure under control. He was not an angry man, prone to these outbursts, but the message he'd received from James Tipping before he'd boarded a flight bound for the United Kingdom had sent him into a blind rage.

When he'd calmed himself a little, Zed opened his eyes and surveyed his office. A lifetime of treasured possessions were strewn like so much rubble and there was little left untouched by his anger. The bookshelves and coffee table had been given a similar treatment. Whatever Zed's tornado of destruction had lacked in speed had been more than made up for by blind fury.

His eyes paused for a second in the middle of the room, where his walking cane lay. There was nothing left to destroy unless Zed wanted to take his campaign beyond his office, though not even his legendary standing with university administration could survive that. He picked up the last thing on his desk – a pen – and dropped it onto the floor with a sigh.

Zed was mad that he'd lost his man inside the White House. While he didn't know how, he assumed that Tipping's latest leak must have contained some kind of poison pill. Tipping was alive, sure, but his usefulness to Zed was now zero. Tipping was the piece that had helped Zed to reach check against the peace agreement, but had been removed from the board before achieving checkmate.

Although it was impossible for any leader to not suffer a few losses over nearly fifty years of such work, Zed considered Tipping a larger loss. He'd risen higher than most and his mother had been Zed's lifelong friend until her death. Losing Tipping was like losing a son. He hadn't anticipated the loss, nor had he prepared himself for the personal consequences.

Zed wiped the single tear from his eye then staggered to his feet and used the edge of the desk to steady himself. He supported himself using furniture as he moved slowly to the door. While he did, he thought hard about what came next. He needed to cool down, despite his every instinct telling him to destroy and pillage to soothe his anger.

In truth, he was mad at himself. He'd overused

Tipping's access and it had burned the young man. Zed had wanted to ramp up the media pressure on the signatories to the peace agreement to make them walk away or delay implementation, but so far he'd failed to achieve either. Tipping was gone and now it looked as if the only way to destroy the peace was to nuke three cities.

He'd seen the Samson Option as a last resort, but now he wondered if it was the only option left. The Israelis and the Palestinians had proven surprisingly resilient in the face of great pressure, while the response of the McGhinnist administration had been baffling. Zed had expected some degree of retreat by the US, but the President had escalated matters instead.

Zed reached the door to his office, opened it and stuck his head out the door. "I'd like you to head home early today."

His assistant looked up from her computer, the confusion on her face clear. "Is everything okay, professor?"

Zed nodded but kept quiet. She clearly knew something was wrong and had probably heard the noise, but knew better than to ask. She smiled at him and started to gather her things. Zed waited, propped against the doorframe and breathing heavily while she made her way out of the office. Soon he was alone and Zed returned to his office, picking up his phone from the floor.

He collapsed back into his chair, as exhausted from his journey as he was by his campaign of destruction. It had been many years since he'd moved without his walking stick. He waited a moment or two while he gathered himself, then dialed a number from memory, raised the phone to his ear and waited for the call to be picked up. When it was, there was the single beep of a voicemail.

"This is Zed." He spoke softly, trying not to let his sadness and the gravity of the situation divert him from the correct decision. "Knight 2 is off the board."

The message was enough for business to be taken care of. Zed knew that if Tipping was captured anywhere in a Western country he'd be arrested, extradited to the US and questioned. If that happened, Zed's place in the Zionist hierarchy could be revealed. He didn't care about his own freedom or his own life, given no court would jail a man of his age. He did fear that the authorities would figure out how to stop the Zionists in their holy cause.

There were cells, dozens of them, which faced exposure or destruction. But his ability to conduct the orchestra would be lost if he was caught. It wouldn't do. Tipping had to die and Zed had just ordered it. The decision was like a lance through his heart. But it was necessary for the safety of the entire Zionist cause and their important mission.

He'd honestly thought the nuclear option was the last resort and that the peace agreement would unravel against such a threat. But it had proven resilient. He'd been prepared for the use of the weapons, but given the exposure of Tipping, he wondered now if it was best to issue one final ultimatum and then use the weapons if his demands weren't met. He dialed another number.

"Hello?" The voice on the other end of the line didn't have any of the stress that Zed had coiled up inside of him. "Ariel speaking."

"Ariel." Zed smiled. Just hearing the young man's voice was proof that his work was not yet done, his campaign hadn't yet concluded. "How are you?"

"Fine, professor." Ariel paused. "Is everything okay? Do you need me to call someone?"

Zed nearly laughed at the success of his charade. Though his body was failing him, clearly the act that his mind was doing the same was proving wildly successful. He had everyone fooled, even his secretary and one of his closest students. A student he was also grooming to form part of his network. A minor part, at first, but with some potential.

"I'd like you to come to my office, Ariel. I've had a bit of an issue here and I could use your help cleaning it up." Zed sighed. "But only if you don't mind."

There was no hesitation. "Of course, professor, give me half an hour and I'll be over."

"Excellent. Thank you, Ariel. I'll see you soon." Zed hung up the phone and placed it on the desk.

He allowed himself one last flicker of anger before he dampened down the flame. Tipping had to die, but not in vain. He was determined that there would be retaliation, but he still needed to decide on the form of it. It could come in the form of another nuclear ultimatum or he could come up with something else.

The choice was his, but he needed to decide before Ariel arrived.

9

The White House is in damage control after the shock resignation of National Security Advisor James Tipping. Washington is awash with speculation that Tipping, a three-year veteran of the McGhinnist administration, was the leak inside the White House that has plagued the President for weeks now. The timing of the resignation isn't ideal, with less than two weeks to go before peace between Israel and Palestine, nuclear-armed Zionist extremists threatening major cities and other states in the Middle East starting to talk tough. Though a White House spokesperson this morning claimed the resignation was an amicable, mutually agreed parting of ways, it's quite possible that Tipping walked before he was forced out.

New York Standard

Captain Joseph Cohen nodded as the printer began its urgent clatter. When the message was complete, the operator ripped the printout from the machine and read it. Satisfied that the message was genuine, she passed it to Tim Jennings – Joseph's executive officer – who turned and immediately left the radio room, arm held high.

Joseph followed a few steps behind Jennings and the other officer with him, whose job it was to make sure the message wasn't substituted on the way to the control room. Joseph didn't say a word or interrupt them. It was important that the process play out, without interference from him. His crew knew what they were doing.

Only once they reached the operations room did Joseph step closer to Jennings. "Open the safe, XO."

"Yes, sir."

Leaning in close to the code panel, Joseph entered the eight-digits that made up his part of the code. He looked left to Jennings, who was a little slower, but within a few seconds the other half of the code was in and the safe unlocked with a click. Joseph opened it and pulled out the cryptographic codes that would tell them whether the order to launch was legitimate.

Before he closed the safe, he glanced quickly at the second safe, inside the first. It contained the Dead Man Letter – a weapon potentially far more destructive than the codes that he'd just extracted. With a quick shake of his head, he closed the safe and put his mind back on the job. There was time later to think about other matters.

Joseph handed one code sheet to Jennings and the other to the Weapons Engineering Officer, Ray Burroughs, who stepped forward to receive it. They looked down at their crypto sheets and compared them against the message that had come in from the boomer command bunker at Northwood, deep under the Chilterns.

"XO!" Jennings' shout reverberated around the interior of the operations room. "My half authenticates, sir!"

"WEO!" Burroughs' voice was deeper but not as loud, the rolling thunder after a lightning strike. "My half authenticates, sir!"

Joseph looked at them both. Their faces were stern, uncompromising. "The message authenticates correctly. XO, bring the submarine to launch station."

He stood back again, watching. His role was complete for the time being, and it was important that he allowed both men the space to complete theirs. He let out a long exhale, calming himself. Though he'd trained for this moment for years, it was his first time doing it in command of a boat. He needed to be stone. He needed to *show* that he was in command.

"Ship control. Pipe the boat to launch station." Jennings' voice was quieter now.

The crewman pressed a button and spoke loudly into the microphone. "Action stations! Missile for strategic launch!"

"Very good." Jennings nodded. "Full rise on the fore planes. Two up. Stop engine."

Joseph watched as the submarine – his submarine – was brought to its launch position closer to the surface. One of his crew held out a small earpiece, and Joseph placed it into his ear and nodded. Just as the submarine reached position, Burroughs left the operations center and moved to take his place in the missile center.

"Boat at launch position." Jennings' voice broke the silence.

"WEO in the missile control center." Burroughs' voice crackled in Joseph's earpiece. "Stand by, operations."

"Check." Jennings reached up and scratched the back of his neck.

Joseph knew that in the missile center, the target package would be being shifted onto target, the right number of missiles readied and coordinates confirmed. Only once the weapons were ready would the weapons officer unlock a safe above his console, open it and remove the trigger that fired the weapons. It had always amused Joseph that the trigger was the handle of a Colt .45 pistol.

The mood in the operations center was of intense concentration, as men and women stared at their screens and worked complex controls. Joseph found that, despite being the captain of the ship, he actually had very little to do when it came to launching the weapons. He carried the pressure – the load on his shoulder – but it was his crew who pressed the buttons in the leadup.

Finally, after another few moments, Burroughs spoke. "Command, weapons systems in condition one for strategic launch."

Joseph nodded, stepped forward and leaned in to the microphone on one of the consoles. "This is the captain, the WEO has my permission to fire."

Joseph stepped back and crossed his arms as Burroughs' voice crackled in his headset again. "Supervisor WEO, initiate fire one."

Joseph waited one more second, then nodded at a member of crew who so far had done nothing. She pressed a button and every light in the operations center – and the entire submarine – flashed on, breaking the strange trance that the drill had created among the crew. Joseph reached into his pocket as his eyes adjusted, then looked down at the old gold fob watch, a gift from his father.

"Too long." Joseph shook his head and closed the watch before returning it to his pocket. "Better, but still too slow on the verification."

The crew sagged as one as Jennings nodded and started the debriefing in the observation room, pointing out where they could improve and where they'd done well. Joseph turned on his heel and started the walk back to his cabin. He needed to freshen up, but he also needed to reflect on where things could be improved or where they could go wrong.

It was quite possible that in a few weeks he'd have to do the exercise for real. He was glad his crew was well oiled and knew their jobs. When the order came down from command, they'd follow his instructions. He'd drill them several times over the coming weeks, because in the event of a launch, he wanted things to move faster and he knew that events didn't always work out easily.

He thought again of the Dead Man Letter and wondered if, when the letter was opened, his crew would follow him.

Jack found it a bit insulting that, after all he'd been through in helping the United States fight extremists and terrorists, Delta Airlines didn't trust him to use a real knife and fork. It was just one of the problems with being stuck on a commercial flight instead of an official one – a condition that the President had placed on sending Jack overseas to find Tipping in order to keep attention off him.

He stabbed at the small piece of overcooked beef with his plastic knife. Though the meat was slicked with some kind of congealed brown sauce, the knife bent as if repelled by steel armor plating. Jack held the knife in front of him and frowned at the ninety-degree bend of the blade. Taking over the plane with the dead cow would be more dangerous to the flight crew than proper cutlery.

"Should have gone for the salad." He gave up on the food and placed it on the vacant tray table next to him.

With a sigh, he pulled out his iPad. If nothing else, the flight had wifi. He downloaded his emails and started to work through them. It was autopilot. If you worked a white-collar job for long enough, wading through emails became as easy as a carpenter hammering a nail, if less enjoyable. It was actually a great time to think about the days ahead.

McGhinnist had finally agreed to let him chase Tipping after he'd been caught on CCTV footage at Heathrow Airport in the United Kingdom. Tipping was traveling on false papers, so he'd waltzed through immigration, but a bright kid at the CIA had spotted him on the footage a few hours after Tipping had entered the country. Jack was now flying to that same airport, hoping he could catch up.

"You're fussy."

Jack laughed and looked up at Chen Shubian, who gestured with his chin toward the food Jack had left aside. "I might have chipped a tooth on that beef."

Chen smiled. "When I finished my special forces training in Taiwan, I had to survive for two days in the Dawu Mountains with a tin of beans and my wits."

Jack dismissed Chen's statement with a wave of his hand. "Well, if you survive the White House press corps you can survive anything except airline food."

Chen shook his head and picked up his magazine. The conversation was over. The man remained an enigma to Jack and their relationship was complicated. Chen was a special forces soldier-turned-terrorist who'd blown up a fair amount of Shanghai and killed Jack's wife in the process. He'd also shot Jack's old boss and friend, Ernest McDowell. On the other hand, just like Jack, Chen had been duped, threatened and nearly killed by the Foundation for a New America, and he'd lost his own wife. Only Jack's efforts to convince Chen to provide evidence against the Foundation's leader, Michelle Dominique, had saved Jack's life and kept her from controlling Congress and a large portion of the world's media.

After stopping Dominique, they'd gone their separate ways. Jack hadn't thought much about Chen during the years following, until he'd joined McGhinnist's administration and learned that Chen was still in the United States. It made sense, given Chen's native Taiwan was a no-go zone for him, but Jack had assumed he'd left America. Instead, the FBI had kept him on retainer, probably as much to keep an eye on him as to occasionally extract information from him. Or to make use of his skillset, as Jack now was. He'd spoken to the other man at the airport and, though the details were scarce, it was clear Chen had been undertaking some work for the United States on American soil. He'd shrugged his shoulders and simply said that it was the cost to keep his children safe.

Having Chen along as an escort had been McGhinnist's other condition for approving Jack's request to go after Tipping. Jack was still a United States Government employee and, as such, he was unarmed. That made Chen useful. If they ran into any trouble with rampaging Zionists the ex-Taiwanese special forces soldier had skills that didn't require a firearm.

Jack's eyes shot open. He must have dozed off and now the plane was rattling in some fairly severe turbulence. He looked at Chen. "You okay?"

Chen was gripping his armrests with both hands, his knuckles white. He turned to Jack. "I'm not a fan of flying."

Jack laughed, loud and long, to the extent that several other passengers cast a glance their way. "So Mr. Special Forces is human. Why agree to come?"

Chen gritted his teeth. "My children are in New York. Their school. Their friends. I could move them, but I'd just as rather save the city."

Jack nodded at Chen's words. He was as dry and as self-motivated as ever, yet on rare occasions Jack had found it possible to work with Chen toward a mutual goal. It was quite possible that Tipping was in with the Zionists, who'd proven they had a fairly decent ability to break shit and blow it up, so it was nice to have Chen along.

Jack looked across the aisle and locked eyes with Chen.

"I'm doing this for Celeste, but we'll make sure your kids are okay too."

"I nearly blew her up once, I hear, so I probably owe her one." Chen's face was impassive. "We'll catch your man and find the bombs."

S AMIH HELD his hand high in the air and kept a wide smile on his face, even though his cheeks were starting to hurt. The applause was rapturous. His arm was linked with Ben Ebron's, who had his other arm linked with Karl Long. The triad in charge of the peace negotiations were receiving a rock-star reception in a community hall in Jerusalem – the latest event to build support for the peace.

Finally, the applause started to subside. Samih gave one last wave and then moved with Long to take his seat slightly behind the lectern, leaving Ebron at the front to speak. It was the same format they'd used a dozen times at events in the past few days. Samih had never smiled and waved so much, nor felt as welcome in Israel after the initial trouble with the protestors.

The vision of him handing his mints to the Israeli girl had gone viral. Suddenly, he'd been thrust into the popular imagination far more prominently than at any time during his career fighting for Palestine or, later, attempting to negotiate a political settlement with Israel. He was now a celebrity. It gave him hope that the world had some interest in what they were trying to achieve.

He'd felt the balance begin to tip. Since broadcasting their threats, the Zionists had gone quiet. Samih knew they were serious and that they had the weapons they claimed, but he felt they were losing the public imagination. It was hard not to worry, but he knew there was no point: the CIA, Mossad and plenty of others were looking for the group and their bombs. He couldn't help with that.

What he could do was try to build public support for the agreement and keep minds on the positives – for Israel, Palestine and the whole world. He shook his head and tuned in to what Ebron was saying. Though Samih had heard it several times already today, it was important to pay attention in case the Israeli negotiator changed his message and required Samih to do the same.

"I call on those Zionists, who call themselves Jews and say they're acting in the interests of Israel, to listen." Ebron held his hands out. "Listen to me. Listen to your people. You save nothing by threatening to destroy cities and kill millions. All you'll do is bring ruin to your spiritual homeland.

"Peace with the Palestinians will secure Israel a long-term, sustainable future in the region. We will no longer have to live with one hand on our guns. We can talk." Ebron shook his head. "Or, if you go through with your threats, we will be fighting for our very existence, against neighbors who'll rightly wish us gone."

On it went, until Ebron was finished and Long stood to make his speech. He spoke the usual lines about the level of US support for the agreement, that America was doing everything in its power to support the peace and catch the Zionists, and that the normal citizens of Israel and Palestine had the most to gain from peace. He was not a commanding speaker but his message was strong.

As more applause rang out, Samih stood and took his turn at the lectern. "Thank you. I want to be brief here today, because I agree with my dear friends and colleagues behind me. My people have fought for their freedom for decades. Despite violence on both sides, we've achieved peace. It's inevitable."

A commotion in the crowd prevented Samih from

continuing. It only took a second to find the source. A man in the front row had stood and ripped his shirt open, revealing some strange rig of explosives strapped to his chest. Security had been tight, but somehow the man had found his way in. Samih raised his hand and screamed, his voice shrill, but the man ignored him as he raised a remote.

"This is a fool's peace!" The man's voice was high and laced with fear as he pressed his thumb down on the button.

Samih turned and dived, taking Ebron down to the floor just as the explosion tore through the small hall. A wave of pressure impacted him even as he hit the ground with Ebron. Dust filled his mouth and nostrils. His ears were ringing, drowning out all other sound around him. He pushed himself off the Israeli and looked around.

The hall was carnage. There were scorch marks on the wooden floor where the man had been. Bodies lay scattered, unmoving and broken. Others writhed in agony like experiments in some strange human abattoir. Samih's eyes were locked on the scene, unblinking, until he felt someone pulling on his shirt. He turned his head and blinked twice.

"We have to go!" Long had one hand gripped on Ebron's arm and the other on Samih's shirt. He let go and held out his hand. "Now!"

Samih grabbed Long's hand, using it as leverage as he started to struggle to his feet. He didn't get the chance, because a gunman approached the American and fired a shotgun blast into his head. As blood and gore sprayed Samih, Long's grip went limp and Samih stumbled back. He looked up, screamed and tried to shuffle away from the gunman.

The attacker turned to Ebron, pumped his shotgun and raised it at the Israeli. Samih watched in horror, frozen, as the barrel slowly came up. His hearing was still muffled, but he could hear other gunshots, booms that sounded to him as if they were underwater and distant rather than in close, lethal proximity. He glanced sideways. Two other gunmen were walking through the hall, terminating anyone who moved. He turned back to the first gunman, who was struggling to unjam his shotgun.

The gunman threw down the shotgun and drew a pistol. Samih scrambled to his feet, shouting, but was too late. The gunman fired a single shot into Ebron's skull and Samih let out a scream as the man he'd been through so much hard, honest negotiations with fell to the floor. Samih surged forward as the gunman started to turn, then leaped onto his back. The man tensed instantly as he tried to buck Samih off. Samih wrapped his arm around the gunman's neck, trying to strangle him, until he felt a hard punch into his side.

He staggered, confused, then turned and saw another man gripping a blade that was protruding from his side. Samih looked down in shock. His eyes narrowed as he tried to comprehend how a blade could enter his side and yet cause no pain. He tried to grip the blade, but his attacker withdrew it before he could grab it. Pressing his hand against the wound did nothing to stem the bleeding, even as he looked up at the other man. The look of hatred on his face was shocking as he thrust the knife into Samih again and again.

Samih's last thought was a prayer that the peace would endure. Ebron, Long and Samih had worked so hard for it. And given their lives.

10

---

*Israeli, Palestinian and American political leaders have
released a joint statement condemning the Zionist attack on
the lead negotiators for the Palestinian–Israeli peace treaty.
Fifty-eight people were killed in the massacre, including the
negotiators, in one of the worst ever terrorist attacks on Israeli
soil. The Zionist terrorist group has claimed responsibility and
downplayed the security camera footage of the Palestinian
lead negotiator, Samih Khaladi, leaping to the defense of
Israeli negotiator Ben Ebron. The footage has gone viral, with
over seventeen million YouTube views.*

New York Standard

Zed's eyes scanned the screen, lapping up the news
like a cat with milk. The analysis was shoddy, but
he was used to that. Gunmen had attacked an
event spruiking the peace agreement and shot the
negotiators and the crowd to pieces. Each of the negotiators
had been killed, along with many members of the crowd. It
had gone perfectly. Just as he'd planned.

He allowed himself an indulgent smile, pleased that the

Israeli negotiator had been dealt with. Though the agreement was signed and he had no further formal role to play, Ben Ebron's cheerleading on behalf of the peace had made Zed's efforts to destroy it harder. Zed would have ordered him killed sooner or later under any circumstances, but Ebron's advocacy had forced his hand.

Unfortunately, the news wasn't all positive and one aspect of the attack had backfired. As he reached the bottom of the article he saw a link to a video he couldn't resist clicking on again. He ground his teeth as he watched the Palestinian, Samih Khaladi, doing his best to protect Ebron from the gunmen. A killing Zed hoped would help to destroy public support for the agreement had instead bolstered it. It was the internet, always the cursed internet. Thirty years ago, the headline would have read 58 dead in massacre in Israel, including peace negotiators. Now? Massacre in peace meeting – you won't believe what happens next!

Things used to be a lot easier. Organize a killing, the media reported it for a day and then the problem went away. He sighed. As much as he was in control of his network, he knew he was kidding himself if he thought he could totally control events. The world didn't work that way. All he could do was keep playing the game, using his pieces and recruiting more to ensure that he won in the end.

He picked up his phone and dialed. "I want the team in Israel dealt with."

Without waiting for confirmation, he hung up. He leaned down with a pained groan, opened the bottom drawer and pulled out a leather-bound folder. He placed it on his desk and slowly flicked through the pages. The names and photos caused memories and regrets to wash over him. So many men and some women – game pieces – expended to protect Israel and the Jewish people.

He finally found the right names and photos. He picked up a marker and sighed as he crossed out each man. They'd been loyal servants, but limited. Thugs. Pawns. They'd played their part and now more capable pieces would end their involvement. It wasn't a question. A move had been ordered and now it would be done. It was how he played the game.

Besides, there were always more pawns. He pressed the intercom to summon his assistant. "Please ask Ariel to come and see me."

"At once, professor."

Zed woke with a start at the knock on the door. He smiled slightly and rubbed his face. He hadn't been sleeping much, which wasn't unusual for him, but the older he got, the less he found he could take the long days and sleepless nights. He found himself dozing off in the strangest places, though thankfully this time it had been in his office and not in public.

"Come!"

The door cracked open and Ariel peered inside. "You asked for me, Zed?"

Zed smiled at Ariel finally using his name. He was one step closer. "Come in."

He struggled to his feet and walked to the chessboard at which they always held their meetings. As he shuffled over, he considered the growth of the young man. He'd made a decision, but he'd play the game first. By the time he'd reached his armchair and eased himself into it, Ariel had made the first move. Zed looked at the board and reached out to move a pawn.

"You're well, professor?"

"Yes, why?"

"No reason." Ariel shrugged. "There's just been some talk about you retiring."

Zed scoffed. "There's been talk about that for twenty

years, Ariel. But I'm still here and they're still trying to get rid of me. For as long as I can continue to get up the nose of the administration, and beat students like you at this game, I'll be around. After that I'll haunt the place, mark my words."

Ariel laughed and looked back down at the board. "Of course you will."

While his student considered his move, Zed considered his student. He'd been working on Ariel for several years now. At first, he'd simply been the young man's teacher. Then, his mentor. Now, perhaps, his friend. While Zed didn't see any great potential in Ariel, he was loyal and smart enough to serve. Everyone had a place and a use.

"Your move, professor."

Zed shook his head. "My apologies, I was just thinking about you."

"Me?" Ariel looked at him quizzically. "What do you mean?"

"You graduate soon." Zed fixed his eyes on his student, who fidgeted under his gaze. "Have you considered your future? It's tough for graduates right now."

"Sure." Ariel shrugged. "I'd thought about doing some post-graduate study, but with the situation in Israel, I feel I might have something to offer as a citizen."

Zed smiled. Though he'd never been a citizen of Israel, everything he'd done as a professional had been aimed at protecting it. Part of that was recruiting the pieces for his board. He'd never expected to need to utilize his army or the great work of his life – the Samson Option – but he was twelve days away from needing both. The destruction of Israel was close.

"You're a remarkable young man, Ariel. I think becoming a citizen and serving in the military would be a wonderful choice for you."

"I've thought about it. But I'm not sure. I don't want to end up as a grunt in the West Bank."

Zed laughed. Maybe the boy wasn't a pawn after all. "I have some contacts in the IDF. I can make some calls and probably work out something better."

"That would be wonderful, professor." Ariel beamed. "Even if I don't sign up, it would be good to know my options."

Zed nodded. Ariel was now his. Though he'd been carefully cultivated over years, there had been no guarantee until now. But the minute Zed made the call to his man inside the Israeli Defense Forces, Ariel would be in his pocket. Zed would make him an offer too good to refuse and then the boy would be in his debt. A piece on the board. Limited, but useful.

He moved another pawn. Though some of his recruits went on to greatness, others fizzled out and some weren't used at all. Though he wasn't sure what he had in Ariel, he was obliged to keep adding pieces. With the stakes so grave and so many pieces being lost, it was nice to add a new one. He wondered how many would be left in a month.

JACK STOOD with his hands tucked into the pockets of his coat as he watched the ferry slowly inch up to the dock and come to a stop. When the ship was still, its air horn let out a long, droning blast. To Jack, it felt like his own personal wail of triumph, a shout to Tipping that his time was up and that he was about to face the consequences of his betrayal.

That betrayal seemed all the more serious now. After landing, Jack had spent several fruitless days searching the United Kingdom for Tipping, even as the pieces fell into place back in the States. Jack had received an email from

Mike Seccombe, head of the Secret Service, which informed him that definitive proof had been found of Tipping's involvement with the Zionists.

Though the proof provided no clue as to who their leader was, it was enough to ratchet up the importance of the search by a few hundred percent. Tipping had to be found. Luckily, Tipping had been spotted boarding a ferry to cross the English Channel that morning. Though tempted to ask the British Special Air Service to nab him, the NSC had picked a different approach.

Jack and Chen had flown by helicopter to Calais, where they now waited with around fifty French police officers, braving the cold and the squally, biting wind in order to get their man. Jack felt an extra sense of urgency, given the negotiators had been killed. It felt like their deaths had frayed the chances of peace even further. The good guys needed a win. They needed Tipping.

Jack looked over at Chen. Icy breath escaped his mouth and he looked miserable. "Like the cold then?"

Chen grimaced. "Winter is winter anywhere, but winter with jetlag is a special kind of miserable."

Jack laughed and turned back to the ferry. By now, the ramp was in place and a large number of people had started to gather on deck. Jack watched as the man in charge of the police detachment ordered his officers forward, ready to foil any attempt by passengers to use the ramp. Their orders were clear: nobody leaves the ferry until Tipping is in cuffs.

When the ramp was finally readied for the police to board, they marched up it five abreast with batons drawn in an obvious show of force. The passengers who'd expected to disembark stood aside, confused, as the phalanx marched past them. Five officers remained at the bottom of the ramp to make sure Tipping couldn't escape.

"Let's go."

Jack and Chen walked up the ramp and onto the deck of the ferry. They waited as the police conducted their search, checking each passenger against a photograph of Tipping. Minutes passed, then more, and Jack began to lose hope of catching their man, when finally the senior police officer told them in broken English that the former National Security Advisor was not on board the ferry.

"Fucking hell!" Jack kicked the wall of the ferry and immediately regretted it. He winced in pain for a couple of seconds, before calming down. "What now?"

"It's no surprise." Chen sighed. "He didn't escape the Secret Service, fly to the UK and board a ferry across the Channel by being stupid."

Jack opened his mouth to respond, but then closed it again. He reached up, scratched his head and turned to face the guardrail on the outside of the ferry. He looked out to the ocean and smiled. Tipping may no longer be his friend, but Jack found it hard to stifle a laugh. He'd been stupid and overconfident. He'd marched in with an army of police officers on the assumption that it'd be enough.

He turned back to one of the crew. "Is there CCTV on board this ferry? Do you have easy access to it?"

The sailor shrugged. "Sure. But you'll need to convince the captain to let you access the tapes."

Jack nodded and gestured for the sailor to lead the way. Another sailor radioed the captain to let him know they were on their way. The small band made their way to the bridge, where the captain had already gathered a handful of laptop computers, ready to stream the footage from the server. He had a grim look on his face.

"Captain." Jack held out his hand. "I'm so sorry for all of this disruption, but we have to find this man."

The captain shook his hand. "So I keep being told. If we can find your man on the camera footage, will you let my passengers off?"

"Of course."

The captain gestured for them to get started. Jack watched one computer, Chen another, and the two police officers took one each. They watched at ten times the normal speed until Jack saw something. He hit the space bar on the machine, causing it to play at normal speed. There was Tipping, jumping overboard with nothing but a backpack and a bright orange floatation device.

Jack shook his head, turning to the others. Everyone except Chen seemed stunned. Jack turned back to the screen and rewound it. He needed to be certain before he could report to McGhinnist and the authorities. Not pretty sure, certain. But the footage was crisp and clear and the person he was looking at was undoubtedly James Tipping.

Jack cursed and slammed the lid of the laptop shut. He turned to the captain.

"You're good to let your passengers off. That's him."

"Thanks. Bad luck." The captain turned and walked away. His concern was clearly for his boat, not the international security crisis playing out on it.

Jack closed his eyes and gripped the table. When he'd scammed the National Security Council with the fake briefing, he'd known there was a chance the gambit would fail: perhaps it wasn't a member of the council leaking, perhaps the leaker would spot the trick, or perhaps Celeste wouldn't print it. But it had worked. Yet Tipping had escaped the White House, America and now the UK.

Who knew where Tipping had swum?

ARON PUSHED the sporty convertible hard out of the corner and drove the final hundred yards to the Jerusalem office of UNICEF, where he braked hard right outside. He gripped the wheel for a moment to compose himself and then killed the engine. Checking his mirrors, he made sure the truck that was following him had pulled up, then climbed out.

"Mr. Yosef!" A well-dressed man greeted him outside the office, a broad smile on his face. "Welcome! I'm Levi Eban, I manage this office."

"Thank you." Aron gave a curt nod. "My apologies for being late, I was delayed slightly by the roadblocks."

"No problem at all. These are troubled times." Eban was clearly doing his best at small talk. "Pleasant drive apart from that, I hope?"

Aron grunted. He'd traveled from Jeddah, near Mecca, to Tel Aviv, where he'd been picked up at the airport by someone in his network. They'd traveled to a warehouse, where Aron had dressed in a suit and taken possession of the sports car. From there, he'd driven the car while two others drove the truck to the office. He wanted this done, given he still had a flight to New York to make today.

"Do you have staff available to help my men unload the truck? I'm afraid there's quite a lot of supplies and I'm keen to do it quickly."

"And what a generous donation!" Eban patted him on the back. "Of course we can help."

"Excellent."

Eban gestured some of the waiting staff forward. "They'll take care of it. Now, if you'd like to come inside, we can have some refresh—"

"I'll wait and watch, if you don't mind." Aron smiled. "My donors were quite insistent that I make sure these supplies reach your hands."

"Of course, of course." Eban waved a hand. "Bring the truck inside and we'll see it unloaded."

Aron nodded and waved at the truck. Its engine roared and it started to move again, directed to the parking bay by a UNICEF staff member. Aron was glad the truck was finally off the main road and inside the grounds of the UNICEF facility, a vital step in what he had planned. He gave Eban another nod. The man shouted orders at members of his staff, who got to work unloading it.

The truck contained dozens of boxes of donated goods for distribution to needy Palestinian children and families. The UNICEF team were joined by Aron's own men – other Zionists – in unloading boxes from the back of the truck for storage at the office. He wasn't sure how often UNICEF received donated goods rather than money, but they hadn't declined the support.

A smirk crossed Aron's lips as he watched them work. Given the money saved on the nuke transaction with the Russians, the cost of the ruse had been a simple affair: an old but reliable truck, a flashy sports car and a few dozens boxes of relief supplies. Not cheap, but nowhere near the cost of a nuclear weapon, especially if he could guarantee the success of the ruse.

The boxes were unloaded onto the ground. It didn't take long, and in ten minutes the back of the truck was empty and the boxes were stacked high, ready for distribution to the needy. Keeping his face passive, he watched as one of the Zionists closed the door at the back of the vehicle while the other moved back to the cabin. A second later, the truck's engine squealed.

"That doesn't sound good." Eban winced as the sound from the truck assaulted their ears.

Aron cursed. "I keep telling them we need to replace that truck. Every time it breaks down, it's out of action for weeks."

Eban's head rotated slightly. "So long?"

"Eastern European truck." Aron shrugged. "Takes that long to get the parts."

"I see." Eban clearly didn't understand, or care to. "Can we help?"

Aron paused for a moment, pretending to consider the office manager's words. "Well, if you don't mind, we could leave the truck parked here until the part arrives in a few weeks. I'd prefer to avoid the cost of towing it, given it reduces the money we're able to donate."

"No problem! We have plenty of space. It's the least I can do."

"Excellent!"

As the other Zionists gave up on starting the truck – an impossible job given they'd sabotaged it – Aron reassured himself that they'd covered everything. He pictured the backpack hidden in the cabin of the truck. The countdown was underway and the device was armed and fully functioning. Only a dedicated search would find the weapon, and that was unlikely.

Two out of three devices were now in place and he had plenty of time left to place the third. He turned to Eban. "I'll be in touch once we hear from the mechanic."

"Not a problem."

Aron stepped away toward his car. "Yes, thanks to you and your staff for taking such fine care of me."

"Our pleasure, Mr. Yosef, but hold on a second." Eban touched Aron's arm gently. "While my staff move the supplies inside, would you join me for lunch?"

Aron was about to refuse, but then he checked his watch. He thought for a second and decided it would be better to eat here than at the airport. "Sure."

Eban beamed. "Do you like curry? There's an excellent Indian place just down the road."

"Sounds fine." When you'd eaten from tins for many years, any restaurant meal was acceptable. He glanced at the sports car. "But I'm driving."

"Excellent! They have a vindaloo that's explosive!"

11

French police were left red-faced yesterday when a large number of officers raided a Channel ferry at the Calais docks but came up empty-handed. The police have refused to comment on the purpose of the raid, except that they were looking to apprehend a suspect believed to be on board. The police left less than an hour after they boarded, leaving passengers and crew concerned about a possible connection between the raids and the Zionist terrorists currently being sought by authorities around the world.

New York Standard

J ack clenched his jaw tightly as he smiled at the cop, declining to say anything else given how close he'd already come to being arrested. Tapping the car's window frame impatiently, he waited for the Belgian officer to finish writing the ticket, taking it silently when it was handed to him. He watched as the officer walked back to his police car.

"You don't learn, do you?" Chen laughed from the seat

beside him. "I can see the headline now: White House staffer busted for speeding. Again."

Jack exhaled loudly through his nose. "We've got a job to do. Treasury will sort out the bills we rack up along the way."

"Well, that's three fines and counting." Chen laughed again. "You sound very much like someone leading an authoritarian state."

"What's the saying? Omelettes and eggshells and all that?" Jack turned to Chen and smiled.

Chen grunted as, for the third time since they'd left Calais, Jack screwed up the ticket and tossed it in the back seat. They'd hired a car and driven after Tipping, following intelligence that he had come ashore in Belgium and was headed inland on the continent. The occasional piece of intelligence was enough to keep them on the trail, but the lack of any specific knowledge about where Tipping was headed was starting to bother Jack. He had the resources of the United States government on his side, but that didn't seem to be enough.

Jack sighed, started the car and pulled back onto the highway. Though it felt like they were traveling blind, onward they went, because if they didn't find Tipping then there was no chance of stopping the Zionists. His teleconference a few hours ago with the NSC had said as much. More evidence of Tipping's support for the Zionists had been found on the former staffer's computer, but there were few other leads to help with tracking down the backpack bombs. It seemed like it was Tipping or bust.

Minutes passed, then hours. Jack listened to the one English radio station he'd found, at least until Chen reached to switch it off.

"Hey! I was listening to that!"

Chen's face was impassive. "My life is too short for bad radio."

Jack let it go as his phone started to ring. He glanced at it in the cradle and waited for it to pick up automatically. "Hello?"

"Hi, Jack." Celeste sounded stressed. "Chen there too?"

"Yep." Jack smiled at the sound of her voice.

"Okay." Her voice told him it wasn't, but she kept talking. "How are you both?"

Chen turned his head and looked out the window.

"We're good. Chasing a phantom, though."

Jack probably shouldn't have told her, but he was too tired to care. Tipping had been a valuable source for Celeste, yet as far as he knew, she hadn't connected with him since he'd gone on the run. Though Tipping probably had stories left to tell, there was every chance a signals intercept would find him the minute he reached out. Until then, they were searching blind.

"Well, I might be able to help with that."

The strange tone of her voice made Jack sit up, while Chen also turned his attention back to the phone. "What do you mean?"

"I know where he is, Jack. I know where Tipping is." Celeste paused. He knew she'd be weighing up each word carefully. "I've got a choice to make."

"Okay."

"He's given me a beast of a story, Jack. The Zionists are trying to kill him and he knows you're on his tail."

Jack looked over at Chen, who shrugged. "What's he offering? What does he want in return?"

"He's offered me a one-hour meeting where he'll answer any questions. On the table are details on anything that's happened inside the White House for the entirety of the McGhinnist administration, Jack, as well as anything I want to know about the Zionists." She sighed. "He's scared and wants money. In cash."

Jack tried to process the different angles on this news.

Tipping could give Celeste a torrent of information – most classified, some embarrassing – that would swamp the President's entire agenda, including the peace agreement. And giving him cash would allow him to disappear, removing the best and possibly only chance of finding the leadership of the Zionists and the nuclear weapons.

"You can't do it, Celeste." He swallowed hard. "I know we've argued about it, but you're putting whole cities and millions of lives at risk."

There was a long pause. "I know."

He was surprised by her words. Though she'd rightfully dug her heels in on this matter so many times, something had changed. "What's your move?"

"I've given him a meeting time and place. I've told him a journalist will meet him with a bag of cash and all the questions I need answered in return for it."

Jack looked at Chen again, who nodded. "We'll intercept him. Give me the details and this is a step closer to ending."

She laughed. "I've told him there's a journalist coming. I bet he'll lay an egg when he sees you. The meeting is at the lobby of the Grand Hyatt in Berlin at 7pm tonight."

"I'll take care of it, Celeste."

"Be careful." She paused again. "I love you."

"I love you too."

Jack grinned as Celeste ended the call. Berlin. They were about seven hours away from the city and within striking distance of Tipping. He looked at his watch and did the math in his head. They could be there with just enough time to spare. There was risk, not the least of which was a Zionist hit team in the vicinity, but it was their only chance.

Jack was a reporter and could play the part, but Tipping would recognize him instantly. He turned to Chen. "You're not going to like this."

"What?" Chen's eyes narrowed.

"I've got a few hours to teach you how to be a convincing reporter."

ANNA FOWLER KNOCKED on the door and waited. Within a second, a gruff voice called for her to enter. She opened the door and stepped inside the office of Sir Andrew Cunningham, Director-General of the British Security Intelligence Service – MI6. While it wasn't the first time she'd met him, it was her first time in his office. It was dour, full of hardwood and portraits of royals, living and dead.

"Agent Fowler." Cunningham was all business as he indicated the other man in the room. "This is Admiral Fraser."

"I know, sir." Anna smiled a fraction. "Nice to meet you, admiral."

"And you, Ms. Fowler." Fraser nodded at her. "Sit."

Anna sat attentively, opening her notepad and waiting for the briefing to begin. She usually received her assignments from her section commander and wasn't used to this sort of treatment. It meant that, whatever the assignment, it was big. Sitting down with the head of MI6 and Admiral Duncan Fraser, First Sea Lord and Chief of the Naval Staff, was a huge step up for her.

"Ms. Fowler." The admiral turned in his seat to face her with his whole body. "What I'm about to tell you is restricted to three people in the United Kingdom: the two of us in this room with you and the Prime Minister. You'll be the fourth and final. I trust you understand how sensitive this matter is?"

Anna nodded with some frustration, given she'd signed the Official Secrets Act and had no need for the lecture. The halls of the SIS building were never the most humorous place on earth, but this was taking it to a new level. Whatever had happened, whatever job she was about to be given, it had both men stressed. As much as she couldn't wait to receive the assignment, part of her dreaded it.

Cunningham leaned forward, rested his elbows on his desk and stared straight at Anna. "One of our Vanguard-class ballistic missile submarines – HMS *Vigilant* – is currently at sea, captained by someone we believe may be a deep cover Mossad agent."

Anna's eyes widened. "Surely not, sir. I think—"

"This isn't up for debate, Ms. Fowler." Cunningham spoke over her. "We believe, further, that said Mossad agent may have recently left their service, but maintained his links to the Zionist group currently threatening to attack several cities in the Middle East and the United States using nuclear weapons."

Fraser cut in deftly, holding a hand up to forestall Cunningham. "Our problem is greater than you might think, though, Agent Fowler. As you know, and as is on the public record, we're relatively certain the Zionists have stolen Russian weapons, which your service and many others are trying to find."

Anna inhaled sharply, connecting the dots. "But even if we manage to track down those weapons, the Zionists having a nuclear submarine makes it all moot. And worse, the damage the boat could cause would be far greater than the backpack devices, and the finger would be pointed right at us."

"Precisely." Cunningham nodded. "And then the missiles would really start flying. All over the world. "

Anna had been an MI6 agent since leaving Oxford. A week after her graduation, she'd responded to an ad offering adventure and work. In post-GFC Britain, those opportunities were few and far between for arts graduates. The years she'd spent inside the organization had been professionally and personally rewarding, though none of her assignments had been as explosive as this one.

"Not to ask the silly question, sirs, but why can't we just call the sub back?" Anna looked at Cunningham, whose faced remained impassive. "Even if the captain is crooked, surely the crew will turn around if a direct order comes down the line from command?"

Cunningham's lips pursed slightly before he spoke. "Usually, that would work, but it turns out the Zionists had moles higher up the chain. Admiral Graham Sinclair, until recently in charge of our submarine forces, ordered the boat to remain at sea regardless of countervailing orders until the end of its tour."

"The submarine is at sea for three months, unless they suffer mechanical failure, there's no point thinking otherwise." Fraser sighed. "Sinclair has been arrested, but the damage is done. We need to find out who the leader of the Zionists is, and confirm whether or not Captain Cohen is one of their number."

"Can't we just ask Admiral Sinclair?" Amy felt stupid for asking. "He'd know, wouldn't he?"

The two men looked at each other. Cunningham gave a small nod and Fraser sighed. "The admiral is dead."

Anna groaned. It would have been all too simple. "So where and when do I start then?"

"There's no 'start' on this mission." Cunningham's eyes bored into her. "We have a small number of days to avert disaster for Britain and the world."

"Okay." She nodded.

"Your mission is to track down Mr. James Tipping, former National Security Advisor to the President of the United States. He's currently somewhere in continental Europe. The Americans have sent assets to track him down, but I need you to find him first."

She nodded again. It all sounded pretty

straightforward, if she could move quickly enough. "What's the catch?"

Cunningham smiled. "We believe James Tipping is an active member of the Zionist group. Our hope – our *only* hope – is that we can catch him and he can point us at their leader. We thought we had him in London, but he boarded a Channel ferry and escaped. We need to locate and acquire him."

Anna crossed her arms. "Will there be any other assets working on this, either with me or independently? It could get hot."

"You'll be operating alone." Cunningham shrugged. "Any associated action being taken is classified, as you well know, Agent Fowler."

She smiled and nodded. "I—"

She was surprised by a large bang behind her. She turned in her chair and was shocked to see the door open and Prime Minister Katherine Huxley moving into the room. Anna's mouth opened slightly, but she caught herself before it became an embarrassment. She shot to her feet and looked around, not surprised to see Cunningham and Fraser already standing.

"Sit down, you lot." Huxley eased herself in to the last vacant seat around the desk. She then turned to Anna. "Are you Fowler?"

"Yes, Prime Minister."

"Good, good. I've heard good things." She turned back to the broader group. "I've just hung up the phone from the Americans. They still haven't contained Tipping, so there's a chance we might get to him first. Until we can do that and find the head of the Zionists, news about the submarine doesn't leave this room."

"How do I find him?" Anna looked at each of the others in turn.

Cunningham smiled. "Have you heard of Jack Emery?"

Anna nodded. Emery was well known in the United States – the Australian who'd foiled several deep plots against the United States and then been invited into the inner sanctum of the McGhinnist administration. His exploits were known to MI6 as well, but he was regarded as a surprisingly successful amateur with some chutzpah.

"Emery tried to detain Tipping in Calais, with French help, but he escaped." Cunningham sighed. "The best way to find Tipping is to track Emery. He's headed toward Berlin in a French car, which we're tracking. Tipping was Emery's friend. It's personal between those two."

"Now, it's time for you to get going." Fraser leaned in and placed a hand on her knee. "How do you feel about very fast aircraft?"

～

JACK KEPT HIS HEAD DOWN, facing the bar, his back to the room. It was taking all his willpower not to turn around and stare at Chen, but he made do with the occasional glance in the reflection of the mirrored sunglasses he'd placed on the bar. It was risky to be here at all, given how easily he'd be recognized by Tipping, but Jack had been unwilling to let Chen fly solo. There was too much at stake.

They were in the Vox Bar of the Grand Hyatt in Berlin, which boasted 300 whiskies that Jack wished he had the time to sample. Chen was posing as a *New York Standard* reporter and waiting for Tipping to appear while Jack, for his part, was seated at the far end of the bar. He occasionally sipped his whisky, but was taking it easy because he needed to keep a clear head.

"Show time." Jack kept his voice soft as he spied Tipping approaching Chen in the reflection of the sunglasses.

Tipping looked sharp, suited up like any other well-dressed professional. It took all of Jack's self-control to resist turning around, crossing the bar and punching the other man in the mouth. He had to wait another few minutes, at least, to find out whether Tipping would reveal anything. Then Jack would help to detain him.

They'd deliberately kept the police out of it. When they took Tipping into custody, they'd drive straight to the US Embassy in Berlin, where assets were in place to question him immediately. If the German police were allowed to arrest him it would be weeks before he could be questioned by US authorities or extradited, which would leave cities glowing in the dark.

It was also imperative that they scoop Tipping up quietly. While the US could send some Navy SEALs into Africa, or a CIA agent into Southeast Asia, operations on allied soil needed to be done with a little more care. Germany had the means to give America a hard time if its assets were caught misbehaving, including Jack and Chen.

Jack's eyes narrowed as he stared at them. Chen stood and shook hands with Tipping. Both men sat and started to talk, until a waiter came to take their order. They spoke for a minute or two and Chen wrote down the lot. Jack didn't take his eyes off Chen's pen. The minute the Taiwanese man put it down it would be time for them to strike.

They never got the chance. Jack's eyes widened as he saw four men closing in on Chen and Tipping from behind. He turned in his chair and shouted, "Chen!"

As Chen looked up at him, Jack rushed forward. Tipping glanced at him, surprised, and they locked eyes for only a second. Jack's lips curled up in fury, while Tipping smiled sadly and then turned to run. He didn't get far. One of the four men wrapped him up in a bear hug and another pulled a hood over his head. The two others moved to deal with Chen.

Adrenaline pushed Jack on and he made it to the sofas

in a few long strides. He pushed down his fear as he vaulted an armchair, aiming straight at one of the black-clad men. Though the man Jack leaped at tried to dodge out of the way, he failed, and Jack landed a solid tackle. They crashed to the ground and Jack heard the other man heave as the oxygen was forced out of him.

The man beneath him hissed as he punched out at Jack. Jack tried to fend off the blows, while swinging a few of his own at the midsection of the other man. He felt the rage caused by Tipping's betrayal fuel his punches and he landed several on the man, including one great blow to the jaw. The man's eyes went glassy and Jack was about to finish the job when he felt a blow to the side of his head.

He fell to the floor and curled into a ball as several kicks punished him in the midsection. With each kick, Jack realized that charging into four-to-two odds hadn't been the smartest move. He let out a sharp cry and felt the breath go out of him as one particularly hard kick landed. Finally, the blows stopped and Jack opened his eyes to try to make sense of it.

Chen had stunned the wannabe David Beckham, and things were now quiet in the bar, except for the staff who were cowering in the corner. He looked around. The two who'd stayed to deal with Jack and Chen were down, and Tipping was nowhere to be seen. Unfortunately, the two attackers who'd detained him had re-entered the bar and didn't look to be in the mood for a little *mano a mano*.

As the new arrivals reached into their coats and drew pistols, Chen grabbed his arm and yanked on it. Jack didn't have to be told twice, and they ran through the bar and into the hotel lobby as several shots boomed from behind them. They rushed toward the elevator bay, where one had just opened with a chime. The smiling guests inside fled the violence like panicked sheep.

"What now?" Jack's breath was heaving as he mashed

the button to close the door. "I couldn't see Tipping, could you?"

"He got away." Chen tossed one of the bags abandoned by the tourists into the gap between the doors, leaving them open about a foot.

"How? There were four of them!"

"Five, actually." Chen shrugged. "We saw four initially, but there was a sweeper as well. When we took down the first two, the other pair approached to help and Tipping managed to cheap shot the one left to guard him. He ran off just as I started to get the kicker off you. That means there's several waiting for us."

"Fuck!" Jack pounded the elevator wall. "What now? We were so close to scooping him up!"

"Now?" Chen smiled. "You've got a choice to make. We either go up in the elevator and call for help or we try to fight our way out."

"We need to find him!"

"Okay." Chen pulled Jack's collar until they were facing. "But first you need to cool down. We survive and get past those guys out there, then we find him."

Jack stared into Chen's eyes for several long seconds, unable to believe that the two of them were in a gunfight in a five-star hotel in Germany. But the Taiwanese man was right. Jack had been so fixated on finding Tipping that he'd been ready to charge right at hot lead. There had to be a better way, and if anyone could figure it out, it was the man next to him.

Chen let go of his collar and peered through the small gap in the elevator doors, Jack staying low and to the side. As he watched, gunfire barked from outside the elevator, and the metal door sounded as if the largest hailstones ever seen were hitting it. None of it seemed to bother Chen, who did what he needed to do with complete calm.

"Well?" Jack prompted.

"Three shooters. Luckily they're not too heavily armed."

"Right." Jack scoffed. "Just a machine gun or two, is it?"

"Nine-millimeter Berettas." Chen reached behind his back, pulled out a pistol and hefted it. "Nothing to worry about."

"Where the hell did you get a weapon from?" Jack was incredulous. The Taiwanese man's resourcefulness always surprised him.

"I went for a walk last night and happened across a trustworthy merchant." Chen shrugged. "Thought it might be needed."

"You bloody genius."

Jack regretted not involving the German police, or at least some local US assets. He'd had tunnel vision, expecting that Chen's presence and set of skills would be enough to subdue Tipping. But in truth, Jack and Chen had walked into a bear trap. Now they needed to fight their way out of it. Or Chen had to, anyway.

"Stay there." Chen pointed at the corner of the elevator.

Jack nodded and watched Chen glide into the gap, weapon raised and firing in a flash. He fired three rounds before he was safely on the other side. The enemy gunmen responded again, more hailstones pinging against the elevator doors, though none of the shots penetrated. Chen did the same thing again, moving faster than the attackers could accurately track.

"I hit one of them." Chen looked down at Jack. "That's the good news."

Jack swallowed hard. "And the bad?"

"There's still two more of them. We should surrender and then try to make a break for it. We're in public."

Jack shook his head and stood. "I've got a better idea."

His finger reached toward the elevator panel, ready to press the button for another floor, when the bark of more pistol fire caused him to flinch. But instead of the sound of hailstones against the elevator door, Jack could hear shouting. He looked at Chen, who stared back quizzically then approached the panel. Before Jack could stop him, Chen pressed the button to open the doors.

"Come on." Chen jerked his head toward the door as it groaned open, clearly the worse for wear after being pounded by bullets. "They're gone."

"Okay." Jack followed Chen outside, but was immediately confronted with German police with their weapons drawn. He turned to Chen. "Nice work."

"No other choice." Chen made a show of lowering his pistol to the ground, then raised his hands. "Be careful. They look upset."

Jack nodded and raised his hands. The police swarmed them and in seconds they were both on the ground. Jack winced as they cuffed him roughly, exacerbating the pain from the kicking he'd received. The officers rushed them both outside, past the body of one of the attackers. Jack wondered if the others had escaped, as he was bundled into the back of a police van and the door slammed shut.

"That didn't go to plan." Chen's voice was barely a whisper.

"You're telling me. Tipping is on the run and knows we're after him."

"And we're in here."

Jack grunted but said nothing. They sat in silence for at least an hour. None of the police informed them what was happening, but the sound of sirens told them everything they needed to know – Jack and Chen had been involved in a major international fuckup. Jack could only imagine McGhinnist's reaction when he found out.

Jack's eyes shot open as the door of the van opened, revealing a woman in her late twenties. She wore civilian clothes, but stood too straight and alert to be one. She gestured for them to climb out. Jack and Chen did so.

Whoever she was, taking the offer of help and freedom was better than spending time in a German lockup.

"Gents, you're just the men I'm after." Her accent was so overwhelmingly British she had to be an Oxford or Cambridge graduate. "You're Jack?"

"I am." Jack shrugged. "And you are?"

She ignored him and pointed at Chen. "Who's your friend?"

Chen addressed her. "Chen."

"Chen what?"

"Chen."

She shrugged. "I'm Anna. You boys are free to go."

Jack scoffed, not believing that this woman could exonerate them of anything, let alone have them walk completely free. But when she gestured for the German cops to remove their cuffs – and they complied – Jack started to believe. Soon they were out of custody and in possession of their things, even Chen's pistol. It was some kind of miracle, except Jack didn't believe in those.

He walked over to where Anna was talking to several of the German police officers. "Excuse me, but who are you?

"A friend."

"Why are you helping us?"

"I'm not." Anna smiled. "Her Majesty's government just had a word in the ear of our German friends. You're free to go."

Jack wanted to press her some more, but didn't get the chance. The woman turned her back on them, returned to the German police and dived right into conversation with them. Whoever she was, she had some pull. Getting Jack and Chen out of custody would have taken the State Department days, but it had taken her a few minutes.

Jack walked to his car. Chen had the engine idling and when Jack climbed inside the other man was smiling. Jack raised an eyebrow.

"What?"

"I got these from the pockets of one of the men I injured." Chen held up some papers. "The hit team knew where he was going."

"Dare I ask?" Jack closed his eyes.

"You don't have to." Chen shrugged. "But I know where Tipping is."

12

The shootout in the lobby of the Grand Hyatt Hotel in Berlin is believed to have been the work of Zionist extremists. German police have so far remained tight-lipped about the incident, citing national security reasons, but sources have revealed that a high-ranking member of the Zionist organization was present in the hotel at the time of the attack. Police have not apprehended any additional suspects, but with a man dead and little information forthcoming, there are questions to be answered.

New York Standard

Jack cast his eyes ahead and settled on a lamppost as his finishing line, having reached his limit after running a small handful of miles through Prague. Though he did his best to stay fit, Jack's lungs were burning. He felt good for the effort, despite the bruises he'd suffered from the brawl at the hotel, but would be glad to reach his target.

As he ran the last little bit, he focused his mind on Tipping, trying to find a new angle. Even though Jack and

Chen had missed their chance to scoop him up, at least they'd managed to foil the attempts of the Zionist gunmen to do the same. Better, Chen had nabbed information from one of the Zionists alluding to Tipping's ultimate location – Prague.

With that known, it hadn't taken much to task the apparatus of American intelligence with finding Tipping. The trick was doing it quietly. While Jack had left Washington hoping to find Tipping with little public attention, since the shootout there'd been a heap of it. An Interpol Red Notice had been issued for Tipping's arrest and he was now wanted by every police officer on the continent.

That made things tricky for Jack and Chen, given they wanted to grab him and question him quickly. The search was now a race: Jack, Chen and US authorities versus everyone else. It was likely there was another Zionist hit team nearby, making the stakes even higher for Jack and Chen. They needed a break, but he didn't see where it was going to come from.

Jack started to wheeze as he slowed and after a few more moments he made it to the lamppost. He used the metal column to support himself as he heaved for air, slowly catching his breath. The run had helped clear his head, including the knowledge that, for the third time, Tipping had slipped from his grasp like a salmon from a bear. It was tough to stay calm knowing how close he'd been.

Jack started to stretch. When he was done, he pulled his phone out of his pocket and checked messages and emails. It took a moment to sift through the dross until one message – an update on Tipping's whereabouts – jumped out at him. Best of all, it was less than two minutes old. He read it and then exited his messages and dialed Chen.

"What?" Chen's voice was groggy. He'd still been in bed when Jack had started out on his run.

"I need you to meet me at the Charles Bridge."

"Why?" Chen still didn't sound impressed. "I don't want to sightsee. I need to sleep for another few hours."

"Tipping." Jack's voice was louder than he'd intended. More desperate. "An Interpol alert just blazed over the network. The police will be heading there."

"Let them."

Jack spoke through gritted teeth. "We need to speak with him before the cops get him. Once he's in a Czech cell, we'll lose access to him for weeks."

"Okay."

The phone started to beep. Jack pulled it away from his ear and stared down at the screen. Chen had hung up on him. Worse, Jack had no idea if Chen was going to meet him at the bridge or roll over and go back to sleep. But there was no time to waste. If Jack wanted to get to Tipping before the Czech police or another Zionist hit team, he had to move quickly.

He started into the fastest jog his fatigued body would allow. The few moments of cooldown had done little to help his endurance, and although the Charles Bridge was barely a mile from his location, each step felt like his last and each breath felt like a knife in his lungs. He'd make it, though, no matter what he had to push through.

There were so many things he was outraged about – the betrayal of McGhinnist and their friendship; the danger Tipping had placed Jack's relationship in; the threat to the peace agreement. The greatest insult of all, however, was that Tipping was involved with a group and a plot that had placed the world in grave danger of nuclear annihilation.

Finally, Jack turned onto the bridge and slowed to a stop. Tipping was standing in the middle of the bridge, arms propped against the railing and staring out at the water like any other tourist. Though wearing a jacket and cap, Jack had no doubt it was his former friend, deep in thought and not expecting to be found. Jack balled his fists by his side and strode over to Tipping.

"James." Jack spoke with ragged, heaving breath. "Nice of you to pick a picturesque spot."

Tipping turned quickly, startled, then smiled at Jack in a way that looked nearly like a grimace. "Hi Jack. Sorry I missed you in Berlin."

"Had a bit of a run in with some people trying to shoot me." Jack kept a few feet between the two of them, taking no chances.

"Yeah, sorry about that. There's some dangerous people after me." This time Tipping's smile was genuine. Sad, but genuine. "It's good to see you."

"You bastard." Jack lifted a fist and swung it at Tipping's jaw. The other man backed away, easily dodging the swing.

"Yeah."

"Do you realize what you've done?" Jack stepped closer to Tipping, the rage coursing through his veins like molten fury. "How many lives you've put at risk?"

"Yeah." Tipping didn't break eye contact. "I was working toward something I believe in, Jack. I still am."

"You were my friend. I don't understand." Jack exhaled slowly. "And you had to leak to my girlfriend's paper?"

Another shrug. "It's the best paper in the country and I knew she'd run the story. I assume the cops are on their way?"

Jack snarled. "Not because of me. I wanted you for myself. You've got some mighty fucking hard work to do redeeming yourself."

Tipping glanced over Jack's shoulder and Jack followed his gaze. There were police cars pulling up. Tipping sighed. "It's too late, Jack."

Jack had half expected Tipping to deny the link with

the Zionists, to repent for the leaks and to apologize for all the damage he'd caused. If that had occurred, and Tipping had cooperated, it may have been possible to work out some kind of deal once they returned home. But Tipping wasn't playing that game. It didn't do much to help Jack's anger.

"There's time." Jack did his best to swallow his emotions. "Who is the leader of the Zionists? Tell me and help me fix this before it turns into a catastrophe."

"I'm a dead man. I supported a cause and now I'm no longer useful. I'll be lucky to see out the week." Tipping turned and gripped the stone wall of the bridge, casting his gaze over the water. "I know you want to believe I was conned, Jack, or that I wasn't a real player in the game, but I was."

"Who's the leader?" Jack pressed. "Tell me, James."

"You don't get it. *It's too late.*" Tipping turned back to him, sighed and then opened his mouth. "The Samson Option is live and I—"

Jack bellowed as Tipping's head exploded before his eyes. A split second later Jack heard the tell-tale boom of a high-calibre rifle. As blood sprayed over him, Jack's mind shrieked with fear. He let out a guttural howl and reached out to catch Tipping as he fell. Though he knew it was pointless, he eased Tipping's body to the cobblestoned ground.

Jack looked up, trying to locate the direction of the shooter. He heard something pound into the stones behind him, followed by another boom of the rifle. He ducked his head instinctively and searched for cover, but he was completely exposed in the middle of the bridge. He looked to either end – the police cars had pulled up but the officers were taking cover from the shooter.

Jack started to move but didn't get far, grunting as something heavy hit him in the midsection and pushed him to the ground. He landed hard as his mind registered another shot. Whoever was doing the shooting had missed him twice now. He climbed up onto his hands and knees and looked up. Chen was staring at him. The Taiwanese man had taken him to the ground and probably saved his life.

"You're not very good at staying low when the shooting starts!" Chen was panting and sweaty. "Did you get a name?"

"No." Jack coughed and shook his head, trying to clear his vision. "They shot him before I could get the info."

Chen nodded as he crouched low, gripped Jack's arm and tugged. "We need to go. Now."

Jack shook off the other man's grip. "No! We need to find the shooter and get some answers!"

"No point. The shooter is a long way out." Chen gripped his arm again, tighter this time. "We need to go before the cops over there start asking questions."

Jack nodded and let himself be pulled to his feet. "We just lost our only link to the Zionist leadership. It's over."

ARON DRANK in the view like the finest wine as the wind howled in fury and lashed out at him. He wasn't bothered by heights, but there was something about the view from the Rockefeller Center – Top of the Rock – that awed him. It was a spectacular way to view New York City, spread for miles as far as the eye could see. It made him feel like God.

It was hard to believe that in ten days anyone within ten city blocks of the building would be vaporized. He lifted his camera and took his time framing the shot – given he'd likely never have another chance at it – and then pressed the button. He took a second shot, just to be sure, then lowered the camera with a long sigh.

He looked out at block after block of offices and apartment buildings one last time. If Mecca was one of the spiritual capitals of the world, New York City was one of the temples to human ingenuity. It was a shame to lose the heart of it to the hubris and foolishness of American political leaders who were so intent on crippling a vital ally, but that was on them.

He sighed again and walked back inside the building. Earlier, he'd watched a video about a pioneering man who'd staked his fortune and his reputation on its construction. Aron respected a man who'd believed in something so much that he'd have ruined himself for it. He could think of no more fitting way to farewell New York than placing his bomb near here.

As he took a short elevator ride to the bottom of the building, he sent a text message to his driver. Once at the bottom he made his way outside and waited for the black sedan to pull up. After it did, he opened the trunk to check that his package was safe, then cast one last look at the Rockefeller Center and climbed inside the car.

Getting the backpack nuke here had been hardest of all. From Russia it had been driven to the German port of Bremen, loaded onto a ship bound for Mexico and then smuggled across the border. That had all been taken care of by others, who could be trusted with transport but not with placement. Aron had taken possession of the weapon in Charlotte and driven the ten hours to New York City.

They drove in silence for less than five minutes – in traffic – before Aron was deposited with his bag on the sidewalk in front of the Waldorf Astoria Hotel. He entered and made his way to the room he'd checked in to earlier, pausing only to dig through his wallet for his access card. He swiped the card, pushed down on the handle, opened the door, flicked on the lights and stepped inside.

He walked over to the bed and placed the bag down

gently, glad to be rid of its weight. He briefly checked that the weapon was functioning and the countdown clock was ticking, and then opened the front compartment of the backpack and removed a small zip lock bag. Just like that, he had a fresh passport, a wad of Euros and a brand new cell phone. He was born again.

Aron had shed three identities in as many weeks as a precaution against one of the bombs being found. It was difficult to do this kind of work in the modern world, with all-pervasive electronic intelligence and large counter-terrorism budgets, and the last thing he needed was some lucky cop stumbling upon one of the weapons. All it took was one loose thread and the whole skirt could unravel.

Now it was time to wear his final skin. He pocketed the cash and the passport and turned on the cell phone. It had one number loaded into it – the only number he needed. He stared at it for a long few moments. In his head he worked through every detail of each bomb drop, making certain that there was nothing he'd missed.

He glanced again at the backpack on the bed and then turned his back and walked to the door. Once outside, he placed the do not disturb sign on the handle. He had no doubt that the sign would be heeded. This wasn't the sort of hotel that asked too many questions of its guests, so long as the bill was paid and no fires were lit. He dialed a number.

ZED SMILED as a wave of relief washed over him. "Well done, Aron. You've done incredible work for our cause under very trying circumstances."

"Thank you, professor."

Zed closed his eyes and smiled. Aron had struck an almighty blow for their cause. The devices were now in place in New York, Jerusalem and Mecca. He could guarantee that those cities would be destroyed if the peace wasn't abandoned before the countdown reached zero. The preparations to enact the Samson Option, which he'd designed but hoped never to have to use, were complete.

"Now I need you to move on to the final piece of work." Zed opened his eyes and ran his hand over his face. "You understand what I need you to do?"

"My flight is already booked, professor." Aron's voice was soft, almost tender. "Don't worry about my assignment. I won't let you down."

"You never do, Aron." Zed smiled slightly. "This is quite possibly the last time we'll ever speak. Good luck and goodbye."

Zed reached over and placed the handset back in its cradle. He stared at it for a moment, sad that he'd probably just spoken to Aron Braff for the final time. The young man had always been his favorite student and Aron had repaid that favoritism in spades. He'd risen through the ranks of Mossad like a soaring eagle, all the while silently waiting for the time when Zed might need to make use of his skills for their greater purpose.

When the time had come, he'd entrusted Aron with the most difficult role of the grand game they played. If Zed was the king – slow moving, vulnerable but in command of a vast army – then Aron was the knight, possessing skills few others had, and an ability to move in special ways. He'd been charged with the impossible, acquiring three nuclear devices and then planting them in three different locations, yet he'd had succeeded beyond Zed's wildest hopes.

Now, between the bombs planted by Aron and the British submarine waiting silently under the sea, Zed's ability to execute the Samson Option was guaranteed. There was no doubt in his mind that if the peace wasn't abandoned the world would glow. He'd designed the doctrine with little subtlety – if Israel was destroyed then so too would its enemies be. The force had to match the threat to be taken seriously.

He reached over for his cane, propped against the desk. He felt ancient as he moved, but for the first time in the last couple of years he felt less weight on his shoulders. The announcement of the peace agreement had sent him into a mad rage. Its signing had led him to a coughing fit, where he'd spat up blood. Now he felt like he might actually see the other side of this fiasco intact. Decades of work would all be worthwhile.

He was halfway to his feet when his phone rang again. With a sigh, he eased himself back into his chair and picked it up.

"Hello?"

"The matter in Prague has been dealt with." The man's voice was coarse, like gravel in a cement mixer or a smoker with throat cancer.

Zed glanced at the drawer where he kept his photo album. Another of his students – another piece – had been taken off the board. He'd sent a hit team after James Tipping with a heavy heart, but it had been a necessary step. There had been a setback in Berlin, where one of the team had been killed, but they'd succeeded in Prague. The final weak link in the chain had been dealt with. His pieces were now fully in place, and nothing could be linked to him. He'd won.

"Good work." Zed spoke softly, his heartburn starting to give him trouble. "Go to ground for a few weeks. I'll speak with you once this is over."

Zed's arm went limp and the phone fell from his grasp. He was vaguely aware of it slamming on the desk and of the voice on the other end, still slightly audible. Zed clasped his chest. He'd never felt pain like it. He held out a hand, trying to reach for his cane, but he couldn't get close enough. He gritted his teeth against the pain and tried harder, grazing it with one finger before it slipped and fell to the carpet.

He cried out in pain as he fell to the floor. All the breath left his body as he landed hard. He tried to call for help, but no sound escaped his mouth. The pain in his chest intensified. It felt as if someone had plunged a fist into his chest, gripped his heart and was squeezing. He knew he should call an ambulance, get up and try to make it out of the room or do *something*, but he could barely move an inch.

Zed pushed his feet against the carpet, getting enough purchase to push himself upright against the base of the desk. He clutched his chest, wanting to live but knowing it was his time. It was fitting, really, that God would wait for the Samson Option to be ready before taking him. The clock was ticking, the threat was clear and the ultimate destruction just days away. Either Israel would be saved or retribution for her death would be swift. Zed closed his eyes.

It was time to go.

13

A sad chapter in the history of United States politics has come to a tragic end, with former National Security Advisor James Tipping gunned down on the Charles Bridge in Prague, Czech Republic. Mr. Tipping, wanted on multiple charges relating to several high-profile leaks to this newspaper, was on the run from US authorities. His killers remain at large and no group has claimed responsibility, though several prominent Americans have claimed that the CIA was responsible for his death.

New York Standard

Anna clasped her bra at the front, twisted it around her torso and adjusted it. As always, doing so made her think of the ex-boyfriend who used to mock her for not being able to do it up from behind. It annoyed her that she thought of him at all – how far she'd come since ditching that bastard – but it was hard not to when he messaged her once a week. She snorted and shook her head. Fuck him.

Her hair was freshly washed and she'd chosen the best

outfit she'd packed, but a quick glance in the mirror showed she looked tired, with large bags under her eyes. It wasn't ideal, given the job she had to do. She rummaged through her bag and found some concealer. It would have to do. She put on her blouse, completing her outfit.

After a quick final scan of the room, she grabbed her purse and slid her pistol and a silencer inside. She whistled a soft tune as she walked to the front of the townhouse, opened the door and stepped out with a smile on her face, the result of a job well done. What had seemed like an impossible mission when she'd been briefed had actually gone well.

She'd managed to get to James Tipping in Prague before Emery or the Zionists. After that, she'd simply had to play on his desperation for protection. He'd given her answers to the one question she had in return for all sorts of promises. At precisely the moment Tipping had mouthed the words "Professor Zed Eshkol" he'd become useless to her but potentially very valuable to others.

Despite her promises, she'd left Tipping to the mercy of the Zionist hit team. Though leaving him alive had been a risk, her superiors had thought it better to let others take the blame for murdering the former US National Security Advisor, giving Britain all the information it needed with none of the consequences. The success of the hit would also keep the Zionists confident and dumb.

Now she only had one more piece of business to conduct in Prague. She hailed a cab, climbed into the back seat and spoke in Czech. "Four Seasons Hotel."

The driver grunted, clearly surprised she spoke the language. She checked her emails while they drove. There was a message from Cunningham, noting that as soon as she was done on the continent she was to fly to New York City to complete the job. He made it clear that all options were on the table to get the information about the submarine confirmed. Good. She liked flexibility.

At the end of the trip she paid and climbed out of the vehicle. As she walked into the hotel lobby, she laughed at the thought of hardened killers staying in a hotel room with spa baths and high thread-count sheets. Just before the elevator bay she passed the restaurant, where guests were busy with breakfast. If any of them knew what was about to happen upstairs, they'd choke on their eggs.

Anna pressed the button for the elevator then rummaged around in her purse for a key card, which she used to swipe herself access to the eleventh floor. She took a deep breath before she exited, trying to stay calm as she found her way to one of the housekeeping closets. She used her key card on the door, opened it and stepped inside. Only then did she relax.

"Showtime." Her voice was barely a whisper as she used the light on her cell phone to illuminate the room.

Anna changed into a housekeeping uniform and removed the pistol from her purse. She attached the silencer then placed the bag and her regular clothes into one of the housekeeping trolleys. She gripped the pistol tightly and covered it with a cleaning cloth, then opened the door and pushed the trolley to door 1107. She knocked.

There were footsteps from inside and a few moments later the door cracked open only slightly and an eye peered out. "Who are you?"

Anna flashed her best smile. "Housekeeping."

The eye narrowed. A second later, the door opened fully and Anna had a large revolver in her face. Behind the gun was a member of the Zionist hit team who'd killed Tipping. She let out a small squeal and did her best to show fear, but said nothing. Her muscles stiffened and her hand gripped the pistol tighter, ready to work, but she made no move. She didn't yet have him where she wanted him.

"No sudden movements." The Zionist jerked his head inside the room. "Come inside. Bring the trolley."

She gave a nod and wheeled the trolley forward. The gunman moved aside but kept the weapon trained on her as the door slammed shut. As she inched inside, Anna did her best to sum up the situation. There were three men, one with a gun on her and two others preparing their bags to leave, who both cast a quick glance at her. She could hear the shower, which meant another target.

She slowed to a stop, the trolley inches from the feet of the man with the gun, and grimaced. "Please don't hurt me."

"You're not housekeeping." The Zionist spoke slowly and calmly. "I need you to tell me who you are."

Anna flicked her eyes between his face and the barrel of the gun. "I'm from housekeeping."

"No, you're not." His finger tightened on the trigger only slightly, the message clear. "We asked not to be disturbed."

Anna squeezed the trigger on her pistol four times in quick succession. It kicked slightly and made a sound akin to a champagne cork popping with each shot. She dropped to a crouch as four crimson splotches darkened the man's white shirt. His eyes widened in surprise and the revolver fell to the soft carpet before Anna lifted her pistol and fired one last shot into the man's head.

As his corpse hit the carpet, Anna propelled herself toward the two other men. They'd only just started to turn toward the unexpected sound, but given one had a weapon in hand, she had to prioritize her targets. As she moved, she raised her pistol and fired a single round into the head of the armed Zionist. A perfect shot. Blood and brain matter exited the back of his head.

Two down, two to go. The third Zionist had reached his

weapon, but she fired first. Or tried to. Her pistol jammed as she pulled the trigger so she tossed it at him, vaulted up onto the bed and leaped at him. The jump carried her higher and faster than his weapon could track in time. She tackled him to the ground, earning a grunt from him. Most importantly, he'd dropped the weapon on the way down.

Anna struggled to her feet and reached for his weapon, but as she did, he grabbed her hand and twisted her wrist. A sharp pain shot up her arm and she lost her grip on the pistol, which fell from her hand. She didn't have the chance to pick it up again, because he lowered his head and tackled her in the midriff, using his size and weight advantage to lift her and push her back. He slammed her into the wall and then onto the ground.

She grunted as he sat on top of her and all of the air was forced from her lungs. Her eyes on his, she used one hand to fend off blows as the other felt around for something, anything, to strike back with. Then he connected with a right hook and stars exploded in her vision, just as her hand gripped a leather shoe. As she fended off another hook with her left hand, she shifted her body and brought the shoe swinging hard up into his face.

His nose gave a sickening crunch as the shoe slammed into it. He staggered back and reached up to cover his face, but Anna didn't give him the chance. She swung the shoe at his head again, then dropped it and thrust into his chest with both of her fists, shifting his weight backward. She bucked and slid out from under him as he fell. She looked for his pistol, but it was behind him and he was already climbing to his feet, a look of rage contorting his features.

"Who are you?" He spat the words as he raised his bloodied hands and balled them into fists. "You're meddling in events that you have no understanding of."

She laughed and advanced on him. He threw a series of quick jabs – which she dodged with ease – then tried to kick out at her. Anna moved to his left slightly and kicked out at his leg. The knee buckled at a strange angle and the Zionist let out a vicious scream as he fell to the carpet, clutching his ruined leg. As he writhed in agony and tried to climb back to his feet, she reached for the pistol. It was an unfamiliar model, but it would shoot him dead just fine.

"I'm housekeeping." She raised the pistol and fired into his head, leaving the Zionist dead in a pool of blood on the carpet.

She turned as she heard the shower stop. Her time was nearly up and there was a final player in the game. She moved toward the bathroom, where danger still waited. She pushed down on the handle and kicked the door inward, hard. It bounced back after it hit something and she heard a sharp cry – a mix of alarm and pain. Anna barged her way inside, where the last Zionist was standing in the nude, dripping wet and with his hands to his face as blood spurted from his nose.

She raised the pistol and stayed a few feet back from him, aware that despite his injuries he had a greater reach than her. "Kneel on the tiles, now."

He lowered his hands from his face and held them out, palms upward. "I can give you who you want."

"Not interested. Kneel."

"Very well." The Zionist spoke as he dropped to his knees, never taking his eyes off her. "But please, we can work something—"

Anna pulled the trigger the minute his knees hit the tiles. The weapon popped and kicked slightly. As he fell forward, she emptied the last of her clip into him, just to be sure. She looked in the mirror and let out a long sigh. She'd expected this to be messy, but she'd be feeling that hook to the jaw for days. Her cheek was already starting to swell. She ran the tap, tried her best to wipe the blood from her face and then dried herself.

She walked out of the bathroom and surveyed the bedroom, just to make sure she'd taken care of everything. Three bodies lay lifeless in the bedroom, and one in the bathroom, and there was no hint that anyone outside the room had heard the disturbance. She didn't bother to clean up – she'd be out of Prague before anyone found the bodies. She collected her own pistol, went to the housekeeping trolley, stripped to her underwear and changed back into her regular clothes.

As she dressed, she considered the situation in her head: she knew who the Zionist leader was, Emery was in the dark and both Tipping and the hit team had been eliminated, in case they got arrested and spilled the beans about Eshkol's identity. Her next stop was the United States, where she'd confront the professor and figure out if the submarine was under his control. If it was, things were about to get very bad for the good professor.

Her last act was to use the bloodied housekeeping uniform to wipe the prints off the trolley, the other man's pistol, the bathroom door handle and the tap handle. Her prints weren't in any system, but this simple precaution helped to make sure that remained the case. When she was done, she walked to the door and opened it. She stepped out into the hallway. Nobody else on the floor was visible and MI6 would fry the security footage.

If she hurried, she'd have time for breakfast at the airport before her flight.

～

JACK HELD his arms wide as McGhinnist approached and the two of them embraced for a second or two. Despite Tipping's betrayal, they were both feeling the loss. Tipping had been a friend and a colleague but ended up a traitor and dead. This was the first time they'd seen each other since Jack had arrived home from Prague, and it looked like McGhinnist was struggling as much as he was.

"How are you, Jack?" McGhinnist's gaze was intense, as if assessing whether Jack was going to fall apart on the spot. "You look tired."

"You'd be amazed what coffee and Red Bull can achieve." Jack shrugged. "There's too much work to do to rest."

"I'd call bullshit on that, but I fear you're right." McGhinnist frowned. "Are you getting anywhere with the digging?"

Jack gestured behind him, where dozens of research staff pulled in from across the entire Federal Government were digging into the life of James Tipping. The clues they had to go on – a reference to something called the Samson Option and that the leader of the Zionists was someone Tipping had history with – were enough to get the wheels of a giant research apparatus turning.

"It might not be enough people or enough time." Jack sighed. "I'm not sure we're going to get what we need before the deadline, but we have to try."

He'd left Prague after Tipping had been shot, flying back by private jet with Chen. He'd briefed the President and the NSC from the air and, while everyone had made the right noises about how close Jack had come to succeeding, he knew he'd failed. He'd been a moment away from getting the name, but instead he'd got Tipping's incomplete, dying whisper.

"And there's been nothing come up yet?" McGhinnist was disappointed. He clearly wasn't used to his people coming up short.

"Nothing so far." Jack shook his head, turning back to McGhinnist. "We'll do our best, but I wouldn't be betting the house on it."

"Can't anyway. Taxpayers pay for my house."

McGhinnist sighed. "We've got to work with what we have – a single lead from a dying man's lips."

"Which leads to one needle in a haystack of 321 million people – the entire population of the United States." Jack sighed. "It looks impossible."

"Unless you can find an obvious link."

"Unless we can find an obvious link." Jack nodded. "I need to get back to work. It's not fair to ask these people to give up their evenings if I stand and talk."

"Of course, Jack. Keep me posted." McGhinnist patted him on the shoulder. "Get some rest, too. Red Bull only gives you wings for so long."

Jack gave a short laugh as they turned to go their separate ways – Jack back to the desk he'd commandeered and McGhinnist back to the Oval Office. As he sat in the chair heavily, Jack punched in his password then picked up his takeaway coffee, one among many scattered on his desk. While he waited for his computer to complete its login script he took a sip of coffee then nearly spat it out. It was as cold as a Chicago winter.

He put down the cup and resumed chasing the line of inquiry he'd been working on when McGhinnist had called to say he was coming down – the Samson Option. Tipping had said something about it on the bridge, and Jack had had no idea what it meant until friendly Professor Google had enlightened him. In fifteen minutes of reading, he'd deduced that the Samson Option was an Israeli defensive doctrine that was terrifying but also fit the Zionist rhetoric.

He got lost in the information. The background of the doctrine, its theoretical uses, the times its use hadn't been considered quite so theoretical and when it had been a live option. It spoke to Israel's unique sense of danger and the unique history of the Jewish people that they'd come up with such a no-holds-barred defensive doctrine. The more he read, the more he was convinced that the Samson

Option was exactly the playbook the Zionists were working from.

He'd never heard of anything like it, but one thing nagged at the back of Jack's mind. If the Samson Option called for the complete eradication of the foe, even if it meant self-destruction, then the Zionists stashing a few suitcase nukes around the place wouldn't be enough. They'd put a sizeable dent in New York, Mecca and Jerusalem, but it wouldn't be the knockout punch that the Samson Option called for: overwhelming force to destroy the foe.

He shook his head. Whoever devised it had a screw loose, that was for sure, but whoever was applying the Samson Option on behalf of the Zionists was even crazier. It wasn't mutually assured destruction, it was simply popping off a few nukes to achieve something that was impossible. McGhinnist had shown no signs of buckling under the threat, nor had the Israelis or the Palestinians. No, the Zionist leader – whoever it was – had badly applied the Samson Option.

"Mr. Emery?"

Jack nearly jumped out of his seat. A junior researcher was holding out a fresh cup of coffee for him, which he took. "Sorry, I was a mile away. Thanks."

She gave a shy smile. "Thought you could use a recharge, sir. You haven't slept since you got off the plane. I guess this is the next best thing?"

He nodded. "Thanks. You're dead right, too..."

"Dana."

"Dana, right. Whoever made this is a lifesaver." Jack paused with the cup halfway to his mouth. "Do me a favor?"

She nodded. "Of course."

"I need your entire team to stop what they're doing – no matter how important – and get to work researching the

Samson Option. I need to know who created it and if that person has links to Tipping." Jack couldn't believe he'd been so stupid as to not ask the question earlier. It compounded his failure in Prague.

She nodded. "We'll get on to it."

Jack thanked her and turned back to his computer. He sipped his coffee as the wheels turned in his head. The Zionists were following a playbook and had assets in place as well, even if those assets weren't sufficient to fully complete the job. What Jack hadn't been able to do was link the players to the playbook. It was a long shot, but he was desperate and starting to hope that one of those would pay off. It had to.

Jack's phone beeped and he reached for it, then cursed as he knocked his coffee cup over and onto the floor. He glanced down at the mess, then back at the phone. The message was from Celeste. They'd barely spoken since his return from Prague and he'd promised to call her hours ago. Though she was usually understanding of work pressures, she'd been making noises about him looking after himself. He dialed and tapped the desk while he waited for her to pick up.

"Hi, Jack."

"Hey gorgeous." He smiled at the sound of her voice. "How are you?"

"Missing you and trying to help run the major paper in a city that's nine days away from being nuked, reportedly. You?"

"Sore, tired, frustrated. It feels like I'm close to winning a hand but I keep coming up with a pair of twos. I really need a royal flush."

"You'll come up with it. You always do. You've got a good team working for you." She paused. "Are you looking after yourself?"

"There's too much work for that."

"Jack—"

"Next question."

"Jack." Her voice had an edge. "You need to get eight hours sleep."

"I—"

"Listen to someone who cares about you for once, would you?"

"Okay."

As she started to speak, to tell him how much rest he needed and what he should be eating, Dana returned to his desk with a printout in her hand and a smile on her face. He raised his eyebrows at her, and she offered a giant thumbs-up and an even wider smile in return. She'd uncovered something. He nodded at Dana and returned his attention to the phone just a moment too late, having missed whatever question she'd asked him.

"Jack?" Celeste's voice was approaching pissed off. "Are you even listening?"

"Sorry, what was the question?"

She sighed. "I asked if you'd eaten."

"Sure, a Snickers bar, coffee and Red Bull. And I ate on the plane."

"Seven hours ago."

"Yep. Look, I have to go, Celeste." Saying each word felt like passing a kidney stone, because he knew the likely effect. "Something has come up."

"Bye."

The phone went dead in his ear. He closed his eyes, let out a long sigh, then looked up at Dana. "I hope this is worth it."

"It is." She smiled and placed the paper down on his desk. "Your wife will forgive you."

"Girlfriend."

She blushed. "Sorry."

Jack looked down at the sheet of paper and his eyes

widened. He pounded his fist on the desk. "It was so bloody simple? Why did I need to go to Prague?"

"I—"

"Never mind. We've been too busy chasing after Tipping's future rather than looking into his past. Could you excuse me?"

She nodded. "Good luck."

Jack's hands raced across the keyboard. He searched through the staff database until he found Tipping's file. It was classified, but he had the access to crack it open. He keyed in the code and waited as the large file loaded. Once it did, he skimmed it until he found what he was after. He had to read it twice, and it was like a punch to his face. He pounded the desk again, picked up his phone and dialed. The President's secretary answered and he asked to be put through.

"What's up, Jack?" McGhinnist sounded surprised. It wasn't often someone demanded that he come to the phone right after he'd seen them in person.

"Did you know Tipping was a practicing Jew his entire life?" The words sounded like an accusation, but it was too late to reel them in.

McGhinnist paused. "He never seemed to make a big deal about it in the time I've known him. I thought he was non-practicing."

Jack nodded. "Right, that's why it was such a surprise that he'd joined the Zionists."

"Yes." McGhinnist's voice was cautious, impatient. "So why did you need to interrupt my meeting with the Ghanaian Ambassador, Jack? Where's this going?"

"Sorry. The only thing we know about his faith and the only thing connecting him to active Judaism, at all, is where he went to school."

"Where would that be?" McGhinnist sounded cautious.

"Yeshiva University, where he studied under Professor Zed Eshkol."

There was a pause. "Wait a minute, that pain in the ass from earlier in the month?"

"The very one." Jack leaned back in his chair and spun around. "And, according to the research team, the father of the Samson Option."

JOSEPH COHEN FINISHED FILLING one of the fine bone china cups, then filled the other, careful not to spill any of the tea. When he was done, he placed the pot back on the table and lifted both cups. He handed one to Tim Jennings with a smile and kept the other for himself. He lifted the cup to his mouth and took a small sip, though in truth fresh tea was too hot for him to drink right away.

Jennings had no such problem. He took a long sip, gave a satisfied sigh and then placed the cup down. "Thanks, captain. Makes a nice change to teabags."

"There has to be some perks to command." Joseph laughed. "Not much else to do down here anyway, is there?"

"Suits me." Jennings' face clouded over. "There's plenty going on above the water that makes me want to stay below it."

Joseph nodded, lifted his cup and took another sip of his tea. He couldn't appear eager to pry, though, in truth, he knew plenty about Jennings' gambling and the marital problems that had followed. It was part of the reason he'd hand selected Jennings to serve on the submarine. He took one more sip then placed the cup gently back down on its saucer.

"Need to talk about it, Tim?" Joseph looked straight at the other man, who seemed to wither under the glare.

Jennings ran a hand through his close-cropped brown hair. "It's okay, sir. I won't put you through a psych session."

"No shame in it." Joseph spoke softly. "This life is hard on sailors, let alone their family. We serve our country and hope our family are there at the end of it. I never managed to even meet someone, let alone get married, so you won't get any judgment from me, Tim."

It was a plain lie, but Jennings had no way of knowing that. Joseph's rise through the ranks had been the result of hard work, but he'd had plenty of time to find a life partner if he'd wanted to. In truth, it hadn't been in the plan he'd constructed for his future with Zed Eshkol. He had no interest in settling down and spending his life with someone. Secrets were hard enough to keep alone.

But the lie appeared to work – Jennings' features softened. "It's not all it's cracked up to be. I have a few gambling problems, sure, but I earn a good salary."

"So what's the problem?"

"Well, while I serve my country, she served herself up to her doctor." Jennings sighed. "They've got a good lawyer, too, so she'll clean me out."

"I'm a strong believer that people who serve together need to stick together." Joseph placed his hand on top of Jennings' for just a brief moment and then removed it. "If you need some extra leave when we're back on shore, just say the word."

"Thanks, captain, but I'll be okay." Jennings gave a weak smile. "While I'm down here I'm good to go. I'll do my job."

Joseph was relying on exactly that. Zed Eshkol's Samson Option had so many moving pieces that Joseph worried something would slip between the cracks. The most important were the triggers that he would need to begin the launch procedure, to convince a crew of submariners that things above the waves had gone to hell. All he could do was focus on things he could control.

Things like Jennings. Even if the crew went along with the launch, he still needed his executive officer to co-authorize any strike. He'd spent quite a bit of effort buttering Jennings up in the event that he was required to launch the nukes. He wasn't certain that the other man would support the process, even if it was all above board, but he'd done everything he could to connect with the man.

He leaned forward slightly. "I know you will, Tim, and if all this Israel and Palestine stuff goes to shit, I may just need you to. I need you strong."

While hoping to connect with the man, Joseph had also started putting in place contingencies in the event that Jennings cracked and refused to follow Joseph's legal orders. He'd told the boat's third officer about his concerns and started to document them, so that if Joseph needed to relieve Jennings of his position there was a fair chance his effort would succeed.

Jennings smiled. "Not a problem, captain. I'll do what needs doing. Have to keep the salary coming in so she can take it, don't I?"

Joseph smiled but said nothing else. Jennings took the hint, finished his tea, stood and replaced his hat. He saluted crisply, but smiled as he did. Joseph remained seated as he fired off a quick salute, then watched as Jennings turned on his heel and left the room. Only when the door was closed did Joseph raise his tea again and take another sip.

In a few days, there mightn't even be time for that.

14

With less than a week before the enacting of the peace agreement, Israeli, Saudi and American authorities are no closer to locating the nuclear weapons placed in their countries. In New York, the NYPD and FBI have responded to over 500 leads purporting to have information about the bombs, all of which have amounted to nothing. Saudi and Israeli authorities are more tight-lipped, but sources reveal that they've also made little progress.

New York Standard

Zed sighed.

"Professor, are you saying that, with a week to go and a nuclear weapon placed somewhere in this very city, you support the Zionist extremists in their efforts to unwind the peace deal between Israel and Palestine?"

Zed sighed again. "Not quite. I—"

The dean held up a hand. "Because, if that were the case, then this university would have to reconsider your employment, regardless of your health issues. Such views would be utterly incompatible with our values."

Zed closed his eyes for a moment. Despite there still being a week until the peace agreement deadline, it was hard not to wish it would come sooner. Sitting across from the dean and two of his flunkies, Zed nearly hoped that Israeli, American and Palestinian leadership would stay resolute in the face of his threats, just so he could have the pleasure of nuking this city, this university and the men opposite him.

Zed opened his eyes. "Excuse me, but I'm very tired. The angina attack has taken a lot out of me."

The dean smiled for the first time. "Completely understandable, Professor Eshkol. How is your health?"

Zed expected they'd be thrilled if he just dropped dead, but he wasn't ready to give them that pleasure. "The doctor tells me the angina attack was brought on by stress. But I'm scheduled in for more tests later this week. They're quite concerned, but God willing I'll be around for a while yet."

The dean nodded. "You've had quite the ordeal. But I must insist on knowing your position before we can agree to your continued tenure."

"I understand and support the position of the administration." Zed fiddled with his walking cane, which he gripped in his right hand despite being seated. "However, I have made no secret of the fact that I do have some sympathy for the Zionist message, if not their methods."

Zed nearly laughed at the looks that crossed their faces. They were peacocks, puffing out their feathers in an impressive but ultimately useless form of theatre. They could be placated with lies and feigned deference to their position, but if they knew the truth of Zed's role they'd probably have larger heart attacks than the scare he'd just had. For men in charge of a large Jewish university, their lack of vision for their people and courage to see what needed doing was appalling.

"Very well, professor." The dean nodded, then looked to his colleagues, who mimicked the gesture. "As long as you understand our concerns. Things could get very hairy for Jews in this city."

Zed smiled and pressed down on his cane, using it to help him to stand. "Of course, of course. Now, if you'll excuse me, I have an awful lot of work to catch up on today. I was hoping to get a lot of it done this morning."

"Of course, professor. Don't push it too hard though."

Zed left the dean's meeting room and struggled back to his office. As he walked, he let his anger at being summoned before them simmer down and then cool. While he'd never show them they'd gotten to him, the outrage at being called to such a meeting to have the riot act read to him burned to his core. If it weren't for the easy stream of recruits that the university provided for his work, he'd resign.

When he made it to his office, ten minutes later, his assistant was nowhere to be seen. It was quite early in the morning, but she'd usually be at her desk outside of his office by now. It was unacceptable. He'd expressly told her he needed her close, each and every minute of the day, in case he had another episode with his heart. There was no guarantee that the next one wouldn't be a big one, and he wouldn't survive without help close to hand.

He sighed, started to open the door to his office and then paused. The lights were on. From home, he'd gone straight to the meeting with the dean. It was his first day back at work, his assistant was nowhere to be seen, he hadn't been inside his office and yet the lights were on. It could be a coincidence, but he didn't really believe in those. He took a deep breath, pushed the door open and wasn't surprised to see someone sitting on one of the sofas inside.

"Hi, professor." The woman flashed a pearly smile, stood and approached with an outstretched hand. "I hope you don't mind me waiting in here?"

He stepped inside. "I—"

"Your assistant said it would be fine."

Zed grunted and moved slowly around her, declining to shake her hand and using the time to sum her up. He made his way to the chair behind his desk, his mind racing with possibilities – none of them good. He doubted very much that this woman was interested in studying at Yeshiva, and doubted even more that his assistant would let a stranger into his office in such a manner. Particularly since she wasn't here. It meant trouble.

He collapsed into his chair with relief and then gripped the desk with his thumbs on top and his fingers underneath. Only then did he look at the woman again. He studied her for several moments, but nothing he saw changed his mind. She was a wolf in sheep's clothing, if a sheep wore ballet flats and a pastel dress with shoestring straps. She was dressed to kill and could probably kill in that dress. He could think of no other explanation.

"Professor?"

Zed shook his head and kept his grip on the desk. "Look, I don't know who you are, but you're not one of my students and I'm certain my assistant didn't let you in. I've been alive for a long time and I've learned to recognise the scent of the secret police when they come knocking, so just get on with it."

She tried to maintain her composure, but there was a flash of doubt that let him catch a glimpse of the wolf. "Professor, I—"

"Get on with it or get out. I'm old, sick and tired. And I have a lot of work to do this morning."

"Fine." She stood and opened her purse, then drew a

pistol and pointed it at him. "Guess I need to go back to acting school."

Zed was not surprised she was here to kill him. "If you expect me to beg, you'll be disappointed. I'm a man well in tune with my own mortality."

She laughed and took a step toward him. "I'm after a simple transaction – information for your life."

Zed's eyes narrowed. There were a lot of things she could ask, and some questions he'd provide answers to, but only a few that mattered. "I'm listening."

She reached the other side of the desk and sat in one of the visitor chairs, never taking the pistol off him. "Tell me about HMS *Vigilant*."

So she knew. Zed kept his features even, but inside he was panicking for the first time. He'd known that there was every chance that Aron Braff's nuclear weapons would be found or otherwise compromised, but he'd been certain that his insurance policy – HMS *Vigilant* and Captain Joseph Cohen – would remain in play. A British woman with a pistol asking questions about the British submarine didn't bode well.

"I assume it's a ship in the Royal Navy?"

"Smart guy." She waved the pistol lazily in his direction. "Work with me. The game is up. I know you lead the Zionists. Tell me all about the submarine."

"I was just in a room defending my academic position against claims I supported the Zionists, now you claim I'm their leader." Zed laughed. "I never thought I'd be working this much in my old age."

"I need confirmation of the link between you and Captain Joseph Cohen, the submarine captain." Her voice was as calm, with a hint of menacing authority. "Give me what I need before I have to ruin those nice curtains behind you."

Zed closed his eyes and let out a long, slow sigh. To

come so close and not see the result of his work struck him as a tragedy, but it had always been a chance. He just had to hope that the preparations he'd made to destroy either the peace process or the world would be enough. It needed to be, or else the doctrine he'd developed and advocated for would be for naught. He was staring down the barrel of his death and intellectual irrelevance at the same time.

She grew tired of waiting. "If you've got anything to say to me, Professor Eshkol, you've only got a few seconds."

"Get on with it." Without opening his eyes, he pressed the button on the underside of his desk.

JACK GRIPPED the overhead handle of the Chevy Suburban as its brakes squealed and the vehicle came to a sudden stop.

Agent Warner, commander of the FBI detail he was riding with, turned from the front seat. "Wait here, Mr. Emery."

Jack nodded and watched as Warner and the other agents spewed out of the SUV, a scene repeated in the two other vehicles that had pulled up as well. A total of ten agents armed with carbines swarmed forward in perfect choreography. Jack knew the same scene would be playing out on other parts of the campus, as the entire forty-six–member FBI New York Field Office SWAT force deployed around the university. Not on the front line – but no less important – were the NYPD officers running interference and keeping a two-block radius around the university clear while, up in the air, two NYPD choppers hovered and watched, ready to route the reserve NYPD SWAT teams toward any location requiring extra muscle.

It was a ridiculous show of force to subdue one old man, but given the influence of that old man and the potential he had to cause harm, Jack and McGhinnist had declined to take any chances. Jack had flown in from Washington soon after he'd discovered Tipping's connection to Eshkol and the Samson Option, and when he'd landed he'd been briefed on the operation that had been worked up while he was in the air. Jack was pleased that the NYPD had had no trouble creating a traffic-free path through the city, with uniforms on every street corner and green lights the entire way. The convoy had covered the distance between Federal Plaza in Lower Manhattan all the way up to Yeshiva University in Hudson Heights at record speed.

When Warner turned back to the vehicle and nodded, Jack knew it was safe. He took a deep breath, opened the door and climbed out. As he did, he wondered if this was the beginning of the end. He slammed the door behind him and moved quickly toward where the agents had formed a perimeter around this entrance to the building. As he ran, the pistol he carried in a shoulder holster bounced against his torso. While he'd never had a great love for guns, he'd been licensed to carry since he'd come down from the rooftop after confronting Richard Hall. It was nice to have the option if you needed it, like storming a building with an FBI SWAT team. As always, though, if he needed to use the weapon then he knew the forces of good were having an awfully bad day.

"What's the story?"

"Exits secured and air cover in place." Warner jerked his head toward the university building. "If your information is good and he's in there, we've got him."

"The information is good."

Warner shrugged. "Give the word then."

"Do it."

Warner nodded and fired off orders into his helmet mike. As he did, his team moved toward the entrance and

Jack followed as instructed. They streamed up the stairs with weapons raised, shouting at students to stand aside as they moved. He knew that the same scene was playing out across the rest of the campus. Jack's team would advance straight to Eshkol's scheduled lecture, another would go to his office and another would go to the cafeteria. The other assets would remain in reserve, in case there was any blow up. If all went to plan, they'd have Eshkol in the bag and the nukes secured within hours.

Jack jogged behind the team as they approached the lecture theatre, scanning the hallways and rooms but with no real threat sighted. A few students squealed but most stood aside and got out of the way. The agents didn't seem to notice, given they were focused on Eshkol and any potential threats. After a few turns and some more jogging, they reached the lecture theatre. Jack stood back as two of the agents opened the door and six more streamed inside to secure it. While Jack couldn't see what was happening inside, he found it odd there was no sound – no shrieks of alarm or shouted orders from the raid team.

A few seconds later, Warner held his forefinger up to his earpiece, then turned to Jack. "This room is empty."

Jack's eyes narrowed. "He's scheduled to be in there, along with two hundred of his students."

Warner shrugged. "See for yourself."

Jack nodded and walked to the door. As soon as he looked inside, he knew Warner was right. The room was empty. "Where the fuck is he, then?"

"Office and caf teams came up empty." Warner barked an order and his men moved out. Then he turned back to Jack. "We're conducting secondary sweeps."

"What does that mean?"

"All target locations have come up with zilch, so we search room to room." Warner paused. "But it's a big campus, to be frank."

"We need to find him!" Jack felt all of his earlier hope go up in smoke. "Or else ten square blocks of this city won't be here in a week!"

Warner nodded and gestured for Jack to follow. They moved back outside in silence, as Warner did his best to keep abreast of the situation. This wasn't good. Eshkol was a very old man with very little mobility. He shouldn't have been able to elude so many heavily armed and well-trained agents. Either the information was wrong, or something else was. Jack froze.

"Agent Warner?"

"Yes?"

"What if someone else has him? Or he knew we were coming? This guy had one mole in the National Security Council, who's to say he doesn't have more?"

Warner seemed to chew on Jack's words for a minute. "Fuck."

"What now?"

He didn't hesitate. "I'll keep the secondary sweeps going and move the NYPD assets up to search surrounding streets. We can also get every beat cop in the city on the lookout and splash it across the media, if you like. But if he's slipped our containment then we're in all sorts of trouble. He could be anywhere."

"Yep – do it." Jack paused, trying to think of any other potential holes that Eshkol could slither out of. Then he considered one further thing. It would be universally loathed in New York City, but not as much as a nuke going off in Times Square. He dug into his pocket, pulled out his cell phone and dialed.

"Frank? This is Jack Emery. You're not going to like this."

"Hi, Jack." Frank Howard sounded tired. He'd been working hard since being promoted to National Security Advisor. "What's up?"

"I need every bridge and tunnel connected to Manhattan shut down." It sounded crazy as he said it, but it was necessary. "And I also need every security camera from here to New Jersey tasked with finding Zed Eshkol. He's slipped our net and we need to find him again."

There was a pause. "Jack, this will be a tall order. The blowback will be—"

"I don't care." Jack interrupted. "We're close to the leader of the Zionists."

"I'll take care of it."

He hung up and gestured for Warner to follow. Jack couldn't be sure that the professor was a senior member of the Zionist terrorists, but he was as close as possible to knowing without actually *knowing*. It was a particularly strong likelihood, given Eshkol had been so vocally against the peace agreement, was one of the fathers of the Samson Option and had very strong links to Tipping.

They made their way back to the vehicles and he climbed inside with Warner, ready to move at a second's notice. The rest of the SWAT team stayed behind, searching the university room by room. But Jack's attention was already diverted. Without being prompted, Warner made the vehicle's radio receiver loud enough so they could both hear as updates rolled in from across New York City.

They waited for hours. At some point, the rest of Warner's squad returned to the vehicles, their search of the campus completed. Jack's hopes fell with his energy, at least until an NYPD uniform fetched them coffee and a sandwich each. He started to wonder if he'd been right to suspect that Eshkol had been scooped up by someone else, or if the professor had simply left town.

He closed his eyes and let the radio reports roll over him, not really understanding the law enforcement shop talk but following enough of it to catch the gist: they had nothing. The search continued, with Federal assets working hard and the NYPD clocking some insane overtime, but it seemed like it was all for nothing.

"Turn it off." Jack opened his eyes and looked over at Warner. "He's gone. We've lost him."

"Shame, I thought we'd nailed that prick to the wall." Warner sighed and reached over to turn down the radio. "Now we'll have to—"

"All units, all units, this is Prowler Two-One. Target located. Repeat, we have the target."

Instead of turning down the radio, Warner picked it up. "Prowler Two-One, this is Alpha Actual, report."

"Alpha Actual, target is cornered inside a diner with one unidentified female, armed, on 164th and Broadway."

"Don't let any harm come to him!" Jack hissed.

Warner nodded. "Prowler Two-One. Keep your distance unless the target is under threat. We need him alive. All SWAT converge to that location."

"Confirmed."

Warner put down the radio and nodded to the driver, who started the engine and hit the sirens. Jack held on as the Chevy did a quick one-eighty, tyres screeching and with the other two vehicles close behind. Jack and Warner sucked down the last of their coffee and scoffed some energy bars, rousing themselves after hours of inactivity, even as the vehicle shot past the speed limit.

Jack tried not to get his hopes up, but given how bad the situation had been a moment ago, having any trace of Eshkol at all was positive. Having him under threat by an unknown woman was a negative, sure, but it also meant that his hunch was probably correct: Eshkol was the lynchpin he was after. The man who could end this after he'd failed to catch Tipping.

"We're one block out." Warner turned his head to look at Jack. "I want you to wait in the car and—"

"No way." Jack shook his head. "I'm coming with you."

Warner looked like he might argue the point, but then relented and nodded. "Okay."

Jack's heart pounded as the vehicle pulled to a stop in the middle of Broadway. There were already four NYPD squad cars at the scene, with a dozen uniforms and a few plain clothes officers taking cover with weapons drawn. The scene was like something out of a movie, even before the Feds showed up. Jack just hoped they could end this with the professor still breathing.

He opened the door and followed Warner over to a waiting NYPD area commander. Given the body language of the two men, it was clear that once Warner arrived on scene, the show was his to run. Jack, invoking the President's authority, had made it clear that there would be no jurisdictional spats. This one had to be clean. Given the nuke in their city, the NYPD were happy to cooperate.

"I'm Agent Lance Warner." Warner crouched down behind the NYPD cruiser that the area commander was using as shelter. "This is Jack Emery."

Jack did the same, but felt a little stupid doing so. If the woman inside the diner wanted a shootout, she wouldn't have waited for the cavalry to arrive. "Hi."

"Lieutenant Henry Dillon." The NYPD man nodded. "Target is seated in a booth with unidentified female. She's armed. They're talking."

Jack glanced over the hood of the car at the diner. He could clearly see Zed Eshkol sitting opposite a woman. He smiled. "I'm just glad we found him."

"It's not that simple." Warner frowned, as SWAT teams kept arriving and flooding the scene with firepower. "What's her game?"

"Hell if I know." Dillon shrugged. "How do you gentleman want to handle this? She only has a pistol, from what we can see, and we can go in and get them."

"Too risky." Warner shook his head. "Sniper?"

"Impossible." Dillon laughed. "Would you believe it used to be a gun store? The windows are bullet proof."

"Almost like she planned it." Jack chanced another peek over the police cruiser. It was an unremarkable coffee and sandwich joint in a city full of them. The woman was seated with Eshkol in one of the front booths, talking with him as easy as you like. She didn't seemed concerned by the army of cops outside.

Warner looked over at Jack. "How do you want to play this, Jack? We can try to talk her out, or we can go in hot. There's not much else on offer if you want to get your boy out in one piece. And even those options don't come with a guarantee."

Jack didn't take his eyes off the woman. His eyes narrowed. Then they widened. "Motherfucker!"

"What?"

Jack stood, removed his pistol and handed it to Warner. "I'm going in. Don't shoot under any circumstances."

"I—"

Jack didn't give him a chance to respond, as he quickly rounded the cruiser and made for the diner. As he walked, he heard Warner curse after him, but Jack didn't look back. Once he reached the door, he opened it and stepped inside. Zed Eshkol looked in his direction, as did the woman who'd bailed Jack and Chen out of the German police van in Berlin, who he'd later discovered the identity of.

He approached the booth. "You better have a *fucking* good explanation for this, Anna."

"Looks like my cover wasn't as good as I thought it was." She smiled. "Hi again. I was just enjoying a sandwich and a cuppa with my good friend Zed here."

Eshkol had less humor. "I've been abducted by this woman and I want to go back to my university."

Jack pointed at Eshkol. "You. Shut up."

"I—"

He turned to Anna. "You. Talk."

She crossed her arms. "Hey, fuck you."

Jack flared. "Your dinner companion here might be the key to preventing a nuclear strike on this city. I need to take him in."

She reached for the pistol, which until now had been on the table. "Yeah, well, I've got my own problems."

"There's a lot of armed men outside."

She smiled and waved the pistol. "I've got the only gun that matters."

Jack exhaled through his teeth. He had to get Eshkol out of there, but couldn't quite see a way to do it without the professor ending up dead.

Eshkol started to laugh, long and deep and nasty. "This is too funny."

Jack glared at Eshkol. "What the fuck are you laughing at?"

The professor laughed so hard he coughed. "You're both fools. I've admitted that I'm the leader of the Zionists. Arrest me. But you're wasting time arguing. You can't stop the Samson Option. You'd be much better served applying your intellect on how to end the peace agreement."

Jack scoffed. "That's not going to happen, professor. I'm going to take you in and get the answers I need to end this."

"Is that so?" Anna pointed the pistol at Jack. "I need him for a little while longer, Mr. Emery, but I don't need you."

Jack suddenly regretted leaving his own pistol back with Agent Warner. He glanced outside, where SWAT were surrounding the building in ever increasing numbers. If he gave a nod, they'd storm the building in a second, but he'd be dead and Eshkol would fall in the crossfire. He was used to hairy situations, but this one seemed hopeless.

"So what do we do here?" He held his hands out. "We both need Eshkol, but we're stalemated."

"We both walk out of here. Equal access to Eshkol.

That's the only thing I can agree to that my government will accept."

He considered it for a moment. He wasn't sure why Britain was so interested in the Zionists, but he didn't care. He needed Eshkol alive and needed to know where the nukes were. Nothing else would save the peace process and millions of lives. "Okay, we'll go with that. I suppose that's fair, since you found him."

"Stand down your goons."

"Pistol first."

Eshkol sighed. "You're both fools."

Anna glared at Eshkol then turned to Jack and lowered the pistol. "Okay. I—"

"*Freeze! Freeze!*"

Jack tensed. An FBI SWAT team was surging into the room through the kitchen with guns trained on each of them. Jack held his hands in place but cast a glance toward Anna. She looked down at her pistol, as if assessing her chances, then up to Jack. The look of fury on her face was terrifying. She held her hands up and let herself be subdued.

The scene froze for a few seconds, nobody moving or saying anything under the watchful guns of the SWAT team. Except Eshkol. The professor laughed and laughed and laughed until he started to cough and wheeze. Jack wanted to clobber the man, except it might earn him a bullet or two. Luckily his rage was interrupted by Warner entering the diner through the front door.

"You bastard." Jack scowled. "You could have ruined everything."

"I didn't." Warner shrugged. "Turns out the back door was open."

"What now?" Anna spoke softly.

"That's up to Mr. Emery." Warner looked to Jack. "I've

disobeyed the President's man once today, I won't do it twice."

Jack exhaled slowly. It was time to take back the initiative. "Leave the pistol where it is, walk out of here and you'll be escorted to the airport. If you make a fuss, you'll be arrested and not even the special relationship between America and Britain will keep you out of prison for the next twenty years."

"Okay." Anna nodded and stood. Before she left, escorted by a pair of agents, she turned back. "Good luck. He's a tough old cookie."

Jack nodded and walked over to Eshkol. "Now, I think we got off on the wrong foot, professor. We've got a lot to talk about."

ARON WOKE with a sigh and fumbled for the lamp. He squinted as the light pierced his solitude, nearly as irritating as the beeping that had woken him. He sat up in bed, rubbed his face and ran a hand through his hair. He looked down at his phone and read the message. There was only one thing that was permitted to override the do not disturb setting on his phone.

Zed Eshkol's emergency button.

He read the message again to confirm it, but he'd known as soon as he heard the phone beep. He didn't know what had happened to Zed Eshkol, nor did he have any care in finding out. The protocols were clear: the professor was compromised, so every single Zionist asset was to be activated. Now it was necessary to proceed with the contingency plan.

His work was not yet done.

ACT III

15

The Federal Bureau of Investigation has so far resisted calls to reveal the identity of the Zionist leader, believed to have been detained after a massive manhunt through the streets of New York City. Sources have revealed that more than 300 police officers and Federal agents were involved in the arrest, which caused chaos across the city. The FBI has reiterated calls from the President for all Zionist members to hand themselves in and offered the largest reward in United States' history for information about the location of the three nuclear devices.

New York Standard

Jack closed his eyes and enjoyed the rest for just a moment. He took a few slow breaths, resisting the urge to sleep, though it tempted him like the final drink on a big night. It was never a good idea to be snoozing when the President walked into a National Security Council meeting, particularly with the world seven days away from nuclear catastrophe. Not even the fact he'd played a lead role in the scooping up of Zed Eshkol would get him off the hook for that one.

As if on cue, McGhinnist's voice boomed. "Thanks for coming in everyone. We ready to get started?"

Jack's eyes shot open and he caught sympathetic glances from a few of the other attendees. They'd all been burning the midnight oil, but some of the others had made a point of praising him for the work he'd put in and the progress he'd made. The recognition was nice, but felt a bit hollow at the moment. He'd only be satisfied when the good professor spilled the beans and they got their hands on the nuclear weapons.

He was still irritated that the SWAT unit had stormed the diner, putting everyone at risk. He thought he'd be able to talk Anna into handing Eshkol over, but instead they'd gone in hot. The professor had been bundled into an armored van and driven off, while Anna had been released and told in no uncertain terms to get on a plane. If she was from any other country, she'd have been locked up. The special relationship between the US and the UK still counted for something.

McGhinnist sat. "Lou, what do you have for us?"

Lou McColl – the FBI Director – removed his glasses, placed them on top of his papers and then smiled. "After the SWAT unit snapped up Eshkol, we moved him to a secure facility. He's currently being interrogated. He's holding out so far, but we could achieve more with enhanced techniques."

Jack snorted. "Torture, you mean?"

"Yes, Jack." McColl glared at him. "We don't have the luxury of a conscience when ten city blocks will soon be gone."

"Enough of that, gentlemen." McGhinnist sighed. "I won't authorize torture. Not while I'm still president. Has he told us where the bombs are yet?"

McColl placed both hands on the table, shook his head

and let out a sigh. It was clear he thought Jack and the President were naive. "Not yet."

McGhinnist nodded. "We have seven days, but I want the weapons secured in one. If we wait any longer we're leaving it too close. Get it done."

"Yes, sir." McColl nodded then replaced his glasses, before scribbling a few notes on his pad. "We'll continue to rely on regular techniques."

"Okay." McGhinnist looked down at his papers. "Next item is the evacuation of Manhattan, twenty-four hours from now, should we fail to break Eshkol."

Jack winced. The thought of removing a few million people from the island was daunting. There would be panic, looting and chaos, at the end of which the greatest metropolis on Earth would resemble a ghost town. But there was a real chance they'd need to do it, given they didn't yet have the slightest clue where the weapon was. If they waited much longer there was no guarantee that the evacuation would be completed in time.

Admiral Bryson Tannenbaum – Chairman of the Joint Chiefs – nodded. "We've got several army and marine units readying to deploy to the city, if need be, along with every helicopter this side of the Atlantic. All assets will be at the disposal of the civilian authorities, sir, even if it's just to help direct people where to go."

"Can we pull it off?"

"Not a question for me, sir." Tannenbaum shrugged. "But the military can help get people out of the city and secure it when it's empty."

Jack leaned in. "Secure it how?"

"A small guard detail at each bridge along with helicopter and river patrols." Tannenbaum paused. "The minimum force required to keep people out."

The next question was obvious to Jack. "Men who could die if the bomb goes off in their vicinity?"

"Volunteers, Mr. Emery." Tannenbaum's look was hard. "These are extreme circumstances, but we've had plans in place to deal with them for seventy years."

Jack shook his head, but kept quiet. He understood the need to keep the city clamped down in the event of the bomb not being found. He spared a thought for the authorities going through the same preparations in Jerusalem and Mecca. It was far easier to button down a metropolis on an island, with all the resources of the United States government, than it was in those other locations. There would be lots of lives lost if the bombs couldn't be found.

"We have to break Eshkol." Jack was surprised by the pitch of his voice. "We can't let those devices go off. It'll be a catastrophe."

His words hung in the air until the phone in front of McGhinnist rang. Everyone at the meeting stared at it and Jack thought it unusual. Very few calls made it through to the President when the council was in session. McGhinnist frowned, lifted the handset and pressed the button to put the call onto speaker. It only took a moment for the President's secretary to announce that the Iranian President was on the line.

"Put him through, Steph." McGhinnist ran a hand through his hair. "President Gharazi, you're on the line with my National Security Council."

There was a slight pause, before a man spoke in heavily accented English. "Mr. President, this is a warning. Iran will launch nuclear weapons at Israel if you can't guarantee the safety of Mecca. We will do it two hours before the peace agreement is due to come into force. I can't tolerate this threat to Mecca."

McGhinnist sighed, as if this was the last thing he needed. "President Gharazi, I can assure you we're doing everything we can to find the weapons. Such an act by Iran, against an ally, would be considered an act of war by the United States and we'd be forced to retaliate."

"I'm aware of all of this, Mr. President, but I can imagine the reaction if a Muslim had a nuke in Vatican City." The Iranian laughed. "We've made reforms and drawn closer to your country in some ways, but some things remain the same. This risk can't be tolerated."

"What good will nuking Israel do?"

"If there's no Israel, there's no peace agreement. Mecca will be spared."

Jack shook his head and shared a look with some other council members. It was a strange arithmetic the Iranian President was engaging in, but it made a mad sort of sense. Iran had been strong-armed by the United States to support the agreement – or at least turn a blind eye – and McGhinnist had hoped that untangling the Israeli–Palestinian mess would help to end the worst conflict in the region. Instead, it looked as if it might do the opposite.

"That's strange logic, Mr. President." McGhinnist seemed to read Jack's mind. "My understanding was that your country supported the peace process."

"We consider the agreement acceptable, if the weapons can be found." Gharazi's voice hardened. "If not, the whole region will go to hell, Mr. President. Palestine has no nuclear weapons, but it does have friends. It's Zionists who hold this dagger to our hearts, and it's Israel that will pay if it isn't dealt with."

The phone started to beep, indicating the call had been ended. Before anyone could speak, McGhinnist slammed a fist down on the table.

"Find those weapons!"

～

ANNA LOOKED down – a long way down – then stepped back

and pulled the balaclava over her head. Once it was comfortably in place, she checked her weapons were on her hip, that her harness and combat vest were tight and secure, and that the small black remote with the single button that she carried was still showing a green light. Satisfied that she was as ready as she could be, she took a few long, deep breaths and then stepped to the ledge again.

Though she was usually okay with heights, the prospect of jumping off a perfectly good ledge and hanging from a zip line seventy-one stories above Broadway didn't really appeal to her. But, as she'd often found since joining MI6, the agent went where the work was to be found. In this case, the work was on the sixty-third level, in a small, off-the-books office that the FBI kept for interviewing important prisoners like Zed Eshkol.

As she connected the zip line to the metal ring on her harness, she cursed herself again for letting Eshkol slip out of her grasp. She'd taken a risk by questioning him in the open after she'd got him away from the campus. She'd wagered that there was no harm being seen with an academic in a diner and that, when he realized the jig was up, the professor would be forthcoming. Following that, he could be easily disposed of – an old man whose heart gave out.

But taking the risk had bitten her. She'd failed and he was now in American custody. What she hadn't counted on was Jack Emery linking Tipping to Eshkol and then Eshkol to the Zionists. Given the hit team had taken care of Tipping, she'd made a mistake in thinking her lead safe. Uncovering Eshkol's link with the Zionists had been a first-rate bit of research by Emery, which had unfortunately cost her dearly. Her overconfidence may have cost her country and the world.

Luckily, she had another chance. She'd easily escaped the security detail tasked with seeing her onto a plane, and

Cunningham had made it clear any action she deemed necessary was on the board in order to get to Eshkol again and get the information out of him. Though he was in American hands, with the full menu of options at her disposal and the permission to use them, she was confident she could get to him.

That's how she found herself on top of a building, about to rappel down it. Eshkol was alive and she intended to make her claim on him. She gave the zip line a tug and eased herself over the side of the building. She winced at the strength of the wind that blew against her. Once she was suspended by nothing other than the line, she let her rubber shoes rest against the glass windows and started to lower herself slowly.

She knew the darkness was her friend and that there was little chance she'd be seen, but she still hurried as much as she dared. All it would take to expose her was one office worker staying back late. If that happened, she'd likely never make it out of the building and this part of the world would be radioactive in a week's time. As her confidence with the abseil grew, so did the speed of her descent.

Seventy-one.

Seventy.

She scanned each floor as she descended, reflecting on the huge disparity in office layout.

Sixty-nine.

Sixty-eight.

A third of the way there, and she hadn't seen a soul. With each floor lit by security lights and empty of people, her assessment of the situation improved.

Sixty-seven.

Sixty-six.

She started to slow her descent, but continued to

bounce softly off of windows with her feet as she rappelled down.

Sixty-five.

Sixty-four.

Sixty-three.

Touching her feet to the window, she slowed to a stop. She pulled a lever on her rig to apply the brake, which freed her hands to get on with the job. After a quick dig in one of the many pockets on her combat vest, she found a small but powerful glass cutter. She fired it up, held it in one hand and reached for her remote with the other. The light on the remote was still green, meaning the security responsible for monitoring this window were still occupied.

After one final glance inside, she set to work creating a large enough circle to fit through. As the cutter bit into the glass, she winced at the noise it made, hoping that nobody was in a position to hear it. The work only took a few minutes, then she put the cutter back in her pocket and used a suction device to remove and secure the glass. Once she was done, she swung inside, careful not to make too much noise and alert security.

She unclipped the zip line and removed her harness, placing it near the window, then drew her pistol and scanned the room. Though MI6 had known about this location for years, nobody ever expected to use the information. Given they knew most of the possible locations that the FBI would use to question Eshkol, simple signal interception had told MI6 which one Eshkol was being taken to. Now it was up to her.

She raised the pistol and advanced through the cubicle jungle, which looked like any other. If all went to plan, the floor should be deserted except for the agent on the security desk – who her little green light told her was under control – and however many agents were interrogating Eshkol. Her weapon swept from side to side, alert to any potential ambush from one of the vacant cubicles, but nothing pricked her senses amid darkness and silence.

She moved toward the target office, relaxed but alert for any movement or trouble. The first office had its door closed and no lights on, so she kept moving past. It was a process she repeated four more times, until she reached the sixth office. The curtains were drawn and the door was similarly shut, but this time light blazed at the edges of the window, where the curtains couldn't totally block it. She allowed herself a small smile and prepared for the violence to come.

There was no subtle way to do this, so she got on with it. She holstered her pistol and pulled out a taser, never taking her eyes off the door. Next she grabbed one of the metal cylinders attached to her combat vest, kicked the bottom of the door a few times, lifted the cylinder to her mouth and pulled out the pin. The door opened and she fired the taser. The contractor who'd opened the door dropped – courtesy of 50,000 volts – at the same time as she threw the cylinder inside and retreated from the doorway.

The flashbang exploded with noise and light, but she was shielded from the worst of it by the door frame. Once the fireworks concluded she rounded back into the doorway, her eyes scanning the small interview room. She made her way toward the second and final contractor, who was rubbing his eyes and in no position to threaten her, and aimed a kick at his knee. The man crumpled and she pulled some cuffs from her vest, restrained him and forced him outside. A few seconds later and the man she'd tasered was likewise restrained.

All was clear except for Eshkol.

She stood in front of the professor, savoring the look of fear and confusion on his face. He was seated with one hand cuffed to a steel ring on the table, but was too busy reacting to the flashbang to notice her enter. She sat opposite and stared at him, waiting for him to regain his composure and wishing he'd be quicker about it. The FBI didn't know she was here, but she was still in very hostile territory. That she'd been authorized to take this action showed how much Fraser and Cunningham wanted Eshkol's information. She drew her pistol.

"Hi again." She kept the weapon on him as she lifted the balaclava off her face. "I'm sorry our nice lunch was interrupted. We've got a lot to discuss."

The second his eyes adjusted to her, they narrowed. He glanced around for the Americans then back at Anna. "You."

"Me." She smiled, never taking the pistol off him. "I'm so glad to see you too, professor."

"You're going to kill me, then?" He continued to blink and spoke louder than normal, the flashbang having affected his hearing. "I gave you the location of the backpack weapons. There's nothing else I can tell you, no matter how fanciful your claims about a nuclear submarine."

"That you did." Anna stood and walked around the table. "And rest assured that I'll pass the location on to my American friends, but I need something else."

"What would that be?"

"Confirmation that HMS *Vigilant* has been compromised and an explanation on how you planned to activate the launch."

"This again?" He gave a sharp laugh. "You're wrong. The backpack nukes were the play. Get those, and you've silenced me."

She sighed. "You have an unknown number of minions, able to enact multiple plans at once. Redundancy."

"If you're so convinced then nothing I can say will change your mind." He closed his eyes and turned his head away. "Shoot me."

Anna had no intention of doing that, not until she had the information she needed. Despite his denials, she knew he had more to tell her. She placed the pistol down on the table, out of his reach but close enough to grab if they were interrupted. She unzipped one of the pockets on her vest and dug around inside, pulling out a small case not unlike one used to hold reading glasses. She opened the case, removing the syringe and a small flask with a rubber stopper. The stopper gave a small pop, then she filled the syringe with liquid.

"Last chance, professor." She pressed down on the plunger and squirted a small amount of the liquid in front of his face. "This won't be pleasant."

"I was in a Nazi camp for two years and came out the other side." He spat at her. "I'm not scared of you."

"You should be."

"My life is irrelevant. What matters is securing Israel." He paused. "Seven days from now a travesty will take place that I don't want to see occur. Kill me."

She shrugged, stabbed the needle into his arm and pressed down on the plunger. The liquid inside emptied out and she threw the empty vessel onto the floor. He had no reaction for the first few seconds, but then his eyes widened and he let out a small whimper. In the seconds that followed, he started to struggle against the handcuffs. Then he started to scream.

The poison was one of the most lethal on Earth and was completely fatal. What made it helpful, however, was the speed at which it acted. It caused immense, crippling pain within seconds of injection, but took a long while to bring the body to its eventual death. It was an eternity to be subjected to the pain of your nervous system dying, given the poison could take eight hours to kill.

She shook her head. Two hours, given his age. Still, a very long time.

"Professor, I know it hurts and it's going to get worse. You're going to die. But if you tell me what I need, a bullet will end you. If not, you'll slowly decay and your nervous system will tell your brain all about it for the next few hours. It really is your choice."

"Okay!" His shriek was piercing. "I'll tell you! Make it stop!"

"I can't stop it until I kill you, professor. Answer my questions." She leaned in to him. "Has the HMS *Vigilant* been compromised?"

"Yes!" he howled. "Joseph Cohen was my student and friend! He's the captain of the submarine!"

She ignored the upward inflection in his voice. He was getting desperate. "How is the launch activated?"

"By using the normal process!"

"That's impossible." She picked up the pistol. "No British Prime Minister would order the launch."

"No, not that way." His eyes were bulging now and saliva started to dribble from his mouth. "The Dead Man Letter!"

Her eyes widened. It was as if she'd found the missing piece to a jigsaw lying under the table. "You fucking bastard."

He laughed, a terrible sight given the pain he was in. "If only you knew. I've activated pieces all throughout your government. The world will burn with nuclear fire, and you'll watch as everything you thought secure is compromised before your eyes."

She raised the pistol and pulled the trigger. His head slumped forward. She gave a moment's thought to killing the men outside, but decided there was no point. They didn't know who she was and she didn't want to end the lives of men just doing their jobs. She stood and prepared to leave the lifeless corpse of one of the most brilliant minds the Western world had seen.

An intellect that may well end the world.

JACK CLINKED his champagne glass against Celeste's then took a sip. The vintage Dom Perignon fizzed in his mouth and he savored the taste. But, more than that, he was savoring the first real meal he'd had with Celeste in over a week. It had been the busiest week in a crazy month and he was feeling the fatigue in his muscles and his bones, in his mind and in his heart. The end of the twenty-eight–day countdown to the peace agreement couldn't come soon enough, if the nukes could be found, anyway.

"Thanks for coming up here for this, Celeste." He put his glass down and looked across the table at her. "I needed it."

"I don't mind bringing the party to you." She took a second sip of her own drink and then winked at him, a twinkle in her eye. "Are you okay?"

He opened his mouth to answer, then paused. It was a loaded question, akin to asking a rabbit staring into the headlights of an oncoming car if it was doing fine. He was tired, sure, and he was counting down the minutes until the peace, but until the nukes were found he'd have no rest. Now that Eshkol had been captured, that should only take a short while, but he couldn't relax until that moment. There was too much work to do, too much at stake and too many lives that could be lost.

"I'm fine." He smiled.

"Liar." She raised her eyebrows. "You need to look after yourself, Jack."

He shrugged. "There are a few million reasons for me to keep working. Once we find those bombs and we've got peace, I'll rest."

"Promise?"

"In fact, I'll do you one better." He paused, reached down into his pocket and pulled out a small box.

She gasped and her eyes flickered between his face and the box. "What're you doing?"

He never took his eyes off her as he stood and lowered himself to one knee. He opened the box, revealing the ring. "Marry me, Celeste?"

"Seriously?" She shook her head and gave a small laugh. "I had no idea this was coming."

"Seriously." He moved the box closer to her. "I know there's a bunch of trouble that comes with being with me, but I want you in my life forever. Marry me?"

He took a deep breath as she stared at the ring, then at him, then back again. It was if she was transfixed, and with each passing second the feeling in the pit of his stomach worsened. He hadn't planned this, not really, and had only purchased the ring in the afternoon after she'd told him she was coming to visit. There were so many reasons that marrying Celeste made sense to him, but he also knew that he was asking a lot. Trouble stalked him, and they'd had their own problems. It seemed unlikely that those two things would cease, but he knew he needed her.

"Sorry." She shook her head. "I was just thinking about how far we've come – both individually and together – since we first met."

He cracked a smile. "We definitely don't do boring. Stick with me, and there'll be more entertainment to come. That I can promise."

"It feels like I've packed in a million lifetimes worth of excitement with you already, Jack."

"Okay." He saw where this was going and started to lower the box. When he'd asked Erin to marry him, years ago, she'd said yes instantly. He felt like someone had punched him in the stomach. He swallowed hard and struggled to find some words, unable to believe he'd misread their relationship so badly. "I—"

"Give me that!" She reached out and plucked the box from his hand. "You didn't let me finish!"

He relinquished the package. "Okay."

"As I was saying, it's been exciting so far, and I wouldn't have it any other way." She pulled the ring from the box. "Of course I'll marry you."

He let out a small laugh and smiled so wide it hurt. He helped her with the ring. "Hope it fits."

She slid it on. "Perfect."

He leaned in to kiss her, but paused when Celeste's eyes flicked behind him and narrowed. "Jack, we've got company."

Jack followed her gaze and was surprised to see four Chevy Suburbans pulled up out the front, with DC Metro Police motorbikes along as outriders. Several black-suited Secret Service agents had taken up station outside the restaurant and one had the door to the restaurant open. Jack stood and waited for the agent to approach, even as Celeste tensed and reached for his hand.

"Evening." He smiled at the agent as he squeezed Celeste's hand. "This is quite a bit of a show to wish me congratulations on my engagement, isn't it?"

The agent acted like he didn't even hear the joke. He was all business. "Mr. Emery, you need to come with us, sir."

"Something wrong?"

"You need to come now, sir."

Jack nodded and turned back to Celeste. He leaned in to kiss her. "Sorry."

"I'll finish my meal and the bottle, but it's going on your card." She gave a small laugh as she pecked him on the lips. "Go save the world. I love you."

"I love you too."

He nodded at the agent and they walked outside the restaurant to the waiting convoy. He hoped whatever had interrupted his proposal was important, given that Celeste had flown from New York to be with him. He waited for the agent to indicate which vehicle he was to get inside, then climbed in. The agent closed the door behind him, and Jack wasn't surprised to see the President, given the size of the security detail. But he was surprised by the presence of a second man.

"Mr. President." Jack nodded at McGhinnist, then shifted his gaze to the other man. "Ambassador Hutchens."

David Hutchens had been UK Ambassador to the United States for the better part of a decade. In that time, he'd been a steady hand at the helm of the most important alliance both countries shared, during a time when the US had dealt with both Michelle Dominique and her Foundation for a New America and Richard Hall's authoritarian takeover. Since McGhinnist had won the Presidency, Hutchens had been a strong supporter. He'd also been at the forefront of the peace negotiations.

"Good to see you again, Jack." The ambassador held out his hand. "Wish it was under better circumstances."

Jack shook Hutchens' hand. "Likewise. Something's come up? I assume it's not good?"

"Sorry to interrupt your dinner, Jack." McGhinnist sounded like he meant it. "This one is on me."

"It'll be an expensive one to cover, Mr. President." Jack smiled. "There was a diamond on the menu."

"You proposed?" McGhinnist's eyes widened slightly and he gave a tired smile. "Good move."

Hutchens grinned at McGhinnist then at Jack. "Fantastic news, Jack. I wish I were congratulating you under better circumstances."

McGhinnist cleared his throat, cutting the celebrations short. "We know where some of the bombs are. A team in

New York has already secured one and Jerusalem will be safe soon. Unfortunately, Mecca came up empty. Looks like the Zionists left that weapon with someone who has moved it somewhere else."

"Eshkol?" Jack's gaze moved between the other two men. He felt the temperature in the vehicle drop to freezing, but neither man spoke. "Well?"

Finally, the ambassador broke the silence. "He's dead. But he did give us the location of the bombs."

Jack started to speak. "How—"

"Leave it, Jack." McGhinnist's voice was laced with threat. Something bad had to have happened, leading to tension between the President and Hutchens.

Hutchens leaned forward. "Unfortunately, we're out of the frying pan and into the fire. We've received intelligence indicating that HMS *Vigilant* is under the command of an agent of the Zionists. Worse, it looks like the Zionists might have a plan to get off a launch. Needless to say this is thoroughly bad news."

Jack's eyes narrowed as he chewed on the ambassador's words. "Wait a minute, isn't that a—"

"A ballistic missile submarine capable of annihilating a fair percentage of humanity." The ambassador nodded. "Yes."

"Fuck."

Jack couldn't believe it. His heart had soared in the moment after McGhinnist had revealed the bombs had been found, but the taste of triumph after all his hard work had turned to ashes in his mouth. A British boomer was waiting silently beneath the ocean to unleash Zed Eshkol's wrath from beyond the grave. After all the effort to find them, the backpack bombs had been a plot shouted to the world, when in reality the larger danger was lurking as quiet as a whisper beneath the ocean.

Hutchens sighed. "It can't be hunted down and it can't

be ordered to the surface, so we've got seven days to figure out how to prevent a launch."

Jack scoffed. "Can it be done?"

"There's one way." Hutchens shrugged. "We're working on it, along with some of your people, but it won't be easy. It looks like Eshkol has agents all the way through Britain and the British Government. I imagine it's the same story in America – Tipping was just the start."

"Nor is it the only issue." McGhinnist's voice was nearly a whisper. "Iran hasn't changed its position."

Jack nearly laughed at the gall of the Iranian President. "Turns out they're playing realpolitik like everyone else."

"It'll take some concessions to get them to back down, I think. Until we can find the bomb in Mecca, they're playing hardball." McGhinnist placed a hand on his knee. "In the meantime, we're going to DEFCON 2. If we can't find a way to deal with that sub, and Iran, we need to be ready."

Jack nodded. The world was on the verge of catastrophe. "What can I do?"

McGhinnist smiled.

16

The State Department has confirmed Israeli reports that the backpack nuclear device planted by the Zionist terrorists in Jerusalem has been secured, five days before the deadline. This follows a similar announcement by the Department of Homeland Security, confirming that the device in New York City has been found. State Department officials remain tight-lipped about the bomb in Mecca, suggesting that it has yet to be found, even as reports emerge of troop movements across the Middle East as enactment of the peace agreement draws near.

New York Standard

J oseph held his coffee in one hand and gripped the safety rail with the other, as the _Vigilant_ ascended toward the surface. Though he didn't have to hold on and there was no danger of falling over, the practice was as instinctive as breathing, drilled into him over many years in the submarine service. As he looked around the bridge, he could see those who weren't seated doing the same thing. He gave a small smile as he felt the boat reach an even plane.

"We're at depth and level, captain." Jennings' voice broke the silence.

Joseph released the rail. "Unfurl the array and download communications."

Jennings nodded and started to fire off commands to the bridge crew, as Joseph sipped his tea and waited for the first batch of messages to come in. While at sea, British nuclear submarines never surfaced and communication with them was difficult, possible only in very short bursts – such as launch orders. They only climbed to periscope depth to receive longer messages a small handful of time during their tour. It was no coincidence that Joseph had chosen this date to do so.

Joseph hoped the first news they'd receive would be about the peace agreement being abandoned. Failing that, he hoped to read that Eshkol's main plan was proceeding well, with nuclear weapons ready for use in the event of the peace agreement being enacted. Though that would mean Israel was a step closer to being divided, it would be the next best result for Joseph. By far the worst would be news that the agreement was close and that Eshkol's plan had failed. In that case, Joseph would become the primary defender of Israel.

"Captain?"

Joseph shook his head, clearing the gloomy thoughts. "Report."

Jennings smiled and winked at his captain, like they shared a little secret. Since their chat in the wardroom, the other man had continued to confide in Joseph about his personal life, to the point where Joseph thought Jennings would walk over hot coals if asked to by his captain. He couldn't be totally sure, of course, but if the *Vigilant* and its warheads did have to become the final act in Eshkol's plan, with Jennings in hand Joseph considered it likely he'd be able to hold up his end. The rest of the crew would follow.

"Attention crew." Jennings spoke over the boat intercom. "News as follows: The separation of Israel and Palestine is five days away. The Zionist leader has been arrested and two of the nuclear weapons found, but Iran has threatened to attack Israel if the Mecca device isn't. In sport, Ipswich Town has been relegated."

Joseph cursed to himself. Even though there were no new orders from British command, the news contained all the orders he needed from his other master. He was now the last person standing in the way of Israel's destruction. Eshkol was incapacitated and two of the backpack bombs were off the board. The Iranian declaration was a surprise, but not relevant to his mission. All that was clear was that the start gun had fired for him and he now had some work to do in order to get ready.

He shook his head and focused on the deck. He turned to Jennings, who'd continued to read the less important news. "Tim?"

Jennings stopped mid-sentence and looked at Joseph, a confused look on his face. He took his finger off the intercom transmit button. "Captain?"

"I want to speak to the crew." Joseph stepped closer to the intercom and Jennings stepped back. Joseph pressed the button. "This is the captain. This news is unexpected, but not a surprise. The world was an unstable, dangerous place when we set out and it looks to have gotten worse. I'm not sure the world has ever faced such a strong possibility of nuclear war. It's important that we stay safe and that we look after each other, because we have a vital job to do. Amid this uncertainty, we're the only thing protecting Britain, however she may get caught up in this. Remain vigilant, do your jobs and we'll get through this."

Joseph took his finger off the intercom button and

looked around the bridge. A few of the crew wore determined looks and Jennings nodded at him. Joseph considered the little speech as necessary in preparing Jennings for the eventuality of the launch. He trusted Eshkol to have things sorted, but nothing above the ocean would matter if Joseph failed to do his job below it. Enactment of the Samson Option and the prevention of the peace agreement now required two plans to proceed, one after the other, with no room for failure. It required choreography more difficult than stashing some nukes around the place.

He exhaled deeply at the burden. "Immediate drill: dive to launch depth and prepare a package with standard incoming orders. Two minutes."

Jennings' eyes narrowed. "I hadn't finished the news yet, sir. Maybe we should wait until—"

Joseph looked at his watch. "Fifteen seconds down, XO. I suggest you get moving."

ARON SMILED at the flight attendant, whose own smile was plastered on with practiced ease, then stepped past her and onto the skybridge. The cool, artificial air was replaced with the crisper air of a London morning and he strolled into the terminal humming a nameless tune. Since Eshkol's alert had sprung him into action he'd taken a slow and ponderous route to London to make sure he didn't appear on the radar of the authorities.

He regretted that two of the three backpack bombs he'd deployed had been located. So much effort had gone into their acquisition and placement that it seemed very anticlimactic to have them scooped up, but that had always been a risk. He hadn't counted on Eshkol being exposed and revealing their location, but there was no use worrying about it. There was still one bomb in place, which threatened to make Mecca glow.

The minute the New York bomb had been found it had been plastered all over the media and, hours later, the Jerusalem bomb had also been secured. Aron had expected to see coverage from Mecca not long after, but it hadn't happened. It meant the only bomb he'd left with a human being, rather than in a supposedly secure location, had been moved at the discretion of its caretaker. Aron hoped the man could keep from being found.

He couldn't count on it though, so he still had work to do. Aron was always restless on aircraft, but knowing the job that waited for him in London had made him all the more anxious to arrive and get started. He made his way through immigration and toward the luggage carousel. As he did, he thought about what needed doing over the next five days, whether or not the weapon in Mecca was located by the authorities.

He still hoped the agreement would be abandoned, but now considered it unlikely. The situation was ridiculous and the answer obvious, yet the signatories to the agreement had failed to blink as they were supposed to so more had to be done. A threat was only as good as the intent behind it and Eshkol wasn't bluffing. The professor's instructions had been clear and Aron intended to serve him faithfully.

By using the emergency button, Aron knew that Eshkol had activated every single asset he had. It was not a step taken lightly. Aron had his own assignment, for which he'd join up with others, but he knew that assets all around the world would have their jobs. Some may assist Aron, others may occur without him even knowing, but it would be the final flourish of a great mind who, in some way or another, had been compromised.

He reached the luggage carousel and his bag emerged

quickly. With the large backpack over his shoulder, it didn't take him too long to clear customs and make his way to the exit. The sliding doors opened and he stepped outside and into the fresh air. He took a deep breath as he looked up at the overcast skies. If all went to plan, he might have emerged from an airport for the last time in his life. As odd as it felt to think it, he was at ease with his fate. Only the mission counted.

"It's good to see you again, my friend."

Aron smiled at the sound of the voice, which he hadn't heard in weeks. He turned and took in the sight of her for several moments. It felt like so much had changed since they'd parted in Russia. They'd studied together under Zed Eshkol, years ago, becoming fast friends and allies in the professor's network – two of the key pieces on his board. That they were both here now spoke to the gravity of the situation. All assets were in play.

"Miri." Aron placed his bag on the ground and held his arms wide. "I had no idea you'd be beside me for this final effort."

Miri Shaked laughed as she stepped into his hug. "You were the golden child, Aron, but you don't really think he'd trust you alone with this, do you?"

He pulled away and shrugged. "You know the plan?"

Her eyes twinkled. "I know my part in it."

Aron nearly laughed. Zed Eshkol's compartmentalization was legendary. "You're in contact with the local network?"

"Yes. That's what I've been doing while you were busy planting bombs. I don't know much about them." She paused. "Zed trusted them, though."

"Let's get going." Aron smiled and jerked his head toward the taxi line, keen to waste no time.

He'd flown in expecting to have to deal with a list of difficult targets with the help of strangers. Now he had

Miri. Though he'd still be relying on Eshkol's local network for most of the heavy lifting, having one friend at his side made him all the more confident. She had skills that he lacked, but was also good at most of the things he was. He'd always found that quite frustrating, in truth, but now it would be an asset.

They climbed into the first available cab and rode in silence. Though they were both too experienced to speak in front of prying ears, they did share a few easy smiles. Aron closed his eyes, knowing he had some time before they reached their destination. He didn't sleep, but used the time to cycle through the list of targets in his head. He had five days to hit them all, with Miri and the local team available for support.

They arrived about an hour after they'd departed, which included being caught in some traffic. As the cab pulled up, Aron looked at the studios of BBC Radio 4 for the first time. Broadcasting House was a mix of the old and the new, a century-old building modernized with steel and glass. After he'd soaked it up, he looked at Miri, who was staring at him intently. It felt as if her eyes were asking hard questions, even if her mouth remained closed.

"What?" He unbuckled his belt.

"Just making sure you're focused."

Aron shrugged, paid the driver and climbed out of the cab. He collected his bag from the trunk, then hefted it over his shoulder and walked toward the building. Miri followed, and he felt her summing up him as much as the building. He couldn't blame her. The targets were ambitious, to say the least, and Aron actually considered the likelihood of success to be slim. He was dedicated to trying and dying, if need be. He wasn't sure she had the same commitment.

Knocking BBC Radio 4 off the air was not even the most difficult of the jobs, but it was one of the first. It was impossible for a pair of them to do it, and that's where Eshkol's local assets would come into play – warm bodies with lots of explosives and a few particular skills. Aron wasn't overly worried about the first target, he was concerned about the ones that followed. Even with all those men and guns and bombs, the size of the task seemed impossible.

"What're you thinking?" Miri placed a hand on his shoulder.

"How much I hate public broadcasting."

~

JACK GAVE a deep sigh as he looked out the window of the car, then spoke into his cell phone. "Anything else, sir?"

McGhinnist laughed from the other end of the line. "You'll be fine, Jack. Stop worrying and remember: I sent you there. Any failure is mine."

Jack snorted. "I'm struggling to see things the same way, knowing that if I leave here empty-handed we'll either lose the peace or watch Israel get glassed."

McGhinnist said nothing for a moment. Jack knew the President well enough to know that he was looking for the right thing to say, the thing that would convince a man in hostile territory on the other side of the world that he could achieve the impossible. In this case, the impossible was convincing nuclear-armed Iranians not to take matters into their own hands, flattening Israel to ostensibly save Mecca, but probably starting a global nuclear war in the process.

"Sir?"

"I'd love to tell you that it doesn't matter if you succeed or not, Jack, but that'd be a lie." McGhinnist paused again. "You've been caught up in a whole bunch of crises in recent years, but now I need you to help solve another. With Karl gone and Zionists popping up all over the place, you're the one I trust for this."

"I'll do my best." He hoped his best would be good enough.

"Do whatever you need to do to get them to back down, Jack. Good luck."

The line went dead and Jack put the phone in his top pocket. He sat back in the soft leather seat and closed his eyes, feeling the weight of the expectation on him. The warning in the car outside the restaurant had been apt, and Eshkol's moles were turning everywhere. As they acted, they were exposed, but the damage had been done. It was terrifying how deep Eshkol's assets had burrowed into the American and British governments.

He sighed and tried to focus on the job. Before he'd called McGhinnist, the driver had told him he was ten minutes out from the Presidential palace. He'd hoped that McGhinnist would have good news – that the bomb in Mecca had been found – but Saudi authorities were still searching for it. He laughed at the ridiculousness of it all: the Iranians were prepared to nuke Israel over Mecca, and a small number of Israelis were prepared to nuke Mecca over Palestine.

The car stopped and Jack opened his eyes as the door was opened for him. Camera flashes greeted him as he climbed out of the vehicle. An honor guard greeted him – the Iranian Republican Guard, which he'd been forewarned about, and the Iranian President, which he hadn't been. Despite the location, he'd half expected to be meeting with a minor official, but the President's presence meant there was hope. He closed the distance between them, deliberately avoiding the temptation to look around too much. He couldn't let himself be overwhelmed.

"Mr. Emery." The President held out his hand. "Welcome to Iran."

Jack shook his hand. "President Gharazi, thanks for welcoming me."

"These are dire days, but there's still some time to eat. Join me."

Gharazi turned on his heel, gesturing for Jack to follow. As they walked, they made small talk while surrounded by the President's army of retainers and hangers on. They eventually reached a small dining room dominated by a six-seater table. Jack was pleased to see there were only two places set. He stood inside the door and waited for whatever was to come. Gharazi dismissed the support staff, leaving just the two of them.

"What now, Mr. President?" Jack felt a little prompting was necessary, given the situation. "I'm quite short on time."

"Aren't we all?" Gharazi smiled as he gestured toward the table. "Please, sit. It's just the two of us. We'll have to serve ourselves."

Jack nodded and sat in the seat the President had gestured him to. In a weaker moment, he might have made a wise crack about being alone with the President and his spy agencies, but he held his tongue. Gharazi had his secrets and Jack had his – such as the fact that a British nuclear submarine had been hijacked and posed a far greater threat to the world – and Mecca – than either backpack nukes or Iranian ones. Adding more fuel to this fire was not something he wanted to do.

"Now, Mr. Emery, you've come a long way." Gharazi rested his elbows on the table, his fingers steepled in front of his face. "I know why you're here, but you needn't have bothered. My terms were clear: the threat to Mecca must be removed or the peace abandoned."

Jack took a sip of water. He'd have preferred to have something stronger, but Gharazi was not a drinker. "Mr. President, I hope you appreciate the bind the United States is in. We've worked to broker a peace that makes everyone happy – including Iran – only to have it threatened by extremists."

Gharazi nodded. "I—"

Jack held up a hand. "Please, let me finish. As I said, this is a deal that's good for everybody, yet having your government make inflammatory threats places the peace and the whole world in danger. I'm simply here to ask that you take your threats, and your nuclear weapons, off the table."

Jack sat back. The other man's features were as hard as granite and his face showed no hint that Jack's words had influenced him at all. While in a sane world what he'd said to Gharazi would be enough, events had spiraled out of control. It was possible that Jack coming here could make things worse. Thankfully, McGhinnist had armed him with more than appeals to reason. The United States could throw a huge amount of resources at diplomatic problems when needed.

"If Iran agrees to take such action, President McGhinnist is willing to remove the last of the economic sanctions against Iran and to also normalize relations between the two countries." Jack smiled. "This is as tough a concession for a Republican president to offer as possible."

Gharazi's features cracked for the first time, as he gave the slightest hint of a smile. "I knew you'd come equipped with platitudes, threats and maybe baubles to dangle in front of me, Mr. Emery, but it appears your boss is more serious about this peace than I gave him credit for."

"He's taken us to the brink of nuclear catastrophe for it. We don't negotiate with terrorists as a matter of policy, but even if we did the President would stand behind the deal and ignore the Zionist demands. Their threat must be dealt with, because we won't relinquish the peace."

Gharazi nodded. "That answers my next question: Why

not walk away? But I appreciate and respect a man of conviction."

Jack was pleased at not having to dwell on that point for too long. McGhinnist had repeatedly stated and shown that abandoning the peace was not an option, through dealing with the initial leaks to chasing Tipping to finding Eshkol and the first two bombs. Iranian brinkmanship was just another step along that road, at the end of which would either be a more peaceful Middle East, or a glowing one. Jack doubted he'd have the stones to be as resolute as McGhinnist had been.

They spoke for several hours, through three courses, dessert and coffee. While Jack appreciated the difficult position Gharazi was in, he was determined to do whatever he needed to in order to buy America, Israel and Palestine some extra time. They circled around the same terms, Jack sweetened them a little, Gharazi blustered and Jack bristled until, eventually, Jack felt he had gone as far as he could.

"Those are the best terms I can offer, Mr. President. The only thing I can add is that the US would consider a pre-emptive attack on Israel to be an act of war."

Gharazi laughed. "My people would consider an attack on Mecca to be the same."

"Then we're at a decision point." Jack held out his hands. "This is the chance to make the right decision, to try our best – together – to end the threat to Mecca and also lock in the two-state solution that has eluded us for generations. You don't like Israel, fine, but I suggest you can live with it if all else is put right."

"You ask much of me. If my people don't revolt at this deal, the spiritual leaders are likely to. You might see me on CNN hanging from my neck tomorrow." Gharazi lifted his water glass and took a long sip, but never took his eyes off Jack. "But we all must take risks to avert catastrophe."

Jack raised an eyebrow. "We have a deal?"

"We have a deal." Gharazi nodded. "But not exactly the one you wanted. Twenty-three hours is all I can give you. If I don't have a guarantee that Mecca is safe one hour prior to the expiry of the agreement, then I'll have no choice but to strike pre-emptively."

Jack stood and held out his hand, which Gharazi shook. Others would work out the detail of the deal, but it had been agreed in principle. It was good enough. It would have to be. Jack had bought McGhinnist, the peace process and the world an extra day. He'd given up nearly a day to do so, as well as mountains of US influence and treasure. But in the world of geopolitics, Jack thought it might just count as a win.

They'd had precious few of those recently.

17

With less than 72 hours before the peace agreement between Israel and Palestine is enacted and a two-state solution realized, the nuclear device that Zionist extremists have placed near Mecca has still not been found. The bomb, which the Zionists claim will be detonated if the countdown expires, threatens to level the most holy Islamic site in the world. Saudi Arabia has already begun mass evacuations from the area, but the saving of lives is of little comfort to leaders in the Islamic world, who are facing the strongest possible demands from their people that something be done to prevent the peace and the explosion of the bomb.

New York Standard

J ack laughed. "It's hardly the Pentagon, is it?"

As the car he'd been riding in pulled to a stop, Jack's judgment of the UK Ministry of Defence headquarters was met with a few nods of agreement by his companions. Squat and grey, the building was about a dozen stories tall and offered little to distinguish itself from other government buildings the convoy had driven past. There was plenty to see in London, but the administration buildings of Whitehall weren't high on the list.

He waited while two of his escorts climbed out of the vehicle and secured the surrounds, an action mimicked by pairs from the other two vehicles. When prompted by the security detail, Jack opened the door and exited the vehicle, pulling his coat tight to guard against the chill. Careful not to get in the way of his guards, Jack started toward the entrance as the six Navy SEALS fanned out, weapons gripped tightly as they scanned their surroundings.

Jack wasn't used to heavily armed SEALs escorting him wherever he went, but he didn't have a choice in the matter. As soon as he'd left the meeting with Gharazi, Jack had flown to the United Kingdom aboard a US Government jet. He'd never expected to be alone on a jet with a fighter escort, and upon landing there had been more surprises – Chen and a US Navy SEAL team waiting for him at Heathrow Airport.

"You're kidding me!" Jack put his hands on his hips when he saw who was waiting for them at the entrance of the building. His alarm caused several of the SEALs to raise their weapons at the woman – an entirely bad idea. "Cool it, guys, she's a friendly."

Anna Fowler glanced at the SEALs as they lowered their weapons, then smiled at him. "Hi, Jack. I should introduce myself. I'm Anna Fowler"

"The surprises keep on coming, don't they?" Jack sighed. "At least I know your surname now. Though I guess I shouldn't be surprised that you skulked back."

She winked at him. "Actually, I flew home first class. Not as nice as the jet you flew in on, but better than I usually get. Follow me. These guys stay outside."

Jack wanted to take issue with her ordering him around, given the mischief she'd caused, but he fell in behind her.

Chen followed too, but the SEAL team remained outside. As they walked deeper into the bowels of the Ministry of Defence, the group caught some sideways glances from military and civilian staff. Jack barely noticed. His mind felt cloudy and he was struggling to process how Anna was back in his life after screwing him over so heartily.

She appeared to have landed on her feet, in her job, back home. While he had no proof, he was certain she was behind the death of Zed Eshkol. It was also very likely she was the one who'd found out about the location of the bombs and the Zionist plot to launch the missiles aboard HMS *Vigilant*. Swings and roundabouts. It made sense now, but he felt it would have been nice of McGhinnist or the NSC to tell him the whole story.

"We're here." Anna stopped outside an office, which had no sign or nameplate on the door she knocked on.

"What's the story?" Jack's eyes narrowed, searching her face for an indication of what she was up to. He didn't like being in the dark.

The door opened and two men stepped into the hallway. One of them, in a simple black suit, spoke to Anna. "This them?"

Anna took a small step back. "Jack Emery, sirs, along with Chen Shubian and a half-dozen Navy SEAL troops waiting outside."

"Mr. Emery, good to meet you. Your exploits have made for very interesting reading over the years." A British naval officer with a fruit salad worth of medals on his chest held out his hand. "Shame it's not under better circumstances, but we're glad you're here."

Jack shook the other man's hand. "Nice to meet you, Mr ..."

"Admiral Duncan Fraser, First Sea Lord and Chief of the Naval Staff." Fraser gestured toward his suited companion. "And this is Director Cunningham, MI6."

"Good to meet you, gentlemen." Jack shook Cunningham's hand. "This is Chen, my advisor."

"Advisor? Okay. Let's go with that." Cunningham raised an eyebrow and gave a slight smirk, showing he knew some of Chen's past. "We should get to work."

Jack nodded and followed them into a deceptively large office, where the five of them took seats on the large sofas inside. The UK Ambassador to the United States had ensured McGhinnist that Jack would have all necessary briefings and information once he arrived in London. Here, he'd find out exactly what was at stake over the next seventy-two hours. And how to stop it. Both governments were united in their effort to stop the Zionists, despite the moles in their ranks.

Cunningham spoke first. "As you know, Mr. Emery, we've got a missing ballistic missile submarine – HMS *Vigilant* – with a rogue commander aboard. Our fears were confirmed thanks to Ms. Fowler's efforts on US soil. This has potentially catastrophic ramifications."

Jack decided to leave the topic of Anna's actions to his superiors. Spy games between friendly powers wasn't the major issue here. "The ambassador wasn't clear about how the boat could launch in the absence of a clear, verified order. I was speaking to some of the SEALs, and US subs can't—"

"Britain isn't America." Fraser's voice was sharp. "Not all of our launch protocols are the same."

Jack shrugged. "Okay, explain it to me then. How can the submarine fire off a few nukes without an order to do so?"

Fraser let out a long breath and then leaned forward. "Your escorts were right about one aspect of a launch: under normal circumstances a British nuclear launch is as restricted as an American one. An order must be sent from the Prime Minister down through the chain of command to the sub, verified at each step along the way."

"It feels like there's a 'but' at the end of that."

Fraser nodded. "British ballistic missile submarines have a secondary safe, inside the safe holding the usual launch codes. Inside that safe is what's called a Dead Man Letter. These letters are written by the Prime Minister and personally addressed to the submarine's captain."

"This sounds ominous." Jack sighed.

"The letter contains orders for what action the captain should take in the event that Britain is attacked and command structures compromised."

"So it's like one giant dead man switch, then?" Jack scoffed. "No offence, but that sounds mad."

"Exactly." Cunningham ran a hand through his hair. "Revenge from beyond the grave. Not all that far removed from the Israeli Samson Option that's plaguing us."

"So how does this apply here? Unless the Zionists have turned the Prime Minister, or they have the capability to flatten Britain, there's no way to trigger either a launch order or the Dead Man Letter. If the captain tries to do it in the absence of an order, his crew will see right through him." Jack paused. "Right?"

"Not quite, and what I'm about to tell you has never been shared with a non-British citizen." Cunningham glanced at Chen and then back to Jack. "Despite my better judgment, I've been instructed to do so here. But this information is highly classified, as is your role in what's to come. Understood?"

Jack nodded and then looked left at Chen, who did the same. "Consider the riot act read."

Cunningham nodded. "Okay. Associated with the Dead Man Letters are a set of conditions that act as a test for our submarine captains, to tell them whether or not Britain is still intact. If all of those conditions are tested by the captain, and each fails, then he's to open the safe and the letter and proceed as ordered."

Jack's eyes widened. He couldn't quite believe that a king-sized salvo of nukes could be launched from a British sub by reading a letter. But, as Cunningham spoke, it became clear that the conditions for such a launch were quite specific. Cunningham detailed each, but Jack was unable to make notes or do anything but memorize them. The more Cunningham spoke, the more daunting a challenge was painted in Jack's head. Finally, the MI6 boss fell silent.

"It's clear that, in the absence of a launch order from the Prime Minister, the Zionists are going to create the preconditions for a launch using Cohen's Dead Man Letter." Jack looked from Fraser to Cunningham to Chen to Anna. "Do we know what the letter says?"

"Yes, we do." Fraser smiled sadly. "Turns out the lady we have isn't for turning, as it were. The Prime Minister has informed us that the letter orders a launch."

Jack sighed. "So we need to fight like hell to defend a few of those things and stop the letter from being opened."

Cunningham smiled. "Our thoughts exactly. Unfortunately, several targets have already been assaulted by Zionist attackers."

Jack frowned. "How did we not know about—"

"The British secret services still have much to be proud of." Cunningham waved a hand. "I suggest we focus on those targets that remain to be protected."

Cunningham spent thirty minutes detailing nearly a dozen targets that the Zionists would need to hit in order to make a Dead Man Letter launch viable. Some had already been hit, but only one needed to still be standing in seventy-two hours to deny Cohen the conditions he needed to open that safe, convince his crew and launch his missiles. The task was daunting, but Jack thought a country like Britain, with all its resources, should be able to pull it off.

"Why not just drop a battalion on top of each target? Put so many guns between the Zionists and their targets, it's impossible?"

Fraser shrugged. "Several targets have already been attacked by Zionist hit teams. Others have been hit by those who were supposed to be guarding them – friendly fire. We're doing our best to pick out any Zionist weeds from our security apparatus, but we're not sure who we can trust. We've found dozens already."

Jack whistled slowly as his mind processed the new information. He'd underestimated the extent of the Zionist penetration, particularly given they'd turned Tipping and a nuclear submarine captain, but the prospect of not being able to deploy armies or police forces because of that infiltration was terrifying. It was no surprise that the British had asked for America's help – there was no other way they could guarantee full coverage of the targets by friendly forces.

"So if we can't guarantee that the good guys are good guys, how can we defend the targets needed to activate the Dead Man Letters?"

"Pick two or three and focus on those." Chen spoke for the first time. "Against a capable infiltrator, if you try to protect all of them, you'll end up protecting none."

Cunningham and Fraser smiled at each other, then the admiral spoke. "Our thoughts exactly. We will deploy trusted assets at as many sites as we can, knowing that they could fall to direct Zionist assault or friendly infiltration. If we can keep a few standing, we'll win."

Cunningham smiled, then turned to the others. "On the most vital targets I intend to use you three, your SEAL team and the most reliable MI6 agents I have."

Jack turned and stared at Chen, who nodded, then turned back to the Britons. "Makes sense to me."

"All the other targets are expendable if we focus on three." Cunningham held up three fingers. "Our focus must be, firstly, protecting BBC Radio 4. Its longwave broadcasts are one of the preconditions required to open the letter. Second, we protect the Prime Minister, whose death or incapacitation is another."

"And third?" Jack raised an eyebrow.

Fraser smiled. "The Prime Minister's designated second."

"Who would that be?"

"Classified." Cunningham's voice was matter of fact.

Jack laughed. "Nice to know you'll use us, but won't fully trust us."

Fraser was completely deadpan. "We're British, Mr. Emery. We don't trust anyone. You wouldn't be in this room at all if the situation weren't so dire, but we need your help. Unfortunately, at this moment, for protecting these targets, I trust my own countrymen even less."

"Where to now, then?" Jack felt everything was getting a bit too heavy. "Any idea where they'll hit first?"

Fraser's eyes bored into him. "You'll head to the BBC shortly, once we finish your briefing. We hope the PM's security is enough, and her second isn't known."

"Like it or not, Jack." Anna placed a hand on his knee. "You and I may well be the last line of defense."

ARON GRUNTED at the strain of lifting the heavy toolbox out of the back of the utility, then turned to face the rest of his team. The ten of them were all dressed in coveralls and had a variety of tools, bags and toolboxes in their hands. They looked like a very large maintenance team. Miri Shaked was the only one he knew well, but Zed Eshkol had hand selected the others for this job, which was good enough for Aron.

"You look good in a uniform." Miri smiled. "I think you missed your calling in life, Aron."

Aron laughed. "I much prefer the line of work I'm in. There's more chance to see the world."

"For another few days, anyway." Miri turned to Broadcasting House. "Let's get going?"

Aron nodded and gestured for the others to follow. They fell in behind him, leaving their three utilities parked on All Souls' Place, and crossed the street to the entrance of Broadcasting House. As he walked, Aron noted the number of heavily armed police outside the building, hoping again that Zed had selected the right crew. Though the attack on the BBC required precision rather than brute force, he'd still prefer to have talented people along if things went poorly.

As he walked deeper inside the horseshoe-shaped grounds, Aron smiled at the old sandstone architecture that was mixed with modern steel and glass. As they drew closer to the entrance, one police officer stepped forward while several of his colleagues half-raised their submachine guns toward Aron and his team. Aron held up a hand. The entire team stopped and waited for the police to act.

"Hold it there." The lead officer stopped squarely in front of them. "I'll need to see identification and a work order."

Aron placed his toolbox on the ground. "Something wrong, officer? The administration booked us for this job a month ago."

"Precautions." The officer gestured at all of the contractors. "Must be a big job you guys are doing?"

"You could say that." Aron made a show of digging around in the pockets of his coveralls. He pulled out his wallet and some sheets of paper he'd folded up and handed them to the officer. As he did, the other members of the team dug out their identification.

"Okay, we'll just be a minute." The officer turned and walked back to his colleagues.

Aron waited, a little nervously, as several police officers checked the orders and the identification. The officer who'd taken their papers used his radio, no doubt checking the legitimacy of the work order and the identification of the contractors. While he was confident that it would all check out, Aron never liked jobs that were quite so public, because all it took was one mistake for the bullets to start flying.

Not today, though. The officer walked over to them and handed back the identification and the work orders. "Everything checks out."

Aron smiled as he found his fake identification and pocketed it, along with the work orders. "Lot of you guys here today. Security drill?"

"If only." The officer didn't share the humor. "I'll leave you all to it, you're free to enter. Have a good day and please keep to your designated areas."

Aron nodded, lifted the toolbox and resumed his walk. Once they were inside the lobby, it became clear that the majority of the extra security was outside – a very public show of force. While Eshkol's selection of the BBC as a target was somewhat confusing, Aron didn't question it. It was clear that British authorities were beefing up security at key sites in London. That changed nothing. He had intelligence from other moles and the team to get the job done.

They made their way through the lobby and into a relatively quiet hallway. Aron placed his toolbox on the ground for the last time. He opened it and pulled out the pair of machine pistols inside, then looked around to make sure the rest of his team were preparing themselves. Each of them had armed themselves with whatever small firearm they preferred. In addition, Aron spotted blades, grenades and explosives. They all pulled on balaclavas, then gathered tightly.

"Everyone ready?" Aron hefted the machine pistols and was answered by a set of nods. "We meet back at the utilities in ten minutes. Let's go."

The team split off into pairs. Two went to guard the front entrance. Another pair went to kill the alarms. The remaining groups prepared for the assault. Aron jogged toward his assigned target with Miri right behind him. They were there within moments, passing only a few shocked staff members along the way. Apart from squealing, the BBC employees hugged the walls and did nothing to stop them as they passed.

He paused near a door and looked at Miri, who lifted her pistol and gave a nod. Aron pushed the door open and entered the room, firing a couple of shots into the air from each of his machine pistols. The effect was instantaneous. Staff looked up from their desks and meeting tables, shock and fear painted on their faces, then either ran away or cowered in corners or under their desks. It didn't matter to Aron which they chose, the end result was inevitable.

He mowed down every member of the radio production staff he could find. The machine pistol in his left hand found a young blond woman. The one in his right found an older man. Left and right. Some ran, others cowered. He didn't worry about those who he'd missed, because Miri picked each off with a single shot before they could escape the room. It was over in less than a minute. The room fell silent and no alarms rang out.

"Take care of this equipment?" Aron turned to Miri as he reloaded both of his pistols in turn. "I'll take care of the studio."

Aron turned and walked to the end of the floor, where a closed door had an on air sign lit brightly above it. He pushed the door open and kept his machine pistol raised as he walked inside. The studio was dimly lit, but he could see one man cowering under the desk in the room. Aron fired a long burst toward him, then stepped inside and placed one of his pistols down on the desk as he dug the explosives out of the pockets of his coveralls.

As he placed the bombs on the equipment, he absentmindedly looked around the studio. It was hard to understand why Eshkol wanted this target flattened as part of his contingency plan, but it had proven easier than Aron had expected. The other members of his team who'd paired off were similarly gunning down key staff and destroying equipment. At the end of the raid, the intent was to take BBC Radio 4 off the air.

He placed two charges at opposite sides of the room, then left the studio. Back in the office spaces, Miri had finished her demolition job on other equipment and was waiting for him. He checked his watch – seven minutes down – then pointed at the door they'd entered through. She nodded and they walked together into the hall and back to the lobby. As they drew closer, Aron could hear gunfire – probably the police trying to force their way into the building.

He paused near the end of the hallway that led into the lobby. He tossed his machine pistols into the trash and then did the same with his balaclava. A quick check of his pockets showed that he had nothing incriminating left. When Miri had done the same, he held up a hand and they waited in silence. After a few moments, the gunfire ceased, only screams and piercing cries of fear and warning able to be heard.

He looked at his watch – ten minutes. "Time to go."

"Do it." Miri's voice was hard.

They ran out of the hallway and into the lobby, where a stream of civilians were rushing toward police, who shouted at them to freeze and put up their hands. Aron raised his hands high and stayed in the middle of the pack streaming toward the exit. The police had a choice – get out of the way or start shooting – and they chose the predictable path. They stepped aside and let the civilians move past them, out of the lobby and into the streets.

Aron spotted the police officer who'd let them in – his face was cut. He stopped next to the man. "What's going on?"

The officer glanced at Aron but didn't really look at him, his eyes scanning for threats as he gripped his submachine gun. "Terrorists. Get out of here."

Aron smiled slightly and nodded. He didn't look back as he made his way out of Broadcasting House and toward the utilities. Miri was alongside him and he could see another pair already at the vehicles. With some luck, there would only be a few lives lost among his team. But whatever the result, there wouldn't be much time to rest, because the assault on the next target was scheduled for tomorrow.

Mentally, he checked one more item off Zed Eshkol's list. He didn't envy the British authorities trying to figure it all out.

JACK WALKED BEHIND ANNA, Chen and the Navy SEALs as they approached Broadcasting House, which was surrounded by armed police and vehicles with flashing lights and blaring sirens. The BBC headquarters had been attacked while he'd been in briefings. On the way over, the radio reports had been bleak – many were dead and critical equipment had been destroyed. The minute they'd seen the building, Jack had known it was too late.

"This is pointless." Jack gestured to the building, where police officers were doing their best to manage the throng of civilians that milled outside and the rush of emergency services in and out. "We need to move on to protecting the next target."

"Hold up." Anna placed an arm on his shoulder. "We don't know the situation yet, we can't rush in. The Prime Minister is okay, for now, and the terrorists don't know who her second is. We need to find out what happened here before we move on. The information about this attack might be the key to stopping the next."

Jack pushed her arm away. "The BBC is done for as far as the Dead Man Letters are concerned, but we can still stop the next attack!"

"Be patient, Jack. You're panicking." Her eyes narrowed. She handed him the pistol she was carrying. "Take this, I've got another. We work out what happened here and then move out to defend the next target. That's how we're going to play this, okay?"

He nodded, but didn't like it. If he was in charge, they'd rush straight on to defend either the PM or her designated second, but Anna was the boss. He took the weapon. A few years ago, he'd have been horrified by the idea of handling it, but now it was a no-brainer. It felt good having some steel in his hand, and he hefted the weapon as one of the SEALs handed Chen a pistol. They kept moving until they reached the outer checkpoint.

"*Stop and drop the weapons!*" Several police officers manning the checkpoint aimed their weapons and shouted at Jack and his group. "*This area is restricted!*"

"Take it easy!" Jack screamed as loudly as he could, to be heard over the shouts of the police officers. "We're friendlies!"

The police continued to target them, while the SEALs pointed carbines right back. Jack cursed. Though they'd probably win a firefight, they didn't have time for this – with each passing second there was more chance of the Zionists attacking their next target. He lifted his pistol with his thumb through the trigger guard, and kept his palms pointed out. It did no good – the SEALs didn't back down and the police didn't budge.

Anna mimicked his actions and slowly stepped forward. "We're here under authorization of the director of MI6. Can I show you?"

Several of the officers hesitated and a couple of them looked at each other, until one waved Anna forward. Jack stood, frozen in place, watching her cross no-man's-land to talk to the police. He couldn't hear what was being said, but after a moment she dug into her pocket and flashed some identification. As if by magic, the police attention melted away – the cops lowered their weapons and waved Jack and the others forward.

Jack led the group into the lobby of Broadcasting House. It was chaos. Police were everywhere, paramedics treated the wounded, several bodies lay uncovered and the few BBC staff who hadn't been allowed to leave appeared to be in shock. Jack looked at Anna. She nodded and led him toward the largest bunch of people in the room – a group of two police and a handful of BBC staff. The SEALs fanned out to cover the room while Chen looked around.

"Anna Fowler, MI6." Anna flashed the ID again – probably a rare occurrence for a secret agent – then jerked a thumb at Jack. "This is Jack Emery."

The most senior of the police officers nodded at Anna, though his eyes narrowed at the presence of a British secret service agent. "DCI Fiskin."

"What's the situation?" Jack slid his pistol down the back of his jeans. "We're in a bit of a hurry."

Fiskin nodded. "We're still trying to figure that out, Mr. Emery, but around ten attackers shot up the staff and studios. We've contained the scene and two of the attackers are dead, but it's all a bit chaotic. There's been significant damage to the facility and we've no idea where the other gunmen went."

Anna frowned. "You didn't capture or kill the attackers? How did that happen, exactly?"

"A mistake from one of my officers." Fiskin shrugged. "He tried to save civilians by letting those inside evacuate, but it looks like he let the terrorists escape as well."

Jack cursed. "Any chance of—"

An officer interrupted Jack, running up to the group with an iPad in his hand. "DCI Fiskin, we've got the footage from the camera feed."

"Show us." Fiskin gestured for them to gather round the officer, who played the video.

The video feed showed several gunmen with balaclavas mowing down civilians indiscriminately. Man, woman, old, young – everyone received the same treatment. If Jack hadn't known the Zionist endgame in attacking the BBC – the eradication of the entire network, but particularly longwave Radio 4 broadcasts – it would look like an indiscriminate office massacre. Instead, it just looked like they'd been thorough.

"They weren't messing around." Jack ran a hand through his hair. He'd worked in enough news rooms for all this to feel a bit too real. He thought of Celeste.

"Is the network compromised?" Anna looked up from the iPad. "Is the main broadcasting equipment intact?"

One of the BBC staff standing near Fiskin spoke up. "You're worried about the World Service? A hundred people just got killed!"

Jack glared at the man. "And a whole lot more will die if

you don't get on with it. What's the status of BBC radio, particularly the longwave?"

The man snarled, but Fiskin put a hand on his arm and the BBC employee took a deep breath. Once he'd composed himself, he spoke. "It's all down. The equipment is as dead as most of the people who know how to use it, not that you care about them."

Jack ignored the crack. "We need to get it back online. I know it sounds callous, but you can't comprehend how important this is."

The man shook his head and turned away from Jack. It was hard not to feel sorry for him, given he'd just had his workplace shot up and his colleagues killed, but there was no time for sentiment. With each passing minute the chances of the Zionists bringing down the list of targets required to activate the Dead Man Letters increased. The minute that happened, there would be nothing that could be done to prevent a launch. They'd witness the end of the world.

Anna sighed, stepped forward and placed a hand on the man's shoulder. "What are the chances?"

"Of getting back online now?" The man shrugged off her touch and had tears streaking down his cheeks as he turned to face them. "None. We'll be lucky if we're up in a week. I don't think any of you understand the damage they've caused here."

She took half a step back. "Can we get the longwave signal up again?"

"No."

The longwave BBC Radio 4 signal was one of the checks British submarine captains went through to determine whether British society had been annihilated. If the signal was down, and Joseph Cohen did the check, he was one step closer to being able to crack open the safe and use the Dead

Man Letter. Cunningham, Fraser, Anna, Chen and Jack had agreed to focus on preventing three of the preconditions from being met and, less than an hour later, one had already fallen.

"We're wasting our time here, Anna." Jack exhaled deeply. "We need to focus on the other two."

She nodded and then addressed DCI Fiskin and his colleagues. "Thanks for your time and good luck with the clean-up."

Jack stepped to the side and waited for her to join him. He spoke as firmly as he could. "I know the PM is the next target we're meant to be protecting, but I need to know the third. We can't act if we're not on the same page, and I'm out of the loop here."

She frowned. "Fraser and Cunningham swore me to secrecy, Jack. Nobody else in the entire United Kingdom besides the PM, the four captains, Cunningham, Fraser and I know who it is. I thought we'd deal with it if and when something happened to the PM."

"I need the name, Anna." Jack crossed his arms. He wasn't taking no for an answer. "The Prime Minister has a shit-ton of protection around her, I'm sure. If the attack against her succeeds, it will be in spite of anything we can do to help. But we can help to protect her second, if you let us."

Anna's eyes bored into him, then she nodded. She pulled a cell phone from her pocket, dialed and lifted it to her ear. In muted tones, she spoke about orders and about how much she could tell Jack. He assumed it was Cunningham on the other end, and the uptight director of MI6 was doing his best to stonewall her, until right at the end of the call she cursed loudly and hung up. She closed her eyes and took a deep breath.

"What's wrong?"

"Two more targets hit by traitors. We're running out of

parachutes on this one, Jack." She shook her head. "Cunningham authorized me to tell you."

"Tell me what?"

"It's Patrick Ho. The PM's second is the Minister of State for Employment. We're to protect him at all costs."

18

With potential nuclear catastrophe just a few days away, the attack on Broadcasting House has tipped the United Kingdom into outright panic. The Zionists have claimed responsibility for this and other attacks, though their motive is unclear. Added to this are reports of Zionist moles being uncovered throughout the government, causing havoc. In response to the attacks and nuclear threat, Britain has raised its threat level to Critical. Prime Minister Katherine Huxley has called for Britons and the world to remain resolute in the face of tyranny.

New York Standard

Jack handed the binoculars to Anna. "Seems quiet. Want to take a look?"

She nodded and used the binoculars to scan their surroundings – the front of the building, its visible windows, the surrounding rooftops and the street below – then lowered them, apparently satisfied that things were safe. Jack was glad he hadn't missed anything, but she was a professional with years of experience. As Anna placed the binoculars on the ground beside him and rubbed her eyes, he wondered how many times she'd been the one trying to crack security just like this during her time in MI6.

Jack didn't know how cops did this for a living, because every minute felt like torture. Cunningham and Fraser had been adamant: the Minister for Employment couldn't be told about the threat unless it was absolutely necessary. Instead, Jack and Anna had been camped out since the previous evening, watching his office for any signs of danger. The SEAL team were similarly placed and a few trustworthy MI6 assets had also covered the minister's home. Minister Ho was wrapped tight in a security blanket he didn't know existed.

While they'd waited, cooling their heels and protecting the minister, other Zionist targets had fallen. Though the PM and Minister Ho were safe, a mix of armed assaults and infiltrations had steadily shrunk the safety net underneath the tightrope they were walking on. Each time Anna received a notification, her anger seemed to increase slightly, along with Jack's determination. He'd realized quickly that Fraser and Cunningham had been right to fear the extent of Zionist infiltration of Britain. He was feeling paranoid himself.

"You alright?" Jack studied Anna's face and saw deep bags under her eyes.

She took a sip of the coffee and winced. "Cold."

"It was cold an hour ago." He laughed. "You should rest."

"I'll rest when the world survives the greatest threat to its existence since the Cuban Missile Crisis." She took a second sip of the coffee, obviously deciding caffeine was more important than taste or temperature. "We fucked up, letting them hit the BBC."

Jack nodded. The result of the attack had been

immediate. All BBC radio broadcasts had been affected and the likelihood of them returning before deadline were slim. Even though other assets were covering other likely Zionist targets, Cunningham had placed the only people he could fully trust in one place – protecting Minister Ho. It was a gutsy call, but Jack figured Cunningham was used to those. He wondered if he'd have made the same decisions as McGhinnist, Huxley, Schiller and others along the way, but parked the thought.

"He's pulling up." Anna edged closer to the window. "I can see the chase car, no sign of a threat, all looking good."

"Fingers crossed it stays that way." Jack glanced out the window to see the minister's sedan pulling to a stop in front of his office building.

The radio on the floor next to Anna and Jack crackled. *"This is Defender Four. The package is on site. Over."*

Anna picked up the radio. "Confirmed Defender Four, we'll take it from here. Over."

Jack watched as the black sedan that had been trailing the minister's SUV kept driving, even as the minister started to climb out of his vehicle. It seemed a stupid risk not to squirrel him away somewhere to protect him from the Zionists, or at least tell the minister that his life was in danger, but the orders had been clear. Jack caressed the pistol Anna had given him back at the BBC studios and had made no effort to reclaim. If things got hairy here, there'd be nobody but him, Chen, Anna and a team of SEALs to protect the minister.

"Is it possible the Zionists don't know who the Prime Minister's designated second is?" Jack turned from watching the car and raised his eyebrows at Anna.

"Possible, sure." She shrugged her shoulders. "But they've shown a knack for kicking us in the teeth, so I'm not banking on it."

"Let's make a bet?" Jack smiled. "If we get out of this and the entire world isn't irradiated, I'll buy you a beer."

"Are you good for it?" She laughed. "I wouldn't want to—"

Jack instinctively turned his head and shielded his eyes as the world in front of him exploded in light and fire. The flash was followed by a terrible boom and sudden pain as the shattered window cut into his arms. He dropped to his hands and knees, his ears ringing and his lungs on fire. He coughed several times, but couldn't expel the dust and the other debris. He shook his head and tried to clear it, then glanced at Anna. She fumbled with the radio and Jack watched her speak into it but, strangely, couldn't hear what she was saying.

He crawled to the windowsill, which he gripped and used to pull himself up. As he did, the ringing in his ears slowly subsided. Once his eyes were level with the window he stared, mouth wide open, at the scene on the street below. Where the minister's car had been there was now just a blackened, flaming metal husk. The street was filled with smoke and victims splayed on the ground, while those who could still move ran from the scene. His eyes scanned the area for the minister, but Jack couldn't see him.

Anna gripped his shoulder and shouted close to his ear. "Grab your gun, Jack, we need to get down there."

He nodded and searched for the pistol, which he'd dropped as he'd gone down. He found it and then looked at her. "I'm ready."

"One more thing." She tore at her white blouse, which was stained and grimy from the explosion. She grabbed hold of his arm. "Hold still."

"Okay."

She wrapped a strip of cloth around the cuts on his arm, pulled it tight and then tied it. "It's only a temporary solution, but it'll do. Let's go."

He gripped the pistol as he followed her out of the stakeout and down the fire stairs. He pulled up short at the emergency exit, where Anna had paused to look at him. She raised an eyebrow, as if asking if he was ready, and Jack nodded. The door opened with a tortured squeal and Jack followed Anna out, down the lane and onto the main street. It was chaos. Flames licked the carcass of the minister's vehicle and debris was scattered throughout the street.

"Defender Actual is heading for the minister." Anna spoke into the radio in her hand as she ran, holding the pistol in the other.

"Defender One, no hostiles."

"Defender Two, we got nothing."

"Defender Three, nothing."

"Copy." She clipped the radio onto her belt, gripped her pistol with both hands and kept moving forward, a look of grim determination on her face.

Jack and Anna crossed the street and rounded the minister's vehicle, which continued to burn. Jack wanted to know how the Zionists had rigged the bomb in the minister's car, but it was moot now. Ho was face down on the pavement twenty feet from his vehicle, bloodied and unmoving. A couple of other casualties from the blast were scattered about, but there was no time to worry about anyone other than the minister – the world depended on it.

"I'll check him out." Jack pointed at the minister and then glanced at Anna. "You work on getting us some help."

"On it." She turned away from Jack, talking into her radio but never lowering her pistol.

Jack crouched beside Minister Ho, placing the pistol on the pavement beside the downed man. He gripped the other man's wrist and exhaled deeply when he felt a strong, steady pulse. Jack rolled the minister over, opened his suit jacket and felt around for any major wounds caused by shrapnel from the exploding vehicle. Thankfully, despite the blood, the wounds appeared minor. Ho had been knocked unconscious by the blast but was otherwise remarkably lucky.

"How is he?" Anna slid down alongside Jack. "Is he alive?"

"Fine, as far as I can tell." Jack looked sideways at her. "We need to move."

"Support is two minutes out and your SEALs are converging on our posit—"

"Who are you people?"

Jack's eyes darted back to the minister, who was blinking quickly and looking back and forth between him and Anna. "Minister, you're okay."

Anna leaned in closer. "Your vehicle exploded, sir. We've secured the scene and we're working to get you out of here."

"Oh, I understand."

Jack wasn't sure the minister could comprehend anything right now, judging from the look in his eyes. "Just relax, sir."

Jack could hear the hint of sirens off into the distance. He looked at Anna, who nodded. Help was on the way. They smiled at each other. Both knew that as long as either the PM or the Minister for Employment was alive and in contact, then all the terrorist attacks in the world couldn't get HMS *Vigilant* to launch its payload. As it was, he doubted they'd manage to get another bomb this close to Minister Ho, meaning that the Zionists had given the launch their best shot and failed. It had been a close call, but Jack felt like they'd caught a break.

And without that launch, the Zionist plot couldn't succeed, no matter how much chaos they caused in Britain.

~

Aron looked down at his watch and then up at his team. "Any moment now. Make sure you're ready. We'll only have a small window."

He was met with nods and grim faces as his six men and Miri went to work, checking their weapons and body armor. He looked down at his own weapon, a carbine far larger than the machine pistols he preferred. As he checked the weapon, he was glad for the distraction. It helped to keep his mind off the fact that this was most likely a one-way mission for all of them – a Hail Mary pass that had almost no chance of success but had to be thrown if they were going to win the game. Aron didn't know the reason, but the order was enough.

"Everyone is ready, Aron." Miri seemed to read his mind, but spoke softly enough that only the two of them could hear. "Trust in Eshkol, in us and yourself."

He looked at her and searched her eyes for doubt, but found none. He cursed himself for his weakness. Before he'd met Zed Eshkol, Aron would have found fanciful the idea that a small team on foot could assassinate the British Prime Minister, but he had to trust in the professor. Aron swallowed hard and warded off the negative thoughts. Eshkol knew what he was doing and Aron's team would succeed. They had to. To come this far and then fail was not a possibility he was prepared to entertain.

After the attack on Broadcasting House, they'd driven away in their utilities and then dumped them after less than five minutes on the road. They'd gone to ground in a nearby apartment building, where they'd cleaned up and rested in preparation for another attack. The apartment had been long readied for this purpose, less than a five-minute walk to Downing Street and packed full of guns and ammo. It was the perfect staging post for an attack on the Prime Minister of the United Kingdom.

It had one other thing of immense value. Aron gripped

his gun and crossed the room to where a number of desktop PCs displayed feeds from webcams placed around the city. He leaned in to look and a smile broke out across his face as he watched a portion of the extra security forces around Downing Street rush away. It had all gone perfectly – a bomb timed to injure but not kill the Minister for Employment, stripping enough security away from the Prime Minister to let Aron and his team do what needed doing.

Aron smiled wider. "They're not sure who they can trust, so there's only a handful of men and women they can throw at problems."

"That's the problem when everything you know has been infiltrated and compromised." Miri laughed. "Zed has played it well."

"Time to go." He lifted his carbine again and turned to his team. "I don't know why Eshkol wants these two dead so badly, but it's not our job to ask why."

"We're ready, Aron." Miri touched his arm. "We'll take out Huxley and then deal with the Minister for Employment."

Aron nodded and led his team downstairs, where black sedans were idling with additional Zionists, fresh from other jobs, at the wheel. They drove in silence to Downing Street. Less than half a mile from the target, Aron gripped the overhead handle with one hand and his carbine with the other, shocked that they'd been able to get this close without being intercepted. He looked at his watch one last time, then lowered the gas mask resting on his head over his face.

As the sedans skidded to a halt next to a large yellow bulldozer, Aron nodded at Miri then opened the door and led his team out of their ride. Those in the other sedan did likewise, and shouts and gunfire started to boom out from the remaining defenders of Downing Street as the Zionists made for safety behind the construction vehicle. The minute he was joined behind the slab of steel by the rest of his team, Aron readied the underslung grenade launcher on his carbine.

"Launch tear gas." Aron spoke softly into his voice-activated headset. "And get the 'dozer moving."

Aron looked around. As the large bulldozer's engine turned over and started, Aron lifted his carbine and joined his team in lobbing gas canisters over the steel security fence blocking them from Downing Street. Each round launched with a *thunk*, exploded with a pop and hissed as they released the gas inside. The team had fired several dozen canisters inside of thirty seconds and when Aron peeked around the bulldozer he could see little but the gas.

The bulldozer's engine roared and the vehicle rolled forward. Already Aron could hear the rattle of gunfire and the hail-on-the-roof pinging of rounds against the bulldozer's scoop. Aron and the other Zionists advanced behind the giant slab of steel, unable to see anything past the bucket, but the crude cover worked to get them right to the gate. The bulldozer hit the fence with a crunch, which gave a sickening squeal as it strained against the force.

As the bulldozer shifted up a gear and pushed harder against the fence, Aron turned his attention to the defenders. It was a slaughter. Gunfire roared from his team as police and other security forces staggered in the street and were cut down. Aron wondered if the attack on the Minister for Employment had even been necessary. With such a brute display of force, it was possible that this would have worked without the ruse.

The gate groaned one final time, crashing against the road as the bulldozer came to a stop and the driver killed the engine. Aron peeked around it as silence fell in the street. Nothing moved except for the final wisps of dissipating tear gas. He grinned like a hyena as he reached up, removed his gas mask and tossed it to the ground. His team did likewise and started to advance, weapons raised, toward the famed tenth house on this very special street.

The team rushed the short distance between the gate and the Prime Minister's residence in a few seconds, then paired off and covered Miri as she moved to the door. Aron half expected another threat to emerge – snipers or reinforcements – but all was calm until he heard two dull thumps as the shaped charges did their work. He turned to face the door. It was wide open and Miri was standing next to it.

"Miri, Vadim, Abram – with me." Aron ejected the magazine from his weapon and reloaded. "The rest of you, cover our rear."

As those left outside took up defensive positions, Aron looked at his watch and led the smaller team inside with his carbine raised. They rushed through the house quicker than he'd like, but the clock was ticking. He fired a quick burst at one defender – dropping him – and Miri dropped two targets before they reached the back of the house. Aron breathed a sigh of relief when he saw British Prime Minister Katherine Huxley standing with her hands held out, showing no threat.

"Ms. Prime Minister." Aron halted a few steps away from her.

"Just who the hell are you?" Huxley hissed at them.

"It doesn't matter." Aron raised his carbine and pointed it at Huxley's chest.

"Britain doesn't negotiate with terrorists." Huxley nearly spat the words.

"Oh, I don't want to negotiate." Aron laughed. "I just want you dead."

"I—"

Aron squeezed the trigger of his carbine. The weapon chattered as it delivered a three-round burst into the Prime

Minister's chest, a process repeated by his colleagues. Huxley's body toppled to the ground. A pool of blood was already forming and Aron could smell the stench of death – evacuated bowels – but he had to be sure. He took a step closer and fired a single round into her head.

"Time to go." Aron started toward the entrance as he looked down at his watch. "We're thirty seconds behind schedule."

He ran to the front of the house as quickly as he could while still being alert for any threat. Once outside, he was relieved to see the helicopters already grounded and half of his team already onboard. He rushed toward the second chopper and was the last inside after Miri. He slid the door shut and the pilot didn't waste one second in taking off. Less than a minute after they'd killed the PM, they were in the air.

Miri smiled at him and gave him a quizzical look. He knew instinctively what she was asking – whether it was safe to fly above London, having just killed the British PM. He nodded back to her, gave a thumbs-up and then turned away. Even if the Royal Air Force was zooming around in the sky, Aron was confident that Zed Eshkol had taken care of it. He had students – assets – everywhere and had proven to be in control.

Aron knew, whatever the final plan, it would succeed.

JACK'S EYES shot open and he sat up in a flash, looking for the source of the loud bang that had woken him from the deepest sleep he'd had in days. He slowly let out the breath he'd sucked in as he turned his head to stare at Anna Fowler. She had her head in her hands and was visibly shaking. He sighed and rubbed his eyes, then glanced down at the phone she'd tossed onto the floor of the vehicle. It was still lit up brightly as he leaned down and picked it up.

"Sorry." She opened her eyes and looked at him, then reached up and ran a hand over her face as she looked away. "Didn't realize you were asleep."

"What's wrong?" He held the phone out to her, but she wasn't watching him. "Anna? Is something wrong?"

"Cunningham just called." Anna turned and stared at the phone, then snatched it from him. "The Prime Minister is dead."

Jack's head spun with the news. They'd left the Minister for Employment's office building in a small convoy of vehicles and made their way straight out of London. Anna had coordinated it all, making sure the minister was well guarded for the drive and that nothing got in their way. Now they were speeding through the Welsh countryside, making their way to an abandoned manor kept off books by MI6.

It was incomprehensible to Jack that the Prime Minister, with all of her protection, could have been killed. That changed the game and significantly increased the danger their little convoy was in, given Ho was now the only thing standing in the way of the Zionist threat to let the nukes fly. The decision by Cunningham, Fraser, Jack and Anna to focus on protecting only three targets had backfired.

"When?" He shook his head. "How did it happen?"

"Less than an hour ago. We pulled security from Downing Street to help protect the minister after the bomb." Anna sighed. "And the Zionists kicked us in the teeth."

"There wasn't enough to go around?" In the States, there would have been enough friendlies with guns to protect the President three times over.

She shrugged. "We can count on a very limited number

of hands the amount of people we trust totally right now. Cohen's treachery has shocked the system."

Jack started to speak, then paused. It made so much sense. "If that's the case, why don't we just get more US boots on the ground to help protect the minister? We can surround the house with so much firepower that an army couldn't get through. All it will take is a phone call."

Anna shook her head. "I floated the idea, but Cunningham is as worried about US forces as he is about British ones. Our best chance, with the restrictions, is to keep everyone a mile away from Ho except those people already in this convoy. That means secrecy."

Jack turned and stared out the window, tapping his leg as he thought. Though the isolated location and the limited size of their convoy should have been enough to protect the minister, it all felt a bit tenuous. Eshkol had been one step ahead of them, and now Jack felt the caress of the professor from beyond the grave – a chill down his spine, a churn in his stomach. It felt impossible to believe that by hiding in the Welsh countryside it would all be over.

He made a decision. He dug into his pocket and dialed a number he knew by heart. It rang, over and over, until finally the line connected.

"Mr. President, it's Jack."

"Jack." There was a heavy dose of sleep in McGhinnist's voice. "How are you? What's the situation?"

"Prime Minister Huxley is dead."

"What?" McGhinnist suddenly sounded as if he had a drip line of black coffee hooked up to wake him. "How do you know this and we don't?"

Jack removed the phone from his ear and pressed the speaker button. "You're on speaker with Anna Fowler and I. There's another MI6 agent driving."

"Mr. President." Anna spoke close to the phone. "Wish we were speaking on better terms."

"Ms. Fowler." McGhinnist's voice was cold. "Tell me what's going on and why I don't know about it."

"The one and only, sir." Anna smiled darkly. "The Prime Minister was assassinated less than an hour ago by the Zionists. It'll hit the news any minute."

"Fucking hell." McGhinnist paused. "What's the situation?"

Jack leaned in to the phone. "We're one dead minister away from doom, sir."

"What support do you need, Jack? Name it."

Jack exhaled deeply. He wanted the next words he said to be a request for additional special forces troops, helicopters, warplanes and armored vehicles. He wanted a twenty-mile exclusion zone around the house they were nearing and satellites covering every inch of it. Finally, he wanted US missiles ready at a moment's notice to flatten anything that was spotted moving inside that exclusion zone. But he didn't ask for any of that.

One glance at Anna told him the only possible answer. The Zionists had so effectively infiltrated the British and US governments that nobody could guarantee any help would be worth the risk of exposure. Eshkol's network had everyone jumping at shadows, afraid of their own people and doubting plans designed to prevent attacks like the very ones they'd been facing. Jack couldn't risk asking the President for anything and revealing their location.

"Nothing, sir." Jack paused. "We're going off grid."

McGhinnist scoffed. "I've got armies on speed dial, you guys know?"

"We know." Jack and Anna spoke at the same time, but Jack kept speaking. "But the Zionists have played our security like a fiddle and we don't know who, or what assets, are compromised. We need secrecy and anonymity, not guns and heavy metal."

"Okay, Jack. I don't agree, but we'll go with your plan."

Jack smiled. "Thanks, Mr. President."

"Good luck. And let me know if you need support."

Jack turned to Anna as the line went dead. "There's not much I can do if you don't let me call in the cavalry."

She nodded. "We've done all we can, Jack. We just have to hope that they can't find us."

Jack crossed his arms and closed his eyes. He considered it highly unlikely that the attackers would be caught if they hadn't already been. The Zionist team had proven so immensely capable and a mile ahead of the British and American forces trying, desperately, to prevent nuclear disaster. That meant hiding was their only hope, but he wasn't sure that would work. As he drifted off to sleep, he wrapped his hand around the pistol resting on the seat beside him.

He hoped that in the next twenty-four hours, he wouldn't need it.

19

With less than a day until the peace agreement between Israel and the soon-to-be-created state of Palestine is enacted, there is no sign that either signatory nor the United States intends to blink in the face of Zionist threats. US and Saudi authorities have stressed that they're close to locating the backpack nuclear device that threatens Mecca, though precautionary evacuations of the area are well underway. A strange silence has descended over Mecca as its doom approaches.

New York Standard

J ack cursed as his finger started to bleed, the fingernail bitten down so far it had started to seep at the edge. He sucked the blood as he glanced at his watch. The turn of the hour approached and, with it, the threat of an Iranian nuclear launch that would render all the blood and effort over the past few days pointless. An attack by Iran on Israel was likely to set off a chain reaction of launches across the world, though at least a manor house in the Welsh countryside might be safe.

"What's wrong?" Anna stared at him from across the table. "You've been on edge for twenty minutes."

Jack had to lie. "Nothing. Just feel like this is the first time we've stopped to catch our breath in weeks."

She smiled wearily, heavy bags under her eyes and a hollow look on her face. "You get used to it. We're okay here, Jack."

They'd arrived at the house late the previous evening. Anna had been right – it was deserted for miles around and still in relatively good upkeep. The SEALs and MI6 agents had made their position more defensible, the minister had gone to sleep, and Jack and Anna had set up in the dining hall with their phones at the ready. He hadn't told her about the Iranian launch threats, but the constant glances at his watch and his cell phone had obviously made her suspicious.

A lot of experiences had combined to make Jack the man he was – a lot of conflict, a lot of danger and a lot of alcohol – but he'd never felt more afraid than the moment his watch ticked over to 10.01pm GMT. He picked up his phone and unlocked it, then scanned the NSC feed for any launch activity originating in Iran. There were a few items, but nothing that looked like what Jack feared. After a few minutes, he tossed the phone on the table, leaned back and closed his eyes.

Then the phone rang. His eyes shot open and he stared at the caller ID for a moment, then answered. "Mr. President?"

"We've found it, Jack. We've found the bomb in Mecca." McGhinnist's voice had never sounded so good. "The Saudis called a few moments ago to tell us."

Jack laughed for several moments. "Did the Iranians indicate if they were going to launch or not? If I had any impact by going there?"

"Best we never know." McGhinnist laughed. "Let's focus

on what matters. In two hours, we're through this. Stay safe and speak soon."

"Amen to that." Jack hung up the phone and tossed it on the table, where it rested next to the pistol he'd acquired from Anna.

"What was that about?"

"Oh, nothing." Jack smiled at her. "We just had a second potential nuclear disaster hanging over our heads. But don't worry, I sorted that one."

Anna's eyes narrowed and she looked like she might ask more, but she left it. "Well, I better make sure I take care of this one. I'd hate to owe you."

"I'll collect once this is all over." He smiled and closed his eyes. One disaster averted, one left to avoid, he felt himself starting to doze off.

His eyes shot open when he heard a popping sound. It was unmistakable – the chatter of automatic weapons fire. The chair he'd been sitting on fell back as he sprang to his feet, grabbed his phone and pistol and bolted toward the sound. He had no idea where Anna was, but he didn't care – there were six American special forces soldiers, a handful of MI6 agents and Chen standing between the attackers and the minister. He needed to help.

He ran down one of the four corridors, each of which had a pair of defenders posted at all times. They'd fortified the house as best they could, had eyes on all approaches and some excellent cover. On the downside, the defenders only had a mix of carbines and small arms, the Navy SEALs not having prepared for a full-blown defensive firefight. Their preparations were the best they could be with so few defenders. Secrecy had been their armor, which seemed to have failed them – another victim of Zionist infiltration of the British security services. Now, any sort of focused attack from any direction would stretch them. He reached the bedroom they were using as a defensive post and saw Chen and an MI6 agent on guard. They were crouched low, peering out windows with weapons ready.

"What's going on?" He slid down next to Chen and gripped the pistol tightly. "Are they here?"

"Yes." Chen glanced over his shoulder at Jack, then gestured at one of the windows. "Take that window."

Jack nodded and took up position. He glanced at his watch. 11.36pm GMT. "We hold for twenty-four minutes."

The others nodded and Jack turned his attention to the grounds outside the manor. A quick glance over the window frame showed Jack what he feared – complete darkness. But it was also met with a short burst of gunfire, which he heard slam into the stone on the outside of the house. Jack gripped the pistol and rested on his knees. After a deep breath, then another, Jack huffed and turned to peer over the window again, the pistol pointed out in front of him.

Automatic fire barked at him and in the dim light, Jack could see someone move in the distance. He squeezed the trigger, again and again, the pistol kicking slightly with each shot. No voices cried out in alarm or pain, so he'd probably hit dirt. He hesitated for just a second too long, and something ricocheted off the windowsill and cut into his cheek. Jack ducked down again and reached up to touch his face, where he could feel the slick of blood.

"Fuck." He pulled his hand away and considered the moisture on his palm. "Something hit me."

"It's nothing. You'll be alright." The MI6 agent squeezed off a few shots. "Get back on the job!"

Jack nodded. "Reloading!"

As he ejected the clip from the pistol and slid in another, Jack glanced at Chen. The ex-Taiwanese special forces soldier had rested a carbine on the windowsill and was as calm as ever as he waited for their enemy to emerge. Chen seemed to have infinite patience, firing off short bursts only when necessary and otherwise playing for time. Jack suddenly felt stupid for blazing away at the darkness, given the patience of the other defenders.

He felt useless, unable to see anything and unsure whether his adversaries could see him.

ARON WATCHED, safe in the darkness, as gunfire rattled back and forth between his comrades and the defenders. While it did, he held his fire and waited, with Miri and a pair of others by his side. They were all dressed in black and armed with their favorite weapons. Aron had reacquired his machine pistols but added a rather nasty combat knife. He had the feeling that this one was going to get up close and personal before the night was done.

They'd left Downing Street by helicopter, landed outside London and acquired vehicles. While on the road, he'd called the contact Eshkol had entrusted to him. With as much difficulty as ordering a pizza, the mole inside the bureaucracy had told Aron who'd taken the minister and where he was being taken. Though they were a few hours behind, the information had allowed Aron and his team to arrive at the house in the Welsh countryside with enough time to get the job done.

His team had halted their drive two miles from the house, then waited until darkness before embarking on their walk. They'd covered the distance quickly and then split up and moved to their assigned positions in silence. Planning had been completed on the road and there were no words to be said, only a job to be done. If anything, Aron felt like the hardest tasks were behind them and that this was the victory lap – the final target that Eshkol had asked him to take care of.

"We should move." Miri spoke softly from beside him. "The minister is there for the taking."

"Not yet." He could sense his team growing restless to join the fray and help their comrades.

A larger group of his men were attacking the house from the north, east and west. Ideally, one of the attacks would succeed and the feints wouldn't matter, but he doubted it. The British would have some of their best defending the minister, which meant something special was required to take him down. So Aron and his squad cooled their heels on the southern approach to the house, watching and waiting for the right moment to strike.

Though he had no more men than the defenders and they were dug in, he had tactical advantages they didn't enjoy. Timing was everything if his attack were to succeed. If he moved too early, his small squad would struggle to penetrate the defenses protecting their target. Too late, and he might have lost too many men for it to matter. He had his eyes locked on to one of the defenders, crouched low behind a window. The second they moved, so would Aron.

As if on cue with his thoughts, one of the figures in the window moved out of sight. They'd pulled assets from the south to reinforce elsewhere.

He smiled. "Go."

Next to him, Miri prepared her rifle for the most important shot of this engagement. Aron watched as she breathed, taking her time, then turned his head to the house as Miri took the shot. The suppressed rifle made barely a sound and the final defender, who'd only peeked over the windowsill, dropped suddenly. Miri threw the rifle on the ground and flashed him a grin. She was still every bit as good as advertised.

The small team stood and moved quickly to close the distance between their position and the house. As they drew closer, with Aron in the lead, there was no sign of a single defender – they'd left the back door open to stop the front door from blowing in. Aron and Miri crouched low, waiting as the other pair moved in first. They approached and climbed through the window, then peeked back and waved Aron and Miri forward.

Aron reached the window and leaped through, keeping low as he landed, eyes scanning the room for any threat. There was none and the room was quiet, except for the muted footsteps of his small squad as they started to move out of the corridor and deeper into the house. Aron and Miri cut north and the other pair moved for the eastern end of the house. In seconds they were behind the defenders and ready to end this.

Gripping his machine pistol in one hand and the combat knife in the other, Aron stalked toward the two defenders he could see. They were apparently so busy keeping his other forces outside that they had no clue what was inside. As he moved closer, he listened as the pair of them shouted at each other in between gunfire. One – an American – wanted to rush to help the others, while the man with the British accent wanted to hold firm.

Aron considered the quirk of circumstance that had brought US forces to defend a British minister in the Welsh countryside, and worried for a moment there might be more US forces close, but quickly disregarded the thought. If the US had more than a token force here, they'd have played their hand already. Aron raised the knife to strike just as the Briton glanced sideways, catching Miri in his peripheral vision.

"They're here!" The British man's shout ruined Aron and Miri's chance of doing this cleanly.

Aron lifted the knife and struck quickly as the American started to turn. The blade ran across the American's throat and Aron heard a gargling sound as blood gushed over the carpet in front of them. To be sure of it, he dug the knife into the base of the man's neck as he fell, going hilt deep and probably severing his spinal cord. As the American hit the floor, Aron glanced left and saw that Miri had already taken care of the British defender.

A gunshot boomed and Miri shrieked in agony. Aron raised the machine pistol and fired off a long burst at the woman who'd just put down his comrade, but she'd ducked back behind the doorframe. Aron cursed and dived behind a sofa, then looked beside him to see if Miri was alright. She was still moving, but was nursing a wound to her arm. Aron gritted his teeth, peered over the sofa and fired off another long burst at the woman who'd shot Miri down.

Any tactical advantage he'd gained through the feint would be lost if they got stuck in here, on the outskirts of the house and kept from his target.

ANNA GRUNTED as the wooden doorframe continued to splinter and shatter under the withering gunfire from the other side. Never more thankful for stone walls, she reloaded her pistol and gritted her teeth, safe for now but under no illusions that would last. She'd left Jack to cover one of the approaches to the house and moved to reinforce another herself, but little had she known that the Zionists were already inside the house and some of her people were dead.

She'd reached the position just as the attackers had engaged her comrades. Though she'd ruined their ambush and winged one of them, it might not make a difference. They'd turned on her and unleashed a withering barrage of fire, forcing her back behind cover. All she had to fire back with was her pistol, but if nothing else her interruption had made their path toward the minister a bit more difficult.

As she shied away from the gunfire, she lifted the radio

clipped to her hip. "They're inside! They're inside the house! At least two attackers! North side!"

Following her report, the radio crackled with more from the other pairings: Emery and a SEAL were holding one direction; a pair of SEALs were holding another; and Chen had peeled off to protect the minister. There was silence from the other rooms, which probably explained how these Zionists had gained entry. Things were going to hell quickly, and she needed to think about more than the Zionist firing at her. She had to salvage the situation.

She spoke into the radio again. "All forces disengage. Everyone fall back to defend the minister."

She tossed the radio on to the ground. The tactical situation was dire. She breathed a sigh of relief that Chen had had the foresight to head straight to Ho, despite the pressure they were under elsewhere, but every other defender left breathing was fully engaged. There was nobody to help her hold off this group. All she could do was keep them here for a few crucial moments, to buy time for the others to reach Chen and the minister for the final stand.

They had to try to defend the inner corridors of the house and, if it came to it, the dining room. If the Zionists made it that far, there was an extremely high likelihood that the minister would eat a bullet, yet the defenders had no other choice. They'd gambled everything on keeping the Zionists outside. Failing that, they were now spread too thin against an unknown number of hostiles. They were probably fucked. She was definitely fucked.

She took a deep breath, peered round the doorframe and squeezed off two quick shots. She wasn't sure if she'd hit anything, because she was already back behind the wall. From the other side, a machine pistol chattered and a pistol barked in response. Anna wished she had a grenade handy. If she made it out of here, she'd be sure to tell MI6 to make them standard issue. As it was, all she had was her pistol and her wits.

"We're not here for you!" a voice shouted from inside the other room. "Bring the minister to me and you can go home."

She laughed. Talking was good – it bought time. "And let you nuke the whole planet? We didn't find your baby bombs only to let you fire ICBMs."

"There's no plan to nuke anyone. We're only after the minister."

"Come and get him then!"

There was silence, then the first attacker rushed through the door. The female Zionist went down quickly, two rounds through the chest, but in the time that took another was upon her. Anna squeezed the trigger one more time but missed. A long chain of machine pistol fire filled her ears and a burning pain seared her legs. She shrieked and fell to the ground, dropping the pistol on the way down before landing hard.

"Stupid bitch." The Zionist with the machine pistol kicked her pistol away then stomped on her chest, driving the wind from her.

"*Home plate secure.*" The long forgotten radio. It was Jack's voice. "*The minister is safe but we're under assault. Where are you, Anna?*"

Anna smiled and closed her eyes. "Hear that? You lose, you giant fucking wanker."

She heard a guttural growl then blackness overcame her.

20

The New York Standard Online has reporters on the streets of Jerusalem, Gaza City and other population centers in Israel and Palestine less than ten minutes before the peace agreement enters into law. Crowds fill the streets, keen to witness history and send off one of the most divisive and heated conflicts of the past century. It appears as if the Zionist terrorists have failed in their efforts to divide the world with hatred and bigotry, in what looks to be a triumph for the future of a newly divided Israel and Palestine.

New York Standard

J ack kept his pistol trained on the doorway of the dining room. He glanced left, then right. Chen and one of the Navy SEALs were doing the same from behind the upturned oak dining table that they claimed might stop a bullet. It was the best cover they could manage in the circumstances. Behind them, deeper inside the room, Minister Ho lay underneath a few spare Kevlar vests. This was very much the final stand – for Jack, the peace agreement and civilization.

After Anna Fowler's radio warning, he'd withdrawn to help secure the dining room, where Chen and the minister were already busy. When he'd reached the room, he'd found it well prepared for a final stand. Unfortunately, only one SEAL had joined them since. He'd radioed Anna a moment ago, but there'd been no response. He didn't know how many Zionists were left, but he'd bet there were more attackers than defenders.

They might not have numbers, but they did have time on their side. If they could hold out for another eight minutes or so, the deed would be done, though it was unlikely Jack, Chen or the others would survive to be labeled heroes. They'd be anonymous to everyone except the uppermost leadership of the United States and Britain – anonymous men and women who'd spared the world nuclear armageddon and improved the lives of millions, but at the cost of their own.

Jack heard a series of pounding bangs on the wooden floor that grew louder as the attackers approached. "They're coming."

"Nice knowing you guys." The SEAL smiled, not taking his eyes off the door as he stared down his iron sights.

Jack looked at his watch as he continued to grip his pistol. "Seven minutes until midnight."

"That's only 420 seconds." The SEAL shouted as he squeezed the trigger of his carbine. "Contact!"

Gunfire erupted. The SEAL's carbine boomed in three-round bursts. Chen's more patient firing added to the cacophony in less frequent intervals. Jack, for his part, was careful only to fire when he had something to fire at. He squeezed off two shots at a Zionist who briefly appeared in his sights, but wasn't confident he'd hit anything. He didn't know how many attackers were left, but he'd be happy if he could take down one of them and help out those trained to do this.

Jack's breathing was fast, in, out, in, out, as he tried to stay calm. He focused on keeping as low a profile behind the upturned table as he could while maintaining his aim. He gasped when rounds fired from the attackers pounded into the hardwood table and he half expected to feel hot lead penetrate his body, but the cover held firm. He wasn't sure how many attackers there were, but he felt confident they might just be able to hold them for the next few minutes.

Until he watched a small, oval-shaped object fly overhead.

"Grenade!" the SEAL shouted.

Jack's eyes involuntarily tracked the grenade in flight, taking his focus off the hallway. A shout of alarm got stuck in his throat as he watched the SEAL drop his carbine and spring to his feet. As the grenade landed near the minister, the SEAL dived on top of it. There was an ear-splitting boom and the SEAL's body lifted slightly off the ground with the impact, but his sacrifice had saved the rest of them, the Minister and probably the world.

Jack turned back to the hallway, but the damage had been done. A pair of Zionists had forced their way inside the room and one was aiming at Chen. Jack swung his pistol and fired at the new threat just as Chen did the same thing. The Zionist dropped, bearing multiple bullet wounds, but Chen grunted and reached for his shoulder too. Jack ducked a little lower as he turned his gun toward what must have been the final attacker. Too slow.

The Zionist leaped over the table and kicked out at Jack's hand, striking hard and causing the pistol to drop to the ground. With a curse, Jack fell on his ass, but wasted no time in backing away from the new threat. As he did, the Zionist aimed a kick at Chen, who was in no position to block it. The blow connected with the head of Jack's last remaining ally and Chen slumped forward, unconscious from the blow to the head and bleeding from the gunshot wound to his shoulder.

Jack was on his own. With two or three minutes left before the deadline.

The Zionist advanced, his machine pistol pointed at Jack and with a nasty-looking knife in his other hand. "Come out, minister, and save this brave man."

"Stay where you are!" Jack shouted at Ho, who'd been told to stay behind cover no matter what happened. "I'll protect you!"

"You're joking." The Zionist let out a laugh as he tossed the machine pistol at Jack's feet.

Jack snarled as he picked up the machine pistol. The Zionist approached him with the knife as Jack lifted the weapon. "Confident, aren't you?"

The other man grinned as he flicked the knife into an underhand grip and stalked forward. "Why wouldn't I be? I've still got two minutes to kill my target."

Jack shouted at him to stop, but the Zionist kept coming. He gripped the machine pistol tight and then squeezed the trigger. He heard a click. "Fuck."

The Zionist slashed out at his face with the knife. Jack flinched and came away with a nasty cut, which was better than losing half of his face. He retreated, blood dripping from his cheek as he reached up to press his palm against the cut, but the Zionist didn't let up. He kicked out at Jack's knee, which buckled under the blow. Jack screamed in pain and fell to the floor, his mind protesting at the pain even as he tried to think about a way out of this.

"You lose." The Zionist raised the knife with the point facing downward, ready to pierce him.

"Do you know the consequences of killing him?" Jack sucked in breath. "Annihilation."

The Zionist laughed. "This is where I pause for twenty

minutes to tell you my evil plan, is it? It's simple: kill the minister, because those are my orders."

Jack's eyes widened. "You don't know, do you? If you kill him, a British nuclear submarine launches enough nukes to end the world."

"It doesn't matter." The Zionist raised his arm then brought the blade down on Jack's thigh.

Jack screamed in agony as the blade went deep. He reached for the hilt and gripped it, but stopped short of pulling it out, remembering that doing so only increased your chance of bleeding out. His eyes locked on the Zionist, who'd picked up the machine pistol and reloaded it. At no point did the man show any hesitation or doubt about what Jack had told him. He pointed the weapon at the minister and fired a long burst.

All Jack could do was scream.

COHEN WAS GROWING FRUSTRATED with the communications officer, who was clearly stalling him. He gripped the man's chair and leaned his head next to the young seaman. "Anything? Is there any sign of broadcast on the longwave band? BBC Radio 4?"

To his credit, the young man didn't shy away. He turned in his chair, removed his headset and ran a hand over his face. "No signal on the longwave band, sir."

Cohen frowned and nodded. It was looking increasingly likely that he had a launch to conduct. "Check on the PM and the Minister for Employment."

With a slight nod, the officer replaced his headset and turned back to his console, fingers dancing across the keyboard at a speed Joseph could never hope to replicate. He left the man to his work, crossed the small bridge and stood alongside Jennings, who waited in silence for orders from his captain. His executive officer was as tense as the rest of the men and women on the bridge, a mood Joseph was sure would be replicated through the entire boat.

Launch prep.

A situation that all ballistic missile submariners prepare for but never really expect to do for real – end the world from safely beneath the ocean, knowing that minutes after pressing the button other states would do likewise. Once that happened friends, family and homes were as like as not to be reduced to ash. Simply contemplating it left a coppery taste in the mouth, but to actually go through with it would feel quite a lot worse. Or so Joseph imagined.

"No proper authentication from the Prime Minister on national command channels, captain." The comms officer turned and stared at his captain, then at the executive officer, then at a few of his crewmates. "The PM is dead or not able to authenticate."

To their credit, the crew kept their composure – the only reaction Joseph could hear was a few sharp intakes of breath – though it did feel like the temperature had dropped. The men and women aboard continued with their jobs. He was proud of them, though they were unwitting puppets in his own mission – acting on the orders Zed Eshkol had given him. He did sense an expectation that he should say or do something, though.

"Carry on with your jobs." Joseph did his best to project an air of calm. "Comms, try to make contact with the PM's second. XO, inform the crew."

As the crew went about their jobs, Joseph closed his eyes. In the few seconds he had to spare, he searched his soul and his heart for confirmation that he'd really go through with this – launch nuclear missiles as a final invocation of Zed Eshkol's Samson Option. That doctrine, developed decades ago by a fiery young Jew, was now the order of a man who was so old he wouldn't live to see the consequences.

Eshkol's age changed nothing, though. A younger Joseph had been taught by a younger professor, nearly two decades prior. He'd been a student of Eshkol's, then a friend, then a confidant and, finally, an agent. With a simple word from his lips, he had confirmed to the elderly Zionist that he'd do whatever was necessary should the existence of Israel ever be seriously threatened. He'd sworn a life of service and, in return, Eshkol's network had opened doors for Joseph.

"Captain?" The comms officer's voice was grave. "We have no proper authentication from the Prime Minister's second."

"Thank you. Stand by everyone." Joseph opened his eyes. He turned to Jennings. "Do you concur that command authority has been compromised?"

Jennings smiled sadly, as if the world had already gone to ash. "I concur, captain."

They went to the safe, wordlessly going through a process that was nearly automatic. Once it was open, Joseph ignored the contents of the safe and instead worked to open the second safe, inside the first. He turned the dial several times, using a code that only he knew to open the door. Inside was one crisp, white envelope. As he reached inside for the envelope, he still couldn't be sure if he'd go through with this.

He opened the envelope and extracted the letter, which was on good-quality paper and folded neatly into thirds. Once the letter was unfolded, his eyes scanned the words but his mind was already made up. The Prime Minister, Joseph wasn't surprised to read, had written to her submarine commanders and ordered them to launch. Not that it would have mattered if the letter said otherwise, given Joseph had no need to show anyone else.

The order was his.

He returned to the bridge and made his way to the ship's address system and picked up the radio. "Attention all crew. I regret to inform you all that the United Kingdom has been attacked and quite possibly rendered helpless. All tests we use to ascertain the viability of the UK government have failed.

"As a result, protocol dictates we open the Dead Man Letter, which dictates the action I'm to take in these circumstances. I've done so, and the Prime Minister's orders were to launch on those states deemed responsible for the destruction of Britain. We will now commence preparations for that launch."

Joseph replaced the radio and turned around. Jennings had his eyes locked on his captain, as did the rest of the crew. He nodded at them. "We have jobs to do."

"The targets, sir?" Jennings' voice had a slight break in it.

Joseph spoke as confidently as he could. "Jerusalem and Mecca."

The other man hesitated, then nodded. "Yes, sir."

The comms officer cut in. "Sir, I've run another check on the Minister for—"

Joseph glared at the junior officer. "Nobody told you—"

"He's alive!" The comms officer let out a cry of relief. "The minister is alive."

"We launch!" Joseph clenched his fists. "Nobody told you to run that check."

"But, sir, he's—"

Joseph held up a hand to cut the other man off, then turned to Jennings. "We proceed as planned."

"I don't think that's wise, sir. The government is still intact." Jennings reached a hand out, moving to place it on Joseph's shoulder.

Joseph reached for his pistol in its holster and raised it